THE COMPLETE LEATHERSTOCKING TALES

VOLUME I

# THE COMPLETE
# LEATHERSTOCKING TALES

## VOLUME I

BEING THE ADVENTURES OF NATTY BUMPPO,

SOMETIMES CALLED "DEERSLAYER," "HAWKEYE," "PATHFINDER," AND "LEATHERSTOCKING"

WRITTEN BY

## JAMES FENIMORE COOPER

THE FIRST TWO NOVELS

*THE DEERSLAYER*

*THE LAST OF THE MOHICANS*

EX FONTIBUS CO., 2015

Taking all that was best in the Greco-Roman world into itself, Western tradition has given us the thousand good books as preparation for the great ones. . . . For us today, the [useful] cutoff point is World War I, before which cars and the electric light had not yet come to dominate our lives and the experience of nature had not been distorted by speed and the destruction of shadows....[These books are] part of the ordinary cultural matter essential for an English-speaking person to grow in.

—Professor John Senior (1923–1999)
*Founder, Integrated Humanities Program*
*University of Kansas*

The novels reproduced in this volume were published as follows:

| | | |
|---|---|---|
| *The Deerslayer.* | Published 1841. | Set in 1740–1755. |
| *The Last of the Mohicans.* | Published 1826. | Set in 1757. |

*Visit Us*

EXFONTIBUSCOMPANY@GMAIL.COM; MAIL@EXFONTIBUS.COM; WWW.EXFONTIBUS.COM

# CONTENTS

# THE DEERSLAYER: OR, THE FIRST WAR-PATH

"There is a pleasure in the pathless woods,
There is a rapture on the lonely shore.
There is society where none intrudes,
By the deep sea, and music in its roar:
I love not man the less, but nature more,
From these our interviews, in which I steal
From all I may be, or have been before,
To mingle with the universe, and feel
What I can ne'er express, yet cannot all conceal"

Childe Harold.

N the human imagination events produce the effects of time. Thus, he who has travelled far and seen much is apt to fancy that he has lived long; and the history that most abounds in important incidents soonest assumes the aspect of antiquity. In no other way can we account for the venerable air that is already gathering around American annals. When the mind reverts to the earliest days of colonial history, the period seems remote and obscure, the thousand changes that thicken along the links of recollections, throwing back the origin of the nation to a day so distant as seemingly to reach the mists of time; and yet four lives of ordinary duration would suffice to transmit, from mouth to mouth, in the form of tradition, all that civilized man has achieved within the limits of the republic. Although New York alone possesses a population materially exceeding that of either of the four smallest kingdoms of Europe, or materially exceeding that of the entire Swiss Confederation, it is little more than two centuries since the Dutch commenced their settlement, rescuing the region from the savage state. Thus, what seems venerable by an accumulation of changes is reduced to familiarity when we come seriously to consider it solely in connection with time.

This glance into the perspective of the past will prepare the reader to look at the pictures we are about to sketch, with less surprise than he might otherwise feel; and a few additional explanations may carry him back in imagination to the precise condition of society that we desire to delineate. It is matter of history that the settlements on the eastern shores of the Hudson, such as Claverack, Kinderhook, and even Poughkeepsie, were not regarded as safe from Indian incursions a century since; and there is still standing on the banks of the same river, and within musket-shot of the wharves of Albany, a residence of a younger branch of the Van Rensselaers, that has loopholes constructed for defence against the same crafty enemy, although it dates from a period scarcely so distant. Other similar memorials of the infancy of the country are to be found, scattered through what is now deemed the very centre of American civilization, affording the plainest proofs that all we possess of security from invasion and hostile violence is the growth of but little more than the time that is frequently fulfilled by a single human life.

The incidents of this tale occurred between the years 1740 and 1745, when the settled portions of the colony of New York were confined to the four Atlantic counties, a narrow belt of country on each side of the Hudson, extending from its mouth to the falls near its head, and to a few advanced "neighborhoods" on the Mohawk and the Schoharie. Broad belts of the virgin wilderness not only reached the shores of the first river, but they even crossed it, stretching away into New England, and affording forest covers to the noiseless moccasin of the native warrior, as he trod the secret and bloody war-path. A bird's-eye view of the whole region east of the Mississippi must then have offered one vast expanse of woods, relieved by a comparatively narrow fringe of cultivation along the sea, dotted by the glittering surfaces of lakes, and intersected by the waving lines of river. In such a vast picture of solemn solitude, the district of country we design to paint sinks into insignificance, though we feel encouraged to proceed by the conviction that, with slight and immaterial distinctions, he who succeeds in giving an accurate idea of any portion of this wild region must necessarily convey a tolerably correct notion of the whole.

Whatever may be the changes produced by man, the eternal round of the seasons is unbroken. Summer and winter, seed-time and harvest, return in their stated order with a sublime precision, affording to man one of the noblest of all the occasions he enjoys of proving the high powers of his far-reaching mind, in compassing the laws that control their exact uniformity, and in calculating their never-ending revolutions.

Centuries of summer suns had warmed the tops of the same noble oaks and pines, sending their heats even to the tenacious roots, when voices were heard calling to each other, in the depths of a forest, of which the leafy surface lay bathed in the brilliant light of a cloudless day in June, while the trunks of the trees rose in gloomy grandeur in the shades beneath. The calls were in different tones, evidently proceeding from two men who had lost their way, and were searching in different directions for their path. At length a shout proclaimed success, and presently a man of gigantic mould broke out of the tangled labyrinth of a small swamp, emerging into an opening that appeared to have been formed partly by the ravages of the wind, and partly by those of fire. This little area, which afforded a good view of the sky, although it was pretty well filled with dead trees, lay on the side of one of the high hills, or low mountains, into which nearly the whole surface of the adjacent country was broken.

"Here is room to breathe in!" exclaimed the liberated forester, as soon as he found himself under a clear sky, shaking his huge frame like a mastiff that has just escaped from a snowbank. "Hurrah! Deerslayer; here is daylight, at last, and yonder is the lake."

These words were scarcely uttered when the second forester dashed aside the bushes of the swamp, and appeared in the area. After making a hurried adjustment of his arms and disordered dress, he joined his companion, who had already begun his disposition for a halt.

"Do you know this spot!" demanded the one called Deerslayer, "or do you shout at the sight of the sun?"

"Both, lad, both; I know the spot, and am not sorry to see so useful a fri'nd as the sun. Now we have got the p'ints of the compass in our minds once more, and 't will be our own faults if we let anything turn them topsy-turvy ag'in, as has just happened. My name is not Hurry Harry, if this be not the very spot where the land-hunters camped the last summer, and passed a week. See I yonder are the dead bushes of their bower, and here is the spring. Much as I like the sun, boy, I've no occasion for it to tell me it is noon; this stomach of mine is as good a time-piece as is to be found in the colony, and it already p'ints to half-past twelve. So open the wallet, and let us wind up for another six hours' run."

At this suggestion, both set themselves about making the preparations necessary for their usual frugal but hearty meal. We will profit by this pause in the discourse to give the reader some idea of the appearance of the men, each of whom is destined to enact no insignificant part in our legend.

It would not have been easy to find a more noble specimen of vigorous manhood than was offered in the person of him who called himself Hurry Harry. His real name was Henry March but the frontiersmen having caught the practice of giving sobriquets from the Indians, the appellation of Hurry was far oftener applied to him than his proper designation, and not unfrequently he was termed Hurry Skurry, a nickname he had obtained from a dashing, reckless offhand manner, and a physical restlessness that kept him so constantly on the move, as to cause him to be known along the whole line of scattered habitations that lay between the province and the Canadas. The stature of Hurry Harry exceeded six feet four, and being unusually well proportioned, his strength fully realized the idea created by his gigantic frame. The face did no discredit to the rest of the man, for it was both good-humored and handsome. His air was free, and though his manner necessarily partook of the rudeness of a border life, the grandeur that pervaded so noble a physique prevented it from becoming altogether vulgar.

Deerslayer, as Hurry called his companion, was a very different person in appearance, as well as in character. In stature he stood about six feet in his moccasins, but his frame was comparatively light and slender, showing muscles, however, that promised unusual agility, if not unusual strength. His face would have had little to recommend it except youth, were it not for an expression that seldom failed to win upon those who had leisure to examine it, and to yield to the feeling of confidence it created. This expression was simply that of guileless truth, sustained by an earnestness of purpose, and a sincerity of feeling, that rendered it remarkable. At times this air of integrity seemed to be so simple as to awaken the suspicion of a want of the usual means to discriminate between artifice and truth; but few came in serious contact with the man, without losing this distrust in respect for his opinions and motives.

Both these frontiersmen were still young, Hurry having reached the age of six or eight and twenty, while Deerslayer was several years his junior. Their attire needs no particular description, though it may be well to add that it was composed in no small degree of dressed deer-skins, and had the usual signs of belonging to those who pass their time between the skirts of civilized society and the boundless forests. There was, notwithstanding, some attention to smartness and the picturesque in the arrangements of Deerslayer's dress, more particularly in the part connected with his arms and accoutrements. His rifle was in perfect condition, the handle of his hunting-knife was neatly carved, his powder-horn was ornamented with suitable devices lightly cut into the material, and his shot-pouch was decorated with wampum.

On the other hand, Hurry Harry, either from constitutional recklessness, or from a secret consciousness how little his appearance required artificial aids, wore everything in a careless, slovenly manner, as if he felt a noble scorn for the trifling accessories of dress and ornaments. Perhaps the peculiar effect of his fine form and great stature was increased rather than lessened, by this unstudied and disdainful air of indifference.

"Come, Deerslayer, fall to, and prove that you have a Delaware stomach, as you say you have had a Delaware edication," cried Hurry, setting the example by opening his mouth to receive a slice of cold venison steak that would have made an entire meal for a European peasant; "fall to, lad, and prove your manhood on this poor devil of a doe with your teeth, as you've already done with your rifle."

"Nay, nay, Hurry, there's little manhood in killing a doe, and that too out of season; though there might be some in bringing down a painter or a catamount," returned the other, disposing himself to comply. "The Delawares have given me my name, not so much on account of a bold heart, as on account of a quick eye, and an actyve foot. There may not be any cowardyce in overcoming a deer, but sartain it is, there's no great valor."

"The Delawares themselves are no heroes," muttered Hurry through his teeth, the mouth being too full to permit it to be fairly opened, "or they would never have allowed them loping vagabonds, the Mingos, to make them women."

"That matter is not rightly understood—has never been rightly explained," said Deerslayer earnestly, for he was as zealous a friend as his companion was dangerous as an enemy; "the Mengwe fill the woods with their lies, and misconstruct words and treaties. I have now lived ten years with the Delawares, and know them to be as manful as any other nation, when the proper time to strike comes."

"Harkee, Master Deerslayer, since we are on the subject, we may as well open our minds to each other in a man-to-man way; answer me one question; you have had so much luck among the game as to have gotten a title, it would seem, but did you ever hit anything human or intelligible: did you ever pull trigger on an inimy that was capable of pulling one upon you?"

This question produced a singular collision between mortification and correct feeling, in the bosom of the youth, that was easily to be traced in the workings of his ingenuous countenance. The struggle was short, however; uprightness of heart soon getting the better of false pride and frontier boastfulness.

"To own the truth, I never did," answered Deerslayer; "seeing that a fitting occasion never offered. The Delawares have been peaceable since my sojourn with 'em, and I hold it to be onlawful to take the life of man, except in open and generous warfare."

"What! did you never find a fellow thieving among your traps and skins, and do the law on him with your own hands, by way of saving the magistrates trouble in the settlements, and the rogue himself the cost of the suit!"

"I am no trapper, Hurry," returned the young man proudly: "I live by the rifle, a we'pon at which I will not turn my back on any man of my years, atween the Hudson and the St. Lawrence. I never offer a skin that has not a hole in its head besides them which natur' made to see with or to breathe through."

"Ay, ay, this is all very well, in the animal way, though it makes but a poor figure alongside of scalps and ambushes. Shooting an Indian from an ambush is acting up to his own principles, and now we have what you call a lawful war on our hands, the sooner you wipe that disgrace off your character, the sounder will be your sleep; if it only come from knowing there is one inimy the less prowling in the woods. I shall not frequent your society long, friend Natty, unless you look higher than four-footed beasts to practice your rifle on."

"Our journey is nearly ended, you say, Master March, and we can part to-night, if you see occasion. I have a fri'nd waiting for me, who will think it no disgrace to consort with a fellow-creatur' that has never yet slain his kind."

"I wish I knew what has brought that skulking Delaware into this part of the country so early in the season," muttered Hurry to himself, in a way to show equally distrust and a recklessness of its betrayal. "Where did you say the young chief was to give you the meeting?"

"At a small round rock, near the foot of the lake, where they tell me, the tribes are given to resorting to make their treaties, and to bury their hatchets. This rock have I often heard the Delawares mention, though lake and rock are equally strangers to me. The country is claimed by both Mingos and Mohicans, and is a sort of common territory to fish and hunt through, in time of peace, though what it may become in war-time, the Lord only knows!"

"Common territory" exclaimed Hurry, laughing aloud. "I should like to know what Floating Tom Hutter would say to that! He claims the lake as his own property, in vartue of fifteen years' possession, and will not be likely to give it up to either Mingo or Delaware without a battle for it!"

"And what will the colony say to such a quarrel—all this country must have some owner, the gentry pushing their cravings into the wilderness, even where they never dare to ventur', in their own persons, to look at the land they own."

"That may do in other quarters of the colony, Deerslayer, but it will not do here. Not a human being, the Lord excepted, owns a foot of sile in this part of the country. Pen was never put to paper consarning either hill or valley hereaway, as I've heard old Tom say time and ag'in, and so he claims the best right to it of any man breathing; and what Tom claims, he'll be very likely to maintain."

"By what I've heard you say, Hurry, this Floating Tom must be an oncommon mortal; neither Mingo, Delaware, nor pale-face. His possession, too, has been long, by your tell, and altogether beyond frontier endurance. What's the man's history and natur'?"

"Why, as to old Tom's human natur', it is not much like other men's human natur', but more like a muskrat's human natar', seeing that he takes more to the ways of that animal than to the ways of any other fellow-creatur'. Some think he was a free liver on the salt water, in his youth, and a companion of a sartain Kidd, who was hanged for piracy, long afore you and I were born or acquainted, and that he came up into these regions, thinking that the king's cruisers could never cross the mountains, and that he might enjoy the plunder peaceably in the woods."

"Then he was wrong, Hurry; very wrong. A man can enjoy plunder peaceably nowhere."

"That's much as his turn of mind may happen to be. I've known them that never could enjoy it at all, unless it was in the midst of a jollification, and them again that enjoyed it best in a corner. Some men have no peace if they don't find plunder, and some if they do. Human nature' is crooked in these matters. Old Tom seems to belong to neither set, as he enjoys his, if plunder he has really got, with his darters, in a very quiet and comfortable way, and wishes for no more."

"Ay, he has darters, too; I've heard the Delawares, who've hunted this a way, tell their histories of these young women. Is there no mother, Hurry?"

"There was once, as in reason; but she has now been dead and sunk these two good years."

"Anan?" said Deerslayer, looking up at his companion in a little surprise.

"Dead and sunk, I say, and I hope that's good English. The old fellow lowered his wife into the lake, by way of seeing the last of her, as I can testify, being an eye-witness of the ceremony; but whether Tom did it to save digging, which is no easy job among roots, or out of a consait that water washes away sin sooner than 'arth, is more than I can say."

"Was the poor woman oncommon wicked, that her husband should take so much pains with her body?"

"Not onreasonable; though she had her faults. I consider Judith Hutter to have been as graceful, and about as likely to make a good ind as any woman who had lived so long beyond the sound of church bells; and I conclude old Tom sunk her as much by way of saving pains, as by way of taking it. There was a little steel in her temper, it's true, and, as old Hutter is pretty much flint, they struck out sparks once-and-a-while; but, on the whole, they might be said to live amicable like. When they did kindle, the listeners got some such insights into their past lives, as one gets into the darker parts of the woods, when a stray gleam of sunshine finds its way down to the roots of the trees. But Judith I shall always esteem, as it's recommend enough to one woman to be the mother of such a creatur' as her darter, Judith Hutter!"

"Ay, Judith was the name the Delawares mentioned, though it was pronounced after a fashion of their own. From their discourse, I do not think the girl would much please my fancy."

"Thy fancy!" exclaimed March, taking fire equally at the indifference and at the presumption of his companion, "what the devil have you to do with a fancy, and that, too, consarning one like Judith? You are but a boy—a sapling, that has scarce got root. Judith has had men among her suitors, ever since she was fifteen; which is now near five years; and will not be apt even to cast a look upon a half-grown creatur' like you!"

"It is June, and there is not a cloud atween us and the sun, Hurry, so all this heat is not wanted," answered the other, altogether undisturbed; "any one may have a fancy, and a squirrel has a right to make up his mind touching a catamount."

"Ay, but it might not be wise, always, to let the catamount know it," growled March. "But you're young and thoughtless, and I'll overlook your ignorance. Come, Deerslayer," he added, with a good-natured laugh, after pausing a moment to reflect, "come, Deerslayer, we are sworn friends, and will not quarrel about a light-minded, jilting jade, just because she happens to be handsome; more especially as you have never seen her. Judith is only for a man whose teeth show the full marks, and it's foolish to be afeard of a boy. What did the Delawares say of the hussy? for an Indian, after all, has his notions of woman-kind, as well as a white man."

"They said she was fair to look on, and pleasant of speech; but over-given to admirers, and light-minded."

"They are devils incarnate! After all, what schoolmaster is a match for an Indian, in looking into natur'! Some people think they are only good on a trail or the war-path, but I say that they are philosophers, and understand a man as well as they understand a beaver, and a woman as well as they understand either. Now that's Judith's character to a ribbon! To own the truth to you, Deerslayer, I should have married the gal two years since, if it had not been for two particular things, one of which was this very lightmindedness."

"And what may have been the other?" demanded the hunter, who continued to eat like one that took very little interest in the subject.

"T'other was an insartainty about her having me. The hussy is handsome, and she knows it. Boy, not a tree that is growing in these hills is straighter, or waves in the wind with an easier bend, nor did you ever see the doe that bounded with a more nat'ral motion. If that was all, every tongue would sound her praises; but she has such failings that I find it hard to overlook them, and sometimes I swear I'll never visit the lake again."

"Which is the reason that you always come back? Nothing is ever made more sure by swearing about it."

"Ah, Deerslayer, you are a novelty in these particulars; keeping as true to education as if you had never left the settlements. With me the case is different, and I never want to clinch an idee, that I do not feel a wish to swear about it. If you know'd all that I know consarning Judith, you'd find a justification for a little cussing. Now, the officers sometimes stray over to the lake, from the forts on the Mohawk, to fish and hunt, and then the creatur' seems beside herself! You can see in the manner which she wears her finery, and the airs she gives herself with the gallants."

"That is unseemly in a poor man's darter," returned Deerslayer gravely, "the officers are all gentry, and can only look on such as Judith with evil intentions."

"There's the unsartainty, and the damper! I have my misgivings about a particular captain, and Jude has no one to blame but her own folly, if I'm right. On the whole, I wish to look upon her as modest and becoming, and yet the clouds that drive among these hills are not more unsartain. Not a dozen white men have ever laid eyes upon her since she was a child, and yet her airs, with two or three of these officers, are extinguishers!"

"I would think no more of such a woman, but turn my mind altogether to the forest; that will not deceive you, being ordered and ruled by a hand that never wavers."

"If you know'd Judith, you would see how much easier it is to say this than it would be to do it. Could I bring my mind to be easy about the officers, I would carry the gal off to the Mohawk by force, make her marry me in spite of her whiffling, and leave old Tom to the care of Hetty, his other child, who, if she be not as handsome or as quick-witted as her sister, is much the most dutiful."

"Is there another bird in the same nest!" asked Deerslayer, raising his eyes with a species of half-awakened curiosity, "the Delawares spoke to me only of one."

"That's nat'ral enough, when Judith Hutter and Hetty Hutter are in question. Hetty is only comely, while her sister, I tell thee, boy, is such another as is not to be found atween this and the sea: Judith is as full of wit, and talk, and cunning, as an old Indian orator, while poor Hetty is at the best but 'compass' meant us."

"Anan?" inquired, again, the Deerslayer.

"Why, what the officers call 'compass meant us,' which I understand to signify that she means always to go in the right direction, but sometimes does not know how. 'Compass' for the p'int, and 'meant us' for the intention. No, poor Hetty is what I call on the verge of ignorance, and sometimes she stumbles on one side of the line, and sometimes on t'other."

"Them are beings that the Lord has in his special care," said Deerslayer, solemnly; "for he looks carefully to all who fall short of their proper share of reason. The red-skins honor and respect them who are so gifted, knowing that the Evil Spirit delights more to dwell in an artful body, than in one that has no cunning to work upon."

"I'll answer for it, then, that he will not remain long with poor Hetty; for the child is just 'compass meant us,' as I have told you. Old Tom has a feeling for the gal, and so has Judith, quick-witted and glorious as she is herself; else would I not answer for her being altogether safe among the sort of men that sometimes meet on the lake shore."

"I thought this water an unknown and little-frequented sheet," observed the Deerslayer, evidently uneasy at the idea of being too near the world.

"It's all that, lad, the eyes of twenty white men never having been laid on it; still, twenty true-bred frontiersmen—hunters and trappers, and scouts, and the like,—can do a deal of mischief if they try. 'T would be an awful thing to me, Deerslayer, did I find Judith married, after an absence of six months!"

"Have you the gal's faith, to encourage you to hope otherwise?"

"Not at all. I know not how it is: I'm good-looking, boy,—that much I can see in any spring on which the sun shines,—and yet I could not get the hussy to a promise, or even a cordial willing smile, though she will laugh by the hour. If she has dared to marry in my absence, she'd be like to know the pleasures of widowhood afore she is twenty!"

"You would not harm the man she has chosen, Hurry, simply because she found him more to her liking than yourself!"

"Why not! If an enemy crosses my path, will I not beat him out of it! Look at me! am I a man like to let any sneaking, crawling, skin-trader get the better of me in a matter that touches me as near as the kindness of Judith Hutter! Besides, when we live beyond law, we must be our own judges and executioners. And if a man should be found dead in the woods, who is there to say who slew him, even admitting that the colony took the matter in hand and made a stir about it?"

"If that man should be Judith Hutter's husband, after what has passed, I might tell enough, at least, to put the colony on the trail."

"You!—half-grown, venison-hunting bantling! You dare to think of informing against Hurry Harry in so much as a matter touching a mink or a woodchuck!"

"I would dare to speak truth, Hurry, consarning you or any man that ever lived."

March looked at his companion, for a moment, in silent amazement; then seizing him by the throat with both hands, he shook his comparatively slight frame with a violence that menaced the dislocation of some of the bones. Nor was this done jocularly, for anger flashed from the giant's eyes, and there were certain signs that seemed to threaten much more earnestness than the occasion would appear to call for. Whatever might be the real intention of March, and it is probable there was none settled in his mind, it is certain that he was unusually aroused; and most men who found themselves throttled by one of a mould so gigantic, in such a mood, and in a solitude so deep and helpless, would have felt intimidated, and tempted to yield even the right. Not so, however, with Deerslayer. His countenance remained unmoved; his hand did not shake, and his answer was given in a voice that did not resort to the artifice of louder tones, even by way of proving its owner's resolution.

"You may shake, Hurry, until you bring down the mountain," he said quietly, "but nothing beside truth will you shake from me. It is probable that Judith Hutter has no husband to slay, and you may never have a chance to waylay one, else would I tell her of your threat, in the first conversation I held with the gal."

March released his grip, and sat regarding the other in silent astonishment.

"I thought we had been friends," he at length added; "but you've got the last secret of mine that will ever enter your ears."

"I want none, if they are to be like this. I know we live in the woods, Hurry, and are thought to be beyond human laws,—and perhaps we are so, in fact, whatever it may be in right,—but there is a law and a law-maker, that rule across the whole continent. He that flies in the face of either need not call me a friend."

"Damme, Deerslayer, if I do not believe you are at heart a Moravian, and no fair-minded, plain-dealing hunter, as you've pretended to be!"

"Fair-minded or not, Hurry, you will find me as plaindealing in deeds as I am in words. But this giving way to sudden anger is foolish, and proves how little you have sojourned with the red man. Judith Hutter no doubt is still single, and you spoke but as the tongue ran, and not as the heart felt. There's my hand, and we will say and think no more about it."

Hurry seemed more surprised than ever; then he burst forth in a loud, good-natured laugh, which brought tears to his eyes. After this he accepted the offered hand, and the parties became friends.

"'T would have been foolish to quarrel about an idee," March cried, as he resumed his meal, "and more like lawyers in the towns than like sensible men in the woods. They tell me, Deerslayer, much ill-blood grows out of idees among the people in the lower counties, and that they sometimes get to extremities upon them."

"That do they,—that do they; and about other matters that might better be left to take care of themselves. I have heard the Moravians say that there are lands in which men quarrel even consarning their religion; and if they can get their tempers up on such a subject, Hurry, the Lord have Marcy on 'em. Howsoever, there is no occasion for our following their example, and more especially about a husband that this Judith Hutter may never see, or never wish to see. For my part, I feel more cur'osity about the feeble-witted sister than about your beauty. There's something that comes close to a man's feelin's, when he meets with a fellow-creatur' that has all the outward show of an accountable mortal, and who fails of being what he seems, only through a lack of reason. This is bad enough in a man, but when it comes to a woman, and she a young, and maybe a winning creatur' it touches all the pitiful thoughts his natur' has. God knows, Hurry, that such poor things be defenceless enough with all their wits about 'em; but it's a cruel fortun' when that great protector and guide fails 'em."

"Hark, Deerslayer,—you know what the hunters, and trappers, and peltry-men in general be; and their best friends will not deny that they are headstrong and given to having their own way, without much bethinking 'em of other people's rights or feelin's,—and yet I don't think the man is to be found, in all this region, who would harm Hetty Hutter, if he could; no, not even a red-skin."

"Therein, fri'nd Hurry, you do the Delawares, at least, and all their allied tribes, only justice, for a red-skin looks upon a being thus struck by God's power as especially under his care. I rejoice to hear what you say, however, I rejoice to hear it; but as the sun is beginning to turn towards the afternoon's sky, had we not better strike the trail again, and make forward, that we may get an opportunity of seeing these wonderful sisters?"

Harry March giving a cheerful assent, the remnants of the meal were soon collected; then the travelers shouldered their packs, resumed their arms, and, quitting the little area of light, they again plunged into the deep shadows of the forest.

## CHAPTER II.

"Thou'rt passing from the lake's green side,
And the hunter's hearth away;
For the time of flowers, for the summer's pride,
Daughter! thou canst not stay."

Mrs. Hemans, "Edith. A Tale of the Woods" II. 191—94

Our two adventurers had not far to go. Hurry knew the direction, as soon as he had found the open spot and the spring, and he now led on with the confident step of a man assured of his object. The forest was dark, as a matter of course, but it was no longer obstructed by underbrush, and the footing was firm and dry. After proceeding near a mile, March stopped, and began to cast about him with an inquiring look, examining the different objects with care, and occasionally turning his eyes on the trunks of the fallen trees, with which the ground was well sprinkled, as is usually the case in an American wood, especially in those parts of the country where timber has not yet become valuable.

"This must be the place, Deerslayer," March at length observed; "here is a beech by the side of a hemlock, with three pines at hand, and yonder is a white birch with a broken top; and yet I see no rock, nor any of the branches bent down, as I told you would be the case."

"Broken branches are onskilful landmarks, as the least exper'enced know that branches don't often break of themselves," returned the other; "and they also lead to suspicion and discoveries. The

Delawares never trust to broken branches, unless it is in friendly times, and on an open trail. As for the beeches, and pines, and hemlocks, why, they are to be seen on all sides of us, not only by twos and threes, but by forties, and fifties, and hundreds."

"Very true, Deerslayer, but you never calculate on position. Here is a beech and a hemlock——"

"Yes, and there is another beech and a hemlock, as loving as two brothers, or, for that matter, more loving than some brothers; and yonder are others, for neither tree is a rarity in these woods. I fear me, Hurry, you are better at trapping beaver and shooting bears, than at leading on a blindish sort of a trail. Ha! there's what you wish to find, a'ter all!"

"Now, Deerslayer, this is one of your Delaware pretensions, for hang me if I see anything but these trees, which do seem to start up around us in a most onaccountable and perplexing manner."

"Look this-a-way, Hurry—here, in a line with the black oak—don't you see the crooked sapling that is hooked up in the branches of the bass-wood, near it? Now, that sapling was once snow-ridden, and got the bend by its weight; but it never straightened itself, and fastened itself in among the bass-wood branches in the way you see. The hand of man did that act of kindness for it."

"That hand was mine!" exclaimed Hurry; "I found the slender young thing bent to the airth, like an unfortunate creatur' borne down by misfortune, and stuck it up where you see it. After all, Deerslayer, I must allow, you're getting to have an oncommon good eye for the woods!"

"'Tis improving, Hurry—'tis improving I will acknowledge; but 'tis only a child's eye, compared to some I know. There's Tamenund, now, though a man so old that few remember when he was in his prime, Tamenund lets nothing escape his look, which is more like the scent of a hound than the sight of an eye. Then Uncas, the father of Chingachgook, and the lawful chief of the Mohicans, is another that it is almost hopeless to pass unseen. I'm improving, I will allow—I'm improving, but far from being perfect, as yet."

"And who is this Chingachgook, of whom you talk so much, Deerslayer!" asked Hurry, as he moved off in the direction of the righted sapling; "a loping red-skin, at the best, I make no question."

"Not so, Hurry, but the best of loping red-skins, as you call 'em. If he had his rights, he would be a great chief; but, as it is, he is only a brave and just-minded Delaware; respected, and even obeyed in some things,'tis true, but of a fallen race, and belonging to a fallen people. Ah! Harry March, 'twould warm the heart within you to sit in their lodges of a winter's night, and listen to the traditions of the ancient greatness and power of the Mohicans!"

"Harkee, fri'nd Nathaniel," said Hurry, stopping short to face his companion, in order that his words might carry greater weight with them, "if a man believed all that other people choose to say in their own favor, he might get an oversized opinion of them, and an undersized opinion of himself. These red-skins are notable boasters, and I set down more than half of their traditions as pure talk."

"There is truth in what you say, Hurry, I'll not deny it, for I've seen it, and believe it. They do boast, but then that is a gift from natur'; and it's sinful to withstand nat'ral gifts. See; this is the spot you come to find!" This remark cut short the discourse, and both the men now gave all their attention to the object immediately before them. Deerslayer pointed out to his companion the trunk of a huge linden, or bass-wood, as it is termed in the language of the country, which had filled its time, and fallen by its own weight. This tree, like so many millions of its brethren, lay where it had fallen, and was mouldering under the slow but certain influence of the seasons. The decay, however, had attacked its centre, even while it stood erect in the pride of vegetation, bellowing out its heart, as disease sometimes destroys the vitals of animal life, even while a fair exterior is presented to the observer. As the trunk lay stretched for near a hundred feet along the earth, the quick eye of the hunter detected this peculiarity, and from this and other circumstances, he knew it to be the tree of which March was in search.

"Ay, here we have what we want," cried Hurry, looking in at the larger end of the linden; "everything is as snug as if it had been left in an old woman's cupboard. Come, lend me a hand, Deerslayer, and we'll be afloat in half an hour."

At this call the hunter joined his companion, and the two went to work deliberately and regularly, like men accustomed to the sort of thing in which they were employed. In the first place, Hurry removed some pieces of bark that lay before the large opening in the tree, and which the other declared to be disposed in a way that would have been more likely to attract attention than to conceal the cover, had any straggler passed that way. The two then drew out a bark canoe, containing its seats, paddles, and other appliances, even to fishing-lines and rods. This vessel was by no means small; but such was its comparative lightness, and so gigantic was the strength of Hurry, that the latter shouldered it with seeming ease, declining all assistance, even in the act of raising it to the awkward position in which he was obliged to hold it.

"Lead ahead, Deerslayer," said March, "and open the bushes; the rest I can do for myself."

The other obeyed, and the men left the spot, Deerslayer clearing the way for his companion, and inclining to the right or to the left, as the latter directed. In about ten minutes they both broke suddenly into the brilliant light of the sun, on a low gravelly point, that was washed by water on quite half its outline.

An exclamation of surprise broke from the lips of Deerslayer, an exclamation that was low and guardedly made, however, for his habits were much more thoughtful and regulated than those of the reckless Hurry, when on reaching the margin of the lake, he beheld the view that unexpectedly met his gaze. It was, in truth, sufficiently striking to merit a brief description. On a level with the point lay a broad sheet of water, so placid and limpid that it resembled a bed of the pure mountain atmosphere, compressed into a setting of hills and woods. Its length was about three leagues, while its breadth was irregular, expanding to half a league, or even more, opposite to the point, and contracting to less than half that distance, more to the southward. Of course, its margin was irregular, being indented by bays, and broken by many projecting, low points. At its northern, or nearest end, it was bounded by an isolated mountain, lower land falling off east and west, gracefully relieving the sweep of the outline. Still the character of the country was mountainous; high hills, or low mountains, rising abruptly from the water, on quite nine tenths of its circuit. The exceptions, indeed, only served a little to vary the scene; and even beyond the parts of the shore that were comparatively low, the background was high, though more distant.

But the most striking peculiarities of this scene were its solemn solitude and sweet repose. On all sides, wherever the eye turned, nothing met it but the mirror-like surface of the lake, the placid view of heaven, and the dense setting of woods. So rich and fleecy were the outlines of the forest, that scarce an opening could be seen, the whole visible earth, from the rounded mountain-top to the water's edge, presenting one unvaried hue of unbroken verdure. As if vegetation were not satisfied with a triumph so complete, the trees overhung the lake itself, shooting out towards the light; and there were miles along its eastern shore, where a boat might have pulled beneath the branches of dark Rembrandt-looking hemlocks, "quivering aspens," and melancholy pines. In a word, the hand of man had never yet defaced or deformed any part of this native scene, which lay bathed in the sunlight, a glorious picture of affluent forest grandeur, softened by the balminess of June, and relieved by the beautiful variety afforded by the presence of so broad an expanse of water.

"This is grand!—'tis solemn!—'tis an edication of itself, to look upon!" exclaimed Deerslayer, as he stood leaning on his rifle, and gazing to the right and left, north and south, above and beneath, in whichever direction his eye could wander; "not a tree disturbed even by red-skin hand, as I can discover, but everything left in the ordering of the Lord, to live and die according to his own designs and laws! Hurry, your Judith ought to be a moral and well disposed young woman, if she has passed half the time you mention in the centre of a spot so favored."

"That's naked truth; and yet the gal has the vagaries. All her time has not been passed here, howsoever, old Tom having the custom, afore I know'd him, of going to spend the winters in the neighborhood of the settlers, or under the guns of the forts. No, no, Jude has caught more than is for her good from the settlers, and especially from the gallantifying officers."

"If she has—if she has, Hurry, this is a school to set her mind right ag'in. But what is this I see off here, abreast of us, that seems too small for an island, and too large for a boat, though it stands in the midst of the water!

"Why, that is what these galantine gentry from the forts call Muskrat Castle; and old Tom himself will grin at the name, though it bears so hard on his own natur' and character. 'Tis the stationary house, there being two; this, which never moves, and the other, that floats, being sometimes in one part of the lake and sometimes in another. The last goes by the name of the ark, though what may be the meaning of the word is more than I can tell you."

"It must come from the missionaries, Hurry, whom I have heard speak and read of such a thing. They say that the 'arth was once covered with water, and that Noah, with his children, was saved from drowning by building a vessel called an ark, in which he embarked in season. Some of the Delawares believe this tradition, and some deny it; but it behooves you and me, as white men born, to put our faith in its truth. Do you see anything of this ark?"

"'Tis down south, no doubt, or anchored in some of the bays. But the canoe is ready, and fifteen minutes will carry two such paddles as your'n and mine to the castle."

At this suggestion, Deerslayer helped his companion to place the different articles in the canoe, which was already afloat. This was no sooner done than the two frontiermen embarked, and by a vigorous push sent the light bark some eight or ten rods from the shore. Hurry now took the seat in the stern, while Deerslayer placed himself forward, and by leisurely but steady strokes of the paddles, the canoe glided across the placid sheet, towards the extraordinary-looking structure that the former had styled Muskrat Castle. Several times the men ceased paddling, and looked about them at the scene, as new glimpses opened from behind points, enabling them to see farther down the lake, or to get broader views of the wooded mountains. The only changes, however, were in the new forms of the hills, the varying curvature of the bays, and the wider reaches of the valley south; the whole earth apparently being clothed in a gala-dress of leaves.

"This is a sight to warm the heart!" exclaimed Deerslayer, when they had thus stopped for the fourth or fifth time; "the lake seems made to let us get an insight into the noble forests; and land and water alike stand in the beauty of God's providence! Do you say, Hurry, that there is no man who calls himself lawful owner of all these glories?"

"None but the King, lad. He may pretend to some right of that natur', but he is so far away that his claim will never trouble old Tom Hutter, who has got possession, and is like to keep it as long as his life lasts. Tom is no squatter, not being on land; I call him a floater."

"I invy that man! I know it's wrong, and I strive ag'in the feelin', but I invy that man! Don't think, Hurry, that I'm consorting any plan to put myself in his moccasins, for such a thought doesn't harbor in my mind; but I can't help a little invy! 'Tis a nat'ral feelin', and the best of us are but nat'ral, a'ter all, and give way to such feelin's at times."

"You've only to marry Hetty to inherit half the estate," cried Hurry, laughing; "the gal is comely; nay, if it wasn't for her sister's beauty she would be even handsome; and then her wits are so small that you may easily convart her into one of your own way of thinking, in all things. Do you take Hetty off the old fellow's hands, and I'll engage he'll give you an interest in every deer you can knock over within five miles of his lake."

"Does game abound!" suddenly demanded the other, who paid but little attention to March's raillery.

"It has the country to itself. Scarce a trigger is pulled on it; and as for the trappers, this is not a region they greatly frequent. I ought not to be so much here myself, but Jude pulls one way, while the beaver pulls another. More than a hundred Spanish dollars has that creatur' cost me the last two seasons, and yet I could not forego the wish to look upon her face once more."

"Do the redmen often visit this lake, Hurry?" continued Deerslayer, pursuing his own train of thought.

"Why, they come and go; sometimes in parties, and sometimes singly. The country seems to belong to no native tribe in particular; and so it has fallen into the hands of the Hutter tribe. The old man tells me that some sharp ones have been wheedling the Mohawks for an Indian deed, in order to get a title out of the colony; but nothing has come of it, seeing that no one heavy enough for such a trade has yet meddled with the matter. The hunters have a good life-lease still of this wilderness."

"So much the better, so much the better, Hurry. If I was King of England, the man that felled one of these trees without good occasion for the timber, should be banished to a desarted and forlorn region, in which no fourfooted animal ever trod. Right glad am I that Chingachgook app'inted our meeting on this lake, for hitherto eye of mine never looked on such a glorious spectacle."

"That's because you've kept so much among the Delawares, in whose country there are no lakes. Now, farther north and farther west these bits of water abound; and you're young, and may yet live to see 'em. But though there be other lakes, Deerslayer, there's no other Judith Hutter!"

At this remark his companion smiled, and then he dropped his paddle into the water, as if in consideration of a lover's haste. Both now pulled vigorously until they got within a hundred yards of the "castle," as Hurry familiarly called the house of Hutter, when they again ceased paddling; the admirer of Judith restraining his impatience the more readily, as he perceived that the building was untenanted, at the moment. This new pause was to enable Deerslayer to survey the singular edifice, which was of a construction so novel as to merit a particular description.

Muskrat Castle, as the house had been facetiously named by some waggish officer, stood in the open lake, at a distance of fully a quarter of a mile from the nearest shore. On every other side the water extended much farther, the precise position being distant about two miles from the northern end of the sheet, and near, if not quite, a mile from its eastern shore. As there was not the smallest appearance of any island, but the house stood on piles, with the water flowing beneath it, and Deerslayer had already discovered that the lake was of a great depth, he was fain to ask an explanation of this singular circumstance. Hurry solved the difficulty by telling him that on this spot alone, a long, narrow shoal, which extended for a few hundred yards in a north and south direction, rose within six or eight feet of the surface of the lake, and that Hutter had driven piles into it, and placed his habitation on them, for the purpose of security.

"The old fellow was burnt out three times, atween the Indians and the hunters; and in one affray with the red-skins he lost his only son, since which time he has taken to the water for safety. No one can attack him here, without coming in a boat, and the plunder and scalps would scarce be worth the trouble of digging out canoes. Then it's by no means sartain which would whip in such a scrimmage, for old Tom is well supplied with arms and ammunition, and the castle, as you may see, is a tight breastwork ag'in light shot."

Deerslayer had some theoretical knowledge of frontier warfare, though he had never yet been called on to raise his hand in anger against a fellow-creature. He saw that Hurry did not overrate the strength of this position in a military point of view, since it would not be easy to attack it without exposing the assailants to the fire of the besieged. A good deal of art had also been manifested in the disposition of the timber of which the building was constructed and which afforded a protection much greater than was usual to the ordinary log-cabins of the frontier. The sides and ends were composed of the trunks of large pines, cut about nine feet long, and placed upright, instead of being laid horizontally, as was the practice of the country. These logs were squared on three sides, and had large tenons on each end. Massive sills were secured on the heads of the piles, with suitable grooves dug out of their upper surfaces, which had been squared for the purpose, and the lower tenons of the upright pieces were placed in these grooves, giving them secure fastening below. Plates had been laid on the upper ends of the upright logs, and were kept in their places by a similar contrivance; the several corners of the structure being well fastened by scarfing and pinning the sills and plates. The doors were made of smaller logs, similarly squared, and the roof was composed of light poles, firmly united, and well covered with bark.

The effect of this ingenious arrangement was to give its owner a house that could be approached only by water, the sides of which were composed of logs closely wedged together, which were two feet thick in their thinnest parts, and which could be separated only by a deliberate and laborious use of human hands, or by the slow operation of time. The outer surface of the building was rude and uneven, the logs being of unequal sizes; but the squared surfaces within gave both the sides and door as uniform an appearance as was desired, either for use or show. The chimney was not the least singular portion of the castle, as Hurry made his companion observe, while he explained the process by which it had been made. The material was a stiff clay, properly worked, which had been put together in a mould of sticks, and suffered to harden, a foot or two at a time, commencing at the bottom. When the entire chimney had thus been raised, and had been properly bound in with outward props, a brisk fire was kindled, and kept going until it was burned to something like a brick-red. This had not been an easy operation, nor had it succeeded entirely; but by dint of filling the cracks with fresh clay, a safe fireplace and chimney had been obtained in the end. This part of the work stood on the log-door, secured beneath by an extra pile. There were a few other peculiarities about this dwelling, which will better appear in the course of the narrative.

"Old Tom is full of contrivances," added Hurry, "and he set his heart on the success of his chimney, which threatened more than once to give out altogether; but perseverance will even overcome smoke; and now he has a comfortable cabin of it, though it did promise, at one time, to be a chinky sort of a flue to carry flames and fire."

"You seem to know the whole history of the castle, Hurry, chimney and sides," said Deerslayer, smiling; "is love so overcoming that it causes a man to study the story of his sweetheart's habitation?"

"Partly that, lad, and partly eyesight," returned the good-natured giant, laughing; "there was a large gang of us in the lake, the summer the old fellow built, and we helped him along with the job. I raised no small part of the weight of them uprights with my own shoulders, and the axes flew, I can inform you, Master Natty, while we were bee-ing it among the trees ashore. The old devil is no way stingy about food, and as we had often eat at his hearth, we thought we would just house him comfortably, afore we went to Albany with our skins. Yes, many is the meal I've swallowed in Tom Hutter's cabins; and Hetty, though so weak in the way of wits, has a wonderful particular way about a frying-pan or a gridiron!

"While the parties were thus discoursing, the canoe had been gradually drawing nearer to the "castle," and was now so close as to require but a single stroke of a paddle to reach the landing. This was at a floored platform in front of the entrance, that might have been some twenty feet square.

"Old Tom calls this sort of a wharf his door-yard," observed Hurry, as he fastened the canoe, after he and his Companion had left it: "and the gallants from the forts have named it the castle court though what a 'court' can have to do here is more than I can tell you, seeing that there is no law. 'Tis as I supposed; not a soul within, but the whole family is off on a v'y'ge of discovery!"

While Hurry was bustling about the "door-yard," examining the fishing-spears, rods, nets, and other similar appliances of a frontier cabin, Deerslayer, whose manner was altogether more rebuked and quiet, entered the building with a curiosity that was not usually exhibited by one so long trained in Indian habits. The interior of the "castle" was as faultlessly neat as its exterior was novel. The entire space, some twenty feet by forty, was subdivided into several small sleeping-rooms; the apartment into which he first entered, serving equally for the ordinary uses of its inmates, and for a kitchen. The furniture was of the strange mixture that it is not uncommon to find in the remotely situated log-tenements of the interior. Most of it was rude, and to the last degree rustic; but there was a clock, with a handsome case of dark wood, in a corner, and two or three chairs, with a table and bureau, that had evidently come from some dwelling of more than usual pretension. The clock was industriously ticking, but its leaden-looking hands did no discredit to their dull aspect, for they pointed to the hour of eleven, though the sun plainly showed it was some time past the turn of the day. There was also a dark, massive chest. The kitchen utensils were of the simplest kind, and far from numerous, but every article was in its place, and showed the nicest care in its condition.

After Deerslayer had cast a look about him in the outer room, he raised a wooden latch, and entered a narrow passage that divided the inner end of the house into two equal parts. Frontier usages being no way scrupulous, and his curiosity being strongly excited, the young man now opened a door, and found himself in a bedroom. A single glance sufficed to show that the apartment belonged to females. The bed was of the feathers of wild geese, and filled nearly to overflowing; but it lay in a rude bunk, raised only a foot from the door. On one side of it were arranged, on pegs, various dresses, of a quality much superior to what one would expect to meet in such a place, with ribbons and other similar articles to correspond. Pretty shoes, with handsome silver buckles, such as were then worn by females in easy circumstances, were not wanting; and no less than six fans, of gay colors, were placed half open, in a way to catch the eye by their conceits and hues. Even the pillow, on this side of the bed, was covered with finer linen than its companion, and it was ornamented with a small ruffle. A cap, coquettishly decorated with ribbons, hung above it, and a pair of long gloves, such as were rarely used in those days by persons of the laboring classes, were pinned ostentatiously to it, as if with an intention to exhibit them there, if they could not be shown on the owner's arms.

All this Deerslayer saw, and noted with a degree of minuteness that would have done credit to the habitual observation of his friends, the Delawares. Nor did he fail to perceive the distinction that existed between the appearances on the different sides of the bed, the head of which stood against the wall. On that opposite to the one just described, everything was homely and uninviting, except through its perfect neatness. The few garments that were hanging from the pegs were of the coarsest materials and of the commonest forms, while nothing seemed made for show. Of ribbons there was not one; nor was there either cap or kerchief beyond those which Hutter's daughters might be fairly entitled to wear.

It was now several years since Deerslayer had been in a spot especially devoted to the uses of females of his own color and race. The sight brought back to his mind a rush of childish recollections; and he lingered in the room with a tenderness of feeling to which he had long been a stranger. He bethought him of his mother, whose homely vestments he remembered to have seen hanging on pegs like those which he felt must belong to Hetty Hutter; and he bethought himself of a sister, whose incipient and native taste for finery had exhibited itself somewhat in the manner of that of Judith, though necessarily in a less degree. These little resemblances opened a long hidden vein of sensations; and as he quitted the room, it was with a saddened mien. He looked no further, but returned slowly and thoughtfully towards the "door-yard."

"If Old Tom has taken to a new calling, and has been trying his hand at the traps," cried Hurry, who had been coolly examining the borderer's implements; "if that is his humor, and you're disposed to remain in these parts, we can make an oncommon comfortable season of it; for, while the old man and I out-knowledge the beaver, you can fish, and knock down the deer, to keep body and soul together. I've always give the poorest hunters half a share, but one as actyve and sartain as yourself might expect a full one."

"Thank'ee, Hurry; thank'ee, with all my heart—but I do a little beavering for myself as occasions offer. 'Tis true, the Delawares call me Deerslayer, but it's not so much because I'm pretty fatal with the venison as because that while I kill so many bucks and does, I've never yet taken the life of a fellow-creatur'. They say their traditions do not tell of another who had shed so much blood of animals that had not shed the blood of man."

"I hope they don't account you chicken-hearted, lad! A faint-hearted man is like a no-tailed beaver."

"I don't believe, Hurry, that they account me as out-of-the-way timorsome, even though they may not account me as out-of-the-way brave. But I'm not quarrelsome; and that goes a great way towards keeping blood off the hands, among the hunters and red-skins; and then, Harry March, it keeps blood off the conscience, too."

"Well, for my part I account game, a red-skin, and a Frenchman as pretty much the same thing; though I'm as onquarrelsome a man, too, as there is in all the colonies. I despise a quarreller as I do a cur-dog; but one has no need to be over-scrupulsome when it's the right time to show the flint."

"I look upon him as the most of a man who acts nearest the right, Hurry. But this is a glorious spot, and my eyes never a-weary looking at it!"

"'Tis your first acquaintance with a lake; and these ideas come over us all at such times. Lakes have a gentle character, as I say, being pretty much water and land, and points and bays."

As this definition by no means met the feelings that were uppermost in the mind of the young hunter, he made no immediate answer, but stood gazing at the dark hills and the glassy water in silent enjoyment.

"Have the Governor's or the King's people given this lake a name?" he suddenly asked, as if struck with a new idea. "If they've not begun to blaze their trees, and set up their compasses, and line off their maps, it's likely they've not bethought them to disturb natur' with a name."

"They've not got to that, yet; and the last time I went in with skins, one of the King's surveyors was questioning me consarning all the region hereabouts. He had heard that there was a lake in this quarter, and had got some general notions about it, such as that there was water and hills; but how much of either, he know'd no more than you know of the Mohawk tongue. I didn't open the trap any wider than was necessary, giving him but poor encouragement in the way of farms and clearings. In short, I left on his mind some such opinion of this country, as a man gets of a spring of dirty water, with a path to it that is so muddy that one mires afore he sets out. He told me they hadn't got the spot down yet on their maps, though I conclude that is a mistake, for he showed me his parchment, and there is a lake down on it, where there is no lake in fact, and which is about fifty miles from the place where it ought to be, if they meant it for this. I don't think my account will encourage him to mark down another, by way of improvement."

Here Hurry laughed heartily, such tricks being particularly grateful to a set of men who dreaded the approaches of civilization as a curtailment of their own lawless empire. The egregious errors that existed in the maps of the day, all of which were made in Europe, were, moreover, a standing topic of ridicule among them; for, if they had not science enough to make any better themselves, they had sufficient local information to detect the gross blunders contained in those that existed. Any one who will take the trouble to compare these unanswerable evidences of the topographical skill of our fathers a century since, with the more accurate sketches of our own time, will at once perceive that the men of the woods had a sufficient justification for all their criticism on this branch of the skill of the colonial governments, which did not at all hesitate to place a river or a lake a degree or two out of the way, even though they lay within a day's march of the inhabited parts of the country.

"I'm glad it has no name," resumed Deerslayer, "or at least, no pale-face name; for their christenings always foretell waste and destruction. No doubt, howsoever, the red-skins have their modes of knowing it, and the hunters and trappers, too; they are likely to call the place by something reasonable and resembling."

"As for the tribes, each has its tongue, and its own way of calling things; and they treat this part of the world just as they treat all others. Among ourselves, we've got to calling the place the 'Glimmerglass,' seeing that its whole basin is so often hinged with pines, cast upward to its face as if it would throw back the hills that hang over it."

"There is an outlet, I know, for all lakes have outlets, and the rock at which I am to meet Chingachgook stands near an outlet. Has that no colony-name yet?"

"In that particular they've got the advantage of us, having one end, and that the biggest, in their own keeping: they've given it a name which has found its way up to its source; names nat'rally working up stream. No doubt, Deerslayer, you've seen the Susquehannah, down in the Delaware country?"

"That have I, and hunted along its banks a hundred times."

"That and this are the same in fact, and, I suppose, the same in sound. I am glad they've been compelled to keep the redmen's name, for it would be too hard to rob them of both land and name!"

Deerslayer made no answer; but he stood leaning on his rifle, gazing at the view which so much delighted him. The reader is not to suppose, however, that it was the picturesque alone which so strongly attracted his attention. The spot was very lovely, of a truth, and it was then seen in one of its most favorable moments, the surface of the lake being as smooth as glass and as limpid as pure air, throwing back the mountains, clothed in dark pines, along the whole of its eastern boundary, the points thrusting forward their trees even to nearly horizontal lines, while the bays were seen glittering through an occasional arch beneath, left by a vault fretted with branches and leaves. It was the air of deep repose—the solitudes, that spoke of scenes and forests untouched by the hands of man—the reign of nature, in a word, that gave so much pure delight to one of his habits and turn of mind. Still, he felt, though it was unconsciously, like a poet also. If he found a pleasure in studying this large, and to him unusual opening into the mysteries and forms of the woods, as one is gratified in getting broader views of any subject that has long occupied his thoughts, he was not insensible to the innate loveliness of such a landscape neither, but felt a portion of that soothing of the spirit which is a common attendant of a scene so thoroughly pervaded by the holy cairn of nature.

CHAPTER III.

"Come, shall we go and kill us venison?
And yet it irks me, the poor dappled foals,—
Being native burghers of this desert city,—
Should, in their own confines, with forked heads
Have their round haunches gored."

As You Like It, II.i.21–25

Hurry Harry thought more of the beauties of Judith Hutter than of those of the Glimmerglass and its accompanying scenery. As soon as he had taken a sufficiently intimate survey of floating Tom's implements, therefore, he summoned his companion to the canoe, that they might go down the lake in quest of the family. Previously to embarking, however, Hurry carefully examined the whole of the northern end of the water with an indifferent ship's glass, that formed a part of Hutter's effects. In this scrutiny, no part of the shore was overlooked; the bays and points in particular being subjected to a closer inquiry than the rest of the wooded boundary.

"'Tis as I thought," said Hurry, laying aside the glass, "the old fellow is drifting about the south end this fine weather, and has left the castle to defend itself. Well, now we know that he is not up this-a-way, 'twill be but a small matter to paddle down and hunt him up in his hiding-place."

"Does Master Hutter think it necessary to burrow on this lake?" inquired Deerslayer, as he followed his companion into the canoe; "to my eye it is such a solitude as one might open his whole soul in, and fear no one to disarrange his thoughts or his worship."

"You forget your friends the Mingos, and all the French savages. Is there a spot on 'arth, Deerslayer, to which them disquiet rogues don't go? Where is the lake, or even the deer lick, that the blackguards don't find out, and having found out, don't, sooner or later, discolour its water with blood."

"I hear no good character of 'em, sartainly, friend Hurry, though I've never been called on, yet, to meet them, or any other mortal, on the warpath. I dare to say that such a lovely spot as this, would not be likely to be overlooked by such plunderers, for, though I've not been in the way of quarreling with them tribes myself, the Delawares give me such an account of 'em that I've pretty much set 'em down in my own mind, as thorough miscreants."

"You may do that with a safe conscience, or for that matter, any other savage you may happen to meet."

Here Deerslayer protested, and as they went paddling down the lake, a hot discussion was maintained concerning the respective merits of the pale-faces and the red-skins. Hurry had all the prejudices and antipathies of a white hunter, who generally regards the Indian as a sort of natural competitor, and not unfrequently as a natural enemy. As a matter of course, he was loud, clamorous, dogmatical and not very argumentative. Deerslayer, on the other hand, manifested a very different temper, proving by the moderation of his language, the fairness of his views, and the simplicity of his distinctions, that he possessed every disposition to hear reason, a strong, innate desire to do justice, and an ingenuousness that was singularly indisposed to have recourse to sophism to maintain an argument; or to defend a prejudice. Still he was not altogether free from the influence of the latter feeling. This tyrant of the human mind, which ruses on it prey through a thousand avenues, almost as soon as men begin to think and feel, and which seldom relinquishes its iron sway until they cease to do either, had made some impression on even the just propensities of this individual, who probably offered in these particulars, a fair specimen of what absence from bad example, the want of temptation to go wrong, and native good feeling can render youth.

"You will allow, Deerslayer, that a Mingo is more than half devil," cried Hurry, following up the discussion with an animation that touched closely on ferocity, "though you want to over-persuade me that the Delaware tribe is pretty much made up of angels. Now, I gainsay that proposal, consarning white men, even. All white men are not faultless, and therefore all Indians can't be faultless. And so your argument is out at the elbow in the start. But this is what I call reason. Here's three colors on 'arth: white, black, and red. White is the highest color, and therefore the best man; black comes next, and is put to live in the neighborhood of the white man, as tolerable, and fit to be made use of; and red comes last, which shows that those that made 'em never expected an Indian to be accounted as more than half human."

"God made all three alike, Hurry."

"Alike! Do you call a nigger like a white man, or me like an Indian?"

"You go off at half-cock, and don't hear me out. God made us all, white, black, and red; and, no doubt, had his own wise intentions in coloring us differently. Still, he made us, in the main, much the same in feelin's; though I'll not deny that he gave each race its gifts. A white man's gifts are Christianized, while a red-skin's are more for the wilderness. Thus, it would be a great offence for a white man to scalp the dead; whereas it's a signal vartue in an Indian. Then ag'in, a white man cannot amboosh women and children in war, while a red-skin may. 'Tis cruel work, I'll allow; but for them it's lawful work; while for us, it would be grievous work."

"That depends on your inimy. As for scalping, or even skinning a savage, I look upon them pretty much the same as cutting off the ears of wolves for the bounty, or stripping a bear of its hide. And then you're out significantly, as to taking the poll of a red-skin in hand, seeing that the very colony has offered a bounty for the job; all the same as it pays for wolves' ears and crows' heads."

"Ay, and a bad business it is, Hurry. Even the Indians themselves cry shame on it, seeing it's ag'in a white man's gifts. I do not pretend that all that white men do, is properly Christianized, and according to the lights given them, for then they would be what they ought to be; which we know they are not; but I will maintain that tradition, and use, and color, and laws, make such a difference in races as to amount to gifts. I do not deny that there are tribes among the Indians that are nat'rally pervarse and wicked, as there are nations among the whites. Now, I account the Mingos as belonging to the first, and the Frenchers, in the Canadas, to the last. In a state of lawful warfare, such as we have lately got into, it is a duty to keep down all compassionate feelin's, so far as life goes, ag'in either; but when it comes to scalps, it's a very different matter."

"Just hearken to reason, if you please, Deerslayer, and tell me if the colony can make an onlawful law? Isn't an onlawful law more ag'in natur' than scalpin' a savage? A law can no more be onlawful, than truth can be a lie."

"That sounds reasonable; but it has a most onreasonable bearing, Hurry. Laws don't all come from the same quarter. God has given us his'n, and some come from the colony, and others come from the King and Parliament. When the colony's laws, or even the King's laws, run ag'in the laws of God, they get to be onlawful, and ought not to be obeyed. I hold to a white man's respecting white laws, so long as they do not cross the track of a law comin' from a higher authority; and for a red man to obey his own red-skin usages, under the same privilege. But, 't is useless talking, as each man will think fir himself, and have his say agreeable to his thoughts. Let us keep a good lookout for your friend Floating Tom, lest we pass him, as he lies hidden under this bushy shore."

Deerslayer had not named the borders of the lake amiss. Along their whole length, the smaller trees overhung the water, with their branches often dipping in the transparent element. The banks were steep, even from the narrow strand; and, as vegetation invariably struggles towards the light, the effect was precisely that at which the lover of the picturesque would have aimed, had the ordering of this glorious setting of forest been submitted to his control. The points and bays, too, were sufficiently numerous to render the outline broken and diversified. As the canoe kept close along the western side of the lake, with a view, as Hurry had explained to his companion, of reconnoitering for enemies, before he trusted himself too openly in sight, the expectations of the two adventurers were kept constantly on the stretch, as neither could foretell what the next turning of a point might reveal. Their progress was swift, the gigantic strength of Hurry enabling him to play with the light bark as if it had been a feather, while the skill of his companion almost equalized their usefulness, notwithstanding the disparity in natural means.

Each time the canoe passed a point, Hurry turned a look behind him, expecting to see the "ark" anchored, or beached in the bay. He was fated to be disappointed, however; and they had got within a mile of the southern end of the lake, or a distance of quite two leagues from the "castle," which was now hidden from view by half a dozen intervening projections of the land, when he suddenly ceased paddling, as if uncertain in what direction next to steer.

"It is possible that the old chap has dropped into the river," said Hurry, after looking carefully along the whole of the eastern shore, which was about a mile distant, and open to his scrutiny for more than half its length; "for he has taken to trapping considerable, of late, and, barring flood-wood, he might drop down it a mile or so; though he would have a most scratching time in getting back again!"

"Where is this outlet?" asked Deerslayer; "I see no opening in the banks or the trees, that looks as if it would let a river like the Susquehannah run through it."

"Ay, Deerslayer, rivers are like human mortals; having small beginnings, and ending with broad shoulders and wide mouths. You don't see the outlet, because it passes atween high, steep banks; and the pines, and hemlocks and bass-woods hang over it, as a roof hangs over a house. If old Tom is not in the 'Rat's Cove,' he must have burrowed in the river; we'll look for him first in the cove, and then we'll cross to the outlet."

As they proceeded, Hurry explained that there was a shallow bay, formed by a long, low point, that had got the name of the "Rat's Cove," from the circumstance of its being a favorite haunt of the muskrat; and which offered so complete a cover for the "ark," that its owner was fond of lying in it, whenever he found it convenient.

"As a man never knows who may be his visitors, in this part of the country," continued Hurry, "it's a great advantage to get a good look at 'em afore they come too near. Now it's war, such caution is more than commonly useful, since a Canada man or a Mingo might get into his hut afore he invited 'em. But Hutter is a first-rate look-outer, and can pretty much scent danger, as a hound scents the deer."

"I should think the castle so open, that it would be sartain to draw inimies, if any happened to find the lake; a thing onlikely enough, I will allow, as it's off the trail of the forts and settlements."

"Why, Deerslayer, I've got to believe that a man meets with inimies easier than he meets with fri'nds. It's skearful to think for how many causes one gets to be your inimy, and for how few your fri'nd. Some take up the hatchet because you don't think just as they think; other some because you run ahead of 'em in the same idees; and I once know'd a vagabond that quarrelled with a fri'nd because he didn't think him handsome. Now, you're no monument in the way of beauty, yourself, Deerslayer, and yet you wouldn't be so onreasonable as to become my inimy for just saying so."

"I'm as the Lord made me; and I wish to be accounted no better, nor any worse. Good looks I may not have; that is to say, to a degree that the light-minded and vain crave; but I hope I'm not altogether without some ricommend in the way of good conduct. There's few nobler looking men to be seen than yourself, Hurry; and I know that I am not to expect any to turn their eyes on me, when such a one as you can be gazed on; but I do not know that a hunter is less expart with the rifle, or less to be relied on for food, because he doesn't wish to stop at every shining spring he may meet, to study his own countenance in the water."

Here Hurry burst into a fit of loud laughter; for while he was too reckless to care much about his own manifest physical superiority, he was well aware of it, and, like most men who derive an advantage from the accidents of birth or nature, he was apt to think complacently on the subject, whenever it happened to cross his mind.

"No, no, Deerslayer, you're no beauty, as you will own yourself, if you'll look over the side of the canoe," he cried; "Jude will say that to your face, if you start her, for a tarter tongue isn't to be found in any gal's head, in or out of the settlements, if you provoke her to use it. My advice to you is, never to aggravate Judith; though you may tell anything to Hetty, and she'll take it as meek as a lamb. No, Jude will be just as like as not to tell you her opinion consarning your looks."

"And if she does, Hurry, she will tell me no more than you have said already."

"You're not thick'ning up about a small remark, I hope, Deerslayer, when no harm is meant. You are not a beauty, as you must know, and why shouldn't fri'nds tell each other these little trifles? If you was handsome, or ever like to be, I'd be one of the first to tell you of it; and that ought to content you. Now, if Jude was to tell me that I'm as ugly as a sinner, I'd take it as a sort of obligation, and try not to believe her."

"It's easy for them that natur' has favored, to jest about such matters, Hurry, though it is sometimes hard for others. I'll not deny but I've had my cravings towards good looks; yes, I have; but then I've always been able to get them down by considering how many I've known with fair outsides, who have had nothing to boast of inwardly. I'll not deny, Hurry, that I often wish I'd been created more comely to the eye, and more like such a one as yourself in them particulars; but then I get the feelin' under by remembering how much better off I am, in a great many respects, than some fellow-mortals. I might have been born lame, and onfit even for a squirrel-hunt, or blind, which would have made me a burden on myself as well as on my fri'nds; or without hearing, which would have totally onqualified me for ever campaigning or scouting; which I look forward to as part of a man's duty in troublesome times. Yes, yes; it's not pleasant, I will allow, to see them that's more comely, and more sought a'ter, and honored than yourself; but it may all be borne, if a man looks the evil in the face, and don't mistake his gifts and his obligations."

Hurry, in the main, was a good-hearted as well as good-natured fellow; and the self-abasement of his companion completely got the better of the passing feeling of personal vanity. He regretted the allusion he had made to the other's appearance, and endeavored to express as much, though it was done in the uncouth manner that belonged to the habits and opinions of the frontier.

"I meant no harm, Deerslayer," he answered, in a deprecating manner, "and hope you'll forget what I've said. If you're not downright handsome, you've a sartain look that says, plainer than any words, that all's right within. Then you set no value by looks, and will the sooner forgive any little slight to your appearance. I will not say that Jude will greatly admire you, for that might raise hopes that would only breed disapp'intment; but there's Hetty, now, would be just as likely to find satisfaction in looking at you, as in looking at any other man. Then you're altogether too grave and considerate-like, to care much about Judith; for, though the gal is oncommon, she is so general in her admiration, that a man need not be exalted because she happens to smile. I sometimes think the hussy loves herself better than she does anything else breathin'."

"If she did, Hurry, she'd do no more, I'm afeard, than most queens on their thrones, and ladies in the towns," answered Deerslayer, smiling, and turning back towards his companion with every trace of feeling banished from his honest-looking and frank countenance. "I never yet know'd even a Delaware of whom you might not say that much. But here is the end of the long p'int you mentioned, and the 'Rat's Cove' can't be far off."

This point, instead of thrusting itself forward, like all the others, ran in a line with the main shore of the lake, which here swept within it, in a deep and retired bay, circling round south again, at the distance of a quarter of a mile, and crossed the valley, forming the southern termination of the water. In this bay Hurry felt almost certain of finding the ark, since, anchored behind the trees that covered the narrow strip of the point, it might have lain concealed from prying eyes an entire summer. So complete, indeed, was the cover, in this spot, that a boat hauled close to the beach, within the point, and near the bottom of the bay, could by any possibility be seen from only one direction; and that was from a densely wooded shore within the sweep of the water, where strangers would be little apt to go.

"We shall soon see the ark," said Hurry, as the canoe glided round the extremity of the point, where the water was so deep as actually to appear black; "he loves to burrow up among the rushes, and we shall be in his nest in five minutes, although the old fellow may be off among the traps himself."

March proved a false prophet. The canoe completely doubled the point, so as to enable the two travellers to command a view of the whole cove or bay, for it was more properly the last, and no object, but those that nature had placed there, became visible. The placid water swept round in a graceful curve, the rushes bent gently towards its surface, and the trees overhung it as usual; but all lay in the soothing and sublime solitude of a wilderness. The scene was such as a poet or an artist would have delighted in, but it had no charm for Hurry Harry, who was burning with impatience to get a sight of his light-minded beauty.

The motion of the canoe had been attended with little or no noise, the frontiermen habitually getting accustomed to caution in most of their movements, and it now lay on the glassy water appearing to float in air, partaking of the breathing stillness that seemed to pervade the entire scene. At this instant a dry stick was heard cracking on the narrow strip of land that concealed the bay from the open lake. Both the adventurers started, and each extended a hand towards his rifle, the weapon never being out of reach of the arm.

"'Twas too heavy for any light creatur'," whispered Hurry, "and it sounded like the tread of a man!"

"Not so—not so," returned Deerslayer; "'t was, as you say, too heavy for one, but it was too light for the other. Put your paddle in the water, and send the canoe in, to that log; I'll land and cut off the creatur's retreat up the p'int, be it a Mingo, or be it a muskrat."

As Hurry complied, Deerslayer was soon on the shore, advancing into the thicket with a moccasined foot, and a caution that prevented the least noise. In a minute he was in the centre of the narrow strip of land, and moving slowly down towards its end, the bushes rendering extreme watchfulness necessary. Just as he reached the centre of the thicket the dried twigs cracked again, and the noise was repeated at short intervals, as if some creature having life walked slowly towards the point. Hurry heard these sounds also, and pushing the canoe off into the bay, he seized his rifle to watch the result. A breathless minute succeeded, after which a noble buck walked out of the thicket, proceeded with a stately step to the sandy extremity of the point, and began to slake his thirst from the water of the lake. Hurry hesitated an instant; then raising his rifle hastily to his shoulder, he took sight and fired. The effect of this sudden interruption of the solemn stillness of such a scene was not its least striking peculiarity. The report of the weapon had the usual sharp, short sound of the rifle: but when a few moments of silence had succeeded the sudden crack, during which the noise was floating in air across the water, it reached the rocks of the opposite mountain, where the vibrations accumulated, and were rolled from cavity to cavity for miles along the hills, seeming to awaken the sleeping thunders of the woods. The buck merely shook his head at the report of the rifle and the whistling of the bullet, for never before had he come in contact with man; but the echoes of the hills awakened his distrust, and leaping forward, with his four legs drawn under his body, he fell at once into deep water, and began to swim towards the foot of the lake. Hurry shouted and dashed forward in chase, and for one or two minutes the water foamed around the pursuer and the pursued. The former was dashing past the point, when Deerslayer appeared on the sand and signed to him to return.

"'Twas inconsiderate to pull a trigger, afore we had reconn'itred the shore, and made sartain that no inimies harbored near it," said the latter, as his companion slowly and reluctantly complied. "This much I have l'arned from the Delawares, in the way of schooling and traditions, even though I've never yet been on a war-path. And, moreover, venison can hardly be called in season now, and we do not want for food. They call me Deerslayer, I'll own, and perhaps I desarve the name, in the way of understanding the creatur's habits, as well as for some sartainty in the aim, but they can't accuse me of killing an animal when there is no occasion for the meat, or the skin. I may be a slayer, it's true, but I'm no slaughterer."

"'Twas an awful mistake to miss that buck!" exclaimed Hurry, doffing his cap and running his fingers through his handsome but matted curls, as if he would loosen his tangled ideas by the process. "I've not done so onhandy a thing since I was fifteen."

"Never lament it, as the creatur's death could have done neither of us any good, and might have done us harm. Them echoes are more awful in my ears, than your mistake, Hurry, for they sound like the voice of natur' calling out ag'in a wasteful and onthinking action."

"You'll hear plenty of such calls, if you tarry long in this quarter of the world, lad," returned the other laughing. "The echoes repeat pretty much all that is said or done on the Glimmerglass, in this calm summer weather. If a paddle falls you hear of it sometimes, ag'in and ag'in, as if the hills were mocking your clumsiness, and a laugh, or a whistle, comes out of them pines, when they're in the humour to speak, in a way to make you believe they can r'ally converse."

"So much the more reason for being prudent and silent. I do not think the inimy can have found their way into these hills yet, for I don't know what they are to gain by it, but all the Delawares tell me that, as courage is a warrior's first vartue, so is prudence his second. One such call from the mountains, is enough to let a whole tribe into the secret of our arrival."

"If it does no other good, it will warn old Tom to put the pot over, and let him know visiters are at hand. Come, lad; get into the canoe, and we will hunt the ark up, while there is yet day."

Deerslayer complied, and the canoe left the spot. Its head was turned diagonally across the lake, pointing towards the south-eastern curvature of the sheet. In that direction, the distance to the shore, or to the termination of the lake, on the course the two were now steering, was not quite a mile, and, their progress being always swift, it was fast lessening under the skilful, but easy sweeps of the paddles. When about half way across, a slight noise drew the eyes of the men towards the nearest land, and they saw that the buck was just emerging from the lake and wading towards the beach. In a minute, the noble animal shook the water from his flanks, gazed up ward at the covering of trees, and, bounding against the bank, plunged into the forest.

"That creatur' goes off with gratitude in his heart," said Deerslayer, "for natur' tells him he has escaped a great danger. You ought to have some of the same feelin's, Hurry, to think your eye wasn't true, or that your hand was onsteady, when no good could come of a shot that was intended onmeaningly rather than in reason."

"I deny the eye and the hand," cried March with some heat. "You've got a little character, down among the Delawares, there, for quickness and sartainty, at a deer, but I should like to see you behind one of them pines, and a full painted Mingo behind another, each with a cock'd rifle and a striving for the chance! Them's the situations, Nathaniel, to try the sight and the hand, for they begin with trying the narves. I never look upon killing a creatur' as an explite; but killing a savage is. The time will come to try your hand, now we've got to blows ag'in, and we shall soon know what a ven'son reputation can do in the field. I deny that either hand or eye was onsteady; it was all a miscalculation of the buck, which stood still when he ought to have kept in motion, and so I shot ahead of him."

"Have it your own way, Hurry; all I contend for is, that it's lucky. I dare say I shall not pull upon a human mortal as steadily or with as light a heart, as I pull upon a deer."

"Who's talking of mortals, or of human beings at all, Deerslayer? I put the matter to you on the supposition of an Injin. I dare say any man would have his feelin's when it got to be life or death, ag'in another human mortal; but there would be no such scruples in regard to an Injin; nothing but the chance of his hitting you, or the chance of your hitting him."

"I look upon the redmen to be quite as human as we are ourselves, Hurry. They have their gifts, and their religion, it's true; but that makes no difference in the end, when each will be judged according to his deeds, and not according to his skin."

"That's downright missionary, and will find little favor up in this part of the country, where the Moravians don't congregate. Now, skin makes the man. This is reason; else how are people to judge of each other. The skin is put on, over all, in order when a creatur', or a mortal, is fairly seen, you may know at once what to make of him. You know a bear from a hog, by his skin, and a gray squirrel from a black."

"True, Hurry," said the other looking back and smiling, "nevertheless, they are both squirrels."

"Who denies it? But you'll not say that a red man and a white man are both Injins?"

"But I do say they are both men. Men of different races and colors, and having different gifts and traditions, but, in the main, with the same natur'. Both have souls; and both will be held accountable for their deeds in this life."

Hurry was one of those theorists who believed in the inferiority of all the human race who were not white. His notions on the subject were not very clear, nor were his definitions at all well settled; but his opinions were none the less dogmatical or fierce. His conscience accused him of sundry lawless acts against the Indians, and he had found it an exceedingly easy mode of quieting it, by putting the whole family of redmen, incontinently, without the category of human rights. Nothing angered him sooner than to deny his proposition, more especially if the denial were accompanied by a show of plausible argument; and he did not listen to his companion's remarks with much composure of either manner or feeling.

"You're a boy, Deerslayer, misled and misconsaited by Delaware arts, and missionary ignorance," he exclaimed, with his usual indifference to the forms of speech, when excited. "You may account yourself as a red-skin's brother, but I hold'em all to be animals; with nothing human about 'em but cunning. That they have, I'll allow; but so has a fox, or even a bear. I'm older than you, and have lived longer in the woods—or, for that matter, have lived always there, and am not to be told what an Injin is or what he is not. If you wish to be considered a savage, you've only to say so, and I'll name you as such to Judith and the old man, and then we'll see how you'll like your welcome."

Here Hurry's imagination did his temper some service, since, by conjuring up the reception his semi-aquatic acquaintance would be likely to bestow on one thus introduced, he burst into a hearty fit of laughter. Deerslayer too well knew the uselessness of attempting to convince such a being of anything against his prejudices, to feel a desire to undertake the task; and he was not sorry that the approach of the canoe to the southeastern curve of the lake gave a new direction to his ideas. They were now, indeed, quite near the place that March had pointed out for the position of the outlet, and both began to look for it with a curiosity that was increased by the expectation of the ark.

It may strike the reader as a little singular, that the place where a stream of any size passed through banks that had an elevation of some twenty feet, should be a matter of doubt with men who could not now have been more than two hundred yards distant from the precise spot. It will be recollected, however, that the trees and bushes here, as elsewhere, fairly overhung the water, making such a fringe to the lake, as to conceal any little variations from its general outline.

"I've not been down at this end of the lake these two summers," said Hurry, standing up in the canoe, the better to look about him. "Ay, there's the rock, showing its chin above the water, and I know that the river begins in its neighborhood."

The men now plied the paddles again, and they were presently within a few yards of the rock, floating towards it, though their efforts were suspended. This rock was not large, being merely some five or six feet high, only half of which elevation rose above the lake. The incessant washing of the water for centuries had so rounded its summit, that it resembled a large beehive in shape, its form being more than usually regular and even. Hurry remarked, as they floated slowly past, that this rock was well known to all the Indians in that part of the country, and that they were in the practice of using it as a mark to designate the place of meeting, when separated by their hunts and marches.

"And here is the river, Deerslayer," he continued, "though so shut in by trees and bushes as to look more like an and-bush, than the outlet of such a sheet as the Glimmerglass."

Hurry had not badly described the place, which did truly seem to be a stream lying in ambush. The high banks might have been a hundred feet asunder; but, on the western side, a small bit of low land extended so far forward as to diminish the breadth of the stream to half that width.

As the bushes hung in the water beneath, and pines that had the stature of church-steeples rose in tall columns above, all inclining towards the light, until their branches intermingled, the eye, at a little distance, could not easily detect any opening in the shore, to mark the egress of the water. In the forest above, no traces of this outlet were to be seen from the lake, the whole presenting the same connected and seemingly interminable carpet of leaves. As the canoe slowly advanced, sucked in by the current, it entered beneath an arch of trees, through which the light from the heavens struggled by casual openings, faintly relieving the gloom beneath.

"This is a nat'ral and-bush," half whispered Hurry, as if he felt that the place was devoted to secrecy and watchfulness; "depend on it, old Tom has burrowed with the ark somewhere in this quarter. We will drop down with the current a short distance, and ferret him out."

"This seems no place for a vessel of any size," returned the other; "it appears to me that we shall have hardly room enough for the canoe."

Hurry laughed at the suggestion, and, as it soon appeared, with reason; for the fringe of bushes immediately on the shore of the lake was no sooner passed, than the adventurers found themselves in a narrow stream, of a sufficient depth of limpid water, with a strong current, and a canopy of leaves upheld by arches composed of the limbs of hoary trees. Bushes lined the shores, as usual, but they left sufficient space between them to admit the passage of anything that did not exceed twenty feet in width, and to allow of a perspective ahead of eight or ten times that distance.

Neither of our two adventurers used his paddle, except to keep the light bark in the centre of the current, but both watched each turning of the stream, of which there were two or three within the first hundred yards, with jealous vigilance. Turn after turn, however, was passed, and the canoe had dropped down with the current some little distance, when Hurry caught a bush, and arrested its movement so suddenly and silently as to denote some unusual motive for the act. Deerslayer laid his hand on the stock of his rifle as soon as he noted this proceeding, but it was quite as much with a hunter's habit as from any feeling of alarm.

"There the old fellow is!" whispered Hurry, pointing with a finger, and laughing heartily, though he carefully avoided making a noise, "ratting it away, just as I supposed; up to his knees in the mud and water, looking to the traps and the bait. But for the life of me I can see nothing of the ark; though I'll bet every skin I take this season, Jude isn't trusting her pretty little feet in the neighborhood of that black mud. The gal's more likely to be braiding her hair by the side of some spring, where she can see her own good looks, and collect scornful feelings ag'in us men."

"You over-judge young women—yes, you do, Hurry—who as often bethink them of their failings as they do of their perfections. I dare to say this Judith, now, is no such admirer of herself, and no such scorner of our sex as you seem to think; and that she is quite as likely to be sarving her father in the house, wherever that may be, as he is to be sarving her among the traps."

"It's a pleasure to hear truth from a man's tongue, if it be only once in a girl's life," cried a pleasant, rich, and yet soft female voice, so near the canoe as to make both the listeners start. "As for you, Master Hurry, fair words are so apt to choke you, that I no longer expect to hear them from your mouth; the last you uttered sticking in your throat, and coming near to death. But I'm glad to see you keep better society than formerly, and that they who know how to esteem and treat women are not ashamed to journey in your company."

As this was said, a singularly handsome and youthful female face was thrust through an opening in the leaves, within reach of Deerslayer's paddle. Its owner smiled graciously on the young man; and the frown that she cast on Hurry, though simulated and pettish, had the effect to render her beauty more striking, by exhibiting the play of an expressive but capricious countenance; one that seemed to change from the soft to the severe, the mirthful to the reproving, with facility and indifference.

A second look explained the nature of the surprise. Unwittingly, the men had dropped alongside of the ark, which had been purposely concealed in bushes cut and arranged for the purpose; and Judith Hutter had merely pushed aside the leaves that lay before a window, in order to show her face, and speak to them.

CHAPTER IV.

"And that timid fawn starts not with fear,
When I steal to her secret bower;
And that young May violet to me is dear,
And I visit the silent streamlet near,
To look on the lovely flower."

Bryant, "An Indian Story," ii.11–15

The ark, as the floating habitation of the Hutters was generally called, was a very simple contrivance. A large flat, or scow, composed the buoyant part of the vessel; and in its centre, occupying the whole of its breadth, and about two thirds of its length, stood a low fabric, resembling the castle in construction, though made of materials so light as barely to be bullet-proof. As the sides of the scow were a little higher than usual, and the interior of the cabin had no more elevation than was necessary for comfort, this unusual addition had neither a very clumsy nor a very obtrusive appearance. It was, in short, little more than a modern canal-boat, though more rudely constructed, of greater breadth than common, and bearing about it the signs of the wilderness, in its bark-covered posts and roof. The scow, however, had been put together with some skill, being comparatively light, for its strength, and sufficiently manageable. The cabin was divided into two apartments, one of which served for a parlor, and the sleeping-room of the father, and the other was appropriated to the uses of the daughters. A very simple arrangement sufficed for the kitchen, which was in one end of the scow, and removed from the cabin, standing in the open air; the ark being altogether a summer habitation.

The "and-bush," as Hurry in his ignorance of English termed it, is quite as easily explained. In many parts of the lake and river, where the banks were steep and high, the smaller trees and larger bushes, as has been already mentioned, fairly overhung the stream, their branches not unfrequently dipping into the water. In some instances they grew out in nearly horizontal lines, for thirty or forty feet. The water being uniformly deepest near the shores, where the banks were highest and the nearest to a perpendicular, Hutter had found no difficulty in letting the ark drop under one of these covers, where it had been anchored with a view to conceal its position; security requiring some such precautions, in his view of the case. Once beneath the trees and bushes, a few stones fastened to the ends of the branches had caused them to bend sufficiently to dip into the river; and a few severed bushes, properly disposed, did the rest. The reader has seen that this cover was so complete as to deceive two men accustomed to the woods, and who were actually in search of those it concealed; a circumstance that will be easily understood by those who are familiar with the matted and wild luxuriance of a virgin American forest, more especially in a rich soil. The discovery of the ark produced very different effects on our two adventurers.

As soon as the canoe could be got round to the proper opening, Hurry leaped on board, and in a minute was closely engaged in a gay, and a sort of recriminating discourse with Judith, apparently forgetful of the existence of all the rest of the world. Not so with Deerslayer. He entered the ark with a slow, cautious step, examining every arrangement of the cover with curious and scrutinizing eyes. It is true, he cast one admiring glance at Judith, which was extorted by her brilliant and singular beauty; but even this could detain him but a single instant from the indulgence of his interest in Hutter's contrivances. Step by step did he look into the construction of the singular abode, investigate its fastenings and strength, ascertain its means of defence, and make every inquiry that would be likely to occur to one whose thoughts dwelt principally on such expedients. Nor was the cover neglected. Of this he examined the whole minutely, his commendation escaping him more than once in audible comments. Frontier usages admitting of this familiarity, he passed through the rooms, as he had previously done at the 'Castle', and opening a door issued into the end of the scow opposite to that where he had left Hurry and Judith. Here he found the other sister, employed at some coarse needle-work, seated beneath the leafy canopy of the cover.

As Deerslayer's examination was by this time ended, he dropped the butt of his rifle, and, leaning on the barrel with both hands, he turned towards the girl with an interest the singular beauty of her sister had not awakened. He had gathered from Hurry's remarks that Hetty was considered to have less intellect than ordinarily falls to the share of human beings, and his education among Indians had taught him to treat those who were thus afflicted by Providence with more than common tenderness. Nor was there any thing in Hetty Hutter's appearance, as so often happens, to weaken the interest her situation excited. An idiot she could not properly be termed, her mind being just enough enfeebled to lose most of those traits that are connected with the more artful qualities, and to retain its ingenuousness and love of truth. It had often been remarked of this girl, by the few who had seen her, and who possessed sufficient knowledge to discriminate, that her perception of the right seemed almost intuitive, while her aversion to the wrong formed so distinctive a feature of her mind, as to surround her with an atmosphere of pure morality; peculiarities that are not infrequent with persons who are termed feeble-minded; as if God had forbidden the evil spirits to invade a precinct so defenceless, with the benign purpose of extending a direct protection to those who had been left without the usual aids of humanity. Her person, too, was agreeable, having a strong resemblance to that of her sister's, of which it was a subdued and humble copy. If it had none of the brilliancy of Judith's, the calm, quiet, almost holy expression of her meek countenance seldom failed to win on the observer, and few noted it long that did not begin to feel a deep and lasting interest in the girl. She had no colour, in common, nor was her simple mind apt to present images that caused her cheek to brighten, though she retained a modesty so innate that it almost raised her to the unsuspecting purity of a being superior to human infirmities. Guileless, innocent, and without distrust, equally by nature and from her mode of life, providence had, nevertheless shielded her from harm, by a halo of moral light, as it is said 'to temper the wind to the shorn lamb.'

"You are Hetty Hutter," said Deerslayer, in the way one puts a question unconsciously to himself, assuming a kindness of tone and manner that were singularly adapted to win the confidence of her he addressed. "Hurry Harry has told me of you, and I know you must be the child?"

"Yes, I'm Hetty Hutter" returned the girl in a low, sweet voice, which nature, aided by some education, had preserved from vulgarity of tone and utterance—"I'm Hetty; Judith Hutter's sister; and Thomas Hutter's youngest daughter."

"I know your history, then, for Hurry Harry talks considerable, and he is free of speech when he can find other people's consarns to dwell on. You pass most of your life on the lake, Hetty."

"Certainly. Mother is dead; father is gone a-trapping, and Judith and I stay at home. What's your name?"

"That's a question more easily asked than it is answered, young woman, seeing that I'm so young, and yet have borne more names than some of the greatest chiefs in all America."

"But you've got a name—you don't throw away one name, before you come honestly by another?"

"I hope not, gal—I hope not. My names have come nat'rally, and I suppose the one I bear now will be of no great lasting, since the Delawares seldom settle on a man's ra'al title, until such time as he has an opportunity of showing his true natur', in the council, or on the warpath; which has never behappened me; seeing firstly, because I'm not born a red-skin and have no right to sit in their councillings, and am much too humble to be called on for opinions from the great of my own colour; and, secondly, because this is the first war that has befallen in my time, and no inimy has yet inroaded far enough into the colony, to be reached by an arm even longer than mine."

"Tell me your names," added Hetty, looking up at him artlessly, "and, maybe, I'll tell you your character."

"There is some truth in that, I'll not deny, though it often fails. Men are deceived in other men's characters, and frequently give 'em names they by no means desarve. You can see the truth of this in the Mingo names, which, in their own tongue, signify the same things as the Delaware names,—at least, so they tell me, for I know little of that tribe, unless it be by report,—and no one can say they are as honest or as upright a nation. I put no great dependence, therefore, on names."

"Tell me all your names," repeated the girl, earnestly, for her mind was too simple to separate things from professions, and she did attach importance to a name; "I want to know what to think of you."

"Well, sartain; I've no objection, and you shall hear them all. In the first place, then, I'm Christian, and white-born, like yourself, and my parents had a name that came down from father to son, as is a part of their gifts. My father was called Bumppo; and I was named after him, of course, the given name being Nathaniel, or Natty, as most people saw fit to tarm it."

"Yes, yes—Natty—and Hetty" interrupted the girl quickly, and looking up from her work again, with a smile: "you are Natty, and I'm Hetty—though you are Bumppo, and I'm Hutter. Bumppo isn't as pretty as Hutter, is it?"

"Why, that's as people fancy. Bumppo has no lofty sound, I admit; and yet men have bumped through the world with it. I did not go by this name, howsoever, very long; for the Delawares soon found out, or thought they found out, that I was not given to lying, and they called me, firstly, 'Straight-tongue.'"

"That's a good name," interrupted Hetty, earnestly, and in a positive manner; "don't tell me there's no virtue in names!"

"I do not say that, for perhaps I desarved to be so called, lies being no favorites with me, as they are with some. After a while they found out I was quick of foot, and then they called me 'The Pigeon'; which, you know, has a swift wing, and flies in a straight line."

"That was a pretty name!" exclaimed Hetty; "pigeons are pretty birds!"

"Most things that God created are pretty in their way, my good gal, though they get to be deformed by mankind, so as to change their natur's, as well as their appearance. From carrying messages, and striking blind trails, I got at last to following the hunters, when it was thought I was quicker and surer at finding the game than most lads, and then they called me the 'Lap-ear'; as, they said, I partook of the sagacity of the hound."

"That's not so pretty," answered Hetty; "I hope you didn't keep that name long."

"Not after I was rich enough to buy a rifle," returned the other, betraying a little pride through his usually quiet and subdued manner; "then it was seen I could keep a wigwam in ven'son; and in time I got the name of 'Deerslayer,' which is that I now bear; homely as some will think it, who set more value on the scalp of a fellow-mortal than on the horns of a buck."

"Well, Deerslayer, I'm not one of them," answered Hetty, simply; "Judith likes soldiers, and flary coats, and fine feathers; but they're all naught to me. She says the officers are great, and gay, and of soft speech; but they make me shudder, for their business is to kill their fellow-creatures. I like your calling better; and your last name is a very good one—better than Natty Bumppo."

"This is nat'ral in one of your turn of mind, Hetty, and much as I should have expected. They tell me your sister is handsome—oncommon, for a mortal; and beauty is apt to seek admiration."

"Did you never see Judith?" demanded the girl, with quick earnestness; "if you never have, go at once and look at her. Even Hurry Harry isn't more pleasant to look at though she is a woman, and he is a man."

Deerslayer regarded the girl for a moment with concern. Her pale-face had flushed a little, and her eye, usually so mild and serene, brightened as she spoke, in the way to betray the inward impulses.

"Ay, Hurry Harry," he muttered to himself, as he walked through the cabin towards the other end of the boat; "this comes of good looks, if a light tongue has had no consarn in it. It's easy to see which way that poor creatur's feelin's are leanin', whatever may be the case with your Jude's."

But an interruption was put to the gallantry of Hurry, the coquetry of his intros, the thoughts of Deerslayer, and the gentle feelings of Hetty, by the sudden appearance of the canoe of the ark's owner, in the narrow opening among the bushes that served as a sort of moat to his position. It would seem that Hutter, or Floating Tom, as he was familiarly called by all the hunters who knew his habits, recognized the canoe of Hurry, for he expressed no surprise at finding him in the scow. On the contrary, his reception was such as to denote not only gratification, but a pleasure, mingled with a little disappointment at his not having made his appearance some days sooner.

"I looked for you last week," he said, in a half-grumbling, half-welcoming manner; "and was disappointed uncommonly that you didn't arrive. There came a runner through, to warn all the trappers and hunters that the colony and the Canadas were again in trouble; and I felt lonesome, up in these mountains, with three scalps to see to, and only one pair of hands to protect them."

"That's reasonable," returned March; "and 't was feeling like a parent. No doubt, if I had two such darters as Judith and Hetty, my exper'ence would tell the same story, though in gin'ral I am just as well satisfied with having the nearest neighbor fifty miles off, as when he is within call."

"Notwithstanding, you didn't choose to come into the wilderness alone, now you knew that the Canada savages are likely to be stirring," returned Hutter, giving a sort of distrustful, and at the same time inquiring glance at Deerslayer.

"Why should I? They say a bad companion, on a journey, helps to shorten the path; and this young man I account to be a reasonably good one. This is Deerslayer, old Tom, a noted hunter among the Delawares, and Christian-born, and Christian-edicated, too, like you and me. The lad is not parfect, perhaps, but there's worse men in the country that he came from, and it's likely he'll find some that's no better, in this part of the world. Should we have occasion to defend our traps, and the territory, he'll be useful in feeding us all; for he's a reg'lar dealer in ven'son."

"Young man, you are welcome," growled Tom, thrusting a hard, bony hand towards the youth, as a pledge of his sincerity; "in such times, a white face is a friend's, and I count on you as a support. Children sometimes make a stout heart feeble, and these two daughters of mine give me more concern than all my traps, and skins, and rights in the country."

"That's nat'ral!" cried Hurry. "Yes, Deerslayer, you and I don't know it yet by experience; but, on the whole, I consider that as nat'ral. If we had darters, it's more than probable we should have some such feelin's; and I honor the man that owns 'em. As for Judith, old man, I enlist, at once, as her soldier, and here is Deerslayer to help you to take care of Hetty."

"Many thanks to you, Master March," returned the beauty, in a full, rich voice, and with an accuracy of intonation and utterance that she shared in common with her sister, and which showed that she had been better taught than her father's life and appearance would give reason to expect. "Many thanks to you; but Judith Hutter has the spirit and the experience that will make her depend more on herself than on good-looking rovers like you. Should there be need to face the savages, do you land with my father, instead of burrowing in the huts, under the show of defending us females and—"

"Girl—girl," interrupted the father, "quiet that glib tongue of thine, and hear the truth. There are savages on the lake shore already, and no man can say how near to us they may be at this very moment, or when we may hear more from them!"

"If this be true, Master Hutter," said Hurry, whose change of countenance denoted how serious he deemed the information, though it did not denote any unmanly alarm, "if this be true, your ark is in a most misfortunate position, for, though the cover did deceive Deerslayer and myself, it would hardly be overlooked by a full-blooded Injin, who was out seriously in s'arch of scalps!"

"I think as you do, Hurry, and wish, with all my heart, we lay anywhere else, at this moment, than in this narrow, crooked stream, which has many advantages to hide in, but which is almost fatal to them that are discovered. The savages are near us, moreover, and the difficulty is, to get out of the river without being shot down like deer standing at a lick!"

"Are you sartain, Master Hutter, that the red-skins you dread are ra'al Canadas?" asked Deerslayer, in a modest but earnest manner. "Have you seen any, and can you describe their paint?"

"I have fallen in with the signs of their being in the neighborhood, but have seen none of 'em. I was down stream a mile or so, looking to my traps, when I struck a fresh trail, crossing the corner of a swamp, and moving northward. The man had not passed an hour; and I know'd it for an Indian footstep, by the size of the foot, and the intoe, even before I found a worn moccasin, which its owner had dropped as useless. For that matter, I found the spot where he halted to make a new one, which was only a few yards from the place where he had dropped the old one."

"That doesn't look much like a red-skin on the war path!" returned the other, shaking his head. "An exper'enced warrior, at least, would have burned, or buried, or sunk in the river such signs of his passage; and your trail is, quite likely, a peaceable trail. But the moccasin may greatly relieve my mind, if you bethought you of bringing it off. I've come here to meet a young chief myself; and his course would be much in the direction you've mentioned. The trail may have been his'n."

"Hurry Harry, you're well acquainted with this young man, I hope, who has meetings with savages in a part of the country where he has never been before?" demanded Hutter, in a tone and in a manner that sufficiently indicated the motive of the question; these rude beings seldom hesitating, on the score of delicacy, to betray their feelings. "Treachery is an Indian virtue; and the whites, that live much in their tribes, soon catch their ways and practices."

"True—true as the Gospel, old Tom; but not personable to Deerslayer, who's a young man of truth, if he has no other ricommend. I'll answer for his honesty, whatever I may do for his valor in battle."

"I should like to know his errand in this strange quarter of the country."

"That is soon told, Master Hutter," said the young man, with the composure of one who kept a clean conscience. "I think, moreover, you've a right to ask it. The father of two such darters, who occupies a lake, after your fashion, has just the same right to inquire into a stranger's business in his neighborhood, as the colony would have to demand the reason why the Frenchers put more rijiments than common along the lines. No, no, I'll not deny your right to know why a stranger comes into your habitation or country, in times as serious as these."

"If such is your way of thinking, friend, let me hear your story without more words."

"'T is soon told, as I said afore; and shall be honestly told. I'm a young man, and, as yet, have never been on a war-path; but no sooner did the news come among the Delawares, that wampum and a hatchet were about to be sent in to the tribe, than they wished me to go out among the people of my own color, and get the exact state of things for 'em. This I did, and, after delivering my talk to the chiefs, on my return, I met an officer of the crown on the Schoharie, who had messages to send to some of the fri'ndly tribes that live farther west. This was thought a good occasion for Chingachgook, a young chief who has never struck a foe, and myself; to go on our first war path in company, and an app'intment was made for us, by an old Delaware, to meet at the rock near the foot of this lake. I'll not deny that Chingachgook has another object in view, but it has no consarn with any here, and is his secret and not mine; therefore I'll say no more about it."

"'Tis something about a young woman," interrupted Judith hastily, then laughing at her own impetuosity, and even having the grace to colour a little, at the manner in which she had betrayed her readiness to impute such a motive. "If 'tis neither war, nor a hunt, it must be love."

"Ay, it comes easy for the young and handsome, who hear so much of them feelin's, to suppose that they lie at the bottom of most proceedin's; but, on that head, I say nothin'. Chingachgook is to meet me at the rock, an hour afore sunset to-morrow evening, after which we shall go our way together, molesting none but the king's inimies, who are lawfully our own. Knowing Hurry of old, who once trapped in our hunting grounds, and falling in with him on the Schoharie, just as he was on the p'int of starting for his summer ha'nts, we agreed to journey in company; not so much from fear of the Mingos, as from good fellowship, and, as he says, to shorten a long road."

"And you think the trail I saw may have been that of your friend, ahead of his time?" said Hutter.

"That's my idee, which may be wrong, but which may be right. If I saw the moccasin, howsever, I could tell, in a minute, whether it is made in the Delaware fashion, or not."

"Here it is, then," said the quick-witted Judith, who had already gone to the canoe in quest of it. "Tell us what it says; friend or enemy. You look honest, and I believe all you say, whatever father may think."

"That's the way with you, Jude; forever finding out friends, where I distrust foes," grumbled Tom: "but, speak out, young man, and tell us what you think of the moccasin."

"That's not Delaware made," returned Deerslayer, examining the worn and rejected covering for the foot with a cautious eye. "I'm too young on a war-path to be positive, but I should say that moccasin has a northern look, and comes from beyond the Great Lakes."

"If such is the case, we ought not to lie here a minute longer than is necessary," said Hutter, glancing through the leaves of his cover, as if he already distrusted the presence of an enemy on the opposite shore of the narrow and sinuous stream. "It wants but an hour or so of night, and to move in the dark will be impossible, without making a noise that would betray us. Did you hear the echo of a piece in the mountains, half-an-hour since?"

"Yes, old man, and heard the piece itself," answered Hurry, who now felt the indiscretion of which he had been guilty, "for the last was fired from my own shoulder."

"I feared it came from the French Indians; still it may put them on the look-out, and be a means of discovering us. You did wrong to fire in war-time, unless there was good occasion.

"So I begin to think myself, Uncle Tom; and yet, if a man can't trust himself to let off his rifle in a wilderness that is a thousand miles square, lest some inimy should hear it, where's the use in carrying one?"

Hutter now held a long consultation with his two guests, in which the parties came to a true understanding of their situation. He explained the difficulty that would exist in attempting to get the ark out of so swift and narrow a stream, in the dark, without making a noise that could not fail to attract Indian ears. Any strollers in their vicinity would keep near the river or the lake; but the former had swampy shores in many places, and was both so crooked and so fringed with bushes, that it was quite possible to move by daylight without incurring much danger of being seen. More was to be apprehended, perhaps, from the ear than from the eye, especially as long as they were in the short, straitened, and canopied reaches of the stream.

"I never drop down into this cover, which is handy to my traps, and safer than the lake from curious eyes, without providing the means of getting out ag'in," continued this singular being; "and that is easier done by a pull than a push. My anchor is now lying above the suction, in the open lake; and here is a line, you see, to haul us up to it. Without some such help, a single pair of hands would make heavy work in forcing a scow like this up stream. I have a sort of a crab, too, that lightens the pull, on occasion. Jude can use the oar astern as well as myself; and when we fear no enemy, to get out of the river gives us but little trouble."

"What should we gain, Master Hutter, by changing the position?" asked Deerslayer, with a good deal of earnestness; "this is a safe cover, and a stout defence might be made from the inside of this cabin. I've never fou't unless in the way of tradition; but it seems to me we might beat off twenty Mingos, with palisades like them afore us."

"Ay, ay; you 've never fought except in traditions, that's plain enough, young man! Did you ever see as broad a sheet of water as this above us, before you came in upon it with Hurry?"

"I can't say that I ever did," Deerslayer answered, modestly. "Youth is the time to l'arn; and I'm far from wishing to raise my voice in counsel, afore it is justified by exper'ence."

"Well, then, I'll teach you the disadvantage of fighting in this position, and the advantage of taking to the open lake. Here, you may see, the savages will know where to aim every shot; and it would be too much to hope that some would not find their way through the crevices of the logs. Now, on the other hand, we should have nothing but a forest to aim at. Then we are not safe from fire, here, the bark of this roof being little better than so much kindling-wood. The castle, too, might be entered and ransacked in my absence, and all my possessions overrun and destroyed. Once in the lake, we can be attacked only in boats or on rafts—shall have a fair chance with the enemy—and can protect the castle with the ark. Do you understand this reasoning, youngster?"

"It sounds well—yes, it has a rational sound; and I'll not gainsay it."

"Well, old Tom," cried Hurry, "If we are to move, the sooner we make a beginning, the sooner we shall know whether we are to have our scalps for night-caps, or not."

As this proposition was self-evident, no one denied its justice. The three men, after a short preliminary explanation, now set about their preparations to move the ark in earnest. The slight fastenings were quickly loosened; and, by hauling on the line, the heavy craft slowly emerged from the cover. It was no sooner free from the incumbrance of the branches, than it swung into the stream, sheering quite close to the western shore, by the force of the current. Not a soul on board heard the rustling of the branches, as the cabin came against the bushes and trees of the western bank, without a feeling of uneasiness; for no one knew at what moment, or in what place, a secret and murderous enemy might unmask himself. Perhaps the gloomy light that still struggled through the impending canopy of leaves, or found its way through the narrow, ribbon-like opening, which seemed to mark, in the air above, the course of the river that flowed beneath, aided in augmenting the appearance of the danger; for it was little more than sufficient to render objects visible, without giving up all their outlines at a glance. Although the sun had not absolutely set, it had withdrawn its direct rays from the valley; and the hues of evening were beginning to gather around objects that stood uncovered, rendering those within the shadows of the woods still more sombre and gloomy.

No interruption followed the movement, however, and, as the men continued to haul on the line, the ark passed steadily ahead, the great breadth of the scow preventing its sinking into the water, and from offering much resistance to the progress of the swift element beneath its bottom. Hutter, too, had adopted a precaution suggested by experience, which might have done credit to a seaman, and which completely prevented any of the annoyances and obstacles which otherwise would have attended the short turns of the river. As the ark descended, heavy stones, attached to the line, were dropped in the centre of the stream, forming local anchors, each of which was kept from dragging by the assistance of those above it, until the uppermost of all was reached, which got its "backing" from the anchor, or grapnel, that lay well out in the lake. In consequence of this expedient, the ark floated clear of the incumbrances of the shore, against which it would otherwise have been unavoidably hauled at every turn, producing embarrassments that Hutter, single-handed, would have found it very difficult to overcome. Favored by this foresight, and stimulated by the apprehension of discovery, Floating Tom and his two athletic companions hauled the ark ahead with quite as much rapidity as comported with the strength of the line. At every turn in the stream, a stone was raised from the bottom, when the direction of the scow changed to one that pointed towards the stone that lay above. In this manner, with the channel buoyed out for him, as a sailor might term it, did Hutter move forward, occasionally urging his friends, in a low and guarded voice, to increase their exertions, and then, as occasions offered, warning them against efforts that might, at particular moments, endanger all by too much zeal. In spite of their long familiarity with the woods, the gloomy character of the shaded river added to the uneasiness that each felt; and when the ark reached the first bend in the Susquehannah, and the eye caught a glimpse of the broader expanse of the lake, all felt a relief, that perhaps none would have been willing to confess. Here the last stone was raised from the bottom, and the line led directly towards the grapnel, which, as Hutter had explained, was dropped above the suction of the current.

"Thank God!" ejaculated Hurry, "there is daylight, and we shall soon have a chance of seeing our inimies, if we are to feel 'em."

"That is more than you or any man can say," growled Hutter. "There is no spot so likely to harbor a party as the shore around the outlet, and the moment we clear these trees and get into open water, will be the most trying time, since it will leave the enemy a cover, while it puts us out of one. Judith, girl, do you and Hetty leave the oar to take care of itself; and go within the cabin; and be mindful not to show your faces at a window; for they who will look at them won't stop to praise their beauty. And now, Hurry, we'll step into this outer room ourselves, and haul through the door, where we shall all be safe, from a surprise, at least. Friend Deerslayer, as the current is lighter, and the line has all the strain on it that is prudent, do you keep moving from window to window, taking care not to let your head be seen, if you set any value on life. No one knows when or where we shall hear from our neighbors."

Deerslayer complied, with a sensation that had nothing in common with fear, but which had all the interest of a perfectly novel and a most exciting situation. For the first time in his life he was in the vicinity of enemies, or had good reason to think so; and that, too, under all the thrilling circumstances of Indian surprises and Indian artifices. As he took his stand at the window, the ark was just passing through the narrowest part of the stream, a point where the water first entered what was properly termed the river, and where the trees fairly interlocked overhead, causing the current to rush into an arch of verdure; a feature as appropriate and peculiar to the country, perhaps, as that of Switzerland, where the rivers come rushing literally from chambers of ice.

The ark was in the act of passing the last curve of this leafy entrance, as Deerslayer, having examined all that could be seen of the eastern bank of the river, crossed the room to look from the opposite window, at the western. His arrival at this aperture was most opportune, for he had no sooner placed his eye at a crack, than a sight met his gaze that might well have alarmed a sentinel so young and inexperienced. A sapling overhung the water, in nearly half a circle, having first grown towards the light, and then been pressed down into this form by the weight of the snows; a circumstance of common occurrence in the American woods. On this no less than six Indians had already appeared, others standing ready to follow them, as they left room; each evidently bent on running out on the trunk, and dropping on the roof of the ark as it passed beneath. This would have been an exploit of no great difficulty, the inclination of the tree admitting of an easy passage, the adjoining branches offering ample support for the hands, and the fall being too trifling to be apprehended. When Deerslayer first saw this party, it was just unmasking itself, by ascending the part of the tree nearest to the earth, or that which was much the most difficult to overcome; and his knowledge of Indian habits told him at once that they were all in their war-paint, and belonged to a hostile tribe.

"Pull, Hurry," he cried; "pull for your life, and as you love Judith Hutter! Pull, man, pull!"

This call was made to one that the young man knew had the strength of a giant. It was so earnest and solemn, that both Hutter and March felt it was not idly given, and they applied all their force to the line simultaneously, and at a most critical moment. The scow redoubled its motion, and seemed to glide from under the tree as if conscious of the danger that was impending overhead. Perceiving that they were discovered, the Indians uttered the fearful war-whoop, and running forward on the tree, leaped desperately towards their fancied prize. There were six on the tree, and each made the effort. All but their leader fell into the river more or less distant from the ark, as they came, sooner or later, to the leaping place. The chief, who had taken the dangerous post in advance, having an earlier opportunity than the others, struck the scow just within the stern. The fall proving so much greater than he had anticipated, he was slightly stunned, and for a moment he remained half bent and unconscious of his situation. At this instant Judith rushed from the cabin, her beauty heightened by the excitement that produced the bold act, which flushed her cheek to crimson, and, throwing all her strength into the effort, she pushed the intruder over the edge of the scow, headlong into the river. This decided feat was no sooner accomplished than the woman resumed her sway; Judith looked over the stern to ascertain what had become of the man, and the expression of her eyes softened to concern, next, her cheek crimsoned between shame and surprise at her own temerity, and then she laughed in her own merry and sweet manner. All this occupied less than a minute, when the arm of Deerslayer was thrown around her waist, and she was dragged swiftly within the protection of the cabin. This retreat was not effected too soon. Scarcely were the two in safety, when the forest was filled with yells, and bullets began to patter against the logs.

The ark being in swift motion all this while, it was beyond the danger of pursuit by the time these little events had occurred; and the savages, as soon as the first burst of their anger had subsided, ceased firing, with the consciousness that they were expending their ammunition in vain. When the scow came up over her grapnel, Hutter tripped the latter in a way not to impede the motion; and being now beyond the influence of the current, the vessel continued to drift ahead, until fairly in the open lake, though still near enough to the land to render exposure to a rifle-bullet dangerous. Hutter and March got out two small sweeps and, covered by the cabin, they soon urged the ark far enough from the shore to leave no inducement to their enemies to make any further attempt to injure them.


CHAPTER V.

"Why, let the strucken deer go weep,
   The hart ungalled play,
For some must watch, while some must sleep,
   Thus runs the world away."

Hamlet, III.ii.271–74


Another consultation took place in the forward part of the scow, at which both Judith and Hetty were present. As no danger could now approach unseen, immediate uneasiness had given place to the concern which attended the conviction that enemies were in considerable force on the shores of the lake, and that they might be sure no practicable means of accomplishing their own destruction would be neglected. As a matter of course Hutter felt these truths the deepest, his daughters having an habitual reliance on his resources, and knowing too little to appreciate fully all the risks they ran; while his male companions were at liberty to quit him at any moment they saw fit. His first remark showed that he had an eye to the latter circumstance, and might have betrayed, to a keen observer, the apprehension that was just then uppermost.

"We've a great advantage over the Iroquois, or the enemy, whoever they are, in being afloat," he said.

"There's not a canoe on the lake that I don't know where it's hid; and now yours is here. Hurry, there are but three more on the land, and they're so snug in hollow logs that I don't believe the Indians could find them, let them try ever so long."

"There's no telling that—no one can say that," put in Deerslayer; "a hound is not more sartain on the scent than a red-skin, when he expects to get anything by it. Let this party see scalps afore 'em, or plunder, or honor accordin' to their idees of what honor is, and 't will be a tight log that hides a canoe from their eyes."

"You're right, Deerslayer," cried Harry March; "you're downright Gospel in this matter, and I rej'ice that my bunch of bark is safe enough here, within reach of my arm. I calculate they'll be at all the rest of the canoes afore to-morrow night, if they are in ra'al 'arnest to smoke you out, old Tom, and we may as well overhaul our paddles for a pull."

Hutter made no immediate reply. He looked about him in silence for quite a minute, examining the sky, the lake, and the belt of forest which inclosed it, as it might be hermetically, like one consulting their signs. Nor did he find any alarming symptoms. The boundless woods were sleeping in the deep repose of nature, the heavens were placid, but still luminous with the light of the retreating sun, while the lake looked more lovely and calm than it had before done that day. It was a scene altogether soothing, and of a character to lull the passions into a species of holy calm. How far this effect was produced, however, on the party in the ark, must appear in the progress of our narrative.

"Judith," called out the father, when he had taken this close but short survey of the omens, "night is at hand; find our friends food; a long march gives a sharp appetite."

"We're not starving, Master Hutter," March observed, "for we filled up just as we reached the lake, and for one, I prefer the company of Jude even to her supper. This quiet evening is very agreeable to sit by her side."

"Natur' is natur'," objected Hutter, "and must be fed. Judith, see to the meal, and take your sister to help you. I've a little discourse to hold with you, friends," he continued, as soon as his daughters were out of hearing, "and wish the girls away. You see my situation, and I should like to hear your opinions concerning what is best to be done. Three times have I been burnt out already, but that was on the shore; and I've considered myself as pretty safe ever since I got the castle built, and the ark afloat. My other accidents, however, happened in peaceable times, being nothing more than such flurries as a man must meet with, in the woods; but this matter looks serious, and your ideas would greatly relieve my mind."

"It's my notion, old Tom, that you, and your huts, and your traps, and your whole possessions, hereaway, are in desperate jippardy," returned the matter-of-fact Hurry, who saw no use in concealment. "Accordin' to my ideas of valie, they're altogether not worth half as much today as they was yesterday, nor would I give more for 'em, taking the pay in skins."

"Then I've children!" continued the father, making the allusion in a way that it might have puzzled even an indifferent observer to say was intended as a bait, or as an exclamation of paternal concern, "daughters, as you know, Hurry, and good girls too, I may say, though I am their father."

"A man may say anything, Master Hutter, particularly when pressed by time and circumstances. You've darters, as you say, and one of them hasn't her equal on the frontiers for good looks, whatever she may have for good behavior. As for poor Hetty, she's Hetty Hutter, and that's as much as one can say about the poor thing. Give me Jude, if her conduct was only equal to her looks!"

"I see, Harry March, I can only count on you as a fair-weather friend; and I suppose that your companion will be of the same way of thinking," returned the other, with a slight show of pride, that was not altogether without dignity; "well, I must depend on Providence, which will not turn a deaf ear, perhaps, to a father's prayers."

"If you've understood Hurry, here, to mean that he intends to desart you," said Deerslayer, with an earnest simplicity that gave double assurance of its truth, "I think you do him injustice, as I know you do me, in supposing I would follow him, was he so ontrue-hearted as to leave a family of his own color in such a strait as this. I've come on this at take, Master Hutter, to rende'vous a fri'nd, and I only wish he was here himself, as I make no doubt he will be at sunset to-morrow, when you'd have another rifle to aid you; an inexper'enced one, I'll allow, like my own, but one that has proved true so often ag'in the game, big and little, that I'll answer for its sarvice ag'in mortals."

"May I depend on you to stand by me and my daughters, then, Deerslayer?" demanded the old man, with a father's anxiety in his countenance.

"That may you, Floating Tom, if that's your name; and as a brother would stand by a sister, a husband his wife, or a suitor his sweetheart. In this strait you may count on me, through all adversities; and I think Hurry does discredit to his natur' and wishes, if you can't count on him."

"Not he," cried Judith, thrusting her handsome face out of the door; "his nature is hurry, as well as his name, and he'll hurry off, as soon as he thinks his fine figure in danger. Neither 'old Tom,' nor his 'gals,' will depend much on Master March, now they know him, but you they will rely on, Deerslayer; for your honest face and honest heart tell us that what you promise you will perform."

This was said, as much, perhaps, in affected scorn for Hurry, as in sincerity. Still, it was not said without feeling. The fine face of Judith sufficiently proved the latter circumstance; and if the conscious March fancied that he had never seen in it a stronger display of contempt—a feeling in which the beauty was apt to indulge—than while she was looking at him, it certainly seldom exhibited more of a womanly softness and sensibility, than when her speaking blue eyes were turned on his travelling companion.

"Leave us, Judith," Hutter ordered sternly, before either of the young men could reply; "leave us; and do not return until you come with the venison and fish. The girl has been spoilt by the flattery of the officers, who sometimes find their way up here, Master March, and you'll not think any harm of her silly words."

"You never said truer syllable, old Tom," retorted Hurry, who smarted under Judith's observations; "the devil-tongued youngsters of the garrison have proved her undoing! I scarce know Jude any longer, and shall soon take to admiring her sister, who is getting to be much more to my fancy."

"I'm glad to hear this, Harry, and look upon it as a sign that you're coming to your right senses. Hetty would make a much safer and more rational companion than Jude, and would be much the most likely to listen to your suit, as the officers have, I greatly fear, unsettled her sister's mind."

"No man needs a safer wife than Hetty," said Hurry, laughing, "though I'll not answer for her being of the most rational. But no matter; Deerslayer has not misconceived me, when he told you I should be found at my post. I'll not quit you, Uncle Tom, just now, whatever may be my feelin's and intentions respecting your eldest darter."

Hurry had a respectable reputation for prowess among his associates, and Hutter heard this pledge with a satisfaction that was not concealed. Even the great personal strength of such an aid became of moment, in moving the ark, as well as in the species of hand-to-hand conflicts, that were not unfrequent in the woods; and no commander who was hard pressed could feel more joy at hearing of the arrival of reinforcements, than the borderer experienced at being told this important auxiliary was not about to quit him. A minute before, Hutter would have been well content to compromise his danger, by entering into a compact to act only on the defensive; but no sooner did he feel some security on this point, than the restlessness of man induced him to think of the means of carrying the war into the enemy's country.

"High prices are offered for scalps on both sides," he observed, with a grim smile, as if he felt the force of the inducement, at the very time he wished to affect a superiority to earning money by means that the ordinary feelings of those who aspire to be civilized men repudiated, even while they were adopted. "It isn't right, perhaps, to take gold for human blood; and yet, when mankind is busy in killing one another, there can be no great harm in adding a little bit of skin to the plunder. What's your sentiments, Hurry, touching these p'ints?"

"That you've made a vast mistake, old man, in calling savage blood human blood, at all. I think no more of a red-skin's scalp than I do of a pair of wolf's ears; and would just as lief finger money for the one as for the other. With white people 't is different, for they've a nat'ral avarsion to being scalped; whereas your Indian shaves his head in readiness for the knife, and leaves a lock of hair by way of braggadocio, that one can lay hold of in the bargain."

"That's manly, however, and I felt from the first that we had only to get you on our side, to have your heart and hand," returned Tom, losing all his reserve, as he gained a renewed confidence in the disposition of his companions. "Something more may turn up from this inroad of the red-skins than they bargained for. Deerslayer, I conclude you're of Hurry's way of thinking, and look upon money 'arned in this way as being as likely to pass as money 'arned in trapping or hunting."

"I've no such feelin', nor any wish to harbor it, not I," returned the other. "My gifts are not scalpers' gifts, but such as belong to my religion and color. I'll stand by you, old man, in the ark or in the castle, the canoe or the woods, but I'll not unhumanize my natur' by falling into ways that God intended for another race. If you and Hurry have got any thoughts that lean towards the colony's gold, go by yourselves in s'arch of it, and leave the females to my care. Much as I must differ from you both on all gifts that do not properly belong to a white man, we shall agree that it is the duty of the strong to take care of the weak, especially when the last belong to them that natur' intended man to protect and console by his gentleness and strength."

"Hurry Harry, that is a lesson you might learn and practise on to some advantage," said the sweet, but spirited voice of Judith, from the cabin; a proof that she had over-heard all that had hitherto been said.

"No more of this, Jude," called out the father angrily. "Move farther off; we are about to talk of matters unfit for a woman to listen to."

Hutter did not take any steps, however, to ascertain whether he was obeyed or not; but dropping his voice a little, he pursued the discourse.

"The young man is right, Hurry," he said; "and we can leave the children in his care. Now, my idea is just this; and I think you'll agree that it is rational and correct. There's a large party of these savages on shore and, though I didn't tell it before the girls, for they're womanish, and apt to be troublesome when anything like real work is to be done, there's women among 'em. This I know from moccasin prints; and 't is likely they are hunters, after all, who have been out so long that they know nothing of the war, or of the bounties."

"In which case, old Tom, why was their first salute an attempt to cut our throats?"

"We don't know that their design was so bloody. It's natural and easy for an Indian to fall into ambushes and surprises; and, no doubt they wished to get on board the ark first, and to make their conditions afterwards. That a disapp'inted savage should fire at us, is in rule; and I think nothing of that. Besides, how often they burned me out, and robbed my traps—ay, and pulled trigger on me, in the most peaceful times?"

"The blackguards will do such things, I must allow; and we pay 'em off pretty much in their own c'ine. Women would not be on the war-path, sartainly; and, so far, there's reason in your idee."

"Nor would a hunter be in his war-paint," returned Deerslayer. "I saw the Mingos, and know that they are out on the trail of mortal men; and not for beaver or deer."

"There you have it ag'in, old fellow," said Hurry. "In the way of an eye, now, I'd as soon trust this young man, as trust the oldest settler in the colony; if he says paint, why paint it was."

"Then a hunting-party and a war-party have met, for women must have been with 'em. It's only a few days since the runner went through with the tidings of the troubles; and it may be that warriors have come out to call in their women and children, to get an early blow."

"That would stand the courts, and is just the truth," cried Hurry; "you've got it now, old Tom, and I should like to hear what you mean to make out of it."

"The bounty," returned the other, looking up at his attentive companion in a cool, sullen manner, in which, however, heartless cupidity and indifference to the means were far more conspicuous than any feelings of animosity or revenge.

"If there's women, there's children; and big and little have scalps; the colony pays for all alike."

"More shame to it, that it should do so," interrupted Deerslayer; "more shame to it, that it don't understand its gifts, and pay greater attention to the will of God."

"Hearken to reason, lad, and don't cry out afore you understand a case," returned the unmoved Hurry; "the savages scalp your fri'nds, the Delawares, or Mohicans whichever they may be, among the rest; and why shouldn't we scalp? I will own, it would be ag'in right for you and me now, to go into the settlements and bring out scalps, but it's a very different matter as concerns Indians. A man shouldn't take scalps, if he isn't ready to be scalped, himself, on fitting occasions. One good turn desarves another, the world over. That's reason, and I believe it to be good religion."

"Ay, Master Hurry," again interrupted the rich voice of Judith, "is it religion to say that one bad turn deserves another?"

"I'll never reason ag'in you, Judy, for you beat me with beauty, if you can't with sense. Here's the Canadas paying their Injins for scalps, and why not we pay——"

"Our Indians!" exclaimed the girl, laughing with a sort of melancholy merriment. "Father, father! think no more of this, and listen to the advice of Deerslayer, who has a conscience; which is more than I can say or think of Harry March."

Hutter now rose, and, entering the cabin, he compelled his daughters to go into the adjoining room, when he secured both the doors, and returned. Then he and Hurry pursued the subject; but, as the purport of all that was material in this discourse will appear in the narrative, it need not be related here in detail. The reader, however, can have no difficulty in comprehending the morality that presided over their conference. It was, in truth, that which, in some form or other, rules most of the acts of men, and in which the controlling principle is that one wrong will justify another. Their enemies paid for scalps, and this was sufficient to justify the colony for retaliating. It is true, the French used the same argument, a circumstance, as Hurry took occasion to observe in answer to one of Deerslayer's objections, that proved its truth, as mortal enemies would not be likely to have recourse to the same reason unless it were a good one. But neither Hutter nor Hurry was a man likely to stick at trifles in matters connected with the right of the aborigines, since it is one of the consequences of aggression that it hardens the conscience, as the only means of quieting it. In the most peaceable state of the country, a species of warfare was carried on between the Indians, especially those of the Canadas, and men of their caste; and the moment an actual and recognized warfare existed, it was regarded as the means of lawfully revenging a thousand wrongs, real and imaginary. Then, again, there was some truth, and a good deal of expediency, in the principle of retaliation, of which they both availed themselves, in particular, to answer the objections of their juster-minded and more scrupulous companion.

"You must fight a man with his own we'pons, Deerslayer," cried Hurry, in his uncouth dialect, and in his dogmatical manner of disposing of all oral propositions; "if he's f'erce you must be f'ercer; if he's stout of heart, you must be stouter. This is the way to get the better of Christian or savage: by keeping up to this trail, you'll get soonest to the ind of your journey."

"That's not Moravian doctrine, which teaches that all are to be judged according to their talents or l'arning; the Injin like an Injin; and the white man like a white man. Some of their teachers say, that if you're struck on the cheek, it's a duty to turn the other side of the face, and take another blow, instead of seeking revenge, whereby I understand——"

"That's enough!" shouted Hurry; "that's all I want, to prove a man's doctrine! How long would it take to kick a man through the colony—in at one ind and out at the other, on that principle?"

"Don't mistake me, March," returned the young hunter, with dignity; "I don't understand by this any more than that it's best to do this, if possible. Revenge is an Injin gift, and forgiveness a white man's. That's all. Overlook all you can is what's meant; and not revenge all you can. As for kicking, Master Hurry," and Deerslayer's sunburnt cheek flushed as he continued, "into the colony, or out of the colony, that's neither here nor there, seeing no one proposes it, and no one would be likely to put up with it. What I wish to say is, that a red-skin's scalping don't justify a pale-face's scalping."

"Do as you're done by, Deerslayer; that's ever the Christian parson's doctrine."

"No, Hurry, I've asked the Moravians consarning that; and it's altogether different. 'Do as you would be done by,' they tell me, is the true saying, while men practyse the false. They think all the colonies wrong that offer bounties for scalps, and believe no blessing will follow the measures. Above all things, they forbid revenge."

"That for your Moravians!" cried March, snapping his fingers; "they're the next thing to Quakers; and if you'd believe all they tell you, not even a 'rat would be skinned, out of marcy. Who ever heard of marcy on a muskrat!"

The disdainful manner of Hurry prevented a reply, and he and the old man resumed the discussion of their plans in a more quiet and confidential manner. This confidence lasted until Judith appeared, bearing the simple but savory supper. March observed, with a little surprise, that she placed the choicest bits before Deerslayer, and that in the little nameless attentions it was in her power to bestow, she quite obviously manifested a desire to let it be seen that she deemed him the honored guest. Accustomed, however, to the waywardness and coquetry of the beauty, this discovery gave him little concern, and he ate with an appetite that was in no degree disturbed by any moral causes. The easily-digested food of the forests offering the fewest possible obstacles to the gratification of this great animal indulgence, Deerslayer, notwithstanding the hearty meal both had taken in the woods, was in no manner behind his companion in doing justice to the viands.

An hour later the scene had greatly changed. The lake was still placid and glassy, but the gloom of the hour had succeeded to the soft twilight of a summer evening, and all within the dark setting of the woods lay in the quiet repose of night. The forests gave up no song, or cry, or even murmur, but looked down from the hills on the lovely basin they encircled, in solemn stillness; and the only sound that was audible was the regular dip of the sweeps, at which Hurry and Deerslayer lazily pushed, impelling the ark towards the castle. Hutter had withdrawn to the stern of the scow, in order to steer, but, finding that the young men kept even strokes, and held the desired course by their own skill, he permitted the oar to drag in the water, took a seat on the end of the vessel, and lighted his pipe. He had not been thus placed many minutes, ere Hetty came stealthily out of the cabin, or house, as they usually termed that part of the ark, and placed herself at his feet, on a little bench that she brought with her. As this movement was by no means unusual in his feeble-minded child, the old man paid no other attention to it than to lay his hand kindly on her head, in an affectionate and approving manner; an act of grace that the girl received in meek silence.

After a pause of several minutes, Hetty began to sing. Her voice was low and tremulous, but it was earnest and solemn. The words and the tune were of the simplest form, the first being a hymn that she had been taught by her mother, and the last one of those natural melodies that find favor with all classes, in every age, coming from and being addressed to the feelings. Hutter never listened to this simple strain without finding his heart and manner softened; facts that his daughter well knew, and by which she had often profited, through the sort of holy instinct that enlightens the weak of mind, more especially in their aims toward good.

Hetty's low, sweet tones had not been raised many moments, when the dip of the oars ceased, and the holy strain arose singly on the breathing silence of the wilderness. As if she gathered courage with the theme, her powers appeared to increase as she proceeded; and though nothing vulgar or noisy mingled in her melody, its strength and melancholy tenderness grew on the ear, until the air was filled with this simple homage of a soul that seemed almost spotless. That the men forward were not indifferent to this touching interruption, was proved by their inaction; nor did their oars again dip until the last of the sweet sounds had actually died among the remarkable shores, which, at that witching hour, would waft even the lowest modulations of the human voice more than a mile. Hutter was much affected; for rude as he was by early habits, and even ruthless as he had got to be by long exposure to the practices of the wilderness, his nature was of that fearful mixture of good and evil that so generally enters into the moral composition of man.

"You are sad to-night, child," said the father, whose manner and language usually assumed some of the gentleness and elevation of the civilized life he had led in youth, when he thus communed with this particular child; "we have just escaped from enemies, and ought rather to rejoice."

"You can never do it, father!" said Hetty, in a low, remonstrating manner, taking his hard, knotty hand into both her own; "you have talked long with Harry March; but neither of you have the heart to do it!"

"This is going beyond your means, foolish child; you must have been naughty enough to have listened, or you could know nothing of our talk."

"Why should you and Hurry kill people—especially women and children?"

"Peace, girl, peace; we are at war, and must do to our enemies as our enemies would do to us."

"That's not it, father! I heard Deerslayer say how it was. You must do to your enemies as you wish your enemies would do to you. No man wishes his enemies to kill him."

"We kill our enemies in war, girl, lest they should kill us. One side or the other must begin; and them that begin first, are most apt to get the victory. You know nothing about these things, poor Hetty, and had best say nothing."

"Judith says it is wrong, father; and Judith has sense though I have none."

"Jude understands better than to talk to me of these matters; for she has sense, as you say, and knows I'll not bear it. Which would you prefer, Hetty; to have your own scalp taken, and sold to the French, or that we should kill our enemies, and keep them from harming us?"

"That's not it, father! Don't kill them, nor let them kill us. Sell your skins, and get more, if you can; but don't sell human blood."

"Come, come, child; let us talk of matters you understand. Are you glad to see our old friend, March, back again? You like Hurry, and must know that one day he may be your brother—if not something nearer."

"That can't be, father," returned the girl, after a considerable pause; "Hurry has had one father, and one mother; and people never have two."

"So much for your weak mind, Hetty. When Jude marries, her husband's father will be her father, and her husband's sister her sister. If she should marry Hurry, then he will be your brother."

"Judith will never have Hurry," returned the girl mildly, but positively; "Judith don't like Hurry."

"That's more than you can know, Hetty. Harry March is the handsomest, and the strongest, and the boldest young man that ever visits the lake; and, as Jude is the greatest beauty, I don't see why they shouldn't come together. He has as much as promised that he will enter into this job with me, on condition that I'll consent."

Hetty began to move her body back and forth, and other-wise to express mental agitation; but she made no answer for more than a minute. Her father, accustomed to her manner, and suspecting no immediate cause of concern, continued to smoke with the apparent phlegm which would seem to belong to that particular species of enjoyment.

"Hurry is handsome, father," said Hetty, with a simple emphasis, that she might have hesitated about using, had her mind been more alive to the inferences of others.

"I told you so, child," muttered old Hutter, without removing the pipe from between his teeth; "he's the likeliest youth in these parts; and Jude is the likeliest young woman I've met with since her poor mother was in her best days."

"Is it wicked to be ugly, father?"

"One might be guilty of worse things—but you're by no means ugly; though not so comely as Jude."

"Is Judith any happier for being so handsome?"

"She may be, child, and she may not be. But talk of other matters now, for you hardly understand these, poor Hetty. How do you like our new acquaintance, Deerslayer?"

"He isn't handsome, father. Hurry is far handsomer than Deerslayer."

"That's true; but they say he is a noted hunter! His fame had reached me before I ever saw him; and I did hope he would prove to be as stout a warrior as he is dexterous with the deer. All men are not alike, howsever, child; and it takes time, as I know by experience, to give a man a true wilderness heart."

"Have I got a wilderness heart, father—and Hurry, is his heart true wilderness?"

"You sometimes ask queer questions, Hetty! Your heart is good, child, and fitter for the settlements than for the woods; while your reason is fitter for the woods than for the settlements."

"Why has Judith more reason than I, father?"

"Heaven help thee, child: this is more than I can answer. God gives sense, and appearance, and all these things; and he grants them as he seeth fit. Dost thou wish for more sense?"

"Not I. The little I have troubles me; for when I think the hardest, then I feel the unhappiest. I don't believe thinking is good for me, though I do wish I was as handsome as Judith!"

"Why so, poor child? Thy sister's beauty may cause her trouble, as it caused her mother before her. It's no advantage, Hetty, to be so marked for anything as to become an object of envy, or to be sought after more than others."

"Mother was good, if she was handsome," returned the girl, the tears starting to her eyes, as usually happened when she adverted to her deceased parent.

Old Hutter, if not equally affected, was moody and silent at this allusion to his wife. He continued smoking, without appearing disposed to make any answer, until his simple-minded daughter repeated her remark, in a way to show that she felt uneasiness lest he might be inclined to deny her assertion. Then he knocked the ashes out of his pipe, and laying his hand in a sort of rough kindness on the girl's head, he made a reply.

"Thy mother was too good for this world," he said; "though others might not think so. Her good looks did not befriend her; and you have no occasion to mourn that you are not as much like her as your sister. Think less of beauty, child, and more of your duty, and you'll be as happy on this lake as you could be in the king's palace."

"I know it, father; but Hurry says beauty is everything in a young woman."

Hutter made an ejaculation expressive of dissatisfaction, and went forward, passing through the house in order to do so. Hetty's simple betrayal of her weakness in behalf of March gave him uneasiness on a subject concerning which he had never felt before, and he determined to come to an explanation at once with his visitor; for directness of speech and decision in conduct were two of the best qualities of this rude being, in whom the seeds of a better education seemed to be constantly struggling upwards, to be choked by the fruits of a life in which his hard struggles for subsistence and security had steeled his feelings and indurated his nature. When he reached the forward end of the scow, he manifested an intention to relieve Deerslayer at the oar, directing the latter to take his own place aft. By these changes, the old man and Hurry were again left alone, while the young hunter was transferred to the other end of the ark.

Hetty had disappeared when Deerslayer reached his new post, and for some little time he directed the course of the slow-moving craft by himself. It was not long, however, before Judith came out of the cabin, as if disposed to do the honors of the place to a stranger engaged in the service of her family. The starlight was sufficient to permit objects to be plainly distinguished when near at hand, and the bright eyes of the girl had an expression of kindness in them, when they met those of the youth, that the latter was easily enabled to discover. Her rich hair shaded her spirited and yet soft countenance, even at that hour rendering it the more beautiful—as the rose is loveliest when reposing amid the shadows and contrasts of its native foliage. Little ceremony is used in the intercourse of the woods; and Judith had acquired a readiness of address, by the admiration that she so generally excited, which, if it did not amount to forwardness, certainly in no degree lent to her charms the aid of that retiring modesty on which poets love to dwell.

"I thought I should have killed myself with laughing, Deerslayer," the beauty abruptly but coquettishly commenced, "when I saw that Indian dive into the river! He was a good-looking savage, too," the girl always dwelt on personal beauty as a sort of merit, "and yet one couldn't stop to consider whether his paint would stand water!"

"And I thought they would have killed you with their we'pons, Judith," returned Deerslayer; "it was an awful risk for a female to run in the face of a dozen Mingos!"

"Did that make you come out of the cabin, in spite of their rifles, too?" asked the girl, with more real interest than she would have cared to betray, though with an indifference of manner that was the result of a good deal of practice united to native readiness.

"Men ar'n't apt to see females in danger, and not come to their assistance. Even a Mingo knows that."

This sentiment was uttered with as much simplicity of manner as of feeling, and Judith rewarded it with a smile so sweet, that even Deerslayer, who had imbibed a prejudice against the girl in consequence of Hurry's suspicions of her levity, felt its charm, notwithstanding half its winning influence was lost in the feeble light. It at once created a sort of confidence between them, and the discourse was continued on the part of the hunter, without the lively consciousness of the character of this coquette of the wilderness, with which it had certainly commenced.

"You are a man of deeds, and not of words, I see plainly, Deerslayer," continued the beauty, taking her seat near the spot where the other stood, "and I foresee we shall be very good friends. Hurry Harry has a tongue, and, giant as he is, he talks more than he performs."

"March is your fri'nd, Judith; and fri'nds should be tender of each other, when apart."

"We all know what Hurry's friendship comes to! Let him have his own way in everything, and he's the best fellow in the colony; but 'head him off,' as you say of the deer, and he is master of everything near him but himself. Hurry is no favorite of mine, Deerslayer; and I dare say, if the truth was known, and his conversation about me repeated, it would be found that he thinks no better of me than I own I do of him."

The latter part of this speech was not uttered without uneasiness. Had the girl's companion been more sophisticated, he might have observed the averted face, the manner in which the pretty little foot was agitated, and other signs that, for some unexplained reason, the opinions of March were not quite as much a matter of indifference to her as she thought fit to pretend. Whether this was no more than the ordinary working of female vanity, feeling keenly even when it affected not to feel at all, or whether it proceeded from that deeply-seated consciousness of right and wrong which God himself has implanted in our breasts that we may know good from evil, will be made more apparent to the reader as we proceed in the tale. Deerslayer felt embarrassed. He well remembered the cruel imputations left by March's distrust; and, while he did not wish to injure his associate's suit by exciting resentment against him, his tongue was one that literally knew no guile. To answer without saying more or less than he wished, was consequently a delicate duty.

"March has his say of all things in natur', whether of fri'nd or foe," slowly and cautiously rejoined the hunter. "He's one of them that speak as they feel while the tongue's a-going, and that's sometimes different from what they'd speak if they took time to consider. Give me a Delaware, Judith, for one that reflects and ruminates on his idees! Inmity has made him thoughtful, and a loose tongue is no ricommend at their council fires."

"I dare say March's tongue goes free enough when it gets on the subject of Judith Hutter and her sister," said the girl, rousing herself as if in careless disdain. "Young women's good names are a pleasant matter of discourse with some that wouldn't dare be so open-mouthed if there was a brother in the way. Master March may find it pleasant to traduce us, but sooner or later he'll repent.

"Nay, Judith, this is taking the matter up too much in 'arnest. Hurry has never whispered a syllable ag'in the good name of Hetty, to begin with—"

"I see how it is—I see how it is," impetuously interrupted Judith. "I am the one he sees fit to scorch with his withering tongue! Hetty, indeed! Poor Hetty!" she continued, her voice sinking into low, husky tones, that seemed nearly to stifle her in the utterance; "she is beyond and above his slanderous malice! Poor Hetty! If God has created her feeble-minded, the weakness lies altogether on the side of errors of which she seems to know nothing. The earth never held a purer being than Hetty Hutter, Deerslayer."

"I can believe it—yes, I can believe that, Judith, and I hope 'arnestly that the same can be said of her handsome sister."

There was a soothing sincerity in the voice of Deerslayer, which touched the girl's feelings; nor did the allusion to her beauty lessen the effect with one who only knew too well the power of her personal charms. Nevertheless, the still, small voice of conscience was not hushed, and it prompted the answer which she made, after giving herself time to reflect.

"I dare say Hurry had some of his vile hints about the people of the garrisons," she added. "He knows they are gentlemen, and can never forgive any one for being what he feels he can never become himself."

"Not in the sense of a king's officer, Judith, sartainly, for March has no turn thataway; but in the sense of reality, why may not a beaver-hunter be as respectable as a governor? Since you speak of it yourself, I'll not deny that he did complain of one as humble as you being so much in the company of scarlet coats and silken sashes. But 't was jealousy that brought it out of him, and I do think he mourned over his own thoughts as a mother would have mourned over her child."

Perhaps Deerslayer was not aware of the full meaning that his earnest language conveyed. It is certain that he did not see the color that crimsoned the whole of Judith's fine face, nor detect the uncontrollable distress that immediately after changed its hue to deadly paleness. A minute or two elapsed in profound stillness, the splash of the water seeming to occupy all the avenues of sound; and then Judith arose, and grasped the hand of the hunter, almost convulsively, with one of her own.

"Deerslayer," she said, hurriedly, "I'm glad the ice is broke between us. They say that sudden friendships lead to long enmities, but I do not believe it will turn out so with us. I know not how it is—but you are the first man I ever met, who did not seem to wish to flatter—to wish my ruin—to be an enemy in disguise—never mind; say nothing to Hurry, and another time we'll talk together again."

As the girl released her grasp, she vanished in the house, leaving the astonished young man standing at the steering-oar, as motionless as one of the pines on the hills. So abstracted, indeed, had his thoughts become, that he was hailed by Hutter to keep the scow's head in the right direction, before he remembered his actual situation.

CHAPTER VI.

> "So spake the apostate Angel, though in pain,
> Vaunting aloud, but racked with deep despair."

Paradise lost, I. 125–26.

Shortly after the disappearance of Judith, a light southerly air arose, and Hutter set a large square sail, that had once been the flying top-sail of an Albany sloop, but which having become threadbare in catching the breezes of Tappan, had been condemned and sold. He had a light, tough spar of tamarack that he could raise on occasion, and with a little contrivance, his duck was spread to the wind in a sufficiently professional manner. The effect on the ark was such as to supersede the necessity of rowing; and in about two hours the castle was seen, in the darkness, rising out of the water, at the distance of a hundred yards. The sail was then lowered, and by slow degrees the scow drifted up to the building, and was secured.

No one had visited the house since Hurry and his companion left it. The place was found in the quiet of midnight, a sort of type of the solitude of a wilderness. As an enemy was known to be near, Hutter directed his daughters to abstain from the use of lights, luxuries in which they seldom indulged during the warm months, lest they might prove beacons to direct their foes where they might be found.

"In open daylight I shouldn't fear a host of savages behind these stout logs, and they without any cover to skulk into," added Hutter, when he had explained to his guests the reasons why he forbade the use of light; "for I've three or four trusty weapons always loaded, and Killdeer, in particular, is a piece that never misses. But it's a different thing at night. A canoe might get upon us unseen, in the dark; and the savages have so many cunning ways of attacking, that I look upon it as bad enough to deal with 'em under a bright sun. I built this dwelling in order to have 'em at arm's length, in case we should ever get to blows again. Some people think it's too open and exposed, but I'm for anchoring out here, clear of underbrush and thickets, as the surest means of making a safe berth."

"You was once a sailor, they tell me, old Tom?" said Hurry, in his abrupt manner, struck by one or two expressions that the other had just used, "and some people believe you could give us strange accounts of inimies and shipwrecks, if you'd a mind to come out with all you know?"

"There are people in this world, Hurry," returned the other, evasively, "who live on other men's thoughts; and some such often find their way into the woods. What I've been, or what I've seen in youth, is of less matter now than what the savages are. It's of more account to find out what will happen in the next twenty-four hours than to talk over what happened twenty-four years since."

"That's judgment, Deerslayer; yes, that's sound judgment. Here's Judith and Hetty to take care of, to say nothing of our own top-knots; and, for my part, I can sleep as well in the dark as I could under a noonday sun. To me it's no great matter whether there is light or not, to see to shut my eyes by."

As Deerslayer seldom thought it necessary to answer his companion's peculiar vein of humor, and Hutter was evidently indisposed to dwell longer on the subject, it's discussion ceased with this remark. The latter had something more on his mind, however, than recollections. His daughters had no sooner left them, with an expressed intention of going to bed, than he invited his two companions to follow him again into the scow. Here the old man opened his project, keeping back the portion that he had reserved for execution by Hurry and himself.

"The great object for people posted like ourselves is to command the water," he commenced. "So long as there is no other craft on the lake, a bark canoe is as good as a man-of-war, since the castle will not be easily taken by swimming. Now, there are but five canoes remaining in these parts, two of which are mine, and one is Hurry's. These three we have with us here; one being fastened in the canoe-dock beneath the house, and the other two being alongside the scow. The other canoes are housed on the shore, in hollow logs, and the savages, who are such venomous enemies, will leave no likely place unexamined in the morning, if they 're serious in s'arch of bounties——"

"Now, friend Hutter," interrupted Hurry, "the Indian don't live that can find a canoe that is suitably wintered. I've done something at this business before now, and Deerslayer here knows that I am one that can hide a craft in such a way that I can't find it myself."

"Very true, Hurry," put in the person to whom the appeal had been made, "but you overlook the sarcumstance that if you couldn't see the trail of the man who did the job, I could. I'm of Master Hutter's mind, that it's far wiser to mistrust a savage's ingenuity, than to build any great expectations on his want of eye-sight. If these two canoes can be got off to the castle, therefore, the sooner it's done the better."

"Will you be of the party that's to do it?" demanded Hutter, in a way to show that the proposal both surprised and pleased him.

"Sartain. I'm ready to enlist in any enterprise that's not ag'in a white man's lawful gifts. Natur' orders us to defend our lives, and the lives of others, too, when there's occasion and opportunity. I'll follow you, Floating Tom, into the Mingo camp, on such an arr'nd, and will strive to do my duty, should we come to blows; though, never having been tried in battle, I don't like to promise more than I may be able to perform. We all know our wishes, but none know their might till put to the proof."

"That's modest and suitable, lad," exclaimed Hurry. "You've never yet heard the crack of an angry rifle; and, let me tell you, 'tis as different from the persuasion of one of your venison speeches, as the laugh of Judith Hutter, in her best humor, is from the scolding of a Dutch house keeper on the Mohawk. I don't expect you'll prove much of a warrior, Deerslayer, though your equal with the bucks and the does don't exist in all these parts. As for the ra'al sarvice, however, you'll turn out rather rearward, according to my consait."

"We'll see, Hurry, we'll see," returned the other, meekly; so far as human eye could discover, not at all disturbed by these expressed doubts concerning his conduct on a point on which men are sensitive, precisely in the degree that they feel the consciousness of demerit; "having never been tried, I'll wait to know, before I form any opinion of myself; and then there'll be sartainty, instead of bragging. I've heard of them that was valiant afore the fight, who did little in it; and of them that waited to know their own tempers, and found that they weren't as bad as some expected, when put to the proof."

"At any rate, we know you can use a paddle, young man," said Hutter, "and that's all we shall ask of you to-night. Let us waste no more time, but get into the canoe, and do, in place of talking."

As Hutter led the way, in the execution of his project, the boat was soon ready, with Hurry and Deerslayer at the paddles. Before the old man embarked himself, however, he held a conference of several minutes with Judith, entering the house for that purpose; then, returning, he took his place in the canoe, which left the side of the ark at the next instant.

Had there been a temple reared to God, in that solitary wilderness, its clock would have told the hour of midnight as the party set forth on their expedition. The darkness had increased, though the night was still clear, and the light of the stars sufficed for all the purposes of the adventurers. Hutter alone knew the places where the canoes were hid, and he directed the course, while his two athletic companions raised and dipped their paddles with proper caution, lest the sound should be carried to the ears of their enemies, across that sheet of placid water, in the stillness of deep night. But the bark was too light to require any extraordinary efforts, and skill supplying the place of strength, in about half an hour they were approaching the shore, at a point near a league from the castle.

"Lay on your paddles, men," said Hutter, in a low voice, "and let us look about us for a moment. We must now be all eyes and ears, for these vermin have noses like bloodhounds."

The shores of the lake were examined closely, in order to discover any glimmering of light that might have been left in a camp; and the men strained their eyes, in the obscurity, to see if some thread of smoke was not still stealing along the mountainside, as it arose from the dying embers of a fire. Nothing unusual could be traced; and as the position was at some distance from the outlet, or the spot where the savages had been met, it was thought safe to land. The paddles were plied again, and the bows of the canoe ground upon the gravelly beach with a gentle motion, and a sound barely audible. Hutter and Hurry immediately landed, the former carrying his own and his friend's rifle, leaving Deerslayer in charge of the canoe. The hollow log lay a little distance up the side of the mountain, and the old man led the way towards it, using so much caution as to stop at every third or fourth step, to listen if any tread betrayed the presence of a foe. The same death-like stillness, however, reigned on the midnight scene, and the desired place was reached without an occurrence to induce alarm.

"This is it," whispered Hutter, laying a foot on the trunk of a fallen linden; "hand me the paddles first, and draw the boat out with care, for the wretches may have left it for a bait, after all."

"Keep my rifle handy, butt towards me, old fellow," answered March. "If they attack me loaded, I shall want to unload the piece at 'em, at least. And feel if the pan is full."

"All's right," muttered the other; "move slow, when you get your load, and let me lead the way."

The canoe was drawn out of the log with the utmost care, raised by Hurry to his shoulder, and the two began to return to the shore, moving but a step at a time, lest they should tumble down the steep declivity. The distance was not great, but the descent was extremely difficult; and, towards the end of their little journey, Deerslayer was obliged to land and meet them, in order to aid in lifting the canoe through the bushes. With his assistance the task was successfully accomplished, and the light craft soon floated by the side of the other canoe. This was no sooner done, than all three turned anxiously towards the forest and the mountain, expecting an enemy to break out of the one, or to come rushing down the other. Still the silence was unbroken, and they all embarked with the caution that had been used in coming ashore.

Hutter now steered broad off towards the centre of the lake. Having got a sufficient distance from the shore, he cast his prize loose, knowing that it would drift slowly up the lake before the light southerly air, and intending to find it on his return. Thus relieved of his tow, the old man held his way down the lake, steering towards the very point where Hurry had made his fruitless attempt on the life of the deer. As the distance from this point to the outlet was less than a mile, it was like entering an enemy's country; and redoubled caution became necessary. They reached the extremity of the point, however, and landed in safety on the little gravelly beach already mentioned. Unlike the last place at which they had gone ashore, here was no acclivity to ascend, the mountains looming up in the darkness quite a quarter of a mile farther west, leaving a margin of level ground between them and the strand. The point itself, though long, and covered with tall trees, was nearly flat, and for some distance only a few yards in width. Hutter and Hurry landed as before, leaving their companion in charge of the boat.

In this instance, the dead tree that contained the canoe of which they had come in quest lay about half-way between the extremity of the narrow slip of land and the place where it joined the main shore; and knowing that there was water so near him on his left, the old man led the way along the eastern side of the belt with some confidence walking boldly, though still with caution. He had landed at the point expressly to get a glimpse into the bay and to make certain that the coast was clear; otherwise he would have come ashore directly abreast of the hollow tree. There was no difficulty in finding the latter, from which the canoe was drawn as before, and instead of carrying it down to the place where Deerslayer lay, it was launched at the nearest favorable spot. As soon as it was in the water, Hurry entered it, and paddled round to the point, whither Hutter also proceeded, following the beach. As the three men had now in their possession all the boats on the lake, their confidence was greatly increased, and there was no longer the same feverish desire to quit the shore, or the same necessity for extreme caution. Their position on the extremity of the long, narrow bit of land added to the feeling of security, as it permitted an enemy to approach in only one direction, that in their front, and under circumstances that would render discovery, with their habitual vigilance, almost certain. The three now landed together, and stood grouped in consultation on the gravelly point.

"We've fairly tree'd the scamps," said Hurry, chuckling at their success; "if they wish to visit the castle, let 'em wade or swim! Old Tom, that idee of your'n, in burrowing out in the lake, was high proof, and carries a fine bead. There be men who would think the land safer than the water; but, after all, reason shows it isn't; the beaver, and rats, and other l'arned creatur's taking to the last when hard pressed. I call our position now, entrenched, and set the Canadas at defiance."

"Let us paddle along this south shore," said Hutter, "and see if there's no sign of an encampment; but, first, let me have a better look into the bay, for no one has been far enough round the inner shore of the point to make suit of that quarter yet."

As Hutter ceased speaking, all three moved in the direction he had named. Scarce had they fairly opened the bottom of the bay, when a general start proved that their eyes had lighted on a common object at the same instant. It was no more than a dying brand, giving out its flickering and failing light; but at that hour, and in that place, it was at once as conspicuous as "a good deed in a naughty world." There was not a shadow of doubt that this fire had been kindled at an encampment of the Indians. The situation, sheltered from observation on all sides but one, and even on that except for a very short distance, proved that more care had been taken to conceal the spot than would be used for ordinary purposes, and Hutter, who knew that a spring was near at hand, as well as one of the best fishing-stations on the lake, immediately inferred that this encampment contained the women and children of the party.

"That's not a warrior's encampment," he growled to Hurry; "and there's bounty enough sleeping round that fire to make a heavy division of head-money. Send the lad to the canoes, for there'll come no good of him in such an onset, and let us take the matter in hand at once, like men."

"There's judgment in your notion, old Tom, and I like it to the backbone. Deerslayer, do you get into the canoe, lad, and paddle off into the lake with the spare one, and set it adrift, as we did with the other; after which you can float along shore, as near as you can get to the head of the bay, keeping outside the point, howsever, and outside the rushes, too. You can hear us when we want you; and if there's any delay, I'll call like a loon—yes, that'll do it—the call of a loon shall be the signal. If you hear rifles, and feel like sogering, why, you may close in, and see if you can make the same hand with the savages that you do with the deer."

"If my wishes could be followed, this matter would not be undertaken, Hurry——"

"Quite true—nobody denies it, boy; but your wishes can't be followed; and that inds the matter. So just canoe yourself off into the middle of the lake, and by the time you get back there'll be movements in that camp!"

The young man set about complying with great reluctance and a heavy heart. He knew the prejudices of the frontiermen too well, however, to attempt a remonstrance. The latter, indeed, under the circumstances, might prove dangerous, as it would certainly prove useless. He paddled the canoe, therefore, silently and with the former caution, to a spot near the centre of the placid sheet of water, and set the boat just recovered adrift, to float towards the castle, before the light southerly air. This expedient had been adopted, in both cases, under the certainty that the drift could not carry the light barks more than a league or two, before the return of light, when they might easily be overtaken in order to prevent any wandering savage from using them, by swimming off and getting possession, a possible but scarcely a probable event, all the paddles were retained.

No sooner had he set the recovered canoe adrift, than Deerslayer turned the bows of his own towards the point on the shore that had been indicated by Hurry. So light was the movement of the little craft, and so steady the sweep of its master's arm, that ten minutes had not elapsed ere it was again approaching the land, having, in that brief time, passed over fully half a mile of distance. As soon as Deerslayer's eye caught a glimpse of the rushes, of which there were many growing in the water a hundred feet from the shore, he arrested the motion of the canoe, and anchored his boat by holding fast to the delicate but tenacious stem of one of the drooping plants. Here he remained, awaiting, with an intensity of suspense that can be easily imagined, the result of the hazardous enterprise.

It would be difficult to convey to the minds of those who have never witnessed it, the sublimity that characterizes the silence of a solitude as deep as that which now reigned over the Glimmerglass. In the present instance, this sublimity was increased by the gloom of night, which threw its shadowy and fantastic forms around the lake, the forest, and the hills. It is not easy, indeed, to conceive of any place more favorable to heighten these natural impressions, than that Deerslayer now occupied. The size of the lake brought all within the reach of human senses, while it displayed so much of the imposing scene at a single view, giving up, as it might be, at a glance, a sufficiency to produce the deepest impressions. As has been said, this was the first lake Deerslayer had ever seen. Hitherto, his experience had been limited to the courses of rivers and smaller streams, and never before had he seen so much of that wilderness, which he so well loved, spread before his gaze. Accustomed to the forest, however, his mind was capable of portraying all its hidden mysteries, as he looked upon its leafy surface. This was also the first time he had been on a trail where human lives depended on the issue. His ears had often drunk in the traditions of frontier warfare, but he had never yet been confronted with an enemy.

The reader will readily understand, therefore, how intense must have been the expectation of the young man, as he sat in his solitary canoe, endeavoring to catch the smallest sound that might denote the course of things on shore. His training had been perfect, so far as theory could go, and his self-possession, notwithstanding the high excitement, that was the fruit of novelty, would have done credit to a veteran. The visible evidences of the existence of the camp, or of the fire could not be detected from the spot where the canoe lay, and he was compelled to depend on the sense of hearing alone. He did not feel impatient, for the lessons he had heard taught him the virtue of patience, and, most of all, inculcated the necessity of wariness in conducting any covert assault on the Indians. Once he thought he heard the cracking of a dried twig, but expectation was so intense it might mislead him. In this manner minute after minute passed, until the whole time since he left his companions was extended to quite an hour. Deerslayer knew not whether to rejoice in or to mourn over this cautious delay, for, if it augured security to his associates, it foretold destruction to the feeble and innocent.

It might have been an hour and a half after his companions and he had parted, when Deerslayer was aroused by a sound that filled him equally with concern and surprise. The quavering call of a loon arose from the opposite side of the lake, evidently at no great distance from its outlet. There was no mistaking the note of this bird, which is so familiar to all who know the sounds of the American lakes. Shrill, tremulous, loud, and sufficiently prolonged, it seems the very cry of warning. It is often raised, also, at night, an exception to the habits of most of the other feathered inmates of the wilderness; a circumstance which had induced Hurry to select it as his own signal. There had been sufficient time, certainly, for the two adventurers to make their way by land from the point where they had been left to that whence the call had come, but it was not probable that they would adopt such a course. Had the camp been deserted they would have summoned Deerslayer to the shore, and, did it prove to be peopled, there could be no sufficient motive for circling it, in order to re-embark at so great a distance. Should he obey the signal, and be drawn away from the landing, the lives of those who depended on him might be the forfeit—and, should he neglect the call, on the supposition that it had been really made, the consequences might be equally disastrous, though from a different cause. In this indecision he waited, trusting that the call, whether feigned or natural, would be speedily renewed. Nor was he mistaken. A very few minutes elapsed before the same shrill warning cry was repeated, and from the same part of the lake. This time, being on the alert, his senses were not deceived. Although he had often heard admirable imitations of this bird, and was no mean adept himself in raising its notes, he felt satisfied that Hurry, to whose efforts in that way he had attended, could never so completely and closely follow nature. He determined, therefore, to disregard that cry, and to wait for one less perfect and nearer at hand.

Deerslayer had hardly come to this determination, when the profound stillness of night and solitude was broken by a cry so startling, as to drive all recollection of the more melancholy call of the loon from the listener's mind. It was a shriek of agony, that came either from one of the female sex, or from a boy so young as not yet to have attained a manly voice. This appeal could not be mistaken. Heart rending terror—if not writhing agony—was in the sounds, and the anguish that had awakened them was as sudden as it was fearful. The young man released his hold of the rush, and dashed his paddle into the water; to do, he knew not what—to steer, he knew not whither. A very few moments, however, removed his indecision. The breaking of branches, the cracking of dried sticks, and the fall of feet were distinctly audible; the sounds appearing to approach the water though in a direction that led diagonally towards the shore, and a little farther north than the spot that Deerslayer had been ordered to keep near. Following this clue, the young man urged the canoe ahead, paying but little attention to the manner in which he might betray its presence. He had reached a part of the shore, where its immediate bank was tolerably high and quite steep. Men were evidently threshing through the bushes and trees on the summit of this bank, following the line of the shore, as if those who fled sought a favorable place for descending. Just at this instant five or six rifles flashed, and the opposite hills gave back, as usual, the sharp reports in prolonged rolling echoes. One or two shrieks, like those which escape the bravest when suddenly overcome by unexpected anguish and alarm, followed; and then the threshing among the bushes was renewed, in a way to show that man was grappling with man.

"Slippery devil!" shouted Hurry with the fury of disappointment—"his skin's greased! I sha'n't grapple! Take that for your cunning!"

The words were followed by the fall of some heavy object among the smaller trees that fringed the bank, appearing to Deerslayer as if his gigantic associate had hurled an enemy from him in this unceremonious manner. Again the flight and pursuit were renewed, and then the young man saw a human form break down the hill, and rush several yards into the water. At this critical moment the canoe was just near enough to the spot to allow this movement, which was accompanied by no little noise, to be seen, and feeling that there he must take in his companion, if anywhere, Deerslayer urged the canoe forward to the rescue. His paddle had not been raised twice, when the voice of Hurry was heard filling the air with imprecations, and he rolled on the narrow beach, literally loaded down with enemies. While prostrate, and almost smothered with his foes, the athletic frontierman gave his loon-call, in a manner that would have excited laughter under circumstances less terrific. The figure in the water seemed suddenly to repent his own flight, and rushed to the shore to aid his companion, but was met and immediately overpowered by half a dozen fresh pursuers, who, just then, came leaping down the bank.

"Let up, you painted riptyles—let up!" cried Hurry, too hard pressed to be particular about the terms he used; "isn't it enough that I am withed like a saw-log that ye must choke too!"

This speech satisfied Deerslayer that his friends were prisoners, and that to land would be to share their fate. He was already within a hundred feet of the shore, when a few timely strokes of the paddle not only arrested his advance, but forced him off to six or eight times that distance from his enemies. Luckily for him, all of the Indians had dropped their rifles in the pursuit, or this retreat might not have been effected with impunity; though no one had noted the canoe in the first confusion of the melee.

"Keep off the land, lad," called out Hutter; "the girls depend only on you, now; you will want all your caution to escape these savages. Keep off, and God prosper you, as you aid my children!"

There was little sympathy in general between Hutter and the young man, but the bodily and mental anguish with which this appeal was made served at the moment to conceal from the latter the former's faults. He saw only the father in his sufferings, and resolved at once to give a pledge of fidelity to its interests, and to be faithful to his word.

"Put your heart at ease, Master Hutter," he called out; "the gals shall be looked to, as well as the castle. The inimy has got the shore, 'tis no use to deny, but he hasn't got the water. Providence has the charge of all, and no one can say what will come of it; but, if good-will can sarve you and your'n, depend on that much. My exper'ence is small, but my will is good."

"Ay, ay, Deerslayer," returned Hurry, in this stentorian voice, which was losing some of its heartiness, notwithstanding,—"Ay, ay, Deerslayer. You mean well enough, but what can you do? You're no great matter in the best of times, and such a person is not likely to turn out a miracle in the worst. If there's one savage on this lake shore, there's forty, and that's an army you ar'n't the man to overcome. The best way, in my judgment, will be to make a straight course to the castle; get the gals into the canoe, with a few eatables; then strike off for the corner of the lake where we came in, and take the best trail for the Mohawk. These devils won't know where to look for you for some hours, and if they did, and went off hot in the pursuit, they must turn either the foot or the head of the lake to get at you. That's my judgment in the matter; and if old Tom here wishes to make his last will and testament in a manner favorable to his darters, he'll say the same."

"'Twill never do, young man," rejoined Hutter. "The enemy has scouts out at this moment, looking for canoes, and you'll be seen and taken. Trust to the castle; and above all things, keep clear of the land. Hold out a week, and parties from the garrisons will drive the savages off."

"'Twon't be four-and-twenty hours, old fellow, afore these foxes will be rafting off to storm your castle," interrupted Hurry, with more of the heat of argument than might be expected from a man who was bound and a captive, and about whom nothing could be called free but his opinions and his tongue. "Your advice has a stout sound, but it will have a fatal tarmination. If you or I was in the house, we might hold out a few days, but remember that this lad has never seen an inimy afore to-night, and is what you yourself called settlement-conscienced; though for my part, I think the consciences in the settlements pretty much the same as they are out here in the woods. These savages are making signs, Deerslayer, for me to encourage you to come ashore with the canoe; but that I'll never do, as it's ag'in reason and natur'. As for old Tom and myself, whether they'll scalp us to-night, keep us for the torture by fire, or carry us to Canada, is more than any one knows but the devil that advises them how to act. I've such a big and bushy head that it's quite likely they'll indivor to get two scalps off it, for the bounty is a tempting thing, or old Tom and I wouldn't be in this scrape. Ay— there they go with their signs ag'in, but if I advise you to land may they eat me as well as roast me. No, no, Deerslayer—do you keep off where you are, and after daylight, on no account come within two hundred yards—"

This injunction of Hurry's was stopped by a hand being rudely slapped against his mouth, the certain sign that some one in the party sufficiently understood English to have at length detected the drift of his discourse. Immediately after, the whole group entered the forest, Hutter and Hurry apparently making no resistance to the movement. Just as the sounds of the cracking bushes were ceasing, however, the voice of the father was again heard.

"As you're true to my children, God prosper you, young man!" were the words that reached Deerslayer's ears; after which he found himself left to follow the dictates of his own discretion.

Several minutes elapsed, in death-like stillness, when the party on the shore had disappeared in the woods. Owing to the distance—rather more than two hundred yards—and the obscurity, Deerslayer had been able barely to distinguish the group, and to see it retiring; but even this dim connection with human forms gave an animation to the scene that was strongly in contrast to the absolute solitude that remained. Although the young man leaned forward to listen, holding his breath and condensing every faculty in the single sense of hearing, not another sound reached his ears to denote the vicinity of human beings. It seemed as if a silence that had never been broken reigned on the spot again; and, for an instant, even that piercing shriek, which had so lately broken the stillness of the forest, or the execrations of March, would have been a relief to the feeling of desertion to which it gave rise.

This paralysis of mind and body, however, could not last long in one constituted mentally and physically like Deerslayer. Dropping his paddle into the water, he turned the head of the canoe, and proceeded slowly, as one walks who thinks intently, towards the centre of the lake. When he believed himself to have reached a point in a line with that where he had set the last canoe adrift, he changed his direction northward, keeping the light air as nearly on his back as possible. After paddling a quarter of a mile in this direction, a dark object became visible on the lake, a little to the right; and turning on one side for the purpose, he had soon secured his lost prize to his own boat. Deerslayer now examined the heavens, the course of the air, and the position of the two canoes. Finding nothing in either to induce a change of plan, he lay down, and prepared to catch a few hours' sleep, that the morrow might find him equal to its exigencies.

Although the hardy and the tired sleep profoundly, even in scenes of danger, it was some time before Deerslayer lost his recollection. His mind dwelt on what had passed, and his half-conscious faculties kept figuring the events of the night, in a sort of waking dream. Suddenly he was up and alert, for he fancied he heard the preconcerted signal of Hurry summoning him to the shore. But all was still as the grave again. The canoes were slowly drifting northward, the thoughtful stars were glimmering in their mild glory over his head, and the forest-bound sheet of water lay embedded between its mountains, as calm and melancholy as if never troubled by the winds, or brightened by a noonday sun. Once more the loon raised his tremulous cry, near the foot of the lake, and the mystery of the alarm was explained. Deerslayer adjusted his hard pillow, stretched his form in the bottom of the canoe, and slept.

## CHAPTER VII.

"Clear, placid Leman I Thy contrasted lake
With the wild world I dwelt in, is a thing
Which warns me, with its stillness, to forsake
Earth's troubled waters for a purer spring.
This quiet sail is as a noiseless wing
To waft me from distraction; once I loved
Torn ocean's roar, but thy soft murmuring
Sounds sweet as if a sister's voice reproved,
That I with stern delights should e'er have been so moved."

BYRON.

Day had fairly dawned before the young man, whom we have left in the situation described in the last chapter, again opened his eyes. This was no sooner done, than he started up, and looked about him with the eagerness of one who suddenly felt the importance of accurately ascertaining his precise position. His rest had been deep and undisturbed; and when he awoke, it was with a clearness of intellect and a readiness of resources that were very much needed at that particular moment. The sun had not risen, it is true, but the vault of heaven was rich with the winning softness that "brings and shuts the day," while the whole air was filled with the carols of birds, the hymns of the feathered tribe. These sounds first told Deerslayer the risks he ran. The air, for wind it could scarce be called, was still light, it is true, but it had increased a little in the course of the night, and as the canoes were feathers on the water, they had drifted twice the expected distance; and, what was still more dangerous, had approached so near the base of the mountain that here rose precipitously from the eastern shore, as to render the carols of the birds plainly audible. This was not the worst. The third canoe had taken the same direction, and was slowly drifting towards a point where it must inevitably touch, unless turned aside by a shift of wind, or human hands. In other respects, nothing presented itself to attract attention, or to awaken alarm. The castle stood on its shoal, nearly abreast of the canoes, for the drift had amounted to miles in the course of the night, and the ark lay fastened to its piles, as both had been left so many hours before.

As a matter of course, Deerslayer's attention was first given to the canoe ahead. It was already quite near the point, and a very few strokes of the paddle sufficed to tell him that it must touch before he could possibly overtake it. Just at this moment, too, the wind inopportunely freshened, rendering the drift of the light craft much more rapid than certain. Feeling the impossibility of preventing a contact with the land, the young man wisely determined not to heat himself with unnecessary exertions; but first looking to the priming of his piece, he proceeded slowly and warily towards the point, taking care to make a little circuit, that he might be exposed on only one side, as he approached.

The canoe adrift being directed by no such intelligence, pursued its proper way, and grounded on a small sunken rock, at the distance of three or four yards from the shore. Just at that moment, Deerslayer had got abreast of the point, and turned the bows of his own boat to the land; first casting loose his tow, that his movements might be unencumbered. The canoe hung an instant to the rock; then it rose a hair's breadth on an almost imperceptible swell of the water, swung round, floated clear, and reached the strand. All this the young man noted, but it neither quickened his pulses, nor hastened his hand. If any one had been lying in wait for the arrival of the waif, he must be seen, and the utmost caution in approaching the shore became indispensable; if no one was in ambush, hurry was unnecessary. The point being nearly diagonally opposite to the Indian encampment, he hoped the last, though the former was not only possible, but probable; for the savages were prompt in adopting all the expedients of their particular modes of warfare, and quite likely had many scouts searching the shores for craft to carry them off to the castle. As a glance at the lake from any height or projection would expose the smallest object on its surface, there was little hope that either of the canoes would pass unseen; and Indian sagacity needed no instruction to tell which way a boat or a log would drift, when the direction of the wind was known. As Deerslayer drew nearer and nearer to the land, the stroke of his paddle grew slower, his eye became more watchful, and his ears and nostrils almost dilated with the effort to detect any lurking danger. It was a trying moment for a novice, nor was there the encouragement which even the timid sometimes feel, when conscious of being observed and commended. He was entirely alone, thrown on his own resources, and was cheered by no friendly eye, emboldened by no encouraging voice. Notwithstanding all these circumstances, the most experienced veteran in forest warfare could not have behaved better. Equally free from recklessness and hesitation, his advance was marked by a sort of philosophical prudence that appeared to render him superior to all motives but those which were best calculated to effect his purpose. Such was the commencement of a career in forest exploits, that afterwards rendered this man, in his way, and under the limits of his habits and opportunities, as renowned as many a hero whose name has adorned the pages of works more celebrated than legends simple as ours can ever become.

When about a hundred yards from the shore, Deerslayer rose in the canoe, gave three or four vigorous strokes with the paddle, sufficient of themselves to impel the bark to land, and then quickly laying aside the instrument of labor, he seized that of war. He was in the very act of raising the rifle, when a sharp report was followed by the buzz of a bullet that passed so near his body as to cause him involuntarily to start. The next instant Deerslayer staggered, and fell his whole length in the bottom of the canoe. A yell—it came from a single voice—followed, and an Indian leaped from the bushes upon the open area of the point, bounding towards the canoe. This was the moment the young man desired. He rose on the instant, and levelled his own rifle at his uncovered foe; but his finger hesitated about pulling the trigger on one whom he held at such a disadvantage. This little delay, probably, saved the life of the Indian, who bounded back into the cover as swiftly as he had broken out of it. In the meantime Deerslayer had been swiftly approaching the land, and his own canoe reached the point just as his enemy disappeared. As its movements had not been directed, it touched the shore a few yards from the other boat; and though the rifle of his foe had to be loaded, there was not time to secure his prize, and carry it beyond danger, before he would be exposed to another shot. Under the circumstances, therefore, he did not pause an instant, but dashed into the woods and sought a cover.

On the immediate point there was a small open area, partly in native grass, and partly beach, but a dense fringe of bushes lined its upper side. This narrow belt of dwarf vegetation passed, one issued immediately into the high and gloomy vaults of the forest. The land was tolerably level for a few hundred feet, and then it rose precipitously in a mountainside. The trees were tall, large, and so free from underbrush, that they resembled vast columns, irregularly scattered, upholding a dome of leaves. Although they stood tolerably close together, for their ages and size, the eye could penetrate to considerable distances; and bodies of men, even, might have engaged beneath their cover, with concert and intelligence.

Deerslayer knew that his adversary must be employed in reloading, unless he had fled. The former proved to be the case, for the young man had no sooner placed himself behind a tree, than he caught a glimpse of the arm of the Indian, his body being concealed by an oak, in the very act of forcing the leathered bullet home. Nothing would have been easier than to spring forward, and decide the affair by a close assault on his unprepared foe; but every feeling of Deerslayer revolted at such a step, although his own life had just been attempted from a cover. He was yet unpracticed in the ruthless expedients of savage warfare, of which he knew nothing except by tradition and theory, and it struck him as unfair advantage to assail an unarmed foe. His color had heightened, his eye frowned, his lips were compressed, and all his energies were collected and ready; but, instead of advancing to fire, he dropped his rifle to the usual position of a sportsman in readiness to catch his aim, and muttered to himself, unconscious that he was speaking—

"No, no—that may be red-skin warfare, but it's not a Christian's gifts. Let the miscreant charge, and then we'll take it out like men; for the canoe he must not, and shall not have. No, no; let him have time to load, and God will take care of the right!"

All this time the Indian had been so intent on his own movements, that he was even ignorant that his enemy was in the woods. His only apprehension was, that the canoe would be recovered and carried away before he might be in readiness to prevent it. He had sought the cover from habit, but was within a few feet of the fringe of bushes, and could be at the margin of the forest in readiness to fire in a moment. The distance between him and his enemy was about fifty yards, and the trees were so arranged by nature that the line of sight was not interrupted, except by the particular trees behind which each party stood.

His rifle was no sooner loaded, than the savage glanced around him, and advanced incautiously as regarded the real, but stealthily as respected the fancied position of his enemy, until he was fairly exposed. Then Deerslayer stepped from behind its own cover, and hailed him.

"This-a-way, red-skin; this-a-way, if you're looking for me," he called out. "I'm young in war, but not so young as to stand on an open beach to be shot down like an owl, by daylight. It rests on yourself whether it's peace or war atween us; for my gifts are white gifts, and I'm not one of them that thinks it valiant to slay human mortals, singly, in the woods."

The savage was a good deal startled by this sudden discovery of the danger he ran. He had a little knowledge of English, however, and caught the drift of the other's meaning. He was also too well schooled to betray alarm, but, dropping the butt of his rifle to the earth, with an air of confidence, he made a gesture of lofty courtesy. All this was done with the ease and self-possession of one accustomed to consider no man his superior. In the midst of this consummate acting, however, the volcano that raged within caused his eyes to glare, and his nostrils to dilate, like those of some wild beast that is suddenly prevented from taking the fatal leap.

"Two canoes," he said, in the deep guttural tones of his race, holding up the number of fingers he mentioned, by way of preventing mistakes; "one for you—one for me."

"No, no, Mingo, that will never do. You own neither; and neither shall you have, as long as I can prevent it. I know it's war atween your people and mine, but that's no reason why human mortals should slay each other, like savage creatur's that meet in the woods; go your way, then, and leave me to go mine. The world is large enough for us both; and when we meet fairly in battle, why, the Lord will order the fate of each of us."

"Good!" exclaimed the Indian; "my brother missionary—great talk; all about Manitou."

"Not so—not so, warrior. I'm not good enough for the Moravians, and am too good for most of the other vagabonds that preach about in the woods. No, no; I'm only a hunter, as yet, though afore the peace is made, 'tis like enough there'll be occasion to strike a blow at some of your people. Still, I wish it to be done in fair fight, and not in a quarrel about the ownership of a miserable canoe."

"Good! My brother very young—but he is very wise. Little warrior—great talker. Chief, sometimes, in council."

"I don't know this, nor do I say it, Injin," returned Deerslayer, coloring a little at the ill-concealed sarcasm of the other's manner; "I look forward to a life in the woods, and I only hope it may be a peaceable one. All young men must go on the war-path, when there's occasion, but war isn't needfully massacre. I've seen enough of the last, this very night, to know that Providence frowns on it; and I now invite you to go your own way, while I go mine; and hope that we may part fri'nds."

"Good! My brother has two scalp—gray hair under 'other. Old wisdom—young tongue."

Here the savage advanced with confidence, his hand extended, his face smiling, and his whole bearing denoting amity and respect. Deerslayer met his offered friendship in a proper spirit, and they shook hands cordially, each endeavoring to assure the other of his sincerity and desire to be at peace.

"All have his own," said the Indian; "my canoe, mine; your canoe, your'n. Go look; if your'n, you keep; if mine, I keep."

"That's just, red-skin; thought you must be wrong in thinking the canoe your property. Howsever, seein' is believin', and we'll go down to the shore, where you may look with your own eyes; for it's likely you'll object to trustin' altogether to mine."

The Indian uttered his favorite exclamation of "Good!" and then they walked side by side, towards the shore. There was no apparent distrust in the manner of either, the Indian moving in advance, as if he wished to show his companion that he did not fear turning his back to him. As they reached the open ground, the former pointed towards Deerslayer's boat, and said emphatically—"No mine—pale-face canoe. This red man's. No want other man's canoe—want his own."

"You're wrong, red-skin, you're altogether wrong. This canoe was left in old Hutter's keeping, and is his'n according to law, red or white, till its owner comes to claim it. Here's the seats and the stitching of the bark to speak for themselves. No man ever know'd an Injin to turn off such work."

"Good! My brother little old—big wisdom. Injin no make him. White man's work."

"I'm glad you think so, for holding out to the contrary might have made ill blood atween us, every one having a right to take possession of his own. I'll just shove the canoe out of reach of dispute at once, as the quickest way of settling difficulties."

While Deerslayer was speaking, he put a foot against the end of the light boat, and giving a vigorous shove, he sent it out into the lake a hundred feet or more, where, taking the true current, it would necessarily float past the point, and be in no further danger of coming ashore. The savage started at this ready and decided expedient, and his companion saw that he cast a hurried and fierce glance at his own canoe, or that which contained the paddles. The change of manner, however, was but momentary, and then the Iroquois resumed his air of friendliness, and a smile of satisfaction.

"Good!" he repeated, with stronger emphasis than ever. "Young head, old mind. Know how to settle quarrel. Farewell, brother. He go to house in water—muskrat house—Injin go to camp; tell chiefs no find canoe."

Deerslayer was not sorry to hear this proposal, for he felt anxious to join the females, and he took the offered hand of the Indian very willingly. The parting words were friendly, and while the red man walked calmly towards the wood, with the rifle in the hollow of his arm, without once looking back in uneasiness or distrust, the white man moved towards the remaining canoe, carrying his piece in the same pacific manner, it is true, but keeping his eye fastened on the movements of the other. This distrust, however, seemed to be altogether uncalled for, and as if ashamed to have entertained it, the young man averted his look, and stepped carelessly up to his boat. Here he began to push the canoe from the shore, and to make his other preparations for departing. He might have been thus employed a minute, when, happening to turn his face towards the land, his quick and certain eye told him, at a glance, the imminent jeopardy in which his life was placed. The black, ferocious eyes of the savage were glancing on him, like those of the crouching tiger, through a small opening in the bushes, and the muzzle of his rifle seemed already to be opening in a line with his own body.

Then, indeed, the long practice of Deerslayer, as a hunter did him good service. Accustomed to fire with the deer on the bound, and often when the precise position of the animal's body had in a manner to be guessed at, he used the same expedients here. To cock and poise his rifle were the acts of a single moment and a single motion: then aiming almost without sighting, he fired into the bushes where he knew a body ought to be, in order to sustain the appalling countenance which alone was visible. There was not time to raise the piece any higher, or to take a more deliberate aim. So rapid were his movements that both parties discharged their pieces at the same instant, the concussions mingling in one report. The mountains, indeed, gave back but a single echo. Deerslayer dropped his piece, and stood with head erect, steady as one of the pines in the calm of a June morning, watching the result; while the savage gave the yell that has become historical for its appalling influence, leaped through the bushes, and came bounding across the open ground, flourishing a tomahawk. Still Deerslayer moved not, but stood with his unloaded rifle fallen against his shoulders, while, with a hunter's habits, his hands were mechanically feeling for the powder-horn and charger. When about forty feet from his enemy, the savage hurled his keen weapon; but it was with an eye so vacant, and a hand so unsteady and feeble, that the young man caught it by the handle as it was flying past him. At that instant the Indian staggered and fell his whole length on the ground.

"I know'd it—I know'd it!" exclaimed Deerslayer, who was already preparing to force a fresh bullet into his rifle; "I know'd it must come to this, as soon as I had got the range from the creatur's eyes. A man sights suddenly, and fires quick when his own life's in danger; yes, I know'd it would come to this. I was about the hundredth part of a second too quick for him, or it might have been bad for me! The riptyle's bullet has just grazed my side—but say what you will for or ag'in 'em, a red-skin is by no means as sartain with powder and ball as a white man. Their gifts don't seem to lie that a way. Even Chingachgook, great as he is in other matters, isn't downright deadly with the rifle."

By this time the piece was reloaded, and Deerslayer, after tossing the tomahawk into the canoe, advanced to his victim, and stood over him, leaning on his rifle, in melancholy attention. It was the first instance in which he had seen a man fall in battle—it was the first fellow-creature against whom he had ever seriously raised his own hand. The sensations were novel; and regret, with the freshness of our better feelings, mingled with his triumph. The Indian was not dead, though shot directly through the body. He lay on his back motionless, but his eyes, now full of consciousness, watched each action of his victor—as the fallen bird regards the fowler—jealous of every movement. The man probably expected the fatal blow which was to precede the loss of his scalp; or perhaps he anticipated that this latter act of cruelty would precede his death. Deerslayer read his thoughts; and he found a melancholy satisfaction in relieving the apprehensions of the helpless savage.

"No, no, red-skin," he said; "you've nothing more to fear from me. I am of a Christian stock, and scalping is not of my gifts. I'll just make sartain of your rifle, and then come back and do you what sarvice I can. Though here I can't stay much longer, as the crack of three rifles will be apt to bring some of your devils down upon me."

The close of this was said in a sort of a soliloquy, as the young man went in quest of the fallen rifle. The piece was found where its owner had dropped it, and was immediately put into the canoe. Laying his own rifle at its side, Deerslayer then returned and stood over the Indian again.

"All inmity atween you and me's at an ind red-skin," he said; "and you may set your heart at rest on the score of the scalp, or any further injury. My gifts are white, as I've told you; and I hope my conduct will be white also."

Could looks have conveyed all they meant, it is probable Deerslayer's innocent vanity on the subject of color would have been rebuked a little; but he comprehended the gratitude that was expressed in the eyes of the dying savage, without in the least detecting the bitter sarcasm that struggled with the better feeling.

"Water!" ejaculated the thirsty and unfortunate creature; "give poor Injin water."

"Ay, water you shall have, if you drink the lake dry. I'll just carry you down to it that you may take your fill. This is the way, they tell me, with all wounded people—water is their greatest comfort and delight."

So saying, Deerslayer raised the Indian in his arms, and carried him to the lake. Here he first helped him to take an attitude in which he could appease his burning thirst; after which he seated himself on a stone, and took the head of his wounded adversary in his own lap, and endeavored to soothe his anguish in the best manner he could.

"It would be sinful in me to tell you your time hadn't come, warrior," he commenced, "and therefore I'll not say it. You've passed the middle age already, and, considerin' the sort of lives ye lead, your days have been pretty well filled. The principal thing now, is to look forward to what comes next. Neither red-skin nor pale-face, on the whole, calculates much on sleepin' forever; but both expect to live in another world. Each has his gifts, and will be judged by 'em, and I suppose you've thought these matters over enough not to stand in need of sarmons when the trial comes. You'll find your happy hunting-grounds, if you've been a just Injin; if an onjust, you'll meet your desarts in another way. I've my own idees about these things; but you're too old and exper'enced to need any explanations from one as young as I."

"Good!" ejaculated the Indian, whose voice retained its depth even as life ebbed away; "young head—old wisdom!"

"It's sometimes a consolation, when the ind comes, to know that them we've harmed, or tried to harm, forgive us. I suppose natur' seeks this relief, by way of getting a pardon on 'arth; as we never can know whether He pardons, who is all in all, till judgment itself comes. It's soothing to know that any pardon at such times; and that, I conclude, is the secret. Now, as for myself, I overlook altogether your designs ag'in my life; first, because no harm came of 'em; next, because it's your gifts, and natur', and trainin', and I ought not to have trusted you at all; and, finally and chiefly, because I can bear no ill-will to a dying man, whether heathen or Christian. So put your heart at ease, so far as I'm consarned; you know best what other matters ought to trouble you, or what ought to give you satisfaction in so trying a moment."

It is probable that the Indian had some of the fearful glimpses of the unknown state of being which God, in mercy, seems at times to afford to all the human race; but they were necessarily in conformity with his habits and prejudices. Like most of his people, and like too many of our own, he thought more of dying in a way to gain applause among those he left than to secure a better state of existence hereafter. While Deerslayer was speaking, his mind was a little bewildered, though he felt that the intention was good; and when he had done, a regret passed over his spirit that none of his own tribe were present to witness his stoicism, under extreme bodily suffering, and the firmness with which he met his end. With the high innate courtesy that so often distinguishes the Indian warrior before he becomes corrupted by too much intercourse with the worst class of the white men, he endeavored to express his thankfulness for the other's good intentions, and to let him understand that they were appreciated.

"Good!" he repeated, for this was an English word much used by the savages, "good! young head; young heart, too. Old heart tough; no shed tear. Hear Indian when he die, and no want to lie—what he call him?"

"Deerslayer is the name I bear now, though the Delawares have said that when I get back from this war-path, I shall have a more manly title, provided I can 'arn one."

"That good name for boy—poor name for warrior. He get better quick. No fear there,"—the savage had strength sufficient, under the strong excitement he felt, to raise a hand and tap the young man on his breast,— "eye sartain—finger lightning—aim, death—great warrior soon. No Deerslayer—Hawkeye—Hawkeye—Hawkeye. Shake hand."

Deerslayer—or Hawkeye, as the youth was then first named, for in after years he bore the appellation throughout all that region—Deerslayer took the hand of the savage, whose last breath was drawn in that attitude, gazing in admiration at the countenance of a stranger, who had shown so much readiness, skill, and firmness, in a scene that was equally trying and novel. When the reader remembers it is the highest gratification an Indian can receive to see his enemy betray weakness, he will be better able to appreciate the conduct which had extorted so great a concession at such a moment.

"His spirit has fled!" said Deerslayer, in a suppressed, melancholy voice. "Ah's me! Well, to this we must all come, sooner or later; and he is happiest, let his skin be what color it may, who is best fitted to meet it. Here lies the body of no doubt a brave warrior, and the soul is already flying towards its heaven or hell, whether that be a happy hunting ground, a place scant of game, regions of glory, according to Moravian doctrine, or flames of fire! So it happens, too, as regards other matters! Here have old Hutter and Hurry Harry got themselves into difficulty, if they haven't got themselves into torment and death, and all for a bounty that luck offers to me in what many would think a lawful and suitable manner. But not a farthing of such money shall cross my hand. White I was born, and white will I die; clinging to color to the last, even though the King's majesty, his governors, and all his councils, both at home and in the colonies, forget from what they come, and where they hope to go, and all for a little advantage in warfare. No, no, warrior, hand of mine shall never molest your scalp, and so your soul may rest in peace on the p'int of making a decent appearance when the body comes to join it, in your own land of spirits."

Deerslayer arose as soon as he had spoken. Then he placed the body of the dead man in a sitting posture, with its back against the little rock, taking the necessary care to prevent it from falling or in any way settling into an attitude that might be thought unseemly by the sensitive, though wild notions of a savage. When this duty was performed, the young man stood gazing at the grim countenance of his fallen foe, in a sort of melancholy abstraction. As was his practice, however, a habit gained by living so much alone in the forest, he then began again to give utterance to his thoughts and feelings aloud.

"I didn't wish your life, red-skin," he said "but you left me no choice atween killing or being killed. Each party acted according to his gifts, I suppose, and blame can light on neither. You were treacherous, according to your natur' in war, and I was a little oversightful, as I'm apt to be in trusting others. Well, this is my first battle with a human mortal, though it's not likely to be the last. I have fou't most of the creatur's of the forest, such as bears, wolves, painters, and catamounts, but this is the beginning with the red-skins. If I was Injin born, now, I might tell of this, or carry in the scalp, and boast of the expl'ite afore the whole tribe; or, if my inimy had only been even a bear, 'twould have been nat'ral and proper to let everybody know what had happened; but I don't well see how I'm to let even Chingachgook into this secret, so long as it can be done only by boasting with a white tongue. And why should I wish to boast of it a'ter all? It's slaying a human, although he was a savage; and how do I know that he was a just Injin; and that he has not been taken away suddenly to anything but happy hunting-grounds. When it's onsartain whether good or evil has been done, the wisest way is not to be boastful—still, I should like Chingachgook to know that I haven't discredited the Delawares, or my training!"

Part of this was uttered aloud, while part was merely muttered between the speaker's teeth; his more confident opinions enjoying the first advantage, while his doubts were expressed in the latter mode. Soliloquy and reflection received a startling interruption, however, by the sudden appearance of a second Indian on the lake shore, a few hundred yards from the point. This man, evidently another scout, who had probably been drawn to the place by the reports of the rifles, broke out of the forest with so little caution that Deerslayer caught a view of his person before he was himself discovered. When the latter event did occur, as was the case a moment later, the savage gave a loud yell, which was answered by a dozen voices from different parts of the mountainside. There was no longer any time for delay; in another minute the boat was quitting the shore under long and steady sweeps of the paddle.

As soon as Deerslayer believed himself to be at a safe distance he ceased his efforts, permitting the little bark to drift, while he leisurely took a survey of the state of things. The canoe first sent adrift was floating before the air, quite a quarter of a mile above him, and a little nearer to the shore than he wished, now that he knew more of the savages were so near at hand. The canoe shoved from the point was within a few yards of him, he having directed his own course towards it on quitting the land. The dead Indian lay in grim quiet where he had left him, the warrior who had shown himself from the forest had already vanished, and the woods themselves were as silent and seemingly deserted as the day they came fresh from the hands of their great Creator. This profound stillness, however, lasted but a moment. When time had been given to the scouts of the enemy to reconnoitre, they burst out of the thicket upon the naked point, filling the air with yells of fury at discovering the death of their companion. These cries were immediately succeeded by shouts of delight when they reached the body and clustered eagerly around it. Deerslayer was a sufficient adept in the usages of the natives to understand the reason of the change. The yell was the customary lamentation at the loss of a warrior, the shout a sign of rejoicing that the conqueror had not been able to secure the scalp; the trophy, without which a victory is never considered complete. The distance at which the canoes lay probably prevented any attempts to injure the conqueror, the American Indian, like the panther of his own woods, seldom making any effort against his foe unless tolerably certain it is under circumstances that may be expected to prove effective.

As the young man had no longer any motive to remain near the point, he prepared to collect his canoes, in order to tow them off to the castle. That nearest was soon in tow, when he proceeded in quest of the other, which was all this time floating up the lake. The eye of Deerslayer was no sooner fastened on this last boat, than it struck him that it was nearer to the shore than it would have been had it merely followed the course of the gentle current of air. He began to suspect the influence of some unseen current in the water, and he quickened his exertions, in order to regain possession of it before it could drift into a dangerous proximity to the woods. On getting nearer, he thought that the canoe had a perceptible motion through the water, and, as it lay broadside to the air, that this motion was taking it towards the land. A few vigorous strokes of the paddle carried him still nearer, when the mystery was explained. Something was evidently in motion on the off side of the canoe, or that which was farthest from himself, and closer scrutiny showed that it was a naked human arm. An Indian was lying in the bottom of the canoe, and was propelling it slowly but certainly to the shore, using his hand as a paddle. Deerslayer understood the whole artifice at a glance. A savage had swum off to the boat while he was occupied with his enemy on the point, got possession, and was using these means to urge it to the shore.

Satisfied that the man in the canoe could have no arms, Deerslayer did not hesitate to dash close alongside of the retiring boat, without deeming it necessary to raise his own rifle. As soon as the wash of the water, which he made in approaching, became audible to the prostrate savage, the latter sprang to his feet, and uttered an exclamation that proved how completely he was taken by surprise.

"If you've enj'yed yourself enough in that canoe, red-skin," Deerslayer coolly observed, stopping his own career in sufficient time to prevent an absolute collision between the two boats,—"if you've enj'yed yourself enough in that canoe, you'll do a prudent act by taking to the lake ag'in. I'm reasonable in these matters, and don't crave your blood, though there's them about that would look upon you more as a due-bill for the bounty than a human mortal. Take to the lake this minute, afore we get to hot words."

The savage was one of those who did not understand a word of English, and he was indebted to the gestures of Deerslayer, and to the expression of an eye that did not often deceive, for an imperfect comprehension of his meaning. Perhaps, too, the sight of the rifle that lay so near the hand of the white man quickened his decision. At all events, he crouched like a tiger about to take his leap, uttered a yell, and the next instant his naked body disappeared in the water. When he rose to take breath, it was at the distance of several yards from the canoe, and the hasty glance he threw behind him denoted how much he feared the arrival of a fatal messenger from the rifle of his foe. But the young man made no indication of any hostile intention. Deliberately securing the canoe to the others, he began to paddle from the shore; and by the time the Indian reached the land, and had shaken himself, like a spaniel, on quitting the water, his dreaded enemy was already beyond rifle-shot on his way to the castle. As was so much his practice, Deerslayer did not fail to soliloquize on what had just occurred, while steadily pursuing his course towards the point of destination.

"Well, well,"—he commenced,—"'twould have been wrong to kill a human mortal without an object. Scalps are of no account with me, and life is sweet, and ought not to be taken marcilessly by them that have white gifts. The savage was a Mingo, it's true; and I make no doubt he is, and will be as long as he lives, a ra'al riptyle and vagabond; but that's no reason I should forget my gifts and color. No, no,—let him go; if ever we meet ag'in, rifle in hand, why then 'twill be seen which has the stoutest heart and the quickest eye. Hawkeye! That's not a bad name for a warrior, sounding much more manful and valiant than Deerslayer! 'Twouldn't be a bad title to begin with, and it has been fairly 'arned. If 't was Chingachgook, now, he might go home and boast of his deeds, and the chiefs would name him Hawkeye in a minute; but it don't become white blood to brag, and 't isn't easy to see how the matter can be known unless I do. Well, well,—everything is in the hands of Providence; this affair as well as another; I'll trust to that for getting my desarts in all things."

Having thus betrayed what might be termed his weak spot, the young man continued to paddle in silence, making his way diligently, and as fast as his tows would allow him, towards the castle. By this time the sun had not only risen, but it had appeared over the eastern mountains, and was shedding a flood of glorious light on this as yet unchristened sheet of water. The whole scene was radiant with beauty; and no one unaccustomed to the ordinary history of the woods would fancy it had so lately witnessed incidents so ruthless and barbarous. As he approached the building of old Hutter, Deerslayer thought, or rather felt that its appearance was in singular harmony with all the rest of the scene. Although nothing had been consulted but strength and security, the rude, massive logs, covered with their rough bark, the projecting roof, and the form, would contribute to render the building picturesque in almost any situation, while its actual position added novelty and piquancy to its other points of interest.

When Deerslayer drew nearer to the castle, however, objects of interest presented themselves that at once eclipsed any beauties that might have distinguished the scenery of the lake, and the site of the singular edifice. Judith and Hetty stood on the platform before the door, Hurry's dooryard awaiting his approach with manifest anxiety; the former, from time to time, taking a survey of his person and of the canoes through the old ship's spyglass that has been already mentioned. Never probably did this girl seem more brilliantly beautiful than at that moment; the flush of anxiety and alarm increasing her color to its richest tints, while the softness of her eyes, a charm that even poor Hetty shared with her, was deepened by intense concern. Such, at least, without pausing or pretending to analyze motives, or to draw any other very nice distinction between cause and effect, were the opinions of the young man as his canoes reached the side of the ark, where he carefully fastened all three before he put his foot on the platform.

CHAPTER VIII.

"His words are bonds, his oaths are oracles;
His love sincere, his thoughts immaculate;
His tears pure messengers sent from his heart;
His heart as far from fraud as heaven from earth."

Two Gentlemen of Verona, II. vii, 75–78

Neither of the girls spoke as Deerslayer stood before them alone, his countenance betraying all the apprehension he felt on account of two absent members of their party.

"Father!" Judith at length exclaimed, succeeding in uttering the word, as it might be by a desperate effort.

"He's met with misfortune, and there's no use in concealing it," answered Deerslayer, in his direct and simple minded manner. "He and Hurry are in Mingo hands, and Heaven only knows what's to be the tarmination. I've got the canoes safe, and that's a consolation, since the vagabonds will have to swim for it, or raft off, to come near this place. At sunset we'll be reinforced by Chingachgook, if I can manage to get him into a canoe; and then, I think, we two can answer for the ark and the castle, till some of the officers in the garrisons hear of this war-path, which sooner or later must be the case, when we may look for succor from that quarter, if from no other."

"The officers!" exclaimed Judith, impatiently, her color deepening, and her eye expressing a lively but passing emotion. "Who thinks or speaks of the heartless gallants now? We are sufficient of ourselves to defend the castle. But what of my father, and of poor Hurry Harry?"

"'T is natural you should feel this consarn for your own parent, Judith, and I suppose it's equally so that you should feel it for Hurry Harry, too."

Deerslayer then commenced a succinct but clear narrative of all that occurred during the night, in no manner concealing what had befallen his two companions, or his own opinion of what might prove to be the consequences. The girls listened with profound attention, but neither betrayed that feminine apprehension and concern which would have followed such a communication when made to those who were less accustomed to the hazards and accidents of a frontier life. To the surprise of Deerslayer, Judith seemed the most distressed, Hetty listening eagerly, but appearing to brood over the facts in melancholy silence, rather than betraying any outward signs of feeling. The former's agitation, the young man did not fail to attribute to the interest she felt in Hurry, quite as much as to her filial love, while Hetty's apparent indifference was ascribed to that mental darkness which, in a measure, obscured her intellect, and which possibly prevented her from foreseeing all the consequences. Little was said, however, by either, Judith and her sister busying themselves in making the preparations for the morning meal, as they who habitually attend to such matters toil on mechanically even in the midst of suffering and sorrow. The plain but nutritious breakfast was taken by all three in sombre silence. The girls ate little, but Deerslayer gave proof of possessing one material requisite of a good soldier, that of preserving his appetite in the midst of the most alarming and embarrassing circumstances. The meal was nearly ended before a syllable was uttered; then, however, Judith spoke in the convulsive and hurried manner in which feeling breaks through restraint, after the latter has become more painful than even the betrayal of emotion.

"Father would have relished this fish," she exclaimed; "he says the salmon of the lakes is almost as good as the salmon of the sea."

"Your father has been acquainted with the sea, they tell me, Judith," returned the young man, who could not forbear throwing a glance of inquiry at the girl; for in common with all who knew Hutter, he had some curiosity on the subject of his early history. "Hurry Harry tells me he was once a sailor."

Judith first looked perplexed; then, influenced by feelings that were novel to her, in more ways than one, she became suddenly communicative, and seemingly much interested in the discourse.

"If Hurry knows anything of father's history, I would he had told it to me!" she cried. "Sometimes I think, too, he was once a sailor, and then again I think he was not. If that chest were open, or if it could speak, it might let us into his whole history. But its fastenings are too strong to be broken like pack thread."

Deerslayer turned to the chest in question, and for the first time examined it closely. Although discolored, and bearing proofs of having received much ill-treatment, he saw that it was of materials and workmanship altogether superior to anything of the same sort he had ever before beheld. The wood was dark, rich, and had once been highly polished, though the treatment it had received left little gloss on its surface, and various scratches and indentations proved the rough collisions that it had encountered with substances still harder than itself. The corners were firmly bound with steel, elaborately and richly wrought, while the locks, of which it had no less than three, and the hinges, were of a fashion and workmanship that would have attracted attention even in a warehouse of curious furniture. This chest was quite large; and when Deerslayer arose, and endeavored to raise an end by its massive handle, he found that the weight fully corresponded with the external appearance.

"Did you never see that chest opened, Judith?" the young man demanded with frontier freedom, for delicacy on such subjects was little felt among the people on the verge of civilization, in that age, even if it be today.

"Never. Father has never opened it in my presence, if he ever opens it at all. No one here has ever seen its lid raised, unless it be father; nor do I even know that he has ever seen it."

"Now you're wrong, Judith," Hetty quietly answered. "Father has raised the lid, and I've seen him do it."

A feeling of manliness kept the mouth of Deerslayer shut; for, while he would not have hesitated about going far beyond what would be thought the bounds of propriety, in questioning the older sister, he had just scruples about taking what might be thought an advantage of the feeble intellect of the younger. Judith, being under no such restraint, however, turned quickly to the last speaker and continued the discourse.

"When and where did you ever see that chest opened, Hetty?"

"Here, and again and again. Father often opens it when you are away, though he don't in the least mind my being by, and seeing all he does, as well as hearing all he says."

"And what is it that he does, and what does he say?"

"That I cannot tell you, Judith," returned the other in a low but resolute voice. "Father's secrets are not my secrets."

"Secrets! This is stranger still, Deerslayer, that father should tell them to Hetty, and not tell them to me!"

"There's a good reason for that, Judith, though you're not to know it. Father's not here to answer for himself, and I'll say no more about it."

Judith and Deerslayer looked surprised, and for a minute the first seemed pained. But, suddenly recollecting herself, she turned away from her sister, as if in pity for her weakness and addressed the young man.

"You've told but half your story," she said, "breaking off at the place where you went to sleep in the canoe—or rather where you rose to listen to the cry of the loon. We heard the call of the loons, too, and thought their cries might bring a storm, though we are little used to tempests on this lake at this season of the year."

"The winds blow and the tempests howl as God pleases; sometimes at one season, and sometimes at another," answered Deerslayer; "and the loons speak accordin' to their natur'. Better would it be if men were as honest and frank. After I rose to listen to the birds, finding it could not be Hurry's signal, I lay down and slept. When the day dawned I was up and stirring, as usual, and then I went in chase of the two canoes, lest the Mingos should lay hands on 'em."

"You have not told us all, Deerslayer," said Judith earnestly. "We heard rifles under the eastern mountain; the echoes were full and long, and came so soon after the reports, that the pieces must have been fired on or quite near to the shore. Our ears are used to these signs, and are not to be deceived."

"They've done their duty, gal, this time; yes, they've done their duty. Rifles have been sighted this morning, ay, and triggers pulled, too, though not as often as they might have been. One warrior has gone to his happy hunting-grounds, and that's the whole of it. A man of white blood and white gifts is not to be expected to boast of his expl'ites and to flourish scalps."

Judith listened almost breathlessly; and when Deerslayer, in his quiet, modest manner, seemed disposed to quit the subject, she rose, and crossing the room, took a seat by his side. The manner of the girl had nothing forward about it, though it betrayed the quick instinct of a female's affection, and the sympathizing kindness of a woman's heart. She even took the hard hand of the hunter, and pressed it in both her own, unconsciously to herself, perhaps, while she looked earnestly and even reproachfully into his sun burnt face.

"You have been fighting the savages, Deerslayer, singly and by yourself!" she said. "In your wish to take care of us——of Hetty—of me, perhaps, you've fought the enemy bravely, with no eye to encourage your deeds, or to witness your fall, had it pleased Providence to suffer so great a calamity!"

"I've fou't, Judith; yes, I have fou't the inimy, and that too, for the first time in my life. These things must be, and they bring with 'em a mixed feelin' of sorrow and triumph. Human natur' is a fightin' natur', I suppose, as all nations kill in battle, and we must be true to our rights and gifts. What has yet been done is no great matter, but should Chingachgook come to the rock this evening, as is agreed atween us, and I get him off it onbeknown to the savages or, if known to them, ag'in their wishes and designs, then may we all look to something like warfare, afore the Mingos shall get possession of either the castle, or the ark, or yourselves."

"Who is this Chingachgook; from what place does he come, and why does he come here?"

"The questions are nat'ral and right, I suppose, though the youth has a great name, already, in his own part of the country. Chingachgook is a Mohican by blood, consorting with the Delawares by usage, as is the case with most of his tribe, which has long been broken up by the increase of our color. He is of the family of the great chiefs; Uncas, his father, having been the considerablest warrior and counsellor of his people. Even old Tamenund honors Chingachgook, though he is thought to be yet too young to lead in war; and then the nation is so disparsed and diminished, that chieftainship among 'em has got to be little more than a name.

"Well, this war having commenced in 'arnest, the Delaware and I rendezvous'd an app'intment, to meet this evening at sunset on the rendezvous-rock at the foot of this very lake, intending to come out on our first hostile expedition ag'in the Mingos. Why we come exactly this a way is our own secret; but thoughtful young men on the war-path, as you may suppose, do nothing without a calculation and a design."

"A Delaware can have no unfriendly intentions towards us," said Judith, after a moment's hesitation, "and we know you to be friendly."

"Treachery is the last crime I hope to be accused of," returned Deerslayer, hurt at the gleam of distrust that had shot through Judith's mind; "and least of all, treachery to my own color."

"No one suspects you, Deerslayer," the girl impetuously cried. "No—no—your honest countenance would be sufficient surety for the truth of a thousand hearts! If all men had as honest tongues, and no more promised what they did not mean to perform, there would be less wrong done in the world, and fine feathers and scarlet cloaks would not be excuses for baseness and deception."

The girl spoke with strong, nay, even with convulsed feeling, and her fine eyes, usually so soft and alluring, flashed fire as she concluded. Deerslayer could not but observe this extraordinary emotion; but with the tact of a courtier, he avoided not only any allusion to the circumstance, but succeeded in concealing the effect of his discovery on himself. Judith gradually grew calm again, and as she was obviously anxious to appear to advantage in the eyes of the young man, she was soon able to renew the conversation as composedly as if nothing had occurred to disturb her.

"I have no right to look into your secrets, or the secrets of your friend, Deerslayer," she continued, "and am ready to take all you say on trust. If we can really get another male ally to join us at this trying moment, it will aid us much; and I am not without hope that when the savages find that we are able to keep the lake, they will offer to give up their prisoners in exchange for skins, or at least for the keg of powder that we have in the house."

The young man had the words "scalps" and "bounty" on his lips, but a reluctance to alarm the feelings of the daughters prevented him from making the allusion he had intended to the probable fate of their father. Still, so little was he practised in the arts of deception, that his expressive countenance was, of itself, understood by the quick-witted Judith, whose intelligence had been sharpened by the risks and habits of her life.

"I understand what you mean," she continued, hurriedly, "and what you would say, but for the fear of hurting me—us, I mean; for Hetty loves her father quite as well as I do. But this is not as we think of Indians. They never scalp an unhurt prisoner, but would rather take him away alive, unless, indeed, the fierce wish for torturing should get the mastery of them. I fear nothing for my father's scalp, and little for his life. Could they steal on us in the night, we should all probably suffer in this way; but men taken in open strife are seldom injured; not, at least, until the time of torture comes."

"That's tradition, I'll allow, and it's accordin' to practice—but, Judith, do you know the arr'nd on which your father and Hurry went ag'in the savages?"

"I do; and a cruel errand it was! But what will you have? Men will be men, and some even that flaunt in their gold and silver, and carry the King's commission in their pockets, are not guiltless of equal cruelty." Judith's eye again flashed, but by a desperate struggle she resumed her composure. "I get warm when I think of all the wrong that men do," she added, affecting to smile, an effort in which she only succeeded indifferently well. "All this is silly. What is done is done, and it cannot be mended by complaints. But the Indians think so little of the shedding of blood, and value men so much for the boldness of their undertakings, that, did they know the business on which their prisoners came, they would be more likely to honor than to injure them for it."

"For a time, Judith; yes, I allow that, for a time. But when that feelin' dies away, then will come the love of revenge. We must indivor,—Chingachgook and I,—we must indivor to see what we can do to get Hurry and your father free; for the Mingos will no doubt hover about this lake some days, in order to make the most of their success."

"You think this Delaware can be depended on, Deerslayer?" demanded the girl, thoughtfully.

"As much as I can myself. You say you do not suspect me, Judith?"

"You!" taking his hand again, and pressing it between her own, with a warmth that might have awakened the vanity of one less simple-minded, and more disposed to dwell on his own good qualities, "I would as soon suspect a brother! I have known you but a day, Deerslayer, but it has awakened the confidence of a year. Your name, however, is not unknown to me; for the gallants of the garrisons frequently speak of the lessons you have given them in hunting, and all proclaim your honesty."

"Do they ever talk of the shooting, gal?" inquired the other eagerly, after, however, laughing in a silent but heartfelt manner. "Do they ever talk of the shooting? I want to hear nothing about my own, for if that isn't sartified to by this time, in all these parts, there's little use in being skilful and sure; but what do the officers say of their own—yes, what do they say of their own? Arms, as they call it, is their trade, and yet there's some among 'em that know very little how to use 'em!"

"Such I hope will not be the case with your friend Chingachgook, as you call him—what is the English of his Indian name?"

"Big Sarpent—so called for his wisdom and cunning, Uncas is his ra'al name—all his family being called Uncas until they get a title that has been 'arned by deeds."

"If he has all this wisdom, we may expect a useful friend in him, unless his own business in this part of the country should prevent him from serving us."

"I see no great harm in telling you his arr'nd, a'ter all, and, as you may find means to help us, I will let you and Hetty into the whole matter, trusting that you'll keep the secret as if it was your own. You must know that Chingachgook is a comely Injin, and is much looked upon and admired by the young women of his tribe, both on account of his family, and on account of himself. Now, there is a chief that has a daughter called Wah-ta-Wah, which is intarpreted into Hist-oh-Hist, in the English tongue, the rarest gal among the Delawares, and the one most sought a'ter and craved for a wife by all the young warriors of the nation. Well, Chingachgook, among others, took a fancy to Wah-ta-Wah, and Wah-ta-Wah took a fancy to him." Here Deerslayer paused an instant; for, as he got thus far in his tale, Hetty Hutter arose, approached, and stood attentive at his knee, as a child draws near to listen to the legends of its mother. "Yes, he fancied her, and she fancied him," resumed Deerslayer, casting a friendly and approving glance at the innocent and interested girl; "and when that is the case, and all the elders are agreed, it does not often happen that the young couple keep apart. Chingachgook couldn't well carry off such a prize without making inimies among them that wanted her as much as he did himself. A sartain Briarthorn, as we call him in English, or Yocommon, as he is tarmed in Injin, took it most to heart, and we mistrust him of having a hand in all that followed."

"Wah-ta-Wah went with her father and mother, two moons ago, to fish for salmon on the western streams, where it is agreed by all in these parts that fish most abounds, and while thus empl'yed the gal vanished. For several weeks we could get no tidings of her; but here, ten days since, a runner, that came through the Delaware country, brought us a message, by which we learn that Wah-ta-Wah was stolen from her people, we think, but do not know it, by Briarthorn's sarcumventions,—and that she was now with the inimy, who had adopted her, and wanted her to marry a young Mingo. The message said that the party intended to hunt and forage through this region for a month or two, afore it went back into the Canadas, and that if we could contrive to get on a scent in this quarter, something might turn up that would lead to our getting the maiden off."

"And how does that concern you, Deerslayer?" demanded Judith, a little anxiously.

"It consarns me, as all things that touches a fri'nd consarns a fri'nd. I'm here as Chingachgook's aid and helper, and if we can get the young maiden he likes back ag'in, it will give me almost as much pleasure as if I had got back my own sweetheart."

"And where, then, is your sweetheart, Deerslayer?"

"She's in the forest, Judith—hanging from the boughs of the trees, in a soft rain—in the dew on the open grass—the clouds that float about in the blue heavens—the birds that sing in the woods—the sweet springs where I slake my thirst—and in all the other glorious gifts that come from God's Providence!"

"You mean that, as yet, you've never loved one of my sex, but love best your haunts, and your own manner of life."

"That's it—that's just it. I am white—have a white heart and can't, in reason, love a red-skinned maiden, who must have a red-skin heart and feelin's. No, no, I'm sound enough in them partic'lars, and hope to remain so, at least till this war is over. I find my time too much taken up with Chingachgook's affair, to wish to have one of my own on my hands afore that is settled."

"The girl that finally wins you, Deerslayer, will at least win an honest heart,—one without treachery or guile; and that will be a victory that most of her sex ought to envy."

As Judith uttered this, her beautiful face had a resentful frown on it; while a bitter smile lingered around a mouth that no derangement of the muscles could render anything but handsome. Her companion observed the change, and though little skilled in the workings of the female heart, he had sufficient native delicacy to understand that it might be well to drop the subject.

As the hour when Chingachgook was expected still remained distant, Deerslayer had time enough to examine into the state of the defences, and to make such additional arrangements as were in his power, and the exigency of the moment seemed to require. The experience and foresight of Hutter had left little to be done in these particulars; still, several precautions suggested themselves to the young man, who may be said to have studied the art of frontier warfare, through the traditions and legends of the people among whom he had so long lived. The distance between the castle and the nearest point on the shore, prevented any apprehension on the subject of rifle-bullets thrown from the land. The house was within musket-shot in one sense, it was true, but aim was entirely out of the question, and even Judith professed a perfect disregard of any danger from that source. So long, then, as the party remained in possession of the fortress, they were safe, unless their assailants could find the means to come off and carry it by fire or storm, or by some of the devices of Indian cunning and Indian treachery.

Against the first source of danger Hutter had made ample provision, and the building itself, the bark roof excepted, was not very combustible. The floor was scuttled in several places, and buckets provided with ropes were in daily use, in readiness for any such emergency. One of the girls could easily extinguish any fire that might be lighted, provided it had not time to make much headway. Judith, who appeared to understand all her father's schemes of defence, and who had the spirit to take no unimportant share in the execution of them, explained all these details to the young man, who was thus saved much time and labor in making his investigations.

Little was to be apprehended during the day. In possession of the canoes and of the ark, no other vessel was to be found on the lake. Nevertheless, Deerslayer well knew that a raft was soon made, and, as dead trees were to be found in abundance near the water, did the savages seriously contemplate the risks of an assault, it would not be a very difficult matter to find the necessary means. The celebrated American axe, a tool that is quite unrivalled in its way, was then not very extensively known, and the savages were far from expert in the use of its hatchet-like substitute; still, they had sufficient practice in crossing streams by this mode to render it certain they would construct a raft, should they deem it expedient to expose themselves to the risks of an assault. The death of their warrior might prove a sufficient incentive, or it might act as a caution; but Deerslayer thought it more than possible that the succeeding night would bring matters to a crisis, and in this precise way. This impression caused him to wish ardently for the presence and succor of his Mohican friend, and to look forward to the approach of sunset with an increasing anxiety.

As the day advanced, the party in the castle matured their plans, and made their preparations. Judith was active, and seemed to find a pleasure in consulting and advising with her new acquaintance, whose indifference to danger, manly devotion to herself and sister, guilelessness of manner, and truth of feeling, had won rapidly on both her imagination and her affections. Although the hours appeared long in some respects to Deerslayer, Judith did not find them so, and when the sun began to descend towards the pine-clad summits of the western hills, she felt and expressed her surprise that the day should so soon be drawing to a close. On the other hand, Hetty was moody and silent. She was never loquacious, or if she occasionally became communicative, it was under the influence of some temporary excitement that served to arouse her unsophisticated mind; but, for hours at a time, in the course of this all-important day, she seemed to have absolutely lost the use of her tongue. Nor did apprehension on account of her father materially affect the manner of either sister. Neither appeared seriously to dread any evil greater than captivity, and once or twice, when

Hetty did speak, she intimated the expectation that Hutter would find the means to liberate himself. Although Judith was less sanguine on this head, she too betrayed the hope that propositions for a ransom would come, when the Indians discovered that the castle set their expedients and artifices at defiance. Deerslayer, however, treated these passing suggestions as the ill-digested fancies of girls, making his own arrangements as steadily, and brooding over the future as seriously, as if they had never fallen from their lips.

At length the hour arrived when it became necessary to proceed to the place of rendezvous appointed with the Mohican, or Delaware, as Chingachgook was more commonly called. As the plan had been matured by Deerslayer, and fully communicated to his companions, all three set about its execution, in concert, and intelligently. Hetty passed into the ark, and fastening two of the canoes together, she entered one, and paddled up to a sort of gateway in the palisadoes that surrounded the building, through which she carried both; securing them beneath the house by chains that were fastened within the building. These palisadoes were trunks of trees driven firmly into the mud, and served the double purpose of a small inclosure that was intended to be used in this very manner, and to keep any enemy that might approach in boats at arm's length. Canoes thus docked were, in a measure, hid from sight, and as the gate was properly barred and fastened, it would not be an easy task to remove them, even in the event of their being seen. Previously, however, to closing the gate, Judith also entered within the inclosure with the third canoe, leaving Deerslayer busy in securing the door and windows inside the building, over her head. As everything was massive and strong, and small saplings were used as bars, it would have been the work of an hour or two to break into the building, when Deerslayer had ended his task, even allowing the assailants the use of any tools but the axe, and to be unresisted. This attention to security arose from Hutter's having been robbed once or twice by the lawless whites of the frontiers, during some of his many absences from home.

As soon as all was fast in the inside of the dwelling, Deerslayer appeared at a trap, from which he descended into the canoe of Judith. When this was done, he fastened the door with a massive staple and stout padlock. Hetty was then received in the canoe, which was shoved outside of the palisadoes. The next precaution was to fasten the gate, and the keys were carried into the ark. The three were now fastened out of the dwelling, which could only be entered by violence, or by following the course taken by the young man in quitting it. The glass had been brought outside as a preliminary step, and Deerslayer next took a careful survey of the entire shore of the lake, as far as his own position would allow. Not a living thing was visible, a few birds excepted, and even the last fluttered about in the shades of the trees, as if unwilling to encounter the heat of a sultry afternoon. All the nearest points, in particular, were subjected to severe scrutiny, in order to make certain that no raft was in preparation; the result everywhere giving the same picture of calm solitude. A few words will explain the greatest embarrassment belonging to the situation of our party. Exposed themselves to the observation of any watchful eyes, the movements of their enemies were concealed by the drapery of a dense forest. While the imagination would be very apt to people the latter with more warriors than it really contained, their own weakness must be too apparent to all who might chance to cast a glance in their direction.

"Nothing is stirring, howsever," exclaimed Deerslayer, as he finally lowered the glass, and prepared to enter the ark. "If the vagabonds do harbor mischief in their minds, they are too cunning to let it be seen; it's true, a raft may be in preparation in the woods, but it has not yet been brought down to the lake. They can't guess that we are about to quit the castle, and, if they did, they've no means of knowing where we intend to go."

"This is so true, Deerslayer," returned Judith, "that now all is ready, we may proceed at once, boldly, and without the fear of being followed; else we shall be behind our time."

"No, no; the matter needs management; for, though the savages are in the dark as to Chingachgook and the rock, they've eyes and legs, and will see in what direction we steer, and will be sartain to follow us. I shall strive to baffle 'em, howsever, by heading the scow in all manner of ways, first in one quarter and then in another, until they get to be a-leg-weary, and tired of tramping a'ter us."

So far as it was in his power, Deerslayer was as good as his word. In less than five minutes after this speech was made, the whole party was in the ark, and in motion. There was a gentle breeze from the north, and boldly hoisting the sail, the young man laid the head of the unwieldy craft in such a direction, as, after making a liberal but necessary allowance for leeway, would have brought it ashore a couple of miles down the lake, and on its eastern side. The sailing of the ark was never very swift, though, floating as it did on the surface, it was not difficult to get it in motion, or to urge it along over the water at the rate of some three or four miles in the hour. The distance between the castle and the rock was a little more than two leagues. Knowing the punctuality of an Indian, Deerslayer had made his calculations closely, and had given himself a little more time than was necessary to reach the place of rendezvous, with a view to delay or to press his arrival, as might prove most expedient. When he hoisted the sail, the sun lay above the western hills, at an elevation that promised rather more than two hours of day; and a few minutes satisfied him that the progress of the scow was such as to equal his expectations.

It was a glorious June afternoon, and never did that solitary sheet of water seem less like an arena of strife and bloodshed. The light air scarce descended as low as the bed of the lake, hovering over it, as if unwilling to disturb its deep tranquillity, or to ruffle its mirror-like surface. Even the forests appeared to be slumbering in the sun, and a few piles of fleecy clouds had lain for hours along the northern horizon like fixtures in the atmosphere, placed there purely to embellish the scene. A few aquatic fowls occasionally skimmed along the water, and a single raven was visible, sailing high above the trees, and keeping a watchful eye on the forest beneath him, in order to detect anything having life that the mysterious woods might offer as prey.

The reader will probably have observed, that, amidst the frankness and abruptness of manner which marked the frontier habits of Judith, her language was superior to that used by her male companions, her own father included. This difference extended as well to pronunciation as to the choice of words and phrases. Perhaps nothing so soon betrays the education and association as the modes of speech; and few accomplishments so much aid the charm of female beauty as a graceful and even utterance, while nothing so soon produces the disenchantment that necessarily follows a discrepancy between appearance and manner, as a mean intonation of voice, or a vulgar use of words. Judith and her sister were marked exceptions to all the girls of their class, along that whole frontier; the officers of the nearest garrison having often flattered the former with the belief that few ladies of the towns acquitted themselves better than herself, in this important particular. This was far from being literally true, but it was sufficiently near the fact to give birth to the compliment. The girls were indebted to their mother for this proficiency, having acquired from her, in childhood, an advantage that no subsequent study or labor can give without a drawback, if neglected beyond the earlier periods of life. Who that mother was, or rather had been, no one but Hutter knew. She had now been dead two summers, and, as was stated by Hurry, she had been buried in the lake; whether in indulgence of a prejudice, or from a reluctance to take the trouble to dig her grave, had frequently been a matter of discussion between the rude beings of that region. Judith had never visited the spot, but Hetty was present at the interment, and she often paddled a canoe, about sunset or by the light of the moon, to the place, and gazed down into the limpid water, in the hope of being able to catch a glimpse of the form that she had so tenderly loved from infancy to the sad hour of their parting.

"Must we reach the rock exactly at the moment the sun sets?" Judith demanded of the young man, as they stood near each other, Deerslayer holding the steering-oar, and she working with a needle at some ornament of dress, that much exceeded her station in life, and was altogether a novelty in the woods. "Will a few minutes, sooner or later, alter the matter? It will be very hazardous to remain long as near the shore as that rock!"

"That's it, Judith; that's the very difficulty! The rock's within p'int blank for a shot-gun, and 'twill never do to hover about it too close and too long. When you have to deal with an Injin, you must calculate and manage, for a red natur' dearly likes sarcumvention. Now you see, Judith, that I do not steer towards the rock at all, but here to the eastward of it, whereby the savages will be tramping off in that direction, and get their legs a-wearied, and all for no advantage."

"You think, then, they see us, and watch our movements, Deerslayer? I was in hopes they might have fallen back into the woods, and left us to ourselves for a few hours."

"That's altogether a woman's consait. There's no let-up in an Injin's watchfulness when he's on a war-path, and eyes are on us at this minute, 'though the lake presarves us. We must draw near the rock on a calculation, and indivor to get the miscreants on a false scent. The Mingos have good noses, they tell me; but a white man's reason ought always to equalize their instinct."

Judith now entered into a desultory discourse with Deerslayer, in which the girl betrayed her growing interest in the young man; an interest that his simplicity of mind and her decision of character, sustained as it was by the consciousness awakened by the consideration her personal charms so universally produced, rendered her less anxious to conceal than might otherwise have been the case. She was scarcely forward in her manner, though there was sometimes a freedom in her glances that it required all the aid of her exceeding beauty to prevent from awakening suspicions unfavorable to her discretion, if not to her morals. With Deerslayer, however, these glances were rendered less obnoxious to so unpleasant a construction; for she seldom looked at him without discovering much of the sincerity and nature that accompany the purest emotions of woman. It was a little remarkable that, as his captivity lengthened, neither of the girls manifested any great concern for her father; but, as has been said already, their habits gave them confidence, and they looked forward to his liberation, by means of a ransom, with a confidence that might, in a great degree, account for their apparent indifference. Once before, Hutter had been in the hands of the Iroquois, and a few skins had readily effected his release. This event, however, unknown to the sisters, had occurred in a time of peace between England and France, and when the savages were restrained, instead of being encouraged to commit their excesses, by the policy of the different colonial governments.

While Judith was loquacious and caressing in her manner, Hetty remained thoughtful and silent. Once, indeed, she drew near to Deerslayer, and questioned him a little closely as to his intentions, as well as concerning the mode of effecting his purpose; but her wish to converse went no further. As soon as her simple queries were answered—and answered they all were, in the fullest and kindest manner—she withdrew to her seat, and continued to work on a coarse garment that she was making for her father, sometimes humming a low melancholy air, and frequently sighing.

In this manner the time passed away; and when the sun was beginning to glow behind the fringe of the pines that bounded the western hill, or about twenty minutes before it actually set, the ark was nearly as low as the point where Hutter and Hurry had been made prisoners. By sheering first to one side of the lake, and then to the other, Deerslayer managed to create an uncertainty as to his object; and, doubtless, the savages, who were unquestionably watching his movements, were led to believe that his aim was to communicate with them, at or near this spot, and would hasten in that direction, in order to be in readiness to profit by circumstances. This artifice was well managed; since the sweep of the bay, the curvature of the lake, and the low marshy land that intervened, would probably allow the ark to reach the rock before its pursuers, if really collected near this point, could have time to make the circuit that would be required to get there by land. With a view to aid this deception, Deerslayer stood as near the western shore as was at all prudent; and then causing Judith and Hetty to enter the house, or cabin, and crouching himself so as to conceal his person by the frame of the scow, he suddenly threw the head of the latter round, and began to make the best of his way towards the outlet. Favored by an increase in the wind, the progress of the ark was such as to promise the complete success of this plan, though the crab-like movement of the craft compelled the helmsman to keep its head looking in a direction very different from that in which it was actually moving.

## CHAPTER IX.

"Yet art thou prodigal of smiles—
Smiles, sweeter than thy frowns are stern:
Earth sends from all her thousand isles,
A shout at thy return.
The glory that comes down from thee
Bathes, in deep joy, the land and sea."

Bryant, "The Firmament," 11.19–24

It may assist the reader in understanding the events we are about to record, if he has a rapidly sketched picture of the scene, placed before his eyes at a single view. It will be remembered that the lake was an irregularly shaped basin, of an outline that, in the main, was oval, but with bays and points to relieve its formality and ornament its shores. The surface of this beautiful sheet of water was now glittering like a gem, in the last rays of the evening sun, and the setting of the whole, hills clothed in the richest forest verdure, was lighted up with a sort of radiant smile, that is best described in the beautiful lines we have placed at the head of this chapter. As the banks, with few exceptions, rose abruptly from the water, even where the mountain did not immediately bound the view, there was a nearly unbroken fringe of leaves overhanging the placid lake, the trees starting out of the acclivities, inclining to the light, until, in many instances they extended their long limbs and straight trunks some forty or fifty feet beyond the line of the perpendicular. In these cases we allude only to the giants of the forest, pines of a hundred or a hundred and fifty feet in height, for of the smaller growth, very many inclined so far as to steep their lower branches in the water. In the position in which the Ark had now got, the castle was concealed from view by the projection of a point, as indeed was the northern extremity of the lake itself. A respectable mountain, forest clad, and rounded, like all the rest, limited the view in that direction, stretching immediately across the whole of the fair scene, with the exception of a deep bay that passed the western end, lengthening the basin, for more than a mile.

The manner in which the water flowed out of the lake, beneath the leafy arches of the trees that lined the sides of the stream, has already been mentioned, and it has also been said that the rock, which was a favorite place of rendezvous throughout all that region, and where Deerslayer now expected to meet his friend, stood near this outlet, and at no great distance from the shore. It was a large, isolated stone that rested on the bottom of the lake, apparently left there when the waters tore away the earth from around it, in forcing for themselves a passage down the river, and which had obtained its shape from the action of the elements, during the slow progress of centuries. The height of this rock could scarcely equal six feet, and, as has been said, its shape was not unlike that which is usually given to beehives, or to a hay-cock. The latter, indeed, gives the best idea not only of its form, but of its dimensions. It stood, and still stands, for we are writing of real scenes, within fifty feet of the bank, and in water that was only two feet in depth, though there were seasons in which its rounded apex, if such a term can properly be used, was covered by the lake. Many of the trees stretched so far forward, as almost to blend the rock with the shore, when seen from a little distance, and one tall pine in particular overhung it in a way to form a noble and appropriate canopy to a seat that had held many a forest chieftain, during the long succession of unknown ages, in which America, and all it contained, had existed apart, in mysterious solitude, a world by itself; equally without a familiar history, and without an origin that the annals of man can reach.

When distant some two or three hundred feet from the shore, Deerslayer took in his sail. He dropped his grapnel, as soon as he found the Ark had drifted in a line that was directly to windward of the rock. The motion of the scow was then checked, when it was brought head to wind, by the action of the breeze. As soon as this was done, Deerslayer "paid out line," and suffered the vessel to "set down" upon the rock, as fast as the light air could force it to leeward. Floating entirely on the surface, this was soon effected, and the young man checked the drift when he was told that the stern of the scow was within fifteen or eighteen feet of the desired spot.

In executing this maneuver, Deerslayer had proceeded promptly, for, while he did not in the least doubt that he was both watched and followed by the foe, he believed he distracted their movements, by the apparent uncertainty of his own, and he knew they could have no means of ascertaining that the rock was his aim, unless indeed one of their prisoners had betrayed him; a chance so improbable in itself, as to give him no concern. Notwithstanding the celerity and decision his movements, he did not, however, venture so near the shore without taking due precautions to effect a retreat, in the event of its becoming necessary. He held the line in his hand, and Judith was stationed at a loop, on the side of the cabin next the shore, where she could watch the beach and the rock, and give timely notice of the approach of either friend or foe. Hetty was also placed on watch, but it was to keep the trees overhead in view, lest some enemy might ascend one, and, by completely commanding the interior of the scow render the defence of the hut, or cabin, useless.

The sun had disappeared from the lake and valley, when Deerslayer checked the Ark, in the manner mentioned. Still it wanted a few minutes to the true sunset, and he knew Indian punctuality too well to anticipate any unmanly haste in his friend. The great question was, whether, surrounded by enemies as he was known to be, he had escaped their toils. The occurrences of the last twenty-four hours must be a secret to him, and like himself, Chingachgook was yet young on a path. It was true, he came prepared to encounter the party that withheld his promised bride, but he had no means ascertaining the extent of the danger he ran, or the precise positions occupied by either friends, or foes. In a word, the trained sagacity, and untiring caution of an Indian were all he had to rely on, amid the critical risks he unavoidably ran.

"Is the rock empty, Judith?" inquired Deerslayer, as soon as he had checked the drift of the Ark, deeming it imprudent to venture unnecessarily near the shore. "Is any thing to be seen of the Delaware chief?"

"Nothing, Deerslayer. Neither rock, shore, trees, nor lake seems to have ever held a human form."

'Keep close, Judith—keep close, Hetty—a rifle has a prying eye, a nimble foot, and a desperate fatal tongue. Keep close then, but keep up actyve looks, and be on the alart. 'Twould grieve me to the heart, did any harm befall either of you.'

"And you Deerslayer—" exclaimed Judith, turning her handsome face from the loop, to bestow a gracious and grateful look on the young man—"do you 'keep close', and have a proper care that the savages do not catch a glimpse of you! A bullet might be as fatal to you as to one of us; and the blow that you felt, would be felt by us all."

"No fear of me, Judith—no fear of me, my good gal. Do not look this-a-way, although you look so pleasant and comely, but keep your eyes on the rock, and the shore, and the—"

Deerslayer was interrupted by a slight exclamation from the girl, who, in obedience to his hurried gestures, as much as in obedience to his words, had immediately bent her looks again, in the opposite direction.

"What is't?—What is't, Judith?" he hastily demanded—"Is any thing to be seen?"

"There is a man on the rock!—An Indian warrior, in his paint—and armed!"

"Where does he wear his hawk's feather?" eagerly added Deerslayer, relaxing his hold of the line, in readiness to drift nearer to the place of rendezvous. "Is it fast to the war-lock, or does he carry it above the left ear?"

"'Tis as you say, above the left ear; he smiles, too, and mutters the word 'Mohican.'"

"God be praised, 'tis the Sarpent, at last!" exclaimed the young man, suffering the line to slip through his hands, until hearing a light bound, in the other end of the craft, he instantly checked the rope, and began to haul it in, again, under the assurance that his object was effected. At that moment the door of the cabin was opened hastily, and, a warrior, darting through the little room, stood at Deerslayer's side, simply uttering the exclamation "Hugh!" At the next instant, Judith and Hetty shrieked, and the air was filled with the yell of twenty savages, who came leaping through the branches, down the bank, some actually falling headlong into the water, in their haste.

"Pull, Deerslayer," cried Judith, hastily barring the door, in order to prevent an inroad by the passage through which the Delaware had just entered; "pull, for life and death—the lake is full of savages, wading after us!"

The young men—for Chingachgook immediately came to his friend's assistance—needed no second bidding, but they applied themselves to their task in a way that showed how urgent they deemed the occasion. The great difficulty was in suddenly overcoming the inertia of so large a mass, for once in motion, it was easy to cause the scow to skim the water with all the necessary speed.

"Pull, Deerslayer, for Heaven's sake!" cried Judith, again at the loop. "These wretches rush into the water like hounds following their prey! Ah—the scow moves! and now, the water deepens, to the arm-pits of the foremost, but they reach forward, and will seize the Ark!"

A slight scream, and then a joyous laugh followed from the girl; the first produced by a desperate effort of their pursuers, and the last by its failure; the scow, which had now got fairly in motion gliding ahead into deep water, with a velocity that set the designs of their enemies at nought. As the two men were prevented by the position of the cabin from seeing what passed astern, they were compelled to inquire of the girls into the state of the chase.

"What now, Judith?—What next?—Do the Mingos still follow, or are we quit of 'em, for the present," demanded Deerslayer, when he felt the rope yielding as if the scow was going fast ahead, and heard the scream and the laugh of the girl, almost in the same breath.

"They have vanished!—One—the last—is just burying himself in the bushes of the bank— There, he has disappeared in the shadows of the trees! You have got your friend, and we are all safe!"

The two men now made another great effort, pulled the Ark up swiftly to the grapnel, tripped it, and when the scow had shot some distance and lost its way, they let the anchor drop again. Then, for the first time since their meeting, they ceased their efforts. As the floating house now lay several hundred feet from the shore, and offered a complete protection against bullets, there was no longer any danger or any motive for immediate exertion.

The manner in which the two friends now recognized each other, was highly characteristic. Chingachgook, a noble, tall, handsome and athletic young Indian warrior, first examined his rifle with care, opening the pan to make sure that the priming was not wet, and, assured of this important fact, he next cast furtive but observant glances around him, at the strange habitation and at the two girls. Still he spoke not, and most of all did he avoid the betrayal of a womanish curiosity, by asking questions.

"Judith and Hetty" said Deerslayer, with an untaught, natural courtesy—"this is the Mohican chief of whom you've heard me speak; Chingachgook as he is called; which signifies Big Sarpent; so named for his wisdom and prudence, and cunning, and my 'arliest and latest fri'nd. I know'd it must be he, by the hawk's feather over the left ear, most other warriors wearing 'em on the war-lock."

As Deerslayer ceased speaking, he laughed heartily, excited more perhaps by the delight of having got his friend safe at his side, under circumstances so trying, than by any conceit that happened to cross his fancy, and exhibiting this outbreaking of feeling in a manner that was a little remarkable, since his merriment was not accompanied by any noise. Although Chingachgook both understood and spoke English, he was unwilling to communicate his thoughts in it, like most Indians, and when he had met Judith's cordial shake of the hand, and Hetty's milder salute, in the courteous manner that became a chief, he turned away, apparently to await the moment when it might suit his friend to enter into an explanation of his future intentions, and to give a narrative of what had passed since their separation. The other understood his meaning, and discovered his own mode of reasoning in the matter, by addressing the girls.

"This wind will soon die away altogether, now the sun is down," he said, "and there is no need for rowing ag'in it. In half an hour, or so, it will either be a flat calm, or the air will come off from the south shore, when we will begin our journey back ag'in to the castle; in the meanwhile, the Delaware and I will talk over matters, and get correct idees of each other's notions consarning the course we ought to take."

No one opposed this proposition, and the girls withdrew into the cabin to prepare the evening meal, while the two young men took their seats on the head of the scow and began to converse. The dialogue was in the language of the Delawares. As that dialect, however, is but little understood, even by the learned; we shall not only on this, but on all subsequent occasions render such parts as it may be necessary to give closely, into liberal English; preserving, as far as possible, the idiom and peculiarities of the respective speakers, by way of presenting the pictures in the most graphic forms to the minds of the readers.

It is unnecessary to enter into the details first related by Deerslayer, who gave a brief narrative of the facts that are already familiar to those who have read our pages. In relating these events, however, it may be well to say that the speaker touched only on the outlines, more particularly abstaining from saying anything about his encounter with, and victory over the Iroquois, as well as to his own exertions in behalf of the two deserted young women. When Deerslayer ended, the Delaware took up the narrative, in turn, speaking sententiously and with grave dignity. His account was both clear and short, nor was it embellished by any incidents that did not directly concern the history of his departure from the villages of his people, and his arrival in the valley of the Susquehannah. On reaching the latter, which was at a point only half a mile south of the outlet, he had soon struck a trail, which gave him notice of the probable vicinity of enemies. Being prepared for such an occurrence, the object of the expedition calling him directly into the neighborhood of the party of Iroquois that was known to be out, he considered the discovery as fortunate, rather than the reverse, and took the usual precautions to turn it to account. First following the river to its source, and ascertaining the position of the rock, he met another trail, and had actually been hovering for hours on the flanks of his enemies, watching equally for an opportunity to meet his mistress, and to take a scalp; and it may be questioned which he most ardently desired. He kept near the lake, and occasionally he ventured to some spot where he could get a view of what was passing on its surface. The Ark had been seen and watched, from the moment it hove in sight, though the young chief was necessarily ignorant that it was to be the instrument of his effecting the desired junction with his friend. The uncertainty of its movements, and the fact that it was unquestionably managed by white men, soon led him to conjecture the truth, however, and he held himself in readiness to get on board whenever a suitable occasion might offer. As the sun drew near the horizon he repaired to the rock, where, on emerging from the forest, he was gratified in finding the Ark lying, apparently in readiness to receive him. The manner of his appearance, and of his entrance into the craft is known.

Although Chingachgook had been closely watching his enemies for hours, their sudden and close pursuit as he reached the scow was as much a matter of surprise to himself, as it had been to his friend. He could only account for it by the fact of their being more numerous than he had at first supposed, and by their having out parties of the existence of which he was ignorant. Their regular, and permanent encampment, if the word permanent can be applied to the residence of a party that intended to remain out, in all probability, but a few weeks, was not far from the spot where Hutter and Hurry had fallen into their hands, and, as a matter of course, near a spring.

"Well, Sarpent," asked Deerslayer, when the other had ended his brief but spirited narrative, speaking always in the Delaware tongue, which for the reader's convenience only we render into the peculiar vernacular of the speaker—"Well, Sarpent, as you've been scouting around these Mingos, have you anything to tell us of their captyves, the father of these young women, and of another, who, I somewhat conclude, is the lovyer of one of 'em."

"Chingachgook has seen them. An old man, and a young warrior—the falling hemlock and the tall pine."

"You're not so much out, Delaware; you're not so much out. Old Hutter is decaying, of a sartainty, though many solid blocks might be hewn out of his trunk yet, and, as for Hurry Harry, so far as height and strength and comeliness go, he may be called the pride of the human forest. Were the men bound, or in any manner suffering torture? I ask on account of the young women, who, I dare to say, would be glad to know."

"It is not so, Deerslayer. The Mingos are too many to cage their game. Some watch; some sleep; some scout; some hunt. The pale-faces are treated like brothers to-day; to-morrow they will lose their scalps."

"Yes, that's red natur', and must be submitted to! Judith and Hetty, here's comforting tidings for you, the Delaware telling me that neither your father nor Hurry Harry is in suffering, but, bating the loss of liberty, as well off as we are ourselves. Of course they are kept in the camp; otherwise they do much as they please."

"I rejoice to hear this, Deerslayer," returned Judith, "and now we are joined by your friend, I make no manner of question that we shall find an opportunity to ransom the prisoners. If there are any women in the camp, I have articles of dress that will catch their eyes, and, should the worst come to the worst, we can open the great chest, which I think will be found to hold things that may tempt the chiefs."

"Judith," said the young man, looking up at her with a smile and an expression of earnest curiosity, that in spite of the growing obscurity did not escape the watchful looks of the girl, "can you find it in your heart, to part with your own finery, to release prisoners; even though one be your own father, and the other is your sworn suitor and lovyer?"

The flush on the face of the girl arose in part from resentment, but more perhaps from a gentler and a novel feeling, that, with the capricious waywardness of taste, had been rapidly rendering her more sensitive to the good opinion of the youth who questioned her, than to that of any other person. Suppressing the angry sensation, with instinctive quickness, she answered with a readiness and truth, that caused her sister to draw near to listen, though the obtuse intellect of the latter was far from comprehending the workings of a heart as treacherous, as uncertain, and as impetuous in its feelings, as that of the spoiled and flattered beauty.

"Deerslayer," answered Judith, after a moment's pause, "I shall be honest with you. I confess that the time has been when what you call finery, was to me the dearest thing on earth; but I begin to feel differently. Though Hurry Harry is nought to me nor ever can be, I would give all I own to set him free. If I would do this for blustering, bullying, talking Hurry, who has nothing but good looks to recommend him, you may judge what I would do for my own father."

"This sounds well, and is according to woman's gifts. Ah's, me! The same feelin's is to be found among the young women of the Delawares. I've known 'em, often and often, sacrifice their vanity to their hearts. Tis as it should be—'tis as it should be I suppose, in both colours. Woman was created for the feelin's, and is pretty much ruled by feelin'."

"Would the savages let father go, if Judith and I give them all our best things?" demanded Hetty, in her innocent, mild, manner.

"Their women might interfere, good Hetty; yes, their women might interfere with such an ind in view. But, tell me, Sarpent, how is it as to squaws among the knaves; have they many of their own women in the camp?"

The Delaware heard and understood all that passed, though with Indian gravity and finesse he had sat with averted face, seemingly inattentive to a discourse in which he had no direct concern. Thus appealed to, however, he answered his friend in his ordinary sententious manner.

"Six—" he said, holding up all the fingers of one hand, and the thumb of the other, "besides this." The last number denoted his betrothed, whom, with the poetry and truth of nature, he described by laying his hand on his own heart.

"Did you see her, chief—did you get a glimpse of her pleasant countenance, or come close enough to her ear, to sing in it the song she loves to hear?"

"No, Deerslayer—the trees were too many, and leaves covered their boughs like clouds hiding the heavens in a storm. But"—and the young warrior turned his dark face towards his friend, with a smile on it that illuminated its fierce-looking paint and naturally stern lineaments with a bright gleam of human feeling, "Chingachgook heard the laugh of Wah-ta-Wah, and knew it from the laugh of the women of the Iroquois. It sounded in his ears, like the chirp of the wren."

"Ay, trust a lovyer's ear for that, and a Delaware's ear for all sounds that are ever heard in the woods. I know not why it is so, Judith, but when young men—and I dares to say it may be all the same with young women, too—but when they get to have kind feelin's towards each other, it's wonderful how pleasant the laugh, or the speech becomes, to the other person. I've seen grim warriors listening to the chattering and the laughing of young gals, as if it was church music, such as is heard in the old Dutch church that stands in the great street of Albany, where I've been, more than once, with peltry and game."

"And you, Deerslayer," said Judith quickly, and with more sensibility than marked her usually light and thoughtless manner,—"have you never felt how pleasant it is to listen to the laugh of the girl you love?"

"Lord bless you gal!—Why I've never lived enough among my own colour to drop into them sort of feelin's,—no never! I dares to say, they are nat'ral and right, but to me there's no music so sweet as the sighing of the wind in the tree tops, and the rippling of a stream from a full, sparkling, natyve fountain of pure forest water—unless, indeed," he continued, dropping his head for an instant in a thoughtful manner—"unless indeed it be the open mouth of a sartain hound, when I'm on the track of a fat buck. As for unsartain dogs, I care little for their cries, seein' they are as likely to speak when the deer is not in sight, as when it is."

Judith walked slowly and pensively away, nor was there any of her ordinary calculating coquetry in the light tremulous sigh that, unconsciously to herself, arose to her lips. On the other hand Hetty listened with guileless attention, though it struck her simple mind as singular that the young man should prefer the melody of the woods, to the songs of girls, or even to the laugh of innocence and joy. Accustomed, however, to defer in most things to her sister, she soon followed Judith into the cabin, where she took a seat and remained pondering intensely over some occurrence, or resolution, or opinion—which was a secret to all but herself. Left alone, Deerslayer and his friend resumed their discourse.

"Has the young pale-face hunter been long on this lake?" demanded the Delaware, after courteously waiting for the other to speak first.

"Only since yesterday noon, Sarpent, though that has been long enough to see and do much." The gaze that the Indian fastened on his companion was so keen that it seemed to mock the gathering darkness of the night. As the other furtively returned his look, he saw the two black eyes glistening on him, like the balls of the panther, or those of the penned wolf. He understood the meaning of this glowing gaze, and answered evasively, as he fancied would best become the modesty of a white man's gifts.

"'Tis as you suspect, Sarpent; yes, 'tis somewhat that-a-way. I have fell in with the inimy, and I suppose it may be said I've fou't them, too."

An exclamation of delight and exultation escaped the Indian, and then laying his hand eagerly on the arm of his friend, he asked if there were any scalps taken.

"That I will maintain in the face of all the Delaware tribe, old Tamenund, and your own father the great Uncas, as well as the rest, is ag'in white gifts! My scalp is on my head, as you can see, Sarpent, and that was the only scalp that was in danger, when one side was altogether Christian and white."

"Did no warrior fall?—Deerslayer did not get his name by being slow of sight, or clumsy with the rifle!"

"In that particular, chief, you're nearer reason, and therefore nearer being right. I may say one Mingo fell."

"A chief!" demanded the other with startling vehemence.

"Nay, that's more than I know, or can say. He was artful, and treacherous, and stout-hearted, and may well have gained popularity enough with his people to be named to that rank. The man fou't well, though his eye was'n't quick enough for one who had had his schooling in your company, Delaware."

"My brother and friend struck the body?"

"That was uncalled for, seeing that the Mingo died in my arms. The truth may as well be said, at once; he fou't like a man of red gifts, and I fou't like a man with gifts of my own colour. God gave me the victory; I coul'n't fly in the face of his Providence by forgetting my birth and natur'. White he made me, and white I shall live and die."

"Good! Deerslayer is a pale-face, and has pale-face hands. A Delaware will look for the scalp, and hang it on a pole, and sing a song in his honour, when we go back to our people. The glory belongs to the tribe; it must not be lost."

"This is easy talking, but 'twill not be as easy doing. The Mingo's body is in the hands of his fri'nds and, no doubt, is hid in some hole where Delaware cunning will never be able to get at the scalp."

The young man then gave his friend a succinct, but clear account, of the event of the morning, concealing nothing of any moment, and yet touching on every thing modestly and with a careful attention to avoid the Indian habit of boasting. Chingachgook again expressed his satisfaction at the honour won by his friend, and then both arose, the hour having arrived when it became prudent to move the Ark further from the land.

It was now quite dark, the heavens having become clouded, and the stars hid. The north wind had ceased—as was usual with the setting of the sun, and a light air arose from the south. This change favoring the design of Deerslayer, he lifted his grapnel, and the scow immediately and quite perceptibly began to drift more into the lake. The sail was set, when the motion of the craft increased to a rate not much less than two miles in the hour. As this superseded the necessity of rowing, an occupation that an Indian would not be likely to desire, Deerslayer, Chingachgook and Judith seated themselves in the stern of the scow, where they first governed its movements by holding the oar. Here they discoursed on their future movements, and on the means that ought to be used in order to effect the liberation of their friends.

In this dialogue Judith held a material part, the Delaware readily understanding all she said, while his own replies and remarks, both of which were few and pithy, were occasionally rendered into English by his friend. Judith rose greatly in the estimation of her companions, in the half hour that followed. Prompt of resolution and firm of purpose, her suggestions and expedients partook of her spirit and sagacity, both of which were of a character to find favor with men of the frontier. The events that had occurred since their meeting, as well as her isolated and dependant situation, induced the girl to feel towards Deerslayer like the friend of a year instead of an acquaintance of a day, and so completely had she been won by his guileless truth of character and of feeling, pure novelties in our sex, as respected her own experience, that his peculiarities excited her curiosity, and created a confidence that had never been awakened by any other man. Hitherto she had been compelled to stand on the defensive in her intercourse with men, with what success was best known to herself, but here had she been suddenly thrown into the society and under the protection of a youth, who evidently as little contemplated evil towards herself as if he had been her brother. The freshness of his integrity, the poetry and truth of his feelings, and even the quaintness of his forms of speech, all had their influence, and aided in awakening an interest that she found as pure as it was sudden and deep. Hurry's fine face and manly form had never compensated for his boisterous and vulgar tone, and her intercourse with the officers had prepared her to make comparisons under which even his great natural advantages suffered. But this very intercourse with the officers who occasionally came upon the lake to fish and hunt, had an effect in producing her present sentiments towards the young stranger. With them, while her vanity had been gratified, and her self-love strongly awakened, she had many causes deeply to regret the acquaintance—if not to mourn over it, in secret sorrow—for it was impossible for one of her quick intellect not to perceive how hollow was the association between superior and inferior, and that she was regarded as the play thing of an idle hour, rather than as an equal and a friend, by even the best intentioned and least designing of her scarlet-clad admirers. Deerslayer, on the other hand, had a window in his breast through which the light of his honesty was ever shining; and even his indifference to charms that so rarely failed to produce a sensation, piqued the pride of the girl, and gave him an interest that another, seemingly more favored by nature, might have failed to excite.

In this manner half an hour passed, during which time the Ark had been slowly stealing over the water, the darkness thickening around it; though it was easy to see that the gloom of the forest at the southern end of the lake was getting to be distant, while the mountains that lined the sides of the beautiful basin were overshadowing it, nearly from side to side. There was, indeed, a narrow stripe of water, in the centre of the lake where the dim light that was still shed from the heavens, fell upon its surface in a line extending north and south; and along this faint track, a sort of inverted milky way, in which the obscurity was not quite as dense as in other places, the scow held her course, he who steered well knowing that it led in the direction he wished to go. The reader is not to suppose, however, that any difficulty could exist as to the course. This would have been determined by that of the air, had it not been possible to distinguish the mountains, as well as by the dim opening to the south, which marked the position of the valley in that quarter, above the plain of tall trees, by a sort of lessened obscurity; the difference between the darkness of the forest, and that of the night, as seen only in the air. The peculiarities at length caught the attention of Judith and the Deerslayer, and the conversation ceased, to allow each to gaze at the solemn stillness and deep repose of nature.

"'Tis a gloomy night—" observed the girl, after a pause of several minutes—"I hope we may be able to find the castle."

"Little fear of our missing that, if we keep this path in the middle of the lake," returned the young man. "Natur' has made us a road here, and, dim as it is, there'll be little difficulty following it."

"Do you hear nothing, Deerslayer?—It seemed as if the water was stirring quite near us!"

"Sartainly something did move the water, oncommon like; must have been a fish. Them creatur's prey upon each other like men and animals on the land; one has leaped into the air and fallen hard, back into his own element. 'Tis of little use Judith, for any to strive to get out of their elements, since it's natur' to stay in 'em, and natur' will have its way. Ha! That sounds like a paddle, used with more than common caution!"

At this moment the Delaware bent forward and pointed significantly into the boundary of gloom, as if some object had suddenly caught his eye. Both Deerslayer and Judith followed the direction of his gesture, and each got a view of a canoe at the same instant. The glimpse of this startling neighbor was dim, and to eyes less practised it might have been uncertain, though to those in the Ark the object was evidently a canoe with a single individual in it; the latter standing erect and paddling. How many lay concealed in its bottom, of course could not be known. Flight, by means of oars, from a bark canoe impelled by vigorous and skilful hands, was utterly impracticable, and each of the men seized his rifle in expectation of a conflict.

"I can easily bring down the paddler," whispered Deerslayer, "but we'll first hail him, and ask his arrn'd." Then raising his voice, he continued in a solemn manner—"hold! If ye come nearer, I must fire, though contrary to my wishes, and then sartain death will follow. Stop paddling, and answer."

"Fire, and slay a poor defenseless girl," returned a soft tremulous female voice. "And God will never forgive you! Go your way, Deerslayer, and let me go mine."

"Hetty!" exclaimed the young man and Judith in a breath; and the former sprang instantly to the spot where he had left the canoe they had been towing. It was gone, and he understood the whole affair. As for the fugitive, frightened at the menace she ceased paddling, and remained dimly visible, resembling a spectral outline of a human form, standing on the water. At the next moment the sail was lowered, to prevent the Ark from passing the spot where the canoe lay. This last expedient, however, was not taken in time, for the momentum of so heavy a craft, and the impulsion of the air, soon set her by, bringing Hetty directly to windward, though still visible, as the change in the positions of the two boats now placed her in that species of milky way which has been mentioned.

"What can this mean, Judith?" demanded Deerslayer—"Why has your sister taken the canoe, and left us?"

"You know she is feeble-minded, poor girl!—and she has her own ideas of what ought to be done. She loves her father more than most children love their parents—and—then—"

"Then, what, gal? This is a trying moment; one in which truth must be spoken!"

Judith felt a generous and womanly regret at betraying her sister, and she hesitated ere she spoke again. But once more urged by Deerslayer, and conscious herself of all the risks the whole party was running by the indiscretion of Hetty, she could refrain no longer.

"Then, I fear, poor, weak-minded Hetty has not been altogether able to see all the vanity, and rudeness and folly, that lie hid behind the handsome face and fine form of Hurry Harry. She talks of him in her sleep, and sometimes betrays the inclination in her waking moments."

"You think, Judith, that your sister is now bent on some mad scheme to serve her father and Hurry, which will, in all likelihood, give them riptyles the Mingos, the mastership of a canoe?"

"Such, I fear, will turn out to be the fact, Deerslayer. Poor Hetty has hardly sufficient cunning to outwit a savage."

All this while the canoe, with the form of Hetty erect in one end of it, was dimly perceptible, though the greater drift of the Ark rendered it, at each instant, less and less distinct. It was evident no time was to be lost, lest it should altogether disappear. The rifles were now laid aside as useless, the two men seizing the oars and sweeping the head of the scow round in the direction of the canoe. Judith, accustomed to the office, flew to the other end of the Ark, and placed herself at what might be called the helm. Hetty took the alarm at these preparations, which could not be made without noise, and started off like a bird that had been suddenly put up by the approach of unexpected danger.

As Deerslayer and his companion rowed with the energy of those who felt the necessity of straining every nerve, and Hetty's strength was impaired by a nervous desire to escape, the chase would have quickly terminated in the capture of the fugitive, had not the girl made several short and unlooked-for deviations in her course. These turnings gave her time, and they had also the effect of gradually bringing both canoe and Ark within the deeper gloom, cast by the shadows from the hills. They also gradually increased the distance between the fugitive and her pursuers, until Judith called out to her companions to cease rowing, for she had completely lost sight of the canoe.

When this mortifying announcement was made, Hetty was actually so near as to understand every syllable her sister uttered, though the latter had used the precaution of speaking as low as circumstances would allow her to do, and to make herself heard. Hetty stopped paddling at the same moment, and waited the result with an impatience that was breathless, equally from her late exertions, and her desire to land. A dead silence immediately fell on the lake, during which the three in the Ark were using their senses differently, in order to detect the position of the canoe. Judith bent forward to listen, in the hope of catching some sound that might betray the direction in which her sister was stealing away, while her two companions brought their eyes as near as possible to a level with the water, in order to detect any object that might be floating on its surface. All was vain, however, for neither sound nor sight rewarded their efforts. All this time Hetty, who had not the cunning to sink into the canoe, stood erect, a finger pressed on her lips, gazing in the direction in which the voices had last been heard, resembling a statue of profound and timid attention. Her ingenuity had barely sufficed to enable her to seize the canoe and to quit the Ark, in the noiseless manner related, and then it appeared to be momentarily exhausted. Even the doublings of the canoe had been as much the consequence of an uncertain hand and of nervous agitation, as of any craftiness or calculation.

The pause continued several minutes, during which Deerslayer and the Delaware conferred together in the language of the latter. Then the oars dipped, again, and the Ark moved away, rowing with as little noise as possible. It steered westward, a little southerly, or in the direction of the encampment of the enemy. Having reached a point at no great distance from the shore, and where the obscurity was intense on account of the proximity of the land, it lay there near an hour, in waiting for the expected approach of Hetty, who, it was thought, would make the best of her way to that spot as soon as she believed herself released from the danger of pursuit. No success rewarded this little blockade, however, neither appearance nor sound denoting the passage of the canoe. Disappointed at this failure, and conscious of the importance of getting possession of the fortress before it could be seized by the enemy, Deerslayer now took his way towards the castle, with the apprehension that all his foresight in securing the canoes would be defeated by this unguarded and alarming movement on the part of the feeble-minded Hetty.

CHAPTER X.

"But who in this wild wood
May credit give to either eye, or ear?
From rocky precipice or hollow cave,
'Midst the confused sound of rustling leaves,
And creaking boughs, and cries of nightly birds,
Returning seeming answer!"

Joanna Baihie, "Rayner: A Tragedy," II.L3–4, 6–9.

Fear, as much as calculation, had induced Hetty to cease paddling, when she found that her pursuers did not know in which direction to proceed. She remained stationary until the Ark had pulled in near the encampment, as has been related in the preceding chapter, when she resumed the paddle and with cautious strokes made the best of her way towards the western shore. In order to avoid her pursuers, however, who, she rightly suspected, would soon be rowing along that shore themselves, the head of the canoe was pointed so far north as to bring her to land on a point that thrust itself into the lake, at the distance of near a league from the outlet. Nor was this altogether the result of a desire to escape, for, feeble minded as she was, Hetty Hutter had a good deal of that instinctive caution which so often keeps those whom God has thus visited from harm. She was perfectly aware of the importance of keeping the canoes from falling into the hands of the Iroquois, and long familiarity with the lake had suggested one of the simplest expedients, by which this great object could be rendered compatible with her own purpose.

The point in question was the first projection that offered on that side of the lake, where a canoe, if set adrift with a southerly air would float clear of the land, and where it would be no great violation of probabilities to suppose it might even hit the castle; the latter lying above it, almost in a direct line with the wind. Such then was Hetty's intention, and she landed on the extremity of the gravelly point, beneath an overhanging oak, with the express intention of shoving the canoe off from the shore, in order that it might drift up towards her father's insulated abode. She knew, too, from the logs that occasionally floated about the lake, that did it miss the castle and its appendages the wind would be likely to change before the canoe could reach the northern extremity of the lake, and that Deerslayer might have an opportunity of regaining it in the morning, when no doubt he would be earnestly sweeping the surface of the water, and the whole of its wooded shores, with glass. In all this, too, Hetty was less governed by any chain of reasoning than by her habits, the latter often supplying the place of mind, in human beings, as they perform the same for animals of the inferior classes.

The girl was quite an hour finding her way to the point, the distance and the obscurity equally detaining her, but she was no sooner on the gravelly beach than she prepared to set the canoe adrift, in the manner mentioned. While in the act of pushing it from her, she heard low voices that seemed to come among the trees behind her. Startled at this unexpected danger Hetty was on the point of springing into the canoe in order to seek safety in flight, when she thought she recognized the tones of Judith's melodious voice. Bending forward so as to catch the sounds more directly, they evidently came from the water, and then she understood that the Ark was approaching from the south, and so close in with the western shore, as necessarily to cause it to pass the point within twenty yards of the spot where she stood. Here, then, was all she could desire; the canoe was shoved off into the lake, leaving its late occupant alone on the narrow strand.

When this act of self-devotion was performed, Hetty did not retire. The foliage of the overhanging trees and bushes would have almost concealed her person, had there been light, but in that obscurity it was utterly impossible to discover any object thus shaded, at the distance of a few feet. Flight, too, was perfectly easy, as twenty steps would effectually bury her in the forest. She remained, therefore, watching with intense anxiety the result of her expedient, intending to call the attention of the others to the canoe with her voice, should they appear to pass without observing it. The Ark approached under its sail, again, Deerslayer standing in its bow, with Judith near him, and the Delaware at the helm. It would seem that in the bay below it had got too close to the shore, in the lingering hope of intercepting Hetty, for, as it came nearer, the latter distinctly heard the directions that the young man forward gave to his companion aft, in order to clear the point.

"Lay her head more off the shore, Delaware," said Deerslayer for the third time, speaking in English that his fair companion might understand his words—"Lay her head well off shore. We have got embayed here, and needs keep the mast clear of the trees. Judith, there's a canoe!"

The last words were uttered with great earnestness, and Deerslayer's hand was on his rifle ere they were fairly out of his mouth. But the truth flashed on the mind of the quick-witted girl, and she instantly told her companion that the boat must be that in which her sister had fled.

"Keep the scow straight, Delaware; steer as straight as your bullet flies when sent ag'in a buck; there—I have it."

The canoe was seized, and immediately secured again to the side of the Ark. At the next moment the sail was lowered, and the motion of the Ark arrested by means of the oars.

"Hetty!" called out Judith, concern, even affection betraying itself in her tones. "Are you within hearing, sister—for God's sake answer, and let me hear the sound of your voice, again! Hetty!—dear Hetty."

"I'm here, Judith—here on the shore, where it will be useless to follow me, as I will hide in the woods."

"Oh! Hetty what is't you do! Remember 'tis drawing near midnight, and that the woods are filled with savages and wild beasts!"

"Neither will harm a poor half-witted girl, Judith. God is as much with me, here, as he would be in the Ark or in the hut. I am going to help my father, and poor Hurry Harry, who will be tortured and slain unless some one cares for them."

"We all care for them, and intend to-morrow to send them a flag of truce, to buy their ransom. Come back then, sister; trust to us, who have better heads than you, and who will do all we can for father."

"I know your head is better than mine, Judith, for mine is very weak, to be sure; but I must go to father and poor Hurry. Do you and Deerslayer keep the castle, sister; leave me in the hands of God."

"God is with us all, Hetty—in the castle, or on the shore—father as well as ourselves, and it is sinful not to trust to his goodness. You can do nothing in the dark; will lose your way in the forest, and perish for want of food."

"God will not let that happen to a poor child that goes to serve her father, sister. I must try and find the savages."

"Come back for this night only; in the morning, we will put you ashore, and leave you to do as you may think right."

"You say so, Judith, and you think so; but you would not. Your heart would soften, and you'd see tomahawks and scalping knives in the air. Besides, I've got a thing to tell the Indian chief that will answer all our wishes, and I'm afraid I may forget it, if I don't tell it to him at once. You'll see that he will let father go, as soon as he hears it!"

"Poor Hetty! What can you say to a ferocious savage that will be likely to change his bloody purpose!"

"That which will frighten him, and make him let father go—" returned the simple-minded girl, positively. "You'll see, sister; you'll see, how soon it will bring him to, like a gentle child!"

"Will you tell me, Hetty, what you intend to say?" asked Deerslayer. "I know the savages well, and can form some idee how far fair words will be likely, or not, to work on their bloody natur's. If it's not suited to the gifts of a red-skin, 'twill be of no use; for reason goes by gifts, as well as conduct."

"Well, then," answered Hetty, dropping her voice to a low, confidential, tone, for the stillness of the night, and the nearness of the Ark, permitted her to do this and still to be heard—"Well, then, Deerslayer, as you seem a good and honest young man I will tell you. I mean not to say a word to any of the savages until I get face to face with their head chief, let them plague me with as many questions as they please I'll answer none of them, unless it be to tell them to lead me to their wisest man— Then, Deerslayer, I'll tell him that God will not forgive murder, and thefts; and that if father and Hurry did go after the scalps of the Iroquois, he must return good for evil, for so the Bible commands, else he will go into everlasting punishment. When he hears this, and feels it to be true, as feel it he must, how long will it be before he sends father, and Hurry, and me to the shore, opposite the castle, telling us all three to go our way in peace?"

The last question was put in a triumphant manner, and then the simple-minded girl laughed at the impression she never doubted that her project had made on her auditors. Deerslayer was dumbfounded at this proof of guileless feebleness of mind, but Judith had suddenly bethought her of a means of counteracting this wild project, by acting on the very feelings that had given it birth. Without adverting to the closing question, or the laugh, therefore, she hurriedly called to her sister by name, as one suddenly impressed with the importance of what she had to say. But no answer was given to the call.

By the snapping of twigs, and the rustling of leaves, Hetty had evidently quitted the shore, and was already burying herself in the forest. To follow would have been fruitless, since the darkness, as well as the dense cover that the woods everywhere offered, would have rendered her capture next to impossible, and there was also the never ceasing danger of falling into the hands of their enemies. After a short and melancholy discussion, therefore, the sail was again set, and the Ark pursued its course towards its habitual moorings, Deerslayer silently felicitating himself on the recovery of the canoe, and brooding over his plans for the morrow. The wind rose as the party quitted the point, and in less than an hour they reached the castle. Here all was found as it had been left, and the reverse of the ceremonies had to be taken in entering the building, that had been used on quitting it. Judith occupied a solitary bed that night bedewing the pillow with her tears, as she thought of the innocent and hitherto neglected creature, who had been her companion from childhood, and bitter regrets came over her mind, from more causes than one, as the weary hours passed away, making it nearly morning before she lost her recollection in sleep. Deerslayer and the Delaware took their rest in the Ark, where we shall leave them enjoying the deep sleep of the honest, the healthful and fearless, to return to the girl we have last seen in the midst of the forest.

When Hetty left the shore, she took her way unhesitatingly into the woods, with a nervous apprehension of being followed. Luckily, this course was the best she could have hit on to effect her own purpose, since it was the only one that led her from the point. The night was so intensely dark, beneath the branches of the trees, that her progress was very slow, and the direction she went altogether a matter of chance, after the first few yards. The formation of the ground, however, did not permit her to deviate far from the line in which she desired to proceed. On one hand it was soon bounded by the acclivity of the hill, while the lake, on the other, served as a guide. For two hours did this single-hearted and simple-minded girl toil through the mazes of the forest, sometimes finding herself on the brow of the bank that bounded the water, and at others struggling up an ascent that warned her to go no farther in that direction, since it necessarily ran at right angles to the course on which she wished to proceed. Her feet often slid from beneath her, and she got many falls, though none to do her injury; but, by the end of the period mentioned, she had become so weary as to want strength to go any farther. Rest was indispensable, and she set about preparing a bed, with the readiness and coolness of one to whom the wilderness presented no unnecessary terrors. She knew that wild beasts roamed through all the adjacent forest, but animals that preyed on the human species were rare, and of dangerous serpents there were literally none. These facts had been taught her by her father, and whatever her feeble mind received at all, it received so confidingly as to leave her no uneasiness from any doubts, or scepticism. To her the sublimity of the solitude in which she was placed, was soothing, rather than appalling, and she gathered a bed of leaves, with as much indifference to the circumstances that would have driven the thoughts of sleep entirely from the minds of most of her sex, as if she had been preparing her place of nightly rest beneath the paternal roof. As soon as Hetty had collected a sufficient number of the dried leaves to protect her person from the damps of the ground, she kneeled beside the humble pile, clasped her raised hands in an attitude of deep devotion, and in a soft, low, but audible voice repeated the Lord's Prayer. This was followed by those simple and devout verses, so familiar to children, in which she recommended her soul to God, should it be called away to another state of existence, ere the return of morning. This duty done, she lay down and disposed herself to sleep. The attire of the girl, though suited to the season, was sufficiently warm for all ordinary purposes, but the forest is ever cool, and the nights of that elevated region of country, have always a freshness about them, that renders clothing more necessary than is commonly the case in the summers of a low latitude. This had been foreseen by Hetty, who had brought with her a coarse heavy mantle, which, when laid over her body, answered all the useful purposes of a blanket. Thus protected, she dropped asleep in a few minutes, as tranquilly as if watched over by the guardian care of that mother, who had so recently been taken from her forever, affording in this particular a most striking contrast between her own humble couch, and the sleepless pillow of her sister.

Hour passed after hour, in a tranquility as undisturbed and a rest as sweet as if angels, expressly commissioned for that object, watched around the bed of Hetty Hutter. Not once did her soft eyes open, until the grey of the dawn came struggling through the tops of the trees, falling on their lids, and, united to the freshness of a summer's morning, giving the usual summons to awake. Ordinarily, Hetty was up ere the rays of the sun tipped the summits of the mountains, but on this occasion her fatigue had been so great, and her rest was so profound, that the customary warnings failed of their effect. The girl murmured in her sleep, threw an arm forward, smiled as gently as an infant in its cradle, but still slumbered. In making this unconscious gesture, her hand fell on some object that was warm, and in the half unconscious state in which she lay, she connected the circumstance with her habits. At the next moment, a rude attack was made on her side, as if a rooting animal were thrusting its snout beneath, with a desire to force her position, and then, uttering the name of "Judith" she awoke. As the startled girl arose to a sitting attitude she perceived that some dark object sprang from her, scattering the leaves and snapping the fallen twigs in its haste. Opening her eyes, and recovering from the first confusion and astonishment of her situation, Hetty perceived a cub, of the common American brown bear, balancing itself on its hinder legs, and still looking towards her, as if doubtful whether it would be safe to trust itself near her person again. The first impulse of Hetty, who had been mistress of several of these cubs, was to run and seize the little creature as a prize, but a loud growl warned her of the danger of such a procedure. Recoiling a few steps, the girl looked hurriedly round, and perceived the dam, watching her movements with fiery eyes at no great distance. A hollow tree, that once been the home of bees, having recently fallen, the mother with two more cubs was feasting on the dainty food that this accident had placed within her reach; while the first kept a jealous eye on the situation of its truant and reckless young.

It would exceed all the means of human knowledge to presume to analyze the influences that govern the acts of the lower animals. On this occasion, the dam, though proverbially fierce when its young is thought to be in danger, manifested no intention to attack the girl. It quitted the honey, and advanced to a place within twenty feet of her, where it raised itself on its hind legs and balanced its body in a sort of angry, growling discontent, but approached no nearer. Happily, Hetty did not fly. On the contrary, though not without terror, she knelt with her face towards the animal, and with clasped hands and uplifted eyes, repeated the prayer of the previous night. This act of devotion was not the result of alarm, but it was a duty she never neglected to perform ere she slept, and when the return of consciousness awoke her to the business of the day. As the girl arose from her knees, the bear dropped on its feet again, and collecting its cubs around her, permitted them to draw their natural sustenance. Hetty was delighted with this proof of tenderness in an animal that has but a very indifferent reputation for the gentler feelings, and as a cub would quit its mother to frisk and leap about in wantonness, she felt a strong desire again to catch it up in her arms, and play with it. But admonished by the growl, she had self-command sufficient not to put this dangerous project in execution, and recollecting her errand among the hills, she tore herself away from the group, and proceeded on her course along the margin of the lake, of which she now caught glimpses again through the trees. To her surprise, though not to her alarm, the family of bears arose and followed her steps, keeping a short distance behind her; apparently watching every movement as if they had a near interest in all she did.

In this manner, escorted by the dam and cubs, the girl proceeded nearly a mile, thrice the distance she had been able to achieve in the darkness, during the same period of time. She then reached a brook that had dug a channel for itself into the earth, and went brawling into the lake, between steep and high banks, covered with trees. Here Hetty performed her ablutions; then drinking of the pure mountain water, she went her way, refreshed and lighter of heart, still attended by her singular companions. Her course now lay along a broad and nearly level terrace, which stretched from the top of the bank that bounded the water, to a low acclivity that rose to a second and irregular platform above. This was at a part of the valley where the mountains ran obliquely, forming the commencement of a plain that spread between the hills, southward of the sheet of water. Hetty knew, by this circumstance, that she was getting near to the encampment, and had she not, the bears would have given her warning of the vicinity of human beings. Snuffing the air, the dam refused to follow any further, though the girl looked back and invited her to come by childish signs, and even by direct appeals made in her own sweet voice. It was while making her way slowly through some bushes, in this manner, with averted face and eyes riveted on the immovable animals, that the girl suddenly found her steps arrested by a human hand, that was laid lightly on her shoulder.

"Where go?—" said a soft female voice, speaking hurriedly, and in concern.—"Indian—red man savage—wicked warrior—that-a-way."

This unexpected salutation alarmed the girl no more than the presence of the fierce inhabitants of the woods. It took her a little by surprise, it is true, but she was in a measure prepared for some such meeting, and the creature who stopped her was as little likely to excite terror as any who ever appeared in the guise of an Indian. It was a girl, not much older than herself, whose smile was sunny as Judith's in her brightest moments, whose voice was melody itself, and whose accents and manner had all the rebuked gentleness that characterizes the sex among a people who habitually treat their women as the attendants and servitors of the warriors. Beauty among the women of the aboriginal Americans, before they have become exposed to the hardships of wives and mothers, is by no means uncommon. In this particular, the original owners of the country were not unlike their more civilized successors, nature appearing to have bestowed that delicacy of mien and outline that forms so great a charm in the youthful female, but of which they are so early deprived; and that, too, as much by the habits of domestic life as from any other cause.

The girl who had so suddenly arrested the steps of Hetty was dressed in a calico mantle that effectually protected all the upper part of her person, while a short petticoat of blue cloth edged with gold lace, that fell no lower than her knees, leggings of the same, and moccasins of deer-skin, completed her attire. Her hair fell in long dark braids down her shoulders and back, and was parted above a low smooth forehead, in a way to soften the expression of eyes that were full of archness and natural feeling. Her face was oval, with delicate features, the teeth were even and white, while the mouth expressed a melancholy tenderness, as if it wore this peculiar meaning in intuitive perception of the fate of a being who was doomed from birth to endure a woman's sufferings, relieved by a woman's affections. Her voice, as has been already intimated, was soft as the sighing of the night air, a characteristic of the females of her race, but which was so conspicuous in herself as to have produced for her the name of Wah-ta-Wah; which rendered into English means Hist-oh-Hist.

In a word, this was the betrothed of Chingachgook, who—having succeeded in lulling their suspicions, was permitted to wander around the encampment of her captors. This indulgence was in accordance with the general policy of the red man, who well knew, moreover, that her trail could have been easily followed in the event of flight. It will also be remembered that the Iroquois, or Hurons, as it would be better to call them, were entirely ignorant of the proximity of her lover, a fact, indeed, that she did not know herself.

It is not easy to say which manifested the most self-possession at this unexpected meeting; the pale-face, or the red girl. But, though a little surprised, Wah-ta-Wah was the most willing to speak, and far the readier in foreseeing consequences, as well as in devising means to avert them. Her father, during her childhood, had been much employed as a warrior by the authorities of the Colony, and dwelling for several years near the forts, she had caught a knowledge of the English tongue, which she spoke in the usual, abbreviated manner of an Indian, but fluently, and without any of the ordinary reluctance of her people.

"Where go?—" repeated Wah-ta-Wah, returning the smile of Hetty, in her own gentle, winning, manner—"wicked warrior that-a-way—good warrior, far off."

"What's your name?" asked Hetty, with the simplicity of a child.

"Wah-ta-Wah. I no Mingo—good Delaware—Yengeese friend. Mingo cruel, and love scalp, for blood—Delaware love him, for honor. Come here, where no eyes."

Wah-ta-Wah now led her companion towards the lake, descending the bank so as to place its overhanging trees and bushes between them and any probable observers. Nor did she stop until they were both seated, side by side, on a fallen log, one end of which actually lay buried in the water.

"Why you come for?" the young Indian eagerly inquired—"Where you come for?" Hetty told her tale in her own simple and truth-loving manner. She explained the situation of her father, and stated her desire to serve him, and if possible to procure his release.

"Why your father come to Mingo camp in night?" asked the Indian girl, with a directness, which if not borrowed from the other, partook largely of its sincerity. "He know it war-time, and he no boy—he no want beard—no want to be told Iroquois carry tomahawk, and knife, and rifle. Why he come night time, seize me by hair, and try to scalp Delaware girl?"

"You!" said Hetty, almost sickening with horror—"Did he seize you—did he try to scalp you?"

"Why no? Delaware scalp sell for much as Mingo scalp. Governor no tell difference. Wicked t'ing for pale-face to scalp. No his gifts, as the good Deerslayer always tell me."

"And do you know the Deerslayer?" said Hetty, coloring with delight and surprise; forgetting her regrets, at the moment, in the influence of this new feeling. "I know him, too. He is now in the Ark, with Judith and a Delaware who is called the Big Serpent. A bold and handsome warrior is this Serpent, too!"

Spite of the rich deep colour that nature had bestowed on the Indian beauty, the tell-tale blood deepened on her cheeks, until the blush gave new animation and intelligence to her jet-black eyes. Raising a finger in an attitude of warning, she dropped her voice, already so soft and sweet, nearly to a whisper, as she continued the discourse.

"Chingachgook!" returned the Delaware girl, sighing out the harsh name, in sounds so softly guttural, as to cause it to reach the ear in melody— "His father, Uncas—great chief of the Mahicanni—next to old Tamenund!—More as warrior, not so much gray hair, and less at Council Fire. You know Serpent?"

"He joined us last evening, and was in the Ark with me, for two or three hours before I left it. I'm afraid, Hist——" Hetty could not pronounce the Indian name of her new friend, but having heard Deerslayer give her this familiar appellation, she used it without any of the ceremony of civilized life——"I'm afraid Hist, he has come after scalps, as well as my poor father and Hurry Harry."

"Why he shouldn't—ha? Chingachgook red warrior—very red—scalp make his honor—Be sure he take him."

"Then," said Hetty, earnestly, "he will be as wicked as any other. God will not pardon in a red man, what he will not pardon in a white man.

"No true——" returned the Delaware girl, with a warmth that nearly amounted to passion. "No true, I tell you! The Manitou smile and pleased when he see young warrior come back from the war path, with two, ten, hundred scalp on a pole! Chingachgook father take scalp—grandfather take scalp—all old chief take scalp, and Chingachgook take as many scalp as he can carry, himself."

"Then, Hist, his sleep of nights must be terrible to think of. No one can be cruel, and hope to be forgiven."

"No cruel—plenty forgiven——" returned Wah-ta-Wah, stamping her little foot on the stony strand, and shaking her head in a way to show how completely feminine feeling, in one of its aspects, had gotten the better of feminine feeling in another. "I tell you, Serpent brave; he go home, this time, with four,—yes—two scalp."

"And is that his errand, here?—Did he really come all this distance, across mountain, and valley, rivers and lakes, to torment his fellow creatures, and do so wicked a thing?"

This question at once appeased the growing ire of the half-offended Indian beauty. It completely got the better of the prejudices of education, and turned all her thoughts to a gentler and more feminine channel. At first, she looked around her, suspiciously, as if distrusting eavesdroppers; then she gazed wistfully into the face of her attentive companion; after which this exhibition of girlish coquetry and womanly feeling, terminated by her covering her face with both her hands, and laughing in a strain that might well be termed the melody of the woods. Dread of discovery, however, soon put a stop to this naive exhibition of feeling, and removing her hands, this creature of impulses gazed again wistfully into the face of her companion, as if inquiring how far she might trust a stranger with her secret. Although Hetty had no claims to her sister's extraordinary beauty, many thought her countenance the most winning of the two. It expressed all the undisguised sincerity of her character, and it was totally free from any of the unpleasant physical accompaniments that so frequently attend mental imbecility. It is true that one accustomed to closer observations than common, might have detected the proofs of her feebleness of intellect in the language of her sometimes vacant eyes, but they were signs that attracted sympathy by their total want of guile, rather than by any other feeling. The effect on Hist, to use the English and more familiar translation of the name, was favorable, and yielding to an impulse of tenderness, she threw her arms around Hetty, and embraced her with an outpouring emotion, so natural that it was only equaled by its warmth.

"You good——" whispered the young Indian—"you good, I know; it so long since Wah-ta-Wah have a friend—a sister—any body to speak her heart to! You Hist friend; don't I say trut'?"

"I never had a friend," answered Hetty returning the warm embrace with unfeigned earnestness. "I've a sister, but no friend. Judith loves me, and I love Judith; but that's natural, and as we are taught in the Bible—but I should like to have a friend! I'll be your friend, with all my heart, for I like your voice and your smile, and your way of thinking in every thing, except about the scalps——"

"No t'ink more of him—no say more of scalp—" interrupted Hist, soothingly—"You pale-face, I red-skin; we bring up different fashion. Deerslayer and Chingachgook great friend, and no the same colour, Hist and—what your name, pretty pale-face?"

"I am called Hetty, though when they spell the name in the bible, they always spell it Esther."

"What that make?—no good, no harm. No need to spell name at all—Moravian try to make Wah-ta-Wah spell, but no won't let him. No good for Delaware girl to know too much—know more than warrior some time; that great shame. My name Wah-ta-Wah that say Hist in your tongue; you call him, Hist—I call him, Hetty."

These preliminaries settled to their mutual satisfaction, the two girls began to discourse of their several hopes and projects. Hetty made her new friend more fully acquainted with her intentions in behalf of her father, and, to one in the least addicted to prying into the affairs, Hist would have betrayed her own feelings and expectations in connection with the young warrior of her own tribe. Enough was revealed on both sides, however, to let each party get a tolerable insight into the views of the other, though enough still remained in mental reservation, to give rise to the following questions and answers, with which the interview in effect closed. As the quickest witted, Hist was the first with her interrogatories. Folding an arm about the waist of Hetty, she bent her head so as to look up playfully into the face of the other, and, laughing, as if her meaning were to be extracted from her looks, she spoke more plainly.

"Hetty got broder, as well as fader?—" she said—"Why no talk of broder, as well as fader?"

"I have no brother, Hist. I had one once, they say, but he is dead many a year, and lies buried in the lake, by the side of my mother."

"No got broder—got a young warrior—Love him, almost as much as fader, eh? Very handsome, and brave-looking; fit to be chief, if he good as he seem to be."

"It's wicked to love any man as well as I love my father, and so I strive not to do it, Hist," returned the conscientious Hetty, who knew not how to conceal an emotion, by an approach to an untruth as venial as an evasion, though powerfully tempted by female shame to err, "though I sometimes think wickedness will get the better of me, if Hurry comes so often to the lake. I must tell you the truth, dear Hist, because you ask me, but I should fall down and die in the woods, if he knew it!"

"Why he no ask you, himself?—Brave looking—why not bold speaking? Young warrior ought to ask young girl, no make young girl speak first. Mingo girls too shame for that."

This was said indignantly, and with the generous warmth a young female of spirit would be apt to feel, at what she deemed an invasion of her sex's most valued privilege. It had little influence on the simple-minded, but also just-minded Hetty, who, though inherently feminine in all her impulses, was much more alive to the workings of her own heart, than to any of the usages with which convention has protected the sensitiveness of her sex.

"Ask me what?' the startled girl demanded, with a suddenness that proved how completely her fears had been aroused. 'Ask me, if I like him as well as I do my own father! Oh! I hope he will never put such a question to me, for I should have to answer, and that would kill me!"

"No—no—no kill, quite—almost," returned the other, laughing in spite of herself. "Make blush come—make shame come too; but he no stay great while; then feel happier than ever. Young warrior must tell young girl he want to make wife, else never can live in his wigwam."

"Hurry don't want to marry me—nobody will ever want to marry me, Hist."

"How you can know? P'raps every body want to marry you, and by-and-bye, tongue say what heart feel. Why nobody want to marry you?"

"I am not full witted, they say. Father often tells me this; and so does Judith, sometimes, when she is vexed; but I shouldn't so much mind them, as I did mother. She said so once and then she cried as if her heart would break; and, so, I know I'm not full witted."

Hist gazed at the gentle, simple girl, for quite a minute without speaking, and then the truth appeared to flash all at once on the mind of the young Indian maid. Pity, reverence and tenderness seemed struggling together in her breast, and then rising suddenly, she indicated a wish to her companion that she would accompany her to the camp, which was situated at no great distance. This unexpected change from the precautions that Hist had previously manifested a desire to use, in order to prevent being seen, to an open exposure of the person of her friend, arose from the perfect conviction that no Indian would harm a being whom the Great Spirit had disarmed, by depriving it of its strongest defence, reason. In this respect, nearly all unsophisticated nations resemble each other, appearing to offer spontaneously, by a feeling creditable to human nature, that protection by their own forbearance, which has been withheld by the inscrutable wisdom of Providence. Wah-ta-Wah, indeed, knew that in many tribes the mentally imbecile and the mad were held in a species of religious reverence, receiving from these untutored inhabitants of the forest respect and honors, instead of the contumely and neglect that it is their fortune to meet with among the more pretending and sophisticated.

Hetty accompanied her new friend without apprehension or reluctance. It was her wish to reach the camp, and, sustained by her motives, she felt no more concern for the consequences than did her companion herself, now the latter was apprised of the character of the protection that the pale-face maiden carried with her. Still, as they proceeded slowly along a shore that was tangled with overhanging bushes, Hetty continued the discourse, assuming the office of interrogating which the other had instantly dropped, as soon as she ascertained the character of the mind to which her questions had been addressed.

"But you are not half-witted," said Hetty, "and there's no reason why the Serpent should not marry you."

"Hist prisoner, and Mingo got big ear. No speak of Chingachgook when they by. Promise Hist that, good Hetty."

"I know—I know—" returned Hetty, half-whispering, in her eagerness to let the other see she understood the necessity of caution. "I know—Deerslayer and the Serpent mean to get you away from the Iroquois, and you wish me not to tell the secret."

"How you know?" said Hist, hastily, vexed at the moment that the other was not even more feeble minded than was actually the case. "How you know? Better not talk of any but fader and Hurry— Mingo understand dat; he no understand t'udder. Promise you no talk about what you no understand."

"But I do understand this, Hist, and so I must talk about it. Deerslayer as good as told father all about it, in my presence, and as nobody told me not to listen, I overheard it all, as I did Hurry and father's discourse about the scalps."

"Very bad for pale-faces to talk about scalps, and very bad for young woman to hear! Now you love Hist, I know, Hetty, and so, among Injins, when love hardest never talk most."

"That's not the way among white people, who talk most about them they love best. I suppose it's because I'm only half-witted that I don't see the reason why it should be so different among red people."

"That what Deerslayer call gift. One gift to talk; t'udder gift to hold tongue. Hold tongue your gift, among Mingos. If Sarpent want to see Hist, so Hetty want to see Hurry. Good girl never tell secret of friend."

Hetty understood this appeal, and she promised the Delaware girl not to make any allusion to the presence of Chingachgook, or to the motive of his visit to the lake.

"Maybe he get off Hurry and fader, as well as Hist, if let him have his way," whispered Wah-ta-Wah to her companion, in a confiding flattering way, just as they got near enough to the encampment to hear the voices of several of their own sex, who were apparently occupied in the usual toils of women of their class. "Tink of dat, Hetty, and put two, twenty finger on mouth. No get friend free without Sarpent do it."

A better expedient could not have been adopted, to secure the silence and discretion of Hetty, than that which was now presented to her mind. As the liberation of her father and the young frontier man was the great object of her adventure, she felt the connection between it and the services of the Delaware, and with an innocent laugh, she nodded her head, and in the same suppressed manner, promised a due attention to the wishes of her friend. Thus assured, Hist tarried no longer, but immediately and openly led the way into the encampment of her captors.

CHAPTER XI.

"The great King of Kings
Hath in the table of his law commanded,
That thou shalt do no murder.
Take heed; for he holds vengeance in his hand,
To hurl upon their heads that break his law."

Richard III, I.iv.i95–97 199–200.

That the party to which Hist compulsorily belonged was not one that was regularly on the war path, was evident by the presence of females. It was a small fragment of a tribe that had been hunting and fishing within the English limits, where it was found by the commencement of hostilities, and, after passing the winter and spring by living on what was strictly the property of its enemies, it chose to strike a hostile blow before it finally retired. There was also deep Indian sagacity in the manoeuvre which had led them so far into the territory of their foes. When the runner arrived who announced the breaking out of hostilities between the English and French—a struggle that was certain to carry with it all the tribes that dwelt within the influence of the respective belligerents—this particular party of the Iroquois were posted on the shores of the Oneida, a lake that lies some fifty miles nearer to their own frontier than that which is the scene of our tale.

To have fled in a direct line for the Canadas would have exposed them to the dangers of a direct pursuit, and the chiefs had determined to adopt the expedient of penetrating deeper into a region that had now become dangerous, in the hope of being able to retire in the rear of their pursuers, instead of having them on their trail. The presence of the women had induced the attempt at this ruse, the strength of these feebler members of the party being unequal to the effort of escaping from the pursuit of warriors. When the reader remembers the vast extent of the American wilderness, at that early day, he will perceive that it was possible for even a tribe to remain months undiscovered in particular portions of it; nor was the danger of encountering a foe, the usual precautions being observed, as great in the woods, as it is on the high seas, in a time of active warfare.

The encampment being temporary, it offered to the eye no more than the rude protection of a bivouac, relieved in some slight degree by the ingenious expedients which suggested themselves to the readiness of those who passed their lives amid similar scenes. One fire, that had been kindled against the roots of a living oak, sufficed for the whole party; the weather being too mild to require it for any purpose but cooking. Scattered around this centre of attraction, were some fifteen or twenty low huts, or perhaps kennels would be a better word, into which their different owners crept at night, and which were also intended to meet the exigencies of a storm.

These little huts were made of the branches of trees, put together with some ingenuity, and they were uniformly topped with bark that had been stripped from fallen trees; of which every virgin forest possesses hundreds, in all stages of decay. Of furniture they had next to none. Cooking utensils of the simplest sort were lying near the fire, a few articles of clothing were to be seen in or around the huts, rifles, horns, and pouches leaned against the trees, or were suspended from the lower branches, and the carcasses of two or three deer were stretched to view on the same natural shambles.

As the encampment was in the midst of a dense wood, the eye could not take in its *tout ensemble* at a glance, but hut after hut started out of the gloomy picture, as one gazed about him in quest of objects. There was no centre, unless the fire might be so considered, no open area where the possessors of this rude village might congregate, but all was dark, covert and cunning, like its owners. A few children strayed from hut to hut, giving the spot a little of the air of domestic life, and the suppressed laugh and low voices of the women occasionally broke in upon the deep stillness of the sombre forest. As for the men, they either ate, slept, or examined their arms. They conversed but little, and then usually apart, or in groups withdrawn from the females, whilst an air of untiring, innate watchfulness and apprehension of danger seemed to be blended even with their slumbers.

As the two girls came near the encampment, Hetty uttered a slight exclamation, on catching a view of the person of her father. He was seated on the ground with his back to a tree, and Hurry stood near him indolently whittling a twig. Apparently they were as much at liberty as any others in or about the camp, and one unaccustomed to Indian usages would have mistaken them for visitors, instead of supposing them to be captives. Wah-ta-Wah led her new friend quite near them, and then modestly withdrew, that her own presence might be no restraint on her feelings. But Hetty was not sufficiently familiar with caresses or outward demonstrations of fondness, to indulge in any outbreaking of feeling. She merely approached and stood at her father's side without speaking, resembling a silent statue of filial affection. The old man expressed neither alarm nor surprise at her sudden appearance. In these particulars he had caught the stoicism of the Indians, well knowing that there was no more certain mode of securing their respect than by imitating their self-command. Nor did the savages themselves betray the least sign of surprise at this sudden appearance of a stranger among them. In a word, this arrival produced much less visible sensation, though occurring under circumstances so peculiar, than would be seen in a village of higher pretensions to civilization did an ordinary traveler drive up to the door of its principal inn.

Still a few warriors collected, and it was evident by the manner in which they glanced at Hetty as they conversed together, that she was the subject of their discourse, and probable that the reasons of her unlooked-for appearance were matters of discussion. This phlegm of manner is characteristic of the North American Indian—some say of his white successor also—but, in this case much should be attributed to the peculiar situation in which the party was placed. The force in the Ark, the presence of Chingachgook excepted, was well known, no tribe or body of troops was believed to be near, and vigilant eyes were posted round the entire lake, watching day and night the slightest movement of those whom it would not be exaggerated now to term the besieged.

Hutter was inwardly much moved by the conduct of Hetty, though he affected so much indifference of manner. He recollected her gentle appeal to him before he left the Ark, and misfortune rendered that of weight which might have been forgotten amid the triumph of success. Then he knew the simple, single-hearted fidelity of his child, and understood why she had come, and the total disregard of self that reigned in all her acts.

"This is not well, Hetty," he said, deprecating the consequences to the girl herself more than any other evil. "These are fierce Iroquois, and are as little apt to forget an injury, as a favor."

"Tell me, father—" returned the girl, looking furtively about her as if fearful of being overheard, "did God let you do the cruel errand on which you came? I want much to know this, that I may speak to the Indians plainly, if he did not."

"You should not have come hither, Hetty; these brutes will not understand your nature or your intentions!"

"How was it, father; neither you nor Hurry seems to have any thing that looks like scalps."

"If that will set your mind at peace, child, I can answer you, no. I had caught the young creatur' who came here with you, but her screeches soon brought down upon me a troop of the wild cats, that was too much for any single Christian to withstand. If that will do you any good, we are as innocent of having taken a scalp, this time, as I make no doubt we shall also be innocent of receiving the bounty."

"Thank God for that, father! Now I can speak boldly to the Iroquois, and with an easy conscience. I hope Hurry, too, has not been able to harm any of the Indians?"

"Why, as to that matter, Hetty," returned the individual in question, "you've put it pretty much in the natyve character of the religious truth. Hurry has not been able, and that is the long and short of it. I've seen many squalls, old fellow, both on land and on the water, but never did I feel one as lively and as snappish as that which come down upon us, night afore last, in the shape of an Indian hurrah-boys! Why, Hetty, you're no great matter at a reason, or an idee that lies a little deeper than common, but you're human and have some human notions—now I'll just ask you to look at them circumstances. Here was old Tom, your father, and myself, bent on a legal operation, as is to be seen in the words of the law and the proclamation; thinking no harm; when we were set upon by critturs that were more like a pack of hungry wolves than mortal savages even, and there they had us tethered like two sheep, in less time than it has taken me to tell you the story."

"You are free now, Hurry," returned Hetty, glancing timidly at the fine unfettered limbs of the young giant—"You have no cords, or withes, to pain your arms, or legs, now."

"Not I, Hetty. Natur' is natur', and freedom is natur', too. My limbs have a free look, but that's pretty much the amount of it, sin' I can't use them in the way I should like. Even these trees have eyes; ay, and tongues too; for was the old man, here, or I, to start one single rod beyond our gaol limits, sarvice would be put on the bail afore we could 'gird up our loins' for a race, and, like as not, four or five rifle bullets would be travelling arter us, carrying so many invitations to curb our impatience. There isn't a gaol in the colony as tight as this we are now in; for I've tried the vartues of two or three on 'em, and I know the mater'als they are made of, as well as the men that made 'em; takin' down being the next step in schoolin', to puttin' up, in all such fabrications."

Lest the reader should get an exaggerated opinion of Hurry's demerits from this boastful and indiscreet revelation, it may be well to say that his offences were confined to assaults and batteries, for several of which he had been imprisoned, when, as he has just said, he often escaped by demonstrating the flimsiness of the constructions in which he was confined, by opening for himself doors in spots where the architects had neglected to place them. But Hetty had no knowledge of gaols, and little of the nature of crimes, beyond what her unadulterated and almost instinctive perceptions of right and wrong taught her, and this sally of the rude being who had spoken was lost upon her. She understood his general meaning, however, and answered in reference to that alone.

"It's so best, Hurry," she said. "It is best father and you should be quiet and peaceable, 'till I have spoken to the Iroquois, when all will be well and happy. I don't wish either of you to follow, but leave me to myself. As soon as all is settled, and you are at liberty to go back to the castle, I will come and let you know it."

Hetty spoke with so much simple earnestness, seemed so confident of success, and wore so high an air of moral feeling and truth, that both the listeners felt more disposed to attach an importance to her mediation, than might otherwise have happened. When she manifested an intention to quit them, therefore, they offered no obstacle, though they saw she was about to join the group of chiefs who were consulting apart, seemingly on the manner and motive of her own sudden appearance.

When Hist—for so we love best to call her—quitted her companion, she strayed near one or two of the elder warriors, who had shown her most kindness in her captivity, the principal man of whom had even offered to adopt her as his child if she would consent to become a Huron. In taking this direction, the shrewd girl did so to invite inquiry. She was too well trained in the habits of her people to obtrude the opinions of one of her sex and years on men and warriors, but nature had furnished a tact and ingenuity that enabled her to attract the attention she desired, without wounding the pride of those to whom it was her duty to defer and respect. Even her affected indifference stimulated curiosity, and Hetty had hardly reached the side of her father, before the Delaware girl was brought within the circle of the warriors, by a secret but significant gesture. Here she was questioned as to the person of her companion, and the motives that had brought her to the camp. This was all that Hist desired. She explained the manner in which she had detected the weakness of Hetty's reason, rather exaggerating than lessening the deficiency in her intellect, and then she related in general terms the object of the girl in venturing among her enemies. The effect was all that the speaker expected, her account investing the person and character of their visitor with a sacredness and respect that she well knew would prove her protection. As soon as her own purpose was attained, Hist withdrew to a distance, where, with female consideration and a sisterly tenderness she set about the preparation of a meal, to be offered to her new friend as soon as the latter might be at liberty to partake of it. While thus occupied, however, the ready girl in no degree relaxed in her watchfulness, noting every change of countenance among the chiefs, every movement of Hetty's, and the smallest occurrence that could be likely to affect her own interests, or that of her new friend.

As Hetty approached the chiefs they opened their little circle, with an ease and deference of manner that would have done credit to men of more courtly origin. A fallen tree lay near, and the oldest of the warriors made a quiet sign for the girl to be seated on it, taking his place at her side with the gentleness of a father. The others arranged themselves around the two with grave dignity, and then the girl, who had sufficient observation to perceive that such a course was expected of her, began to reveal the object of her visit. The moment she opened her mouth to speak, however, the old chief gave a gentle sign for her to forbear, said a few words to one of his juniors, and then waited in silent patience until the latter had summoned Hist to the party. This interruption proceeded from the chief's having discovered that there existed a necessity for an interpreter, few of the Hurons present understanding the English language, and they but imperfectly.

Wah-ta-Wah was not sorry to be called upon to be present at the interview, and least of all in the character in which she was now wanted. She was aware of the hazards she ran in attempting to deceive one or two of the party, but was none the less resolved to use every means that offered, and to practice every artifice that an Indian education could supply, to conceal the facts of the vicinity of her betrothed, and of the errand on which he had come. One unpracticed in the expedients and opinions of savage life would not have suspected the readiness of invention, the wariness of action, the high resolution, the noble impulses, the deep self-devotion, and the feminine disregard of self when the affections were concerned, that lay concealed beneath the demure looks, the mild eyes, and the sunny smiles of this young Indian beauty. As she approached them, the grim old warriors regarded her with pleasure, for they had a secret pride in the hope of engrafting so rare a scion on the stock of their own nation; adoption being as regularly practised, and as distinctly recognized among the tribes of America, as it ever had been among those nations that submit to the sway of the Civil Law.

As soon as Hist was seated by the side of Hetty, the old chief desired her to ask "the fair young pale-face" what had brought her among the Iroquois, and what they could do to serve her.

"Tell them, Hist, who I am—Thomas Hutter's youngest daughter; Thomas Hutter, the oldest of their two prisoners; he who owns the castle and the Ark, and who has the best right to be thought the owner of these hills, and that lake, since he has dwelt so long, and trapped so long, and fished so long, among them—They'll know whom you mean by Thomas Hutter, if you tell them, that. And then tell them that I've come here to convince them they ought not to harm father and Hurry, but let them go in peace, and to treat them as brethren rather than as enemies. Now tell them all this plainly, Hist, and fear nothing for yourself or me. God will protect us."

Wah-ta-Wah did as the other desired, taking care to render the words of her friend as literally as possible into the Iroquois tongue, a language she used with a readiness almost equal to that with which she spoke her own. The chiefs heard this opening explanation with grave decorum, the two who had a little knowledge of English intimating their satisfaction with the interpreter by furtive but significant glances of the eyes.

"And, now, Hist," continued Hetty, as soon as it was intimated to her that she might proceed, "and, now, Hist, I wish you to tell these red men, word for word, what I am about to say. Tell them first, that father and Hurry came here with an intention to take as many scalps as they could, for the wicked governor and the province have offered money for scalps, whether of warriors, or women, men or children, and the love of gold was too strong for their hearts to withstand it. Tell them this, dear Hist, just as you have heard it from me, word for word."

Wah-ta-Wah hesitated about rendering this speech as literally as had been desired, but detecting the intelligence of those who understood English, and apprehending even a greater knowledge than they actually possessed she found herself compelled to comply. Contrary to what a civilized man would have expected, the admission of the motives and of the errands of their prisoners produced no visible effect on either the countenances or the feelings of the listeners. They probably considered the act meritorious, and that which neither of them would have hesitated to perform in his own person, he would not be apt to censure in another.

"And, now, Hist," resumed Hetty, as soon as she perceived that her first speeches were understood by the chiefs, "you can tell them more. They know that father and Hurry did not succeed, and therefore they can bear them no grudge for any harm that has been done. If they had slain their children and wives it would not alter the matter, and I'm not certain that what I am about to tell them would not have more weight had there been mischief done. But ask them first, Hist, if they know there is a God, who reigns over the whole earth, and is ruler and chief of all who live, let them be red, or white, or what color they may?"

Wah-ta-Wah looked a little surprised at this question, for the idea of the Great Spirit is seldom long absent from the mind of an Indian girl. She put the question as literally as possible, however, and received a grave answer in the affirmative.

"This is right," continued Hetty, "and my duty will now be light. This Great Spirit, as you call our God, has caused a book to be written, that we call a Bible, and in this book have been set down all his commandments, and his holy will and pleasure, and the rules by which all men are to live, and directions how to govern the thoughts even, and the wishes, and the will. Here, this is one of these holy books, and you must tell the chiefs what I am about to read to them from its sacred pages."

As Hetty concluded, she reverently unrolled a small English Bible from its envelope of coarse calico, treating the volume with the sort of external respect that a Romanist would be apt to show to a religious relic. As she slowly proceeded in her task the grim warriors watched each movement with riveted eyes, and when they saw the little volume appear a slight expression of surprise escaped one or two of them. But Hetty held it out towards them in triumph, as if she expected the sight would produce a visible miracle, and then, without betraying either surprise or mortification at the Stoicism of the Indian, she turned eagerly to her new friend, in order to renew the discourse.

"This is the sacred volume, Hist," she said— "and these words, and lines, and verses, and chapters, all came from God."

"Why Great Spirit no send book to Injin, too?" demanded Hist, with the directness of a mind that was totally unsophisticated.

"Why?" answered Hetty, a little bewildered by a question so unexpected. "Why?—Ah! you know the Indians don't know how to read."

If Hist was not satisfied with this explanation, she did not deem the point of sufficient importance to be pressed. Simply bending her body, in a gentle admission of the truth of what she heard, she sat patiently awaiting the further arguments of the pale-face enthusiast.

"You can tell these chiefs that throughout this book, men are ordered to forgive their enemies; to treat them as they would brethren; and never to injure their fellow creatures, more especially on account of revenge or any evil passions. Do you think you can tell them this, so that they will understand it, Hist?"

"Tell him well enough, but he no very easy to understand." Hist then conveyed the ideas of Hetty, in the best manner she could, to the attentive Indians, who heard her words with some such surprise as an American of our own times would be apt to betray at a suggestion that the great modern but vacillating ruler of things human, public opinion, might be wrong. One or two of their number, however, having met with missionaries, said a few words in explanation, and then the group gave all its attention to the communications that were to follow. Before Hetty resumed she inquired earnestly of Hist if the chiefs had understood her, and receiving an evasive answer, was fain to be satisfied.

"I will now read to the warriors some of the verses that it is good for them to know," continued the girl, whose manner grew more solemn and earnest as she proceeded—"and they will remember that they are the very words of the Great Spirit. First, then, ye are commanded to 'love thy neighbor as Thyself.' Tell them that, dear Hist."

"Neighbor, for Injin, no mean pale-face," answered the Delaware girl, with more decision than she had hitherto thought it necessary to use. "Neighbor mean Iroquois for Iroquois, Mohican for Mohican, Pale-face for pale face. No need tell chief any thing else."

"You forget, Hist, these are the words of the Great Spirit, and the chiefs must obey them as well as others. Here is another commandment—'Whosoever shall smite thee on the right cheek, turn to him the other also.'"

"What that mean?" demanded Hist, with the quickness of lightning.

Hetty explained that it was an order not to resent injuries, but rather to submit to receive fresh wrongs from the offender.

"And hear this, too, Hist," she added. "'Love your enemies, bless them that curse you, do good to them that hate you, and pray for them which despitefully use you and persecute you.'"

By this time Hetty had become excited; her eye gleamed with the earnestness of her feelings, her cheeks flushed, and her voice, usually so low and modulated, became stronger and more impressive. With the Bible she had been early made familiar by her mother, and she now turned from passage to passage with surprising rapidity, taking care to cull such verses as taught the sublime lessons of Christian charity and Christian forgiveness. To translate half she said, in her pious earnestness, Wah-ta-Wah would have found impracticable, had she made the effort, but wonder held her tongue tied, equally with the chiefs, and the young, simple-minded enthusiast had fairly become exhausted with her own efforts, before the other opened her mouth, again, to utter a syllable. Then, indeed, the Delaware girl gave a brief translation of the substance of what had been both read and said, confining herself to one or two of the more striking of the verses, those that had struck her own imagination as the most paradoxical, and which certainly would have been the most applicable to the case, could the uninstructed minds of the listeners embrace the great moral truths they conveyed.

It will be scarcely necessary to tell the reader the effect that such novel duties would be likely to produce among a group of Indian warriors, with whom it was a species of religious principle never to forget a benefit, or to forgive an injury. Fortunately, the previous explanations of Hist had prepared the minds of the Hurons for something extravagant, and most of that which to them seemed inconsistent and paradoxical, was accounted for by the fact that the speaker possessed a mind that was constituted differently from those of most of the human race. Still there were one or two old men who had heard similar doctrines from the missionaries, and these felt a desire to occupy an idle moment by pursuing a subject that they found so curious.

"This is the Good Book of the pale-faces," observed one of these chiefs, taking the volume from the unresisting hands of Hetty, who gazed anxiously at his face while he turned the leaves, as if she expected to witness some visible results from the circumstance. "This is the law by which my white brethren professes to live?"

Hist, to whom this question was addressed, if it might be considered as addressed to any one, in particular, answered simply in the affirmative; adding that both the French of the Canadas, and the Yengeese of the British provinces equally admitted its authority, and affected to revere its principles.

"Tell my young sister," said the Huron, looking directly at Hist, "that I will open my mouth and say a few words."

"The Iroquois chief go to speak—my pale-face friend listen," said Hist.

"I rejoice to hear it!" exclaimed Hetty. "God has touched his heart, and he will now let father and Hurry go."

"This is the pale-face law," resumed the chief. "It tells him to do good to them that hurt him, and when his brother asks him for his rifle to give him the powder horn, too. Such is the pale-face law?"

"Not so—not so—" answered Hetty earnestly, when these words had been interpreted—"There is not a word about rifles in the whole book, and powder and bullets give offence to the Great Spirit."

"Why then does the pale-face use them? If he is ordered to give double to him that asks only for one thing, why does he take double from the poor Indian who ask for no thing. He comes from beyond the rising sun, with this book in his hand, and he teaches the red man to read it, but why does he forget himself all it says? When the Indian gives, he is never satisfied; and now he offers gold for the scalps of our women and children, though he calls us beasts if we take the scalp of a warrior killed in open war. My name is Rivenoak."

When Hetty had got this formidable question fairly presented to her mind in the translation, and Hist did her duty with more than usual readiness on this occasion, it scarcely need be said that she was sorely perplexed. Abler heads than that of this poor girl have frequently been puzzled by questions of a similar drift, and it is not surprising that with all her own earnestness and sincerity she did not know what answer to make.

"What shall I tell them, Hist," she asked imploringly—"I know that all I have read from the book is true, and yet it wouldn't seem so, would it, by the conduct of those to whom the book was given?"

"Give 'em pale-face reason," returned Hist, ironically—"that always good for one side; though he bad for t'other."

"No—no—Hist, there can't be two sides to truth—and yet it does seem strange! I'm certain I have read the verses right, and no one would be so wicked as to print the word of God wrong. That can never be, Hist."

"Well, to poor Injin girl, it seem every thing can be to pale-faces," returned the other, coolly. "One time 'ey say white, and one time 'ey say black. Why never can be?"

Hetty was more and more embarrassed, until overcome with the apprehension that she had failed in her object, and that the lives of her father and Hurry would be the forfeit of some blunder of her own, she burst into tears. From that moment the manner of Hist lost all its irony and cool indifference, and she became the fond caressing friend again. Throwing her arms around the afflicted girl, she attempted to soothe her sorrows by the scarcely ever failing remedy of female sympathy.

"Stop cry—no cry—" she said, wiping the tears from the face of Hetty, as she would have performed the same office for a child, and stopping to press her occasionally to her own warm bosom with the affection of a sister. "Why you so trouble? You no make he book, if he be wrong, and you no make he pale-face if he wicked. There wicked red man, and wicked white man—no colour all good—no colour all wicked. Chiefs know that well enough."

Hetty soon recovered from this sudden burst of grief, and then her mind reverted to the purpose of her visit, with all its single-hearted earnestness. Perceiving that the grim looking chiefs were still standing around her in grave attention, she hoped that another effort to convince them of the right might be successful. "Listen, Hist," she said, struggling to suppress her sobs, and to speak distinctly— "Tell the chiefs that it matters not what the wicked do—right is right—The words of The Great Spirit are the words of The Great Spirit—and no one can go harmless for doing an evil act, because another has done it before him. 'Render good for evil,' says this book, and that is the law for the red man as well as for the white man."

"Never hear such law among Delaware, or among Iroquois—" answered Hist soothingly. "No good to tell chiefs any such laws as dat. Tell 'em somet'ing they believe."

Hist was about to proceed, notwithstanding, when a tap on the shoulder from the finger of the oldest chief caused her to look up. She then perceived that one of the warriors had left the group, and was already returning to it with Hutter and Hurry. Understanding that the two last were to become parties in the inquiry, she became mute, with the unhesitating obedience of an Indian woman. In a few seconds the prisoners stood face to face with the principal men of the captors.

"Daughter," said the senior chief to the young Delaware, "ask this grey beard why he came into our camp?"

The question was put by Hist, in her own imperfect English, but in a way that was easy to be understood. Hutter was too stern and obdurate by nature to shrink from the consequences of any of his acts, and he was also too familiar with the opinions of the savages not to understand that nothing was to be gained by equivocation or an unmanly dread of their anger. Without hesitating, therefore, he avowed the purpose with which he had landed, merely justifying it by the fact that the government of the province had bid high for scalps. This frank avowal was received by the Iroquois with evident satisfaction, not so much, however, on account of the advantage it gave them in a moral point of view, as by its proving that they had captured a man worthy of occupying their thoughts and of becoming a subject of their revenge. Hurry, when interrogated, confessed the truth, though he would have been more disposed to concealment than his sterner companion, did the circumstances very well admit of its adoption. But he had tact enough to discover that equivocation would be useless, at that moment, and he made a merit of necessity by imitating a frankness, which, in the case of Hutter, was the offspring of habits of indifference acting on a disposition that was always ruthless, and reckless of personal consequences.

As soon as the chiefs had received the answers to their questions, they walked away in silence, like men who deemed the matter disposed of, all Hetty's dogmas being thrown away on beings trained in violence from infancy to manhood. Hetty and Hist were now left alone with Hutter and Hurry, no visible restraint being placed on the movements of either; though all four, in fact, were vigilantly and unceasingly watched. As respects the men, care was had to prevent them from getting possession of any of the rifles that lay scattered about, their own included; and there all open manifestations of watchfulness ceased. But they, who were so experienced in Indian practices, knew too well how great was the distance between appearances and reality, to become the dupes of this seeming carelessness. Although both thought incessantly of the means of escape, and this without concert, each was aware of the uselessness of attempting any project of the sort that was not deeply laid, and promptly executed. They had been long enough in the encampment, and were sufficiently observant to have ascertained that Hist, also, was a sort of captive, and, presuming on the circumstance, Hutter spoke in her presence more openly than he might otherwise have thought it prudent to do; inducing Hurry to be equally unguarded by his example.

"I'll not blame you, Hetty, for coming on this errand, which was well meant if not very wisely planned," commenced the father, seating himself by the side of his daughter and taking her hand; a sign of affection that this rude being was accustomed to manifest to this particular child. "But preaching, and the Bible, are not the means to turn an Indian from his ways. Has Deerslayer sent any message; or has he any scheme by which he thinks to get us free?"

"Ay, that's the substance of it!" put in Hurry. "If you can help us, gal, to half a mile of freedom, or even a good start of a short quarter, I'll answer for the rest. Perhaps the old man may want a little more, but for one of my height and years that will meet all objections."

Hetty looked distressed, turning her eyes from one to the other, but she had no answer to give to the question of the reckless Hurry.

"Father," she said, "neither Deerslayer nor Judith knew of my coming until I had left the Ark. They are afraid the Iroquois will make a raft and try to get off to the hut, and think more of defending that than of coming to aid you."

"No—no—no—" said Hist hurriedly, though in a low voice, and with her face bent towards the earth, in order to conceal from those whom she knew to be watching them the fact of her speaking at all. "No—no—no—Deerslayer different man. He no t'ink of defending 'self, with friend in danger. Help one another, and all get to hut."

"This sounds well, old Tom," said Hurry, winking and laughing, though he too used the precaution to speak low——"Give me a ready witted squaw for a fri'nd, and though I'll not downright defy an Iroquois, I think I would defy the devil."

"No talk loud," said Hist. "Some Iroquois got Yengeese tongue, and all got Yengeese ear."

"Have we a friend in you, young woman?" enquired Hutter with an increasing interest in the conference. "If so, you may calculate on a solid reward, and nothing will be easier than to send you to your own tribe, if we can once fairly get you off with us to the castle. Give us the Ark and the canoes, and we can command the lake, spite of all the savages in the Canadas. Nothing but artillery could drive us out of the castle, if we can get back to it.

"S'pose 'ey come ashore to take scalp?" retorted Hist, with cool irony, at which the girl appeared to be more expert than is common for her sex.

"Ay—ay—that was a mistake; but there is little use in lamentations, and less still, young woman, in flings."

"Father," said Hetty, "Judith thinks of breaking open the big chest, in hopes of finding something in that which may buy your freedom of the savages."

A dark look came over Hutter at the announcement of this fact, and he muttered his dissatisfaction in a way to render it intelligible enough.

"What for no break open chest?" put in Hist. "Life sweeter than old chest—scalp sweeter than old chest. If no tell darter to break him open, Wah-ta-Wah no help him to run away."

"Ye know not what ye ask—ye are but silly girls, and the wisest way for ye both is to speak of what ye understand and to speak of nothing else. I little like this cold neglect of the savages, Hurry; it's a proof that they think of something serious, and if we are to do any thing, we must do it soon. Can we count on this young woman, think you?"

"Listen—" said Hist quickly, and with an earnestness that proved how much her feelings were concerned— "Wah-ta-Wah no Iroquois—All over Delaware—got Delaware heart—Delaware feeling. She prisoner, too. One prisoner help t'udder prisoner. No good to talk more, now. Darter stay with fader—Wah-ta-Wah come and see friend—all look right—Then tell what he do."

This was said in a low voice, but distinctly, and in a manner to make an impression. As soon as it was uttered the girl arose and left the group, walking composedly towards the hut she occupied, as if she had no further interest in what might pass between the pale-faces.

CHAPTER XII.

"She speaks much of her father; says she hears,
There's tricks i' the world; and hems, and beats her breast;
Spurns enviously at straws; speaks things in doubt,
That carry but half sense; her speech is nothing,
Yet the unshaped use of it doth move
The hearers to collection;"

Hamlet, IV.v.4–9.

We left the occupants of the castle and the ark, buried in sleep. Once, or twice, in the course of the night, it is true, Deerslayer or the Delaware, arose and looked out upon the tranquil lake; when, finding all safe, each returned to his pallet, and slept like a man who was not easily deprived of his natural rest. At the first signs of the dawn the former arose, however, and made his personal arrangements for the day; though his companion, whose nights had not been tranquil or without disturbances of late, continued on his blanket until the sun had fairly risen; Judith, too, was later than common that morning, for the earlier hours of the night had brought her little of either refreshment or sleep. But ere the sun had shown himself over the eastern hills these too were up and afoot, even the tardy in that region seldom remaining on their pallets after the appearance of the great luminary. Chingachgook was in the act of arranging his forest toilet, when Deerslayer entered the cabin of the Ark and threw him a few coarse but light summer vestments that belonged to Hutter.

"Judith hath given me them for your use, chief," said the latter, as he cast the jacket and trousers at the feet of the Indian, "for it's ag'in all prudence and caution to be seen in your war dress and paint. Wash off all them fiery streaks from your cheeks, put on these garments, and here is a hat, such as it is, that will give you an awful oncivilized sort of civilization, as the missionaries call it. Remember that Hist is at hand, and what we do for the maiden must be done while we are doing for others. I know it's ag'in your gifts and your natur' to wear clothes, unless they are cut and carried in a red man's fashion, but make a virtue of necessity and put these on at once, even if they do rise a little in your throat."

Chingachgook, or the Serpent, eyed the vestments with strong disgust; but he saw the usefulness of the disguise, if not its absolute necessity. Should the Iroquois discover a red man, in or about the Castle, it might, indeed, place them more on their guard, and give their suspicions a direction towards their female captive. Any thing was better than a failure, as it regarded his betrothed, and, after turning the different garments round and round, examining them with a species of grave irony, affecting to draw them on in a way that defeated itself, and otherwise manifesting the reluctance of a young savage to confine his limbs in the usual appliances of civilized life, the chief submitted to the directions of his companion, and finally stood forth, so far as the eye could detect, a red man in colour alone. Little was to be apprehended from this last peculiarity, however, the distance from the shore, and the want of glasses preventing any very close scrutiny, and Deerslayer, himself, though of a brighter and fresher tint, had a countenance that was burnt by the sun to a hue scarcely less red than that of his Mohican companion. The awkwardness of the Delaware in his new attire caused his friend to smile more than once that day, but he carefully abstained from the use of any of those jokes which would have been bandied among white men on such an occasion, the habits of a chief, the dignity of a warrior on his first path, and the gravity of the circumstances in which they were placed uniting to render so much levity out of season.

The meeting at the morning meal of the three islanders, if we may use the term, was silent, grave and thoughtful. Judith showed by her looks that she had passed an unquiet night, while the two men had the future before them, with its unseen and unknown events. A few words of courtesy passed between Deerslayer and the girl, in the course of the breakfast, but no allusion was made to their situation. At length Judith, whose heart was full, and whose novel feelings disposed her to entertain sentiments more gentle and tender than common, introduced the subject, and this in a way to show how much of her thoughts it had occupied, in the course of the last sleepless night.

"It would be dreadful, Deerslayer," the girl abruptly exclaimed, "should anything serious befall my father and Hetty! We cannot remain quietly here and leave them in the hands of the Iroquois, without bethinking us of some means of serving them."

"I'm ready, Judith, to sarve them, and all others who are in trouble, could the way to do it be p'inted out. It's no trifling matter to fall into red-skin hands, when men set out on an ar'n'd like that which took Hutter and Hurry ashore; that I know as well as another, and I wouldn't wish my worst inimy in such a strait, much less them with whom I've journeyed, and eat, and slept. Have you any scheme, that you would like to have the Sarpent and me indivour to carry out?"

"I know of no other means to release the prisoners, than by bribing the Iroquois. They are not proof against presents, and we might offer enough, perhaps, to make them think it better to carry away what to them will be rich gifts, than to carry away poor prisoners; if, indeed, they should carry them away at all!"

"This is well enough, Judith; yes, it's well enough, if the inimy is to be bought, and we can find articles to make the purchase with. Your father has a convenient lodge, and it is most cunningly placed, though it doesn't seem overstock'd with riches that will be likely to buy his ransom. There's the piece he calls Killdeer, might count for something, and I understand there's a keg of powder about, which might be a make-weight, sartain; and yet two able bodied men are not to be bought off for a trifle—besides—"

"Besides what?" demanded Judith impatiently, observing that the other hesitated to proceed, probably from a reluctance to distress her.

"Why, Judith, the Frenchers offer bounties as well as our own side, and the price of two scalps would purchase a keg of powder, and a rifle; though I'll not say one of the latter altogether as good as Killdeer, there, which your father va'nts as uncommon, and unequalled, like. But fair powder, and a pretty sartain rifle; then the red men are not the expartest in fire arms, and don't always know the difference atwixt that which is ra'al, and that which is seeming."

"This is horrible!" muttered the girl, struck by the homely manner in which her companion was accustomed to state his facts. "But you overlook my own clothes, Deerslayer, and they, I think, might go far with the women of the Iroquois."

"No doubt they would; no doubt they would, Judith," returned the other, looking at her keenly, as if he would ascertain whether she were really capable of making such a sacrifice. "But, are you sartain, gal, you could find it in your heart to part with your own finery for such a purpose? Many is the man who has thought he was valiant till danger stared him in the face; I've known them, too, that consaited they were kind and ready to give away all they had to the poor, when they've been listening to other people's hard heartedness; but whose fists have clench'd as tight as the riven hickory when it came to downright offerings of their own. Besides, Judith, you're handsome—uncommon in that way, one might observe and do no harm to the truth—and they that have beauty, like to have that which will adorn it. Are you sartain you could find it in your heart to part with your own finery?"

The soothing allusion to the personal charms of the girl was well timed, to counteract the effect produced by the distrust that the young man expressed of Judith's devotion to her filial duties. Had another said as much as Deerslayer, the compliment would most probably have been overlooked in the indignation awakened by the doubts, but even the unpolished sincerity, that so often made this simple minded hunter bare his thoughts, had a charm for the girl; and while she colored, and for an instant her eyes flashed fire, she could not find it in her heart to be really angry with one whose very soul seemed truth and manly kindness. Look her reproaches she did, but conquering the desire to retort, she succeeded in answering in a mild and friendly manner.

"You must keep all your favorable opinions for the Delaware girls, Deerslayer, if you seriously think thus of those of your own colour," she said, affecting to laugh. "But try me; if you find that I regret either ribbon or feather, silk or muslin, then may you think what you please of my heart, and say what you think."

"That's justice! The rarest thing to find on 'arth is a truly just man. So says Tamenund, the wisest prophet of the Delawares, and so all must think that have occasion to see, and talk, and act among Mankind. I love a just man, Sarpent. His eyes are never covered with darkness towards his inimies, while they are all sunshine and brightness towards his fri'nds. He uses the reason that God has given him, and he uses it with a feelin' of his being ordered to look at, and to consider things as they are, and not as he wants them to be. It's easy enough to find men who call themselves just, but it's wonderful oncommon to find them that are the very thing, in fact. How often have I seen Indians, gal, who believed they were lookin' into a matter agreeable to the will of the Great Spirit, when in truth they were only striving to act up to their own will and pleasure, and this, half the time, with a temptation to go wrong that could no more be seen by themselves, than the stream that runs in the next valley can be seen by us through yonder mountain', though any looker on might have discovered it as plainly as we can discover the parch that are swimming around this hut."

"Very true, Deerslayer," rejoined Judith, losing every trace of displeasure in a bright smile—"very true, and I hope to see you act on this love of justice in all matters in which I am concerned. Above all, I hope you will judge for yourself, and not believe every evil story that a prating idler like Hurry Harry may have to tell, that goes to touch the good name of any young woman, who may not happen to have the same opinion of his face and person that the blustering gallant has of himself."

"Hurry Harry's ideas do not pass for gospel with me, Judith; but even worse than he may have eyes and ears," returned the other gravely.

"Enough of this!" exclaimed Judith, with flashing eye and a flush that mounted to her temples, "and more of my father and his ransom. 'Tis as you say, Deerslayer; the Indians will not be likely to give up their prisoners without a heavier bribe than my clothes can offer, and father's rifle and powder. There is the chest."

"Ay, there is the chest as you say, Judith, and when the question gets to be between a secret and a scalp, I should think most men would prefer keeping the last. Did your father ever give you any downright commands consarning that chist?"

"Never. He has always appeared to think its locks, and its steel bands, and its strength, its best protection."

"'Tis a rare chest, and altogether of curious build," returned Deerslayer, rising and approaching the thing in question, on which he seated himself, with a view to examine it with greater ease. "Chingachgook, this is no wood that comes of any forest that you or I have ever trailed through!

'Tisn't the black walnut, and yet it's quite as comely, if not more so, did the smoke and the treatment give it fair play."

The Delaware drew near, felt of the wood, examined its grain, endeavored to indent the surface with a nail, and passed his hand curiously over the steel bands, the heavy padlocks, and the other novel peculiarities of the massive box.

"No—nothing like this grows in these regions," resumed Deerslayer. "I've seen all the oaks, both the maples, the elms, the bass woods, all the walnuts, the butternuts, and every tree that has a substance and colour, wrought into some form or other, but never have I before seen such a wood as this! Judith, the chest itself would buy your father's freedom, or Iroquois cur'osity isn't as strong as red-skin cur'osity, in general; especially in the matter of woods."

"The purchase might be cheaper made, perhaps, Deerslayer. The chest is full, and it would be better to part with half than to part with the whole. Besides, father—I know not why—but father values that chest highly."

"He would seem to prize what it holds more than the chest, itself, judging by the manner in which he treats the outside, and secures the inside. Here are three locks, Judith; is there no key?"

"I've never seen one, and yet key there must be, since Hetty told us she had often seen the chest opened."

"Keys no more lie in the air, or float on the water, than humans, gal; if there is a key, there must be a place in which it is kept."

"That is true, and it might not be difficult to find it, did we dare to search!"

"This is for you, Judith; it is altogether for you. The chist is your'n, or your father's; and Hutter is your father, not mine. Cur'osity is a woman's, and not a man's failing, and there you have got all the reasons before you. If the chist has articles for ransom, it seems to me they would be wisely used in redeeming their owner's life, or even in saving his scalp; but that is a matter for your judgment, and not for ourn. When the lawful owner of a trap, or a buck, or a canoe, isn't present, his next of kin becomes his riprisentyve by all the laws of the woods. We therefore leave you to say whether the chist shall, or shall not be opened."

"I hope you do not believe I can hesitate, when my father's life's in danger, Deerslayer!"

"Why, it's pretty much putting a scolding ag'in tears and mourning. It's not onreasonable to foretell that old Tom may find fault with what you've done, when he sees himself once more in his hut, here, but there's nothing unusual in men's falling out with what has been done for their own good; I dare to say that even the moon would seem a different thing from what it now does, could we look at it from the other side."

"Deerslayer, if we can find the key, I will authorize you to open the chest, and to take such things from it as you may think will buy father's ransom."

"First find the key, gal; we'll talk of the rest a'terwards. Sarpent, you've eyes like a fly, and a judgment that's seldom out. Can you help us in calculating where Floating Tom would be apt to keep the key of a chist that he holds to be as private as this?"

The Delaware had taken no part in the discourse until he was thus directly appealed to, when he quitted the chest, which had continued to attract his attention, and cast about him for the place in which a key would be likely to be concealed under such circumstances. As Judith and Deerslayer were not idle the while, the whole three were soon engaged in an anxious and spirited search. As it was certain that the desired key was not to be found in any of the common drawers or closets, of which there were several in the building, none looked there, but all turned their inquiries to those places that struck them as ingenious hiding places, and more likely to be used for such a purpose. In this manner the outer room was thoroughly but fruitlessly examined, when they entered the sleeping apartment of Hutter. This part of the rude building was better furnished than the rest of the structure, containing several articles that had been especially devoted to the service of the deceased wife of its owner, but as Judith had all the rest of the keys, it was soon rummaged without bringing to light the particular key desired.

They now entered the bed room of the daughters. Chingachgook was immediately struck with the contrast between the articles and the arrangement of that side of the room that might be called Judith's, and that which more properly belonged to Hetty. A slight exclamation escaped him, and pointing in each direction he alluded to the fact in a low voice, speaking to his friend in the Delaware tongue.

"'Tis as you think, Sarpent," answered Deerslayer, whose remarks we always translate into English, preserving as much as possible of the peculiar phraseology and manner of the man, "'Tis just so, as any one may see, and 'tis all founded in natur'. One sister loves finery, some say overmuch; while t'other is as meek and lowly as God ever created goodness and truth. Yet, after all, I dare say that Judith has her vartues, and Hetty has her failin's."

"And the 'Feeble-Mind' has seen the chist opened?" inquired Chingachgook, with curiosity in his glance.

"Sartain; that much I've heard from her own lips; and, for that matter, so have you. It seems her father doesn't misgive her discretion, though he does that of his eldest darter."

"Then the key is hid only from the Wild Rose?" for so Chingachgook had begun gallantly to term Judith, in his private discourse with his friend.

"That's it! That's just it! One he trusts, and the other he doesn't. There's red and white in that, Sarpent, all tribes and nations agreeing in trusting some, and refusing to trust other some. It depends on character and judgment."

"Where could a key be put, so little likely to be found by the Wild Rose, as among coarse clothes?"

Deerslayer started, and turning to his friend with admiration expressed in every lineament of his face, he fairly laughed, in his silent but hearty manner, at the ingenuity and readiness of the conjecture.

"Your name's well bestowed, Sarpent—yes, 'tis well bestowed! Sure enough, where would a lover of finery be so little likely to s'arch, as among garments as coarse and onseemly as these of poor Hetty's. I dares to say, Judith's delicate fingers haven't touched a bit of cloth as rough and oncomely as that petticoat, now, since she first made acquaintance with the officers! Yet, who knows? The key may be as likely to be on the same peg, as in any other place. Take down the garment, Delaware, and let us see if you are ra'ally a prophet." Chingachgook did as desired, but no key was found. A coarse pocket, apparently empty, hung on the adjoining peg, and this was next examined. By this time, the attention of Judith was called in that direction, and she spoke hurriedly and like one who wished to save unnecessary trouble.

"Those are only the clothes of poor Hetty, dear simple girl!" she said, "Nothing we seek would be likely to be there."

The words were hardly out of the handsome mouth of the speaker, when Chingachgook drew the desired key from the pocket. Judith was too quick of apprehension not to understand the reason a hiding place so simple and exposed had been used. The blood rushed to her face, as much with resentment, perhaps, as with shame, and she bit her lip, though she continued silent. Deerslayer and his friend now discovered the delicacy of men of native refinement, neither smiling or even by a glance betraying how completely he understood the motives and ingenuity of this clever artifice. The former, who had taken the key from the Indian, led the way into the adjoining room, and applying it to a lock ascertained that the right instrument had actually been found. There were three padlocks, each of which however was easily opened by this single key. Deerslayer removed them all, loosened the hasps, raised the lid a little to make certain it was loose, and then he drew back from the chest several feet, signing to his friend to follow.

"This is a family chist, Judith," he said, "and 'tis like to hold family secrets. The Sarpent and I will go into the Ark, and look to the canoes, and paddles, and oars, while you can examine it by yourself, and find out whether any thing that will be a make-weight in a ransom is, or is not, among the articles. When you've got through give us a call, and we'll all sit in council together touching the valie of the articles."

"Stop, Deerslayer," exclaimed the girl, as he was about to withdraw. "Not a single thing will I touch—I will not even raise the lid—unless you are present. Father and Hetty have seen fit to keep the inside of this chest a secret from me, and I am much too proud to pry into their hidden treasures unless it were for their own good. But on no account will I open the chest alone. Stay with me, then; I want witnesses of what I do."

"I rather think, Sarpent, that the gal is right! Confidence and reliance beget security, but suspicion is like to make us all wary. Judith has a right to ask us to be present, and should the chist hold any of Master Hutter's secrets, they will fall into the keeping of two as close mouthed young men as are to be found. We will stay with you, Judith—but first let us take a look at the lake and the shore, for this chist will not be emptied in a minute."

The two men now went out on the platform, and Deerslayer swept the shore with the glass, while the Indian gravely turned his eye on the water and the woods, in quest of any sign that might betray the machinations of their enemies. Nothing was visible, and assured of their temporary security, the three collected around the chest again, with the avowed object of opening it.

Judith had held this chest and its unknown contents in a species of reverence as long as she could remember. Neither her father nor her mother ever mentioned it in her presence, and there appeared to be a silent convention that in naming the different objects that occasionally stood near it, or even lay on its lid, care should be had to avoid any allusion to the chest itself. Habit had rendered this so easy, and so much a matter of course, that it was only quite recently the girl had began even to muse on the singularity of the circumstance. But there had never been sufficient intimacy between Hutter and his eldest daughter to invite confidence. At times he was kind, but in general, with her more especially, he was stern and morose. Least of all had his authority been exercised in a way to embolden his child to venture on the liberty she was about to take, without many misgivings of the consequences, although the liberty proceeded from a desire to serve himself. Then Judith was not altogether free from a little superstition on the subject of this chest, which had stood a sort of tabooed relic before her eyes from childhood to the present hour. Nevertheless the time had come when it would seem that this mystery was to be explained, and that under circumstances, too, which left her very little choice in the matter.

Finding that both her companions were watching her movements, in grave silence, Judith placed a hand on the lid and endeavored to raise it. Her strength, however, was insufficient, and it appeared to the girl, who was fully aware that all the fastenings were removed, that she was resisted in an unhallowed attempt by some supernatural power.

"I cannot raise the lid, Deerslayer!" she said—"Had we not better give up the attempt, and find some other means of releasing the prisoners?"

"Not so—Judith; not so, gal. No means are as sartain and easy, as a good bribe," answered the other. "As for the lid, 'tis held by nothing but its own weight, which is prodigious for so small a piece of wood, loaded with iron as it is."

As Deerslayer spoke, he applied his own strength to the effort, and succeeded in raising the lid against the timbers of the house, where he took care to secure it by a sufficient prop. Judith fairly trembled as she cast her first glance at the interior, and she felt a temporary relief in discovering that a piece of canvas, that was carefully tucked in around the edges, effectually concealed all beneath it. The chest was apparently well stored, however, the canvas lying within an inch of the lid.

"Here's a full cargo," said Deerslayer, eyeing the arrangement, "and we had needs go to work leisurely and at our ease. Sarpent, bring some stools while I spread this blanket on the floor, and then we'll begin work orderly and in comfort."

The Delaware complied, Deerslayer civilly placed a stool for Judith, took one himself, and commenced the removal of the canvas covering. This was done deliberately, and in as cautious a manner as if it were believed that fabrics of a delicate construction lay hidden beneath. When the canvass was removed, the first articles that came in view were some of the habiliments of the male sex. They were of fine materials, and, according to the fashions of the age, were gay in colours and rich in ornaments. One coat in particular was of scarlet, and had button holes worked in gold thread. Still it was not military, but was part of the attire of a civilian of condition, at a period when social rank was rigidly respected in dress. Chingachgook could not refrain from an exclamation of pleasure, as soon as Deerslayer opened this coat and held it up to view, for, notwithstanding all his trained self-command, the splendor of the vestment was too much for the philosophy of an Indian. Deerslayer turned quickly, and he regarded his friend with momentary displeasure as this burst of weakness escaped him, and then he soliloquized, as was his practice whenever any strong feeling suddenly got the ascendancy.

"'Tis his gift!—yes, 'tis the gift of a red-skin to love finery, and he is not to be blamed. This is an extr'ornary garment, too, and extr'ornary things get up extr'ornary feelin's. I think this will do, Judith, for the Indian heart is hardly to be found in all America that can withstand colours like these, and glitter like that. If this coat was ever made for your father, you've come honestly by the taste for finery, you have."

"That coat was never made for father," answered the girl, quickly—"it is much too long, while father is short and square."

"Cloth was plenty if it was, and glitter cheap," answered Deerslayer, with his silent, joyous laugh. "Sarpent, this garment was made for a man of your size, and I should like to see it on your shoulders."

Chingachgook, nothing loath, submitted to the trial, throwing aside the coarse and thread bare jacket of Hutter, to deck his person in a coat that was originally intended for a gentleman. The transformation was ludicrous, but as men are seldom struck with incongruities in their own appearance, any more than in their own conduct, the Delaware studied this change in a common glass, by which Hutter was in the habit of shaving, with grave interest. At that moment he thought of Hist, and we owe it to truth, to say, though it may militate a little against the stern character of a warrior to avow it, that he wished he could be seen by her in his present improved aspect.

"Off with it, Sarpent—off with it," resumed the inflexible Deerslayer. "Such garments as little become you as they would become me. Your gifts are for paint, and hawk's feathers, and blankets, and wampum, and mine are for doublets of skins, tough leggings, and sarviceable moccasins. I say moccasins, Judith, for though white, living as I do in the woods it's necessary to take to some of the practyces of the woods, for comfort's sake and cheapness."

"I see no reason, Deerslayer, why one man may not wear a scarlet coat, as well as another," returned the girl. "I wish I could see you in this handsome garment."

"See me in a coat fit for a Lord!—Well, Judith, if you wait till that day, you'll wait until you see me beyond reason and memory. No—no—gal, my gifts are my gifts, and I'll live and die in 'em, though I never bring down another deer, or spear another salmon. What have I done that you should wish to see me in such a flaunting coat, Judith?"

"Because I think, Deerslayer, that the false-tongued and false-hearted young gallants of the garrisons, ought not alone to appear in fine feathers, but that truth and honesty have their claims to be honored and exalted."

"And what exaltification"—the reader will have remarked that Deerslayer had not very critically studied his dictionary—"and what exaltification would it be to me, Judith, to be bedizened and bescarleted like a Mingo chief that has just got his presents up from Quebec? No—no—I'm well as I am; and if not, I can be no better. Lay the coat down on the blanket, Sarpent, and let us look farther into the chist."

The tempting garment, one surely that was never intended for Hutter, was laid aside, and the examination proceeded. The male attire, all of which corresponded with the coat in quality, was soon exhausted, and then succeeded female. A beautiful dress of brocade, a little the worse from negligent treatment, followed, and this time open exclamations of delight escaped the lips of Judith. Much as the girl had been addicted to dress, and favorable as had been her opportunities of seeing some little pretension in that way among the wives of the different commandants, and other ladies of the forts, never before had she beheld a tissue, or tints, to equal those that were now so unexpectedly placed before her eyes. Her rapture was almost childish, nor would she allow the inquiry to proceed, until she had attired her person in a robe so unsuited to her habits and her abode. With this end, she withdrew into her own room, where with hands practised in such offices, she soon got rid of her own neat gown of linen, and stood forth in the gay tints of the brocade. The dress happened to fit the fine, full person of Judith, and certainly it had never adorned a being better qualified by natural gifts to do credit to its really rich hues and fine texture. When she returned, both Deerslayer and Chingachgook, who had passed the brief time of her absence in taking a second look at the male garments, arose in surprise, each permitting exclamations of wonder and pleasure to escape him, in a way so unequivocal as to add new lustre to the eyes of Judith, by flushing her cheeks with a glow of triumph. Affecting, however, not to notice the impression she had made, the girl seated herself with the stateliness of a queen, desiring that the chest might be looked into, further.

"I don't know a better way to treat with the Mingos, gal," cried Deerslayer, "than to send you ashore as you be, and to tell 'em that a queen has arrived among 'em! They'll give up old Hutter, and Hurry, and Hetty, too, at such a spectacle!"

"I thought your tongue too honest to flatter, Deerslayer," returned the girl, gratified at this admiration more than she would have cared to own. "One of the chief reasons of my respect for you, was your love for truth."

"And 'tis truth, and solemn truth, Judith, and nothing else. Never did eyes of mine gaze on as glorious a lookin' creatur' as you be yourself, at this very moment! I've seen beauties in my time, too, both white and red; and them that was renowned and talk'd of, far and near; but never have I beheld one that could hold any comparison with what you are at this blessed instant, Judith; never."

The glance of delight which the girl bestowed on the frank-speaking hunter in no degree lessened the effect of her charms, and as the humid eyes blended with it a look of sensibility, perhaps Judith never appeared more truly lovely, than at what the young man had called that "blessed instant." He shook his head, held it suspended a moment over the open chest, like one in doubt, and then proceeded with the examination.

Several of the minor articles of female dress came next, all of a quality to correspond with the gown. These were laid at Judith's feet, in silence, as if she had a natural claim to their possession. One or two, such as gloves, and lace, the girl caught up, and appended to her already rich attire in affected playfulness, but with the real design of decorating her person as far as circumstances would allow. When these two remarkable suits, male and female they might be termed, were removed, another canvas covering separated the remainder of the articles from the part of the chest which they had occupied. As soon as Deerslayer perceived this arrangement he paused, doubtful of the propriety of proceeding any further.

"Every man has his secrets, I suppose," he said, "and all men have a right to their enj'yment. We've got low enough in this chist in my judgment to answer our wants, and it seems to me we should do well by going no farther; and by letting Master Hutter have to himself, and his own feelin's, all that's beneath this cover.

"Do you mean, Deerslayer, to offer these clothes to the Iroquois as ransom?" demanded Judith, quickly.

"Sartain. What are we prying into another man's chist for, but to sarve its owner in the best way we can. This coat, alone, would be very apt to gain over the head chief of the riptyles, and if his wife or darter should happen to be out with him, that there gownd would soften the heart of any woman that is to be found atween Albany and Montreal. I do not see that we want a larger stock in trade than them two articles."

"To you it may seem so, Deerslayer," returned the disappointed girl, "but of what use could a dress like this be to any Indian woman? She could not wear it among the branches of the trees, the dirt and smoke of the wigwam would soon soil it, and how would a pair of red arms appear, thrust through these short, laced sleeves!"

"All very true, gal, and you might go on and say it is altogether out of time, and place and season, in this region at all. What is it to us how the finery is treated, so long as it answers our wishes? I do not see that your father can make any use of such clothes, and it's lucky he has things that are of no valie to himself, that will bear a high price with others. We can make no better trade for him, than to offer these duds for his liberty. We'll throw in the light frivol'ties, and get Hurry off in the bargain."

"Then you think, Deerslayer, that Thomas Hutter has no one in his family—no child—no daughter, to whom this dress may be thought becoming, and whom you could wish to see in it, once and awhile, even though it should be at long intervals, and only in playfulness?"

"I understand you, Judith—yes, I now understand your meaning, and I think I can say, your wishes. That you are as glorious in that dress as the sun when it rises or sets in a soft October day, I'm ready to allow, and that you greatly become it is a good deal more sartain than that it becomes you. There's gifts in clothes, as well as in other things. Now I do not think that a warrior on his first path ought to lay on the same awful paints as a chief that has had his virtue tried, and knows from exper'ence he will not disgrace his pretensions. So it is with all of us, red or white. You are Thomas Hutter's darter, and that gownd was made for the child of some governor, or a lady of high station, and it was intended to be worn among fine furniture, and in rich company. In my eyes, Judith, a modest maiden never looks more becoming than when becomingly clad, and nothing is suitable that is out of character. Besides, gal, if there's a creatur' in the colony that can afford to do without finery, and to trust to her own good looks and sweet countenance, it's yourself."

"I'll take off the rubbish this instant, Deerslayer," cried the girl, springing up to leave the room, "and never do I wish to see it on any human being, again."

"So it is with 'em, all, Sarpent," said the other, turning to his friend and laughing, as soon as the beauty had disappeared. "They like finery, but they like their natyve charms most of all. I'm glad the gal has consented to lay aside her furbelows, howsever, for it's ag'in reason for one of her class to wear em; and then she is handsome enough, as I call it, to go alone. Hist would show oncommon likely, too, in such a gownd, Delaware!"

"Wah-ta-Wah is a red-skin girl, Deerslayer," returned the Indian, "like the young of the pigeon, she is to be known by her own feathers. I should pass by without knowing her, were she dressed in such a skin. It's wisest always to be so clad that our friends need not ask us for our names. The 'Wild Rose' is very pleasant, but she is no sweeter for so many colours."

"That's it!—that's natur', and the true foundation for love and protection. When a man stoops to pick a wild strawberry, he does not expect to find a melon; and when he wishes to gather a melon, he's disapp'inted if it proves to be a squash; though squashes be often brighter to the eye than melons. That's it, and it means stick to your gifts, and your gifts will stick to you."

The two men had now a little discussion together, touching the propriety of penetrating any farther into the chest of Hutter, when Judith re-appeared, divested of her robes, and in her own simple linen frock again.

"Thank you, Judith," said Deerslayer, taking her kindly by the hand—"for I know it went a little ag'in the nat'ral cravings of woman, to lay aside so much finery, as it might be in a lump. But you're more pleasing to the eye as you stand, you be, than if you had a crown on your head, and jewels dangling from your hair. The question now is, whether to lift this covering to see what will be ra'ally the best bargain we can make for Master Hutter, for we must do as we think he would be willing to do, did he stand here in our places."

Judith looked very happy. Accustomed as she was to adulation, the homely homage of Deerslayer had given her more true satisfaction, than she had ever yet received from the tongue of man. It was not the terms in which this admiration had been expressed, for they were simple enough, that produced so strong an impression; nor yet their novelty, or their warmth of manner, nor any of those peculiarities that usually give value to praise; but the unflinching truth of the speaker, that carried his words so directly to the heart of the listener. This is one of the great advantages of plain dealing and frankness. The habitual and wily flatterer may succeed until his practices recoil on himself, and like other sweets his aliment cloys by its excess; but he who deals honestly, though he often necessarily offends, possesses a power of praising that no quality but sincerity can bestow, since his words go directly to the heart, finding their support in the understanding. Thus it was with Deerslayer and Judith. So soon and so deeply did this simple hunter impress those who knew him with a conviction of his unbending honesty, that all he uttered in commendation was as certain to please, as all he uttered in the way of rebuke was as certain to rankle and excite enmity, where his character had not awakened a respect and affection, that in another sense rendered it painful. In after life, when the career of this untutored being brought him in contact with officers of rank, and others entrusted with the care of the interests of the state, this same influence was exerted on a wider field, even generals listening to his commendations with a glow of pleasure, that it was not always in the power of their official superiors to awaken. Perhaps Judith was the first individual of his own colour who fairly submitted to this natural consequence of truth and fair-dealing on the part of Deerslayer. She had actually pined for his praise, and she had now received it, and that in the form which was most agreeable to her weaknesses and habits of thought. The result will appear in the course of the narrative.

"If we knew all that chest holds, Deerslayer," returned the girl, when she had a little recovered from the immediate effect produced by his commendations of her personal appearance, "we could better determine on the course we ought to take."

"That's not onreasonable, gal, though it's more a pale-face than a red-skin gift to be prying into other people's secrets."

"Curiosity is natural, and it is expected that all human beings should have human failings. Whenever I've been at the garrisons, I've found that most in and about them had a longing to learn their neighbor's secrets."

"Yes, and sometimes to fancy them, when they couldn't find 'em out! That's the difference atween an Indian gentleman and a white gentleman. The Sarpent, here, would turn his head aside if he found himself onknowingly lookin' into another chief's wigwam, whereas in the settlements while all pretend to be great people, most prove they've got betters, by the manner in which they talk of their consarns. I'll be bound, Judith, you wouldn't get the Sarpent, there, to confess there was another in the tribe so much greater than himself, as to become the subject of his ideas, and to empl'y his tongue in conversations about his movements, and ways, and food, and all the other little matters that occupy a man when he's not empl'y'd in his greater duties. He who does this is but little better than a blackguard, in the grain, and them that encourages him is pretty much of the same kidney, let them wear coats as fine as they may, or of what dye they please."

"But this is not another man's wigwam; it belongs to my father, these are his things, and they are wanted in his service."

"That's true, gal; that's true, and it carries weight with it. Well, when all is before us we may, indeed, best judge which to offer for the ransom, and which to withhold."

Judith was not altogether as disinterested in her feelings as she affected to be. She remembered that the curiosity of Hetty had been indulged in connection with this chest, while her own had been disregarded, and she was not sorry to possess an opportunity of being placed on a level with her less gifted sister in this one particular. It appearing to be admitted all round that the enquiry into the contents of the chest ought to be renewed, Deerslayer proceeded to remove the second covering of canvass.

The articles that lay uppermost, when the curtain was again raised on the secrets of the chest, were a pair of pistols, curiously inlaid with silver. Their value would have been considerable in one of the towns, though as weapons in the woods they were a species of arms seldom employed; never, indeed, unless it might be by some officer from Europe, who visited the colonies, as many were then wont to do, so much impressed with the superiority of the usages of London as to fancy they were not to be laid aside on the frontiers of America. What occurred on the discovery of these weapons will appear in the succeeding chapter.

CHAPTER XIII.

"An oaken, broken, elbow-chair;
A caudle-cup without an ear;
A battered, shattered ash bedstead;
A box of deal without a lid;
A pair of tongs, but out of joint;
A back-sword poker, without point;
A dish which might good meat afford once;
An Ovid, and an old
Concordance."

Thomas Sheridan, "A True and Faithful Inventory of the Goods
belonging to Dr. Swift," II. 1–6, 13–14.

No sooner did Deerslayer raise the pistols, than he turned to the Delaware and held them up for his admiration.

"Child gun," said the Serpent, smiling, while he handled one of the instruments as if it had been a toy.

"Not it, Sarpent; not it— 'twas made for a man and would satisfy a giant, if rightly used. But stop; white men are remarkable for their carelessness in putting away fire arms, in chists and corners. Let me look if care has been given to these."

As Deerslayer spoke, he took the weapon from the hand of his friend and opened the pan. The last was filled with priming, caked like a bit of cinder, by time, moisture and compression. An application of the ramrod showed that both the pistols were charged, although Judith could testify that they had probably lain for years in the chest. It is not easy to portray the surprise of the Indian at this discovery, for he was in the practice of renewing his priming daily, and of looking to the contents of his piece at other short intervals.

"This is white neglect," said Deerslayer, shaking his head, "and scarce a season goes by that some one in the settlements doesn't suffer from it. It's extr'ornary too, Judith—yes, it's downright extr'ornary that the owner shall fire his piece at a deer, or some other game, or perhaps at an inimy, and twice out of three times he'll miss; but let him catch an accident with one of these forgotten charges, and he makes it sartain death to a child, or a brother, or a fri'nd! Well, we shall do a good turn to the owner if we fire these pistols for him, and as they're novelties to you and me, Sarpent, we'll try our hands at a mark. Freshen that priming, and I'll do the same with this, and then we'll see who is the best man with a pistol; as for the rifle, that's long been settled atween us."

Deerslayer laughed heartily at his own conceit, and, in a minute or two, they were both standing on the platform, selecting some object in the Ark for their target. Judith was led by curiosity to their side.

"Stand back, gal, stand a little back; these we'pons have been long loaded," said Deerslayer, "and some accident may happen in the discharge." "Then you shall not fire them! Give them both to the Delaware; or it would be better to unload them without firing."

"That's ag'in usage—and some people say, ag'in manhood; though I hold to no such silly doctrine. We must fire 'em, Judith; yes, we must fire 'em; though I foresee that neither will have any great reason to boast of his skill."

Judith, in the main, was a girl of great personal spirit, and her habits prevented her from feeling any of the terror that is apt to come over her sex at the report of fire arms. She had discharged many a rifle, and had even been known to kill a deer, under circumstances that were favorable to the effort. She submitted therefore, falling a little back by the side of Deerslayer, giving the Indian the front of the platform to himself. Chingachgook raised the weapon several times, endeavored to steady it by using both hands, changed his attitude from one that was awkward to another still more so, and finally drew the trigger with a sort of desperate indifference, without having, in reality, secured any aim at all. The consequence was, that instead of hitting the knot which had been selected for the mark, he missed the ark altogether; the bullet skipping along the water like a stone that was thrown by hand.

"Well done—Sarpent—well done—" cried Deerslayer laughing, with his noiseless glee, "you've hit the lake, and that's an expl'ite for some men! I know'd it, and as much as said it, here, to Judith; for your short we'pons don't belong to red-skin gifts. You've hit the lake, and that's better than only hitting the air! Now, stand back and let us see what white gifts can do with a white we'pon. A pistol isn't a rifle, but colour is colour."

The aim of Deerslayer was both quick and steady, and the report followed almost as soon as the weapon rose. Still the pistol hung fire, as it is termed, and fragments of it flew in a dozen directions, some falling on the roof of the castle, others in the Ark, and one in the water. Judith screamed, and when the two men turned anxiously towards the girl she was as pale as death, trembling in every limb.

"She's wounded—yes, the poor gal's wounded, Sarpent, though one couldn't foresee it, standing where she did. We'll lead her in to a seat, and we must do the best for her that our knowledge and skill can afford."

Judith allowed herself to be supported to a seat, swallowed a mouthful of the water that the Delaware offered her in a gourd, and, after a violent fit of trembling that seemed ready to shake her fine frame to dissolution, she burst into tears.

"The pain must be borne, poor Judith—yes, it must be borne," said Deerslayer, soothingly, "though I am far from wishing you not to weep; for weeping often lightens galish feelin's. Where can she be hurt, Sarpent? I see no signs of blood, nor any rent of skin or garments?"

"I am uninjured, Deerslayer," stammered the girl through her tears. "It's fright—nothing more, I do assure you, and, God be praised! no one, I find, has been harmed by the accident."

"This is extr'ornary!" exclaimed the unsuspecting and simple minded hunter—"I thought, Judith, you'd been above settlement weaknesses, and that you was a gal not to be frightened by the sound of a bursting we'pon—No—I didn't think you so skeary! Hetty might well have been startled; but you've too much judgment and reason to be frightened when the danger's all over. They're pleasant to the eye, chief, and changeful, but very unsartin in their feelin's!"

Shame kept Judith silent. There had been no acting in her agitation, but all had fairly proceeded from sudden and uncontrollable alarm—an alarm that she found almost as inexplicable to herself, as it proved to be to her companions. Wiping away the traces of tears, however, she smiled again, and was soon able to join in the laugh at her own folly.

"And you, Deerslayer," she at length succeeded in saying—"are you, indeed, altogether unhurt? It seems almost miraculous that a pistol should have burst in your hand, and you escape without the loss of a limb, if not of life!"

"Such wonders ar'n't oncommon, at all, among worn out arms. The first rifle they gave me play'd the same trick, and yet I liv'd through it, though not as onharmless as I've got out of this affair.

Thomas Hutter is master of one pistol less than he was this morning, but, as it happened in trying to sarve him, there's no ground of complaint. Now, draw near, and let us look farther into the inside of the chist."

Judith, by this time, had so far gotten the better of her agitation as to resume her seat, and the examination went on. The next article that offered was enveloped in cloth, and on opening it, it proved to be one of the mathematical instruments that were then in use among seamen, possessing the usual ornaments and fastenings in brass. Deerslayer and Chingachgook expressed their admiration and surprise at the appearance of the unknown instrument, which was bright and glittering, having apparently been well cared for.

"This goes beyond the surveyors, Judith!" Deerslayer exclaimed, after turning the instrument several times in his hands. "I've seen all their tools often, and wicked and heartless enough are they, for they never come into the forest but to lead the way to waste and destruction; but none of them have as designing a look as this! I fear me, after all, that Thomas Hutter has journeyed into the wilderness with no fair intentions towards its happiness. Did you ever see any of the cravings of a surveyor about your father, gal?"

"He is no surveyor, Deerslayer, nor does he know the use of that instrument, though he seems to own it. Do you suppose that Thomas Hutter ever wore that coat? It is as much too large for him, as this instrument is beyond his learning."

"That's it—that must be it, Sarpent, and the old fellow, by some onknown means, has fallen heir to another man's goods! They say he has been a mariner, and no doubt this chist, and all it holds—ha! What have we here?—This far out does the brass and black wood of the tool!"

Deerslayer had opened a small bag, from which he was taking, one by one, the pieces of a set of chessmen. They were of ivory, much larger than common, and exquisitely wrought. Each piece represented the character or thing after which it is named; the knights being mounted, the castles stood on elephants, and even the pawns possessed the heads and busts of men. The set was not complete, and a few fractures betrayed bad usage; but all that was left had been carefully put away and preserved. Even Judith expressed wonder, as these novel objects were placed before her eyes, and Chingachgook fairly forgot his Indian dignity in admiration and delight. The latter took up each piece, and examined it with never tiring satisfaction, pointing out to the girl the more ingenious and striking portions of the workmanship. But the elephants gave him the greatest pleasure. The "Hughs!" that he uttered, as he passed his fingers over their trunks, and ears, and tails, were very distinct, nor did he fail to note the pawns, which were armed as archers. This exhibition lasted several minutes, during which time Judith and the Indian had all the rapture to themselves. Deerslayer sat silent, thoughtful, and even gloomy, though his eyes followed each movement of the two principal actors, noting every new peculiarity about the pieces as they were held up to view. Not an exclamation of pleasure, nor a word of condemnation passed his lips. At length his companions observed his silence, and then, for the first time since the chessmen had been discovered, did he speak.

"Judith," he asked earnestly, but with a concern that amounted almost to tenderness of manner, "did your parents ever talk to you of religion?"

The girl coloured, and the flashes of crimson that passed over her beautiful countenance were like the wayward tints of a Neapolitan sky in November. Deerslayer had given her so strong a taste for truth, however, that she did not waver in her answer, replying simply and with sincerity.

"My mother did often," she said, "my father never. I thought it made my mother sorrowful to speak of our prayers and duties, but my father has never opened his mouth on such matters, before or since her death."

"That I can believe—that I can believe. He has no God—no such God as it becomes a man of white skin to worship, or even a red-skin. Them things are idols!"

Judith started, and for a moment she seemed seriously hurt. Then she reflected, and in the end she laughed. "And you think, Deerslayer, that these ivory toys are my father's Gods? I have heard of idols, and know what they are."

"Them are idols!" repeated the other, positively. "Why should your father keep 'em, if he doesn't worship 'em."

"Would he keep his gods in a bag, and locked up in a chest? No, no, Deerslayer; my poor father carries his God with him, wherever he goes, and that is in his own cravings. These things may really be idols—I think they are myself, from what I have heard and read of idolatry, but they have come from some distant country, and like all the other articles, have fallen into Thomas Hutter's hands when he was a sailor."

"I'm glad of it—I am downright glad to hear it, Judith, for I do not think I could have mustered the resolution to strive to help a white idolater out of his difficulties! The old man is of my colour and nation and I wish to sarve him, but as one who denied all his gifts, in the way of religion, it would have come hard to do so. That animal seems to give you great satisfaction, Sarpent, though it's an idolatrous beast at the best."

"It is an elephant," interrupted Judith. "I've often seen pictures of such animals, at the garrisons, and mother had a book in which there was a printed account of the creature. Father burnt that with all the other books, for he said Mother loved reading too well. This was not long before mother died, and I've sometimes thought that the loss hastened her end."

This was said equally without levity and without any very deep feeling. It was said without levity, for Judith was saddened by her recollections, and yet she had been too much accustomed to live for self, and for the indulgence of her own vanities, to feel her mother's wrongs very keenly. It required extraordinary circumstances to awaken a proper sense of her situation, and to stimulate the better feelings of this beautiful, but misguided girl, and those circumstances had not yet occurred in her brief existence.

"Elephant, or no elephant, 'tis an idol," returned the hunter, "and not fit to remain in Christian keeping."

"Good for Iroquois!" said Chingachgook, parting with one of the castles with reluctance, as his friend took it from him to replace it in the bag—"Elephon buy whole tribe—buy Delaware, almost!"

"Ay, that it would, as any one who comprehends red-skin natur' must know," answered Deerslayer, "but the man that passes false money, Sarpent, is as bad as he who makes it. Did you ever know a just Injin that wouldn't scorn to sell a 'coon skin for the true marten, or to pass off a mink for a beaver. I know that a few of these idols, perhaps one of them elephants, would go far towards buying Thomas Hutter's liberty, but it goes ag'in conscience to pass such counterfeit money. Perhaps no Injin tribe, hereaway, is downright idolaters but there's some that come so near it, that white gifts ought to be particular about encouraging them in their mistake."

"If idolatry is a gift, Deerslayer, and gifts are what you seem to think them, idolatry in such people can hardly be a sin," said Judith with more smartness than discrimination.

"God grants no such gifts to any of his creatur's, Judith," returned the hunter, seriously. "He must be adored, under some name or other, and not creatur's of brass or ivory. It matters not whether the Father of All is called God, or Manitou, Deity or Great Spirit, he is none the less our common maker and master; nor does it count for much whether the souls of the just go to Paradise, or Happy Hunting Grounds, since He may send each his own way, as suits his own pleasure and wisdom; but it curdles my blood, when I find human mortals so bound up in darkness and consait, as to fashion the 'arth, or wood, or bones, things made by their own hands, into motionless, senseless effigies, and then fall down afore them, and worship 'em as a Deity!"

"After all, Deerslayer, these pieces of ivory may not be idols, at all. I remember, now, to have seen one of the officers at the garrison with a set of fox and geese made in some such a design as these, and here is something hard, wrapped in cloth, that may belong to your idols."

Deerslayer took the bundle the girl gave him, and unrolling it, he found the board within. Like the pieces it was large, rich, and inlaid with ebony and ivory. Putting the whole in conjunction the hunter, though not without many misgivings, slowly came over to Judith's opinion, and finally admitted that the fancied idols must be merely the curiously carved men of some unknown game. Judith had the tact to use her victory with great moderation, nor did she once, even in the most indirect manner, allude to the ludicrous mistake of her companion.

This discovery of the uses of the extraordinary-looking little images settled the affair of the proposed ransom. It was agreed generally, and all understood the weaknesses and tastes of Indians, that nothing could be more likely to tempt the cupidity of the Iroquois than the elephants, in particular. Luckily the whole of the castles were among the pieces, and these four tower-bearing animals it was finally determined should be the ransom offered. The remainder of the men, and, indeed, all the rest of the articles in the chest, were to be kept out of view, and to be resorted to only as a last appeal. As soon as these preliminaries were settled, everything but those intended for the bribe was carefully replaced in the chest, all the covers were 'tucked in' as they had been found, and it was quite possible, could Hutter have been put in possession of the castle again, that he might have passed the remainder of his days in it without even suspecting the invasion that had been made on the privacy of the chest. The rent pistol would have been the most likely to reveal the secret, but this was placed by the side of its fellow, and all were pressed down as before, some half a dozen packages in the bottom of the chest not having been opened at all. When this was done the lid was lowered, the padlocks replaced, and the key turned. The latter was then replaced in the pocket from which it had been taken.

More than an hour was consumed in settling the course proper to be pursued, and in returning everything to its place. The pauses to converse were frequent, and Judith, who experienced a lively pleasure in the open, undisguised admiration with which Deerslayer's honest eyes gazed at her handsome face, found the means to prolong the interview, with a dexterity that seems to be innate in female coquetry. Deerslayer, indeed, appeared to be the first who was conscious of the time that had been thus wasted, and to call the attention of his companions to the necessity of doing something towards putting the plan of ransoming into execution. Chingachgook had remained in Hutter's bed room, where the elephants were laid, to feast his eyes with the images of animals so wonderful, and so novel. Perhaps an instinct told him that his presence would not be as acceptable to his companions as this holding himself aloof, for Judith had not much reserve in the manifestations of her preferences, and the Delaware had not got so far as one betrothed without acquiring some knowledge of the symptoms of the master passion.

"Well, Judith," said Deerslayer, rising, after the interview had lasted much longer than even he himself suspected, "'tis pleasant conversing with you, and settling all these matters, but duty calls us another way. All this time, Hurry and your father, not to say Hetty—"The word was cut short in the speaker's mouth, for, at that critical moment, a light step was heard on the platform, or 'court-yard', a human figure darkened the doorway, and the person last mentioned stood before him. The low exclamation that escaped Deerslayer and the slight scream of Judith were hardly uttered, when an

Indian youth, between the ages of fifteen and seventeen, stood beside her. These two entrances had been made with moccasined feet, and consequently almost without noise, but, unexpected and stealthy as they were, they had not the effect to disturb Deerslayer's self possession. His first measure was to speak rapidly in Delaware to his friend, cautioning him to keep out of sight, while he stood on his guard; the second was to step to the door to ascertain the extent of the danger. No one else, however, had come, and a simple contrivance, in the shape of a raft, that lay floating at the side of the Ark, at once explained the means that had been used in bringing Hetty off. Two dead and dry, and consequently buoyant, logs of pine were bound together with pins and withes and a little platform of riven chestnut had been rudely placed on their surfaces. Here Hetty had been seated, on a billet of wood, while the young Iroquois had rowed the primitive and slow-moving, but perfectly safe craft from the shore.

As soon as Deerslayer had taken a close survey of this raft, and satisfied himself nothing else was near, he shook his head and muttered in his soliloquizing way—"This comes of prying into another man's chist! Had we been watchful, and keen eyed, such a surprise could never have happened, and, getting this much from a boy teaches us what we may expect when the old warriors set themselves fairly about their sarcumventions. It opens the way, howsever, to a treaty for the ransom, and I will hear what Hetty has to say."

Judith, as soon as her surprise and alarm had a little abated, discovered a proper share of affectionate joy at the return of her sister. She folded her to her bosom, and kissed her, as had been her wont in the days of their childhood and innocence. Hetty herself was less affected, for to her there was no surprise, and her nerves were sustained by the purity and holiness of her purpose. At her sister's request she took a seat, and entered into an account of her adventures since they had parted. Her tale commenced just as Deerslayer returned, and he also became an attentive listener, while the young Iroquois stood near the door, seemingly as indifferent to what was passing as one of its posts.

The narrative of the girl was sufficiently clear, until she reached the time where we left her in the camp, after the interview with the chiefs, and, at the moment when Hist quitted her, in the abrupt manner already related. The sequel of the story may be told in her own language.

"When I read the texts to the chiefs, Judith, you could not have seen that they made any changes on their minds," she said, "but if seed is planted, it will grow. God planted the seeds of all these trees—"

"Ay that did he—that did he—" muttered Deerslayer; "and a goodly harvest has followed."

"God planted the seeds of all these trees," continued Hetty, after a moment's pause, "and you see to what a height and shade they have grown! So it is with the Bible. You may read a verse this year, and forget it, and it will come back to you a year hence, when you least expect to remember it."

"And did you find any thing of this among the savages, poor Hetty?"

"Yes, Judith, and sooner and more fully than I had even hoped. I did not stay long with father and Hurry, but went to get my breakfast with Hist. As soon as we had done the chiefs came to us, and then we found the fruits of the seed that had been planted. They said what I had read from the good book was right—it must be right—it sounded right; like a sweet bird singing in their ears; and they told me to come back and say as much to the great warrior who had slain one of their braves; and to tell it to you, and to say how happy they should be to come to church here, in the castle, or to come out in the sun, and hear me read more of the sacred volume—and to tell you that they wish you would lend them some canoes that they can bring father and Hurry and their women to the castle, that we might all sit on the platform there and listen to the singing of the Pale-face Manitou. There, Judith; did you ever know of any thing that so plainly shows the power of the Bible, as that!"

"If it were true 't would be a miracle, indeed, Hetty. But all this is no more than Indian cunning and Indian treachery, striving to get the better of us by management, when they find it is not to be done by force."

"Do you doubt the Bible, sister, that you judge the savages so harshly!"

"I do not doubt the Bible, poor Hetty, but I much doubt an Indian and an Iroquois. What do you say to this visit, Deerslayer?"

"First let me talk a little with Hetty," returned the party appealed to; "Was the raft made a'ter you had got your breakfast, gal, and did you walk from the camp to the shore opposite to us, here?"

"Oh! no, Deerslayer. The raft was ready made and in the water—could that have been by a miracle, Judith?"

"Yes—yes—an Indian miracle," rejoined the hunter—"They're expart enough in them sort of miracles. And you found the raft ready made to your hands, and in the water, and in waiting like for its cargo?"

"It was all as you say. The raft was near the camp, and the Indians put me on it, and had ropes of bark, and they dragged me to the place opposite to the castle, and then they told that young man to row me off, here."

"And the woods are full of the vagabonds, waiting to know what is to be the upshot of the miracle. We comprehend this affair, now, Judith, but I'll first get rid of this young Canada blood sucker, and then we'll settle our own course. Do you and Hetty leave us together, first bringing me the elephants, which the Sarpent is admiring, for 'twill never do to let this loping deer be alone a minute, or he'll borrow a canoe without asking."

Judith did as desired, first bringing the pieces, and retiring with her sister into their own room. Deerslayer had acquired some knowledge of most of the Indian dialects of that region, and he knew enough of the Iroquois to hold a dialogue in the language. Beckoning to the lad, therefore, he caused him to take a seat on the chest, when he placed two of the castles suddenly before him. Up to that moment, this youthful savage had not expressed a single intelligible emotion, or fancy. There were many things, in and about the place, that were novelties to him, but he had maintained his self-command with philosophical composure. It is true, Deerslayer had detected his dark eye scanning the defences and the arms, but the scrutiny had been made with such an air of innocence, in such a gaping, indolent, boyish manner, that no one but a man who had himself been taught in a similar school, would have even suspected his object. The instant, however, the eyes of the savage fell upon the wrought ivory, and the images of the wonderful, unknown beasts, surprise and admiration got the mastery of him. The manner in which the natives of the South Sea Islands first beheld the toys of civilized life has been often described, but the reader is not to confound it with the manner of an American Indian, under similar circumstances. In this particular case, the young Iroquois or Huron permitted an exclamation of rapture to escape him, and then he checked himself like one who had been guilty of an indecorum. After this, his eyes ceased to wander, but became riveted on the elephants, one of which, after a short hesitation, he even presumed to handle. Deerslayer did not interrupt him for quite ten minutes, knowing that the lad was taking such note of the curiosities, as would enable him to give the most minute and accurate description of their appearance to his seniors, on his return. When he thought sufficient time had been allowed to produce the desired effect, the hunter laid a finger on the naked knee of the youth and drew his attention to himself.

"Listen," he said; "I want to talk with my young friend from the Canadas. Let him forget that wonder for a minute."

"Where t'other pale brother?" demanded the boy, looking up and letting the idea that had been most prominent in his mind, previously to the introduction of the chess men, escape him involuntarily.

"He sleeps, or if he isn't fairly asleep, he is in the room where the men do sleep," returned Deerslayer. "How did my young friend know there was another?"

"See him from the shore. Iroquois have got long eyes—see beyond the clouds—see the bottom of the Great Spring!"

"Well, the Iroquois are welcome. Two pale-faces are prisoners in the camp of your fathers, boy."

The lad nodded, treating the circumstance with great apparent indifference; though a moment after he laughed as if exulting in the superior address of his own tribe.

"Can you tell me, boy, what your chiefs intend to do with these captyves, or haven't they yet made up their minds?"

The lad looked a moment at the hunter with a little surprise. Then he coolly put the end of his fore finger on his own head, just above the left ear, and passed it round his crown with an accuracy and readiness that showed how well he had been drilled in the peculiar art of his race.

"When?" demanded Deerslayer, whose gorge rose at this cool demonstration of indifference to human life. "And why not take them to your wigwams?"

"Road too long, and full of pale-faces. Wigwam full, and scalps sell high. Small scalp, much gold."

"Well that explains it—yes, that does explain it. There's no need of being any plainer. Now you know, lad, that the oldest of your prisoners is the father of these two young women, and the other is the suitor of one of them. The gals nat'rally wish to save the scalps of such fri'nds, and they will give them two ivory creaturs, as ransom. One for each scalp. Go back and tell this to your chiefs, and bring me the answer before the sun sets."

The boy entered zealously into this project, and with a sincerity that left no doubt of his executing his commission with intelligence and promptitude. For a moment he forgot his love of honor, and all his clannish hostility to the British and their Indians, in his wish to have such a treasure in his tribe, and Deerslayer was satisfied with the impression he had made. It is true the lad proposed to carry one of the elephants with him, as a specimen of the other, but to this his brother negotiator was too sagacious to consent; well knowing that it might never reach its destination if confided to such hands. This little difficulty was soon arranged, and the boy prepared to depart. As he stood on the platform, ready to step aboard of the raft, he hesitated, and turned short with a proposal to borrow a canoe, as the means most likely to shorten the negotiations. Deerslayer quietly refused the request, and, after lingering a little longer, the boy rowed slowly away from the castle, taking the direction of a thicket on the shore that lay less than half a mile distant. Deerslayer seated himself on a stool and watched the progress of the ambassador, sometimes closely scanning the whole line of shore, as far as eye could reach, and then placing an elbow on a knee, he remained a long time with his chin resting on the hand.

During the interview between Deerslayer and the lad, a different scene took place in the adjoining room. Hetty had inquired for the Delaware, and being told why and where he remained concealed, she joined him. The reception which Chingachgook gave his visitor was respectful and gentle. He understood her character, and, no doubt, his disposition to be kind to such a being was increased by the hope of learning some tidings of his betrothed. As soon as the girl entered she took a seat, and invited the Indian to place himself near her; then she continued silent, as if she thought it decorous for him to question her, before she consented to speak on the subject she had on her mind. But, as Chingachgook did not understand this feeling, he remained respectfully attentive to any thing she might be pleased to tell him.

"You are Chingachgook, the Great Serpent of the Delawares, ar'n't you?" the girl at length commenced, in her own simple way losing her self-command in the desire to proceed, but anxious first to make sure of the individual. "Chingachgook," returned the Delaware with grave dignity. "That say Great Sarpent, in Deerslayer tongue."

"Well, that is my tongue. Deerslayer, and father, and Judith, and I, and poor Hurry Harry—do you know Henry March, Great Serpent? I know you don't, however, or he would have spoken of you, too."

"Did any tongue name Chingachgook, Drooping-Lily"? for so the chief had named poor Hetty. "Was his name sung by a little bird among Iroquois?"

Hetty did not answer at first, but, with that indescribable feeling that awakens sympathy and intelligence among the youthful and unpracticed of her sex, she hung her head, and the blood suffused her cheek ere she found her tongue. It would have exceeded her stock of intelligence to explain this embarrassment, but, though poor Hetty could not reason, on every emergency, she could always feel. The colour slowly receded from her cheeks, and the girl looked up archly at the Indian, smiling with the innocence of a child, mingled with the interest of a woman.

"My sister, the Drooping Lily, hear such bird!" Chingachgook added, and this with a gentleness of tone and manner that would have astonished those who sometimes heard the discordant cries that often came from the same throat; these transitions from the harsh and guttural, to the soft and melodious not being infrequent in ordinary Indian dialogues. "My sister's ears were open—has she lost her tongue?"

"You are Chingachgook—you must be; for there is no other red man here, and she thought Chingachgook would come."

"Chin-gach-gook," pronouncing the name slowly, and dwelling on each syllable—"Great Sarpent, Yengeese tongue."

[It is singular there should be any question concerning the origin of the well-known sobriquet of "Yankees." Nearly all the old writers who speak of the Indians first known to the colonists make them pronounce the word "English" as "Yengeese." Even at this day, it is a provincialism of New England to say "Anglish" instead of "Inglish," and there is a close conformity of sound between "Anglish" and "yengeese," more especially if the latter word, as was probably the case, be pronounced short. The transition from "Yengeese," thus pronounced, to "Yankees" is quite easy. If the former is pronounced "Yangis," it is almost identical with "Yankees," and Indian words have seldom been spelt as they are pronounced. Thus the scene of this tale is spelt "Otsego," and is properly pronounced "Otsago." The liquids of the Indians would easily convert "En" into "Yen."]

"Chin-gach-gook," repeated Hetty, in the same deliberate manner. "Yes, so Hist called it, and you must be the chief."

"Wah-ta-Wah," added the Delaware.

"Wah-ta-Wah, or Hist-oh-Hist. I think Hist prettier than Wah, and so I call her Hist."

"Wah very sweet in Delaware ears!"

"You make it sound differently from me. But, never mind, I did hear the bird you speak of sing, Great Serpent."

"Will my sister say words of song? What she sing most—how she look—often she laugh?"

"She sang Chin-gach-gook oftener than any thing else; and she laughed heartily, when I told how the Iroquois waded into the water after us, and couldn't catch us. I hope these logs haven't ears, Serpent!"

"No fear logs; fear sister next room. No fear Iroquois; Deerslayer stuff his eyes and ears with strange beast."

"I understand you, Serpent, and I understood Hist. Sometimes I think I'm not half as feeble minded as they say I am. Now, do you look up at the roof, and I'll tell you all. But you frighten me, you look so eager when I speak of Hist."

The Indian controlled his looks, and affected to comply with the simple request of the girl.

"Hist told me to say, in a very low voice, that you mustn't trust the Iroquois in anything. They are more artful than any Indians she knows. Then she says that there is a large bright star that comes over the hill, about an hour after dark"—Hist had pointed out the planet Jupiter, without knowing it—"and just as that star comes in sight, she will be on the point, where I landed last night, and that you must come for her, in a canoe."

"Good—Chingachgook understand well enough, now; but he understand better if my sister sing him ag'in."

Hetty repeated her words, more fully explaining what star was meant, and mentioning the part of the point where he was to venture ashore. She now proceeded in her own unsophisticated way to relate her intercourse with the Indian maid, and to repeat several of her expressions and opinions that gave great delight to the heart of her betrothed. She particularly renewed her injunctions to be on their guard against treachery, a warning that was scarcely needed, however, as addressed to men as wary as those to whom it was sent. She also explained with sufficient clearness, for on all such subjects the mind of the girl seldom failed her, the present state of the enemy, and the movements they had made since morning. Hist had been on the raft with her until it quitted the shore, and was now somewhere in the woods, opposite to the castle, and did not intend to return to the camp until night approached; when she hoped to be able to slip away from her companions, as they followed the shore on their way home, and conceal herself on the point. No one appeared to suspect the presence of Chingachgook, though it was necessarily known that an Indian had entered the Ark the previous night, and it was suspected that he had since appeared in and about the castle in the dress of a pale-face. Still some little doubt existed on the latter point, for, as this was the season when white men might be expected to arrive, there was some fear that the garrison of the castle was increasing by these ordinary means. All this had Hist communicated to Hetty while the Indians were dragging them along shore, the distance, which exceeded six miles, affording abundance of time.

"Hist don't know, herself, whether they suspect her or not, or whether they suspect you, but she hopes neither is the case. And now, Serpent, since I have told you so much from your betrothed," continued Hetty, unconsciously taking one of the Indian's hands, and playing with the fingers, as a child is often seen to play with those of a parent, "you must let me tell you something from myself. When you marry Hist, you must be kind to her, and smile on her, as you do now on me, and not look cross as some of the chiefs do at their squaws. Will you promise this?"

"Alway good to Wah!—too tender to twist hard; else she break."

"Yes, and smile, too; you don't know how much a girl craves smiles from them she loves. Father scarce smiled on me once, while I was with him—and, Hurry—Yes—Hurry talked loud and laughed, but I don't think he smiled once either. You know the difference between a smile and a laugh?"

"Laugh, best. Hear Wah laugh, think bird sing!"

"I know that; her laugh is pleasant, but you must smile. And then, Serpent, you mustn't make her carry burthens and hoe corn, as so many Indians do; but treat her more as the pale-faces treat their wives."

"Wah-ta-Wah no pale-face—got red-skin; red heart, red feelin's. All red; no pale-face. Must carry papoose."

"Every woman is willing to carry her child," said Hetty smiling, "and there is no harm in that. But you must love Hist, and be gentle, and good to her; for she is gentle and good herself."

Chingachgook gravely bowed, and then he seemed to think this part of the subject might be dismissed. Before there was time for Hetty to resume her communications, the voice of Deerslayer was heard calling on his friend, in the outer room. At this summons the Serpent arose to obey, and Hetty joined her sister.

CHAPTER XIV.

"'A stranger animal,' cries one,
'Sure never liv'd beneath the sun;
A lizard's body lean and long,
A fish's head, a serpent's tongue,
Its foot, with triple claw disjoined;
And what a length of tail behind!'"

James Merrick, "The Chameleon," 11.21–26.

The first act of the Delaware, on rejoining his friend, was to proceed gravely to disencumber himself of his civilized attire, and to stand forth an Indian warrior again. The protest of Deerslayer was met by his communicating the fact that the presence of an Indian in the hut was known to the Iroquois, and that maintaining the disguise would be more likely to direct suspicions to his real object, than if he came out openly as a member of a hostile tribe. When the latter understood the truth, and was told that he had been deceived in supposing the chief had succeeded in entering the Ark undiscovered, he cheerfully consented to the change, since further attempt at concealment was useless. A gentler feeling than the one avowed, however, lay at the bottom of the Indian's desire to appear as a son of the forest. He had been told that Hist was on the opposite shore, and nature so far triumphed over all distinctions of habit, and tribes and people, as to reduce this young savage warrior to the level of a feeling which would have been found in the most refined inhabitant of a town, under similar circumstances. There was a mild satisfaction in believing that she he loved could see him, and as he walked out on the platform in his scanty, native attire, an Apollo of the wilderness, a hundred of the tender fancies that fleet through lovers' brains beset his imagination and softened his heart. All this was lost on Deerslayer, who was no great adept in the mysteries of Cupid, but whose mind was far more occupied with the concerns that forced themselves on his attention, than with any of the truant fancies of love. He soon recalled his companion, therefore, to a sense of their actual condition, by summoning him to a sort of council of war, in which they were to settle their future course. In the dialogue that followed, the parties mutually made each other acquainted with what had passed in their several interviews. Chingachgook was told the history of the treaty about the ransom, and Deerslayer heard the whole of Hetty's communications. The latter listened with generous interest to his friend's hopes, and promised cheerfully all the assistance he could lend.

"'Tis our main ar'n'd, Sarpent, as you know, this battling for the castle and old Hutter's darters, coming in as a sort of accident. Yes—yes—I'll be actyve in helping little Hist, who's not only one of the best and handsomest maidens of the tribe, but the very best and handsomest. I've always encouraged you, chief, in that liking, and it's proper, too, that a great and ancient race like your'n shouldn't come to an end. If a woman of red skin and red gifts could get to be near enough to me to wish her for a wife, I'd s'arch for just such another, but that can never be; no, that can never be. I'm glad Hetty has met with Hist, howsever, for though the first is a little short of wit and understanding, the last has enough for both. Yes, Sarpent," laughing heartily—"put 'em together, and two smarter gals isn't to be found in all York Colony!"

"I will go to the Iroquois camp," returned the Delaware, gravely. "No one knows Chingachgook but Wah, and a treaty for lives and scalps should be made by a chief. Give me the strange beasts, and let me take a canoe."

Deerslayer dropped his head and played with the end of a fish-pole in the water, as he sat dangling his legs over the edge of the platform, like a man who was lost in thought by the sudden occurrence of a novel idea. Instead of directly answering the proposal of his friend, he began to soliloquize, a circumstance however that in no manner rendered his words more true, as he was remarkable for saying what he thought, whether the remarks were addressed to himself, or to any one else.

"Yes—yes—" he said—"this must be what they call love! I've heard say that it sometimes upsets reason altogether, leaving a young man as helpless, as to calculation and caution, as a brute beast. To think that the Sarpent should be so lost to reason, and cunning, and wisdom! We must sartainly manage to get Hist off, and have 'em married as soon as we get back to the tribe, or this war will be of no more use to the chief, than a hunt a little oncommon extr'ornary. Yes—Yes—he'll never be the man he was, till this matter is off his mind, and he comes to his senses like all the rest of mankind. Sarpent, you can't be in airnest, and therefore I shall say but little to your offer. But you're a chief, and will soon be sent out on the war path at head of the parties, and I'll just ask if you'd think of putting your forces into the inimy's hands, afore the battle is fou't?"

"Wah!" ejaculated the Indian.

"Ay—Wah—I know well enough it's Wah, and altogether Wah—Ra'ally, Sarpent, I'm consarned and mortified about you! I never heard so weak an idee come from a chief, and he, too, one that's already got a name for being wise, young and inexper'enced as he is. Canoe you sha'n't have, so long as the v'ice of fri'ndship and warning can count for any thing."

"My pale-face friend is right. A cloud came over the face of Chingachgook, and weakness got into his mind, while his eyes were dim. My brother has a good memory for good deeds, and a weak memory for bad. He will forget."

"Yes, that's easy enough. Say no more about it chief, but if another of them clouds blow near you, do your endivours to get out of its way. Clouds are bad enough in the weather, but when they come to the reason, it gets to be serious. Now, sit down by me here, and let us calculate our movements a little, for we shall soon either have a truce and a peace, or we shall come to an actyve and bloody war. You see the vagabonds can make logs sarve their turn, as well as the best raftsmen on the rivers, and it would be no great expl'ite for them to invade us in a body. I've been thinking of the wisdom of putting all old Tom's stores into the Ark, of barring and locking up the Castle, and of taking to the Ark, altogether. That is moveable, and by keeping the sail up, and shifting places, we might worry through a great many nights, without them Canada wolves finding a way into our sheep fold!"

Chingachgook listened to this plan with approbation. Did the negotiation fail, there was now little hope that the night would pass without an assault, and the enemy had sagacity enough to understand that in carrying the castle they would probably become masters of all it contained, the offered ransom included, and still retain the advantages they had hitherto gained. Some precaution of the sort appeared to be absolutely necessary, for now the numbers of the Iroquois were known, a night attack could scarcely be successfully met. It would be impossible to prevent the enemy from getting possession of the canoes and the Ark, and the latter itself would be a hold in which the assailants would be as effectually protected against bullets as were those in the building. For a few minutes, both the men thought of sinking the Ark in the shallow water, of bringing the canoes into the house, and of depending altogether on the castle for protection. But reflection satisfied them that, in the end, this expedient would fail. It was so easy to collect logs on the shore, and to construct a raft of almost any size, that it was certain the Iroquois, now they had turned their attention to such means, would resort to them seriously, so long as there was the certainty of success by perseverance. After deliberating maturely, and placing all the considerations fairly before them, the two young beginners in the art of forest warfare settled down into the opinion that the Ark offered the only available means of security. This decision was no sooner come to, than it was communicated to Judith. The girl had no serious objection to make, and all four set about the measures necessary to carrying the plan into execution.

The reader will readily understand that Floating Tom's worldly goods were of no great amount. A couple of beds, some wearing apparel, the arms and ammunition, a few cooking utensils, with the mysterious and but half examined chest formed the principal items. These were all soon removed, the Ark having been hauled on the eastern side of the building, so that the transfer could be made without being seen from the shore. It was thought unnecessary to disturb the heavier and coarser articles of furniture, as they were not required in the Ark, and were of but little value in themselves. As great caution was necessary in removing the different objects, most of which were passed out of a window with a view to conceal what was going on, it required two or three hours before all could be effected. By the expiration of that time, the raft made its appearance, moving from the shore. Deerslayer immediately had recourse to the glass, by the aid of which he perceived that two warriors were on it, though they appeared to be unarmed. The progress of the raft was slow, a circumstance that formed one of the great advantages that would be possessed by the scow, in any future collision between them, the movements of the latter being comparatively swift and light. As there was time to make the dispositions for the reception of the two dangerous visitors, everything was prepared for them, long before they had got near enough to be hailed. The Serpent and the girls retired into the building, where the former stood near the door, well provided with rifles, while Judith watched the proceedings without through a loop. As for Deerslayer, he had brought a stool to the edge of the platform, at the point towards which the raft was advancing, and taken his seat with his rifle leaning carelessly between his legs.

As the raft drew nearer, every means possessed by the party in the castle was resorted to, in order to ascertain if their visitors had any firearms. Neither Deerslayer nor Chingachgook could discover any, but Judith, unwilling to trust to simple eyesight, thrust the glass through the loop, and directed it towards the hemlock boughs that lay between the two logs of the raft, forming a sort of flooring, as well as a seat for the use of the rowers. When the heavy moving craft was within fifty feet of him, Deerslayer hailed the Hurons, directing them to cease rowing, it not being his intention to permit them to land. Compliance, of course, was necessary, and the two grim-looking warriors instantly quitted their seats, though the raft continued slowly to approach, until it had driven in much nearer to the platform.

"Are ye chiefs?" demanded Deerslayer with dignity—"Are ye chiefs?—Or have the Mingos sent me warriors without names, on such an ar'n'd? If so, the sooner ye go back, the sooner them will be likely to come that a warrior can talk with."

"Hugh!" exclaimed the elder of the two on the raft, rolling his glowing eyes over the different objects that were visible in and about the Castle, with a keenness that showed how little escaped him. "My brother is very proud, but Rivenoak (we use the literal translation of the term, writing as we do in English) is a name to make a Delaware turn pale."

"That's true, or it's a lie, Rivenoak, as it may be; but I am not likely to turn pale, seeing that I was born pale. What's your ar'n'd, and why do you come among light bark canoes, on logs that are not even dug out?"

"The Iroquois are not ducks, to walk on water! Let the pale-faces give them a canoe, and they'll come in a canoe."

"That's more rational, than likely to come to pass. We have but four canoes, and being four persons that's only one for each of us. We thank you for the offer, howsever, though we ask leave not to accept it. You are welcome, Iroquois, on your logs."

"Thanks—My young pale-face warrior—he has got a name—how do the chiefs call him?"

Deerslayer hesitated a moment, and a gleam of pride and human weakness came over him. He smiled, muttered between his teeth, and then looking up proudly, he said—"Mingo, like all who are young and actyve, I've been known by different names, at different times. One of your warriors whose spirit started for the Happy Grounds of your people, as lately as yesterday morning, thought I desarved to be known by the name of Hawkeye, and this because my sight happened to be quicker than his own, when it got to be life or death atween us."

Chingachgook, who was attentively listening to all that passed, heard and understood this proof of passing weakness in his friend, and on a future occasion he questioned him more closely concerning the transaction on the point, where Deerslayer had first taken human life. When he had got the whole truth, he did not fail to communicate it to the tribe, from which time the young hunter was universally known among the Delawares by an appellation so honorably earned. As this, however, was a period posterior to all the incidents of this tale, we shall continue to call the young hunter by the name under which he has been first introduced to the reader. Nor was the Iroquois less struck with the vaunt of the white man. He knew of the death of his comrade, and had no difficulty in understanding the allusion, the intercourse between the conqueror and his victim on that occasion having been seen by several savages on the shore of the lake, who had been stationed at different points just within the margin of bushes to watch the drifting canoes, and who had not time to reach the scene of action, ere the victor had retired. The effect on this rude being of the forest was an exclamation of surprise; then such a smile of courtesy, and wave of the hand, succeeded, as would have done credit to Asiatic diplomacy. The two Iroquois spoke to each other in low tones, and both drew near the end of the raft that was closest to the platform.

"My brother, Hawkeye, has sent a message to the Hurons," resumed Rivenoak, "and it has made their hearts very glad. They hear he has images of beasts with two tails! Will he show them to his friends?"

"Inimies would be truer," returned Deerslayer, "but sound isn't sense, and does little harm. Here is one of the images; I toss it to you under faith of treaties. If it's not returned, the rifle will settle the p'int atween us."

The Iroquois seemed to acquiesce in the conditions, and Deerslayer arose and prepared to toss one of the elephants to the raft, both parties using all the precaution that was necessary to prevent its loss. As practice renders men expert in such things, the little piece of ivory was soon successfully transferred from one hand to the other, and then followed another scene on the raft, in which astonishment and delight got the mastery of Indian stoicism. These two grim old warriors manifested even more feeling, as they examined the curiously wrought chessman, than had been betrayed by the boy; for, in the case of the latter, recent schooling had interposed its influence; while the men, like all who are sustained by well established characters, were not ashamed to let some of their emotions be discovered. For a few minutes they apparently lost the consciousness of their situation, in the intense scrutiny they bestowed on a material so fine, work so highly wrought, and an animal so extraordinary. The lip of the moose is, perhaps, the nearest approach to the trunk of the elephant that is to be found in the American forest, but this resemblance was far from being sufficiently striking to bring the new creature within the range of their habits and ideas, and the more they studied the image, the greater was their astonishment. Nor did these children of the forest mistake the structure on the back of the elephant for a part of the animal. They were familiar with horses and oxen, and had seen towers in the Canadas, and found nothing surprising in creatures of burthen. Still, by a very natural association, they supposed the carving meant to represent that the animal they saw was of a strength sufficient to carry a fort on its back; a circumstance that in no degree lessened their wonder.

"Has my pale-face brother any more such beasts?" at last the senior of the Iroquois asked, in a sort of petitioning manner.

"There's more where them came from, Mingo," was the answer; "one is enough, howsever, to buy off fifty scalps."

"One of my prisoners is a great warrior—tall as a pine—strong as the moose—active as a deer—fierce as the panther! Some day he'll be a great chief, and lead the army of King George!"

"Tut-tut Mingo; Hurry Harry is Hurry Harry, and you'll never make more than a corporal of him, if you do that. He's tall enough, of a sartainty; but that's of no use, as he only hits his head ag'in the branches as he goes through the forest. He's strong too, but a strong body isn't a strong head, and the king's generals are not chosen for their sinews; he's swift, if you will, but a rifle bullet is swifter; and as for f'erceness, it's no great ricommend to a soldier; they that think they feel the stoutest often givin' out at the pinch. No, no, you'll niver make Hurry's scalp pass for more than a good head of curly hair, and a rattle pate beneath it!"

"My old prisoner very wise—king of the lake—great warrior, wise counsellor!"

"Well, there's them that might gainsay all this, too, Mingo. A very wise man wouldn't be apt to be taken in so foolish a manner as befell Master Hutter, and if he gives good counsel, he must have listened to very bad in that affair. There's only one king of this lake, and he's a long way off, and isn't likely ever to see it. Floating Tom is some such king of this region, as the wolf that prowls through the woods is king of the forest. A beast with two tails is well worth two such scalps!"

"But my brother has another beast?—He will give two"—holding up as many fingers, "for old father?"

"Floating Tom is no father of mine, but he'll fare none the worse for that. As for giving two beasts for his scalp, and each beast with two tails, it is quite beyond reason. Think yourself well off, Mingo, if you make a much worse trade."

By this time the self-command of Rivenoak had got the better of his wonder, and he began to fall back on his usual habits of cunning, in order to drive the best bargain he could. It would be useless to relate more than the substance of the desultory dialogue that followed, in which the Indian manifested no little management, in endeavoring to recover the ground lost under the influence of surprise. He even affected to doubt whether any original for the image of the beast existed, and asserted that the oldest Indian had never heard a tradition of any such animal. Little did either of them imagine at the time that long ere a century elapsed, the progress of civilization would bring even much more extraordinary and rare animals into that region, as curiosities to be gazed at by the curious, and that the particular beast, about which the disputants contended, would be seen laving its sides and swimming in the very sheet of water, on which they had met.

[The Otsego is a favorite place for the caravan keepers to let their elephants bathe. The writer has seen two at a time, since the publication of this book, swimming about in company.]

As is not uncommon on such occasions, one of the parties got a little warm in the course of the discussion, for Deerslayer met all the arguments and prevarication of his subtle opponent with his own cool directness of manner, and unmoved love of truth. What an elephant was he knew little better than the savage, but he perfectly understood that the carved pieces of ivory must have some such value in the eyes of an Iroquois as a bag of gold or a package of beaver skins would in those of a trader. Under the circumstances, therefore, he felt it to be prudent not to concede too much at first, since there existed a nearly unconquerable obstacle to making the transfers, even after the contracting parties had actually agreed upon the terms. Keeping this difficulty in view, he held the extra chessmen in reserve, as a means of smoothing any difficulty in the moment of need.

At length the savage pretended that further negotiation was useless, since he could not be so unjust to his tribe as to part with the honor and emoluments of two excellent, full grown male scalps for a consideration so trifling as a toy like that he had seen, and he prepared to take his departure. Both parties now felt as men are wont to feel, when a bargain that each is anxious to conclude is on the eve of being broken off, in consequence of too much pertinacity in the way of management. The effect of the disappointment was very different, however, on the respective individuals. Deerslayer was mortified, and filled with regret, for he not only felt for the prisoners, but he also felt deeply for the two girls. The conclusion of the treaty, therefore, left him melancholy and full of regret. With the savage, his defeat produced the desire of revenge. In a moment of excitement, he had loudly announced his intention to say no more, and he felt equally enraged with himself and with his cool opponent, that he had permitted a pale face to manifest more indifference and self-command than an Indian chief. When he began to urge his raft away from the platform his countenance lowered and his eye glowed, even while he affected a smile of amity and a gesture of courtesy at parting.

It took some little time to overcome the inertia of the logs, and while this was being done by the silent Indian, Rivenoak stalked over the hemlock boughs that lay between the logs in sullen ferocity, eyeing keenly the while the hut, the platform and the person of his late disputant. Once he spoke in low, quick tones to his companion, and he stirred the boughs with his feet like an animal that is restive. At that moment the watchfulness of Deerslayer had a little abated, for he sat musing on the means of renewing the negotiation without giving too much advantage to the other side. It was perhaps fortunate for him that the keen and bright eyes of Judith were as vigilant as ever. At the instant when the young man was least on his guard, and his enemy was the most on the alert, she called out in a warning voice to the former, most opportunely giving the alarm.

"Be on your guard, Deerslayer," the girl cried—"I see rifles with the glass, beneath the hemlock brush, and the Iroquois is loosening them with his feet!"

It would seem that the enemy had carried their artifices so far as to employ an agent who understood English. The previous dialogue had taken place in his own language, but it was evident by the sudden manner in which his feet ceased their treacherous occupation, and in which the countenance of Rivenoak changed from sullen ferocity to a smile of courtesy, that the call of the girl was understood. Signing to his companion to cease his efforts to set the logs in motion, he advanced to the end of the raft which was nearest to the platform, and spoke.

"Why should Rivenoak and his brother leave any cloud between them," he said. "They are both wise, both brave, and both generous; they ought to part friends. One beast shall be the price of one prisoner."

"And, Mingo," answered the other, delighted to renew the negotiations on almost any terms, and determined to clinch the bargain if possible by a little extra liberality, "you'll see that a pale-face knows how to pay a full price, when he trades with an open heart, and an open hand. Keep the beast that you had forgotten to give back to me, as you was about to start, and which I forgot to ask for, on account of consarn at parting in anger. Show it to your chiefs. When you bring us our fri'nds, two more shall be added to it, and," hesitating a moment in distrust of the expediency of so great a concession; then, deciding in its favor—"and, if we see them afore the sun sets, we may find a fourth to make up an even number."

This settled the matter. Every gleam of discontent vanished from the dark countenance of the Iroquois, and he smiled as graciously, if not as sweetly, as Judith Hutter, herself. The piece already in his possession was again examined, and an ejaculation of pleasure showed how much he was pleased with this unexpected termination of the affair. In point of fact, both he and Deerslayer had momentarily forgotten what had become of the subject of their discussion, in the warmth of their feelings, but such had not been the case with Rivenoak's companion. This man retained the piece, and had fully made up his mind, were it claimed under such circumstances as to render its return necessary, to drop it in the lake, trusting to his being able to find it again at some future day. This desperate expedient, however, was no longer necessary, and after repeating the terms of agreement, and professing to understand them, the two Indians finally took their departure, moving slowly towards the shore.

"Can any faith be put in such wretches?" asked Judith, when she and Hetty had come out on the platform, and were standing at the side of Deerslayer, watching the dull movement of the logs. "Will they not rather keep the toy they have, and send us off some bloody proofs of their getting the better of us in cunning, by way of boasting? I've heard of acts as bad as this."

"No doubt, Judith; no manner of doubt, if it wasn't for Indian natur'. But I'm no judge of a red-skin, if that two tail'd beast doesn't set the whole tribe in some such stir as a stick raises in a beehive! Now, there's the Sarpent; a man with narves like flint, and no more cur'osity in every day consarns than is befitting prudence; why he was so overcome with the sight of the creatur', carved as it is in bone, that I felt ashamed for him! That's just their gifts, howsever, and one can't well quarrel with a man for his gifts, when they are lawful. Chingachgook will soon get over his weakness and remember that he's a chief, and that he comes of a great stock, and has a renowned name to support and uphold; but as for yonder scamps, there'll be no peace among 'em until they think they've got possession of every thing of the natur' of that bit of carved bone that's to be found among Thomas Hutter's stores!"

"They only know of the elephants, and can have no hopes about the other things."

"That's true, Judith; still, covetousness is a craving feelin'! They'll say, if the pale-faces have these cur'ous beasts with two tails, who knows but they've got some with three, or for that matter with four! That's what the schoolmasters call nat'ral arithmetic, and 'twill be sartain to beset the feelin's of savages. They'll never be easy, till the truth is known."

"Do you think, Deerslayer," inquired Hetty, in her simple and innocent manner, "that the Iroquois won't let father and Hurry go? I read to them several of the very best verses in the whole Bible, and you see what they have done, already."

The hunter, as he always did, listened kindly and even affectionately to Hetty's remarks; then he mused a moment in silence. There was something like a flush on his cheek as he answered, after quite a minute had passed.

"I don't know whether a white man ought to be ashamed, or not, to own he can't read, but such is my case, Judith. You are skilful, I find, in all such matters, while I have only studied the hand of God as it is seen in the hills and the valleys, the mountain-tops, the streams, the forests and the springs. Much l'arning may be got in this way, as well as out of books; and, yet, I sometimes think it is a white man's gift to read! When I hear from the mouths of the Moravians the words of which Hetty speaks, they raise a longing in my mind, and I then think I will know how to read 'em myself; but the game in summer, and the traditions, and lessons in war, and other matters, have always kept me behind hand."

"Shall I teach you, Deerslayer?" asked Hetty, earnestly. "I'm weak-minded, they say, but I can read as well as Judith. It might save your life to know how to read the Bible to the savages, and it will certainly save your soul; for mother told me that, again and again!"

"Thankee, Hetty—yes, thankee, with all my heart. These are like to be too stirring times for much idleness, but after it's peace, and I come to see you ag'in on this lake, then I'll give myself up to it, as if 'twas pleasure and profit in a single business. Perhaps I ought to be ashamed, Judith, that 'tis so; but truth is truth. As for these Iroquois, 'tisn't very likely they'll forget a beast with two tails, on account of a varse or two from the Bible. I rather expect they'll give up the prisoners, and trust to some sarcumvenion or other to get 'em back ag'in, with us and all in the castle and the Ark in the bargain. Howsever, we must humour the vagabonds, first to get your father and Hurry out of their hands, and next to keep the peace atween us, until such time as the Sarpent there can make out to get off his betrothed wife. If there's any sudden outbreakin' of anger and ferocity, the Indians will send off all their women and children to the camp at once, whereas, by keeping 'em calm and trustful we may manage to meet Hist at the spot she has mentioned. Rather than have the bargain fall through, now, I'd throw in half a dozen of them effigy bow-and-arrow men, such as we've in plenty in the chist."

Judith cheerfully assented, for she would have resigned even the flowered brocade, rather than not redeem her father and please Deerslayer. The prospects of success were now so encouraging as to raise the spirits of all in the castle, though a due watchfulness of the movements of the enemy was maintained. Hour passed after hour, notwithstanding, and the sun had once more begun to fall towards the summits of the western hills, and yet no signs were seen of the return of the raft. By dint of sweeping the shore with the glass, Deerslayer at length discovered a place in the dense and dark woods where, he entertained no doubt, the Iroquois were assembled in considerable numbers. It was near the thicket whence the raft had issued, and a little rill that trickled into the lake announced the vicinity of a spring. Here, then, the savages were probably holding their consultation, and the decision was to be made that went to settle the question of life or death for the prisoners. There was one ground for hope in spite of the delay, however, that Deerslayer did not fail to place before his anxious companions. It was far more probable that the Indians had left their prisoners in the camp, than that they had encumbered themselves by causing them to follow through the woods a party that was out on a merely temporary excursion. If such was the fact, it required considerable time to send a messenger the necessary distance, and to bring the two white men to the spot where they were to embark. Encouraged by these reflections, a new stock of patience was gathered, and the declension of the sun was viewed with less alarm.

The result justified Deerslayer's conjecture. Not long before the sun had finally disappeared, the two logs were seen coming out of the thicket, again, and as it drew near, Judith announced that her father and Hurry, both of them pinioned, lay on the bushes in the centre. As before, the two Indians were rowing. The latter seemed to be conscious that the lateness of the hour demanded unusual exertions, and contrary to the habits of their people, who are ever averse to toil, they labored hard at the rude substitutes for oars. In consequence of this diligence, the raft occupied its old station in about half the time that had been taken in the previous visits.

Even after the conditions were so well understood, and matters had proceeded so far, the actual transfer of the prisoners was not a duty to be executed without difficulty. The Iroquois were compelled to place great reliance on the good faith of their foes, though it was reluctantly given; and was yielded to necessity rather than to confidence. As soon as Hutter and Hurry should be released, the party in the castle numbered two to one, as opposed to those on the raft, and escape by flight was out of the question, as the former had three bark canoes, to say nothing of the defences of the house and the Ark. All this was understood by both parties, and it is probable the arrangement never could have been completed, had not the honest countenance and manner of Deerslayer wrought their usual effect on Rivenoak.

"My brother knows I put faith in him," said the latter, as he advanced with Hutter, whose legs had been released to enable the old man to ascend to the platform. "One scalp—one more beast."

"Stop, Mingo," interrupted the hunter, "keep your prisoner a moment. I have to go and seek the means of payment."

This excuse, however, though true in part, was principally a fetch. Deerslayer left the platform, and entering the house, he directed Judith to collect all the arms and to conceal them in her own room. He then spoke earnestly to the Delaware, who stood on guard as before, near the entrance of the building, put the three remaining castles in his pocket, and returned.

"You are welcome back to your old abode, Master Hutter," said Deerslayer, as he helped the other up on the platform, slyly passing into the hand of Rivenoak, at the same time, another of the castles. "You'll find your darters right glad to see you, and here's Hetty come herself to say as much in her own behalf."

Here the hunter stopped speaking and broke out into a hearty fit of his silent and peculiar laughter. Hurry's legs were just released, and he had been placed on his feet. So tightly had the ligatures been drawn, that the use of his limbs was not immediately recovered, and the young giant presented, in good sooth, a very helpless and a somewhat ludicrous picture. It was this unusual spectacle, particularly the bewildered countenance, that excited the merriment of Deerslayer.

"You look like a girdled pine in a clearin', Hurry Harry, that is rocking in a gale," said Deerslayer, checking his unseasonable mirth, more from delicacy to the others than from any respect to the liberated captive. "I'm glad, howsever, to see that you haven't had your hair dressed by any of the Iroquois barbers, in your late visit to their camp."

"Harkee, Deerslayer," returned the other a little fiercely, "it will be prudent for you to deal less in mirth and more in friendship on this occasion. Act like a Christian, for once, and not like a laughing gal in a country school when the master's back is turned, and just tell me whether there's any feet, or not, at the end of these legs of mine. I think I can see them, but as for feelin' they might as well be down on the banks of the Mohawk, as be where they seem to be."

"You've come off whole, Hurry, and that's not a little," answered the other, secretly passing to the Indian the remainder of the stipulated ransom, and making an earnest sign at the same moment for him to commence his retreat. "You've come off whole, feet and all, and are only a little numb from a tight fit of the withes. Natur'll soon set the blood in motion, and then you may begin to dance, to celebrate what I call a most wonderful and onexpected deliverance from a den of wolves."

Deerslayer released the arms of his friends, as each landed, and the two were now stamping and limping about on the platform, growling and uttering denunciations as they endeavored to help the returning circulation. They had been tethered too long, however, to regain the use of their limbs in a moment, and the Indians being quite as diligent on their return as on their advance, the raft was fully a hundred yards from the castle when Hurry, turning accidentally in that direction, discovered how fast it was getting beyond the reach of his vengeance. By this time he could move with tolerable facility, though still numb and awkward. Without considering his own situation, however, he seized the rifle that leaned against the shoulder of Deerslayer, and attempted to cock and present it. The young hunter was too quick for him. Seizing the piece he wrenched it from the hands of the giant, not, however, until it had gone off in the struggle, when pointed directly upward. It is probable that Deerslayer could have prevailed in such a contest, on account of the condition of Hurry's limbs, but the instant the gun went off, the latter yielded, and stumped towards the house, raising his legs at each step quite a foot from the ground, from an uncertainty of the actual position of his feet. But he had been anticipated by Judith. The whole stock of Hutter's arms, which had been left in the building as a resource in the event of a sudden outbreaking of hostilities, had been removed, and were already secreted, agreeably to Deerslayer's directions. In consequence of this precaution, no means offered by which March could put his designs in execution.

Disappointed in his vengeance, Hurry seated himself, and like Hutter, for half an hour, he was too much occupied in endeavoring to restore the circulation, and in regaining the use of his limbs, to indulge in any other reflections. By the end of this time the raft had disappeared, and night was beginning to throw her shadows once more over the whole sylvan scene. Before darkness had completely set in, and while the girls were preparing the evening meal, Deerslayer related to Hutter an outline of events that had taken place, and gave him a history of the means he had adopted for the security of his children and property.

CHAPTER XV.

"As long as Edwarde rules thys lande,
  Ne quiet you wylle ye know;
Your sonnes and husbandes shall be slayne,
  And brookes with bloode shall 'flowe.'

"You leave youre geode and lawfulle kynge,
  Whenne ynne adversity;
Like me, untoe the true cause stycke,
  And for the true cause dye."

Chatterton.

The calm of evening was again in singular contrast, while its gathering gloom was in as singular unison with the passions of men. The sun was set, and the rays of the retiring luminary had ceased to gild the edges of the few clouds that had sufficient openings to admit the passage of its fading light. The canopy overhead was heavy and dense, promising another night of darkness, but the surface of the lake was scarcely disturbed by a ripple. There was a little air, though it scarce deserved to be termed wind. Still, being damp and heavy, it had a certain force. The party in the castle were as gloomy and silent as the scene. The two ransomed prisoners felt humbled and discoloured, but their humility partook of the rancour of revenge. They were far more disposed to remember the indignity with which they had been treated during the last few hours of their captivity, than to feel grateful for the previous indulgence. Then that keen-sighted monitor, conscience, by reminding them of the retributive justice of all they had endured, goaded them rather to turn the tables on their enemies than to accuse themselves. As for the others, they were thoughtful equally from regret and joy. Deerslayer and Judith felt most of the former sensation, though from very different causes, while Hetty for the moment was perfectly happy. The Delaware had also lively pictures of felicity in the prospect of so soon regaining his betrothed. Under such circumstances, and in this mood, all were taking the evening meal.

"Old Tom!" cried Hurry, bursting into a fit of boisterous laughter, "you look'd amazin'ly like a tethered bear, as you was stretched on them hemlock boughs, and I only wonder you didn't growl more. Well, it's over, and syth's and lamentations won't mend the matter! There's the blackguard Rivenoak, he that brought us off has an oncommon scalp, and I'd give as much for it myself as the Colony. Yes, I feel as rich as the governor in these matters now, and will lay down with them doubloon for doubloon. Judith, darling, did you mourn for me much, when I was in the hands of the Philipsteins?"

The last were a family of German descent on the Mohawk, to whom Hurry had a great antipathy, and whom he had confounded with the enemies of Judea.

"Our tears have raised the lake, Hurry March, as you might have seen by the shore!" returned Judith, with a feigned levity that she was far from feeling. "That Hetty and I should have grieved for father was to be expected; but we fairly rained tears for you."

"We were sorry for poor Hurry, as well as for father, Judith!" put in her innocent and unconscious sister.

"True, girl, true; but we feel sorrow for everybody that's in trouble, you know," returned the other in a quick, admonitory manner and a low tone. "Nevertheless, we are glad to see you, Master March, and out of the hands of the Philipsteins, too."

"Yes, they're a bad set, and so is the other brood of 'em, down on the river. It's a wonderment to me how you got us off, Deerslayer; and I forgive you the interference that prevented my doin' justice on that vagabond, for this small service. Let us into the secret, that we may do you the same good turn, at need. Was it by lying, or by coaxing?"

"By neither, Hurry, but by buying. We paid a ransom for you both, and that, too, at a price so high you had well be on your guard ag'in another captyvement, lest our stock of goods shouldn't hold out."

"A ransom! Old Tom has paid the fiddler, then, for nothing of mine would have bought off the hair, much less the skin. I didn't think men as keen set as them vagabonds would let a fellow up so easy, when they had him fairly at a close hug, and floored. But money is money, and somehow it's unnat'ral hard to withstand. Indian or white man, 'tis pretty much the same. It must be owned, Judith, there's a considerable of human natur' in mankind ginirally, arter all!"

Hutter now rose, and signing to Deerslayer, he led him to an inner room, where, in answer to his questions, he first learned the price that had been paid for his release. The old man expressed neither resentment nor surprise at the inroad that had been made on his chest, though he did manifest some curiosity to know how far the investigation of its contents had been carried. He also inquired where the key had been found. The habitual frankness of Deerslayer prevented any prevarication, and the conference soon terminated by the return of the two to the outer room, or that which served for the double purpose of parlour and kitchen.

"I wonder if it's peace or war, between us and the savages!" exclaimed Hurry, just as Deerslayer, who had paused for a single instant, listened attentively, and was passing through the outer door without stopping. "This givin' up captives has a friendly look, and when men have traded together on a fair and honourable footing they ought to part fri'nds, for that occasion at least. Come back, Deerslayer, and let us have your judgment, for I'm beginnin' to think more of you, since your late behaviour, than I used to do."

"There's an answer to your question, Hurry, since you're in such haste to come ag'in to blows."

As Deerslayer spoke, he threw on the table on which the other was reclining with one elbow a sort of miniature fagot, composed of a dozen sticks bound tightly together with a deer-skin thong. March seized it eagerly, and holding it close to a blazing knot of pine that lay on the hearth, and which gave out all the light there was in the room, ascertained that the ends of the several sticks had been dipped in blood.

"If this isn't plain English," said the reckless frontier man, "it's plain Indian! Here's what they call a dicliration of war, down at York, Judith. How did you come by this defiance, Deerslayer?"

"Fairly enough. It lay not a minut' since, in what you call Floatin' Tom's door-yard."

"How came it there?"

"It never fell from the clouds, Judith, as little toads sometimes do, and then it don't rain."

"You must prove where it come from, Deerslayer, or we shall suspect some design to skear them that would have lost their wits long ago, if fear could drive 'em away."

Deerslayer had approached a window, and cast a glance out of it on the dark aspect of the lake. As if satisfied with what he beheld, he drew near Hurry, and took the bundle of sticks into his own hand, examining it attentively.

"Yes, this is an Indian declaration of war, sure enough," he said, "and it's a proof how little you're suited to be on the path it has travelled, Harry March, that it has got here, and you never the wiser as to the means. The savages may have left the scalp on your head, but they must have taken off the ears; else you'd have heard the stirring of the water made by the lad as he come off ag'in on his two logs. His ar'n'd was to throw these sticks at our door, as much as to say, we've struck the war-post since the trade, and the next thing will be to strike you."

"The prowling wolves! But hand me that rifle, Judith, and I'll send an answer back to the vagabonds through their messenger."

"Not while I stand by, Master March," coolly put in Deerslayer, motioning for the other to forbear. "Faith is faith, whether given to a red-skin, or to a Christian. The lad lighted a knot, and came off fairly under its blaze to give us this warning; and no man here should harm him, while empl'yed on such an ar'n'd. There's no use in words, for the boy is too cunning to leave the knot burning, now his business is done, and the night is already too dark for a rifle to have any sartainty."

"That may be true enough, as to a gun, but there's virtue still in a canoe," answered Hurry, passing towards the door with enormous strides, carrying a rifle in his hands. "The being doesn't live that shall stop me from following and bringing back that riptyle's scalp. The more on 'em that you crush in the egg, the fewer there'll be to dart at you in the woods!"

Judith trembled like the aspen, she scarce knew why herself, though there was the prospect of a scene of violence; for if Hurry was fierce and overbearing in the consciousness of his vast strength, Deerslayer had about him the calm determination that promises greater perseverance, and a resolution more likely to effect its object. It was the stern, resolute eye of the latter, rather than the noisy vehemence of the first, that excited her apprehensions. Hurry soon reached the spot where the canoe was fastened, but not before Deerslayer had spoken in a quick, earnest voice to the Serpent, in Delaware. The latter had been the first, in truth, to hear the sounds of the oars, and he had gone upon the platform in jealous watchfulness. The light satisfied him that a message was coming, and when the boy cast his bundle of sticks at his feet, it neither moved his anger nor induced surprise. He merely stood at watch, rifle in hand, to make certain that no treachery lay behind the defiance. As Deerslayer now called to him, he stepped into the canoe, and quick as thought removed the paddles. Hurry was furious when he found that he was deprived of the means of proceeding. He first approached the Indian with loud menaces, and even Deerslayer stood aghast at the probable consequences. March shook his sledge-hammer fists and flourished his arms as he drew near the Indian, and all expected he would attempt to fell the Delaware to the earth; one of them, at least, was well aware that such an experiment would be followed by immediate bloodshed. But even Hurry was awed by the stern composure of the chief, and he, too, knew that such a man was not to be outraged with impunity; he therefore turned to vent his rage on Deerslayer, where he foresaw no consequences so terrible. What might have been the result of this second demonstration if completed, is unknown, since it was never made.

"Hurry," said a gentle, soothing voice at his elbow, "it's wicked to be so angry, and God will not overlook it. The Iroquois treated you well, and they didn't take your scalp, though you and father wanted to take theirs."

The influence of mildness on passion is well known. Hetty, too, had earned a sort of consideration, that had never before been enjoyed by her, through the self-devotion and decision of her recent conduct. Perhaps her established mental imbecility, by removing all distrust of a wish to control, aided her influence. Let the cause be as questionable as it might, the effect we sufficiently certain. Instead of throttling his old fellow-traveler, Hurry turned to the girl and poured out a portion of his discontent, if none of his anger, in her attentive ears.

"Tis too bad, Hetty!" he exclaimed; "as bad as a county gaol or a lack of beaver, to get a creatur' into your very trap, then to see it get off. As much as six first quality skins, in valie, has paddled off on them clumsy logs, when twenty strokes of a well-turned paddle would overtake 'em. I say in valie, for as to the boy in the way of natur', he is only a boy, and is worth neither more nor less than one. Deerslayer, you've been ontrue to your fri'nds in letting such a chance slip through my fingers well as your own."

The answer was given quietly, but with a voice as steady as a fearless nature and the consciousness of rectitude could make it. "I should have been untrue to the right, had I done otherwise," returned the Deerslayer, steadily; "and neither you, nor any other man has authority to demand that much of me. The lad came on a lawful business, and the meanest red-skin that roams the woods would be ashamed of not respecting his ar'n'd. But he's now far beyond your reach, Master March, and there's little use in talking, like a couple of women, of what can no longer be helped."

So saying, Deerslayer turned away, like one resolved to waste no more words on the subject, while Hutter pulled Harry by the sleeve, and led him into the ark. There they sat long in private conference. In the mean time, the Indian and his friend had their secret consultation; for, though it wanted some three or four hours to the rising of the star, the former could not abstain from canvassing his scheme, and from opening his heart to the other. Judith, too, yielded to her softer feelings, and listened to the whole of Hetty's artless narrative of what occurred after she landed. The woods had few terrors for either of these girls, educated as they had been, and accustomed as they were to look out daily at their rich expanse or to wander beneath their dark shades; but the elder sister felt that she would have hesitated about thus venturing alone into an Iroquois camp. Concerning Hist, Hetty was not very communicative. She spoke of her kindness and gentleness and of the meeting in the forest; but the secret of Chingachgook was guarded with a shrewdness and fidelity that many a sharper-witted girl might have failed to display.

At length the several conferences were broken up by the reappearance of Hutter on the platform. Here he assembled the whole party, and communicated as much of his intentions as he deemed expedient. Of the arrangement made by Deerslayer, to abandon the castle during the night and to take refuge in the ark, he entirely approved. It struck him as it had the others, as the only effectual means of escaping destruction. Now that the savages had turned their attention to the construction of rafts, no doubt could exist of their at least making an attempt to carry the building, and the message of the bloody sticks sufficiently showed their confidence in their own success. In short, the old man viewed the night as critical, and he called on all to get ready as soon as possible, in order to abandon the dwellings temporarily at least, if not forever.

These communications made, everything proceeded promptly and with intelligence; the castle was secured in the manner already described, the canoes were withdrawn from the dock and fastened to the ark by the side of the other; the few necessaries that had been left in the house were transferred to the cabin, the fire was extinguished and all embarked.

The vicinity of the hills, with their drapery of pines, had the effect to render nights that were obscure darker than common on the lake. As usual, however, a belt of comparative light was etched through the centre of the sheet, while it was within the shadows of the mountains that the gloom rested most heavily on the water. The island, or castle, stood in this belt of comparative light, but still the night was so dark as to cover the aperture of the ark. At the distance of an observer on the shore her movements could not be seen at all, more particularly as a background of dark hillside filled up the perspective of every view that was taken diagonally or directly across the water. The prevailing wind on the lakes of that region is west, but owing to the avenues formed by the mountains it is frequently impossible to tell the true direction of the currents, as they often vary within short distances and brief differences of time. This is truer in light fluctuating puffs of air than in steady breezes; though the squalls of even the latter are familiarly known to be uncertain and baffling in all mountainous regions and narrow waters. On the present occasion, Hutter himself (as he shoved the ark from her berth at the side of the platform) was at a loss to pronounce which way the wind blew. In common, this difficulty was solved by the clouds, which, floating high above the hill tops, as a matter of course obeyed the currents; but now the whole vault of heaven seemed a mass of gloomy wall. Not an opening of any sort was visible, and Chingachgook was already trembling lest the non-appearance of the star might prevent his betrothed from being punctual to her appointment. Under these circumstances, Hutter hoisted his sail, seemingly with the sole intention of getting away from the castle, as it might be dangerous to remain much longer in its vicinity. The air soon filled the cloth, and when the scow was got under command, and the sail was properly trimmed, it was found that the direction was southerly, inclining towards the eastern shore. No better course offering for the purposes of the party, the singular craft was suffered to skim the surface of the water in this direction for more than hour, when a change in the currents of the air drove them over towards the camp.

Deerslayer watched all the movements of Hutter and Harry with jealous attention. At first, he did not know whether to ascribe the course they held to accident or to design; but he now began to suspect the latter. Familiar as Hutter was with the lake, it was easy to deceive one who had little practice on the water; and let his intentions be what they might, it was evident, ere two hours had elapsed, that the ark had got sufficient space to be within a hundred rods of the shore, directly abreast of the known position of the camp. For a considerable time previously to reaching this point, Hurry, who had some knowledge of the Algonquin language, had been in close conference with the Indian, and the result was now announced by the latter to Deerslayer, who had been a cold, not to say distrusted, looker-on of all that passed.

"My old father, and my young brother, the Big Pine,"—for so the Delaware had named March—"want to see Huron scalps at their belts," said Chingachgook to his friend. "There is room for some on the girdle of the Sarpent, and his people will look for them when he goes back to his village. Their eyes must not be left long in a fog, but they must see what they look for. I know that my brother has a white hand; he will not strike even the dead. He will wait for us; when we come back, he will not hide his face from shame for his friend. The great Serpent of the Mohicans must be worthy to go on the war-path with Hawkeye."

"Ay, ay, Sarpent, I see how it is; that name's to stick, and in time I shall get to be known by it instead of Deerslayer; well, if such honours will come, the humblest of us all must be willing to abide by 'em. As for your looking for scalps, it belongs to your gifts, and I see no harm in it. Be marciful, Sarpent, howsever; be marciful, I beseech of you. It surely can do no harm to a red-skin's honour to show a little marcy. As for the old man, the father of two young women, who might ripen better feelin's in his heart, and Harry March, here, who, pine as he is, might better bear the fruit of a more Christianized tree, as for them two, I leave them in the hands of the white man's God. Wasn't it for the bloody sticks, no man should go ag'in the Mingos this night, seein' that it would dishonor our faith and characters; but them that crave blood can't complain if blood is shed at their call. Still, Sarpent, you can be marciful. Don't begin your career with the wails of women and the cries of children. Bear yourself so that Hist will smile, and not weep, when she meets you. Go, then; and the Manitou presarve you!"

"My brother will stay here with the scow. Wah will soon be standing on the shore waiting, and Chingachgook must hasten."

The Indian then joined his two co-adventurers, and first lowering the sail, they all three entered the canoe, and left the side of the ark. Neither Hutter nor March spoke to Deerslayer concerning their object, or the probable length of their absence. All this had been confided to the Indian, who had acquitted himself of the trust with characteristic brevity. As soon as the canoe was out of sight, and that occurred ere the paddles had given a dozen strokes, Deerslayer made the best dispositions he could to keep the ark as nearly stationary as possible; and then he sat down in the end of the scow, to chew the cud of his own bitter reflections. It was not long, however, before he was joined by Judith, who sought every occasion to be near him, managing her attack on his affections with the address that was suggested by native coquetry, aided by no little practice, but which received much of its most dangerous power from the touch of feeling that threw around her manner, voice, accents, thoughts, and acts, the indescribable witchery of natural tenderness. Leaving the young hunter exposed to these dangerous assailants, it has become our more immediate business to follow the party in the canoe to the shore.

The controlling influence that led Hutter and Hurry to repeat their experiment against the camp was precisely that which had induced the first attempt, a little heightened, perhaps, by the desire of revenge. But neither of these two rude beings, so ruthless in all things that touched the rights and interests of the red man, thought possessing veins of human feeling on other matters, was much actuated by any other desire than a heartless longing for profit. Hurry had felt angered at his sufferings, when first liberated, it is true, but that emotion soon disappeared in the habitual love of gold, which he sought with the reckless avidity of a needy spendthrift, rather than with the ceaseless longings of a miser. In short, the motive that urged them both so soon to go against the Hurons, was an habitual contempt of their enemy, acting on the unceasing cupidity of prodigality. The additional chances of success, however, had their place in the formation of the second enterprise. It was known that a large portion of the warriors—perhaps all—were encamped for the night abreast of the castle, and it was hoped that the scalps of helpless victims would be the consequence. To confess the truth, Hutter in particular—he who had just left two daughters behind him—expected to find few besides women and children in the camp. The fact had been but slightly alluded to in his communications with Hurry, and with Chingachgook it had been kept entirely out of view. If the Indian thought of it at all, it was known only to himself.

Hutter steered the canoe; Hurry had manfully taken his post in the bows, and Chingachgook stood in the centre. We say stood, for all three were so skilled in the management of that species of frail bark, as to be able to keep erect positions in the midst of the darkness. The approach to the shore was made with great caution, and the landing effected in safety. The three now prepared their arms, and began their tiger-like approach upon the camp. The Indian was on the lead, his two companions treading in his footsteps with a stealthy cautiousness of manner that rendered their progress almost literally noiseless. Occasionally a dried twig snapped under the heavy weight of the gigantic Hurry, or the blundering clumsiness of the old man; but, had the Indian walked on air, his step could not have seemed lighter. The great object was first to discover the position of the fire, which was known to be the centre of the whole encampment. At length the keen eye of Chingachgook caught a glimpse of this important guide. It was glimmering at a distance among the trunks of trees. There was no blaze, but merely a single smouldering brand, as suited the hour; the savages usually retiring and rising with the revolutions of the sun.

As soon as a view was obtained of this beacon, the progress of the adventurers became swifter and more certain. In a few minutes they got to the edge of the circle of little huts. Here they stopped to survey their ground, and to concert their movements. The darkness was so deep as to render it difficult to distinguish anything but the glowing brand, the trunks of the nearest trees, and the endless canopy of leaves that veiled the clouded heaven. It was ascertained, however, that a hut was quite near, and Chingachgook attempted to reconnnoitre its interior. The manner in which the Indian approached the place that was supposed to contain enemies, resembled the wily advances of the cat on the bird. As he drew near, he stooped to his hands and knees, for the entrance was so low as to require this attitude, even as a convenience. Before trusting his head inside, however, he listened long to catch the breathing of sleepers. No sound was audible, and this human Serpent thrust his head in at the door, or opening, as another serpent would have peered in on the nest. Nothing rewarded the hazardous experiment; for, after feeling cautiously with a hand, the place was found to be empty.

The Delaware proceeded in the same guarded manner to one or two more of the huts, finding all in the same situation. He then returned to his companions, and informed them that the Hurons had deserted their camp. A little further inquiry corroborated this fact, and it only remained to return to the canoe. The different manner in which the adventurers bore the disappointment is worthy of a passing remark. The chief, who had landed solely with the hope of acquiring renown, stood stationary, leaning against a tree, waiting the pleasure of his companions. He was mortified, and a little surprised, it is true; but he bore all with dignity, falling back for support on the sweeter expectations that still lay in reserve for that evening. It was true, he could not now hope to meet his mistress with the proofs of his daring and skill on his person, but he might still hope to meet her; and the warrior, who was zealous in the search, might always hope to be honored. On the other hand,

Hutter and Hurry, who had been chiefly instigated by the basest of all human motives, the thirst of gain, could scarce control their feelings. They went prowling among the huts, as if they expected to find some forgotten child or careless sleeper; and again and again did they vent their spite on the insensible huts, several of which were actually torn to pieces, and scattered about the place. Nay, they even quarrelled with each other, and fierce reproaches passed between them. It is possible some serious consequences might have occurred, had not the Delaware interfered to remind them of the danger of being so unguarded, and of the necessity of returning to the ark. This checked the dispute, and in a few minutes they were paddling sullenly back to the spot where they hoped to find that vessel.

It has been said that Judith took her place at the side of Deerslayer, soon after the adventurers departed. For a short time the girl was silent, and the hunter was ignorant which of the sisters had approached him, but he soon recognized the rich, full-spirited voice of the elder, as her feelings escaped in words.

"This is a terrible life for women, Deerslayer!" she exclaimed. "Would to Heaven I could see an end of it!"

"The life is well enough, Judith," was the answer, "being pretty much as it is used or abused. What would you wish to see in its place?"

"I should be a thousand times happier to live nearer to civilized beings—where there are farms and churches, and houses built as it might be by Christian hands; and where my sleep at night would be sweet and tranquil! A dwelling near one of the forts would be far better than this dreary place where we live!"

"Nay, Judith, I can't agree too lightly in the truth of all this. If forts are good to keep off inimies, they sometimes hold inimies of their own. I don't think 'twould be for your good, or the good of Hetty, to live near one; and if I must say what I think, I'm afeard you are a little too near as it is." Deerslayer went on, in his own steady, earnest manner, for the darkness concealed the tints that colored the cheeks of the girl almost to the brightness of crimson, while her own great efforts suppressed the sounds of the breathing that nearly choked her. "As for farms, they have their uses, and there's them that like to pass their lives on 'em; but what comfort can a man look for in a clearin', that he can't find in double quantities in the forest? If air, and room, and light, are a little craved, the windrows and the streams will furnish 'em, or here are the lakes for such as have bigger longings in that way; but where are you to find your shades, and laughing springs, and leaping brooks, and vinerable trees, a thousand years old, in a clearin'? You don't find them, but you find their disabled trunks, marking the 'arth like headstones in a graveyard. It seems to me that the people who live in such places must be always thinkin' of their own inds, and of universal decay; and that, too, not of the decay that is brought about by time and natur', but the decay that follows waste and violence. Then as to churches, they are good, I suppose, else wouldn't good men uphold 'em. But they are not altogether necessary. They call 'em the temples of the Lord; but, Judith, the whole 'arth is a temple of the Lord to such as have the right mind. Neither forts nor churches make people happier of themselves. Moreover, all is contradiction in the settlements, while all is concord in the woods. Forts and churches almost always go together, and yet they're downright contradictions; churches being for peace, and forts for war. No, no—give me the strong places of the wilderness, which is the trees, and the churches, too, which are arbors raised by the hand of natur'."

"Woman is not made for scenes like these, Deerslayer, scenes of which we shall have no end, as long as this war lasts."

"If you mean women of white colour, I rather think you're not far from the truth, gal; but as for the females of the redmen, such visitations are quite in character. Nothing would make Hist, now, the bargained wife of yonder Delaware, happier than to know that he is at this moment prowling around his nat'ral inimies, striving after a scalp."

"Surely, surely, Deerslayer, she cannot be a woman, and not feel concern when she thinks the man she loves is in danger!"

"She doesn't think of the danger, Judith, but of the honor; and when the heart is desperately set on such feelin's, why, there is little room to crowd in fear. Hist is a kind, gentle, laughing, pleasant creatur', but she loves honor, as well as any Delaware gal I ever know'd. She's to meet the Sarpent an hour hence, on the p'int where Hetty landed, and no doubt she has her anxiety about it, like any other woman; but she'd be all the happier did she know that her lover was at this moment waylaying a Mingo for his scalp."

"If you really believe this, Deerslayer, no wonder you lay so much stress on gifts. Certain am I, that no white girl could feel anything but misery while she believed her betrothed in danger of his life! Nor do I suppose even you, unmoved and calm as you ever seem to be, could be at peace if you believed your Hist in danger."

"That's a different matter— 'tis altogether a different matter, Judith. Woman is too weak and gentle to be intended to run such risks, and man must feel for her. Yes, I rather think that's as much red natur' as it's white. But I have no Hist, nor am I like to have; for I hold it wrong to mix colours, any way except in friendship and sarvices."

"In that you are and feel as a white man should! As for Hurry Harry, I do think it would be all the same to him whether his wife were a squaw or a governor's daughter, provided she was a little comely, and could help to keep his craving stomach full."

"You do March injustice, Judith; yes, you do. The poor fellow dotes on you, and when a man has ra'ally set his heart on such a creatur' it isn't a Mingo, or even a Delaware gal, that'll be likely to unsettle his mind. You may laugh at such men as Hurry and I, for we're rough and unteached in the ways of books and other knowledge; but we've our good p'ints, as well as our bad ones. An honest heart is not to be despised, gal, even though it be not varsed in all the niceties that please the female fancy."

"You, Deerslayer! And do you—can you, for an instant, suppose I place you by the side of Harry March? No, no, I am not so far gone in dullness as that. No one—man or woman—could think of naming your honest heart, manly nature, and simple truth, with the boisterous selfishness, greedy avarice, and overbearing ferocity of Harry March. The very best that can be said of him, is to be found in his name of Hurry Skurry, which, if it means no great harm, means no great good. Even my father, following his feelings with the other, as he is doing at this moment, well knows the difference between you. This I know, for he said as much to me, in plain language."

Judith was a girl of quick sensibilities and of impetuous feelings; and, being under few of the restraints that curtail the manifestations of maiden emotions among those who are educated in the habits of civilized life, she sometimes betrayed the latter with a feeling that was so purely natural as to place it as far above the wiles of coquetry as it was superior to its heartlessness. She had now even taken one of the hard hands of the hunter and pressed it between both her own, with a warmth and earnestness that proved how sincere was her language. It was perhaps fortunate that she was checked by the very excess of her feelings, since the same power might have urged her on to avow all that her father had said—the old man not having been satisfied with making a comparison favorable to Deerslayer, as between the hunter and Hurry, but having actually, in his blunt rough way, briefly advised his daughter to cast off the latter entirely, and to think of the former as a husband. Judith would not willingly have said this to any other man, but there was so much confidence awakened by the guileless simplicity of Deerslayer, that one of her nature found it a constant temptation to overstep the bounds of habit. She went no further, however, immediately relinquishing the hand, and falling back on a reserve that was more suited to her sex, and, indeed, to her natural modesty.

"Thankee, Judith, thankee with all my heart," returned the hunter, whose humility prevented him from placing any flattering interpretation on either the conduct or the language of the girl. "Thankee as much as if it was all true. Harry's sightly—yes, he's as sightly as the tallest pine of the mountains, and the Sarpent has named him accordingly; however, some fancy good looks, and some fancy good conduct, only. Hurry has one advantage, and it depends on himself whether he'll have t'other or— Hark! That's your father's voice, gal, and he speaks like a man who's riled at something."

"God save us from any more of these horrible scenes!" exclaimed Judith, bending her face to her knees, and endeavoring to exclude the discordant sounds, by applying her hands to her ears. "I sometimes wish I had no father!"

This was bitterly said, and the repinings which extorted the words were bitterly felt. It is impossible to say what might next have escaped her had not a gentle, low voice spoken at her elbow.

"Judith, I ought to have read a chapter to father and Hurry!" said the innocent but terrified speaker, "and that would have kept them from going again on such an errand. Do you call to them, Deerslayer, and tell them I want them, and that it will be good for them both if they'll return and hearken to my words."

"Ah's me! Poor Hetty, you little know the cravin's for gold and revenge, if you believe they are so easily turned aside from their longin's! But this is an uncommon business in more ways than one, Judith. I hear your father and Hurry growling like bears, and yet no noise comes from the mouth of the young chief. There's an ind of secrecy, and yet his whoop, which ought to ring in the mountains, accordin' to rule in such sarcumstances, is silent!"

"Justice may have alighted on him, and his death have saved the lives of the innocent."

"Not it—not it—the Sarpent is not the one to suffer if that's to be the law. Sartainly there has been no onset, and 'tis most likely that the camp's deserted, and the men are comin' back disapp'inted. That accounts for the growls of Hurry and the silence of the Sarpent."

Just at this instant a fall of a paddle was heard in the canoe, for vexation made March reckless. Deerslayer felt convinced that his conjecture was true. The sail being down, the ark had not drifted far; and ere many minutes he heard Chingachgook, in a low, quiet tone, directing Hutter how to steer in order to reach it. In less time than it takes to tell the fact, the canoe touched the scow, and the adventurers entered the latter. Neither Hutter nor Hurry spoke of what had occurred. But the Delaware, in passing his friend, merely uttered the words "fire's out," which, if not literally true, sufficiently explained the truth to his listener.

It was now a question as to the course to be steered. A short surly conference was held, when Hutter decided that the wisest way would be to keep in motion as the means most likely to defeat any attempt at a surprise—announcing his own and March's intention to requite themselves for the loss of sleep during their captivity, by lying down. As the air still baffled and continued light, it was finally determined to sail before it, let it come in what direction it might, so long as it did not blow the ark upon the strand. This point settled, the released prisoners helped to hoist the sail, and they threw themselves upon two of the pallets, leaving Deerslayer and his friend to look after the movements of the craft. As neither of the latter was disposed to sleep, on account of the appointment with Hist, this arrangement was acceptable to all parties. That Judith and Hetty remained up also, in no manner impaired the agreeable features of this change.

For some time the scow rather drifted than sailed along the western shore, following a light southerly current of the air. The progress was slow—not exceeding a couple of miles in the hour—but the two men perceived that it was not only carrying them towards the point they desired to reach, but at a rate that was quite as fast as the hour yet rendered necessary. But little more was said the while even by the girls; and that little had more reference to the rescue of Hist than to any other subject. The Indian was calm to the eye, but as minute after minute passed, his feelings became more and more excited, until they reached a state that might have satisfied the demands of even the most exacting mistress. Deerslayer kept the craft as much in the bays as was prudent, for the double purpose of sailing within the shadows of the woods, and of detecting any signs of an encampment they might pass on the shore. In this manner they doubled one low point, and were already in the bay that was terminated north by the goal at which they aimed. The latter was still a quarter of a mile distant, when Chingachgook came silently to the side of his friend and pointed to a place directly ahead. A small fire was glimmering just within the verge of the bushes that lined the shore on the southern side of the point—leaving no doubt that the Indians had suddenly removed their camp to the very place, or at least the very projection of land where Hist had given them the rendezvous!

CHAPTER XVI

"I hear thee babbling to the vale
Of sunshine and of flowers,
But unto me thou bring'st a tale
Of visionary hours."

Wordsworth.

One discovery mentioned at the close of the preceding chapter was of great moment in the eyes of Deerslayer and his friend. In the first place, there was the danger, almost the certainty, that Hutter and Hurry would make a fresh attempt on this camp, should they awake and ascertain its position. Then there was the increased risk of landing to bring off Hist; and there were the general uncertainty and additional hazards that must follow from the circumstance that their enemies had begun to change their positions. As the Delaware was aware that the hour was near when he ought to repair to the rendezvous, he no longer thought of trophies torn from his foes, and one of the first things arranged between him and his associate was to permit the two others to sleep on, lest they should disturb the execution of their plans by substituting some of their own. The ark moved slowly, and it would have taken fully a quarter of an hour to reach the point, at the rate at which they were going, thus affording time for a little forethought. The Indians, in the wish to conceal their fire from those who were thought to be still in the castle, had placed it so near the southern side of the point as to render it extremely difficult to shut it in by the bushes, though Deerslayer varied the direction of the scow both to the right and to the left, in the hope of being able to effect that object.

"There's one advantage, Judith, in finding that fire so near the water," he said, while executing these little manoeuvres, "since it shows the Mingos believe we are in the hut, and our coming on 'em from this quarter will be an unlooked for event. But it's lucky Harry March and your father are asleep, else we should have 'em prowling after scalps ag'in. Ha! there—the bushes are beginning to shut in the fire—and now it can't be seen at all!"

Deerslayer waited a little to make certain that he had at last gained the desired position, when he gave the signal agreed on, and Chingachgook let go the grapnel and lowered the sail.

The situation in which the ark now lay had its advantages and its disadvantages. The fire had been hid by sheering towards the shore, and the latter was nearer, perhaps, than was desirable. Still, the water was known to be very deep further off in the lake, and anchoring in deep water, under the circumstances in which the party was placed, was to be avoided, if possible. It was also believed no raft could be within miles; and though the trees in the darkness appeared almost to overhang the scow, it would not be easy to get off to her without using a boat. The intense darkness that prevailed so close in with the forest, too, served as an effectual screen, and so long as care was had not to make a noise, there was little or no danger of being detected. All these things Deerslayer pointed out to Judith, instructing her as to the course she was to follow in the event of an alarm; for it was thought to the last degree inexpedient to arouse the sleepers, unless it might be in the greatest emergency.

"And now, Judith, as we understand one another, it is time the Sarpent and I had taken to the canoe," the hunter concluded. "The star has not risen yet, it's true, but it soon must, though none of us are likely to be any the wiser for it to-night, on account of the clouds. Howsever, Hist has a ready mind, and she's one of them that doesn't always need to have a thing afore her, to see it. I'll warrant you she'll not be either two minutes or two feet out of the way, unless them jealous vagabonds, the Mingos, have taken the alarm, and put her as a stool-pigeon to catch us, or have hid her away, in order to prepare her mind for a Huron instead of a Mohican husband."

"Deerslayer," interrupted the girl, earnestly; "this is a most dangerous service; why do you go on it, at all?"

"Anan!—Why you know, gal, we go to bring off Hist, the Sarpent's betrothed—the maid he means to marry, as soon as we get back to the tribe."

"That is all right for the Indian—but you do not mean to marry Hist—you are not betrothed, and why should two risk their lives and liberties, to do that which one can just as well perform?"

"Ah—now I understand you, Judith—yes, now I begin to take the idee. You think as Hist is the Sarpent's betrothed, as they call it, and not mine, it's altogether his affair; and as one man can paddle a canoe he ought to be left to go after his gal alone! But you forget this is our ar'n'd here on the lake, and it would not tell well to forget an ar'n'd just as the pinch came. Then, if love does count for so much with some people, particularly with young women, fri'ndship counts for something, too, with other some. I dares to say, the Delaware can paddle a canoe by himself, and can bring off Hist by himself, and perhaps he would like that quite as well, as to have me with him; but he couldn't sarcumvent sarcumventions, or stir up an ambushment, or fight with the savages, and get his sweetheart at the same time, as well by himself as if he had a fri'nd with him to depend on, even if that fri'nd is no better than myself. No—no—Judith, you wouldn't desert one that counted on you, at such a moment, and you can't, in reason, expect me to do it."

"I fear—I believe you are right, Deerslayer, and yet I wish you were not to go! Promise me one thing, at least, and that is, not to trust yourself among the savages, or to do anything more than to save the girl. That will be enough for once, and with that you ought to be satisfied."

"Lord bless you! gal; one would think it was Hetty that's talking, and not the quick-witted and wonderful Judith Hutter! But fright makes the wise silly, and the strong weak. Yes, I've seen proofs of that, time and ag'in! Well, it's kind and softhearted in you, Judith, to feel this consarn for a fellow creatur', and I shall always say that you are kind and of true feelings, let them that envy your good looks tell as many idle stories of you as they may."

"Deerslayer!" hastily said the girl, interrupting him, though nearly choked by her own emotions; "do you believe all you hear about a poor, motherless girl? Is the foul tongue of Hurry Harry to blast my life?"

"Not it, Judith—not it. I've told Hurry it wasn't manful to backbite them he couldn't win by fair means; and that even an Indian is always tender, touching a young woman's good name."

"If I had a brother, he wouldn't dare to do it!" exclaimed Judith, with eyes flashing fire. "But, finding me without any protector but an old man, whose ears are getting to be as dull as his feelings, he has his way as he pleases!"

"Not exactly that, Judith; no, not exactly that, neither! No man, brother or stranger, would stand by and see as fair a gal as yourself hunted down, without saying a word in her behalf. Hurry's in 'arnest in wanting to make you his wife, and the little he does let out ag'in you, comes more from jealousy, like, than from any thing else. Smile on him when he awakes, and squeeze his hand only half as hard as you squeezed mine a bit ago, and my life on it, the poor fellow will forget every thing but your comeliness. Hot words don't always come from the heart, but oftener from the stomach than anywhere else. Try him, Judith, when he awakes, and see the virtue of a smile."

Deerslayer laughed, in his own manner, as he concluded, and then he intimated to the patient-looking, but really impatient Chingachgook, his readiness to proceed. As the young man entered the canoe, the girl stood immovable as stone, lost in the musings that the language and manner of the other were likely to produce. The simplicity of the hunter had completely put her at fault; for, in her narrow sphere, Judith was an expert manager of the other sex; though in the present instance she was far more actuated by impulses, in all she had said and done, than by calculation. We shall not deny that some of Judith's reflections were bitter, though the sequel of the tale must be referred to, in order to explain how merited, or how keen were her sufferings.

Chingachgook and his pale-face friend set forth on their hazardous and delicate enterprise, with a coolness and method that would have done credit to men who were on their twentieth, instead of being on their first, war-path. As suited his relation to the pretty fugitive, in whose service they were engaged, the Indian took his place in the head of the canoe; while Deerslayer guided its movements in the stern. By this arrangement, the former would be the first to land, and of course, the first to meet his mistress. The latter had taken his post without comment, but in secret influenced by the reflection that one who had so much at stake as the Indian, might not possibly guide the canoe with the same steadiness and intelligence, as another who had more command of his feelings. From the instant they left the side of the ark, the movements of the two adventurers were like the manoeuvres of highly-drilled soldiers, who, for the first time were called on to meet the enemy in the field. As yet, Chingachgook had never fired a shot in anger, and the debut of his companion in warfare is known to the reader. It is true, the Indian had been hanging about his enemy's camp for a few hours, on his first arrival, and he had even once entered it, as related in the last chapter, but no consequences had followed either experiment. Now, it was certain that an important result was to be effected, or a mortifying failure was to ensue. The rescue, or the continued captivity of Hist, depended on the enterprise. In a word, it was virtually the maiden expedition of these two ambitious young forest soldiers; and while one of them set forth impelled by sentiments that usually carry men so far, both had all their feelings of pride and manhood enlisted in their success.

Instead of steering in a direct line to the point, then distant from the ark less than a quarter of a mile, Deerslayer laid the head of his canoe diagonally towards the centre of the lake, with a view to obtain a position from which he might approach the shore, having his enemies in his front only. The spot where Hetty had landed, and where Hist had promised to meet them, moreover, was on the upper side of the projection rather than on the lower; and to reach it would have required the two adventurers to double nearly the whole point, close in with the shore, had not this preliminary step been taken. So well was the necessity for this measure understood, that Chingachgook quietly paddled on, although it was adopted without consulting him, and apparently was taking him in a direction nearly opposite to that one might think he most wished to go. A few minutes sufficed, however, to carry the canoe the necessary distance, when both the young men ceased paddling as it were by instinctive consent, and the boat became stationary. The darkness increased rather than diminished, but it was still possible, from the place where the adventurers lay, to distinguish the outlines of the mountains. In vain did the Delaware turn his head eastward, to catch a glimpse of the promised star; for, notwithstanding the clouds broke a little near the horizon in that quarter of the heavens, the curtain continued so far drawn as effectually to conceal all behind it. In front, as was known by the formation of land above and behind it, lay the point, at the distance of about a thousand feet. No signs of the castle could be seen, nor could any movement in that quarter of the lake reach the ear. The latter circumstance might have been equally owing to the distance, which was several miles, or to the fact that nothing was in motion. As for the ark, though scarcely farther from the canoe than the point, it lay so completely buried in the shadows of the shore, that it would not have been visible even had there been many degrees more of light than actually existed.

The adventurers now held a conference in low voices, consulting together as to the probable time. Deerslayer thought it wanted yet some minutes to the rising of the star, while the impatience of the chief caused him to fancy the night further advanced, and to believe that his betrothed was already waiting his appearance on the shore. As might have been expected, the opinion of the latter prevailed, and his friend disposed himself to steer for the place of rendezvous. The utmost skill and precaution now became necessary in the management of the canoe. The paddles were lifted and returned to the water in a noiseless manner; and when within a hundred yards of the beach, Chingachgook took in his, altogether laying his hand on his rifle in its stead. As they got still more within the belt of darkness that girded the woods, it was seen that they were steering too far north, and the course was altered accordingly. The canoe now seemed to move by instinct, so cautious and deliberate were all its motions. Still it continued to advance, until its bows grated on the gravel of the beach, at the precise spot where Hetty had landed, and whence her voice had issued, the previous night, as the ark was passing. There was, as usual, a narrow strand, but bushes fringed the woods, and in most places overhung the water.

Chingachgook stepped upon the beach, and cautiously examined it for some distance on each side of the canoe. In order to do this, he was often obliged to wade to his knees in the lake, but no Hist rewarded his search. When he returned, he found his friend also on the shore. They next conferred in whispers, the Indian apprehending that they must have mistaken the place of rendezvous. But Deerslayer thought it was probable they had mistaken the hour. While he was yet speaking, he grasped the arm of the Delaware, caused him to turn his head in the direction of the lake, and pointed towards the summits of the eastern mountains. The clouds had broken a little, apparently behind rather than above the hills, and the evening star was glittering among the branches of a pine. This was every way a flattering omen, and the young men leaned on their rifles, listening intently for the sound of approaching footsteps. Voices they often heard, and mingled with them were the suppressed cries of children, and the low but sweet laugh of Indian women. As the native Americans are habitually cautious, and seldom break out in loud conversation, the adventurers knew by these facts that they must be very near the encampment. It was easy to perceive that there was a fire within the woods, by the manner in which some of the upper branches of the trees were illuminated, but it was not possible, where they stood, to ascertain exactly how near it was to themselves. Once or twice, it seemed as if stragglers from around the fire were approaching the place of rendezvous; but these sounds were either altogether illusion, or those who had drawn near returned again without coming to the shore. A quarter of an hour was passed in this state of intense expectation and anxiety, when Deerslayer proposed that they should circle the point in the canoe; and by getting a position close in, where the camp could be seen, reconnoitre the Indians, and thus enable themselves to form some plausible conjectures for the non-appearance of Hist. The Delaware, however, resolutely refused to quit the spot, reasonably enough offering as a reason the disappointment of the girl, should she arrive in his absence. Deerslayer felt for his friend's concern, and offered to make the circuit of the point by himself, leaving the latter concealed in the bushes to await the occurrence of any fortunate event that might favour his views. With this understanding, then, the parties separated.

As soon as Deerslayer was at his post again, in the stern of the canoe, he left the shore with the same precautions, and in the same noiseless manner, as he had approached it. On this occasion he did not go far from the land, the bushes affording a sufficient cover, by keeping as close in as possible. Indeed, it would not have been easy to devise any means more favourable to reconnoitering round an Indian camp, than those afforded by the actual state of things. The formation of the point permitted the place to be circled on three of its sides, and the progress of the boat was so noiseless as to remove any apprehensions from an alarm through sound. The most practised and guarded foot might stir a bunch of leaves, or snap a dried stick in the dark, but a bark canoe could be made to float over the surface of smooth water, almost with the instinctive readiness, and certainly with the noiseless movements of an aquatic bird.

Deerslayer had got nearly in a line between the camp and the ark before he caught a glimpse of the fire. This came upon him suddenly, and a little unexpectedly, at first causing an alarm, lest he had incautiously ventured within the circle of light it cast. But perceiving at a second glance that he was certainly safe from detection, so long as the Indians kept near the centre of the illumination, he brought the canoe to a state of rest in the most favourable position he could find, and commenced his observations.

We have written much, but in vain, concerning this extraordinary being, if the reader requires now to be told, that, untutored as he was in the learning of the world, and simple as he ever showed himself to be in all matters touching the subtleties of conventional taste, he was a man of strong, native, poetical feeling. He loved the woods for their freshness, their sublime solitudes, their vastness, and the impress that they everywhere bore of the divine hand of their creator. He seldom moved through them, without pausing to dwell on some peculiar beauty that gave him pleasure, though seldom attempting to investigate the causes; and never did a day pass without his communing in spirit, and this, too, without the aid of forms or language, with the infinite source of all he saw, felt, and beheld. Thus constituted, in a moral sense, and of a steadiness that no danger could appall, or any crisis disturb, it is not surprising that the hunter felt a pleasure at looking on the scene he now beheld, that momentarily caused him to forget the object of his visit. This will more fully appear when we describe it.

The canoe lay in front of a natural vista, not only through the bushes that lined the shore, but of the trees also, that afforded a clear view of the camp. It was by means of this same opening that the light had been first seen from the ark. In consequence of their recent change of ground, the Indians had not yet retired to their huts, but had been delayed by their preparations, which included lodging as well as food. A large fire had been made, as much to answer the purpose of torches as for the use of their simple cookery; and at this precise moment it was blazing high and bright, having recently received a large supply of dried brush. The effect was to illuminate the arches of the forest, and to render the whole area occupied by the camp as light as if hundreds of tapers were burning. Most of the toil had ceased, and even the hungriest child had satisfied its appetite. In a word, the time was that moment of relaxation and general indolence which is apt to succeed a hearty meal, and when the labours of the day have ended. The hunters and the fishermen had been totally successful; and food, that one great requisite of savage life, being abundant, every other care appeared to have subsided in the sense of enjoyment dependent on this all-important fact.

Deerslayer saw at a glance that many of the warriors were absent. His acquaintance Rivenoak, however, was present, being seated in the foreground of a picture that Salvator Rosa would have delighted to draw, his swarthy features illuminated as much by pleasure as by the torchlike flame, while he showed another of the tribe one of the elephants that had caused so much sensation among his people. A boy was looking over his shoulder, in dull curiosity, completing the group. More in the background eight or ten warriors lay half recumbent on the ground, or sat with their backs reclining against trees, so many types of indolent repose. Their arms were near them all, sometimes leaning against the same trees as themselves, or were lying across their bodies in careless preparation. But the group that most attracted the attention of Deerslayer was that composed of the women and children. All the females appeared to be collected together, and, almost as a matter of course, their young were near them. The former laughed and chatted in their rebuked and quiet manner, though one who knew the habits of the people might have detected that everything was not going on in its usual train. Most of the young women seemed to be light-hearted enough; but one old hag was seated apart with a watchful soured aspect, which the hunter at once knew betokened that some duty of an unpleasant character had been assigned her by the chiefs. What that duty was, he had no means of knowing; but he felt satisfied it must be in some measure connected with her own sex, the aged among the women generally being chosen for such offices and no other.

As a matter of course, Deerslayer looked eagerly and anxiously for the form of Hist. She was nowhere visible though the light penetrated to considerable distances in all directions around the fire. Once or twice he started, as he thought he recognized her laugh; but his ears were deceived by the soft melody that is so common to the Indian female voice. At length the old woman spoke loud and angrily, and then he caught a glimpse of one or two dark figures in the background of trees, which turned as if obedient to the rebuke, and walked more within the circle of the light. A young warrior's form first came fairly into view; then followed two youthful females, one of whom proved to be the Delaware girl. Deerslayer now comprehended it all. Hist was watched, possibly by her young companion, certainly by the old woman. The youth was probably some suitor of either her or her companion; but even his discretion was distrusted under the influence of his admiration. The known vicinity of those who might be supposed to be her friends, and the arrival of a strange red man on the lake had induced more than the usual care, and the girl had not been able to slip away from those who watched her in order to keep her appointment. Deerslayer traced her uneasiness by her attempting once or twice to look up through the branches of the trees, as if endeavouring to get glimpses of the star she had herself named as the sign for meeting. All was vain, however, and after strolling about the camp a little longer, in affected indifference, the two girls quitted their male escort, and took seats among their own sex. As soon as this was done, the old sentinel changed her place to one more agreeable to herself, a certain proof that she had hitherto been exclusively on watch.

Deerslayer now felt greatly at a loss how to proceed. He well knew that Chingachgook could never be persuaded to return to the ark without making some desperate effort for the recovery of his mistress, and his own generous feelings well disposed him to aid in such an undertaking. He thought he saw the signs of an intention among the females to retire for the night; and should he remain, and the fire continue to give out its light, he might discover the particular hut or arbour under which Hist reposed; a circumstance that would be of infinite use in their future proceedings. Should he remain, however, much longer where he was, there was great danger that the impatience of his friend would drive him into some act of imprudence. At each instant, indeed, he expected to see the swarthy form of the Delaware appearing in the background, like the tiger prowling around the fold. Taking all things into consideration, therefore, he came to the conclusion it would be better to rejoin his friend, and endeavour to temper his impetuosity by some of his own coolness and discretion. It required but a minute or two to put this plan in execution, the canoe returning to the strand some ten or fifteen minutes after it had left it.

Contrary to his expectations, perhaps, Deerslayer found the Indian at his post, from which he had not stirred, fearful that his betrothed might arrive during his absence. A conference followed, in which Chingachgook was made acquainted with the state of things in the camp. When Hist named the point as the place of meeting, it was with the expectation of making her escape from the old position, and of repairing to a spot that she expected to find without any occupants; but the sudden change of localities had disconcerted all her plans. A much greater degree of vigilance than had been previously required was now necessary; and the circumstance that an aged woman was on watch also denoted some special grounds of alarm. All these considerations, and many more that will readily suggest themselves to the reader, were briefly discussed before the young men came to any decision. The occasion, however, being one that required acts instead of words, the course to be pursued was soon chosen.

Disposing of the canoe in such a manner that Hist must see it, should she come to the place of meeting previously to their return, the young men looked to their arms and prepared to enter the wood. The whole projection into the lake contained about two acres of land; and the part that formed the point, and on which the camp was placed, did not compose a surface of more than half that size. It was principally covered with oaks, which, as is usual in the American forests, grew to a great height without throwing out a branch, and then arched in a dense and rich foliage. Beneath, except the fringe of thick bushes along the shore, there was very little underbrush; though, in consequence of their shape, the trees were closer together than is common in regions where the axe has been freely used, resembling tall, straight, rustic columns, upholding the usual canopy of leaves. The surface of the land was tolerably even, but it had a small rise near its centre, which divided it into a northern and southern half. On the latter, the Hurons had built their fire, profiting by the formation to conceal it from their enemies, who, it will be remembered, were supposed to be in the castle, which bore northerly. A brook also came brawling down the sides of the adjacent hills, and found its way into the lake on the southern side of the point. It had cut for itself a deep passage through some of the higher portions of the ground, and, in later days, when this spot has become subjected to the uses of civilization, by its windings and shaded banks, it has become no mean accessory in contributing to the beauty of the place. This brook lay west of the encampment, and its waters found their way into the great reservoir of that region on the same side, and quite near to the spot chosen for the fire. All these peculiarities, so far as circumstances allowed, had been noted by Deerslayer, and explained to his friend.

The reader will understand that the little rise in the ground, that lay behind the Indian encampment, greatly favoured the secret advance of the two adventurers. It prevented the light of the fire diffusing itself on the ground directly in the rear, although the land fell away towards the water, so as to leave what might be termed the left, or eastern flank of the position unprotected by this covering. We have said unprotected, though that is not properly the word, since the knoll behind the huts and the fire offered a cover for those who were now stealthily approaching, rather than any protection to the Indians. Deerslayer did not break through the fringe of bushes immediately abreast of the canoe, which might have brought him too suddenly within the influence of the light, since the hillock did not extend to the water; but he followed the beach northerly until he had got nearly on the opposite side of the tongue of land, which brought him under the shelter of the low acclivity, and consequently more in the shadow.

As soon as the friends emerged from the bushes, they stopped to reconnoitre. The fire was still blazing behind the little ridge, casting its light upward into the tops of the trees, producing an effect that was more pleasing than advantageous. Still the glare had its uses; for, while the background was in obscurity, the foreground was in strong light; exposing the savages and concealing their foes. Profiting by the latter circumstance, the young men advanced cautiously towards the ridge, Deerslayer in front, for he insisted on this arrangement, lest the Delaware should be led by his feelings into some indiscretion. It required but a moment to reach the foot of the little ascent, and then commenced the most critical part of the enterprise. Moving with exceeding caution, and trailing his rifle, both to keep its barrel out of view, and in readiness for service, the hunter put foot before foot, until he had got sufficiently high to overlook the summit, his own head being alone brought into the light. Chingachgook was at his side and both paused to take another close examination of the camp. In order, however, to protect themselves against any straggler in the rear, they placed their bodies against the trunk of an oak, standing on the side next the fire.

The view that Deerslayer now obtained of the camp was exactly the reverse of that he had perceived from the water. The dim figures which he had formerly discovered must have been on the summit of the ridge, a few feet in advance of the spot where he was now posted. The fire was still blazing brightly, and around it were seated on logs thirteen warriors, which accounted for all whom he had seen from the canoe. They were conversing, with much earnestness among themselves, the image of the elephant passing from hand to hand. The first burst of savage wonder had abated, and the question now under discussion was the probable existence, the history and the habits of so extraordinary an animal. We have not leisure to record the opinions of these rude men on a subject so consonant to their lives and experience; but little is hazarded in saying that they were quite as plausible, and far more ingenious, than half the conjectures that precede the demonstrations of science. However much they may have been at fault as to their conclusions and inferences, it is certain that they discussed the questions with a zealous and most undivided attention. For the time being all else was forgotten, and our adventurers could not have approached at a more fortunate instant.

The females were collected near each other, much as Deerslayer had last seen them, nearly in a line between the place where he now stood and the fire. The distance from the oak against which the young men leaned and the warriors was about thirty yards; the women may have been half that number of yards nigher. The latter, indeed, were so near as to make the utmost circumspection, as to motion and noise, indispensable. Although they conversed in their low, soft voices it was possible, in the profound stillness of the woods, even to catch passages of the discourse; and the light-hearted laugh that escaped the girls might occasionally have reached the canoe. Deerslayer felt the tremolo that passed through the frame of his friend when the latter first caught the sweet sounds that issued from the plump, pretty lips of Hist. He even laid a hand on the shoulder of the Indian, as a sort of admonition to command himself. As the conversation grew more earnest, each leaned forward to listen.

"The Hurons have more curious beasts than that," said one of the girls, contemptuously, for, like the men, they conversed of the elephant and his qualities. "The Delawares will think this creature wonderful, but to-morrow no Huron tongue will talk of it. Our young men will find him if the animals dare to come near our wigwams!"

This was, in fact, addressed to Wah-ta-Wah, though she who spoke uttered her words with an assumed diffidence and humility that prevented her looking at the other.

"The Delawares are so far from letting such creatures come into their country," returned Hist, "that no one has even seen their images there! Their young men would frighten away the images as well as the beasts."

"The Delaware young men!—the nation is women—even the deer walk when they hear their hunters coming! Who has ever heard the name of a young Delaware warrior?"

This was said in good-humour, and with a laugh; but it was also said bitingly. That Hist so felt it, was apparent by the spirit betrayed in her answer.

"Who has ever heard the name of a young Delaware?" she repeated earnestly. "Tamenund, himself, though now as old as the pines on the hill, or as the eagles in the air, was once young; his name was heard from the great salt lake to the sweet waters of the west. What is the family of Uncas? Where is another as great, though the pale-faces have ploughed up its grates, and trodden on its bones? Do the eagles fly as high, is the deer as swift or the panther as brave? Is there no young warrior of that race? Let the Huron maidens open their eyes wider, and they may see one called Chingachgook, who is as stately as a young ash, and as tough as the hickory."

As the girl used her figurative language and told her companions to "open their eyes, and they would see" the Delaware, Deerslayer thrust his fingers into the sides of his friend, and indulged in a fit of his hearty, benevolent laughter. The other smiled; but the language of the speaker was too flattering, and the tones of her voice too sweet for him to be led away by any accidental coincidence, however ludicrous. The speech of Hist produced a retort, and the dispute, though conducted in good-humour, and without any of the coarse violence of tone and gesture that often impairs the charms of the sex in what is called civilized life, grew warm and slightly clamorous. In the midst of this scene, the Delaware caused his friend to stoop, so as completely to conceal himself, and then he made a noise so closely resembling the little chirrup of the smallest species of the American squirrel, that Deerslayer himself, though he had heard the imitation a hundred times, actually thought it came from one of the little animals skipping about over his head. The sound is so familiar in the woods, that none of the Hurons paid it the least attention. Hist, however, instantly ceased talking, and sat motionless. Still she had sufficient self-command to abstain from turning her head. She had heard the signal by which her lover so often called her from the wigwam to the stolen interview, and it came over her senses and her heart, as the serenade affects the maiden in the land of song.

From that moment, Chingachgook felt certain that his presence was known. This was effecting much, and he could now hope for a bolder line of conduct on the part of his mistress than she might dare to adopt under an uncertainty of his situation. It left no doubt of her endeavouring to aid him in his effort to release her. Deerslayer arose as soon as the signal was given, and though he had never held that sweet communion which is known only to lovers, he was not slow to detect the great change that had come over the manner of the girl. She still affected to dispute, though it was no longer with spirit and ingenuity, but what she said was uttered more as a lure to draw her antagonists on to an easy conquest, than with any hopes of succeeding herself. Once or twice, it is true, her native readiness suggested a retort, or an argument that raised a laugh, and gave her a momentary advantage; but these little sallies, the offspring of mother-wit, served the better to conceal her real feelings, and to give to the triumph of the other party a more natural air than it might have possessed without them. At length the disputants became wearied, and they rose in a body as if about to separate. It was now that Hist, for the first time, ventured to turn her face in the direction whence the signal had come. In doing this, her movements were natural, but guarded, and she stretched her arm and yawned, as if overcome with a desire to sleep. The chirrup was again heard, and the girl felt satisfied as to the position of her lover, though the strong light in which she herself was placed, and the comparative darkness in which the adventurers stood, prevented her from seeing their heads, the only portions of their forms that appeared above the ridge at all. The tree against which they were posted had a dark shadow cast upon it by the intervention of an enormous pine that grew between it and the fire, a circumstance which alone would have rendered objects within its cloud invisible at any distance. This Deerslayer well knew, and it was one of the reasons why he had selected this particular tree.

The moment was near when it became necessary for Hist to act. She was to sleep in a small hut, or bower, that had been built near where she stood, and her companion was the aged hag already mentioned. Once within the hut, with this sleepless old woman stretched across the entrance, as was her nightly practice, the hope of escape was nearly destroyed, and she might at any moment be summoned to her bed. Luckily, at this instant one of the warriors called to the old woman by name, and bade her bring him water to drink. There was a delicious spring on the northern side of the point, and the hag took a gourd from a branch and, summoning Hist to her side, she moved towards the summit of the ridge, intending to descend and cross the point to the natural fountain. All this was seen and understood by the adventurers, and they fell back into the obscurity, concealing their persons by trees, until the two females had passed them. In walking, Hist was held tightly by the hand. As she moved by the tree that hid Chingachgook and his friend the former felt for his tomahawk, with the intention to bury it in the brain of the woman. But the other saw the hazard of such a measure, since a single scream might bring all the warriors upon them, and he was averse to the act on considerations of humanity. His hand, therefore, prevented the blow. Still as the two moved past, the chirrup was repeated, and the Huron woman stopped and faced the tree whence the sounds seemed to proceed, standing, at the moment, within six feet of her enemies. She expressed her surprise that a squirrel should be in motion at so late an hour, and said it boded evil. Hist answered that she had heard the same squirrel three times within the last twenty minutes, and that she supposed it was waiting to obtain some of the crumbs left from the late supper. This explanation appeared satisfactory, and they moved towards the spring, the men following stealthily and closely. The gourd was filled, and the old woman was hurrying back, her hand still grasping the wrist of the girl, when she was suddenly seized so violently by the throat as to cause her to release her captive, and to prevent her making any other sound than a sort of gurgling, suffocating noise. The Serpent passed his arm round the waist of his mistress and dashed through the bushes with her, on the north side of the point. Here he immediately turned along the beach and ran towards the canoe. A more direct course could have been taken, but it might have led to a discovery of the place of embarking.

Deerslayer kept playing on the throat of the old woman like the keys of an organ, occasionally allowing her to breathe, and then compressing his fingers again nearly to strangling. The brief intervals for breath, however, were well improved, and the hag succeeded in letting out a screech or two that served to alarm the camp. The tramp of the warriors, as they sprang from the fire, was plainly audible, and at the next moment three or four of them appeared on the top of the ridge, drawn against the background of light, resembling the dim shadows of the phantasmagoria. It was now quite time for the hunter to retreat. Tripping up the heels of his captive, and giving her throat a parting squeeze, quite as much in resentment at her indomitable efforts to sound the alarm as from any policy, he left her on her back, and moved towards the bushes, his rifle at a poise, and his head over his shoulders, like a lion at bay.

## CHAPTER XVII.

"There, ye wise saints, behold your light, your star,
  Ye would be dupes and victims and ye are.
  Is it enough?  or, must I, while a thrill
  Lives in your sapient bosoms, cheat you still?"

Thomas Moore, Lalla Rookh, "The Veiled Prophet of Khorassan"

The fire, the canoe, and the spring, near which Deerslayer commenced his retreat, would have stood in the angles of a triangle of tolerably equal sides. The distance from the fire to the boat was a little less than the distance from the fire to the spring, while the distance from the spring to the boat was about equal to that between the two points first named. This, however, was in straight lines, a means of escape to which the fugitives could not resort. They were obliged to have recourse to a detour in order to get the cover of the bushes, and to follow the curvature of the beach. Under these disadvantages, then, the hunter commenced his retreat, disadvantages that he felt to be so much the greater from his knowledge of the habits of all Indians, who rarely fail in cases of sudden alarms, more especially when in the midst of cover, immediately to throw out flankers, with a view to meet their foes at all points, and if possible to turn their rear. That some such course was now adopted he believed from the tramp of feet, which not only came up the ascent, as related, but were also heard, under the first impulse, diverging not only towards the hill in the rear, but towards the extremity of the point, in a direction opposite to that he was about to take himself. Promptitude, consequently became a matter of the last importance, as the parties might meet on the strand, before the fugitive could reach the canoe.

Notwithstanding the pressing nature of the emergency, Deerslayer hesitated a single instant, ere he plunged into the bushes that lined the shore. His feelings had been awakened by the whole scene, and a sternness of purpose had come over him, to which he was ordinarily a stranger. Four dark figures loomed on the ridge, drawn against the brightness of the fire, and an enemy might have been sacrificed at a glance. The Indians had paused to gaze into the gloom, in search of the screeching hag, and with many a man less given to reflection than the hunter, the death of one of them would have been certain. Luckily he was more prudent. Although the rifle dropped a little towards the foremost ter VI.559The Prairie: A Tale560Chapter VI.561The Prairie: A Tale562Chapter VII.563beach, and to round to the place where Chingachgook was already in the canoe, with Hist, anxiously waiting his appearance, occupied but a moment. Laying his rifle in the bottom of the canoe, Deerslayer stooped to give the latter a vigorous shove from the shore, when a powerful Indian leaped through the bushes, alighting like a panther on his back. Everything was now suspended by a hair; a false step ruining all. With a generosity that would have rendered a Roman illustrious throughout all time, but which, in the career of one so simple and humble, would have been forever lost to the world but for this unpretending legend, Deerslayer threw all his force into a desperate effort, shoved the canoe off with a power that sent it a hundred feet from the shore, as it might be in an instant, and fell forward into the lake, himself, face downward; his assailant necessarily following him.

Although the water was deep within a few yards of the beach, it was not more than breast high, as close in as the spot where the two combatants fell. Still this was quite sufficient to destroy one who had sunk, under the great disadvantages in which Deerslayer was placed. His hands were free, however, and the savage was compelled to relinquish his hug, to keep his own face above the surface. For half a minute there was a desperate struggle, like the floundering of an alligator that has just seized some powerful prey, and then both stood erect, grasping each other's arms, in order to prevent the use of the deadly knife in the darkness. What might have been the issue of this severe personal struggle cannot be known, for half a dozen savages came leaping into the water to the aid of their friend, and Deerslayer yielded himself a prisoner, with a dignity that was as remarkable as his self-devotion.

To quit the lake and lead their new captive to the fire occupied the Indians but another minute. So much engaged were they all with the struggle and its consequences, that the canoe was unseen, though it still lay so near the shore as to render every syllable that was uttered perfectly intelligible to the Delaware and his betrothed; and the whole party left the spot, some continuing the pursuit after Hist, along the beach, though most proceeded to the light. Here Deerslayer's antagonist so far recovered his breath and his recollection, for he had been throttled nearly to strangulation, as to relate the manner in which the girl had got off. It was now too late to assail the other fugitives, for no sooner was his friend led into the bushes than the Delaware placed his paddle into the water, and the light canoe glided noiselessly away, holding its course towards the centre of the lake until safe from shot, after which it sought the Ark. When Deerslayer reached the fire, he found himself surrounded by no less than eight grim savages, among whom was his old acquaintance Rivenoak. As soon as the latter caught a glimpse of the captive's countenance, he spoke apart to his companions, and a low but general exclamation of pleasure and surprise escaped them. They knew that the conqueror of their late friend, he who had fallen on the opposite side of the lake, was in their hands, and subject to their mercy, or vengeance. There was no little admiration mingled in the ferocious looks that were thrown on the prisoner; an admiration that was as much excited by his present composure, as by his past deeds. This scene may be said to have been the commencement of the great and terrible reputation that Deerslayer, or Hawkeye, as he was afterwards called, enjoyed among all the tribes of New York and Canada; a reputation that was certainly more limited in its territorial and numerical extent, than those which are possessed in civilized life, but which was compensated for what it wanted in these particulars, perhaps, by its greater justice, and the total absence of mystification and management.

The arms of Deerslayer were not pinioned, and he was left the free use of his hands, his knife having been first removed. The only precaution that was taken to secure his person was untiring watchfulness, and a strong rope of bark that passed from ankle to ankle, not so much to prevent his walking, as to place an obstacle in the way of his attempting to escape by any sudden leap. Even this extra provision against flight was not made until the captive had been brought to the light, and his character ascertained. It was, in fact, a compliment to his prowess, and he felt proud of the distinction. That he might be bound when the warriors slept he thought probable, but to be bound in the moment of capture showed that he was already, and thus early, attaining a name. While the young Indians were fastening the rope, he wondered if Chingachgook would have been treated in the same manner, had he too fallen into the hands of the enemy. Nor did the reputation of the young pale-face rest altogether on his success in the previous combat, or in his discriminating and cool manner of managing the late negotiation, for it had received a great accession by the occurrences of the night. Ignorant of the movements of the Ark, and of the accident that had brought their fire into view, the Iroquois attributed the discovery of their new camp to the vigilance of so shrewd a foe. The manner in which he ventured upon the point, the abstraction or escape of Hist, and most of all the self-devotion of the prisoner, united to the readiness with which he had sent the canoe adrift, were so many important links in the chain of facts, on which his growing fame was founded. Many of these circumstances had been seen, some had been explained, and all were understood.

While this admiration and these honors were so unreservedly bestowed on Deerslayer, he did not escape some of the penalties of his situation. He was permitted to seat himself on the end of a log, near the fire, in order to dry his clothes, his late adversary standing opposite, now holding articles of his own scanty vestments to the heat, and now feeling his throat, on which the marks of his enemy's fingers were still quite visible. The rest of the warriors consulted together, near at hand, all those who had been out having returned to report that no signs of any other prowlers near the camp were to be found. In this state of things, the old woman, whose name was Shebear, in plain English, approached Deerslayer, with her fists clenched and her eyes flashing fire. Hitherto, she had been occupied with screaming, an employment at which she had played her part with no small degree of success, but having succeeded in effectually alarming all within reach of a pair of lungs that had been strengthened by long practice, she next turned her attention to the injuries her own person had sustained in the struggle. These were in no manner material, though they were of a nature to arouse all the fury of a woman who had long ceased to attract by means of the gentler qualities, and who was much disposed to revenge the hardships she had so long endured, as the neglected wife and mother of savages, on all who came within her power. If Deerslayer had not permanently injured her, he had temporarily caused her to suffer, and she was not a person to overlook a wrong of this nature, on account of its motive.

"Skunk of the pale-faces," commenced this exasperated and semi-poetic fury, shaking her fist under the nose of the impassable hunter, "you are not even a woman. Your friends the Delawares are only women, and you are their sheep. Your own people will not own you, and no tribe of redmen would have you in their wigwams; you skulk among petticoated warriors. You slay our brave friend who has left us?—No—his great soul scorned to fight you, and left his body rather than have the shame of slaying you! But the blood that you spilt when the spirit was not looking on, has not sunk into the ground. It must be buried in your groans. What music do I hear? Those are not the wailings of a red man!—no red warrior groans so much like a hog. They come from a pale-face throat—a Yengeese bosom, and sound as pleasant as girls singing—Dog—skunk—woodchuck-mink—hedgehog—pig—toad—spider—yengee—"

Here the old woman, having expended her breath and exhausted her epithets, was fain to pause a moment, though both her fists were shaken in the prisoner's face, and the whole of her wrinkled countenance was filled with fierce resentment. Deerslayer looked upon these impotent attempts to arouse him as indifferently as a gentleman in our own state of society regards the vituperative terms of a blackguard: the one party feeling that the tongue of an old woman could never injure a warrior, and the other knowing that mendacity and vulgarity can only permanently affect those who resort to their use; but he was spared any further attack at present, by the interposition of Rivenoak, who shoved aside the hag, bidding her quit the spot, and prepared to take his seat at the side of his prisoner. The old woman withdrew, but the hunter well understood that he was to be the subject of all her means of annoyance, if not of positive injury, so long as he remained in the power of his enemies, for nothing rankles so deeply as the consciousness that an attempt to irritate has been met by contempt, a feeling that is usually the most passive of any that is harbored in the human breast. Rivenoak quietly took the seat we have mentioned, and, after a short pause, he commenced a dialogue, which we translate as usual, for the benefit of those readers who have not studied the North American languages.

"My pale-face friend is very welcome," said the Indian, with a familiar nod, and a smile so covert that it required all Deerslayer's vigilance to detect, and not a little of his philosophy to detect unmoved; "he is welcome. The Hurons keep a hot fire to dry the white man's clothes by."

"I thank you, Huron—or Mingo, as I most like to call you," returned the other, "I thank you for the welcome, and I thank you for the fire. Each is good in its way, and the last is very good, when one has been in a spring as cold as the Glimmerglass. Even Huron warmth may be pleasant, at such a time, to a man with a Delaware heart."

"The pale-face—but my brother has a name? So great a warrior would not have lived without a name?"

"Mingo," said the hunter, a little of the weakness of human nature exhibiting itself in the glance of his eye, and the colour on his cheek—"Mingo, your brave called me Hawkeye, I suppose on account of a quick and sartain aim, when he was lying with his head in my lap, afore his spirit started for the Happy Hunting Grounds."

"'Tis a good name! The hawk is sure of his blow. Hawkeye is not a woman; why does he live with the Delawares?"

"I understand you, Mingo, but we look on all that as a sarcumvention of some of your subtle devils, and deny the charge. Providence placed me among the Delawares young, and, 'bating what Christian usages demand of my colour and gifts, I hope to live and die in their tribe. Still I do not mean to throw away altogether my natyve rights, and shall strive to do a pale-face's duty, in red-skin society."

"Good; a Huron is a red-skin, as well as a Delaware. Hawkeye is more of a Huron than of a woman."

"I suppose you know, Mingo, your own meaning; if you don't I make no question 'tis well known to Satan. But if you wish to get any thing out of me, speak plainer, for bargains can not be made blindfolded, or tongue tied."

"Good; Hawkeye has not a forked tongue, and he likes to say what he thinks. He is an acquaintance of the Muskrat," this was the name by which all the Indians designated Hutter—"and has lived in his wigwam. But he is not a friend. He wants no scalps, like a miserable Indian, but fights like a stout-hearted pale-face. The Muskrat is neither white, nor red. Neither a beast nor a fish. He is a water snake; sometimes in the spring and sometimes on the land. He looks for scalps, like an outcast. Hawkeye can go back and tell him how he has outwitted the Hurons, how he has escaped, and when his eyes are in a fog, when he can't see as far as from his cabin to the shore, then Hawkeye can open the door for the Hurons. And how will the plunder be divided? Why, Hawkeye, will carry away the most, and the Hurons will take what he may choose to leave behind him. The scalps can go to Canada, for a pale-face has no satisfaction in them."

"Well, well, Rivenoak—for so I hear 'em tarm you—This is plain English, enough, though spoken in Iroquois. I understand all you mean, now, and must say it out-devils even Mingo deviltry! No doubt, 'twould be easy enough to go back and tell the Muskrat that I had got away from you, and gain some credit, too, by the expl'ite."

"Good. That is what I want the pale-face to do."

"Yes—yes—That's plain enough. I know what you want me to do, without more words. When inside the house, and eating the Muskrat's bread, and laughing and talking with his pretty darters, I might put his eyes into so thick a fog, that he couldn't even see the door, much less the land."

"Good! Hawkeye should have been born a Huron! His blood is not more than half white!"

"There you're out, Huron; yes, there you're as much out, as if you mistook a wolf for a catamount. I'm white in blood, heart, natur' and gifts, though a little red-skin in feelin's and habits. But when old Hutter's eyes are well befogged, and his pretty darters perhaps in a deep sleep, and Hurry Harry, the Great Pine as you Indians tarm him, is dreaming of any thing but mischief, and all suppose Hawkeye is acting as a faithful sentinel, all I have to do is set a torch somewhere in sight for a signal, open the door, and let in the Hurons, to knock 'em all on the head."

"Surely my brother is mistaken. He cannot be white! He is worthy to be a great chief among the Hurons!"

"That is true enough, I dares to say, if he could do all this. Now, harkee, Huron, and for once hear a few honest words from the mouth of a plain man. I am Christian born, and them that come of such a stock, and that listen to the words that were spoken to their fathers and will be spoken to their children, until 'arth and all it holds perishes, can never lend themselves to such wickedness. Sarcumventions in war, may be, and are, lawful; but sarcumventions, and deceit, and treachery among fri'inds are fit only for the pale-face devils. I know that there are white men enough to give you this wrong idee of our natur', but such be ontrue to their blood and gifts, and ought to be, if they are not, outcasts and vagabonds. No upright pale-face could do what you wish, and to be as plain with you as I wish to be, in my judgment no upright Delaware either. With a Mingo it may be different."

The Huron listened to this rebuke with obvious disgust, but he had his ends in view, and was too wily to lose all chance of effecting them by a precipitate avowal of resentment. Affecting to smile, he seemed to listen eagerly, and he then pondered on what he had heard.

"Does Hawkeye love the Muskrat?" he abruptly demanded; "Or does he love his daughters?"

"Neither, Mingo. Old Tom is not a man to gain my love, and, as for the darters, they are comely enough to gain the liking of any young man, but there's reason ag'in any very great love for either. Hetty is a good soul, but natur' has laid a heavy hand on her mind, poor thing."

"And the Wild Rose!" exclaimed the Huron—for the fame of Judith's beauty had spread among those who could travel the wilderness, as well as the highway by means of old eagles' nests, rocks, and riven trees known to them by report and tradition, as well as among the white borderers, "And the Wild Rose; is she not sweet enough to be put in the bosom of my brother?"

Deerslayer had far too much of the innate gentleman to insinuate aught against the fair fame of one who, by nature and position was so helpless, and as he did not choose to utter an untruth, he preferred being silent. The Huron mistook the motive, and supposed that disappointed affection lay at the bottom of his reserve. Still bent on corrupting or bribing his captive, in order to obtain possession of the treasures with which his imagination filled the Castle, he persevered in his attack.

"Hawkeye is talking with a friend," he continued. "He knows that Rivenoak is a man of his word, for they have traded together, and trade opens the soul. My friend has come here on account of a little string held by a girl, that can pull the whole body of the sternest warrior?"

"You are nearer the truth, now, Huron, than you've been afore, since we began to talk. This is true. But one end of that string was not fast to my heart, nor did the Wild Rose hold the other."

"This is wonderful! Does my brother love in his head, and not in his heart? And can the Feeble Mind pull so hard against so stout a warrior?"

"There it is ag'in; sometimes right, and sometimes wrong! The string you mean is fast to the heart of a great Delaware; one of Mohican stock in fact, living among the Delawares since the disparsion of his own people, and of the family of Uncas—Chingachgook by name, or Great Sarpent. He has come here, led by the string, and I've followed, or rather come afore, for I got here first, pulled by nothing stronger than fri'ndship; which is strong enough for such as are not niggardly of their feelin's, and are willing to live a little for their fellow creatur's, as well as for themselves."

"But a string has two ends—one is fast to the mind of a Mohican; and the other?"

"Why the other was here close to the fire, half an hour since. Wah-ta-Wah held it in her hand, if she didn't hold it to her heart."

"I understand what you mean, my brother," returned the Indian gravely, for the first time catching a direct clue to the adventures of the evening. "The Great Serpent, being strongest, pulled the hardest, and Hist was forced to leave us."

"I don't think there was much pulling about it," answered the other, laughing, always in his silent manner, with as much heartiness as if he were not a captive, and in danger of torture or death—"I don't think there was much pulling about it; no I don't. Lord help you, Huron! He likes the gal, and the gal likes him, and it surpassed Huron sarcumventions to keep two young people apart, where there was so strong a feelin' to bring 'em together."

"And Hawkeye and Chingachgook came into our camp on this errand, only?"

"That's a question that'll answer itself, Mingo! Yes, if a question could talk it would answer itself, to your parfect satisfaction. For what else should we come? And yet, it isn't exactly so, neither; for we didn't come into your camp at all, but only as far as that pine, there, that you see on the other side of the ridge, where we stood watching your movements, and conduct, as long as we liked. When we were ready, the Sarpent gave his signal, and then all went just as it should, down to the moment when yonder vagabond leaped upon my back. Sartain; we come for that, and for no other purpose, and we got what we come for; there's no use in pretending otherwise. Hist is off with a man who's the next thing to her husband, and come what will to me, that's one good thing determined."

"What sign, or signal, told the young maiden that her lover was nigh?" asked the Huron with more curiosity than it was usual for him to betray.

Deerslayer laughed again, and seem'd to enjoy the success of the exploit, with as much glee as if he had not been its victim.

"Your squirrels are great gadabouts, Mingo," he cried still laughing—"yes, they're sartainly great gadabouts! When other folk's squirrels are at home and asleep, yourn keep in motion among the trees, and chirrup and sing, in a way that even a Delaware gal can understand their musick! Well, there's four legged squirrels, and there's two legged squirrels, and give me the last, when there's a good tight string atween two hearts. If one brings 'em together, t'other tells when to pull hardest!"

The Huron looked vexed, though he succeeded in suppressing any violent exhibition of resentment. He now quitted his prisoner and, joining the rest of the warriors, he communicated the substance of what he had learned. As in his own case, admiration was mingled with anger at the boldness and success of their enemies. Three or four of them ascended the little acclivity and gazed at the tree where it was understood the adventurers had posted themselves, and one even descended to it, and examined for foot prints around its roots, in order to make sure that the statement was true. The result confirmed the story of the captive, and they all returned to the fire with increased wonder and respect. The messenger who had arrived with some communication from the party above, while the two adventurers were watching the camp, was now despatched with some answer, and doubtless bore with him the intelligence of all that had happened.

Down to this moment, the young Indian who had been seen walking in company with Hist and another female had made no advances to any communication with Deerslayer. He had held himself aloof from his friends, even, passing near the bevy of younger women, who were clustering together, apart as usual, and conversed in low tones on the subject of the escape of their late companion. Perhaps it would be true to say that these last were pleased as well as vexed at what had just occurred. Their female sympathies were with the lovers, while their pride was bound up in the success of their own tribe. It is possible, too, that the superior personal advantages of Hist rendered her dangerous to some of the younger part of the group, and they were not sorry to find she was no longer in the way of their own ascendency. On the whole, however, the better feeling was most prevalent, for neither the wild condition in which they lived, the clannish prejudices of tribes, nor their hard fortunes as Indian women, could entirely conquer the inextinguishable leaning of their sex to the affections. One of the girls even laughed at the disconsolate look of the swain who might fancy himself deserted, a circumstance that seemed suddenly to arouse his energies, and induce him to move towards the log, on which the prisoner was still seated, drying his clothes.

"This is Catamount!" said the Indian, striking his hand boastfully on his naked breast, as he uttered the words in a manner to show how much weight he expected them to carry.

"This is Hawkeye," quietly returned Deerslayer, adopting the name by which he knew he would be known in future, among all the tribes of the Iroquois. "My sight is keen; is my brother's leap long?"

"From here to the Delaware villages. Hawkeye has stolen my wife; he must bring her back, or his scalp will hang on a pole, and dry in my wigwam."

"Hawkeye has stolen nothing, Huron. He doesn't come of a thieving breed, nor has he thieving gifts. Your wife, as you call Wah-ta-Wah, will never be the wife of any red-skin of the Canadas; her mind is in the cabin of a Delaware, and her body has gone to find it. The catamount is actyve I know, but its legs can't keep pace with a woman's wishes."

"The Serpent of the Delawares is a dog—he is a poor bull trout that keeps in the water; he is afraid to stand on the hard earth, like a brave Indian!"

"Well, well, Huron, that's pretty impudent, considering it's not an hour since the Sarpent stood within a hundred feet of you, and would have tried the toughness of your skin with a rifle bullet, when I pointed you out to him, hadn't I laid the weight of a little judgment on his hand. You may take in timorsome gals in the settlements, with your catamount whine, but the ears of a man can tell truth from ontruth."

"Hist laughs at him! She sees he is lame, and a poor hunter, and he has never been on a war path. She will take a man for a husband, and not a fish."

"How do you know that, Catamount? how do you know that?" returned Deerslayer laughing. "She has gone into the lake, you see, and maybe she prefars a trout to a mongrel cat. As for war paths, neither the Sarpent nor I have much exper'ence, we are ready to own, but if you don't call this one, you must tarm it, what the gals in the settlements tarm it, the high road to matrimony. Take my advice, Catamount, and s'arch for a wife among the Huron women; you'll never get one with a willing mind from among the Delawares."

Catamount's hand felt for his tomahawk, and when the fingers reached the handle they worked convulsively, as if their owner hesitated between policy and resentment. At this critical moment Rivenoak approached, and by a gesture of authority, induced the young man to retire, assuming his former position, himself, on the log at the side of Deerslayer. Here he continued silent for a little time, maintaining the grave reserve of an Indian chief.

"Hawkeye is right," the Iroquois at length began; "his sight is so strong that he can see truth in a dark night, and our eyes have been blinded. He is an owl, darkness hiding nothing from him. He ought not to strike his friends. He is right."

"I'm glad you think so, Mingo," returned the other, "for a traitor, in my judgment, is worse than a coward. I care as little for the Muskrat, as one pale-face ought to care for another, but I care too much for him to ambush him in the way you wished. In short, according to my idees, any sarcumventions, except open-war sarcumventions, are ag'in both law, and what we whites call 'gospel', too."

"My pale-face brother is right; he is no Indian, to forget his Manitou and his colour. The Hurons know that they have a great warrior for their prisoner, and they will treat him as one. If he is to be tortured, his torments shall be such as no common man can bear; if he is to be treated as a friend, it will be the friendship of chiefs."

As the Huron uttered this extraordinary assurance of consideration, his eye furtively glanced at the countenance of his listener, in order to discover how he stood the compliment, though his gravity and apparent sincerity would have prevented any man but one practised in artifices, from detecting his motives. Deerslayer belonged to the class of the unsuspicious, and acquainted with the Indian notions of what constitutes respect, in matters connected with the treatment of captives, he felt his blood chill at the announcement, even while he maintained an aspect so steeled that his quick sighted enemy could discover in it no signs of weakness.

"God has put me in your hands, Huron," the captive at length answered, "and I suppose you will act your will on me. I shall not boast of what I can do, under torment, for I've never been tried, and no man can say till he has been; but I'll do my endivours not to disgrace the people among whom I got my training. Howsever, I wish you now to bear witness that I'm altogether of white blood, and, in a nat'ral way of white gifts too; so, should I be overcome and forget myself, I hope you'll lay the fault where it properly belongs, and in no manner put it on the Delawares, or their allies and friends the Mohicans. We're all created with more or less weakness, and I'm afeard it's a pale-face's to give in under great bodily torment, when a red-skin will sing his songs, and boast of his deeds in the very teeth of his foes."

"We shall see. Hawkeye has a good countenance, and he is tough—but why should he be tormented, when the Hurons love him? He is not born their enemy, and the death of one warrior will not cast a cloud between them forever."

"So much the better, Huron; so much the better. Still I don't wish to owe any thing to a mistake about each other's meaning. It is so much the better that you bear no malice for the loss of a warrior who fell in war, and yet it is ontrue that there is no inmity—lawful inmity I mean—atween us. So far as I have red-skin feelin's at all, I've Delaware feelin's, and I leave you to judge for yourself how far they are likely to be fri'ndly to the Mingos—"

Deerslayer ceased, for a sort of spectre stood before him, that put a stop to his words, and, indeed, caused him for a moment to doubt the fidelity of his boasted vision. Hetty Hutter was standing at the side of the fire as quietly as if she belonged to the tribe.

As the hunter and the Indian sat watching the emotions that were betrayed in each other's countenance, the girl had approached unnoticed, doubtless ascending from the beach on the southern side of the point, or that next to the spot where the Ark had anchored, and had advanced to the fire with the fearlessness that belonged to her simplicity, and which was certainly justified by the treatment formerly received from the Indians. As soon as Rivenoak perceived the girl, she was recognised, and calling to two or three of the younger warriors, the chief sent them out to reconnoitre, lest her appearance should be the forerunner of another attack. He then motioned to Hetty to draw near.

"I hope your visit is a sign that the Sarpent and Hist are in safety, Hetty," said Deerslayer, as soon as the girl had complied with the Huron's request. "I don't think you'd come ashore ag'in, on the arr'nd that brought you here afore."

"Judith told me to come this time, Deerslayer," Hetty replied, "she paddled me ashore herself, in a canoe, as soon as the Serpent had shown her Hist and told his story. How handsome Hist is to-night, Deerslayer, and how much happier she looks than when she was with the Hurons!"

"That's natur' gal; yes, that may be set down as human natur'. She's with her betrothed, and no longer fears a Mingo husband. In my judgment Judith, herself, would lose most of her beauty if she thought she was to bestow it all on a Mingo! Content is a great fortifier of good looks, and I'll warrant you, Hist is contented enough, now she is out of the hands of these miscreants, and with her chosen warrior! Did you say that Judith told you to come ashore—why should your sister do that?"

"She bid me come to see you, and to try and persuade the savages to take more elephants to let you off, but I've brought the Bible with me—that will do more than all the elephants in father's chest!"

"And your father, good little Hetty—and Hurry; did they know of your arr'nd?"

"Not they. Both are asleep, and Judith and the Serpent thought it best they should not be woke, lest they might want to come again after scalps, when Hist had told them how few warriors, and how many women and children there were in the camp. Judith would give me no peace, till I had come ashore to see what had happened to you."

"Well, that's remarkable as consarns Judith! Whey should she feel so much unsartainty about me?—Ah—-I see how it is, now; yes, I see into the whole matter, now. You must understand, Hetty, that your sister is oneasy lest Harry March should wake, and come blundering here into the hands of the inimy ag'in, under some idee that, being a travelling comrade, he ought to help me in this matter! Hurry is a blunderer, I will allow, but I don't think he'd risk as much for my sake, as he would for his own."

"Judith don't care for Hurry, though Hurry cares for her," replied Hetty innocently, but quite positively.

"I've heard you say as much as that afore; yes, I've heard that from you, afore, gal, and yet it isn't true. One don't live in a tribe, not to see something of the way in which liking works in a woman's heart. Though no way given to marrying myself, I've been a looker on among the Delawares, and this is a matter in which pale-face and red-skin gifts are all as one as the same. When the feelin' begins, the young woman is thoughtful, and has no eyes or ears onless for the warrior that has taken her fancy; then follows melancholy and sighing, and such sort of actions; after which, especially if matters don't come to plain discourse, she often flies round to back biting and fault finding, blaming the youth for the very things she likes best in him. Some young creatur's are forward in this way of showing their love, and I'm of opinion Judith is one of 'em. Now, I've heard her as much as deny that Hurry was good-looking, and the young woman who could do that, must be far gone indeed!"

"The young woman who liked Hurry would own that he is handsome. I think Hurry very handsome, Deerslayer, and I'm sure everybody must think so, that has eyes. Judith don't like Harry March, and that's the reason she finds fault with him."

"Well—well—my good little Hetty, have it your own way. If we should talk from now till winter, each would think as at present, and there's no use in words. I must believe that Judith is much wrapped up in Hurry, and that, sooner or later, she'll have him; and this, too, all the more from the manner in which she abuses him; and I dare to say, you think just the contrary. But mind what I now tell you, gal, and pretend not to know it," continued this being, who was so obtuse on a point on which men are usually quick enough to make discoveries, and so acute in matters that would baffle the observation of much the greater portion of mankind, "I see how it is, with them vagabonds. Rivenoak has left us, you see, and is talking yonder with his young men, and though too far to be heard, I can see what he is telling them. Their orders is to watch your movements, and to find where the canoe is to meet you, to take you back to the Ark, and then to seize all and what they can. I'm sorry Judith sent you, for I suppose she wants you to go back ag'in."

"All that's settled, Deerslayer," returned the girl, in a low, confidential and meaning manner, "and you may trust me to outwit the best Indian of them all. I know I am feeble minded, but I've got some sense, and you'll see how I'll use it in getting back, when my errand is done!"

"Ahs! me, poor girl; I'm afeard all that's easier said than done. They're a venomous set of riptyles and their p'ison's none the milder, for the loss of Hist. Well, I'm glad the Sarpent was the one to get off with the gal, for now there'll be two happy at least, whereas had he fallen into the hands of the Mingos, there'd been two miserable, and another far from feelin' as a man likes to feel."

"Now you put me in mind of a part of my errand that I had almost forgotten, Deerslayer. Judith told me to ask you what you thought the Hurons would do with you, if you couldn't be bought off, and what she had best do to serve you. Yes, this was the most important part of the errand—what she had best do, in order to serve you?"

"That's as you think, Hetty; but it's no matter. Young women are apt to lay most stress on what most touches their feelin's; but no matter; have it your own way, so you be but careful not to let the vagabonds get the mastery of a canoe. When you get back to the Ark, tell 'em to keep close, and to keep moving too, most especially at night. Many hours can't go by without the troops on the river hearing of this party, and then your fri'nds may look for relief. 'Tis but a day's march from the nearest garrison, and true soldiers will never lie idle with the foe in their neighborhood. This is my advice, and you may say to your father and Hurry that scalp-hunting will be a poor business now, as the Mingos are up and awake, and nothing can save 'em, 'till the troops come, except keeping a good belt of water atween 'em and the savages."

"What shall I tell Judith about you, Deerslayer; I know she will send me back again, if I don't bring her the truth about you."

"Then tell her the truth. I see no reason Judith Hutter shouldn't hear the truth about me, as well as a lie. I'm a captyve in Indian hands, and Providence only knows what will come of it! Harkee, Hetty," dropping his voice and speaking still more confidentially, "you are a little weak minded, it must be allowed, but you know something of Injins. Here I am in their hands, after having slain one of their stoutest warriors, and they've been endivouring to work upon me through fear of consequences, to betray your father, and all in the Ark. I understand the blackguards as well as if they'd told it all out plainly, with their tongues. They hold up avarice afore me, on one side, and fear on t'other, and think honesty will give way atween 'em both. But let your father and Hurry know, 'tis all useless; as for the Sarpent, he knows it already."

"But what shall I tell Judith? She will certainly send me back, if I don't satisfy her mind."

"Well, tell Judith the same. No doubt the savages will try the torments, to make me give in, and to revenge the loss of their warrior, but I must hold out ag'in nat'ral weakness in the best manner I can. You may tell Judith to feel no consarn on my account—it will come hard I know, seeing that a white man's gifts don't run to boasting and singing under torment, for he generally feels smallest when he suffers most—but you may tell her not to have any consarn. I think I shall make out to stand it, and she may rely on this, let me give in, as much as I may, and prove completely that I am white, by wailings, and howlings, and even tears, yet I'll never fall so far as to betray my fri'nds. When it gets to burning holes in the flesh, with heated ramrods, and to hacking the body, and tearing the hair out by the roots, natur' may get the upperhand, so far as groans, and complaints are consarned, but there the triumph of the vagabonds will ind; nothing short of God's abandoning him to the devils can make an honest man ontrue to his colour and duty."

Hetty listened with great attention, and her mild but speaking countenance manifested a strong sympathy in the anticipated agony of the supposititious sufferer. At first she seemed at a loss how to act; then, taking a hand of Deerslayer's she affectionately recommended to him to borrow her Bible, and to read it while the savages were inflicting their torments. When the other honestly admitted that it exceeded his power to read, she even volunteered to remain with him, and to perform this holy office in person. The offer was gently declined, and Rivenoak being about to join them, Deerslayer requested the girl to leave him, first enjoining her again to tell those in the Ark to have full confidence in his fidelity. Hetty now walked away, and approached the group of females with as much confidence and self-possession as if she were a native of the tribe. On the other hand the Huron resumed his seat by the side of his prisoner, the one continuing to ask questions with all the wily ingenuity of a practised Indian counsellor, and the other baffling him by the very means that are known to be the most efficacious in defeating the finesse of the more pretending diplomacy of civilization, or by confining his answers to the truth, and the truth only.

## CHAPTER XVIII

> "Thus died she; never more on her
> Shall sorrow light, or shame. She was not made
> Through years or moons the inner weight to bear,
> Which colder hearts endure till they are laid
> By age in earth; her days and pleasure were
> Brief but delightful—such as had not stayed
> Long with her destiny; but she sleeps well
> By the sea-shore whereon she loved to dwell."

Byron. Don Juan, IV, lxxi.

The young men who had been sent out to reconnoitre, on the sudden appearance of Hetty, soon returned to report their want of success in making any discovery. One of them had even been along the beach as far as the spot opposite to the ark, but the darkness had completely concealed that vessel from his notice. Others had examined in different directions, and everywhere the stillness of night was added to the silence and solitude of the woods.

It was consequently believed that the girl had come alone, as on her former visit, and on some similar errand. The Iroquois were ignorant that the ark had left the castle, and there were movements projected, if not in the course of actual execution, by this time, which also greatly added to the sense of security. A watch was set, therefore, and all but the sentinels disposed themselves to sleep. Sufficient care was had to the safe keeping of the captive, without inflicting on him any unnecessary suffering; and, as for Hetty, she was permitted to find a place among the Indian girls in the best manner she could. She did not find the friendly offices of Hist, though her character not only bestowed impunity from pain and captivity, but it procured for her a consideration and an attention that placed her, on the score of comfort, quite on a level with the wild but gentle beings around her. She was supplied with a skin, and made her own bed on a pile of boughs a little apart from the huts. Here she was soon in a profound sleep, like all around her.

There were now thirteen men in the party, and three kept watch at a time. One remained in shadow, not far from the fire, however. His duty was to guard the captive, to take care that the fire neither blazed up so as to illuminate the spot, nor yet became wholly extinguished, and to keep an eye generally on the state of the camp. Another passed from one beach to the other, crossing the base of the point, while the third kept moving slowly around the strand on its outer extremity, to prevent a repetition of the surprise that had already taken place that night. This arrangement was far from being usual among savages, who ordinarily rely more on the secrecy of their movements, than on vigilance of this nature; but it had been called for by the peculiarity of the circumstances in which the Hurons were now placed. Their position was known to their foes, and it could not easily be changed at an hour which demanded rest. Perhaps, too, they placed most of their confidence on the knowledge of what they believed to be passing higher up the lake, and which, it was thought, would fully occupy the whole of the pale-faces who were at liberty, with their solitary Indian ally. It was also probable Rivenoak was aware that, in holding his captive, he had in his own hands the most dangerous of all his enemies.

The precision with which those accustomed to watchfulness, or lives of disturbed rest, sleep, is not the least of the phenomena of our mysterious being. The head is no sooner on the pillow than consciousness is lost; and yet, at a necessary hour, the mind appears to arouse the body, as promptly as if it had stood sentinel the while over it. There can be no doubt that they who are thus roused awake by the influence of thought over matter, though the mode in which this influence is exercised must remain hidden from our curiosity until it shall be explained, should that hour ever arrive, by the entire enlightenment of the soul on the subject of all human mysteries. Thus it was with Hetty Hutter. Feeble as the immaterial portion of her existence was thought to be, it was sufficiently active to cause her to open her eyes at midnight. At that hour she awoke, and leaving her bed of skin and boughs she walked innocently and openly to the embers of the fire, stirring the latter, as the coolness of the night and the woods, in connection with an exceedingly unsophisticated bed, had a little chilled her. As the flame shot up, it lighted the swarthy countenance of the Huron on watch, whose dark eyes glistened under its light like the balls of the panther that is pursued to his den with burning brands. But Hetty felt no fear, and she approached the spot where the Indian stood. Her movements were so natural, and so perfectly devoid of any of the stealthiness of cunning or deception, that he imagined she had merely arisen on account of the coolness of the night, a common occurrence in a bivouac, and the one of all others, perhaps, the least likely to excite suspicion. Hetty spoke to him, but he understood no English. She then gazed near a minute at the sleeping captive, and moved slowly away in a sad and melancholy manner. The girl took no pains to conceal her movements. Any ingenious expedient of this nature quite likely exceeded her powers; still her step was habitually light, and scarcely audible. As she took the direction of the extremity of the point, or the place where she had landed in the first adventure, and where Hist had embarked, the sentinel saw her light form gradually disappear in the gloom without uneasiness or changing his own position. He knew that others were on the look-out, and he did not believe that one who had twice come into the camp voluntarily, and had already left it openly, would take refuge in flight. In short, the conduct of the girl excited no more attention that that of any person of feeble intellect would excite in civilized society, while her person met with more consideration and respect.

Hetty certainly had no very distinct notions of the localities, but she found her way to the beach, which she reached on the same side of the point as that on which the camp had been made. By following the margin of the water, taking a northern direction, she soon encountered the Indian who paced the strand as sentinel. This was a young warrior, and when he heard her light tread coming along the gravel he approached swiftly, though with anything but menace in his manner. The darkness was so intense that it was not easy to discover forms within the shadows of the woods at the distance of twenty feet, and quite impossible to distinguish persons until near enough to touch them. The young Huron manifested disappointment when he found whom he had met; for, truth to say, he was expecting his favourite, who had promised to relieve the ennui of a midnight watch with her presence. This man was also ignorant of English, but he was at no loss to understand why the girl should be up at that hour. Such things were usual in an Indian village and camp, where sleep is as irregular as the meals. Then poor Hetty's known imbecility, as in most things connected with the savages, stood her friend on this occasion. Vexed at his disappointment, and impatient of the presence of one he thought an intruder, the young warrior signed for the girl to move forward, holding the direction of the beach. Hetty complied; but as she walked away she spoke aloud in English in her usual soft tones, which the stillness of the night made audible at some little distance.

"If you took me for a Huron girl, warrior," she said, "I don't wonder you are so little pleased. I am Hetty Hutter, Thomas Hutter's daughter, and have never met any man at night, for mother always said it was wrong, and modest young women should never do it; modest young women of the pale-faces, I mean; for customs are different in different parts of the world, I know. No, no; I'm Hetty Hutter, and wouldn't meet even Hurry Harry, though he should fall down on his knees and ask me! Mother said it was wrong."

By the time Hetty had said this, she reached the place where the canoes had come ashore, and, owing to the curvature of the land and the bushes, would have been completely hid from the sight of the sentinel, had it been broad day. But another footstep had caught the lover's ear, and he was already nearly beyond the sound of the girl's silvery voice. Still Hetty, bent only on her own thoughts and purposes, continued to speak, though the gentleness of her tones prevented the sounds from penetrating far into the woods. On the water they were more widely diffused.

"Here I am, Judith," she added, "and there is no one near me. The Huron on watch has gone to meet his sweetheart, who is an Indian girl you know, and never had a Christian mother to tell her how wrong it is to meet a man at night."

Hetty's voice was hushed by a "Hist!" that came from the water, and then she caught a dim view of the canoe, which approached noiselessly, and soon grated on the shingle with its bow. The moment the weight of Hetty was felt in the light craft the canoe withdrew, stern foremost, as if possessed of life and volition, until it was a hundred yards from the shore. Then it turned and, making a wide sweep, as much to prolong the passage as to get beyond the sound of voices, it held its way towards the ark. For several minutes nothing was uttered; but, believing herself to be in a favourable position to confer with her sister, Judith, who alone sat in the stern, managing the canoe with a skill little short of that of a man, began a discourse which she had been burning to commence ever since they had quitted the point.

"Here we are safe, Hetty," she said, "and may talk without the fear of being overheard. You must speak low, however, for sounds are heard far on the water in a still night. I was so close to the point some of the time while you were on it, that I have heard the voices of the warriors, and I heard your shoes on the gravel of the beach, even before you spoke."

"I don't believe, Judith, the Hurons know I have left them."

"Quite likely they do not, for a lover makes a poor sentry, unless it be to watch for his sweetheart! But tell me, Hetty, did you see and speak with Deerslayer?"

"Oh, yes—there he was seated near the fire, with his legs tied, though they left his arms free, to move them as he pleased."

"Well, what did he tell you, child? Speak quick; I am dying to know what message he sent me."

"What did he tell me? why, what do you think, Judith; he told me that he couldn't read! Only think of that! a white man, and not know how to read his Bible even! He never could have had a mother, sister!"

"Never mind that, Hetty. All men can't read; though mother knew so much and taught us so much, father knows very little about books, and he can barely read the Bible you know."

"Oh! I never thought fathers could read much, but mothers ought all to read, else how can they teach their children? Depend on it, Judith, Deerslayer could never have had a mother, else he would know how to read."

"Did you tell him I sent you ashore, Hetty, and how much concern I feel for his misfortune?" asked the other, impatiently.

"I believe I did, Judith; but you know I am feeble-minded, and I may have forgotten. I did tell him you brought me ashore. And he told me a great deal that I was to say to you, which I remember well, for it made my blood run cold to hear him. He told me to say that his friends—I suppose you are one of them, sister?"

"How can you torment me thus, Hetty! Certainly, I am one of the truest friends he has on earth."

"Torment you! yes, now I remember all about it. I am glad you used that word, Judith, for it brings it all back to my mind. Well, he said he might be tormented by the savages, but he would try to bear it as becomes a Christian white man, and that no one need be afeard—why does Deerslayer call it afeard, when mother always taught us to say afraid?"

"Never mind, dear Hetty, never mind that, now," cried the other, almost gasping for breath. "Did Deerslayer really tell you that he thought the savages would put him to the torture? Recollect now, well, Hetty, for this is a most awful and serious thing."

"Yes he did; and I remember it by your speaking about my tormenting you. Oh! I felt very sorry for him, and Deerslayer took all so quietly and without noise! Deerslayer is not as handsome as Hurry Harry, Judith, but he is more quiet."

"He's worth a million Hurrys! yes, he's worth all the young men who ever came upon the lake put together," said Judith, with an energy and positiveness that caused her sister to wonder. "He is true. There is no lie about Deerslayer. You, Hetty, may not know what a merit it is in a man to have truth, but when you get—no—I hope you will never know it. Why should one like you be ever made to learn the hard lesson to distrust and hate!"

Judith bowed her face, dark as it was, and unseen as she must have been by any eye but that of Omniscience, between her hands, and groaned. This sudden paroxysm of feeling, however, lasted but for a moment, and she continued more calmly, still speaking frankly to her sister, whose intelligence, and whose discretion in any thing that related to herself, she did not in the least distrust. Her voice, however, was low and husky, instead of having its former clearness and animation.

"It is a hard thing to fear truth, Hetty," she said, "and yet do I more dread Deerslayer's truth, than any enemy! One cannot tamper with such truth—so much honesty—such obstinate uprightness! But we are not altogether unequal, sister—Deerslayer and I? He is not altogether my superior?"

It was not usual for Judith so far to demean herself as to appeal to Hetty's judgment. Nor did she often address her by the title of sister, a distinction that is commonly given by the junior to the senior, even where there is perfect equality in all other respects. As trifling departures from habitual deportment oftener strike the imagination than more important changes, Hetty perceived the circumstances, and wondered at them in her own simple way. Her ambition was a little quickened, and the answer was as much out of the usual course of things as the question; the poor girl attempting to refine beyond her strength.

"Superior, Judith!" she repeated with pride. "In what can Deerslayer be your superior? Are you not mother's child—and does he know how to read—and wasn't mother before any woman in all this part of the world? I should think, so far from supposing himself your superior, he would hardly believe himself mine. You are handsome, and he is ugly—"

"No, not ugly, Hetty," interrupted Judith. "Only plain. But his honest face has a look in it that is far better than beauty. In my eyes, Deerslayer is handsomer than Hurry Harry."

"Judith Hutter! you frighten me. Hurry is the handsomest mortal in the world—even handsomer than you are yourself; because a man's good looks, you know, are always better than a woman's good looks."

This little innocent touch of natural taste did not please the elder sister at the moment, and she did not scruple to betray it. "Hetty, you now speak foolishly, and had better say no more on this subject," she answered. "Hurry is not the handsomest mortal in the world, by many; and there are officers in the garrisons—" Judith stammered at the words—"there are officers in the garrisons, near us, far comelier than he. But why do you think me the equal of Deerslayer—speak of that, for I do not like to hear you show so much admiration of a man like Hurry Harry, who has neither feelings, manners, nor conscience. You are too good for him, and he ought to be told it, at once."

"I! Judith, how you forget! Why I am not beautiful, and am feeble-minded."

"You are good, Hetty, and that is more than can be said of Harry March. He may have a face, and a body, but he has no heart. But enough of this, for the present. Tell me what raises me to an equality with Deerslayer."

"To think of you asking me this, Judith! He can't read, and you can. He don't know how to talk, but speaks worse than Hurry even;—for, sister, Harry doesn't always pronounce his words right! Did you ever notice that?"

"Certainly, he is as coarse in speech as in everything else. But I fear you flatter me, Hetty, when you think I can be justly called the equal of a man like Deerslayer. It is true, I have been better taught; in one sense am more comely; and perhaps might look higher; but then his truth—his truth—makes a fearful difference between us! Well, I will talk no more of this; and we will bethink us of the means of getting him out of the hands of the Hurons. We have father's chest in the ark, Hetty, and might try the temptation of more elephants; though I fear such baubles will not buy the liberty of a man like Deerslayer. I am afraid father and Hurry will not be as willing to ransom Deerslayer, as Deerslayer was to ransom them!"

"Why not, Judith? Hurry and Deerslayer are friends, and friends should always help one another."

"Alas! poor Hetty, you little know mankind! Seeming friends are often more to be dreaded than open enemies; particularly by females. But you'll have to land in the morning, and try again what can be done for Deerslayer. Tortured he shall not be, while Judith Hutter lives, and can find means to prevent it."

The conversation now grew desultory, and was drawn out, until the elder sister had extracted from the younger every fact that the feeble faculties of the latter permitted her to retain, and to communicate. When Judith was satisfied—though she could never be said to be satisfied, whose feelings seemed to be so interwoven with all that related to the subject, as to have excited a nearly inappeasable curiosity—but, when Judith could think of no more questions to ask, without resorting to repetition, the canoe was paddled towards the scow. The intense darkness of the night, and the deep shadows which the hills and forest cast upon the water, rendered it difficult to find the vessel, anchored, as it had been, as close to the shore as a regard to safety rendered prudent. Judith was expert in the management of a bark canoe, the lightness of which demanded skill rather than strength; and she forced her own little vessel swiftly over the water, the moment she had ended her conference with Hetty, and had come to the determination to return. Still no ark was seen. Several times the sisters fancied they saw it, looming up in the obscurity, like a low black rock; but on each occasion it was found to be either an optical illusion, or some swell of the foliage on the shore. After a search that lasted half an hour, the girls were forced to the unwelcome conviction that the ark had departed. Most young women would have felt the awkwardness of their situation, in a physical sense, under the circumstances in which the sisters were left, more than any apprehensions of a different nature. Not so with Judith, however; and even Hetty felt more concern about the motives that might have influenced her father and Hurry, than any fears for her own safety.

"It cannot be, Hetty," said Judith, when a thorough search had satisfied them both that no ark was to be found; "it cannot be that the Indians have rafted, or swum off and surprised our friends as they slept?"

"I don't believe that Hist and Chingachgook would sleep until they had told each other all they had to say after so long a separation—do you, sister?"

"Perhaps not, child. There was much to keep them awake, but one Indian may have been surprised even when not asleep, especially as his thoughts may have been on other things. Still we should have heard a noise; for in a night like this, an oath of Hurry Harry's would have echoed in the eastern hills like a clap of thunder."

"Hurry is sinful and thoughtless about his words, Judith," Hetty meekly and sorrowfully answered.

"No—no; 'tis impossible the ark could be taken and I not hear the noise. It is not an hour since I left it, and the whole time I have been attentive to the smallest sound. And yet, it is not easy to believe a father would willingly abandon his children!"

"Perhaps father has thought us in our cabin asleep, Judith, and has moved away to go home. You know we often move the ark in the night."

"This is true, Hetty, and it must be as you suppose. There is a little more southern air than there was, and they have gone up the lake—" Judith stopped, for, as the last word was on her tongue, the scene was suddenly lighted, though only for a single instant, by a flash. The crack of a rifle succeeded, and then followed the roll of the echo along the eastern mountains. Almost at the same moment a piercing female cry rose in the air in a prolonged shriek. The awful stillness that succeeded was, if possible, more appalling than the fierce and sudden interruption of the deep silence of midnight. Resolute as she was both by nature and habit, Judith scarce breathed, while poor Hetty hid her face and trembled.

"That was a woman's cry, Hetty," said the former solemnly, "and it was a cry of anguish! If the ark has moved from this spot it can only have gone north with this air, and the gun and shriek came from the point. Can any thing have befallen Hist?"

"Let us go and see, Judith; she may want our assistance—for, besides herself, there are none but men in the ark."

It was not a moment for hesitation, and ere Judith had ceased speaking her paddle was in the water. The distance to the point, in a direct line, was not great, and the impulses under which the girls worked were too exciting to allow them to waste the precious moments in useless precautions. They paddled incautiously for them, but the same excitement kept others from noting their movements. Presently a glare of light caught the eye of Judith through an opening in the bushes, and steering by it, she so directed the canoe as to keep it visible, while she got as near the land as was either prudent or necessary.

The scene that was now presented to the observation of the girls was within the woods, on the side of the declivity so often mentioned, and in plain view from the boat. Here all in the camp were collected, some six or eight carrying torches of fat-pine, which cast a strong but funereal light on all beneath the arches of the forest. With her back supported against a tree, and sustained on one side by the young sentinel whose remissness had suffered Hetty to escape, sat the female whose expected visit had produced his delinquency. By the glare of the torch that was held near her face, it was evident that she was in the agonies of death, while the blood that trickled from her bared bosom betrayed the nature of the injury she had received. The pungent, peculiar smell of gunpowder, too, was still quite perceptible in the heavy, damp night air. There could be no question that she had been shot. Judith understood it all at a glance. The streak of light had appeared on the water a short distance from the point, and either the rifle had been discharged from a canoe hovering near the land, or it had been fired from the ark in passing. An incautious exclamation, or laugh, may have produced the assault, for it was barely possible that the aim had been assisted by any other agent than sound. As to the effect, that was soon still more apparent, the head of the victim dropping, and the body sinking in death. Then all the torches but one were extinguished—a measure of prudence; and the melancholy train that bore the body to the camp was just to be distinguished by the glimmering light that remained. Judith sighed heavily and shuddered, as her paddle again dipped, and the canoe moved cautiously around the point. A sight had afflicted her senses, and now haunted her imagination, that was still harder to be borne, than even the untimely fate and passing agony of the deceased girl.

She had seen, under the strong glare of all the torches, the erect form of Deerslayer, standing with commiseration, and as she thought, with shame depicted on his countenance, near the dying female. He betrayed neither fear nor backwardness himself; but it was apparent by the glances cast at him by the warriors, that fierce passions were struggling in their bosoms. All this seemed to be unheeded by the captive, but it remained impressed on the memory of Judith throughout the night. No canoe was met hovering near the point. A stillness and darkness, as complete as if the silence of the forest had never been disturbed, or the sun had never shone on that retired region, now reigned on the point, and on the gloomy water, the slumbering woods, and even the murky sky. No more could be done, therefore, than to seek a place of safety; and this was only to be found in the centre of the lake. Paddling in silence to that spot, the canoe was suffered to drift northerly, while the girls sought such repose as their situation and feelings would permit.

CHAPTER XIX.

"Stand to your arms, and guard the door—all's lost
Unless that fearful bell be silenced soon.
The officer hath miss'd his path, or purpose,
Or met some unforeseen and hideous obstacle.
Anselmo, with thy company proceed
Straight to the tower; the rest remain with me."

Byron, Marino Faliero, IV.ii.230–35.

The conjecture of Judith Hutter, concerning the manner in which the Indian girl had met her death, was accurate in the main. After sleeping several hours, her father and March awoke. This occurred a few minutes after she had left the Ark to go in quest of her sister, and when of course Chingachgook and his betrothed were on board. From the Delaware the old man learned the position of the camp, and the recent events, as well as the absence of his daughters. The latter gave him no concern, for he relied greatly on the sagacity of the elder, and the known impunity with which the younger passed among the savages. Long familiarity with danger, too, had blunted his sensibilities. Nor did he seem much to regret the captivity of Deerslayer, for, while he knew how material his aid might be in a defence, the difference in their views on the morality of the woods, had not left much sympathy between them. He would have rejoiced to know the position of the camp before it had been alarmed by the escape of Hist, but it would be too hazardous now to venture to land, and he reluctantly relinquished for the night the ruthless designs that cupidity and revenge had excited him to entertain. In this mood Hutter took a seat in the head of the scow, where he was quickly joined by Hurry, leaving the Serpent and Hist in quiet possession of the other extremity of the vessel.

"Deerslayer has shown himself a boy, in going among the savages at this hour, and letting himself fall into their hands like a deer that tumbles into a pit," growled the old man, perceiving as usual the mote in his neighbor's eyes, while he overlooked the beam in his own; "if he is left to pay for his stupidity with his own flesh, he can blame no one but himself."

"That's the way of the world, old Tom," returned Hurry. "Every man must meet his own debts, and answer for his own sins. I'm amazed, howsever, that a lad as skilful and watchful as Deerslayer should have been caught in such a trap! Didn't he know any better than to go prowling about a Huron camp at midnight, with no place to retreat to but a lake? or did he think himself a buck, that by taking to the water could throw off the scent and swim himself out of difficulty? I had a better opinion of the boy's judgment, I'll own; but we must overlook a little ignorance in a raw hand. I say, Master Hutter, do you happen to know what has become of the gals—I see no signs of Judith, or Hetty, though I've been through the Ark, and looked into all its living creatur's."

Hutter briefly explained the manner in which his daughters had taken to the canoe, as it had been related by the Delaware, as well as the return of Judith after landing her sister, and her second departure.

"This comes of a smooth tongue, Floating Tom," exclaimed Hurry, grating his teeth in pure resentment—"This comes of a smooth tongue, and a silly gal's inclinations, and you had best look into the matter! You and I were both prisoners—" Hurry could recall that circumstance now—"you and I were both prisoners and yet Judith never stirred an inch to do us any sarvice! She is bewitched with this lank-looking Deerslayer, and he, and she, and you, and all of us, had best look to it. I am not a man to put up with such a wrong quietly, and I say, all the parties had best look to it! Let's up kedge, old fellow, and move nearer to this p'int, and see how matters are getting on."

Hutter had no objections to this movement, and the Ark was got under way in the usual manner; care being taken to make no noise. The wind was passing northward, and the sail soon swept the scow so far up the lake as to render the dark outlines of the trees that clothed the point dimly visible. Floating Tom steered, and he sailed along as near the land as the depth of the water and the overhanging branches would allow. It was impossible to distinguish anything that stood within the shadows of the shore, but the forms of the sail and of the hut were discerned by the young sentinel on the beach, who has already been mentioned. In the moment of sudden surprise, a deep Indian exclamation escaped him. In that spirit of recklessness and ferocity that formed the essence of Hurry's character, this man dropped his rifle and fired. The ball was sped by accident, or by that overruling providence which decides the fates of all, and the girl fell. Then followed the scene with the torches, which has just been described.

At the precise moment when Hurry committed this act of unthinking cruelty, the canoe of Judith was within a hundred feet of the spot from which the Ark had so lately moved. Her own course has been described, and it has now become our office to follow that of her father and his companions. The shriek announced the effects of the random shot of March, and it also proclaimed that the victim was a woman. Hurry himself was startled at these unlooked for consequences, and for a moment he was sorely disturbed by conflicting sensations. At first he laughed, in reckless and rude-minded exultation; and then conscience, that monitor planted in our breasts by God, and which receives its more general growth from the training bestowed in the tillage of childhood, shot a pang to his heart. For a minute, the mind of this creature equally of civilization and of barbarism, was a sort of chaos as to feeling, not knowing what to think of its own act; and then the obstinacy and pride of one of his habits, interposed to assert their usual ascendency. He struck the butt of his rifle on the bottom of the scow, with a species of defiance, and began to whistle a low air with an affectation of indifference. All this time the Ark was in motion, and it was already opening the bay above the point, and was consequently quitting the land.

Hurry's companions did not view his conduct with the same indulgence as that with which he appeared disposed to regard it himself. Hutter growled out his dissatisfaction, for the act led to no advantage, while it threatened to render the warfare more vindictive than ever, and none censure motiveless departures from the right more severely than the mercenary and unprincipled. Still he commanded himself, the captivity of Deerslayer rendering the arm of the offender of double consequence to him at that moment. Chingachgook arose, and for a single instant the ancient animosity of tribes was forgotten, in a feeling of colour; but he recollected himself in season to prevent any of the fierce consequences that, for a passing moment, he certainly meditated. Not so with Hist. Rushing through the hut, or cabin, the girl stood at the side of Hurry, almost as soon as his rifle touched the bottom of the scow, and with a fearlessness that did credit to her heart, she poured out her reproaches with the generous warmth of a woman.

"What for you shoot?" she said. "What Huron gal do, dat you kill him? What you t'ink Manitou say? What you t'ink Manitou feel? What Iroquois do? No get honour—no get camp—no get prisoner—no get battle—no get scalp—no get not'ing at all! Blood come after blood! How you feel, your wife killed? Who pity you, when tear come for moder, or sister? You big as great pine—Huron gal little slender birch—why you fall on her and crush her? You t'ink Huron forget it? No; red-skin never forget! Never forget friend; never forget enemy. Red man Manitou in dat. Why you so wicked, great pale-face?"

Hurry had never been so daunted as by this close and warm attack of the Indian girl. It is true that she had a powerful ally in his conscience, and while she spoke earnestly, it was in tones so feminine as to deprive him of any pretext for unmanly anger. The softness of her voice added to the weight of her remonstrance, by lending to the latter an air of purity and truth. Like most vulgar minded men, he had only regarded the Indians through the medium of their coarser and fiercer characteristics. It had never struck him that the affections are human, that even high principles— modified by habits and prejudices, but not the less elevated within their circle—can exist in the savage state, and that the warrior who is most ruthless in the field, can submit to the softest and gentlest influences in the moments of domestic quiet. In a word, it was the habit of his mind to regard all Indians as being only a slight degree removed from the wild beasts that roamed the woods, and to feel disposed to treat them accordingly, whenever interest or caprice supplied a motive or an impulse. Still, though daunted by these reproaches, the handsome barbarian could hardly be said to be penitent. He was too much rebuked by conscience to suffer an outbreak of temper to escape him, and perhaps he felt that he had already committed an act that might justly bring his manhood in question. Instead of resenting, or answering the simple but natural appeal of Hist, he walked away, like one who disdained entering into a controversy with a woman.

In the mean while the Ark swept onward, and by the time the scene with the torches was enacting beneath the trees, it had reached the open lake, Floating Tom causing it to sheer further from the land with a sort of instinctive dread of retaliation. An hour now passed in gloomy silence, no one appearing disposed to break it. Hist had retired to her pallet, and Chingachgook lay sleeping in the forward part of the scow. Hutter and Hurry alone remained awake, the former at the steering oar, while the latter brooded over his own conduct, with the stubbornness of one little given to a confession of his errors, and the secret goadings of the worm that never dies. This was at the moment when Judith and Hetty reached the centre of the lake, and had lain down to endeavor to sleep in their drifting canoe.

The night was calm, though so much obscured by clouds. The season was not one of storms, and those which did occur in the month of June, on that embedded water, though frequently violent were always of short continuance. Nevertheless, there was the usual current of heavy, damp night air, which, passing over the summits of the trees, scarcely appeared to descend as low as the surface of the glassy lake, but kept moving a short distance above it, saturated with the humidity that constantly arose from the woods, and apparently never proceeding far in any one direction. The currents were influenced by the formation of the hills, as a matter of course, a circumstance that rendered even fresh breezes baffling, and which reduced the feebler efforts of the night air to be a sort of capricious and fickle sighings of the woods. Several times the head of the Ark pointed east, and once it was actually turned towards the south, again; but, on the whole, it worked its way north; Hutter making always a fair wind, if wind it could be called, his principal motive appearing to keep in motion, in order to defeat any treacherous design of his enemies. He now felt some little concern about his daughters, and perhaps as much about the canoe; but, on the whole, this uncertainty did not much disturb him, as he had the reliance already mentioned on the intelligence of Judith.

It was the season of the shortest nights, and it was not long before the deep obscurity which precedes the day began to yield to the returning light. If any earthly scene could be presented to the senses of man that might soothe his passions and temper his ferocity, it was that which grew upon the eyes of Hutter and Hurry as the hours advanced, changing night to morning. There were the usual soft tints of the sky, in which neither the gloom of darkness nor the brilliancy of the sun prevails, and under which objects appear more unearthly, and we might add holy, than at any other portion of the twenty four hours. The beautiful and soothing calm of eventide has been extolled by a thousand poets, and yet it does not bring with it the far-reaching and sublime thoughts of the half hour that precedes the rising of a summer sun. In the one case the panorama is gradually hid from the sight, while in the other its objects start out from the unfolding picture, first dim and misty; then marked in, in solemn background; next seen in the witchery of an increasing, a thing as different as possible from the decreasing twilight, and finally mellow, distinct and luminous, as the rays of the great centre of light diffuse themselves in the atmosphere. The hymns of birds, too, have no moral counterpart in the retreat to the roost, or the flight to the nest, and these invariably accompany the advent of the day, until the appearance of the sun itself—

"Bathes in deep joy, the land and sea."

All this, however, Hutter and Hurry witnessed without experiencing any of that calm delight which the spectacle is wont to bring, when the thoughts are just and the aspirations pure. They not only witnessed it, but they witnessed it under circumstances that had a tendency to increase its power, and to heighten its charms. Only one solitary object became visible in the returning light that had received its form or uses from human taste or human desires, which as often deform as beautify a landscape. This was the castle, all the rest being native, and fresh from the hand of God. That singular residence, too, was in keeping with the natural objects of the view, starting out from the gloom, quaint, picturesque and ornamental. Nevertheless the whole was lost on the observers, who knew no feeling of poetry, had lost their sense of natural devotion in lives of obdurate and narrow selfishness, and had little other sympathy with nature, than that which originated with her lowest wants.

As soon as the light was sufficiently strong to allow of a distinct view of the lake, and more particularly of its shores, Hutter turned the head of the Ark directly towards the castle, with the avowed intention of taking possession, for the day at least, as the place most favorable for meeting his daughters and for carrying on his operations against the Indians. By this time, Chingachgook was up, and Hist was heard stirring among the furniture of the kitchen. The place for which they steered was distant only a mile, and the air was sufficiently favorable to permit it to be reached by means of the sail. At this moment, too, to render the appearances generally auspicious, the canoe of Judith was seen floating northward in the broadest part of the lake; having actually passed the scow in the darkness, in obedience to no other power than that of the elements. Hutter got his glass, and took a long and anxious survey, to ascertain if his daughters were in the light craft or not, and a slight exclamation like that of joy escaped him, as he caught a glimpse of what he rightly conceived to be a part of Judith's dress above the top of the canoe. At the next instant the girl arose and was seen gazing about her, like one assuring herself of her situation. A minute later, Hetty was seen on her knees in the other end of the canoe, repeating the prayers that had been taught her in childhood by a misguided but repentant mother. As Hutter laid down the glass, still drawn to its focus, the Serpent raised it to his eye and turned it towards the canoe. It was the first time he had ever used such an instrument, and Hist understood by his "Hugh!," the expression of his face, and his entire mien, that something wonderful had excited his admiration. It is well known that the American Indians, more particularly those of superior characters and stations, singularly maintain their self-possession and stoicism, in the midst of the flood of marvels that present themselves in their occasional visits to the abodes of civilization, and Chingachgook had imbibed enough of this impassibility to suppress any very undignified manifestation of surprise. With Hist, however, no such law was binding, and when her lover managed to bring the glass in a line with the canoe, and her eye was applied to the smaller end, the girl started back in alarm; then she clapped her hands with delight, and a laugh, the usual attendant of untutored admiration, followed. A few minutes sufficed to enable this quick witted girl to manage the instrument for herself, and she directed it at every prominent object that struck her fancy. Finding a rest in one of the windows, she and the Delaware first surveyed the lake; then the shores, the hills, and, finally, the castle attracted their attention. After a long steady gaze at the latter, Hist took away her eye, and spoke to her lover in a low, earnest manner. Chingachgook immediately placed his eye to the glass, and his look even exceeded that of his betrothed in length and intensity. Again they spoke together, confidentially, appearing to compare opinions, after which the glass was laid aside, and the young warrior quitted the cabin to join Hutter and Hurry.

The Ark was slowly but steadily advancing, and the castle was materially within half a mile, when Chingachgook joined the two white men in the stern of the scow. His manner was calm, but it was evident to the others, who were familiar with the habits of the Indians, that he had something to communicate. Hurry was generally prompt to speak and, according to custom, he took the lead on this occasion.

"Out with it, red-skin," he cried, in his usual rough manner. "Have you discovered a chipmunk in a tree, or is there a salmon-trout swimming under the bottom of the scow? You find what a pale-face can do in the way of eyes, now, Sarpent, and mustn't wonder that they can see the land of the Indians from afar off."

"No good to go to Castle," put in Chingachgook with emphasis, the moment the other gave him an opportunity of speaking. "Huron there."

"The devil he is!—If this should turn out to be true, Floating Tom, a pretty trap were we about to pull down on our heads! Huron, there!—Well, this may be so; but no signs can I see of any thing, near or about the old hut, but logs, water, and bark—bating two or three windows, and one door."

Hutter called for the glass, and took a careful survey of the spot, before he ventured an opinion, at all; then he somewhat cavalierly expressed his dissent from that given by the Indian.

"You've got this glass wrong end foremost, Delaware," continued Hurry. "Neither the old man nor I can see any trail in the lake."

"No trail—water make no trail," said Hist, eagerly. "Stop boat—no go too near. Huron there!"

"Ay, that's it!—Stick to the same tale, and more people will believe you. I hope, Sarpent, you and your gal will agree in telling the same story arter marriage, as well as you do now. 'Huron, there!'— Whereabouts is he to be seen—in the padlock, or the chains, or the logs. There isn't a gaol in the colony that has a more lock up look about it, than old Tom's chiente, and I know something about gaols from exper'ence."

"No see moccasin," said Hist, impatiently "why no look—and see him."

"Give me the glass, Harry," interrupted Hutter, "and lower the sail. It is seldom that an Indian woman meddles, and when she does, there is generally a cause for it. There is, truly, a moccasin floating against one of the piles, and it may or may not be a sign that the castle hasn't escaped visitors in our absence. Moccasins are no rarities, however, for I wear 'em myself; and Deerslayer wears 'em, and you wear 'em, March, and, for that matter so does Hetty, quite as often as she wears shoes, though I never yet saw Judith trust her pretty foot in a moccasin."

Hurry had lowered the sail, and by this time the Ark was within two hundred yards of the castle, setting in, nearer and nearer, each moment, but at a rate too slow to excite any uneasiness. Each now took the glass in turn, and the castle, and every thing near it, was subjected to a scrutiny still more rigid than ever. There the moccasin lay, beyond a question, floating so lightly, and preserving its form so well, that it was scarcely wet. It had caught by a piece of the rough bark of one of the piles, on the exterior of the water-palisade that formed the dock already mentioned, which circumstance alone prevented it from drifting away before the air. There were many modes, however, of accounting for the presence of the moccasin, without supposing it to have been dropped by an enemy. It might have fallen from the platform, even while Hutter was in possession of the place, and drifted to the spot where it was now seen, remaining unnoticed until detected by the acute vision of Hist. It might have drifted from a distance, up or down the lake, and accidentally become attached to the pile, or palisade. It might have been thrown from a window, and alighted in that particular place; or it might certainly have fallen from a scout, or an assailant, during the past night, who was obliged to abandon it to the lake, in the deep obscurity which then prevailed.

All these conjectures passed from Hutter to Hurry, the former appearing disposed to regard the omen as a little sinister, while the latter treated it with his usual reckless disdain. As for the Indian, he was of opinion that the moccasin should be viewed as one would regard a trail in the woods, which might, or might not, equally, prove to be threatening. Hist, however, had something available to propose. She declared her readiness to take a canoe, to proceed to the palisade and bring away the moccasin, when its ornaments would show whether it came from the Canadas or not. Both the white men were disposed to accept this offer, but the Delaware interfered to prevent the risk. If such a service was to be undertaken, it best became a warrior to expose himself in its execution, and he gave his refusal to let his betrothed proceed, much in the quiet but brief manner in which an Indian husband issues his commands.

"Well then, Delaware, go yourself if you're so tender of your squaw," put in the unceremonious Hurry. "That moccasin must be had, or Floating Tom will keep off, here, at arm's length, till the hearth cools in his cabin. It's but a little deerskin, a'ter all, and cut this-a-way or that-a-way, it's not a skear-crow to frighten true hunters from their game. What say you, Sarpent, shall you or I canoe it?"

"Let red man go.—Better eyes than pale-face—know Huron trick better, too."

"That I'll gainsay, to the hour of my death! A white man's eyes, and a white man's nose, and for that matter his sight and ears are all better than an Injin's when fairly tried. Time and ag'in have I put that to the proof, and what is proved is sartain. Still I suppose the poorest vagabond going, whether Delaware or Huron, can find his way to yonder hut and back ag'in, and so, Sarpent, use your paddle and welcome."

Chingachgook was already in the canoe, and he dipped the implement the other named into the water, just as Hurry's limber tongue ceased. Wah-ta-Wah saw the departure of her warrior on this occasion with the submissive silence of an Indian girl, but with most of the misgivings and apprehensions of her sex. Throughout the whole of the past night, and down to the moment, when they used the glass together in the hut, Chingachgook had manifested as much manly tenderness towards his betrothed as one of the most refined sentiment could have shown under similar circumstances, but now every sign of weakness was lost in an appearance of stern resolution. Although Hist timidly endeavored to catch his eye as the canoe left the side of the Ark, the pride of a warrior would not permit him to meet her fond and anxious looks. The canoe departed and not a wandering glance rewarded her solicitude.

Nor were the Delaware's care and gravity misplaced, under the impressions with which he proceeded on this enterprise. If the enemy had really gained possession of the building he was obliged to put himself under the very muzzles of their rifles, as it were, and this too without the protection of any of that cover which forms so essential an ally in Indian warfare. It is scarcely possible to conceive of a service more dangerous, and had the Serpent been fortified by the experience of ten more years, or had his friend the Deerslayer been present, it would never have been attempted; the advantages in no degree compensating for the risk. But the pride of an Indian chief was acted on by the rivalry of colour, and it is not unlikely that the presence of the very creature from whom his ideas of manhood prevented his receiving a single glance, overflowing as he was with the love she so well merited, had no small influence on his determination.

Chingachgook paddled steadily towards the palisades, keeping his eyes on the different loops of the building. Each instant he expected to see the muzzle of a rifle protruded, or to hear its sharp crack; but he succeeded in reaching the piles in safety. Here he was, in a measure, protected, having the heads of the palisades between him and the hut, and the chances of any attempt on his life while thus covered, were greatly diminished. The canoe had reached the piles with its head inclining northward, and at a short distance from the moccasin. Instead of turning to pick up the latter, the Delaware slowly made the circuit of the whole building, deliberately examining every object that should betray the presence of enemies, or the commission of violence. Not a single sign could he discover, however, to confirm the suspicions that had been awakened. The stillness of desertion pervaded the building; not a fastening was displaced, not a window had been broken. The door looked as secure as at the hour when it was closed by Hutter, and even the gate of the dock had all the customary fastenings. In short, the most wary and jealous eye could detect no other evidence of the visit of enemies, than that which was connected with the appearance of the floating moccasin.

The Delaware was now greatly at a loss how to proceed. At one moment, as he came round in front of the castle, he was on the point of stepping up on the platform and of applying his eye to one of the loops, with a view of taking a direct personal inspection of the state of things within; but he hesitated. Though of little experience in such matters, himself, he had heard so much of Indian artifices through traditions, had listened with such breathless interest to the narration of the escapes of the elder warriors, and, in short, was so well schooled in the theory of his calling, that it was almost as impossible for him to make any gross blunder on such an occasion, as it was for a well grounded scholar, who had commenced correctly, to fail in solving his problem in mathematics. Relinquishing the momentary intention to land, the chief slowly pursued his course round the palisades. As he approached the moccasin, having now nearly completed the circuit of the building, he threw the ominous article into the canoe, by a dexterous and almost imperceptible movement of his paddle. He was now ready to depart, but retreat was even more dangerous than the approach, as the eye could no longer be riveted on the loops. If there was really any one in the castle, the motive of the Delaware in reconnoitering must be understood, and it was the wisest way, however perilous it might be, to retire with an air of confidence, as if all distrust were terminated by the examination. Such, accordingly, was the course adopted by the Indian, who paddled deliberately away, taking the direction of the Ark, suffering no nervous impulse to quicken the motions of his arms, or to induce him to turn even a furtive glance behind him.

No tender wife, reared in the refinements of the highest civilization, ever met a husband on his return from the field with more of sensibility in her countenance than Hist discovered, as she saw the Great Serpent of the Delawares step, unharmed, into the Ark. Still she repressed her emotion, though the joy that sparkled in her dark eyes, and the smile that lighted her pretty mouth, spoke a language that her betrothed could understand.

"Well, Sarpent," cried Hurry, always the first to speak, "what news from the muskrats? Did they shew their teeth, as you surrounded their dwelling?"

"I no like him," sententiously returned the Delaware. "Too still. So still, can see silence!"

"That's downright Injin—as if any thing could make less noise than nothing! If you've no better reason than this to give, old Tom had better hoist his sail, and go and get his breakfast under his own roof. What has become of the moccasin?"

"Here," returned Chingachgook, holding up his prize for the general inspection. The moccasin was examined, and Hist confidently pronounced it to be Huron, by the manner in which the porcupine's quills were arranged on its front. Hutter and the Delaware, too, were decidedly of the same opinion. Admitting all this, however, it did not necessarily follow that its owners were in the castle. The moccasin might have drifted from a distance, or it might have fallen from the foot of some scout, who had quitted the place when his errand was accomplished. In short it explained nothing, while it awakened so much distrust.

Under the circumstances, Hutter and Hurry were not men to be long deterred from proceeding by proofs as slight as that of the moccasin. They hoisted the sail again, and the Ark was soon in motion, heading towards the castle. The wind or air continued light, and the movement was sufficiently slow to allow of a deliberate survey of the building, as the scow approached. The same death-like silence reigned, and it was difficult to fancy that any thing possessing animal life could be in or around the place. Unlike the Serpent, whose imagination had acted through his traditions until he was ready to perceive an artificial, in a natural stillness, the others saw nothing to apprehend in a tranquility that, in truth, merely denoted the repose of inanimate objects. The accessories of the scene, too, were soothing and calm, rather than exciting. The day had not yet advanced so far as to bring the sun above the horizon, but the heavens, the atmosphere, and the woods and lake were all seen under that softened light which immediately precedes his appearance, and which perhaps is the most witching period of the four and twenty hours. It is the moment when every thing is distinct, even the atmosphere seeming to possess a liquid lucidity, the hues appearing gray and softened, with the outlines of objects defined, and the perspective just as moral truths that are presented in their simplicity, without the meretricious aids of ornament or glitter. In a word, it is the moment when the senses seem to recover their powers, in the simplest and most accurate forms, like the mind emerging from the obscurity of doubts into the tranquility and peace of demonstration. Most of the influence that such a scene is apt to produce on those who are properly constituted in a moral sense, was lost on Hutter and Hurry; but both the Delawares, though too much accustomed to witness the loveliness of morning-tide to stop to analyze their feelings, were equally sensible of the beauties of the hour, though it was probably in a way unknown to themselves. It disposed the young warrior to peace, and never had he felt less longings for the glory of the combat, than when he joined Hist in the cabin, the instant the scow rubbed against the side of the platform. From the indulgence of such gentle emotions, however, he was aroused by a rude summons from Hurry, who called on him to come forth and help to take in the sail, and to secure the Ark.

Chingachgook obeyed, and by the time he had reached the head of the scow, Hurry was on the platform, stamping his feet, like one glad to touch what, by comparison, might be called terra firma, and proclaiming his indifference to the whole Huron tribe in his customary noisy, dogmatical manner. Hutter had hauled a canoe up to the head of the scow, and was already about to undo the fastenings of the gate, in order to enter within the 'dock.' March had no other motive in landing than a senseless bravado, and having shaken the door in a manner to put its solidity to the proof, he joined Hutter in the canoe and began to aid him in opening the gate. The reader will remember that this mode of entrance was rendered necessary by the manner in which the owner of this singular residence habitually secured it, whenever it was left empty; more particularly at moments when danger was apprehended. Hutter had placed a line in the Delaware's hand, on entering the canoe, intimating that the other was to fasten the Ark to the platform and to lower the sail. Instead of following these directions, however, Chingachgook left the sail standing, and throwing the bight of the rope over the head of a pile, he permitted the Ark to drift round until it lay against the defences, in a position where it could be entered only by means of a boat, or by passing along the summits of the palisades; the latter being an exploit that required some command of the feet, and which was not to be attempted in the face of a resolute enemy.

In consequence of this change in the position of the scow, which was effected before Hutter had succeeded in opening the gate of his dock, the Ark and the Castle lay, as sailors would express it, yard-arm and yard-arm, kept asunder some ten or twelve feet by means of the piles. As the scow pressed close against the latter, their tops formed a species of breast work that rose to the height of a man's head, covering in a certain degree the parts of the scow that were not protected by the cabin. The Delaware surveyed this arrangement with great satisfaction and, as the canoe of Hutter passed through the gate into the dock, he thought that he might defend his position against any garrison in the castle, for a sufficient time, could he but have had the helping arm of his friend Deerslayer. As it was, he felt comparatively secure, and no longer suffered the keen apprehensions he had lately experienced in behalf of Hist.

A single shove sent the canoe from the gate to the trap beneath the castle. Here Hutter found all fast, neither padlock nor chain nor bar having been molested. The key was produced, the locks removed, the chain loosened, and the trap pushed upward. Hurry now thrust his head in at the opening; the arms followed, and the colossal legs rose without any apparent effort. At the next instant, his heavy foot was heard stamping in the passage above; that which separated the chambers of the father and daughters, and into which the trap opened. He then gave a shout of triumph.

"Come on, old Tom," the reckless woodsman called out from within the building—"here's your tenement, safe and sound; ay, and as empty as a nut that has passed half an hour in the paws of a squirrel! The Delaware brags of being able to see silence; let him come here, and he may feel it, in the bargain."

"Any silence where you are, Hurry Harry," returned Hutter, thrusting his head in at the hole as he uttered the last word, which instantly caused his voice to sound smothered to those without—"Any silence where you are, ought to be both seen and felt, for it's unlike any other silence."

"Come, come, old fellow; hoist yourself up, and we'll open doors and windows and let in the fresh air to brighten up matters. Few words in troublesome times, make men the best fri'nds. Your darter Judith is what I call a misbehaving young woman, and the hold of the whole family on me is so much weakened by her late conduct, that it wouldn't take a speech as long as the ten commandments to send me off to the river, leaving you and your traps, your Ark and your children, your man servants and your maid servants, your oxen and your asses, to fight this battle with the Iroquois by yourselves. Open that window, Floating Tom, and I'll blunder through and do the same job to the front door."

A moment of silence succeeded, and a noise like that produced by the fall of a heavy body followed. A deep execration from Hurry succeeded, and then the whole interior of the building seemed alive. The noises that now so suddenly, and we may add so unexpectedly even to the Delaware, broke the stillness within, could not be mistaken. They resembled those that would be produced by a struggle between tigers in a cage. Once or twice the Indian yell was given, but it seemed smothered, and as if it proceeded from exhausted or compressed throats, and, in a single instance, a deep and another shockingly revolting execration came from the throat of Hurry. It appeared as if bodies were constantly thrown upon the floor with violence, as often rising to renew the struggle. Chingachgook felt greatly at a loss what to do. He had all the arms in the Ark, Hutter and Hurry having proceeded without their rifles, but there was no means of using them, or of passing them to the hands of their owners. The combatants were literally caged, rendering it almost as impossible under the circumstances to get out, as to get into the building. Then there was Hist to embarrass his movements, and to cripple his efforts. With a view to relieve himself from this disadvantage, he told the girl to take the remaining canoe and to join Hutter's daughters, who were incautiously but deliberately approaching, in order to save herself, and to warn the others of their danger. But the girl positively and firmly refused to comply. At that moment no human power, short of an exercise of superior physical force, could have induced her to quit the Ark. The exigency of the moment did not admit of delay, and the Delaware seeing no possibility of serving his friends, cut the line and by a strong shove forced the scow some twenty feet clear of the piles. Here he took the sweeps and succeeded in getting a short distance to windward, if any direction could be thus termed in so light an air, but neither the time, nor his skill at the oars, allowed the distance to be great. When he ceased rowing, the Ark might have been a hundred yards from the platform, and half that distance to the southward of it, the sail being lowered. Judith and Hetty had now discovered that something was wrong, and were stationary a thousand feet farther north.

All this while the furious struggle continued within the house. In scenes like these, events thicken in less time than they can be related. From the moment when the first fall was heard within the building to that when the Delaware ceased his awkward attempts to row, it might have been three or four minutes, but it had evidently served to weaken the combatants. The oaths and execrations of Hurry were no longer heard, and even the struggles had lost some of their force and fury. Nevertheless they still continued with unabated perseverance. At this instant the door flew open, and the fight was transferred to the platform, the light and the open air. A Huron had undone the fastenings of the door, and three or four of his tribe rushed after him upon the narrow space, as if glad to escape from some terrible scene within. The body of another followed, pitched headlong through the door with terrific violence. Then March appeared, raging like a lion at bay, and for an instant freed from his numerous enemies. Hutter was already a captive and bound. There was now a pause in the struggle, which resembled a lull in a tempest. The necessity of breathing was common to all, and the combatants stood watching each other, like mastiffs that have been driven from their holds, and are waiting for a favorable opportunity of renewing them. We shall profit by this pause to relate the manner in which the Indians had obtained possession of the castle, and this the more willingly because it may be necessary to explain to the reader why a conflict which had been so close and fierce, should have also been so comparatively bloodless.

Rivenoak and his companion, particularly the latter who had appeared to be a subordinate and occupied solely with his raft, had made the closest observations in their visits to the castle. Even the boy had brought away minute and valuable information. By these means the Hurons obtained a general idea of the manner in which the place was constructed and secured, as well as of details that enabled them to act intelligently in the dark. Notwithstanding the care that Hutter had taken to drop the Ark on the east side of the building when he was in the act of transferring the furniture from the former to the latter, he had been watched in a way to render the precaution useless. Scouts were on the look-out on the eastern as well as on the western shore of the lake, and the whole proceeding had been noted. As soon as it was dark, rafts like that already described approached from both shores to reconnoitre, and the Ark had passed within fifty feet of one of them without its being discovered; the men it held lying at their length on the logs, so as to blend themselves and their slow moving machine with the water. When these two sets of adventurers drew near the castle they encountered each other, and after communicating their respective observations, they unhesitatingly approached the building. As had been expected, it was found empty. The rafts were immediately sent for a reinforcement to the shore, and two of the savages remained to profit by their situation. These men succeeded in getting on the roof, and by removing some of the bark, in entering what might be termed the garret. Here they were found by their companions. Hatchets now opened a hole through the squared logs of the upper floor, through which no less than eight of the most athletic of the Indians dropped into the rooms beneath. Here they were left, well supplied with arms and provisions, either to stand a siege, or to make a sortie, as the case might require. The night was passed in sleep, as is usual with Indians in a state of inactivity. The returning day brought them a view of the approach of the Ark through the loops, the only manner in which light and air were now admitted, the windows being closed most effectually with plank, rudely fashioned to fit. As soon as it was ascertained that the two white men were about to enter by the trap, the chief who directed the proceedings of the Hurons took his measures accordingly. He removed all the arms from his own people, even to the knives, in distrust of savage ferocity when awakened by personal injuries, and he hid them where they could not be found without a search. Ropes of bark were then prepared, and taking their stations in the three different rooms, they all waited for the signal to fall upon their intended captives. As soon as the party had entered the building, men without replaced the bark of the roof, removed every sign of their visit, with care, and then departed for the shore. It was one of these who had dropped his moccasin, which he had not been able to find again in the dark. Had the death of the girl been known, it is probable nothing could have saved the lives of Hurry and Hutter, but that event occurred after the ambush was laid, and at a distance of several miles from the encampment near the castle. Such were the means that had been employed to produce the state of things we shall continue to describe.

CHAPTER XX.

"Now all is done that man can do,
And all is done in vain!
My love! my native land, adieu
For I must cross the main, My dear,
For I must cross the main."

Robert Burns, "It was a' for our Rightfu' King," ll. 7–12.

The last chapter we left the combatants breathing in their narrow lists. Accustomed to the rude sports of wrestling and jumping, then so common in America, more especially on the frontiers, Hurry possessed an advantage, in addition to his prodigious strength, that had rendered the struggle less unequal than it might otherwise appear to be. This alone had enabled him to hold out so long, against so many enemies, for the Indian is by no means remarkable for his skill, or force, in athletic exercises. As yet, no one had been seriously hurt, though several of the savages had received severe falls, and he, in particular, who had been thrown bodily upon the platform, might be said to be temporarily hors de combat. Some of the rest were limping, and March himself had not entirely escaped from bruises, though want of breath was the principal loss that both sides wished to repair.

Under circumstances like those in which the parties were placed, a truce, let it come from what cause it might, could not well be of long continuance. The arena was too confined, and the distrust of treachery too great, to admit of this. Contrary to what might be expected in his situation, Hurry was the first to recommence hostilities. Whether this proceeded from policy, an idea that he might gain some advantage by making a sudden and unexpected assault, or was the fruit of irritation and his undying hatred of an Indian, it is impossible to say. His onset was furious, however, and at first it carried all before it. He seized the nearest Huron by the waist, raised him entirely from the platform, and hurled him into the water, as if he had been a child. In half a minute, two more were at his side, one of whom received a grave injury by the friend who had just preceded him. But four enemies remained, and, in a hand to hand conflict, in which no arms were used but those which nature had furnished, Hurry believed himself fully able to cope with that number of red-skins.

"Hurrah! Old Tom," he shouted—"The rascals are taking to the lake, and I'll soon have 'em all swimming!" As these words were uttered a violent kick in the face sent back the injured Indian, who had caught at the edge of the platform, and was endeavoring to raise himself to its level, helplessly and hopelessly into the water. When the affray was over, his dark body was seen, through the limpid element of the Glimmerglass, lying, with outstretched arms, extended on the bottom of the shoal on which the Castle stood, clinging to the sands and weeds, as if life were to be retained by this frenzied grasp of death. A blow sent into the pit of another's stomach doubled him up like a worm that had been trodden on, and but two able bodied foes remained to be dealt with. One of these, however, was not only the largest and strongest of the Hurons, but he was also the most experienced of their warriors present, and that one whose sinews were the best strung in fights, and by marches on the warpath. This man fully appreciated the gigantic strength of his opponent, and had carefully husbanded his own. He was also equipped in the best manner for such a conflict, standing in nothing but his breech-cloth, the model of a naked and beautiful statue of agility and strength. To grasp him required additional dexterity and unusual force. Still Hurry did not hesitate, but the kick that had actually destroyed one fellow creature was no sooner given, than he closed in with this formidable antagonist, endeavoring to force him into the water, also. The struggle that succeeded was truly frightful. So fierce did it immediately become, and so quick and changeful were the evolutions of the athletes, that the remaining savage had no chance for interfering, had he possessed the desire; but wonder and apprehension held him spell bound. He was an inexperienced youth, and his blood curdled as he witnessed the fell strife of human passions, exhibited too, in an unaccustomed form.

Hurry first attempted to throw his antagonist. With this view he seized him by the throat, and an arm, and tripped with the quickness and force of an American borderer. The effect was frustrated by the agile movements of the Huron, who had clothes to grasp by, and whose feet avoided the attempt with a nimbleness equal to that with which it was made. Then followed a sort of melee, if such a term can be applied to a struggle between two in which no efforts were strictly visible, the limbs and bodies of the combatants assuming so many attitudes and contortions as to defeat observation. This confused but fierce rally lasted less than a minute, however; when, Hurry, furious at having his strength baffled by the agility and nakedness of his foe, made a desperate effort, which sent the Huron from him, hurling his body violently against the logs of the hut. The concussion was so great as momentarily to confuse the latter's faculties. The pain, too, extorted a deep groan; an unusual concession to agony to escape a red man in the heat of battle. Still he rushed forward again to meet his enemy, conscious that his safety rested on it's resolution. Hurry now seized the other by the waist, raised him bodily from the platform, and fell with his own great weight on the form beneath. This additional shock so stunned the sufferer, that his gigantic white opponent now had him completely at his mercy. Passing his hands around the throat of his victim, he compressed them with the strength of a vice, fairly doubling the head of the Huron over the edge of the platform, until the chin was uppermost, with the infernal strength he expended. An instant sufficed to show the consequences. The eyes of the sufferer seemed to start forward, his tongue protruded, and his nostrils dilated nearly to splitting. At this instant a rope of bark, having an eye, was passed dexterously within the two arms of Hurry, the end threaded the eye, forming a noose, and his elbows were drawn together behind his back, with a power that all his gigantic strength could not resist. Reluctantly, even under such circumstances, did the exasperated borderer see his hands drawn from their deadly grasp, for all the evil passions were then in the ascendant. Almost at the same instant a similar fastening secured his ankles, and his body was rolled to the centre of the platform as helplessly, and as cavalierly, as if it were a log of wood. His rescued antagonist, however, did not rise, for while he began again to breathe, his head still hung helplessly over the edge of the logs, and it was thought at first that his neck was dislocated. He recovered gradually only, and it was hours before he could walk. Some fancied that neither his body, nor his mind, ever totally recovered from this near approach to death.

Hurry owed his defeat and capture to the intensity with which he had concentrated all his powers on his fallen foe. While thus occupied, the two Indians he had hurled into the water mounted to the heads of the piles, along which they passed, and joined their companion on the platform. The latter had so far rallied his faculties as to have gotten the ropes, which were in readiness for use as the others appeared, and they were applied in the manner related, as Hurry lay pressing his enemy down with his whole weight, intent only on the horrible office of strangling him. Thus were the tables turned, in a single moment; he who had been so near achieving a victory that would have been renowned for ages, by means of traditions, throughout all that region, lying helpless, bound and a captive. So fearful had been the efforts of the pale-face, and so prodigious the strength he exhibited, that even as he lay tethered like a sheep before them, they regarded him with respect, and not without dread. The helpless body of their stoutest warrior was still stretched on the platform, and, as they cast their eyes towards the lake, in quest of the comrade that had been hurled into it so unceremoniously, and of whom they had lost sight in the confusion of the fray, they perceived his lifeless form clinging to the grass on the bottom, as already described. These several circumstances contributed to render the victory of the Hurons almost as astounding to themselves as a defeat.

Chingachgook and his betrothed witnessed the whole of this struggle from the Ark. When the three Hurons were about to pass the cords around the arms of the prostrate Hurry the Delaware sought his rifle, but, before he could use it the white man was bound and the mischief was done. He might still bring down an enemy, but to obtain the scalp was impossible, and the young chief, who would so freely risk his own life to obtain such a trophy, hesitated about taking that of a foe without such an object in view. A glance at Hist, and the recollection of what might follow, checked any transient wish for revenge. The reader has been told that Chingachgook could scarcely be said to know how to manage the oars of the Ark at all, however expert he might be in the use of the paddle. Perhaps there is no manual labor at which men are so bungling and awkward, as in their first attempts to pull oar, even the experienced mariner, or boat man, breaking down in his efforts to figure with the celebrated rullock of the gondolier. In short it is, temporarily, an impracticable thing for a new beginner to succeed with a single oar, but in this case it was necessary to handle two at the same time, and those of great size. Sweeps, or large oars, however, are sooner rendered of use by the raw hand than lighter implements, and this was the reason that the Delaware had succeeded in moving the Ark as well as he did in a first trial. That trial, notwithstanding, sufficed to produce distrust, and he was fully aware of the critical situation in which Hist and himself were now placed, should the Hurons take to the canoe that was still lying beneath the trap, and come against them. At the moment he thought of putting Hist into the canoe in his own possession, and of taking to the eastern mountain in the hope of reaching the Delaware villages by direct flight. But many considerations suggested themselves to put a stop to this indiscreet step. It was almost certain that scouts watched the lake on both sides, and no canoe could possibly approach shore without being seen from the hills. Then a trail could not be concealed from Indian eyes, and the strength of Hist was unequal to a flight sufficiently sustained to outstrip the pursuit of trained warriors. This was a part of America in which the Indians did not know the use of horses, and everything would depend on the physical energies of the fugitives. Last, but far from being least, were the thoughts connected with the situation of Deerslayer, a friend who was not to be deserted in his extremity.

Hist in some particulars reasoned, and even felt, differently though she arrived at the same conclusions. Her own anger disturbed her less than her concern for the two sisters, on whose behalf her womanly sympathies were now strongly enlisted. The canoe of the girls, by the time the struggle on the platform had ceased, was within three hundred yards of the castle, and here Judith ceased paddling, the evidences of strife first becoming apparent to the eyes. She and Hetty were standing erect, anxiously endeavoring to ascertain what had occurred, but unable to satisfy their doubts from the circumstance that the building, in a great measure, concealed the scene of action.

The parties in the Ark, and in the canoe, were indebted to the ferocity of Hurry's attack for their momentary security. In any ordinary case, the girls would have been immediately captured, a measure easy of execution now the savages had a canoe, were it not for the rude check the audacity of the Hurons had received in the recent struggle. It required some little time to recover from the effects of this violent scene, and this so much the more, because the principal man of the party, in the way of personal prowess at least, had been so great a sufferer. Still it was of the last importance that Judith and her sister should seek immediate refuge in the Ark, where the defences offered a temporary shelter at least, and the first step was to devise the means of inducing them to do so. Hist showed herself in the stern of the scow, and made many gestures and signs, in vain, in order to induce the girls to make a circuit to avoid the Castle, and to approach the Ark from the eastward. But these signs were distrusted or misunderstood. It is probable Judith was not yet sufficiently aware of the real state of things to put full confidence in either party. Instead of doing as desired, she rather kept more aloof, paddling slowly back to the north, or into the broadest part of the lake, where she could command the widest view, and had the fairest field for flight before her. At this instant the sun appeared above the pines of the eastern range of mountains and a light southerly breeze arose, as was usual enough at that season and hour. Chingachgook lost no time in hoisting the sail. Whatever might be in reserve for him, there could be no question that it was every way desirable to get the Ark at such a distance from the castle as to reduce his enemies to the necessity of approaching the former in the canoe, which the chances of war had so inopportunely, for his wishes and security, thrown into their hands. The appearance of the opening duck seemed first to arouse the Hurons from their apathy, and by the time the head of the scow had fallen off before the wind, which it did unfortunately in the wrong direction, bringing it within a few yards of the platform, Hist found it necessary to warn her lover of the importance of covering his person against the rifles of his foes. This was a danger to be avoided under all circumstances, and so much the more, because the Delaware found that Hist would not take to the cover herself so long as he remained exposed. Accordingly, Chingachgook abandoned the scow to its own movements, forced Hist into the cabin, the doors of which he immediately secured, and then he looked about him for the rifles. The situation of the parties was now so singular as to merit a particular description. The Ark was within sixty yards of the castle, a little to the southward, or to windward of it, with its sail full, and the steering oar abandoned. The latter, fortunately, was loose, so that it produced no great influence on the crab like movements of the unwieldy craft. The sail being as sailors term it, flying, or having no braces, the air forced the yard forward, though both sheets were fast. The effect was threefold on a boat with a bottom that was perfectly flat, and which drew merely some three or four inches water. It pressed the head slowly round to leeward, it forced the whole fabric bodily in the same direction at the same time, and the water that unavoidably gathered under the lee gave the scow also a forward movement. All these changes were exceedingly slow, however, for the wind was not only light, but it was baffling as usual, and twice or thrice the sail shook. Once it was absolutely taken aback.

Had there been any keel to the Ark, it would inevitably have run foul of the platform, bows on, when it is probable nothing could have prevented the Hurons from carrying it; more particularly as the sail would have enabled them to approach under cover. As it was, the scow wore slowly round, barely clearing that part of the building. The piles projecting several feet, they were not cleared, but the head of the slow moving craft caught between two of them, by one of its square corners, and hung. At this moment the Delaware was vigilantly watching through a loop for an opportunity to fire, while the Hurons kept within the building, similarly occupied. The exhausted warrior reclined against the hut, there having been no time to remove him, and Hurry lay, almost as helpless as a log, tethered like a sheep on its way to the slaughter, near the middle of the platform. Chingachgook could have slain the first, at any moment, but his scalp would have been safe, and the young chief disdained to strike a blow that could lead to neither honor nor advantage.

"Run out one of the poles, Sarpent, if Sarpent you be," said Hurry, amid the groans that the tightness of the ligatures was beginning to extort from him—"run out one of the poles, and shove the head of the scow off, and you'll drift clear of us—and, when you've done that good turn for yourself just finish this gagging blackguard for me."

The appeal of Hurry, however, had no other effect than to draw the attention of Hist to his situation. This quick witted creature comprehended it at a glance. His ankles were bound with several turns of stout bark rope, and his arms, above the elbows, were similarly secured behind his back; barely leaving him a little play of the hands and wrists. Putting her mouth near a loop she said in a low but distinct voice—"Why you don't roll here, and fall in scow? Chingachgook shoot Huron, if he chase!"

"By the Lord, gal, that's a judgematical thought, and it shall be tried, if the starn of your scow will come a little nearer. Put a bed at the bottom, for me to fall on."

This was said at a happy moment, for, tired of waiting, all the Indians made a rapid discharge of their rifles, almost simultaneously, injuring no one; though several bullets passed through the loops. Hist had heard part of Hurry's words, but most of what he said was lost in the sharp reports of the firearms. She undid the bar of the door that led to the stern of the scow, but did not dare to expose her person. All this time, the head of the Ark hung, but by a gradually decreasing hold as the other end swung slowly round, nearer and nearer to the platform. Hurry, who now lay with his face towards the Ark, occasionally writhing and turning over like one in pain, evolutions he had performed ever since he was secured, watched every change, and, at last, he saw that the whole vessel was free, and was beginning to grate slowly along the sides of the piles. The attempt was desperate, but it seemed to be the only chance for escaping torture and death, and it suited the reckless daring of the man's character. Waiting to the last moment, in order that the stern of the scow might fairly rub against the platform, he began to writhe again, as if in intolerable suffering, execrating all Indians in general, and the Hurons in particular, and then he suddenly and rapidly rolled over and over, taking the direction of the stern of the scow. Unfortunately, Hurry's shoulders required more space to revolve in than his feet, and by the time he reached the edge of the platform his direction had so far changed as to carry him clear of the Ark altogether, and the rapidity of his revolutions and the emergency admitting of no delay, he fell into the water. At this instant, Chingachgook, by an understanding with his betrothed, drew the fire of the Hurons again, not a man of whom saw the manner in which one whom they knew to be effectually tethered, had disappeared. But Hist's feelings were strongly interested in the success of so bold a scheme, and she watched the movements of Hurry as the cat watches the mouse. The moment he was in motion she foresaw the consequences, and this the more readily, as the scow was now beginning to move with some steadiness, and she bethought her of the means of saving him. With a sort of instinctive readiness, she opened the door at the very moment the rifles were ringing in her ears, and protected by the intervening cabin, she stepped into the stem of the scow in time to witness the fall of Hurry into the lake. Her foot was unconsciously placed on the end of one of the sheets of the sail, which was fastened aft, and catching up all the spare rope with the awkwardness, but also with the generous resolution of a woman, she threw it in the direction of the helpless Hurry. The line fell on the head and body of the sinking man and he not only succeeded in grasping separate parts of it with his hands, but he actually got a portion of it between his teeth. Hurry was an expert swimmer, and tethered as he was he resorted to the very expedient that philosophy and reflection would have suggested. He had fallen on his back, and instead of floundering and drowning himself by desperate efforts to walk on the water, he permitted his body to sink as low as possible, and was already submerged, with the exception of his face, when the line reached him. In this situation he might possibly have remained until rescued by the Hurons, using his hands as fishes use their fins, had he received no other succour, but the movement of the Ark soon tightened the rope, and of course he was dragged gently ahead holding even pace with the scow. The motion aided in keeping his face above the surface of the water, and it would have been possible for one accustomed to endurance to have been towed a mile in this singular but simple manner.

It has been said that the Hurons did not observe the sudden disappearance of Hurry. In his present situation he was not only hid from view by the platform, but, as the Ark drew slowly ahead, impelled by a sail that was now filled, he received the same friendly service from the piles. The Hurons, indeed, were too intent on endeavoring to slay their Delaware foe, by sending a bullet through some one of the loops or crevices of the cabin, to bethink them at all of one whom they fancied so thoroughly tied. Their great concern was the manner in which the Ark rubbed past the piles, although its motion was lessened at least one half by the friction, and they passed into the northern end of the castle in order to catch opportunities of firing through the loops of that part of the building. Chingachgook was similarly occupied, and remained as ignorant as his enemies of the situation of Hurry. As the Ark grated along the rifles sent their little clouds of smoke from one cover to the other, but the eyes and movements of the opposing parties were too quick to permit any injury to be done. At length one side had the mortification and the other the pleasure of seeing the scow swing clear of the piles altogether, when it immediately moved away, with a materially accelerated motion, towards the north.

Chingachgook now first learned from Hist the critical condition of Hurry. To have exposed either of their persons in the stern of the scow would have been certain death, but fortunately the sheet to which the man clung led forward to the foot of the sail. The Delaware found means to unloosen it from the cleet aft, and Hist, who was already forward for that purpose, immediately began to pull upon the line. At this moment Hurry was towing fifty or sixty feet astern, with nothing but his face above water. As he was dragged out clear of the castle and the piles he was first perceived by the Hurons, who raised a hideous yell and commenced a fire on, what may very well be termed the floating mass. It was at the same instant that Hist began to pull upon the line forward—a circumstance that probably saved Hurry's life, aided by his own self-possession and border readiness. The first bullet struck the water directly on the spot where the broad chest of the young giant was visible through the pure element, and might have pierced his heart had the angle at which it was fired been less acute. Instead of penetrating the lake, however, it glanced from its smooth surface, rose, and buried itself in the logs of the cabin near the spot at which Chingachgook had shown himself the minute before, while clearing the line from the cleet. A second, and a third, and a fourth bullet followed, all meeting with the same resistance of the water, though Hurry sensibly felt the violence of the blows they struck upon the lake so immediately above, and so near his breast. Discovering their mistake, the Hurons now changed their plan, and aimed at the uncovered face; but by this time Hist was pulling on the line, the target advanced and the deadly missiles still fell upon the water. In another moment the body was dragged past the end of the scow and became concealed. As for the Delaware and Hist, they worked perfectly covered by the cabin, and in less time than it requires to tell it, they had hauled the huge frame of Harry to the place they occupied. Chingachgook stood in readiness with his keen knife, and bending over the side of the scow he soon severed the bark that bound the limbs of the borderer. To raise him high enough to reach the edge of the boat and to aid him in entering were less easy, as Hurry's arms were still nearly useless, but both were done in time, when the liberated man staggered forward and fell exhausted and helpless into the bottom of the scow. Here we shall leave him to recover his strength and the due circulation of his blood, while we proceed with the narrative of events that crowd upon us too fast to admit of any postponement. The moment the Hurons lost sight of the body of Hurry they gave a common yell of disappointment, and three of the most active of their number ran to the trap and entered the canoe. It required some little delay, however, to embark with their weapons, to find the paddles and, if we may use a phrase so purely technical, "to get out of dock." By this time Hurry was in the scow, and the Delaware had his rifles again in readiness. As the Ark necessarily sailed before the wind, it had got by this time quite two hundred yards from the castle, and was sliding away each instant, farther and farther, though with a motion so easy as scarcely to stir the water. The canoe of the girls was quite a quarter of a mile distant from the Ark, obviously keeping aloof, in ignorance of what had occurred, and in apprehension of the consequences of venturing too near. They had taken the direction of the eastern shore, endeavoring at the same time to get to windward of the Ark, and in a manner between the two parties, as if distrusting which was to be considered a friend, and which an enemy. The girls, from long habit, used the paddles with great dexterity, and Judith, in particular, had often sportively gained races, in trials of speed with the youths that occasionally visited the lake.

When the three Hurons emerged from behind the palisades, and found themselves on the open lake, and under the necessity of advancing unprotected on the Ark, if they persevered in the original design, their ardor sensibly cooled. In a bark canoe they were totally without cover, and Indian discretion was entirely opposed to such a sacrifice of life as would most probably follow any attempt to assault an enemy entrenched as effectually as the Delaware. Instead of following the Ark, therefore, these three warriors inclined towards the eastern shore, keeping at a safe distance from the rifles of Chingachgook. But this manoeuvre rendered the position of the girls exceedingly critical. It threatened to place them if not between two fires, at least between two dangers, or what they conceived to be dangers, and instead of permitting the Hurons to enclose her, in what she fancied a sort of net, Judith immediately commenced her retreat in a southern direction, at no very great distance from the shore. She did not dare to land; if such an expedient were to be resorted to at all, she could only venture on it in the last extremity. At first the Indians paid little or no attention to the other canoe, for, fully apprised of its contents, they deemed its capture of comparatively little moment, while the Ark, with its imaginary treasures, the persons of the Delaware and of Hurry, and its means of movement on a large scale, was before them. But this Ark had its dangers as well as its temptations, and after wasting near an hour in vacillating evolutions, always at a safe distance from the rifle, the Hurons seemed suddenly to take their resolution, and began to display it by giving eager chase to the girls.

When this last design was adopted, the circumstances of all parties, as connected with their relative positions, were materially changed. The Ark had sailed and drifted quite half a mile, and was nearly that distance due north of the castle. As soon as the Delaware perceived that the girls avoided him, unable to manage his unwieldy craft, and knowing that flight from a bark canoe, in the event of pursuit, would be a useless expedient if attempted, he had lowered his sail, in the hope it might induce the sisters to change their plan and to seek refuge in the scow. This demonstration produced no other effect than to keep the Ark nearer to the scene of action, and to enable those in her to become witnesses of the chase. The canoe of Judith was about a quarter of a mile south of that of the Hurons, a little nearer to the east shore, and about the same distance to the southward of the castle as it was from the hostile canoe, a circumstance which necessarily put the last nearly abreast of Hutter's fortress. With the several parties thus situated the chase commenced.

At the moment when the Hurons so suddenly changed their mode of attack their canoe was not in the best possible racing trim. There were but two paddles, and the third man so much extra and useless cargo. Then the difference in weight between the sisters and the other two men, more especially in vessels so extremely light, almost neutralized any difference that might proceed from the greater strength of the Hurons, and rendered the trial of speed far from being as unequal as it might seem. Judith did not commence her exertions until the near approach of the other canoe rendered the object of the movement certain, and then she exhorted Hetty to aid her with her utmost skill and strength.

"Why should we run, Judith?" asked the simple minded girl. "The Hurons have never harmed me, nor do I think they ever will."

"That may be true as to you, Hetty, but it will prove very different with me. Kneel down and say your prayer, and then rise and do your utmost to help escape. Think of me, dear girl, too, as you pray."

Judith gave these directions from a mixed feeling; first because she knew that her sister ever sought the support of her great ally in trouble, and next because a sensation of feebleness and dependance suddenly came over her own proud spirit, in that moment of apparent desertion and trial. The prayer was quickly said, however, and the canoe was soon in rapid motion. Still, neither party resorted to their greatest exertions from the outset, both knowing that the chase was likely to be arduous and long. Like two vessels of war that are preparing for an encounter, they seemed desirous of first ascertaining their respective rates of speed, in order that they might know how to graduate their exertions, previously to the great effort. A few minutes sufficed to show the Hurons that the girls were expert, and that it would require all their skill and energies to overtake them.

Judith had inclined towards the eastern shore at the commencement of the chase, with a vague determination of landing and flying to the woods as a last resort, but as she approached the land, the certainty that scouts must be watching her movements made her reluctance to adopt such an expedient unconquerable. Then she was still fresh, and had sanguine hopes of being able to tire out her pursuers. With such feelings she gave a sweep with her paddle, and sheered off from the fringe of dark hemlocks beneath the shades of which she was so near entering, and held her way again, more towards the centre of the lake. This seemed the instant favorable for the Hurons to make their push, as it gave them the entire breadth of the sheet to do it in; and this too in the widest part, as soon as they had got between the fugitives and the land. The canoes now flew, Judith making up for what she wanted in strength by her great dexterity and self command. For half a mile the Indians gained no material advantage, but the continuance of so great exertions for so many minutes sensibly affected all concerned. Here the Indians resorted to an expedient that enabled them to give one of their party time to breathe, by shifting their paddles from hand to hand, and this too without sensibly relaxing their efforts.

Judith occasionally looked behind her, and she saw this expedient practised. It caused her immediately to distrust the result, since her powers of endurance were not likely to hold out against those of men who had the means of relieving each other. Still she persevered, allowing no very visible consequences immediately to follow the change.

As yet the Indians had not been able to get nearer to the girls than two hundred yards, though they were what seamen would term "in their wake"; or in a direct line behind them, passing over the same track of water. This made the pursuit what is technically called a "stern chase", which is proverbially a "long chase": the meaning of which is that, in consequence of the relative positions of the parties, no change becomes apparent except that which is a direct gain in the nearest possible approach. "Long" as this species of chase is admitted to be, however, Judith was enabled to perceive that the Hurons were sensibly drawing nearer and nearer, before she had gained the centre of the lake. She was not a girl to despair, but there was an instant when she thought of yielding, with the wish of being carried to the camp where she knew the Deerslayer to be a captive; but the considerations connected with the means she hoped to be able to employ in order to procure his release immediately interposed, in order to stimulate her to renewed exertions. Had there been any one there to note the progress of the two canoes, he would have seen that of Judith flying swiftly away from its pursuers, as the girl gave it freshly impelled speed, while her mind was thus dwelling on her own ardent and generous schemes. So material, indeed, was the difference in the rate of going between the two canoes for the next five minutes, that the Hurons began to be convinced all their powers must be exerted or they would suffer the disgrace of being baffled by women. Making a furious effort under the mortification of such a conviction, one of the strongest of their party broke his paddle at the very moment when he had taken it from the hand of a comrade to relieve him. This at once decided the matter, a canoe containing three men and having but one paddle being utterly unable to overtake fugitives like the daughters of Thomas Hutter.

"There, Judith!" exclaimed Hetty, who saw the accident, "I hope now you will own, that praying is useful! The Hurons have broke a paddle, and they never can overtake us."

"I never denied it, poor Hetty, and sometimes wish in bitterness of spirit that I had prayed more myself, and thought less of my beauty! As you say, we are now safe and need only go a little south and take breath."

This was done; the enemy giving up the pursuit, as suddenly as a ship that has lost an important spar, the instant the accident occurred. Instead of following Judith's canoe, which was now lightly skimming over the water towards the south, the Hurons turned their bows towards the castle, where they soon arrived and landed. The girls, fearful that some spare paddles might be found in or about the buildings, continued on, nor did they stop until so distant from their enemies as to give them every chance of escape, should the chase be renewed. It would seem that the savages meditated no such design, but at the end of an hour their canoe, filled with men, was seen quitting the castle and steering towards the shore. The girls were without food, and they now drew nearer to the buildings and the Ark, having finally made up their minds from its manoeuvres that the latter contained friends.

Notwithstanding the seeming desertion of the castle, Judith approached it with extreme caution. The Ark was now quite a mile to the northward, but sweeping up towards the buildings, and this, too, with a regularity of motion that satisfied Judith a white man was at the oars. When within a hundred yards of the building the girls began to encircle it, in order to make sure that it was empty. No canoe was nigh, and this emboldened them to draw nearer and nearer, until they had gone round the piles and reached the platform.

"Do you go into the house, Hetty," said Judith, "and see that the savages are gone. They will not harm you, and if any of them are still here you can give me the alarm. I do not think they will fire on a poor defenceless girl, and I at least may escape, until I shall be ready to go among them of my own accord."

Hetty did as desired, Judith retiring a few yards from the platform the instant her sister landed, in readiness for flight. But the last was unnecessary, not a minute elapsing before Hetty returned to communicate that all was safe.

"I've been in all the rooms, Judith," said the latter earnestly, "and they are empty, except father's; he is in his own chamber, sleeping, though not as quietly as we could wish."

"Has any thing happened to father?" demanded Judith, as her foot touched the platform; speaking quickly, for her nerves were in a state to be easily alarmed.

Hetty seemed concerned, and she looked furtively about her as if unwilling any one but a child should hear what she had to communicate, and even that she should learn it abruptly.

"You know how it is with father sometimes, Judith," she said, "When overtaken with liquor he doesn't always know what he says or does, and he seems to be overtaken with liquor now."

"That is strange! Would the savages have drunk with him, and then leave him behind? But 'tis a grievous sight to a child, Hetty, to witness such a failing in a parent, and we will not go near him 'til he wakes."

A groan from the inner room, however, changed this resolution, and the girls ventured near a parent whom it was no unusual thing for them to find in a condition that lowers a man to the level of brutes. He was seated, reclining in a corner of the narrow room with his shoulders supported by the angle, and his head fallen heavily on his chest. Judith moved forward with a sudden impulse, and removed a canvass cap that was forced so low on his head as to conceal his face, and indeed all but his shoulders. The instant this obstacle was taken away, the quivering and raw flesh, the bared veins and muscles, and all the other disgusting signs of mortality, as they are revealed by tearing away the skin, showed he had been scalped, though still living.

CHAPTER XXI.

> "Lightly they'll talk of the spirit that's gone,
> And o'er his cold ashes upbraid him;
> But nothing he'll reck, if they'll let him sleep on,
> In the grave where a Briton has laid him."

Charles Wolfe, "The Burial of Sir John Moore," vi.

The reader must imagine the horror that daughters would experience, at unexpectedly beholding the shocking spectacle that was placed before the eyes of Judith and Esther, as related in the close of the last chapter. We shall pass over the first emotions, the first acts of filial piety, and proceed with the narrative by imagining rather than relating most of the revolting features of the scene. The mutilated and ragged head was bound up, the unseemly blood was wiped from the face of the sufferer, the other appliances required by appearances and care were resorted to, and there was time to enquire into the more serious circumstances of the case. The facts were never known until years later in all their details, simple as they were, but they may as well be related here, as it can be done in a few words. In the struggle with the Hurons, Hutter had been stabbed by the knife of the old warrior, who had used the discretion to remove the arms of every one but himself. Being hard pushed by his sturdy foe, his knife had settled the matter. This occurred just as the door was opened, and Hurry burst out upon the platform, as has been previously related. This was the secret of neither party's having appeared in the subsequent struggle; Hutter having been literally disabled, and his conqueror being ashamed to be seen with the traces of blood about him, after having used so many injunctions to convince his young warriors of the necessity of taking their prisoners alive. When the three Hurons returned from the chase, and it was determined to abandon the castle and join the party on the land, Hutter was simply scalped to secure the usual trophy, and was left to die by inches, as has been done in a thousand similar instances by the ruthless warriors of this part of the American continent. Had the injury of Hutter been confined to his head, he might have recovered, however, for it was the blow of the knife that proved mortal. There are moments of vivid consciousness, when the stern justice of God stands forth in colours so prominent as to defy any attempts to veil them from the sight, however unpleasant they may appear, or however anxious we may be to avoid recognising it. Such was now the fact with Judith and Hetty, who both perceived the decrees of a retributive Providence, in the manner of their father's suffering, as a punishment for his own recent attempts on the Iroquois. This was seen and felt by Judith with the keenness of perception and sensibility that were suited to her character, while the impression made on the simpler mind of her sister was perhaps less lively, though it might well have proved more lasting.

"Oh! Judith," exclaimed the weak minded girl, as soon as their first care had been bestowed on sufferer. "Father went for scalps, himself, and now where is his own? The Bible might have foretold this dreadful punishment!"

"Hush, Hetty—hush, poor sister—He opens his eyes; he may hear and understand you. 'Tis as you say and think, but 'tis too dreadful to speak."

"Water," ejaculated Hutter, as it might be by a desperate effort, that rendered his voice frightfully deep and strong for one as near death as he evidently was—"Water—foolish girls—will you let me die of thirst?"

Water was brought and administered to the sufferer; the first he had tasted in hours of physical anguish. It had the double effect of clearing his throat and of momentarily reviving his sinking system. His eyes opened with that anxious, distended gaze which is apt to accompany the passage of a soul surprised by death, and he seemed disposed to speak.

"Father," said Judith, inexpressibly pained by his deplorable situation, and this so much the more from her ignorance of what remedies ought to be applied—"Father, can we do any thing for you? Can Hetty and I relieve your pain?"

"Father!" slowly repeated the old man. "No, Judith; no, Hetty—I'm no father. She was your mother, but I'm no father. Look in the chest—'Tis all there—give me more water."

The girls complied, and Judith, whose early recollections extended farther back than her sister's, and who on every account had more distinct impressions of the past, felt an uncontrollable impulse of joy as she heard these words. There had never been much sympathy between her reputed father and herself, and suspicions of this very truth had often glanced across her mind, in consequence of dialogues she had overheard between Hutter and her mother. It might be going too far to say she had never loved him, but it is not so to add that she rejoiced it was no longer a duty. With Hetty the feeling was different. Incapable of making all the distinctions of her sister, her very nature was full of affection, and she had loved her reputed parent, though far less tenderly than the real parent, and it grieved her now to hear him declare he was not naturally entitled to that love. She felt a double grief, as if his death and his words together were twice depriving her of parents. Yielding to her feelings, the poor girl went aside and wept.

The very opposite emotions of the two girls kept both silent for a long time. Judith gave water to the sufferer frequently, but she forbore to urge him with questions, in some measure out of consideration for his condition, but, if truth must be said, quite as much lest something he should add in the way of explanation might disturb her pleasing belief that she was not Thomas Hutter's child. At length Hetty dried her tears, and came and seated herself on a stool by the side of the dying man, who had been placed at his length on the floor, with his head supported by some coarse vestments that had been left in the house.

"Father," she said "you will let me call you father, though you say you are not one—Father, shall I read the Bible to you—mother always said the Bible was good for people in trouble. She was often in trouble herself, and then she made me read the Bible to her—for Judith wasn't as fond of the Bible as I am—and it always did her good. Many is the time I've known mother begin to listen with the tears streaming from her eyes, and end with smiles and gladness. Oh! father, you don't know how much good the Bible can do, for you've never tried it. Now, I'll read a chapter and it will soften your heart as it softened the hearts of the Hurons."

While poor Hetty had so much reverence for, and faith in, the virtues of the Bible, her intellect was too shallow to enable her fully to appreciate its beauties, or to fathom its profound and sometimes mysterious wisdom. That instinctive sense of right which appeared to shield her from the commission of wrong, and even cast a mantle of moral loveliness and truth around her character, could not penetrate abstrusities, or trace the nice affinities between cause and effect, beyond their more obvious and indisputable connection, though she seldom failed to see all the latter, and to defer to all their just consequences. In a word, she was one of those who feel and act correctly without being able to give a logical reason for it, even admitting revelation as her authority. Her selections from the Bible, therefore, were commonly distinguished by the simplicity of her own mind, and were oftener marked for containing images of known and palpable things than for any of the higher cast of moral truths with which the pages of that wonderful book abound—wonderful, and unequalled, even without referring to its divine origin, as a work replete with the profoundest philosophy, expressed in the noblest language. Her mother, with a connection that will probably strike the reader, had been fond of the book of Job, and Hetty had, in a great measure, learned to read by the frequent lessons she had received from the different chapters of this venerable and sublime poem—now believed to be the oldest book in the world. On this occasion the poor girl was submissive to her training, and she turned to that well known part of the sacred volume, with the readiness with which the practised counsel would cite his authorities from the stores of legal wisdom. In selecting the particular chapter, she was influenced by the caption, and she chose that which stands in our English version as "Job excuseth his desire of death." This she read steadily, from beginning to end, in a sweet, low and plaintive voice; hoping devoutly that the allegorical and abstruse sentences might convey to the heart of the sufferer the consolation he needed. It is another peculiarity of the comprehensive wisdom of the Bible that scarce a chapter, unless it be strictly narration, can be turned to, that does not contain some searching truth that is applicable to the condition of every human heart, as well as to the temporal state of its owner, either through the workings of that heart, or even in a still more direct form. In this instance, the very opening sentence—"Is there not an appointed time to man on earth?" was startling, and as Hetty proceeded, Hutter applied, or fancied he could apply many aphorisms and figures to his own worldly and mental condition. As life is ebbing fast, the mind clings eagerly to hope when it is not absolutely crushed by despair. The solemn words "I have sinned; what shall I do unto thee, O thou preserver of men? Why hast thou set me as a mark against thee, so that I am a burden to myself," struck Hutter more perceptibly than the others, and, though too obscure for one of his blunted feelings and obtuse mind either to feel or to comprehend in their fullest extent, they had a directness of application to his own state that caused him to wince under them.

"Don't you feel better now, father?" asked Hetty, closing the volume. "Mother was always better when she had read the Bible."

"Water," returned Hutter—"give me water, Judith. I wonder if my tongue will always be so hot! Hetty, isn't there something in the Bible about cooling the tongue of a man who was burning in Hell fire?"

Judith turned away shocked, but Hetty eagerly sought the passage, which she read aloud to the conscience stricken victim of his own avaricious longings.

"That's it, poor Hetty; yes, that's it. My tongue wants cooling, now—what will it be hereafter?"

This appeal silenced even the confiding Hetty, for she had no answer ready for a confession so fraught with despair. Water, so long as it could relieve the sufferer, it was in the power of the sisters to give, and from time to time it was offered to the lips of the sufferer as he asked for it. Even Judith prayed. As for Hetty, as soon as she found that her efforts to make her father listen to her texts were no longer rewarded with success, she knelt at his side and devoutly repeated the words which the Saviour has left behind him as a model for human petitions. This she continued to do, at intervals, as long as it seemed to her that the act could benefit the dying man. Hutter, however, lingered longer than the girls had believed possible when they first found him. At times he spoke intelligibly, though his lips oftener moved in utterance of sounds that carried no distinct impressions to the mind. Judith listened intently, and she heard the words—"husband"—"death"—"pirate"—"law"—"scalps"—and several others of similar import, though there was no sentence to tell the precise connection in which they were used. Still they were sufficiently expressive to be understood by one whose ears had not escaped all the rumours that had been circulated to her reputed father's discredit, and whose comprehension was as quick as her faculties were attentive.

During the whole of the painful hour that succeeded, neither of the sisters bethought her sufficiently of the Hurons to dread their return. It seemed as if their desolation and grief placed them above the danger of such an interruption, and when the sound of oars was at length heard, even Judith, who alone had any reason to apprehend the enemy, did not start, but at once understood that the Ark was near. She went upon the platform fearlessly, for should it turn out that Hurry was not there, and that the Hurons were masters of the scow also, escape was impossible. Then she had the sort of confidence that is inspired by extreme misery. But there was no cause for any new alarm, Chingachgook, Hist, and Hurry all standing in the open part of the scow, cautiously examining the building to make certain of the absence of the enemy. They, too, had seen the departure of the Hurons, as well as the approach of the canoe of the girls to the castle, and presuming on the latter fact, March had swept the scow up to the platform. A word sufficed to explain that there was nothing to be apprehended, and the Ark was soon moored in her old berth.

Judith said not a word concerning the condition of her father, but Hurry knew her too well not to understand that something was more than usually wrong. He led the way, though with less of his confident bold manner than usual, into the house, and penetrating to the inner room, found Hutter lying on his back with Hetty sitting at his side, fanning him with pious care. The events of the morning had sensibly changed the manner of Hurry. Notwithstanding his skill as a swimmer, and the readiness with which he had adopted the only expedient that could possibly save him, the helplessness of being in the water, bound hand and foot, had produced some such effect on him, as the near approach of punishment is known to produce on most criminals, leaving a vivid impression of the horrors of death upon his mind, and this too in connection with a picture of bodily helplessness; the daring of this man being far more the offspring of vast physical powers, than of the energy of the will, or even of natural spirit. Such heroes invariably lose a large portion of their courage with the failure of their strength, and though Hurry was now unfettered and as vigorous as ever, events were too recent to permit the recollection of his late deplorable condition to be at all weakened. Had he lived a century, the occurrences of the few momentous minutes during which he was in the lake would have produced a chastening effect on his character, if not always on his manner.

Hurry was not only shocked when he found his late associate in this desperate situation, but he was greatly surprised. During the struggle in the building, he had been far too much occupied himself to learn what had befallen his comrade, and, as no deadly weapon had been used in his particular case, but every effort had been made to capture him without injury, he naturally believed that Hutter had been overcome, while he owed his own escape to his great bodily strength, and to a fortunate concurrence of extraordinary circumstances. Death, in the silence and solemnity of a chamber, was a novelty to him. Though accustomed to scenes of violence, he had been unused to sit by the bedside and watch the slow beating of the pulse, as it gradually grew weaker and weaker. Notwithstanding the change in his feelings, the manners of a life could not be altogether cast aside in a moment, and the unexpected scene extorted a characteristic speech from the borderer.

"How now! old Tom," he said, "have the vagabonds got you at an advantage, where you're not only down, but are likely to be kept down! I thought you a captyve it's true, but never supposed you so hard run as this!"

Hutter opened his glassy eyes, and stared wildly at the speaker. A flood of confused recollections rushed on his wavering mind at the sight of his late comrade. It was evident that he struggled with his own images, and knew not the real from the unreal.

"Who are you?" he asked in a husky whisper, his failing strength refusing to aid him in a louder effort of his voice.

"Who are you?—You look like the mate of 'The Snow'—he was a giant, too, and near overcoming us."

"I'm your mate, Floating Tom, and your comrade, but have nothing to do with any snow. It's summer now, and Harry March always quits the hills as soon after the frosts set in, as is convenient."

"I know you—Hurry Skurry—I'll sell you a scalp!—a sound one, and of a full grown man— What'll you give?"

"Poor Tom! That scalp business hasn't turned out at all profitable, and I've pretty much concluded to give it up; and to follow a less bloody calling."

"Have you got any scalp? Mine's gone—How does it feel to have a scalp? I know how it feels to lose one—fire and flames about the brain—and a wrenching at the heart—no—no—kill first, Hurry, and scalp afterwards."

"What does the old fellow mean, Judith? He talks like one that is getting tired of the business as well as myself. Why have you bound up his head? or, have the savages tomahawked him about the brains?"

"They have done that for him which you and he, Harry March, would have so gladly done for them. His skin and hair have been torn from his head to gain money from the governor of Canada, as you would have torn theirs from the heads of the Hurons, to gain money from the Governor of York."

Judith spoke with a strong effort to appear composed, but it was neither in her nature, nor in the feeling of the moment to speak altogether without bitterness. The strength of her emphasis, indeed, as well as her manner, caused Hetty to look up reproachfully.

"These are high words to come from Thomas Hutter's darter, as Thomas Hutter lies dying before her eyes," retorted Hurry.

"God be praised for that!—whatever reproach it may bring on my poor mother, I am not Thomas Hutter's daughter."

"Not Thomas Hutter's darter!—Don't disown the old fellow in his last moments, Judith, for that's a sin the Lord will never overlook. If you're not Thomas Hutter's darter, whose darter be you?"

This question rebuked the rebellious spirit of Judith, for, in getting rid of a parent whom she felt it was a relief to find she might own she had never loved, she overlooked the important circumstance that no substitute was ready to supply his place.

"I cannot tell you, Harry, who my father was," she answered more mildly; "I hope he was an honest man, at least."

"Which is more than you think was the case with old Hutter? Well, Judith, I'll not deny that hard stories were in circulation consarning Floating Tom, but who is there that doesn't get a scratch, when an inimy holds the rake? There's them that say hard things of me, and even you, beauty as you be, don't always escape."

This was said with a view to set up a species of community of character between the parties, and as the politicians are wont to express it, with ulterior intentions. What might have been the consequences with one of Judith's known spirit, as well as her assured antipathy to the speaker, it is not easy to say, for, just then, Hutter gave unequivocal signs that his last moment was nigh. Judith and Hetty had stood by the dying bed of their mother, and neither needed a monitor to warn them of the crisis, and every sign of resentment vanished from the face of the first. Hutter opened his eyes, and even tried to feel about him with his hands, a sign that sight was failing. A minute later, his breathing grew ghastly; a pause totally without respiration followed; and, then, succeeded the last, long drawn sigh, on which the spirit is supposed to quit the body. This sudden termination of the life of one who had hitherto filled so important a place in the narrow scene on which he had been an actor, put an end to all discussion.

The day passed by without further interruption, the Hurons, though possessed of a canoe, appearing so far satisfied with their success as to have relinquished all immediate designs on the castle. It would not have been a safe undertaking, indeed, to approach it under the rifles of those it was now known to contain, and it is probable that the truce was more owing to this circumstance than to any other. In the mean while the preparations were made for the interment of Hutter. To bury him on the land was impracticable, and it was Hetty's wish that his body should lie by the side of that of her mother, in the lake. She had it in her power to quote one of his speeches, in which he himself had called the lake the "family burying ground," and luckily this was done without the knowledge of her sister, who would have opposed the plan, had she known it, with unconquerable disgust. But Judith had not meddled with the arrangement, and every necessary disposition was made without her privity or advice.

The hour chosen for the rude ceremony was just as the sun was setting, and a moment and a scene more suited to paying the last offices to one of calm and pure spirit could not have been chosen. There are a mystery and a solemn dignity in death, that dispose the living to regard the remains of even a malefactor with a certain degree of reverence. All worldly distinctions have ceased; it is thought that the veil has been removed, and that the character and destiny of the departed are now as much beyond human opinions, as they are beyond human ken. In nothing is death more truly a leveller than in this, since, while it may be impossible absolutely to confound the great with the low, the worthy with the unworthy, the mind feels it to be arrogant to assume a right to judge of those who are believed to be standing at the judgment seat of God. When Judith was told that all was ready, she went upon the platform, passive to the request of her sister, and then she first took heed of the arrangement. The body was in the scow, enveloped in a sheet, and quite a hundred weight of stones, that had been taken from the fire place, were enclosed with it, in order that it might sink. No other preparation seemed to be thought necessary, though Hetty carried her Bible beneath her arm.

When all were on board the Ark, the singular habitation of the man whose body it now bore to its final abode, was set in motion. Hurry was at the oars. In his powerful hands, indeed, they seemed little more than a pair of sculls, which were wielded without effort, and, as he was expert in their use, the Delaware remained a passive spectator of the proceedings. The progress of the Ark had something of the stately solemnity of a funeral procession, the dip of the oars being measured, and the movement slow and steady. The wash of the water, as the blades rose and fell, kept time with the efforts of Hurry, and might have been likened to the measured tread of mourners. Then the tranquil scene was in beautiful accordance with a rite that ever associates with itself the idea of God. At that instant, the lake had not even a single ripple on its glassy surface, and the broad panorama of woods seemed to look down on the holy tranquillity of the hour and ceremony in melancholy stillness. Judith was affected to tears, and even Hurry, though he hardly knew why, was troubled. Hetty preserved the outward signs of tranquillity, but her inward grief greatly surpassed that of her sister, since her affectionate heart loved more from habit and long association, than from the usual connections of sentiment and taste. She was sustained by religious hope, however, which in her simple mind usually occupied the space that worldly feelings filled in that of Judith, and she was not without an expectation of witnessing some open manifestation of divine power, on an occasion so solemn. Still she was neither mystical nor exaggerated; her mental imbecility denying both. Nevertheless her thoughts had generally so much of the purity of a better world about them that it was easy for her to forget earth altogether, and to think only of heaven. Hist was serious, attentive and interested, for she had often seen the interments of the pale-faces, though never one that promised to be as peculiar as this; while the Delaware, though grave, and also observant, in his demeanor was stoical and calm.

Hetty acted as pilot, directing Hurry how to proceed, to find that spot in the lake which she was in the habit of terming "mother's grave." The reader will remember that the castle stood near the southern extremity of a shoal that extended near half a mile northerly, and it was at the farthest end of this shallow water that Floating Tom had seen fit to deposit the remains of his wife and child. His own were now in the course of being placed at their side. Hetty had marks on the land by which she usually found the spot, although the position of the buildings, the general direction of the shoal, and the beautiful transparency of the water all aided her, the latter even allowing the bottom to be seen. By these means the girl was enabled to note their progress, and at the proper time she approached March, whispering, "Now, Hurry you can stop rowing. We have passed the stone on the bottom, and mother's grave is near."

March ceased his efforts, immediately dropping the kedge and taking the warp in his hand in order to check the scow. The Ark turned slowly round under this restraint, and when it was quite stationary, Hetty was seen at its stern, pointing into the water, the tears streaming from her eyes, in ungovernable natural feeling. Judith had been present at the interment of her mother, but she had never visited the spot since. The neglect proceeded from no indifference to the memory of the deceased; for she had loved her mother, and bitterly had she found occasion to mourn her loss; but she was averse to the contemplation of death; and there had been passages in her own life since the day of that interment which increased this feeling, and rendered her, if possible, still more reluctant to approach the spot that contained the remains of one whose severe lessons of female morality and propriety had been deepened and rendered doubly impressive by remorse for her own failings. With Hetty, the case had been very different. To her simple and innocent mind, the remembrance of her mother brought no other feeling than one of gentle sorrow; a grief that is so often termed luxurious even, because it associates with itself the images of excellence and the purity of a better state of existence. For an entire summer, she had been in the habit of repairing to the place after night-fall; and carefully anchoring her canoe so as not to disturb the body, she would sit and hold fancied conversations with the deceased, sing sweet hymns to the evening air, and repeat the orisons that the being who now slumbered below had taught her in infancy. Hetty had passed her happiest hours in this indirect communion with the spirit of her mother; the wildness of Indian traditions and Indian opinions, unconsciously to herself, mingling with the Christian lore received in childhood. Once she had even been so far influenced by the former as to have bethought her of performing some of those physical rites at her mother's grave which the redmen are known to observe; but the passing feeling had been obscured by the steady, though mild light of Christianity, which never ceased to burn in her gentle bosom. Now her emotions were merely the natural outpourings of a daughter that wept for a mother whose love was indelibly impressed on the heart, and whose lessons had been too earnestly taught to be easily forgotten by one who had so little temptation to err.

There was no other priest than nature at that wild and singular funeral rite. March cast his eyes below, and through the transparent medium of the clear water, which was almost as pure as air, he saw what Hetty was accustomed to call "mother's grave." It was a low, straggling mound of earth, fashioned by no spade, out of a corner of which gleamed a bit of the white cloth that formed the shroud of the dead. The body had been lowered to the bottom, and Hutter brought earth from the shore and let it fall upon it, until all was concealed. In this state the place had remained until the movement of the waters revealed the solitary sign of the uses of the spot that has just been mentioned.

Even the most rude and brawling are chastened by the ceremonies of a funeral. March felt no desire to indulge his voice in any of its coarse outbreakings, and was disposed to complete the office he had undertaken in decent sobriety. Perhaps he reflected on the retribution that had alighted on his late comrade, and bethought him of the frightful jeopardy in which his own life had so lately been placed. He signified to Judith that all was ready, received her directions to proceed, and, with no other assistant than his own vast strength, raised the body and bore it to the end of the scow. Two parts of a rope were passed beneath the legs and shoulders, as they are placed beneath coffins, and then the corpse was slowly lowered beneath the surface of the lake.

"Not there—Harry March—no, not there," said Judith, shuddering involuntarily; "do not lower it quite so near the spot where mother lies!"

"Why not, Judith?" asked Hetty, earnestly. "They lived together in life, and should lie together in death."

"No—no—Harry March, further off—further off. Poor Hetty, you know not what you say. Leave me to order this."

"I know I am weak-minded, Judith, and that you are clever—but, surely a husband should be placed near a wife. Mother always said that this was the way they bury in Christian churchyards."

This little controversy was conducted earnestly, but in smothered voices, as if the speakers feared that the dead might overhear them. Judith could not contend with her sister at such a moment, but a significant gesture induced March to lower the body at a little distance from that of his wife; when he withdrew the cords, and the act was performed.

"There's an end of Floating Tom!" exclaimed Hurry, bending over the scow, and gazing through the water at the body. "He was a brave companion on a scout, and a notable hand with traps. Don't weep, Judith, don't be overcome, Hetty, for the righteousest of us all must die; and when the time comes, lamentations and tears can't bring the dead to life. Your father will be a loss to you, no doubt; most fathers are a loss, especially to onmarried darters; but there's a way to cure that evil, and you're both too young and handsome to live long without finding it out. When it's agreeable to hear what an honest and onpretending man has to say, Judith, I should like to talk a little with you, apart."

Judith had scarce attended to this rude attempt of Hurry's at consolation, although she necessarily understood its general drift, and had a tolerably accurate notion of its manner. She was weeping at the recollection of her mother's early tenderness, and painful images of long forgotten lessons and neglected precepts were crowding her mind. The words of Hurry, however, recalled her to the present time, and abrupt and unseasonable as was their import, they did not produce those signs of distaste that one might have expected from the girl's character. On the contrary, she appeared to be struck with some sudden idea, gazed intently for a moment at the young man, dried her eyes, and led the way to the other end of the scow, signifying her wish for him to follow. Here she took a seat and motioned for March to place himself at her side. The decision and earnestness with which all this was done a little intimidated her companion, and Judith found it necessary to open the subject herself.

"You wish to speak to me of marriage, Harry March," she said, "and I have come here, over the grave of my parents, as it might be—no—no—over the grave of my poor, dear, dear, mother, to hear what you have to say."

"This is oncommon, and you have a skearful way with you this evening, Judith," answered Hurry, more disturbed than he would have cared to own, "but truth is truth, and it shall come out, let what will follow. You well know, gal, that I've long thought you the comeliest young woman my eyes ever beheld, and that I've made no secret of that fact, either here on the lake, out among the hunters and trappers, or in the settlements."

"Yes—yes, I've heard this before, and I suppose it to be true," answered Judith with a sort of feverish impatience.

"When a young man holds such language of any particular young woman, it's reasonable to calculate he sets store by her."

"True—true, Hurry—all this you've told me, again and again."

"Well, if it's agreeable, I should think a woman coul'n't hear it too often. They all tell me this is the way with your sex, that nothing pleases them more than to repeat over and over, for the hundredth time, how much you like 'em, unless it be to talk to 'em of their good looks!"

"No doubt—we like both, on most occasions, but this is an uncommon moment, Hurry, and vain words should not be too freely used. I would rather hear you speak plainly."

"You shall have your own way, Judith, and I some suspect you always will. I've often told you that I not only like you better than any other young woman going, or, for that matter, better than all the young women going, but you must have observed, Judith, that I've never asked you, in up and down tarms, to marry me."

"I have observed both," returned the girl, a smile struggling about her beautiful mouth, in spite of the singular and engrossing intentness which caused her cheeks to flush and lighted her eyes with a brilliancy that was almost dazzling—"I have observed both, and have thought the last remarkable for a man of Harry March's decision and fearlessness."

"There's been a reason, gal, and it's one that troubles me even now—nay, don't flush up so, and look fiery like, for there are thoughts which will stick long in any man's mind, as there be words that will stick in his throat—but, then ag'in, there's feelin's that will get the better of 'em all, and to these feelin's I find I must submit. You've no longer a father, or a mother, Judith, and it's morally unpossible that you and Hetty could live here, alone, allowing it was peace and the Iroquois was quiet; but, as matters stand, not only would you starve, but you'd both be prisoners, or scalped, afore a week was out. It's time to think of a change and a husband, and, if you'll accept of me, all that's past shall be forgotten, and there's an end on't."

Judith had difficulty in repressing her impatience until this rude declaration and offer were made, which she evidently wished to hear, and which she now listened to with a willingness that might well have excited hope. She hardly allowed the young man to conclude, so eager was she to bring him to the point, and so ready to answer.

"There—Hurry—that's enough," she said, raising a hand as if to stop him—"I understand you as well as if you were to talk a month. You prefer me to other girls, and you wish me to become your wife."

"You put it in better words than I can do, Judith, and I wish you to fancy them said just as you most like to hear 'em."

"They're plain enough, Harry, and 'tis fitting they should be so. This is no place to trifle or deceive in. Now, listen to my answer, which shall be, in every tittle, as sincere as your offer. There is a reason, March, why I should never—

"I suppose I understand you, Judith, but if I'm willing to overlook that reason, it's no one's consarn but mine—Now, don't brighten up like the sky at sundown, for no offence is meant, and none should be taken."

"I do not brighten up, and will not take offence," said Judith, struggling to repress her indignation, in a way she had never found it necessary to exert before. "There is a reason why I should not, cannot, ever be your wife, Hurry, that you seem to overlook, and which it is my duty now to tell you, as plainly as you have asked me to consent to become so. I do not, and I am certain that I never shall, love you well enough to marry you. No man can wish for a wife who does not prefer him to all other men, and when I tell you this frankly, I suppose you yourself will thank me for my sincerity."

"Ah! Judith, them flaunting, gay, scarlet-coated officers of the garrisons have done all this mischief!"

"Hush, March; do not calumniate a daughter over her mother's grave! Do not, when I only wish to treat you fairly, give me reason to call for evil on your head in bitterness of heart! Do not forget that I am a woman, and that you are a man; and that I have neither father, nor brother, to revenge your words!"

"Well, there is something in the last, and I'll say no more. Take time, Judith, and think better on this."

"I want no time—my mind has long been made up, and I have only waited for you to speak plainly, to answer plainly. We now understand each other, and there is no use in saying any more."

The impetuous earnestness of the girl awed the young man, for never before had he seen her so serious and determined. In most, of their previous interviews she had met his advances with evasion or sarcasm, but these Hurry had mistaken for female coquetry, and had supposed might easily be converted into consent. The struggle had been with himself, about offering, nor had he ever seriously believed it possible that Judith would refuse to become the wife of the handsomest man on all that frontier. Now that the refusal came, and that in terms so decided as to put all cavilling out of the question; if not absolutely dumbfounded, he was so much mortified and surprised as to feel no wish to attempt to change her resolution.

"The Glimmerglass has now no great call for me," he exclaimed after a minute's silence. "Old Tom is gone, the Hurons are as plenty on the shore as pigeons in the woods, and altogether it is getting to be an onsuitable place."

"Then leave it. You see it is surrounded by dangers, and there is no reason why you should risk your life for others. Nor do I know that you can be of any service to us. Go, to-night; we'll never accuse you of having done any thing forgetful, or unmanly."

"If I do go, 'twill be with a heavy heart on your account, Judith; I would rather take you with me."

"That is not to be spoken of any longer, March; but, I will land you in one of the canoes, as soon as it is dark and you can strike a trail for the nearest garrison. When you reach the fort, if you send a party—"

Judith smothered the words, for she felt that it was humiliating to be thus exposing herself to the comments and reflections of one who was not disposed to view her conduct in connection with all in those garrisons, with an eye of favor. Hurry, however, caught the idea, and without perverting it, as the girl dreaded, he answered to the purpose.

"I understand what you would say, and why you don't say it." he replied. "If I get safe to the fort, a party shall start on the trail of these vagabonds, and I'll come with it, myself, for I should like to see you and Hetty in a place of safety, before we part forever."

"Ah, Harry March, had you always spoken thus, felt thus, my feelings towards you might have been different!"

"Is it too late, now, Judith? I'm rough and a woodsman, but we all change under different treatment from what we have been used to."

"It is too late, March. I can never feel towards you, or any other man but one, as you would wish to have me. There, I've said enough, surely, and you will question me no further. As soon as it is dark, I or the Delaware will put you on the shore. You will make the best of your way to the Mohawk, and the nearest garrison, and send all you can to our assistance. And, Hurry, we are now friends, and I may trust in you, may I not?"

"Sartain, Judith; though our fri'ndship would have been all the warmer, could you look upon me as I look upon you."

Judith hesitated, and some powerful emotion was struggling within her. Then, as if determined to look down all weaknesses, and accomplish her purposes at every hazard, she spoke more plainly.

"You will find a captain of the name of Warley at the nearest post," she said, pale as death, and even trembling as she spoke; "I think it likely he will wish to head the party, but I would greatly prefer it should be another. If Captain Warley can be kept back, 't would make me very happy!"

"That's easier said than done, Judith, for these officers do pretty much as they please. The Major will order, and captains, and lieutenants, and ensigns must obey. I know the officer you mean, a red faced, gay, oh! be joyful sort of a gentleman, who swallows madeira enough to drown the Mohawk, and yet a pleasant talker. All the gals in the valley admire him, and they say he admires all the gals. I don't wonder he is your dislike, Judith, for he's a very gin'ral lover, if he isn't a gin'ral officer."

Judith did not answer, though her frame shook, and her colour changed from pale to crimson, and from crimson back again to the hue of death.

"Alas! my poor mother!" she ejaculated mentally instead of uttering it aloud, "We are over thy grave, but little dost thou know how much thy lessons have been forgotten; thy care neglected; thy love defeated!"

As this goading of the worm that never dies was felt, she arose and signified to Hurry, that she had no more to communicate.

## CHAPTER XXII.

"That point in misery, which makes the oppressed man regardless
  of his own life, makes him too Lord of the oppressor's."

Coleridge, Remorse, V. i. 201–04.

All this time Hetty had remained seated in the head of the scow, looking sorrowfully into the water which held the body of her mother, as well as that of the man whom she had been taught to consider her father. Hist stood near her in gentle quiet, but had no consolation to offer in words. The habits of her people taught her reserve in this respect, and the habits of her sex induced her to wait patiently for a moment when she might manifest some soothing sympathy by means of acts, rather than of speech. Chingachgook held himself a little aloof, in grave reserve, looking like a warrior, but feeling like a man.

Judith joined her sister with an air of dignity and solemnity it was not her practice to show, and, though the gleamings of anguish were still visible on her beautiful face, when she spoke it was firmly and without tremor. At that instant Hist and the Delaware withdrew, moving towards Hurry, in the other end of the boat.

"Sister," said Judith kindly, "I have much to say to you; we will get into this canoe, and paddle off to a distance from the Ark—The secrets of two orphans ought not to be heard by every ear."

"Certainly, Judith, by the ears of their parents? Let Hurry lift the grapnel and move away with the Ark, and leave us here, near the graves of father and mother, to say what we may have to say."

"Father!" repeated Judith slowly, the blood for the first time since her parting with March mounting to her cheeks—"He was no father of ours, Hetty! That we had from his own mouth, and in his dying moments."

"Are you glad, Judith, to find you had no father! He took care of us, and fed us, and clothed us, and loved us; a father could have done no more. I don't understand why he wasn't a father."

"Never mind, dear child, but let us do as you have said. It may be well to remain here, and let the Ark move a little away. Do you prepare the canoe, and I will tell Hurry and the Indians our wishes."

This was soon and simply done, the Ark moving with measured strokes of the sweeps a hundred yards from the spot, leaving the girls floating, seemingly in air, above the place of the dead; so buoyant was the light vessel that held them, and so limpid the element by which it was sustained.

"The death of Thomas Hutter," Judith commenced, after a short pause had prepared her sister to receive her communications, "has altered all our prospects, Hetty. If he was not our father, we are sisters, and must feel alike and live together."

"How do I know, Judith, that you wouldn't be as glad to find I am not your sister, as you are in finding that Thomas Hutter, as you call him, was not your father. I am only half witted, and few people like to have half witted relations; and then I'm not handsome—at least, not as handsome as you—and you may wish a handsomer sister."

"No, no Hetty. You and you only are my sister—my heart, and my love for you tell me that—and mother was my mother—of that too am I glad, and proud; for she was a mother to be proud of—but father was not father!"

"Hush, Judith! His spirit may be near; it would grieve it to hear his children talking so, and that, too, over his very grave. Children should never grieve parents, mother often told me, and especially when they are dead!"

"Poor Hetty! They are happily removed beyond all cares on our account. Nothing that I can do or say will cause mother any sorrow now—there is some consolation in that, at least! And nothing you can say or do will make her smile, as she used to smile on your good conduct when living."

"You don't know that, Judith. Spirits can see, and mother may see as well as any spirit. She always told us that God saw all we did, and that we should do nothing to offend him; and now she has left us, I strive to do nothing that can displease her. Think how her spirit would mourn and feel sorrow, Judith, did it see either of us doing what is not right; and spirits may see, after all; especially the spirits of parents that feel anxious about their children."

"Hetty—Hetty—you know not what you say!" murmured Judith, almost livid with emotion—"The dead cannot see, and know nothing of what passes here! But, we will not talk of this any longer. The bodies of Mother and Thomas Hutter lie together in the lake, and we will hope that the spirits of both are with God. That we, the children of one of them, remain on earth is certain; it is now proper to know what we are to do in future."

"If we are not Thomas Hutter's children, Judith, no one will dispute our right to his property. We have the castle and the Ark, and the canoes, and the woods, and the lakes, the same as when he was living, and what can prevent us from staying here, and passing our lives just as we ever have done?"

"No, no poor sister—this can no longer be. Two girls would not be safe here, even should these Hurons fail in getting us into their power. Even father had as much as he could sometimes do, to keep peace upon the lake, and we should fail altogether. We must quit this spot, Hetty, and remove into the settlements."

"I am sorry you think so, Judith," returned Hetty, dropping her head on her bosom, and looking thoughtfully down at the spot where the funeral pile of her mother could just be seen. "I am very sorry to hear it. I would rather stay here, where, if I wasn't born, I've passed my life. I don't like the settlements—they are full of wickedness and heart burnings, while God dwells unoffended in these hills! I love the trees, and the mountains, and the lake, and the springs; all that his bounty has given us, and it would grieve me sorely, Judith, to be forced to quit them. You are handsome, and not at all half-witted, and one day you will marry, and then you will have a husband, and I a brother to take care of us, if women can't really take care of themselves in such a place as this."

"Ah! if this could be so, Hetty, then, indeed, I could now be a thousand times happier in these woods, than in the settlements. Once I did not feel thus, but now I do. Yet where is the man to turn this beautiful place into such a garden of Eden for us?"

"Harry March loves you, sister," returned poor Hetty, unconsciously picking the bark off the canoe as she spoke. "He would be glad to be your husband, I'm sure, and a stouter and a braver youth is not to be met with the whole country round."

"Harry March and I understand each other, and no more need be said about him. There is one—but no matter. It is all in the hands of providence, and we must shortly come to some conclusion about our future manner of living. Remain here—that is, remain here, alone, we cannot—and perhaps no occasion will ever offer for remaining in the manner you think of. It is time, too, Hetty, we should learn all we can concerning our relations and family. It is not probable we are altogether without relations, and they may be glad to see us. The old chest is now our property, and we have a right to look into it, and learn all we can by what it holds. Mother was so very different from Thomas Hutter, that, now I know we are not his children, I burn with a desire to know whose children we can be. There are papers in that chest, I am certain, and those papers may tell us all about our parents and natural friends."

"Well, Judith, you know best, for you are cleverer than common, mother always said, and I am only half-witted. Now father and mother are dead, I don't much care for any relation but you, and don't think I could love them I never saw, as well as I ought. If you don't like to marry Hurry, I don't see who you can choose for a husband, and then I fear we shall have to quit the lake, after all."

"What do you think of Deerslayer, Hetty?" asked Judith, bending forward like her unsophisticated sister, and endeavoring to conceal her embarrassment in a similar manner. "Would he not make a brother-in-law to your liking?"

"Deerslayer!" repeated the other, looking up in unfeigned surprise. "Why, Judith, Deerslayer isn't in the least comely, and is altogether unfit for one like you!"

"He is not ill-looking, Hetty, and beauty in a man is not of much matter."

"Do you think so, Judith? I know that beauty is of no great matter, in man or woman, in the eyes of God, for mother has often told me so, when she thought I might have been sorry I was not as handsome as you, though she needn't have been uneasy on that account, for I never coveted any thing that is yours, sister—but, tell me so she did—still, beauty is very pleasant to the eye, in both! I think, if I were a man, I should pine more for good looks than I do as a girl. A handsome man is a more pleasing sight than a handsome woman."

"Poor child! You scarce know what you say, or what you mean! Beauty in our sex is something, but in men, it passes for little. To be sure, a man ought to be tall, but others are tall, as well as Hurry; and active—and I think I know those that are more active—and strong; well, he hasn't all the strength in the world—and brave—I am certain I can name a youth who is braver!"

"This is strange, Judith!—I didn't think the earth held a handsomer, or a stronger, or a more active or a braver man than Hurry Harry! I'm sure I never met his equal in either of these things."

"Well, well, Hetty—say no more of this. I dislike to hear you talking in this manner. 'Tis not suitable to your innocence, and truth, and warm-hearted sincerity. Let Harry March go. He quits us to-night, and no regret of mine will follow him, unless it be that he has staid so long, and to so little purpose."

"Ah! Judith; that is what I've long feared—and I did so hope he might be my brother-in-law!"

"Never mind it now. Let us talk of our poor mother—and of Thomas Hutter."

"Speak kindly then, sister, for you can't be quite certain that spirits don't both hear and see. If father wasn't father, he was good to us, and gave us food and shelter. We can't put any stones over their graves, here in the water, to tell people all this, and so we ought to say it with our tongues."

"They will care little for that, girl. 'Tis a great consolation to know, Hetty, that if mother ever did commit any heavy fault when young, she lived sincerely to repent of it; no doubt her sins were forgiven her."

"Tisn't right, Judith, for children to talk of their parents' sins. We had better talk of our own."

"Talk of your sins, Hetty!—If there ever was a creature on earth without sin, it is you! I wish I could say, or think the same of myself; but we shall see. No one knows what changes affection for a good husband can make in a woman's heart. I don't think, child, I have even now the same love for finery I once had."

"It would be a pity, Judith, if you did think of clothes, over your parents' graves! We will never quit this spot, if you say so, and will let Hurry go where he pleases."

"I am willing enough to consent to the last, but cannot answer for the first, Hetty. We must live, in future, as becomes respectable young women, and cannot remain here, to be the talk and jest of all the rude and foul tongu'd trappers and hunters that may come upon the lake. Let Hurry go by himself, and then I'll find the means to see Deerslayer, when the future shall be soon settled. Come, girl, the sun has set, and the Ark is drifting away from us; let us paddle up to the scow, and consult with our friends. This night I shall look into the chest, and to-morrow shall determine what we are to do. As for the Hurons, now we can use our stores without fear of Thomas Hutter, they will be easily bought off. Let me get Deerslayer once out of their hands, and a single hour shall bring things to an understanding."

Judith spoke with decision, and she spoke with authority, a habit she had long practised towards her feeble-minded sister. But, while thus accustomed to have her way, by the aid of manner and a readier command of words, Hetty occasionally checked her impetuous feelings and hasty acts by the aid of those simple moral truths that were so deeply engrafted in all her own thoughts and feelings; shining through both with a mild and beautiful lustre that threw a sort of holy halo around so much of what she both said and did. On the present occasion, this healthful ascendancy of the girl of weak intellect, over her of a capacity that, in other situations, might have become brilliant and admired, was exhibited in the usual simple and earnest manner.

"You forget, Judith, what has brought us here," she said reproachfully. "This is mother's grave, and we have just laid the body of father by her side. We have done wrong to talk so much of ourselves at such a spot, and ought now to pray God to forgive us, and ask him to teach us where we are to go, and what we are to do."

Judith involuntarily laid aside her paddle, while Hetty dropped on her knees, and was soon lost in her devout but simple petitions. Her sister did not pray. This she had long ceased to do directly, though anguish of spirit frequently wrung from her mental and hasty appeals to the great source of benevolence, for support, if not for a change of spirit. Still she never beheld Hetty on her knees, that a feeling of tender recollection, as well as of profound regret at the deadness of her own heart, did not come over her. Thus had she herself done in childhood, and even down to the hour of her ill fated visits to the garrisons, and she would willingly have given worlds, at such moments, to be able to exchange her present sensations for the confiding faith, those pure aspirations, and the gentle hope that shone through every lineament and movement of her otherwise, less favored sister. All she could do, however, was to drop her head to her bosom, and assume in her attitude some of that devotion in which her stubborn spirit refused to unite. When Hetty rose from her knees, her countenance had a glow and serenity that rendered a face that was always agreeable, positively handsome. Her mind was at peace, and her conscience acquitted her of a neglect of duty.

"Now, you may go if you want to, Judith," she said, "for God has been kind to me, and lifted a burden off my heart. Mother had many such burdens, she used to tell me, and she always took them off in this way. 'Tis the only way, sister, such things can be done. You may raise a stone, or a log, with your hands; but the heart must be lightened by prayer. I don't think you pray as often as you used to do, when younger, Judith!"

"Never mind—never mind, child," answered the other huskily, "'tis no matter, now. Mother is gone, and Thomas Hutter is gone, and the time has come when we must think and act for ourselves."

As the canoe moved slowly away from the place, under the gentle impulsion of the elder sister's paddle, the younger sat musing, as was her wont whenever her mind was perplexed by any idea more abstract and difficult of comprehension than common.

"I don't know what you mean by 'future', Judith," she at length, suddenly observed. "Mother used to call Heaven the future, but you seem to think it means next week, or to-morrow!"

"It means both, dear sister—every thing that is yet to come, whether in this world or another. It is a solemn word, Hetty, and most so, I fear, to them that think the least about it. Mother's future is eternity; ours may yet mean what will happen while we live in this world—Is not that a canoe just passing behind the castle—here, more in the direction of the point, I mean; it is hid, now; but certainly I saw a canoe stealing behind the logs!"

"I've seen it some time," Hetty quietly answered, for the Indians had few terrors for her, "but I didn't think it right to talk about such things over mother's grave! The canoe came from the camp, Judith, and was paddled by a single man. He seemed to be Deerslayer, and no Iroquois."

"Deerslayer!" returned the other, with much of her native impetuosity— "That cannot be! Deerslayer is a prisoner, and I have been thinking of the means of setting him free. Why did you fancy it Deerslayer, child?"

"You can look for yourself, sister, for there comes the canoe in sight, again, on this side of the hut."

Sure enough, the light boat had passed the building, and was now steadily advancing towards the Ark; the persons on board of which were already collecting in the head of the scow to receive their visitor. A single glance sufficed to assure Judith that her sister was right, and that Deerslayer was alone in the canoe. His approach was so calm and leisurely, however, as to fill her with wonder, since a man who had effected his escape from enemies by either artifice or violence, would not be apt to move with the steadiness and deliberation with which his paddle swept the water. By this time the day was fairly departing, and objects were already seen dimly under the shores. In the broad lake, however, the light still lingered, and around the immediate scene of the present incidents, which was less shaded than most of the sheet, being in its broadest part, it cast a glow that bore some faint resemblance to the warm tints of an Italian or Grecian sunset. The logs of the hut and Ark had a sort of purple hue, blended with the growing obscurity, and the bark of the hunter's boat was losing its distinctness in colours richer, but more mellowed, than those it showed under a bright sun. As the two canoes approached each other—for Judith and her sister had plied their paddles so as to intercept the unexpected visiter ere he reached the Ark—even Deerslayer's sun-burned countenance wore a brighter aspect than common, under the pleasing tints that seemed to dance in the atmosphere. Judith fancied that delight at meeting her had some share in this unusual and agreeable expression. She was not aware that her own beauty appeared to more advantage than common, from the same natural cause, nor did she understand what it would have given her so much pleasure to know, that the young man actually thought her, as she drew nearer, the loveliest creature of her sex his eyes had ever dwelt on.

"Welcome—welcome, Deerslayer!" exclaimed the girl, as the canoes floated at each other's side; "we have had a melancholy—a frightful day—but your return is, at least, one misfortune the less! Have the Hurons become more human, and let you go; or have you escaped from the wretches, by your own courage and skill?"

"Neither, Judith—neither one nor t'other. The Mingos are Mingos still, and will live and die Mingos; it is not likely their natur's will ever undergo much improvement. Well! They've their gifts, and we've our'n, Judith, and it doesn't much become either to speak ill of what the Lord has created;

though, if the truth must be said, I find it a sore trial to think kindly or to talk kindly of them vagabonds. As for outwitting them, that might have been done, and it was done, too, atween the Sarpent, yonder, and me, when we were on the trail of Hist—" here the hunter stopped to laugh in his own silent fashion—"but it's no easy matter to sarcumvent the sarcumvented. Even the fa'ans get to know the tricks of the hunters afore a single season is over, and an Indian whose eyes have once been opened by a sarcumvention never shuts them ag'in in precisely the same spot. I've known whites to do that, but never a red-skin. What they l'arn comes by practice, and not by books, and of all schoolmasters exper'ence gives lessons that are the longest remembered."

"All this is true, Deerslayer, but if you have not escaped from the savages, how came you here?"

"That's a nat'ral question, and charmingly put. You are wonderful handsome this evening, Judith, or Wild Rose, as the Sarpent calls you, and I may as well say it, since I honestly think it! You may well call them Mingos, savages too, for savage enough do they feel, and savage enough will they act, if you once give them an opportunity. They feel their loss here, in the late skrimmage, to their hearts' cores, and are ready to revenge it on any creatur' of English blood that may fall in their way. Nor, for that matter do I much think they would stand at taking their satisfaction out of a Dutch man."

"They have killed father; that ought to satisfy their wicked cravings for blood," observed Hetty reproachfully.

"I know it, gal—I know the whole story—partly from what I've seen from the shore, since they brought me up from the point, and partly from their threats ag'in myself, and their other discourse. Well, life is unsartain at the best, and we all depend on the breath of our nostrils for it, from day to day. If you've lost a staunch fri'nd, as I make no doubt you have, Providence will raise up new ones in his stead, and since our acquaintance has begun in this oncommon manner, I shall take it as a hint that it will be a part of my duty in futur', should the occasion offer, to see you don't suffer for want of food in the wigwam. I can't bring the dead to life, but as to feeding the living, there's few on all this frontier can outdo me, though I say it in the way of pity and consolation, like, and in no particular, in the way of boasting."

"We understand you, Deerslayer," returned Judith, hastily, "and take all that falls from your lips, as it is meant, in kindness and friendship. Would to Heaven all men had tongues as true, and hearts as honest!"

"In that respect men do differ, of a sartainty, Judith. I've known them that wasn't to be trusted any farther than you can see them; and others ag'in whose messages, sent with a small piece of wampum, perhaps, might just as much be depended on, as if the whole business was finished afore your face. Yes, Judith, you never said truer word, than when you said some men might be depended on, and other some might not."

"You are an unaccountable being, Deerslayer," returned the girl, not a little puzzled with the childish simplicity of character that the hunter so often betrayed—a simplicity so striking that it frequently appeared to place him nearly on a level with the fatuity of poor Hetty, though always relieved by the beautiful moral truth that shone through all that this unfortunate girl both said and did—"You are a most unaccountable man, and I often do not know how to understand you. But never mind, just now; you have forgotten to tell us by what means you are here."

"I!—Oh! That's not very onaccountable, if I am myself, Judith. I'm out on furlough."

"Furlough!—That word has a meaning among the soldiers that I understand; but I cannot tell what it signifies when used by a prisoner."

"It means just the same. You're right enough; the soldiers do use it, and just in the same way as I use it. A furlough is when a man has leave to quit a camp or a garrison for a sartain specified time; at the end of which he is to come back and shoulder his musket, or submit to his torments, just as he may happen to be a soldier, or a captyve. Being the last, I must take the chances of a prisoner."

"Have the Hurons suffered you to quit them in this manner, without watch or guard."

"Sartain—I woul'n't have come in any other manner, unless indeed it had been by a bold rising, or a sarcumvention."

"What pledge have they that you will ever return?"

"My word," answered the hunter simply. "Yes, I own I gave 'em that, and big fools would they have been to let me come without it! Why in that case, I shouldn't have been obliged to go back and ondergo any deviltries their fury may invent, but might have shouldered my rifle, and made the best of my way to the Delaware villages. But, Lord! Judith, they know'd this, just as well as you and I do, and would no more let me come away, without a promise to go back, than they would let the wolves dig up the bones of their fathers!"

"Is it possible you mean to do this act of extraordinary self-destruction and recklessness?"

"Anan!"

"I ask if it can be possible that you expect to be able to put yourself again in the power of such ruthless enemies, by keeping your word."

Deerslayer looked at his fair questioner for a moment with stern displeasure. Then the expression of his honest and guileless face suddenly changed, lighting as by a quick illumination of thought, after which he laughed in his ordinary manner.

"I didn't understand you, at first, Judith; no, I didn't! You believe that Chingachgook and Hurry Harry won't suffer it; but you don't know mankind thoroughly yet, I see. The Delaware would be the last man on 'arth to offer any objections to what he knows is a duty, and, as for March, he doesn't care enough about any creatur' but himself to spend many words on such a subject. If he did, 'twould make no great difference howsever; but not he, for he thinks more of his gains than of even his own word. As for my promises, or your'n, Judith, or any body else's, they give him no consarn. Don't be under any oneasiness, therefore, gal; I shall be allowed to go back according to the furlough; and if difficulties was made, I've not been brought up, and edicated as one may say, in the woods, without knowing how to look 'em down."

Judith made no answer for some little time. All her feelings as a woman, and as a woman who, for the first time in her life was beginning to submit to that sentiment which has so much influence on the happiness or misery of her sex, revolted at the cruel fate that she fancied Deerslayer was drawing down upon himself, while the sense of right, which God has implanted in every human breast, told her to admire an integrity as indomitable and as unpretending as that which the other so unconsciously displayed. Argument, she felt, would be useless, nor was she at that moment disposed to lessen the dignity and high principle that were so striking in the intentions of the hunter, by any attempt to turn him from his purpose. That something might yet occur to supersede the necessity for this self immolation she tried to hope, and then she proceeded to ascertain the facts in order that her own conduct might be regulated by her knowledge of circumstances.

"When is your furlough out, Deerslayer," she asked, after both canoes were heading towards the Ark, and moving, with scarcely a perceptible effort of the paddles, through the water.

"To-morrow noon; not a minute afore; and you may depend on it, Judith, I shan't quit what I call Christian company, to go and give myself up to them vagabonds, an instant sooner than is downright necessary. They begin to fear a visit from the garrisons, and wouldn't lengthen the time a moment, and it's pretty well understood atween us that, should I fail in my ar'n'd, the torments are to take place when the sun begins to fall, that they may strike upon their home trail as soon as it is dark."

This was said solemnly, as if the thought of what was believed to be in reserve duly weighed on the prisoner's mind, and yet so simply, and without a parade of suffering, as rather to repel than to invite any open manifestations of sympathy.

"Are they bent on revenging their losses?" Judith asked faintly, her own high spirit yielding to the influence of the other's quiet but dignified integrity of purpose.

"Downright, if I can judge of Indian inclinations by the symptoms. They think howsever I don't suspect their designs, I do believe, but one that has lived so long among men of red-skin gifts, is no more likely to be misled in Injin feelin's, than a true hunter is like to lose his trail, or a stanch hound his scent. My own judgment is greatly ag'in my own escape, for I see the women are a good deal enraged on behalf of Hist, though I say it, perhaps, that shouldn't say it, seein' that I had a considerable hand myself in getting the gal off. Then there was a cruel murder in their camp last night, and that shot might just as well have been fired into my breast. Howsever, come what will, the Sarpent and his wife will be safe, and that is some happiness in any case."

"Oh! Deerslayer, they will think better of this, since they have given you until to-morrow noon to make up your mind!"

"I judge not, Judith; yes, I judge not. An Injin is an Injin, gal, and it's pretty much hopeless to think of swarving him, when he's got the scent and follows it with his nose in the air. The Delawares, now, are a half Christianized tribe—not that I think such sort of Christians much better than your whole blooded onbelievers—but, nevertheless, what good half Christianizing can do to a man, some among 'em have got, and yet revenge clings to their hearts like the wild creepers here to the tree! Then, I slew one of the best and boldest of their warriors, they say, and it is too much to expect that they should captivate the man who did this deed, in the very same scouting on which it was performed, and they take no account of the matter. Had a month, or so, gone by, their feelin's would have been softened down, and we might have met in a more friendly way, but it is as it is. Judith, this is talking of nothing but myself, and my own consarns, when you have had trouble enough, and may want to consult a fri'nd a little about your own matters. Is the old man laid in the water, where I should think his body would like to rest?"

"It is, Deerslayer," answered Judith, almost inaudibly. "That duty has just been performed. You are right in thinking that I wish to consult a friend; and that friend is yourself. Hurry Harry is about to leave us; when he is gone, and we have got a little over the feelings of this solemn office, I hope you will give me an hour alone. Hetty and I are at a loss what to do."

"That's quite nat'ral, coming as things have, suddenly and fearfully. But here's the Ark, and we'll say more of this when there is a better opportunity."

CHAPTER XXIII.

"The winde is great upon the highest hilles;
The quiet life is in the dale below;
Who tread on ice shall slide against their willes;
They want not cares, that curious arts should know.
Who lives at ease and can content him so,
 Is perfect wise, and sets us all to schoole:
Who hates this lore may well be called a foole."

Thomas Churchyard, "Shore's Wife," xlvii.

The meeting between Deerslayer and his friends in the Ark was grave and anxious. The two Indians, in particular, read in his manner that he was not a successful fugitive, and a few sententious words sufficed to let them comprehend the nature of what their friend had termed his 'furlough.' Chingachgook immediately became thoughtful, while Hist, as usual, had no better mode of expressing her sympathy than by those little attentions which mark the affectionate manner of woman.

In a few minutes, however, something like a general plan for the proceedings of the night was adopted, and to the eye of an uninstructed observer things would be thought to move in their ordinary train. It was now getting to be dark, and it was decided to sweep the Ark up to the castle, and secure it in its ordinary berth. This decision was come to, in some measure on account of the fact that all the canoes were again in the possession of their proper owners, but principally, from the security that was created by the representations of Deerslayer. He had examined the state of things among the Hurons, and felt satisfied that they meditated no further hostilities during the night, the loss they had met having indisposed them to further exertions for the moment. Then, he had a proposition to make; the object of his visit; and, if this were accepted, the war would at once terminate between the parties; and it was improbable that the Hurons would anticipate the failure of a project on which their chiefs had apparently set their hearts, by having recourse to violence previously to the return of their messenger. As soon as the Ark was properly secured, the different members of the party occupied themselves in their several peculiar manners, haste in council, or in decision, no more characterizing the proceedings of these border whites, than it did those of their red neighbors. The women busied themselves in preparations for the evening meal, sad and silent, but ever attentive to the first wants of nature. Hurry set about repairing his moccasins, by the light of a blazing knot; Chingachgook seated himself in gloomy thought, while Deerslayer proceeded, in a manner equally free from affectation and concern, to examine 'Killdeer', the rifle of Hutter that has been already mentioned, and which subsequently became so celebrated, in the hands of the individual who was now making a survey of its merits. The piece was a little longer than usual, and had evidently been turned out from the work shops of some manufacturer of a superior order. It had a few silver ornaments, though, on the whole, it would have been deemed a plain piece by most frontier men, its great merit consisting in the accuracy of its bore, the perfection of the details, and the excellence of the metal. Again and again did the hunter apply the breech to his shoulder, and glance his eye along the sights, and as often did he poise his body and raise the weapon slowly, as if about to catch an aim at a deer, in order to try the weight, and to ascertain its fitness for quick and accurate firing. All this was done, by the aid of Hurry's torch, simply, but with an earnestness and abstraction that would have been found touching by any spectator who happened to know the real situation of the man.

"'Tis a glorious we'pon, Hurry!" Deerslayer at length exclaimed, "and it may be thought a pity that it has fallen into the hands of women. The hunters have told me of its expl'ites, and by all I have heard, I should set it down as sartain death in exper'enced hands. Hearken to the tick of this lock—a wolf trap has'n't a livelier spring; pan and cock speak together, like two singing masters undertaking a psalm in meetin'. I never did see so true a bore, Hurry, that's sartain!"

"Ay, Old Tom used to give the piece a character, though he wasn't the man to particularize the ra'al natur' of any sort of fire arms, in practise," returned March, passing the deer's thongs through the moccasin with the coolness of a cobbler. "He was no marksman, that we must all allow; but he had his good p'ints, as well as his bad ones. I have had hopes that Judith might consait the idee of giving Killdeer to me."

"There's no saying what young women may do, that's a truth, Hurry, and I suppose you're as likely to own the rifle as another. Still, when things are so very near perfection, it's a pity not to reach it entirely."

"What do you mean by that?—Would not that piece look as well on my shoulder, as on any man's?"

"As for looks, I say nothing. You are both good-looking, and might make what is called a good-looking couple. But the true p'int is as to conduct. More deer would fall in one day, by that piece, in some man's hands, than would fall in a week in your'n, Hurry! I've seen you try; yes, remember the buck t'other day."

"That buck was out of season, and who wishes to kill venison out of season. I was merely trying to frighten the creatur', and I think you will own that he was pretty well skeared, at any rate."

"Well, well, have it as you say. But this is a lordly piece, and would make a steady hand and quick eye the King of the Woods!"

"Then keep it, Deerslayer, and become King of the Woods," said Judith, earnestly, who had heard the conversation, and whose eye was never long averted from the honest countenance of the hunter. "It can never be in better hands than it is, at this moment, and there I hope it will remain these fifty years.

"Judith you can't be in 'arnest!" exclaimed Deerslayer, taken so much by surprise, as to betray more emotion than it was usual for him to manifest on ordinary occasions. "Such a gift would be fit for a ra'al King to make; yes, and for a ra'al King to receive."

"I never was more in earnest, in my life, Deerslayer, and I am as much in earnest in the wish as in the gift."

"Well, gal, well; we'll find time to talk of this ag'in. You mustn't be down hearted, Hurry, for Judith is a sprightly young woman, and she has a quick reason; she knows that the credit of her father's rifle is safer in my hands, than it can possibly be in yourn; and, therefore, you mustn't be down hearted. In other matters, more to your liking, too, you'll find she'll give you the preference."

Hurry growled out his dissatisfaction, but he was too intent on quitting the lake, and in making his preparations, to waste his breath on a subject of this nature. Shortly after, the supper was ready, and it was eaten in silence as is so much the habit of those who consider the table as merely a place of animal refreshment. On this occasion, however, sadness and thought contributed their share to the general desire not to converse, for Deerslayer was so far an exception to the usages of men of his cast, as not only to wish to hold discourse on such occasions, but as often to create a similar desire in his companions.

The meal ended, and the humble preparations removed, the whole party assembled on the platform to hear the expected intelligence from Deerslayer on the subject of his visit. It had been evident he was in no haste to make his communication, but the feelings of Judith would no longer admit of delay. Stools were brought from the Ark and the hut, and the whole six placed themselves in a circle, near the door, watching each other's countenances, as best they could, by the scanty means that were furnished by a lovely star-light night. Along the shores, beneath the mountains, lay the usual body of gloom, but in the broad lake no shadow was cast, and a thousand mimic stars were dancing in the limpid element, that was just stirred enough by the evening air to set them all in motion.

"Now, Deerslayer," commenced Judith, whose impatience resisted further restraint— "now, Deerslayer, tell us all the Hurons have to say, and the reason why they have sent you on parole, to make us some offer."

"Furlough, Judith; furlough is the word; and it carries the same meaning with a captyve at large, as it does with a soldier who has leave to quit his colors. In both cases the word is passed to come back, and now I remember to have heard that's the ra'al signification; 'furlough' meaning a 'word' passed for the doing of any thing of the like. Parole I rather think is Dutch, and has something to do with the tattoos of the garrisons. But this makes no great difference, since the vartue of a pledge lies in the idee, and not in the word. Well, then, if the message must be given, it must; and perhaps there is no use in putting it off. Hurry will soon be wanting to set out on his journey to the river, and the stars rise and set, just as if they cared for neither Injin nor message. Ah's! me; 'Tisn't a pleasant, and I know it's a useless ar'n'd, but it must be told."

"Harkee, Deerslayer," put in Hurry, a little authoritatively—"You're a sensible man in a hunt, and as good a fellow on a march, as a sixty-miler-a-day could wish to meet with, but you're oncommon slow about messages; especially them that you think won't be likely to be well received. When a thing is to be told, why tell it; and don't hang back like a Yankee lawyer pretending he can't understand a Dutchman's English, just to get a double fee out of him."

"I understand you, Hurry, and well are you named to-night, seeing you've no time to lose. But let us come at once to the p'int, seeing that's the object of this council—for council it may be called, though women have seats among us. The simple fact is this. When the party came back from the castle, the Mingos held a council, and bitter thoughts were uppermost, as was plain to be seen by their gloomy faces. No one likes to be beaten, and a red-skin as little as a pale-face. Well, when they had smoked upon it, and made their speeches, and their council fire had burnt low, the matter came out. It seems the elders among 'em consaited I was a man to be trusted on a furlough—They're wonderful obsarvant, them Mingos; that their worst mimics must allow—but they consaited I was such a man; and it isn't often—" added the hunter, with a pleasing consciousness that his previous life justified this implicit reliance on his good faith—"it isn't often they consait any thing so good of a pale-face; but so they did with me, and, therefore, they didn't hesitate to speak their minds, which is just this: You see the state of things. The lake, and all on it, they fancy, lie at their marcy. Thomas Hutter is deceased, and, as for Hurry, they've got the idee he has been near enough to death to-day, not to wish to take another look at him this summer. Therefore, they account all your forces as reduced to Chingachgook and the two young women, and, while they know the Delaware to be of a high race, and a born warrior, they know he's now on his first war path. As for the gals, of course they set them down much as they do women in gin'ral."

"You mean that they despise us!" interrupted Judith, with eyes that flashed so brightly as to be observed by all present.

"That will be seen in the end. They hold that all on the lake lies at their marcy, and, therefore, they send by me this belt of wampum," showing the article in question to the Delaware, as he spoke, "with these words. 'Tell the Sarpent, they say, that he has done well for a beginner; he may now strike across the mountains for his own villages, and no one shall look for his trail. If he has found a scalp, let him take it with him, for the Huron braves have hearts, and can feel for a young warrior who doesn't wish to go home empty-handed. If he is nimble, he is welcome to lead out a party in pursuit. Hist, howsever, must go back to the Hurons, for, when she left there in the night, she carried away by mistake, that which doesn't belong to her."

"That can't be true!" said Hetty earnestly. "Hist is no such girl, but one that gives every body his due——"

How much more she would have said in remonstrance cannot be known, inasmuch as Hist, partly laughing and partly hiding her face in shame, passed her own hand across the speaker's mouth in a way to check the words.

"You don't understand Mingo messages, poor Hetty——" resumed Deerslayer, "which seldom mean what lies exactly uppermost. Hist has brought away with her the inclinations of a young Huron, and they want her back again, that the poor young man may find them where he last saw them! The Sarpent they say is too promising a young warrior not to find as many wives as he wants, but this one he cannot have. That's their meaning, and nothing else, as I understand it."

"They are very obliging and thoughtful, in supposing a young woman can forget all her own inclinations in order to let this unhappy youth find his!" said Judith, ironically; though her manner became more bitter as she proceeded. "I suppose a woman is a woman, let her colour be white, or red, and your chiefs know little of a woman's heart, Deerslayer, if they think it can ever forgive when wronged, or ever forget when it fairly loves."

"I suppose that's pretty much the truth with some women, Judith, though I've known them that could do both. The next message is to you. They say the Muskrat, as they called your father, has dove to the bottom of the lake; that he will never come up again, and that his young will soon be in want of wigwams if not of food. The Huron huts, they think, are better than the huts of York, and they wish you to come and try them. Your colour is white, they own, but they think young women who've lived so long in the woods would lose their way in the clearin's. A great warrior among them has lately lost his wife, and he would be glad to put the Wild Rose on her bench at his fireside. As for the Feeble Mind, she will always be honored and taken care of by red warriors. Your father's goods they think ought to go to enrich the tribe, but your own property, which is to include everything of a female natur', will go like that of all wives, into the wigwam of the husband. Moreover, they've lost a young maiden by violence, lately, and 'twill take two pale-faces to fill her seat."

"And do you bring such a message to me," exclaimed Judith, though the tone in which the words were uttered had more in it of sorrow than of anger. "Am I a girl to be an Indian's slave?"

"If you wish my honest thoughts on this p'int, Judith, I shall answer that I don't think you'll, willingly, ever become any man's slave; red-skin or white. You're not to think hard, howsever, of my bringing the message, as near as I could, in the very words in which it was given to me. Them was the conditions on which I got my furlough, and a bargain is a bargain, though it is made with a vagabond. I've told you what they've said, but I've not yet told you what I think you ought, one and all, to answer."

"Ay; let's hear that, Deerslayer," put in Hurry. "My cur'osity is up on that consideration, and I should like, right well, to hear your ideas of the reasonableness of the reply. For my part, though, my own mind is pretty much settled on the p'int of my own answer, which shall be made known as soon as necessary."

"And so is mine, Hurry, on all the different heads, and on no one is it more sartainly settled that on your'n. If I was you, I should say—'Deerslayer, tell them scamps they don't know Harry March! He is human; and having a white skin, he has also a white natur', which natur' won't let him desart females of his own race and gifts in their greatest need. So set me down as one that will refuse to come into your treaty, though you should smoke a hogshead of tobacco over it.'"

March was a little embarrassed at this rebuke, which was uttered with sufficient warmth of manner, and with a point that left no doubt of the meaning. Had Judith encouraged him, he would not have hesitated about remaining to defend her and her sister, but under the circumstances a feeling of resentment rather urged him to abandon them. At all events, there was not a sufficiency of chivalry in Hurry Harry to induce him to hazard the safety of his own person unless he could see a direct connection between the probable consequences and his own interests. It is no wonder, therefore, that his answer partook equally of his intention, and of the reliance he so boastingly placed on his gigantic strength, which if it did not always make him outrageous, usually made him impudent, as respects those with whom he conversed.

"Fair words make long friendships, Master Deerslayer," he said a little menacingly. "You're but a stripling, and you know by exper'ence what you are in the hands of a man. As you're not me, but only a go between sent by the savages to us Christians, you may tell your empl'yers that they do know Harry March, which is a proof of their sense as well as his. He's human enough to follow human natur', and that tells him to see the folly of one man's fighting a whole tribe. If females desart him, they must expect to be desarted by him, whether they're of his own gifts or another man's gifts. Should Judith see fit to change her mind, she's welcome to my company to the river, and Hetty with her; but shouldn't she come to this conclusion, I start as soon as I think the enemy's scouts are beginning to nestle themselves in among the brush and leaves for the night."

"Judith will not change her mind, and she does not ask your company, Master March," returned the girl with spirit.

"That p'int's settled, then," resumed Deerslayer, unmoved by the other's warmth. "Hurry Harry must act for himself, and do that which will be most likely to suit his own fancy. The course he means to take will give him an easy race, if it don't give him an easy conscience. Next comes the question with Hist—what say you gal?—Will you desart your duty, too, and go back to the Mingos and take a Huron husband, and all not for the love of the man you're to marry, but for the love of your own scalp?"

"Why you talk so to Hist!" demanded the girl half-offended. "You t'ink a red-skin girl made like captain's lady, to laugh and joke with any officer that come."

"What I think, Hist, is neither here nor there in this matter. I must carry back your answer, and in order to do so it is necessary that you should send it. A faithful messenger gives his ar'n'd, word for word."

Hist no longer hesitated to speak her mind fully. In the excitement she rose from her bench, and naturally recurring to that language in which she expressed herself the most readily, she delivered her thoughts and intentions, beautifully and with dignity, in the tongue of her own people.

"Tell the Hurons, Deerslayer," she said, "that they are as ignorant as moles; they don't know the wolf from the dog. Among my people, the rose dies on the stem where it budded, the tears of the child fall on the graves of its parents; the corn grows where the seed has been planted. The Delaware girls are not messengers to be sent, like belts of wampum, from tribe to tribe. They are honeysuckles, that are sweetest in their own woods; their own young men carry them away in their bosoms, because they are fragrant; they are sweetest when plucked from their native stems. Even the robin and the martin come back, year after year, to their old nests; shall a woman be less true hearted than a bird? Set the pine in the clay and it will turn yellow; the willow will not flourish on the hill; the tamarack is healthiest in the swamp; the tribes of the sea love best to hear the winds that blow over the salt water. As for a Huron youth, what is he to a maiden of the Lenni Lenape. He may be fleet, but her eyes do not follow him in the race; they look back towards the lodges of the Delawares. He may sing a sweet song for the girls of Canada, but there is no music for Wah, but in the tongue she has listened to from childhood. Were the Huron born of the people that once owned the shores of the salt lake, it would be in vain, unless he were of the family of Uncas. The young pine will rise to be as high as any of its fathers. Wah-ta-Wah has but one heart, and it can love but one husband."

Deerslayer listened to this characteristic message, which was given with an earnestness suited to the feelings from which it sprung, with undisguised delight, meeting the ardent eloquence of the girl, as she concluded, with one of his own heartfelt, silent, and peculiar fits of laughter.

"That's worth all the wampum in the woods!" he exclaimed. "You don't understand it, I suppose, Judith, but if you'll look into your feelin's, and fancy that an inimy had sent to tell you to give up the man of your ch'ice, and to take up with another that wasn't the man of your ch'ice, you'll get the substance of it, I'll warrant! Give me a woman for ra'al eloquence, if they'll only make up their minds to speak what they feel. By speakin', I don't mean chatterin', howsever; for most of them will do that by the hour; but comm' out with their honest, deepest feelin's in proper words. And now, Judith, having got the answer of a red-skin girl, it is fit I should get that of a pale-face, if, indeed, a countenance that is as blooming as your'n can in any wise so be tarmed. You are well named the Wild Rose, and so far as colour goes, Hetty ought to be called the Honeysuckle."

"Did this language come from one of the garrison gallants, I should deride it, Deerslayer, but coming from you, I know it can be depended on," returned Judith, deeply gratified by his unmeditated and characteristic compliments. "It is too soon, however, to ask my answer; the Great Serpent has not yet spoken."

"The Sarpent! Lord; I could carry back his speech without hearing a word of it! I didn't think of putting the question to him at all, I will allow; though 'twould be hardly right either, seeing that truth is truth, and I'm bound to tell these Mingos the fact and nothing else. So, Chingachgook, let us hear your mind on this matter—are you inclined to strike across the hills towards your village, to give up Hist to a Huron, and to tell the chiefs at home that, if they're actyve and successful, they may possibly get on the end of the Iroquois trail some two or three days a'ter the inimy has got off of it?"

Like his betrothed, the young chief arose, that his answer might be given with due distinctness and dignity. Hist had spoken with her hands crossed upon her bosom, as if to suppress the emotions within, but the warrior stretched an arm before him with a calm energy that aided in giving emphasis to his expressions. "Wampum should be sent for wampum," he said; "a message must be answered by a message. Hear what the Great Serpent of the Delawares has to say to the pretended wolves from the great lakes, that are howling through our woods. They are no wolves; they are dogs that have come to get their tails and ears cropped by the hands of the Delawares. They are good at stealing young women; bad at keeping them. Chingachgook takes his own where he finds it; he asks leave of no cur from the Canadas. If he has a tender feeling in his heart, it is no business of the Hurons. He tells it to her who most likes to know it; he will not bellow it in the forest, for the ears of those that only understand yells of terror. What passes in his lodge is not for the chiefs of his own people to know; still less for Mingo rogues—"

"Call 'em vagabonds, Sarpent——" interrupted Deerslayer, unable to restrain his delight——"yes, just call 'em up-and-down vagabonds, which is a word easily intarpreted, and the most hateful of all to their ears, it's so true. Never fear me; I'll give em your message, syllable for syllable, sneer for sneer, idee for idee, scorn for scorn, and they desarve no better at your hands——only call 'em vagabonds, once or twice, and that will set the sap mounting in 'em, from their lowest roots to the uppermost branches!"

"Still less for Mingo vagabonds," resumed Chingachgook, quite willingly complying with his friend's request. "Tell the Huron dogs to howl louder, if they wish a Delaware to find them in the woods, where they burrow like foxes, instead of hunting like warriors. When they had a Delaware maiden in their camp, there was a reason for hunting them up; now they will be forgotten unless they make a noise. Chingachgook don't like the trouble of going to his villages for more warriors; he can strike their run-a-way trail; unless they hide it under ground, he will follow it to Canada alone. He will keep Wah-ta-Wah with him to cook his game; they two will be Delawares enough to scare all the Hurons back to their own country."

"That's a grand despatch, as the officers call them things!" cried Deerslayer; "'twill set all the Huron blood in motion; most particularily that part where he tells 'em Hist, too, will keep on their heels 'til they're fairly driven out of the country. Ahs! me; big words ain't always big deeds, notwithstanding! The Lord send that we be able to be only one half as good as we promise to be! And now, Judith, it's your turn to speak, for them miscreants will expect an answer from each person, poor Hetty, perhaps, excepted."

"And why not Hetty, Deerslayer? She often speaks to the purpose; the Indians may respect her words, for they feel for people in her condition."

"That is true, Judith, and quick-thoughted in you. The red-skins do respect misfortunes of all kinds, and Hetty's in particular. So, Hetty, if you have any thing to say, I'll carry it to the Hurons as faithfully as if it was spoken by a schoolmaster, or a missionary."

The girl hesitated a moment, and then she answered in her own gentle, soft tones, as earnestly as any who had preceded her.

"The Hurons can't understand the difference between white people and themselves," she said, "or they wouldn't ask Judith and me to go and live in their villages. God has given one country to the red men and another to us. He meant us to live apart. Then mother always said that we should never dwell with any but Christians, if possible, and that is a reason why we can't go. This lake is ours, and we won't leave it. Father and mother's graves are in it, and even the worst Indians love to stay near the graves of their fathers. I will come and see them again, if they wish me to, and read more out of the Bible to them, but I can't quit father's and mother's graves."

"That will do——that will do, Hetty, just as well as if you sent them a message twice as long," interrupted the hunter. "I'll tell 'em all you've said, and all you mean, and I'll answer for it that they'll be easily satisfied. Now, Judith, your turn comes next, and then this part of my ar'n'd will be tarminated for the night."

Judith manifested a reluctance to give her reply, that had awakened a little curiosity in the messenger. Judging from her known spirit, he had never supposed the girl would be less true to her feelings and principles than Hist, or Hetty, and yet there was a visible wavering of purpose that rendered him slightly uneasy. Even now when directly required to speak, she seemed to hesitate, nor did she open her lips until the profound silence told her how anxiously her words were expected. Then, indeed, she spoke, but it was doubtingly and with reluctance.

"Tell me, first—tell us, first, Deerslayer," she commenced, repeating the words merely to change the emphasis—"what effect will our answers have on your fate? If you are to be the sacrifice of our spirit, it would have been better had we all been more wary as to the language we use. What, then, are likely to be the consequences to yourself?"

"Lord, Judith, you might as well ask me which way the wind will blow next week, or what will be the age of the next deer that will be shot! I can only say that their faces look a little dark upon me, but it doesn't thunder every time a black cloud rises, nor does every puff of wind blow up rain. That's a question, therefore, much more easily put than answered."

"So is this message of the Iroquois to me," answered Judith rising, as if she had determined on her own course for the present. "My answer shall be given, Deerslayer, after you and I have talked together alone, when the others have laid themselves down for the night."

There was a decision in the manner of the girl that disposed Deerslayer to comply, and this he did the more readily as the delay could produce no material consequences one way or the other. The meeting now broke up, Hurry announcing his resolution to leave them speedily. During the hour that was suffered to intervene, in order that the darkness might deepen before the frontierman took his departure, the different individuals occupied themselves in their customary modes, the hunter, in particular, passing most of the time in making further enquiries into the perfection of the rifle already mentioned.

The hour of nine soon arrived, however, and then it had been determined that Hurry should commence his journey. Instead of making his adieus frankly, and in a generous spirit, the little he thought it necessary to say was uttered sullenly and in coldness. Resentment at what he considered Judith's obstinacy was blended with mortification at the career he had since reaching the lake, and, as is usual with the vulgar and narrow-minded, he was more disposed to reproach others with his failures than to censure himself. Judith gave him her hand, but it was quite as much in gladness as with regret, while the two Delawares were not sorry to find he was leaving them. Of the whole party, Hetty alone betrayed any real feeling. Bashfulness, and the timidity of her sex and character, kept even her aloof, so that Hurry entered the canoe, where Deerslayer was already waiting for him, before she ventured near enough to be observed. Then, indeed, the girl came into the Ark and approached its end, just as the little bark was turning from it, with a movement so light and steady as to be almost imperceptible. An impulse of feeling now overcame her timidity, and Hetty spoke.

"Goodbye Hurry—" she called out, in her sweet voice—"goodbye, dear Hurry. Take care of yourself in the woods, and don't stop once, 'til you reach the garrison. The leaves on the trees are scarcely plentier than the Hurons round the lake, and they'll not treat a strong man like you as kindly as they treat me."

The ascendency which March had obtained over this feebleminded, but right-thinking, and right-feeling girl, arose from a law of nature. Her senses had been captivated by his personal advantages, and her moral communications with him had never been sufficiently intimate to counteract an effect that must have been otherwise lessened, even with one whose mind was as obtuse as her own. Hetty's instinct of right, if such a term can be applied to one who seemed taught by some kind spirit how to steer her course with unerring accuracy, between good and evil, would have revolted at Hurry's character on a thousand points, had there been opportunities to enlighten her, but while he conversed and trifled with her sister, at a distance from herself, his perfection of form and feature had been left to produce their influence on her simple imagination and naturally tender feelings, without suffering by the alloy of his opinions and coarseness. It is true she found him rough and rude; but her father was that, and most of the other men she had seen, and that which she believed to belong to all of the sex struck her less unfavorably in Hurry's character than it might otherwise have done. Still, it was not absolutely love that Hetty felt for Hurry, nor do we wish so to portray it, but merely that awakening sensibility and admiration, which, under more propitious circumstances, and always supposing no untoward revelations of character on the part of the young man had supervened to prevent it, might soon have ripened into that engrossing feeling. She felt for him an incipient tenderness, but scarcely any passion. Perhaps the nearest approach to the latter that Hetty had manifested was to be seen in the sensitiveness which had caused her to detect March's predilection for her sister, for, among Judith's many admirers, this was the only instance in which the dull mind of the girl had been quickened into an observation of the circumstances.

Hurry received so little sympathy at his departure that the gentle tones of Hetty, as she thus called after him, sounded soothingly. He checked the canoe, and with one sweep of his powerful arm brought it back to the side of the Ark. This was more than Hetty, whose courage had risen with the departure of her hero, expected, and she now shrunk timidly back at this unexpected return.

"You're a good gal, Hetty, and I can't quit you without shaking hands," said March kindly. "Judith, a'ter all, isn't worth as much as you, though she may be a trifle better looking. As to wits, if honesty and fair dealing with a young man is a sign of sense in a young woman, you're worth a dozen Judiths; ay, and for that matter, most young women of my acquaintance."

"Don't say any thing against Judith, Harry," returned Hetty imploringly. "Father's gone, and mother's gone, and nobody's left but Judith and me, and it isn't right for sisters to speak evil, or to hear evil of each other. Father's in the lake, and so is mother, and we should all fear God, for we don't know when we may be in the lake, too."

"That sounds reasonable, child, as does most you say. Well, if we ever meet ag'in, Hetty, you'll find a fri'nd in me, let your sister do what she may. I was no great fri'nd of your mother I'll allow, for we didn't think alike on most p'ints, but then your father, Old Tom, and I, fitted each other as remarkably as a buckskin garment will fit any reasonable-built man. I've always been unanimous of opinion that Old Floating Tom Hutter, at the bottom, was a good fellow, and will maintain that ag'in all inimies for his sake, as well as for your'n."

"Goodbye, Hurry," said Hetty, who now wanted to hasten the young man off, as ardently as she had wished to keep him only the moment before, though she could give no clearer account of the latter than of the former feeling; "goodbye, Hurry; take care of yourself in the woods; don't halt 'til you reach the garrison. I'll read a chapter in the Bible for you before I go to bed, and think of you in my prayers."

This was touching a point on which March had no sympathies, and without more words, he shook the girl cordially by the hand and re-entered the canoe. In another minute the two adventurers were a hundred feet from the Ark, and half a dozen had not elapsed before they were completely lost to view. Hetty sighed deeply, and rejoined her sister and Hist.

For some time Deerslayer and his companion paddled ahead in silence. It had been determined to land Hurry at the precise point where he is represented, in the commencement of our tale, as having embarked, not only as a place little likely to be watched by the Hurons, but because he was sufficiently familiar with the signs of the woods, at that spot, to thread his way through them in the dark. Thither, then, the light craft proceeded, being urged as diligently and as swiftly as two vigorous and skilful canoemen could force their little vessel through, or rather over, the water. Less than a quarter of an hour sufficed for the object, and, at the end of that time, being within the shadows of the shore, and quite near the point they sought, each ceased his efforts in order to make their parting communications out of earshot of any straggler who might happen to be in the neighborhood.

"You will do well to persuade the officers at the garrison to lead out a party ag'in these vagabonds as soon as you git in, Hurry," Deerslayer commenced; "and you'll do better if you volunteer to guide it up yourself. You know the paths, and the shape of the lake, and the natur' of the land, and can do it better than a common, gin'ralizing scout. Strike at the Huron camp first, and follow the signs that will then show themselves. A few looks at the hut and the Ark will satisfy you as to the state of the Delaware and the women, and, at any rate, there'll be a fine opportunity to fall on the Mingo trail, and to make a mark on the memories of the blackguards that they'll be apt to carry with 'em a long time. It won't be likely to make much difference with me, since that matter will be determined afore to-morrow's sun has set, but it may make a great change in Judith and Hetty's hopes and prospects!"

"And as for yourself, Nathaniel," Hurry enquired with more interest than he was accustomed to betray in the welfare of others—"And, as for yourself, what do you think is likely to turn up?"

"The Lord, in his wisdom, only can tell, Henry March! The clouds look black and threatening, and I keep my mind in a state to meet the worst. Vengeful feelin's are uppermost in the hearts of the Mingos, and any little disapp'intment about the plunder, or the prisoners, or Hist, may make the torments sartain. The Lord, in his wisdom, can only determine my fate, or your'n!"

"This is a black business, and ought to be put a stop to in some way or other—" answered Hurry, confounding the distinctions between right and wrong, as is usual with selfish and vulgar men. "I heartily wish old Hutter and I had scalped every creatur' in their camp, the night we first landed with that capital object! Had you not held back, Deerslayer, it might have been done, and then you wouldn't have found yourself, at the last moment, in the desperate condition you mention."

"'Twould have been better had you said you wished you had never attempted to do what it little becomes any white man's gifts to undertake; in which case, not only might we have kept from coming to blows, but Thomas Hutter would now have been living, and the hearts of the savages would be less given to vengeance. The death of that young woman, too, was on-called for, Henry March, and leaves a heavy load on our names if not on our consciences!"

This was so apparent, and it seemed so obvious to Hurry himself, at the moment, that he dashed his paddle into the water, and began to urge the canoe towards the shore, as if bent only on running away from his own lively remorse. His companion humoured this feverish desire for change, and, in a minute or two, the bows of the boat grated lightly on the shingle of the beach. To land, shoulder his pack and rifle, and to get ready for his march occupied Hurry but an instant, and with a growling adieu, he had already commenced his march, when a sudden twinge of feeling brought him to a dead stop, and immediately after to the other's side.

"You cannot mean to give yourself up ag'in to them murdering savages, Deerslayer!" he said, quite as much in angry remonstrance, as with generous feeling. "'Twould be the act of a madman or a fool!"

"There's them that thinks it madness to keep their words, and there's them that don't, Hurry Harry. You may be one of the first, but I'm one of the last. No red-skin breathing shall have it in his power to say that a Mingo minds his word more than a man of white blood and white gifts, in any thing that consarns me. I'm out on a furlough, and if I've strength and reason, I'll go in on a furlough afore noon to-morrow!"

"What's an Injin, or a word passed, or a furlough taken from creatur's like them, that have neither souls, nor reason!"

"If they've got neither souls nor reason, you and I have both, Henry March, and one is accountable for the other. This furlough is not, as you seem to think, a matter altogether atween me and the Mingos, seeing it is a solemn bargain made atween me and God. He who thinks that he can say what he pleases, in his distress, and that twill all pass for nothing, because 'tis uttered in the forest, and into red men's ears, knows little of his situation, and hopes, and wants. The woods are but the ears of the Almighty, the air is his breath, and the light of the sun is little more than a glance of his eye. Farewell, Harry; we may not meet ag'in, but I would wish you never to treat a furlough, or any other solemn thing that your Christian God has been called on to witness, as a duty so light that it may be forgotten according to the wants of the body, or even accordin' to the cravings of the spirit."

March was now glad again to escape. It was quite impossible that he could enter into the sentiments that ennobled his companion, and he broke away from both with an impatience that caused him secretly to curse the folly that could induce a man to rush, as it were, on his own destruction. Deerslayer, on the contrary, manifested no such excitement. Sustained by his principles, inflexible in the purpose of acting up to them, and superior to any unmanly apprehension, he regarded all before him as a matter of course, and no more thought of making any unworthy attempt to avoid it, than a Mussulman thinks of counteracting the decrees of Providence. He stood calmly on the shore, listening to the reckless tread with which Hurry betrayed his progress through the bushes, shook his head in dissatisfaction at the want of caution, and then stepped quietly into his canoe. Before he dropped the paddle again into the water, the young man gazed about him at the scene presented by the star-lit night. This was the spot where he had first laid his eyes on the beautiful sheet of water on which he floated. If it was then glorious in the bright light of a summer's noon-tide, it was now sad and melancholy under the shadows of night. The mountains rose around it like black barriers to exclude the outer world, and the gleams of pale light that rested on the broader parts of the basin were no bad symbols of the faintness of the hopes that were so dimly visible in his own future. Sighing heavily, he pushed the canoe from the land, and took his way back with steady diligence towards the Ark and the castle.

CHAPTER XXIV.

"Thy secret pleasure turns to open shame;
Thy private feasting to a public fast;
Thy smoothing titles to a ragged name;
Thy sugar'd tongue to bitter worm wood taste:
Thy violent vanities can never last."

Shakespeare, Rape of Lucrece, 11. 890–94.

Judith was waiting the return of Deerslayer on the platform, with stifled impatience, when the latter reached the hut. Hist and Hetty were both in a deep sleep, on the bed usually occupied by the two daughters of the house, and the Delaware was stretched on the floor of the adjoining room, his rifle at side, and a blanket over him, already dreaming of the events of the last few days. There was a lamp burning in the Ark, for the family was accustomed to indulge in this luxury on extraordinary occasions, and possessed the means, the vessel being of a form and material to render it probable it had once been an occupant of the chest.

As soon as the girl got a glimpse of the canoe, she ceased her hurried walk up and down the platform and stood ready to receive the young man, whose return she had now been anxiously expecting for some time. She helped him to fasten the canoe, and by aiding in the other little similar employments, manifested her desire to reach a moment of liberty as soon as possible. When this was done, in answer to an inquiry of his, she informed him of the manner in which their companions had disposed of themselves. He listened attentively, for the manner of the girl was so earnest and impressive as to apprise him that she had something on her mind of more than common concern.

"And now, Deerslayer," Judith continued, "you see I have lighted the lamp, and put it in the cabin of the Ark. That is never done with us, unless on great occasions, and I consider this night as the most important of my life. Will you follow me and see what I have to show you—hear what I have to say."

The hunter was a little surprised, but, making no objections, both were soon in the scow, and in the room that contained the light. Here two stools were placed at the side of the chest, with the lamp on another, and a table near by to receive the different articles as they might be brought to view. This arrangement had its rise in the feverish impatience of the girl, which could brook no delay that it was in her power to obviate. Even all the padlocks were removed, and it only remained to raise the heavy lid, again, to expose all the treasures of this long secreted hoard.

"I see, in part, what all this means," observed Deerslayer—"yes, I see through it, in part. But why is not Hetty present? Now Thomas Hutter is gone, she is one of the owners of these cur'osities, and ought to see them opened and handled."

"Hetty sleeps—" answered Judith, huskily. "Happily for her, fine clothes and riches have no charms. Besides she has this night given her share of all that the chest may hold to me, that I may do with it as I please."

"Is poor Hetty compass enough for that, Judith?" demanded the just-minded young man. "It's a good rule and a righteous one, never to take when them that give don't know the valie of their gifts; and such as God has visited heavily in their wits ought to be dealt with as carefully as children that haven't yet come to their understandings."

Judith was hurt at this rebuke, coming from the person it did, but she would have felt it far more keenly had not her conscience fully acquitted her of any unjust intentions towards her feeble-minded but confiding sister. It was not a moment, however, to betray any of her usual mountings of the spirit, and she smothered the passing sensation in the desire to come to the great object she had in view.

"Hetty will not be wronged," she mildly answered; "she even knows not only what I am about to do, Deerslayer, but why I do it. So take your seat, raise the lid of the chest, and this time we will go to the bottom. I shall be disappointed if something is not found to tell us more of the history of Thomas Hutter and my mother."

"Why Thomas Hutter, Judith, and not your father? The dead ought to meet with as much reverence as the living!"

"I have long suspected that Thomas Hutter was not my father, though I did think he might have been Hetty's, but now we know he was the father of neither. He acknowledged that much in his dying moments. I am old enough to remember better things than we have seen on this lake, though they are so faintly impressed on my memory that the earlier part of my life seems like a dream."

"Dreams are but miserable guides when one has to detarmine about realities, Judith," returned the other admonishingly. "Fancy nothing and hope nothing on their account, though I've known chiefs that thought 'em useful."

"I expect nothing for the future from them, my good friend, but cannot help remembering what has been. This is idle, however, when half an hour of examination may tell us all, or even more than I want to know."

Deerslayer, who comprehended the girl's impatience, now took his seat and proceeded once more to bring to light the different articles that the chest contained. As a matter of course, all that had been previously examined were found where they had been last deposited, and they excited much less interest or comment than when formerly exposed to view. Even Judith laid aside the rich brocade with an air of indifference, for she had a far higher aim before her than the indulgence of vanity, and was impatient to come at the still hidden, or rather unknown, treasures.

"All these we have seen before," she said, "and will not stop to open. The bundle under your hand, Deerslayer, is a fresh one; that we will look into. God send it may contain something to tell poor Hetty and myself who we really are!"

"Ay, if some bundles could speak, they might tell wonderful secrets," returned the young man deliberately undoing the folds of another piece of course canvass, in order to come at the contents of the roll that lay on his knees: "though this doesn't seem to be one of that family, seeing 'tis neither more nor less than a sort of flag, though of what nation, it passes my l'arnin' to say."

"That flag must have some meaning to it—" Judith hurriedly interposed. "Open it wider, Deerslayer, that we may see the colours."

"Well, I pity the ensign that has to shoulder this cloth, and to parade it about on the field. Why 'tis large enough, Judith, to make a dozen of them colours the King's officers set so much store by. These can be no ensign's colours, but a gin'ral's!"

"A ship might carry it, Deerslayer, and ships I know do use such things. Have you never heard any fearful stories about Thomas Hutter's having once been concerned with the people they call buccaneers?"

"Buck-ah-near! Not I—not I—I never heard him mentioned as good at a buck far off, or near by. Hurry Harry did till me something about its being supposed that he had formerly, in some way or other, dealings with sartain sea robbers, but, Lord, Judith, it can't surely give you any satisfaction to make out that ag'in your mother's own husband, though he isn't your father."

"Anything will give me satisfaction that tells me who I am, and helps to explain the dreams of childhood. My mother's husband! Yes, he must have been that, though why a woman like her, should have chosen a man like him, is more than mortal reason can explain. You never saw mother, Deerslayer, and can't feel the vast, vast difference there was between them!"

"Such things do happen, howsever;—yes, they do happen; though why providence lets them come to pass is more than I understand. I've knew the f'ercest warriors with the gentlest wives of any in the tribe, and awful scolds fall to the lot of Injins fit to be missionaries."

"That was not it, Deerslayer; that was not it. Oh! if it should prove that—no; I cannot wish she should not have been his wife at all. That no daughter can wish for her own mother! Go on, now, and let us see what the square looking bundle holds."

Deerslayer complied, and he found that it contained a small trunk of pretty workmanship, but fastened. The next point was to find a key; but, search proving ineffectual, it was determined to force the lock. This Deerslayer soon effected by the aid of an iron instrument, and it was found that the interior was nearly filled with papers. Many were letters; some fragments of manuscripts, memorandums, accounts, and other similar documents. The hawk does not pounce upon the chicken with a more sudden swoop than Judith sprang forward to seize this mine of hitherto concealed knowledge. Her education, as the reader will have perceived, was far superior to her situation in life, and her eye glanced over page after page of the letters with a readiness that her schooling supplied, and with an avidity that found its origin in her feelings. At first it was evident that the girl was gratified; and we may add with reason, for the letters written by females, in innocence and affection, were of a character to cause her to feel proud of those with whom she had every reason to think she was closely connected by the ties of blood. It does not come within the scope of our plan to give more of these epistles, however, than a general idea of their contents, and this will best be done by describing the effect they produced on the manner, appearance, and feeling of her who was so eagerly perusing them.

It has been said, already, that Judith was much gratified with the letters that first met her eye. They contained the correspondence of an affectionate and intelligent mother to an absent daughter, with such allusions to the answers as served in a great measure to fill up the vacuum left by the replies. They were not without admonitions and warnings, however, and Judith felt the blood mounting to her temples, and a cold shudder succeeding, as she read one in which the propriety of the daughter's indulging in as much intimacy as had evidently been described in one of the daughter's own letters, with an officer "who came from Europe, and who could hardly be supposed to wish to form an honorable connection in America," was rather coldly commented on by the mother. What rendered it singular was the fact that the signatures had been carefully cut from every one of these letters, and wherever a name occurred in the body of the epistles it had been erased with so much diligence as to render it impossible to read it. They had all been enclosed in envelopes, according to the fashion of the age, and not an address either was to be found. Still the letters themselves had been religiously preserved, and Judith thought she could discover traces of tears remaining on several. She now remembered to have seen the little trunk in her mother's keeping, previously to her death, and she supposed it had first been deposited in the chest, along with the other forgotten or concealed objects, when the letters could no longer contribute to that parent's grief or happiness.

Next came another bundle, and these were filled with the protestations of love, written with passion certainly, but also with that deceit which men so often think it justifiable to use to the other sex. Judith had shed tears abundantly over the first packet, but now she felt a sentiment of indignation and pride better sustaining her. Her hand shook, however, and cold shivers again passed through her frame, as she discovered a few points of strong resemblance between these letters and some it had been her own fate to receive. Once, indeed, she laid the packet down, bowed her head to her knees, and seemed nearly convulsed. All this time Deerslayer sat a silent but attentive observer of every thing that passed. As Judith read a letter she put it into his hands to hold until she could peruse the next; but this served in no degree to enlighten her companion, as he was totally unable to read. Nevertheless he was not entirely at fault in discovering the passions that were contending in the bosom of the fair creature by his side, and, as occasional sentences escaped her in murmurs, he was nearer the truth, in his divinations, or conjectures, than the girl would have been pleased at discovering.

Judith had commenced with the earliest letters, luckily for a ready comprehension of the tale they told, for they were carefully arranged in chronological order, and to any one who would take the trouble to peruse them, would have revealed a sad history of gratified passion, coldness, and finally of aversion. As she obtained the clue to their import, her impatience would not admit of delay, and she soon got to glancing her eyes over a page by way of coming at the truth in the briefest manner possible. By adopting this expedient, one to which all who are eager to arrive at results without encumbering themselves with details are so apt to resort, Judith made a rapid progress in these melancholy revelations of her mother's failing and punishment. She saw that the period of her own birth was distinctly referred to, and even learned that the homely name she bore was given her by the father, of whose person she retained so faint an impression as to resemble a dream. This name was not obliterated from the text of the letters, but stood as if nothing was to be gained by erasing it. Hetty's birth was mentioned once, and in that instance the name was the mother's, but ere this period was reached came the signs of coldness, shadowing forth the desertion that was so soon to follow. It was in this stage of the correspondence that her mother had recourse to the plan of copying her own epistles. They were but few, but were eloquent with the feelings of blighted affection, and contrition. Judith sobbed over them, until again and again she felt compelled to lay them aside from sheer physical inability to see; her eyes being literally obscured with tears. Still she returned to the task, with increasing interest, and finally succeeded in reaching the end of the latest communication that had probably ever passed between her parents.

All this occupied fully an hour, for near a hundred letters were glanced at, and some twenty had been closely read. The truth now shone clear upon the acute mind of Judith, so far as her own birth and that of Hetty were concerned. She sickened at the conviction, and for the moment the rest of the world seemed to be cut off from her, and she had now additional reasons for wishing to pass the remainder of her life on the lake, where she had already seen so many bright and so many sorrowing days.

There yet remained more letters to examine. Judith found these were a correspondence between her mother and Thomas Hovey. The originals of both parties were carefully arranged, letter and answer, side by side; and they told the early history of the connection between the ill-assorted pair far more plainly than Judith wished to learn it. Her mother made the advances towards a marriage, to the surprise, not to say horror of her daughter, and she actually found a relief when she discovered traces of what struck her as insanity—or a morbid desperation, bordering on that dire calamity—in the earlier letters of that ill-fated woman. The answers of Hovey were coarse and illiterate, though they manifested a sufficient desire to obtain the hand of a woman of singular personal attractions, and whose great error he was willing to overlook for the advantage of possessing one every way so much his superior, and who it also appeared was not altogether destitute of money. The remainder of this part of the correspondence was brief, and it was soon confined to a few communications on business, in which the miserable wife hastened the absent husband in his preparations to abandon a world which there was a sufficient reason to think was as dangerous to one of the parties as it was disagreeable to the other. But a sincere expression had escaped her mother, by which Judith could get a clue to the motives that had induced her to marry Hovey, or Hutter, and this she found was that feeling of resentment which so often tempts the injured to inflict wrongs on themselves by way of heaping coals on the heads of those through whom they have suffered. Judith had enough of the spirit of that mother to comprehend this sentiment, and for a moment did she see the exceeding folly which permitted such revengeful feelings to get the ascendancy.

There what may be called the historical part of the papers ceased. Among the loose fragments, however, was an old newspaper that contained a proclamation offering a reward for the apprehension of certain free-booters by name, among which was that of Thomas Hovey. The attention of the girl was drawn to the proclamation and to this particular name by the circumstance that black lines had been drawn under both, in ink. Nothing else was found among the papers that could lead to a discovery of either the name or the place of residence of the wife of Hutter. All the dates, signatures, and addresses had been cut from the letters, and wherever a word occurred in the body of the communications that might furnish a clue, it was scrupulously erased. Thus Judith found all her hopes of ascertaining who her parents were defeated, and she was obliged to fall back on her own resources and habits for everything connected with the future. Her recollection of her mother's manners, conversation, and sufferings filled up many a gap in the historical facts she had now discovered, and the truth, in its outlines, stood sufficiently distinct before her to take away all desire, indeed, to possess any more details. Throwing herself back in her seat, she simply desired her companion to finish the examination of the other articles in the chest, as it might yet contain something of importance.

"I'll do it, Judith; I'll do it," returned the patient Deerslayer, "but if there's many more letters to read, we shall see the sun ag'in afore you've got through with the reading of them! Two good hours have you been looking at them bits of papers!"

"They tell me of my parents, Deerslayer, and have settled my plans for life. A girl may be excused, who reads about her own father and mother, and that too for the first time in her life! I am sorry to have kept you waiting."

"Never mind me, gal; never mind me. It matters little whether I sleep or watch; but though you be pleasant to look at, and are so handsome, Judith, it is not altogether agreeable to sit so long to behold you shedding tears. I know that tears don't kill, and that some people are better for shedding a few now and then, especially young women; but I'd rather see you smile any time, Judith, than see you weep."

This gallant speech was rewarded with a sweet, though a melancholy smile; and then the girl again desired her companion to finish the examination of the chest. The search necessarily continued some time, during which Judith collected her thoughts and regained her composure. She took no part in the search, leaving everything to the young man, looking listlessly herself at the different articles that came uppermost. Nothing further of much interest or value, however, was found. A sword or two, such as were then worn by gentlemen, some buckles of silver, or so richly plated as to appear silver, and a few handsome articles of female dress, composed the principal discoveries. It struck both Judith and the Deerslayer, notwithstanding, that some of these things might be made useful in effecting a negotiation with the Iroquois, though the latter saw a difficulty in the way that was not so apparent to the former. The conversation was first renewed in connection with this point.

"And now, Deerslayer," said Judith, "we may talk of yourself, and of the means of getting you out of the hands of the Hurons. Any part, or all of what you have seen in the chest, will be cheerfully given by me and Hetty to set you at liberty."

"Well, that's gin'rous,—yes, 'tis downright free-hearted, and free-handed, and gin'rous. This is the way with women; when they take up a fri'ndship, they do nothing by halves, but are as willing to part with their property as if it had no value in their eyes. However, while I thank you both, just as much as if the bargain was made, and Rivenoak, or any of the other vagabonds, was here to accept and close the treaty, there's two principal reasons why it can never come to pass, which may be as well told at once, in order no onlikely expectations may be raised in you, or any onjustifiable hopes in me."

"What reason can there be, if Hetty and I are willing to part with the trifles for your sake, and the savages are willing to receive them?"

"That's it, Judith; you've got the ideas, but they're a little out of their places, as if a hound should take the back'ard instead of the leading scent. That the Mingos will be willing to receive them things, or any more like 'em you may have to offer is probable enough, but whether they'll pay valie for 'em is quite another matter. Ask yourself, Judith, if any one should send you a message to say that, for such or such a price, you and Hetty might have that chist and all it holds, whether you'd think it worth your while to waste many words on the bargain?"

"But this chest and all it holds, are already ours; there is no reason why we should purchase what is already our own."

"Just so the Mingos caculate! They say the chist is theirn, already; or, as good as theirn, and they'll not thank anybody for the key."

"I understand you, Deerslayer; surely we are yet in possession of the lake, and we can keep possession of it until Hurry sends troops to drive off the enemy. This we may certainly do provided you will stay with us, instead of going back and giving yourself up a prisoner, again, as you now seem determined on."

"That Hurry Harry should talk in this-a-way, is nat'ral, and according to the gifts of the man. He knows no better, and, therefore, he is little likely to feel or to act any better; but, Judith, I put it to your heart and conscience—would you, could you think of me as favorably, as I hope and believe you now do, was I to forget my furlough and not go back to the camp?"

"To think more favorably of you than I now do, Deerslayer, would not be easy; but I might continue to think as favorably—at least it seems so—I hope I could, for a world wouldn't tempt me to let you do anything that might change my real opinion of you."

"Then don't try to entice me to overlook my furlough, gal! A furlough is a sacred thing among warriors and men that carry their lives in their hands, as we of the forests do, and what a grievous disapp'intment would it be to old Tamenund, and to Uncas, the father of the Sarpent, and to my other fri'nds in the tribe, if I was so to disgrace myself on my very first war-path. This you will pairceive, moreover, Judith, is without laying any stress on nat'ral gifts, and a white man's duties, to say nothing of conscience. The last is king with me, and I try never to dispute his orders."

"I believe you are right, Deerslayer," returned the girl, after a little reflection and in a saddened voice: "a man like you ought not to act as the selfish and dishonest would be apt to act; you must, indeed, go back. We will talk no more of this, then. Should I persuade you to anything for which you would be sorry hereafter, my own regret would not be less than yours. You shall not have it to say, Judith—I scarce know by what name to call myself, now!"

"And why not? Why not, gal? Children take the names of their parents, nat'rally, and by a sort of gift, like, and why shouldn't you and Hetty do as others have done afore ye? Hutter was the old man's name, and Hutter should be the name of his darters;—at least until you are given away in lawful and holy wedlock."

"I am Judith, and Judith only," returned the girl positively—"until the law gives me a right to another name. Never will I use that of Thomas Hutter again; nor, with my consent, shall Hetty! Hutter was not even his own name, I find, but had he a thousand rights to it, it would give none to me. He was not my father, thank heaven; though I may have no reason to be proud of him that was!"

"This is strange!" said Deerslayer, looking steadily at the excited girl, anxious to know more, but unwilling to inquire into matters that did not properly concern him; "yes, this is very strange and oncommon! Thomas Hutter wasn't Thomas Hutter, and his darters weren't his darters! Who, then, could Thomas Hutter be, and who are his darters?"

"Did you never hear anything whispered against the former life of this person, Deerslayer?" demanded Judith "Passing, as I did, for his child, such reports reached even me."

"I'll not deny it, Judith; no, I'll not deny it. Sartain things have been said, as I've told you, but I'm not very credible as to reports. Young as I am, I've lived long enough to l'arn there's two sorts of characters in the world—them that is 'arned by deeds, and them that is 'arned by tongues, and so I prefar to see and judge for myself, instead of letting every jaw that chooses to wag become my judgment. Hurry Harry spoke pretty plainly of the whole family, as we journeyed this-a-way, and he did hint something consarning Thomas Hutter's having been a free-liver on the water, in his younger days. By free-liver, I mean that he made free to live on other men's goods."

"He told you he was a pirate—there is no need of mincing matters between friends. Read that, Deerslayer, and you will see that he told you no more than the truth. This Thomas Hovey was the Thomas Hutter you knew, as is seen by these letters."

As Judith spoke, with a flushed cheek and eyes dazzling with the brilliancy of excitement, she held the newspaper towards her companion, pointing to the proclamation of a Colonial Governor, already mentioned.

"Bless you, Judith!" answered the other laughing, "you might as well ask me to print that—or, for that matter to write it. My edication has been altogether in the woods; the only book I read, or care about reading, is the one which God has opened afore all his creatur's in the noble forests, broad lakes, rolling rivers, blue skies, and the winds and tempests, and sunshine, and other glorious marvels of the land! This book I can read, and I find it full of wisdom and knowledge."

"I crave your pardon, Deerslayer," said Judith, earnestly, more abashed than was her wont, in finding that she had in advertently made an appeal that might wound her companion's pride. "I had forgotten your manner of life, and least of all did I wish to hurt your feelings."

"Hurt my feelin's? Why should it hurt my feelin's to ask me to read, when I can't read. I'm a hunter—and I may now begin to say a warrior, and no missionary, and therefore books and papers are of no account with such as I—No, no—Judith," and here the young man laughed cordially, "not even for wads, seeing that your true deerkiller always uses the hide of a fa'a'n, if he's got one, or some other bit of leather suitably prepared. There's some that do say, all that stands in print is true, in which case I'll own an unl'arned man must be somewhat of a loser; nevertheless, it can't be truer than that which God has printed with his own hand in the sky, and the woods, and the rivers, and the springs."

"Well, then, Hutter, or Hovey, was a pirate, and being no father of mine, I cannot wish to call him one. His name shall no longer be my name."

"If you dislike the name of that man, there's the name of your mother, Judith. Her'n may sarve you just as good a turn."

"I do not know it. I've look'd through those papers, Deerslayer, in the hope of finding some hint by which I might discover who my mother was, but there is no more trace of the past, in that respect, than the bird leaves in the air."

"That's both oncommon, and onreasonable. Parents are bound to give their offspring a name, even though they give 'em nothing else. Now I come of a humble stock, though we have white gifts and a white natur', but we are not so poorly off as to have no name. Bumppo we are called, and I've heard it said—" a touch of human vanity glowing on his cheek, "that the time has been when the Bumppos had more standing and note among mankind than they have just now."

"They never deserved them more, Deerslayer, and the name is a good one; either Hetty, or myself, would a thousand times rather be called Hetty Bumppo, or Judith Bumppo, than to be called Hetty or Judith Hutter."

"That's a moral impossible," returned the hunter, good humouredly, "onless one of you should so far demean herself as to marry me."

Judith could not refrain from smiling, when she found how simply and naturally the conversation had come round to the very point at which she had aimed to bring it. Although far from unfeminine or forward, either in her feelings or her habits, the girl was goaded by a sense of wrongs not altogether merited, incited by the hopelessness of a future that seemed to contain no resting place, and still more influenced by feelings that were as novel to her as they proved to be active and engrossing. The opening was too good, therefore, to be neglected, though she came to the subject with much of the indirectness and perhaps justifiable address of a woman.

"I do not think Hetty will ever marry, Deerslayer," she said, "and if your name is to be borne by either of us, it must be borne by me."

"There's been handsome women too, they tell me, among the Bumppos, Judith, afore now, and should you take up with the name, oncommon as you be in this particular, them that knows the family won't be altogether surprised."

"This is not talking as becomes either of us, Deerslayer, for whatever is said on such a subject, between man and woman, should be said seriously and in sincerity of heart. Forgetting the shame that ought to keep girls silent until spoken to, in most cases, I will deal with you as frankly as I know one of your generous nature will most like to be dealt by. Can you—do you think, Deerslayer, that you could be happy with such a wife as a woman like myself would make?"

"A woman like you, Judith! But where's the sense in trifling about such a thing? A woman like you, that is handsome enough to be a captain's lady, and fine enough, and so far as I know edicated enough, would be little apt to think of becoming my wife. I suppose young gals that feel themselves to be smart, and know themselves to be handsome, find a sartain satisfaction in passing their jokes ag'in them that's neither, like a poor Delaware hunter."

This was said good naturedly, but not without a betrayal of feeling which showed that something like mortified sensibility was blended with the reply. Nothing could have occurred more likely to awaken all Judith's generous regrets, or to aid her in her purpose, by adding the stimulant of a disinterested desire to atone to her other impulses, and cloaking all under a guise so winning and natural, as greatly to lessen the unpleasant feature of a forwardness unbecoming the sex.

"You do me injustice if you suppose I have any such thought, or wish," she answered, earnestly. "Never was I more serious in my life, or more willing to abide by any agreement that we may make to-night. I have had many suitors, Deerslayer—nay, scarce an unmarried trapper or hunter has been in at the Lake these four years, who has not offered to take me away with him, and I fear some that were married, too."

"Ay, I'll warrant that!" interrupted the other—"I'll warrant all that! Take 'em as a body, Judith, 'arth don't hold a set of men more given to theirselves, and less given to God and the law."

"Not one of them would I—could I listen to; happily for myself perhaps, has it been that such was the case. There have been well looking youths among them too, as you may have seen in your acquaintance, Henry March."

"Yes, Harry is sightly to the eye, though, to my idees, less so to the judgment. I thought, at first, you meant to have him, Judith, I did; but afore he went, it was easy enough to verify that the same lodge wouldn't be big enough for you both."

"You have done me justice in that at least, Deerslayer. Hurry is a man I could never marry, though he were ten times more comely to the eye, and a hundred times more stout of heart than he really is."

"Why not, Judith, why not? I own I'm cur'ous to know why a youth like Hurry shouldn't find favor with a maiden like you?"

"Then you shall know, Deerslayer," returned the girl, gladly availing herself of the opportunity of indirectly extolling the qualities which had so strongly interested her in her listener; hoping by these means covertly to approach the subject nearest her heart. "In the first place, looks in a man are of no importance with a woman, provided he is manly, and not disfigured, or deformed."

"There I can't altogether agree with you," returned the other thoughtfully, for he had a very humble opinion of his own personal appearance; "I have noticed that the comeliest warriors commonly get the best-looking maidens of the tribe for wives, and the Sarpent, yonder, who is sometimes wonderful in his paint, is a gineral favorite with all the Delaware young women, though he takes to Hist, himself, as if she was the only beauty on 'arth!"

"It may be so with Indians; but it is different with white girls. So long as a young man has a straight and manly frame, that promises to make him able to protect a woman, and to keep want from the door, it is all they ask of the figure. Giants like Hurry may do for grenadiers, but are of little account as lovers. Then as to the face, an honest look, one that answers for the heart within, is of more value than any shape or colour, or eyes, or teeth, or trifles like them. The last may do for girls, but who thinks of them at all, in a hunter, or a warrior, or a husband? If there are women so silly, Judith is not among them."

"Well, this is wonderful! I always thought that handsome liked handsome, as riches love riches!"

"It may be so with you men, Deerslayer, but it is not always so with us women. We like stout-hearted men, but we wish to see them modest; sure on a hunt, or the war-path, ready to die for the right, and unwilling to yield to the wrong. Above all we wish for honesty—tongues that are not used to say what the mind does not mean, and hearts that feel a little for others, as well as for themselves. A true-hearted girl could die for such a husband! while the boaster, and the double-tongued suitor gets to be as hateful to the sight, as he is to the mind."

Judith spoke bitterly, and with her usual force, but her listener was too much struck with the novelty of the sensations he experienced to advert to her manner. There was something so soothing to the humility of a man of his temperament, to hear qualities that he could not but know he possessed himself, thus highly extolled by the loveliest female he had ever beheld, that, for the moment, his faculties seemed suspended in a natural and excusable pride. Then it was that the idea of the possibility of such a creature as Judith becoming his companion for life first crossed his mind. The image was so pleasant, and so novel, that he continued completely absorbed by it for more than a minute, totally regardless of the beautiful reality that was seated before him, watching the expression of his upright and truth-telling countenance with a keenness that gave her a very fair, if not an absolutely accurate clue to his thoughts. Never before had so pleasing a vision floated before the mind's eye of the young hunter, but, accustomed most to practical things, and little addicted to submitting to the power of his imagination, even while possessed of so much true poetical feeling in connection with natural objects in particular, he soon recovered his reason, and smiled at his own weakness, as the fancied picture faded from his mental sight, and left him the simple, untaught, but highly moral being he was, seated in the Ark of Thomas Hutter, at midnight, with the lovely countenance of its late owner's reputed daughter, beaming on him with anxious scrutiny, by the light of the solitary lamp.

"You're wonderful handsome, and enticing, and pleasing to look on, Judith!" he exclaimed, in his simplicity, as fact resumed its ascendency over fancy. "Wonderful! I don't remember ever to have seen so beautiful a gal, even among the Delawares; and I'm not astonished that Hurry Harry went away soured as well as disapp'inted!"

"Would you have had me, Deerslayer, become the wife of such a man as Henry March?"

"There's that which is in his favor, and there's that which is ag'in him. To my taste, Hurry wouldn't make the best of husbands, but I fear that the tastes of most young women, hereaway, wouldn't be so hard upon him."

"No—no—Judith without a name would never consent to be called Judith March! Anything would be better than that."

"Judith Bumppo wouldn't sound as well, gal; and there's many names that would fall short of March, in pleasing the ear."

"Ah! Deerslayer, the pleasantness of the sound, in such cases, doesn't come through the ear, but through the heart. Everything is agreeable, when the heart is satisfied. Were Natty Bumppo, Henry March, and Henry March, Natty Bumppo, I might think the name of March better than it is; or were he, you, I should fancy the name of Bumppo horrible!"

"That's just it—yes, that's the reason of the matter. Now, I'm nat'rally avarse to sarpents, and I hate even the word, which, the missionaries tell me, comes from human natur', on account of a sartain sarpent at the creation of the 'arth, that outwitted the first woman; yet, ever since Chingachgook has 'arned the title he bears, why the sound is as pleasant to my ears as the whistle of the whippoorwill of a calm evening—it is. The feelin's make all the difference in the world, Judith, in the natur' of sounds; ay, even in that of looks, too."

"This is so true, Deerslayer, that I am surprised you should think it remarkable a girl, who may have some comeliness herself, should not think it necessary that her husband should have the same advantage, or what you fancy an advantage. To me, looks in a man is nothing provided his countenance be as honest as his heart."

"Yes, honesty is a great advantage, in the long run; and they that are the most apt to forget it in the beginning, are the most apt to l'arn it in the ind. Nevertheless, there's more, Judith, that look to present profit than to the benefit that is to come after a time. One they think a sartainty, and the other an onsartainty. I'm glad, howsever, that you look at the thing in its true light, and not in the way in which so many is apt to deceive themselves."

"I do thus look at it, Deerslayer," returned the girl with emphasis, still shrinking with a woman's sensitiveness from a direct offer of her hand, "and can say, from the bottom of my heart, that I would rather trust my happiness to a man whose truth and feelings may be depended on, than to a false-tongued and false-hearted wretch that had chests of gold, and houses and lands—yes, though he were even seated on a throne!"

"These are brave words, Judith; they're downright brave words; but do you think that the feelin's would keep 'em company, did the ch'ice actually lie afore you? If a gay gallant in a scarlet coat stood on one side, with his head smelling like a deer's foot, his face smooth and blooming as your own, his hands as white and soft as if God hadn't bestowed 'em that man might live by the sweat of his brow, and his step as lofty as dancing-teachers and a light heart could make it; and the other side stood one that has passed his days in the open air till his forehead is as red as his cheek; had cut his way through swamps and bushes till his hand was as rugged as the oaks he slept under; had trodden on the scent of game till his step was as stealthy as the catamount's, and had no other pleasant odor about him than such as natur' gives in the free air and the forest—now, if both these men stood here, as suitors for your feelin's, which do you think would win your favor?"

Judith's fine face flushed, for the picture that her companion had so simply drawn of a gay officer of the garrisons had once been particularly grateful to her imagination, though experience and disappointment had not only chilled all her affections, but given them a backward current, and the passing image had a momentary influence on her feelings; but the mounting colour was succeeded by a paleness so deadly, as to make her appear ghastly.

"As God is my judge," the girl solemnly answered, "did both these men stand before me, as I may say one of them does, my choice, if I know my own heart, would be the latter. I have no wish for a husband who is any way better than myself."

"This is pleasant to listen to, and might lead a young man in time to forget his own onworthiness, Judith! Howsever, you hardly think all that you say. A man like me is too rude and ignorant for one that has had such a mother to teach her. Vanity is nat'ral, I do believe, but vanity like that, would surpass reason."

"Then you do not know of what a woman's heart is capable! Rude you are not, Deerslayer, nor can one be called ignorant that has studied what is before his eyes as closely as you have done. When the affections are concerned, all things appear in their pleasantest colors, and trifles are overlooked, or are forgotten. When the heart feels sunshine, nothing is gloomy, even dull looking objects, seeming gay and bright, and so it would be between you and the woman who should love you, even though your wife might happen, in some matters, to possess what the world calls the advantage over you."

"Judith, you come of people altogether above mine, in the world, and onequal matches, like onequal fri'ndships can't often tarminate kindly. I speak of this matter altogether as a fanciful thing, since it's not very likely that you, at least, would be apt to treat it as a matter that can ever come to pass."

Judith fastened her deep blue eyes on the open, frank countenance of her companion, as if she would read his soul. Nothing there betrayed any covert meaning, and she was obliged to admit to herself, that he regarded the conversation as argumentative, rather than positive, and that he was still without any active suspicion that her feelings were seriously involved in the issue. At first, she felt offended; then she saw the injustice of making the self-abasement and modesty of the hunter a charge against him, and this novel difficulty gave a piquancy to the state of affairs that rather increased her interest in the young man. At that critical instant, a change of plan flashed on her mind, and with a readiness of invention that is peculiar to the quick-witted and ingenious, she adopted a scheme by which she hoped effectually to bind him to her person. This scheme partook equally of her fertility of invention, and of the decision and boldness of her character. That the conversation might not terminate too abruptly, however, or any suspicion of her design exist, she answered the last remark of Deerslayer, as earnestly and as truly as if her original intention remained unaltered.

"I, certainly, have no reason to boast of parentage, after what I have seen this night," said the girl, in a saddened voice. "I had a mother, it is true; but of her name even, I am ignorant—and, as for my father, it is better, perhaps, that I should never know who he was, lest I speak too bitterly of him!"

"Judith," said Deerslayer, taking her hand kindly, and with a manly sincerity that went directly to the girl's heart, "tis better to say no more to-night. Sleep on what you've seen and felt; in the morning things that now look gloomy, may look more che'rful. Above all, never do anything in bitterness, or because you feel as if you'd like to take revenge on yourself for other people's backslidings. All that has been said or done atween us, this night, is your secret, and shall never be talked of by me, even with the Sarpent, and you may be sartain if he can't get it out of me no man can. If your parents have been faulty, let the darter be less so; remember that you're young, and the youthful may always hope for better times; that you're more quick-witted than usual, and such gin'rally get the better of difficulties, and that, as for beauty, you're oncommon, which is an advantage with all. It is time to get a little rest, for to-morrow is like to prove a trying day to some of us."

Deerslayer arose as he spoke, and Judith had no choice but to comply. The chest was closed and secured, and they parted in silence, she to take her place by the side of Hist and Hetty, and he to seek a blanket on the floor of the cabin he was in. It was not five minutes ere the young man was in a deep sleep, but the girl continued awake for a long time. She scarce knew whether to lament, or to rejoice, at having failed in making herself understood. On the one hand were her womanly sensibilities spared; on the other was the disappointment of defeated, or at least of delayed expectations, and the uncertainty of a future that looked so dark. Then came the new resolution, and the bold project for the morrow, and when drowsiness finally shut her eyes, they closed on a scene of success and happiness, that was pictured by the fancy, under the influence of a sanguine temperament, and a happy invention.

CHAPTER XXV.

> "But, mother, now a shade has past,
> Athwart my brightest visions here,
> A cloud of darkest gloom has wrapt,
> The remnant of my brief career!
> No song, no echo can I win,
> The sparkling fount has died within."

Margaret Davidson, "To my Mother," 11. 7–12.

Hist and Hetty arose with the return of light, leaving Judith still buried in sleep. It took but a minute for the first to complete her toilet. Her long coal-black hair was soon adjusted in a simple knot, the calico dress belted tight to her slender waist, and her little feet concealed in their gaudily ornamented moccasins. When attired, she left her companion employed in household affairs, and went herself on the platform to breathe the pure air of the morning. Here she found Chingachgook studying the shores of the lake, the mountains and the heavens, with the sagacity of a man of the woods, and the gravity of an Indian.

The meeting between the two lovers was simple, but affectionate. The chief showed a manly kindness, equally removed from boyish weakness and haste, while the girl betrayed, in her smile and half averted looks, the bashful tenderness of her sex. Neither spoke, unless it were with the eyes, though each understood the other as fully as if a vocabulary of words and protestations had been poured out. Hist seldom appeared to more advantage than at that moment, for just from her rest and ablutions, there was a freshness about her youthful form and face that the toils of the wood do not always permit to be exhibited, by even the juvenile and pretty. Then Judith had not only imparted some of her own skill in the toilet, during their short intercourse, but she had actually bestowed a few well selected ornaments from her own stores, that contributed not a little to set off the natural graces of the Indian maid. All this the lover saw and felt, and for a moment his countenance was illuminated with a look of pleasure, but it soon grew grave again, and became saddened and anxious. The stools used the previous night were still standing on the platform; placing two against the walls of the hut, he seated himself on one, making a gesture to his companion to take the other. This done, he continued thoughtful and silent for quite a minute, maintaining the reflecting dignity of one born to take his seat at the council-fire, while Hist was furtively watching the expression of his face, patient and submissive, as became a woman of her people. Then the young warrior stretched his arm before him, as if to point out the glories of the scene at that witching hour, when the whole panorama, as usual, was adorned by the mellow distinctness of early morning, sweeping with his hand slowly over lake, hills and heavens. The girl followed the movement with pleased wonder, smiling as each new beauty met her gaze.

"Hugh!" exclaimed the chief, in admiration of a scene so unusual even to him, for this was the first lake he had ever beheld. "This is the country of the Manitou! It is too good for Mingos, Hist; but the curs of that tribe are howling in packs through the woods. They think that the Delawares are asleep, over the mountains."

"All but one of them is, Chingachgook. There is one here; and he is of the blood of Uncas!"

"What is one warrior against a tribe? The path to our villages is very long and crooked, and we shall travel it under a cloudy sky. I am afraid, too, Honeysuckle of the Hills, that we shall travel it alone!"

Hist understood the allusion, and it made her sad; though it sounded sweet to her ears to be compared, by the warrior she so loved, to the most fragrant and the pleasantest of all the wild flowers of her native woods. Still she continued silent, as became her when the allusion was to a grave interest that men could best control, though it exceeded the power of education to conceal the smile that gratified feeling brought to her pretty mouth.

"When the sun is thus," continued the Delaware, pointing to the zenith, by simply casting upward a hand and finger, by a play of the wrist, "the great hunter of our tribe will go back to the Hurons to be treated like a bear, that they roast and skin even on full stomachs."

"The Great Spirit may soften their hearts, and not suffer them to be so bloody minded. I have lived among the Hurons, and know them. They have hearts, and will not forget their own children, should they fall into the hands of the Delawares."

"A wolf is forever howling; a hog will always eat. They have lost warriors; even their women will call out for vengeance. The pale-face has the eyes of an eagle, and can see into a Mingo's heart; he looks for no mercy. There is a cloud over his spirit, though it is not before his face."

A long, thoughtful pause succeeded, during which Hist stealthily took the hand of the chief, as if seeking his support, though she scarce ventured to raise her eyes to a countenance that was now literally becoming terrible, under the conflicting passions and stern resolution that were struggling in the breast of its owner.

"What will the Son of Uncas do?" the girl at length timidly asked. "He is a chief, and is already celebrated in council, though so young; what does his heart tell him is wisest; does the head, too, speak the same words as the heart?"

"What does Wah-ta-Wah say, at a moment when my dearest friend is in such danger. The smallest birds sing the sweetest; it is always pleasant to hearken to their songs. I wish I could hear the Wren of the Woods in my difficulty; its note would reach deeper than the ear."

Again Hist experienced the profound gratification that the language of praise can always awaken when uttered by those we love. The 'Honeysuckle of the Hills' was a term often applied to the girl by the young men of the Delawares, though it never sounded so sweet in her ears as from the lips of Chingachgook; but the latter alone had ever styled her the Wren of the Woods. With him, however, it had got to be a familiar phrase, and it was past expression pleasant to the listener, since it conveyed to her mind the idea that her advice and sentiments were as acceptable to her future husband, as the tones of her voice and modes of conveying them were agreeable; uniting the two things most prized by an Indian girl, as coming from her betrothed, admiration for a valued physical advantage, with respect for her opinion. She pressed the hand she held between both her own, and answered—

"Wah-ta-Wah says that neither she nor the Great Serpent could ever laugh again, or ever sleep without dreaming of the Hurons, should the Deerslayer die under a Mingo tomahawk, and they do nothing to save him. She would rather go back, and start on her long path alone, than let such a dark cloud pass before her happiness."

"Good! The husband and the wife will have but one heart; they will see with the same eyes, and feel with the same feelings."

What further was said need not be related here. That the conversation was of Deerslayer, and his hopes, has been seen already, but the decision that was come to will better appear in the course of the narrative. The youthful pair were yet conversing when the sun appeared above the tops of the pines, and the light of a brilliant American day streamed down into the valley, bathing "in deep joy" the lake, the forests and the mountain sides. Just at this instant Deerslayer came out of the cabin of the Ark and stepped upon the platform. His first look was at the cloudless heavens, then his rapid glance took in the entire panorama of land and water, when he had leisure for a friendly nod at his friends, and a cheerful smile for Hist.

"Well," he said, in his usual, composed manner, and pleasant voice, "he that sees the sun set in the west, and wakes 'arly enough in the morning will be sartain to find him coming back ag'in in the east, like a buck that is hunted round his ha'nt. I dare say, now, Hist, you've beheld this, time and ag'in, and yet it never entered into your galish mind to ask the reason?"

Both Chingachgook and his betrothed looked up at the luminary, with an air that betokened sudden wonder, and then they gazed at each other, as if to seek the solution of the difficulty. Familiarity deadens the sensibilities even as connected with the gravest natural phenomena, and never before had these simple beings thought of enquiring into a movement that was of daily occurrence, however puzzling it might appear on investigation. When the subject was thus suddenly started, it struck both alike, and at the same instant, with some such force, as any new and brilliant proposition in the natural sciences would strike the scholar. Chingachgook alone saw fit to answer.

"The pale-faces know everything," he said; "can they tell us why the sun hides his face, when he goes back, at night."

"Ay, that is downright red-skin l'arnin'" returned the other, laughing, though he was not altogether insensible to the pleasure of proving the superiority of his race by solving the difficulty, which he set about doing in his own peculiar manner. "Harkee, Sarpent," he continued more gravely, though too simply for affectation; "this is easierly explained than an Indian brain may fancy. The sun, while he seems to keep traveling in the heavens, never budges, but it is the 'arth that turns round, and any one can understand, if he is placed on the side of a mill-wheel, for instance, when it's in motion, that he must some times see the heavens, while he is at other times under water. There's no great secret in that; but plain natur'; the difficulty being in setting the 'arth in motion."

"How does my brother know that the earth turns round?" demanded the Indian. "Can he see it?"

"Well, that's been a puzzler, I will own, Delaware, for I've often tried, but never could fairly make it out. Sometimes I've consaited that I could; and then ag'in, I've been obliged to own it an onpossibility. Howsever, turn it does, as all my people say, and you ought to believe 'em, since they can foretell eclipses, and other prodigies, that used to fill the tribes with terror, according to your own traditions of such things."

"Good. This is true; no red man will deny it. When a wheel turns, my eyes can see it—they do not see the earth turn."

"Ay, that's what I call sense obstinacy! Seeing is believing, they say, and what they can't see, some men won't in the least give credit to. Nevertheless, chief, that isn't quite as good reason as it mayat first seem. You believe in the Great Spirit, I know, and yet, I conclude, it would puzzle you to show where you see him!"

"Chingachgook can see Him everywhere—everywhere in good things—the Evil Spirit in bad. Here, in the lake; there, in the forest; yonder, in the clouds; in Hist, in the Son of Uncas, in

Tannemund, in Deerslayer. The Evil Spirit is in the Mingos. That I see; I do not see the earth turn round."

"I don't wonder they call you the Sarpent, Delaware; no, I don't! There's always a meaning in your words, and there's often a meaning in your countenance, too! Notwithstanding, your answers doesn't quite meet my idee. That God is observable in all nat'ral objects is allowable, but then he is not perceptible in the way I mean. You know there is a Great Spirit by his works, and the pale-faces know that the 'arth turns round by its works. This is the reason of the matter, though how it is to be explained is more than I can exactly tell you. This I know; all my people consait that fact, and what all the pale-faces consait, is very likely to be true."

"When the sun is in the top of that pine to-morrow, where will my brother Deerslayer be?"

The hunter started, and he looked intently, though totally without alarm, at his friend. Then he signed for him to follow, and led the way into the Ark, where he might pursue the subject unheard by those whose feelings he feared might get the mastery over their reason. Here he stopped, and pursued the conversation in a more confidential tone.

"'Twas a little onreasonable in you Sarpent," he said, "to bring up such a subject afore Hist, and when the young women of my own colour might overhear what was said. Yes, 'twas a little more onreasonable than most things that you do. No matter; Hist didn't comprehend, and the other didn't hear. Howsever, the question is easier put than answered. No mortal can say where he will be when the sun rises to-morrow. I will ask you the same question, Sarpent, and should like to hear what answer you can give."

"Chingachgook will be with his friend Deerslayer—if he be in the land of spirits, the Great Serpent will crawl at his side; if beneath yonder sun, its warmth and light shall fall on both."

"I understand you, Delaware," returned the other, touched with the simple self-devotion of his friend, "Such language is as plain in one tongue as in another. It comes from the heart, and goes to the heart, too. 'Tis well to think so, and it may be well to say so, for that matter, but it would not be well to do so, Sarpent. You are no longer alone in life, for though you have the lodges to change, and other ceremonies to go through, afore Hist becomes your lawful wife, yet are you as good as married in all that bears on the feelin's, and joy, and misery. No—no—Hist must not be desarted, because a cloud is passing atween you and me, a little onexpectedly and a little darker than we may have looked for."

"Hist is a daughter of the Mohicans. She knows how to obey her husband. Where he goes, she will follow. Both will be with the Great Hunter of the Delawares, when the sun shall be in the pine to-morrow."

"The Lord bless and protect you! Chief, this is downright madness. Can either, or both of you, alter a Mingo natur'? Will your grand looks, or Hist's tears and beauty, change a wolf into a squirrel, or make a catamount as innocent as a fa'an? No—Sarpent, you will think better of this matter, and leave me in the hands of God. A'ter all, it's by no means sartain that the scamps design the torments, for they may yet be pitiful, and bethink them of the wickedness of such a course—though it is but a hopeless expectation to look forward to a Mingo's turning aside from evil, and letting marcy get uppermost in his heart. Nevertheless, no one knows to a sartainty what will happen, and young creatur's, like Hist, a'n't to be risked on onsartainties. This marrying is altogether a different undertaking from what some young men fancy. Now, if you was single, or as good as single, Delaware, I should expect you to be actyve and stirring about the camp of the vagabonds, from sunrise to sunset, sarcumventing and contriving, as restless as a hound off the scent, and doing all manner of things to help me, and to distract the inimy, but two are oftener feebler than one, and we must take things as they are, and not as we want 'em to be."

"Listen, Deerslayer," returned the Indian with an emphasis so decided as to show how much he was in earnest. "If Chingachgook was in the hands of the Hurons, what would my pale-face brother do? Sneak off to the Delaware villages, and say to the chiefs, and old men, and young warriors—'see, here is Wah-ta-Wah; she is safe, but a little tired; and here is the Son of Uncas, not as tired as the Honeysuckle, being stronger, but just as safe.' Would he do this?"

"Well, that's oncommon ingen'ous; it's cunning enough for a Mingo, himself! The Lord only knows what put it into your head to ask such a question. What would I do? Why, in the first place, Hist wouldn't be likely to be in my company at all, for she would stay as near you as possible, and therefore all that part about her couldn't be said without talking nonsense. As for her being tired, that would fall through too, if she didn't go, and no part of your speech would be likely to come from me; so, you see, Sarpent, reason is ag'in you, and you may as well give it up, since to hold out ag'in reason, is no way becoming a chief of your character and repitation."

"My brother is not himself; he forgets that he is talking to one who has sat at the Council Fire of his nation," returned the other kindly. "When men speak, they should say that which does not go in at one side of the head and out at the other. Their words shouldn't be feathers, so light that a wind which does not ruffle the water can blow them away. He has not answered my question; when a chief puts a question, his friend should not talk of other things."

"I understand you, Delaware; I understand well enough what you mean, and truth won't allow me to say otherwise. Still it's not as easy to answer as you seem to think, for this plain reason. You wish me to say what I would do if I had a betrothed as you have, here, on the lake, and a fri'nd yonder in the Huron camp, in danger of the torments. That's it, isn't it?"

The Indian bowed his head silently, and always with unmoved gravity, though his eye twinkled at the sight of the other's embarrassment.

"Well, I never had a betrothed—never had the kind of feelin's toward any young woman that you have towards Hist, though the Lord knows my feelin's are kind enough towards 'em all! Still my heart, as they call it in such matters, isn't touched, and therefore I can't say what I would do. A fri'nd pulls strong, that I know by exper'ence, Sarpent, but, by all that I've seen and heard consarning love, I'm led to think that a betrothed pulls stronger."

"True; but the betrothed of Chingachgook does not pull towards the lodges of the Delawares; she pulls towards the camp of the Hurons."

"She's a noble gal, for all her little feet, and hands that an't bigger than a child's, and a voice that is as pleasant as a mocker's; she's a noble gal, and like the stock of her sires! Well, what is it, Sarpent; for I conclude she hasn't changed her mind, and means to give herself up, and turn Huron wife. What is it you want?"

"Wah-ta-Wah will never live in the wigwam of an Iroquois," answered the Delaware drily. "She has little feet, but they can carry her to the villages of her people; she has small hands, too, but her mind is large. My brother will see what we can do, when the time shall come, rather than let him die under Mingo torments."

"Attempt nothing heedlessly, Delaware," said the other earnestly; "I suppose you must and will have your way; and, on the whole it's right you should, for you'd neither be happy, unless something was undertaken. But attempt nothing heedlessly—I didn't expect you'd quit the lake, while my matter remained in unsartainty, but remember, Sarpent, that no torments that Mingo ingenuity can invent, no ta'ntings and revilings; no burnings and roastings and nail-tearings, nor any other onhuman contrivances can so soon break down my spirit, as to find that you and Hist have fallen into the power of the inimy in striving to do something for my good."

"The Delawares are prudent. The Deerslayer will not find them running into a strange camp with their eyes shut."

Here the dialogue terminated. Hetty announced that the breakfast was ready, and the whole party was soon seated around the simple board, in the usual primitive manner of borderers. Judith was the last to take her seat, pale, silent, and betraying in her countenance that she had passed a painful, if not a sleepless, night. At this meal scarce a syllable was exchanged, all the females manifesting want of appetites, though the two men were unchanged in this particular. It was early when the party arose, and there still remained several hours before it would be necessary for the prisoner to leave his friends. The knowledge of this circumstance, and the interest all felt in his welfare, induced the whole to assemble on the platform again, in the desire to be near the expected victim, to listen to his discourse, and if possible to show their interest in him by anticipating his wishes. Deerslayer, himself, so far as human eyes could penetrate, was wholly unmoved, conversing cheerfully and naturally, though he avoided any direct allusions to the expected and great event of the day. If any evidence could be discovered of his thought's reverting to that painful subject at all, it was in the manner in which he spoke of death and the last great change.

"Grieve not, Hetty," he said, for it was while consoling this simple-minded girl for the loss of her parents that he thus betrayed his feelings, "since God has app'inted that all must die. Your parents, or them you fancied your parents, which is the same thing, have gone afore you; this is only in the order of natur', my good gal, for the aged go first, and the young follow. But one that had a mother like your'n, Hetty, can be at no loss to hope the best, as to how matters will turn out in another world. The Delaware, here, and Hist, believe in happy hunting grounds, and have idees befitting their notions and gifts as red-skins, but we who are of white blood hold altogether to a different doctrine. Still, I rather conclude our heaven is their land of spirits, and that the path which leads to it will be travelled by all colours alike. 'Tis onpossible for the wicked to enter on it, I will allow, but fri'nds can scarce be separated, though they are not of the same race on 'arth. Keep up your spirits, poor Hetty, and look forward to the day when you will meet your mother ag'in, and that without pain, or sorrowing."

"I do expect to see mother," returned the truth-telling and simple girl, "but what will become of father?"

"That's a non-plusser, Delaware," said the hunter, in the Indian dialect—"yes, that is a downright non-plusser! The Muskrat was not a saint on 'arth, and it's fair to guess he'll not be much of one, hereafter! Howsever, Hetty," dropping into the English by an easy transition, "howsever, Hetty, we must all hope for the best. That is wisest, and it is much the easiest to the mind, if one can only do it. I ricommend to you, trusting to God, and putting down all misgivings and fainthearted feelin's. It's wonderful, Judith, how different people have different notions about the futur', some fancying one change, and some fancying another. I've known white teachers that have thought all was spirit, hereafter, and them, ag'in, that believed the body will be transported to another world, much as the red-skins themselves imagine, and that we shall walk about in the flesh, and know each other, and talk together, and be fri'nds there as we've been fri'nds here."

"Which of these opinions is most pleasing to you, Deerslayer?" asked the girl, willing to indulge his melancholy mood, and far from being free from its influence herself. "Would it be disagreeable to think that you should meet all who are now on this platform in another world? Or have you known enough of us here, to be glad to see us no more.

"The last would make death a bitter portion; yes it would. It's eight good years since the Sarpent and I began to hunt together, and the thought that we were never to meet ag'in would be a hard thought to me. He looks forward to the time when he shall chase a sort of spirit-deer, in company, on plains where there's no thorns, or brambles, or marshes, or other hardships to overcome, whereas I can't fall into all these notions, seeing that they appear to be ag'in reason. Spirits can't eat, nor have they any use for clothes, and deer can only rightfully be chased to be slain, or slain, unless it be for the venison or the hides. Now, I find it hard to suppose that blessed spirits can be put to chasing game without an object, tormenting the dumb animals just for the pleasure and agreeableness of their own amusements. I never yet pulled a trigger on buck or doe, Judith, unless when food or clothes was wanting."

"The recollection of which, Deerslayer, must now be a great consolation to you."

"It is the thought of such things, my fri'nds, that enables a man to keep his furlough. It might be done without it, I own; for the worst red-skins sometimes do their duty in this matter; but it makes that which might otherwise be hard, easy, if not altogether to our liking. Nothing truly makes a bolder heart than a light conscience."

Judith turned paler than ever, but she struggled for self-command, and succeeded in obtaining it. The conflict had been severe, however, and it left her so little disposed to speak that Hetty pursued the subject. This was done in the simple manner natural to the girl.

"It would be cruel to kill the poor deer," she said, "in this world, or any other, when you don't want their venison, or their skins. No good white man, and no good red man would do it. But it's wicked for a Christian to talk about chasing anything in heaven. Such things are not done before the face of God, and the missionary that teaches these doctrines can't be a true missionary. He must be a wolf in sheep's clothing. I suppose you know what a sheep is, Deerslayer."

"That I do, gal, and a useful creatur' it is, to such as like cloths better than skins for winter garments. I understand the natur' of sheep, though I've had but little to do with 'em, and the natur' of wolves too, and can take the idee of a wolf in the fleece of a sheep, though I think it would be like to prove a hot jacket for such a beast, in the warm months!"

"And sin and hypocrisy are hot jackets, as they will find who put them on," returned Hetty, positively, "so the wolf would be no worse off than the sinner. Spirits don't hunt, nor trap, nor fish, nor do anything that vain men undertake, since they've none of the longings of this world to feed. Oh! Mother told me all that, years ago, and I don't wish to hear it denied."

"Well, my good Hetty, in that case you'd better not broach your doctrine to Hist, when she and you are alone, and the young Delaware maiden is inclined to talk religion. It's her fixed idee, I know, that the good warriors do nothing but hunt and fish in the other world, though I don't believe that she fancies any of them are brought down to trapping, which is no empl'yment for a brave. But of hunting and fishing, accordin' to her notion, they've their fill, and that, too, over the most agreeablest hunting grounds, and among game that is never out of season, and which is just actyve and instinctyve enough to give a pleasure to death. So I wouldn't ricommend it to you to start Hist on that idee."

"Hist can't be so wicked as to believe any such thing," returned the other, earnestly. "No Indian hunts after he is dead."

"No wicked Indian, I grant you; no wicked Indian, sartainly. He is obliged to carry the ammunition, and to look on without sharing in the sport, and to cook, and to light the fires, and to do every thing that isn't manful. Now, mind; I don't tell you these are my ideas, but they are Hist's ideas, and, therefore, for the sake of peace the less you say to her ag'in 'em, the better."

"And what are your ideas of the fate of an Indian, in the other world?" demanded Judith, who had just found her voice.

"Ah! gal, any thing but that! I am too Christianized to expect any thing so fanciful as hunting and fishing after death, nor do I believe there is one Manitou for the red-skin and another for a pale-face. You find different colours on 'arth, as any one may see, but you don't find different natur's. Different gifts, but only one natur'."

"In what is a gift different from a nature? Is not nature itself a gift from God?"

"Sartain; that's quick-thoughted, and creditable, Judith, though the main idee is wrong. A natur' is the creatur' itself; its wishes, wants, ideas and feelin's, as all are born in him. This natur' never can be changed, in the main, though it may undergo some increase, or lessening. Now, gifts come of sarcumstances. Thus, if you put a man in a town, he gets town gifts; in a settlement, settlement gifts; in a forest, gifts of the woods. A soldier has soldierly gifts, and a missionary preaching gifts. All these increase and strengthen, until they get to fortify natur', as it might be, and excuse a thousand acts and idees. Still the creatur' is the same at the bottom; just as a man who is clad in regimentals is the same as the man that is clad in skins. The garments make a change to the eye, and some change in the conduct, perhaps; but none in the man. Herein lies the apology for gifts; seein' that you expect different conduct from one in silks and satins, from one in homespun; though the Lord, who didn't make the dresses, but who made the creatur's themselves, looks only at his own work. This isn't ra'al missionary doctrine, but it's as near it as a man of white colour need be. Ah's! me; little did I think to be talking of such matters, to-day, but it's one of our weaknesses never to know what will come to pass. Step into the Ark with me, Judith, for a minute; I wish to converse with you."

Judith complied with a willingness she could scarce conceal. Following the hunter into the cabin, she took a seat on a stool, while the young man brought Killdeer, the rifle she had given him, out of a corner, and placed himself on another, with the weapon laid upon his knees. After turning the piece round and round, and examining its lock and its breech with a sort of affectionate assiduity, he laid it down and proceeded to the subject which had induced him to desire the interview.

"I understand you, Judith, to say that you gave me this rifle," he said. "I agreed to take it, because a young woman can have no particular use for firearms. The we'pon has a great name, and it desarves it, and ought of right to be carried by some known and sure hand, for the best repitation may be lost by careless and thoughtless handling."

"Can it be in better hands than those in which it is now, Deerslayer? Thomas Hutter seldom missed with it; with you it must turn out to be——"

"Sartain death!" interrupted the hunter, laughing. "I once know'd a beaver-man that had a piece he called by that very name, but 'twas all boastfulness, for I've seen Delawares that were as true with arrows, at a short range. Howsever, I'll not deny my gifts—for this is a gift, Judith, and not natur'—but, I'll not deny my gifts, and therefore allow that the rifle couldn't well be in better hands than it is at present. But, how long will it be likely to remain there? Atween us, the truth may be said, though I shouldn't like to have it known to the Sarpent and Hist; but, to you the truth may be spoken, since your feelin's will not be as likely to be tormented by it, as those of them that have known me longer and better. How long am I like to own this rifle or any other? That is a serious question for our thoughts to rest on, and should that happen which is so likely to happen, Killdeer would be without an owner."

Judith listened with apparent composure, though the conflict within came near overpowering her. Appreciating the singular character of her companion, however, she succeeded in appearing calm, though, had not his attention been drawn exclusively to the rifle, a man of his keenness of observation could scarce have failed to detect the agony of mind with which the girl had hearkened to his words.

Her great self-command, notwithstanding, enabled her to pursue the subject in a way still to deceive him.

"What would you have me do with the weapon," she asked, "should that which you seem to expect take place?"

"That's just what I wanted to speak to you about, Judith; that's just it. There's Chingachgook, now, though far from being parfect sartainty, with a rifle—for few red-skins ever get to be that—though far from being parfect sartainty, he is respectable, and is coming on. Nevertheless, he is my fri'nd, and all the better fri'nd, perhaps, because there never can be any hard feelin's atween us, touchin' our gifts, his'n bein' red, and mine bein' altogether white. Now, I should like to leave Killdeer to the Sarpent, should any thing happen to keep me from doing credit and honor to your precious gift, Judith."

"Leave it to whom you please, Deerslayer. The rifle is your own, to do with as you please. Chingachgook shall have it, should you never return to claim it, if that be your wish."

"Has Hetty been consulted in this matter? Property goes from the parent to the children, and not to one child, in partic'lar!"

"If you place your right on that of the law, Deerslayer, I fear none of us can claim to be the owner. Thomas Hutter was no more the father of Esther, than he was the father of Judith. Judith and Esther we are truly, having no other name!"

"There may be law in that, but there's no great reason, gal. Accordin' to the custom of families, the goods are your'n, and there's no one here to gainsay it. If Hetty would only say that she is willing, my mind would be quite at ease in the matter. It's true, Judith, that your sister has neither your beauty, nor your wit; but we should be the tenderest of the rights and welfare of the most weak-minded."

The girl made no answer but placing herself at a window, she summoned her sister to her side. When the question was put to Hetty, that simple-minded and affectionate creature cheerfully assented to the proposal to confer on Deerslayer a full right of ownership to the much-coveted rifle. The latter now seemed perfectly happy, for the time being at least, and after again examining and re-examining his prize, he expressed a determination to put its merits to a practical test, before he left the spot. No boy could have been more eager to exhibit the qualities of his trumpet, or his crossbow, than this simple forester was to prove those of his rifle. Returning to the platform, he first took the Delaware aside, and informed him that this celebrated piece was to become his property, in the event of any thing serious befalling himself.

"This is a new reason why you should be wary, Sarpent, and not run into any oncalculated danger," the hunter added, "for, it will be a victory of itself to a tribe to own such a piece as this! The Mingos will turn green with envy, and, what is more, they will not ventur' heedlessly near a village where it is known to be kept. So, look well to it, Delaware, and remember that you've now to watch over a thing that has all the valie of a creatur', without its failin's. Hist may be, and should be precious to you, but Killdeer will have the love and veneration of your whole people."

"One rifle like another, Deerslayer," returned the Indian, in English, the language used by the other, a little hurt at his friend's lowering his betrothed to the level of a gun. "All kill; all wood and iron. Wife dear to heart; rifle good to shoot."

"And what is a man in the woods without something to shoot with?—a miserable trapper, or a forlorn broom and basket maker, at the best. Such a man may hoe corn, and keep soul and body together, but he can never know the savory morsels of venison, or tell a bear's ham from a hog's. Come, my fri'nd, such another occasion may never offer ag'in, and I feel a strong craving for a trial with this celebrated piece. You shall bring out your own rifle, and I will just sight Killdeer in a careless way, in order that we may know a few of its secret vartues."

As this proposition served to relieve the thoughts of the whole party, by giving them a new direction, while it was likely to produce no unpleasant results, every one was willing to enter into it; the girls bringing forth the firearms with an alacrity bordering on cheerfulness. Hutter's armory was well supplied, possessing several rifles, all of which were habitually kept loaded in readiness to meet any sudden demand for their use. On the present occasion it only remained to freshen the primings, and each piece was in a state for service. This was soon done, as all assisted in it, the females being as expert in this part of the system of defence as their male companions.

"Now, Sarpent, we'll begin in a humble way, using Old Tom's commoners first, and coming to your we'pon and Killdeer as the winding up observations," said Deerslayer, delighted to be again, weapon in hand, ready to display his skill. "Here's birds in abundance, some in, and some over the lake, and they keep at just a good range, hovering round the hut. Speak your mind, Delaware, and p'int out the creatur' you wish to alarm. Here's a diver nearest in, off to the eastward, and that's a creatur' that buries itself at the flash, and will be like enough to try both piece and powder."

Chingachgook was a man of few words. No sooner was the bird pointed out to him than he took his aim and fired. The duck dove at the flash, as had been expected, and the bullet skipped harmlessly along the surface of the lake, first striking the water within a few inches of the spot where the bird had so lately swam. Deerslayer laughed, cordially and naturally, but at the same time he threw himself into an attitude of preparation and stood keenly watching the sheet of placid water. Presently a dark spot appeared, and then the duck arose to breathe, and shook its wings. While in this act, a bullet passed directly through its breast, actually turning it over lifeless on its back. At the next moment, Deerslayer stood with the breech of his rifle on the platform, as tranquil as if nothing had happened, though laughing in his own peculiar manner.

"There's no great trial of the pieces in that!" he said, as if anxious to prevent a false impression of his own merit. "No, that proof's neither for nor ag'in the rifles, seeing it was all quickness of hand and eye. I took the bird at a disadvantage, or he might have got under, again, afore the bullet reached him. But the Sarpent is too wise to mind such tricks, having long been used to them. Do you remember the time, chief, when you thought yourself sartain of the wild-goose, and I took him out of your very eyes, as it might be with a little smoke! Howsever, such things pass for nothing atween fri'nds, and young folk will have their fun, Judith. Ay; here's just the bird we want, for it's as good for the fire, as it is for the aim, and nothing should be lost that can be turned to just account. There, further north, Delaware."

The latter looked in the required direction, and he soon saw a large black duck floating in stately repose on the water. At that distant day, when so few men were present to derange the harmony of the wilderness, all the smaller lakes with which the interior of New York so abounds were places of resort for the migratory aquatic birds, and this sheet like the others had once been much frequented by all the varieties of the duck, by the goose, the gull, and the loon. On the appearance of Hutter, the spot was comparatively deserted for other sheets, more retired and remote, though some of each species continued to resort thither, as indeed they do to the present hour. At that instant, a hundred birds were visible from the castle, sleeping on the water or laying their feathers in the limpid element, though no other offered so favorable a mark as that Deerslayer had just pointed out to his friend. Chingachgook, as usual, spared his words, and proceeded to execution. This time his aim was more careful than before, and his success in proportion. The bird had a wing crippled, and fluttered along the water screaming, materially increasing its distance from its enemies.

"That bird must be put out of pain," exclaimed Deerslayer, the moment the animal endeavored to rise on the wing, "and this is the rifle and the eye to do it."

The duck was still floundering along, when the fatal bullet overtook it, severing the head from the neck as neatly as if it had been done with an axe. Hist had indulged in a low cry of delight at the success of the young Indian, but now she affected to frown and resent the greater skill of his friend. The chief, on the contrary, uttered the usual exclamation of pleasure, and his smile proved how much he admired, and how little he envied.

"Never mind the gal, Sarpent, never mind Hist's feelin's, which will neither choke, nor drown, slay nor beautify," said Deerslayer, laughing. "'Tis nat'ral for women to enter into their husband's victories and defeats, and you are as good as man and wife, so far as prejudyce and fri'ndship go. Here is a bird over head that will put the pieces to the proof. I challenge you to an upward aim, with a flying target. That's a ra'al proof, and one that needs sartain rifles, as well as sartain eyes."

The species of eagle that frequents the water, and lives on fish, was also present, and one was hovering at a considerable height above the hut, greedily watching for an opportunity to make a swoop; its hungry young elevating their heads from a nest that was in sight, in the naked summit of a dead pine. Chingachgook silently turned a new piece against this bird, and after carefully watching his time, fired. A wider circuit than common denoted that the messenger had passed through the air at no great distance from the bird, though it missed its object. Deerslayer, whose aim was not more true than it was quick, fired as soon as it was certain his friend had missed, and the deep swoop that followed left it momentarily doubtful whether the eagle was hit or not. The marksman himself, however, proclaimed his own want of success, calling on his friend to seize another rifle, for he saw signs on the part of the bird of an intention to quit the spot.

"I made him wink, Sarpent, I do think his feathers were ruffled, but no blood has yet been drawn, nor is that old piece fit for so nice and quick a sight. Quick, Delaware, you've now a better rifle, and, Judith, bring out Killdeer, for this is the occasion to try his merits, if he has 'em."

A general movement followed, each of the competitors got ready, and the girls stood in eager expectation of the result. The eagle had made a wide circuit after his low swoop, and fanning his way upward, once more hovered nearly over the hut, at a distance even greater than before. Chingachgook gazed at him, and then expressed his opinion of the impossibility of striking a bird at that great height, and while he was so nearly perpendicular, as to the range. But a low murmur from Hist produced a sudden impulse and he fired. The result showed how well he had calculated, the eagle not even varying his flight, sailing round and round in his airy circle, and looking down, as if in contempt, at his foes.

"Now, Judith," cried Deerslayer, laughing, with glistening and delighted eyes, "we'll see if Killdeer isn't Killeagle, too! Give me room Sarpent, and watch the reason of the aim, for by reason any thing may be l'arned."

A careful sight followed, and was repeated again and again, the bird continuing to rise higher and higher. Then followed the flash and the report. The swift messenger sped upward, and, at the next instant, the bird turned on its side, and came swooping down, now struggling with one wing and then with the other, sometimes whirling in a circuit, next fanning desperately as if conscious of its injury, until, having described several complete circles around the spot, it fell heavily into the end of the Ark. On examining the body, it was found that the bullet had pierced it about half way between one of its wings and the breast-bone.

## CHAPTER XXVI.

"Upon two stony tables, spread before her,
 She lean'd her bosom, more than stony hard,
 There slept th' impartial judge, and strict restorer
 Of wrong, or right, with pain or with reward;
 There hung the score of all our debts, the card
 Where good, and bad, and life, and death, were painted;
 Was never heart of mortal so untainted,
 But when the roll was read, with thousand terrors fainted."

Giles Fletcher, Christ's Victory in Heaven, lxv.

"We've done an unthoughtful thing, Sarpent—yes, Judith, we've done an unthoughtful thing in taking life with an object no better than vanity!" exclaimed Deerslayer, when the Delaware held up the enormous bird, by its wings, and exhibited the dying eyes riveted on its enemies with the gaze that the helpless ever fasten on their destroyers. "'Twas more becomin' two boys to gratify their feelin's in this onthoughtful manner, than two warriors on a warpath, even though it be their first. Ah's! me; well, as a punishment I'll quit you at once, and when I find myself alone with them bloody-minded Mingos, it's more than like I'll have occasion to remember that life is sweet, even to the beasts of the woods and the fowls of the air. There, Judith; there's Kildeer; take him back, ag'in, and keep him for some hand that's more desarving to own such a piece."

"I know of none as deserving as your own, Deerslayer," answered the girl in haste; "none but yours shall keep the rifle."

"If it depended on skill, you might be right enough, gal, but we should know when to use firearms, as well as how to use 'em. I haven't l'arnt the first duty yet, it seems; so keep the piece till I have. The sight of a dyin' and distressed creatur', even though it be only a bird, brings wholesome thoughts to a man who don't know how soon his own time may come, and who is pretty sartain that it will come afore the sun sets; I'd give back all my vain feelin's, and rej'icin's in hand and eye, if that poor eagle was only on its nest ag'in, with its young, praisin' the Lord for anything that we can know about the matter, for health and strength!"

The listeners were confounded with this proof of sudden repentance in the hunter, and that too for an indulgence so very common, that men seldom stop to weigh its consequences, or the physical suffering it may bring on the unoffending and helpless. The Delaware understood what was said, though he scarce understood the feelings which had prompted the words, and by way of disposing of the difficulty, he drew his keen knife, and severed the head of the sufferer from its body.

"What a thing is power!" continued the hunter, "and what a thing it is to have it, and not to know how to use it. It's no wonder, Judith, that the great so often fail of their duties, when even the little and the humble find it so hard to do what's right, and not to do what's wrong. Then, how one evil act brings others a'ter it! Now, wasn't it for this furlough of mine, which must soon take me back to the Mingos, I'd find this creatur's nest, if I travelled the woods a fortnight—though an eagle's nest is soon found by them that understands the bird's natur',—but I'd travel a fortnight rather than not find it, just to put the young, too, out of their pain."

"I'm glad to hear you say this, Deerslayer," observed Hetty, "and God will be more apt to remember your sorrow for what you've done, than the wickedness itself. I thought how wicked it was to kill harmless birds, while you were shooting, and meant to tell you so; but, I don't know how it happened,—I was so curious to see if you could hit an eagle at so great a height, that I forgot altogether to speak, 'till the mischief was done."

"That's it; that's just it, my good Hetty. We can all see our faults and mistakes when it's too late to help them! Howsever I'm glad you didn't speak, for I don't think a word or two would have stopped me, just at that moment, and so the sin stands in its nakedness, and not aggravated by any unheeded calls to forbear. Well, well, bitter thoughts are hard to be borne at all times, but there's times when they're harder than at others."

Little did Deerslayer know, while thus indulging in feelings that were natural to the man, and so strictly in accordance with his own unsophisticated and just principles, that, in the course of the inscrutable providence, which so uniformly and yet so mysteriously covers all events with its mantle, the very fault he was disposed so severely to censure was to be made the means of determining his own earthly fate. The mode and the moment in which he was to feel the influence of this interference, it would be premature to relate, but both will appear in the course of the succeeding chapters. As for the young man, he now slowly left the Ark, like one sorrowing for his misdeeds, and seated himself in silence on the platform. By this time the sun had ascended to some height, and its appearance, taken in connection with his present feelings, induced him to prepare to depart. The Delaware got the canoe ready for his friend, as soon as apprised of his intention, while Hist busied herself in making the few arrangements that were thought necessary to his comfort. All this was done without ostentation, but in a way that left Deerslayer fully acquainted with, and equally disposed to appreciate, the motive. When all was ready, both returned to the side of Judith and Hetty, neither of whom had moved from the spot where the young hunter sat.

"The best fri'nds must often part," the last began, when he saw the whole party grouped around him—"yes, fri'ndship can't alter the ways of Providence, and let our feelin's be as they may, we must part. I've often thought there's moments when our words dwell longer on the mind than common, and when advice is remembered, just because the mouth that gives it isn't likely to give it ag'in. No one knows what will happen in this world, and therefore it may be well, when fri'nds separate under a likelihood that the parting may be long, to say a few words in kindness, as a sort of keepsakes. If all but one will go into the Ark, I'll talk to each in turn, and what is more, I'll listen to what you may have to say back ag'in, for it's a poor counsellor that won't take as well as give."

As the meaning of the speaker was understood, the two Indians immediately withdrew as desired, leaving the sisters, however, still standing at the young man's side. A look of Deerslayer's induced Judith to explain.

"You can advise Hetty as you land," she said hastily, "for I intend that she shall accompany you to the shore."

"Is this wise, Judith? It's true, that under common sarcumstances a feeble mind is a great protection among red-skins, but when their feelin's are up, and they're bent on revenge, it's hard to say what may come to pass. Besides—"

"What were you about to say, Deerslayer?" asked Judith, whose gentleness of voice and manner amounted nearly to tenderness, though she struggled hard to keep her emotions and apprehensions in subjection.

"Why, simply that there are sights and doin's that one even as little gifted with reason and memory as Hetty here, might better not witness. So, Judith, you would do well to let me land alone, and to keep your sister back."

"Never fear for me, Deerslayer," put in Hetty, who comprehended enough of the discourse to know its general drift, "I'm feeble minded, and that they say is an excuse for going anywhere; and what that won't excuse, will be overlooked on account of the Bible I always carry. It is wonderful, Judith, how all sorts of men; the trappers as well as the hunters; red-men as well as white; Mingos as well as Delawares do reverence and fear the Bible!"

"I think you have not the least ground to fear any injury, Hetty," answered the sister, "and therefore I shall insist on your going to the Huron camp with our friend. Your being there can do no harm, not even to yourself, and may do great good to Deerslayer."

"This is not a moment, Judith, to dispute, and so have the matter your own way," returned the young man. "Get yourself ready, Hetty, and go into the canoe, for I've a few parting words to say to your sister, which can do you no good."

Judith and her companion continued silent, until Hetty had so far complied as to leave them alone, when Deerslayer took up the subject, as if it had been interrupted by some ordinary occurrence, and in a very matter of fact way.

"Words spoken at parting, and which may be the last we ever hear from a fri'nd are not soon forgotten," he repeated, "and so Judith, I intend to speak to you like a brother, seein' I'm not old enough to be your father. In the first place, I wish to caution you ag'in your inimies, of which two may be said to ha'nt your very footsteps, and to beset your ways. The first is oncommon good looks, which is as dangerous a foe to some young women, as a whole tribe of Mingos could prove, and which calls for great watchfulness—not to admire and praise—but to distrust and sarcumvent. Yes, good looks may be sarcumvented, and fairly outwitted, too. In order to do this you've only to remember that they melt like the snows, and, when once gone, they never come back ag'in. The seasons come and go, Judith, and if we have winter, with storms and frosts, and spring with chills and leafless trees, we have summer with its sun and glorious skies, and fall with its fruits, and a garment thrown over the forest, that no beauty of the town could rummage out of all the shops in America. 'Arth is in an etarnal round, the goodness of God bringing back the pleasant when we've had enough of the onpleasant. But it's not so with good looks. They are lent for a short time in youth, to be used and not abused, and, as I never met with a young woman to whom providence has been as bountiful as it has to you, Judith, in this partic'lar, I warn you, as it might be with my dyin' breath, to beware of the inimy—fri'nd, or inimy, as we deal with the gift."

It was so grateful to Judith to hear these unequivocal admissions of her personal charms, that much would have been forgiven to the man who made them, let him be who he might. But, at that moment, and from a far better feeling, it would not have been easy for Deerslayer seriously to offend her, and she listened with a patience, which, had it been foretold only a week earlier, it would have excited her indignation to hear.

"I understand your meaning, Deerslayer," returned the girl, with a meekness and humility that a little surprised her listener, "and hope to be able to profit by it. But, you have mentioned only one of the enemies I have to fear; who, or what is the other."

"The other is givin' way afore your own good sense and judgment, I find, Judith; yes, he's not as dangerous as I supposed. Howsever, havin' opened the subject, it will be as well to end it honestly. The first inimy you have to be watchful of, as I've already told you, Judith, is oncommon good looks, and the next is an oncommon knowledge of the sarcumstance. If the first is bad, the last doesn't, in any way, mend the matter, so far as safety and peace of mind are consarned."

How much longer the young man would have gone on in his simple and unsuspecting, but well intentioned manner, it might not be easy to say, had he not been interrupted by his listener's bursting into tears, and giving way to an outbreak of feeling, which was so much the more violent from the fact that it had been with so much difficulty suppressed. At first her sobs were so violent and uncontrollable that Deerslayer was a little appalled, and he was abundantly repentant from the instant that he discovered how much greater was the effect produced by his words than he had anticipated. Even the austere and exacting are usually appeased by the signs of contrition, but the nature of Deerslayer did not require proofs of intense feelings so strong in order to bring him down to a level with the regrets felt by the girl herself. He arose, as if an adder had stung him, and the accents of the mother that soothes her child were scarcely more gentle and winning than the tones of his voice, as he now expressed his contrition at having gone so far.

"It was well meant, Judith," he said, "but it was not intended to hurt your feelin's so much. I have overdone the advice, I see; yes, I've overdone it, and I crave your pardon for the same. Fri'ndship's an awful thing! Sometimes it chides us for not having done enough; and then, ag'in it speaks in strong words for havin' done too much. Howsever, I acknowledge I've overdone the matter, and as I've a ra'al and strong regard for you, I rej'ice to say it, inasmuch as it proves how much better you are, than my own vanity and consaits had made you out to be."

Judith now removed her hands from her face, her tears had ceased, and she unveiled a countenance so winning with the smile which rendered it even radiant, that the young man gazed at her, for a moment, with speechless delight.

"Say no more, Deerslayer," she hastily interposed; "it pains me to hear you find fault with yourself. I know my own weakness, all the better, now I see that you have discovered it; the lesson, bitter as I have found it for a moment, shall not be forgotten. We will not talk any longer of these things, for I do not feel myself brave enough for the undertaking, and I should not like the Delaware, or Hist, or even Hetty, to notice my weakness. Farewell, Deerslayer; may God bless and protect you as your honest heart deserves blessings and protection, and as I must think he will."

Judith had so far regained the superiority that properly belonged to her better education, high spirit, and surpassing personal advantages, as to preserve the ascendancy she had thus accidentally obtained, and effectually prevented any return to the subject that was as singularly interrupted, as it had been singularly introduced. The young man permitted her to have every thing her own way, and when she pressed his hard hand in both her own, he made no resistance, but submitted to the homage as quietly, and with quite as matter of course a manner, as a sovereign would have received a similar tribute from a subject, or the mistress from her suitor. Feeling had flushed the face and illuminated the whole countenance of the girl, and her beauty was never more resplendant than when she cast a parting glance at the youth. That glance was filled with anxiety, interest and gentle pity. At the next instant, she darted into the hut and was seen no more, though she spoke to Hist from a window, to inform her that their friend expected her appearance.

"You know enough of red-skin natur', and red-skin usages, Wah-ta-Wah, to see the condition I am in on account of this furlough," commenced the hunter in Delaware, as soon as the patient and submissive girl of that people had moved quietly to his side; "you will therefore best onderstand how onlikely I am ever to talk with you ag'in. I've but little to say; but that little comes from long livin' among your people, and from havin' obsarved and noted their usages. The life of a woman is hard at the best, but I must own, though I'm not opinionated in favor of my own colour, that it is harder among the red men than it is among the pale-faces. This is a p'int on which Christians may well boast, if boasting can be set down for Christianity in any manner or form, which I rather think it cannot. Howsever, all women have their trials. Red women have their'n in what I should call the nat'ral way, while white women take 'em innoculated like. Bear your burthen, Hist, becomingly, and remember if it be a little toilsome, how much lighter it is than that of most Indian women. I know the Sarpent well—what I call cordially—and he will never be a tyrant to any thing he loves, though he will expect to be treated himself like a Mohican Chief. There will be cloudy days in your lodge I suppose, for they happen under all usages, and among all people, but, by keepin' the windows of the heart open there will always be room for the sunshine to enter. You come of a great stock yourself, and so does Chingachgook. It's not very likely that either will ever forget the sarcumstance and do any thing to disgrace your forefathers. Nevertheless, likin' is a tender plant, and never thrives long when watered with tears. Let the 'arth around your married happiness be moistened by the dews of kindness."

"My pale brother is very wise; Wah will keep in her mind all that his wisdom tells her."

"That's judicious and womanly, Hist. Care in listening, and stout-heartedness in holding to good counsel, is a wife's great protection. And, now, ask the Sarpent to come and speak with me, for a moment, and carry away with you all my best wishes and prayers. I shall think of you, Hist, and of your intended husband, let what may come to pass, and always wish you well, here and hereafter, whether the last is to be according to Indian idees, or Christian doctrines."

Hist shed no tear at parting. She was sustained by the high resolution of one who had decided on her course, but her dark eyes were luminous with the feelings that glowed within, and her pretty countenance beamed with an expression of determination that was in marked and singular contrast to its ordinary gentleness. It was but a minute ere the Delaware advanced to the side of his friend with the light, noiseless tread of an Indian.

"Come this-a-way, Sarpent, here more out of sight of the women," commenced the Deerslayer, "for I've several things to say that mustn't so much as be suspected, much less overheard. You know too well the natur' of furloughs and Mingos to have any doubts or misgivin's consarnin' what is like to happen, when I get back to the camp. On them two p'ints therefore, a few words will go a great way. In the first place, chief, I wish to say a little about Hist, and the manner in which you red men treat your wives. I suppose it's accordin' to the gifts of your people that the women should work, and the men hunt; but there's such a thing as moderation in all matters. As for huntin', I see no good reason why any limits need be set to that, but Hist comes of too good a stock to toil like a common drudge. One of your means and standin' need never want for corn, or potatoes, or anything that the fields yield; therefore, I hope the hoe will never be put into the hands of any wife of yourn. You know I am not quite a beggar, and all I own, whether in ammunition, skins, arms, or calicoes, I give to Hist, should I not come back to claim them by the end of the season. This will set the maiden up, and will buy labor for her, for a long time to come. I suppose I needn't tell you to love the young woman, for that you do already, and whomsoever the man ra'ally loves, he'll be likely enough to cherish. Nevertheless, it can do no harm to say that kind words never rankle, while bitter words do. I know you're a man, Sarpent, that is less apt to talk in his own lodge, than to speak at the Council Fire; but forgetful moments may overtake us all, and the practyse of kind doin', and kind talkin', is a wonderful advantage in keepin' peace in a cabin, as well as on a hunt."

"My ears are open," returned the Delaware gravely; "the words of my brother have entered so far that they never can fall out again. They are like rings, that have no end, and cannot drop. Let him speak on; the song of the wren and the voice of a friend never tire."

"I will speak a little longer, chief, but you will excuse it for the sake of old companionship, should I now talk about myself. If the worst comes to the worst, it's not likely there'll be much left of me but ashes, so a grave would be useless, and a sort of vanity. On that score I'm no way partic'lar, though it might be well enough to take a look at the remains of the pile, and should any bones, or pieces be found, 'twould be more decent to gather them together, and bury them, than to let them lie for the wolves to gnaw at, and howl over. These matters can make no great difference in the mind, but men of white blood and Christian feelin's have rather a gift for graves."

"It shall be done as my brother says," returned the Indian, gravely. "If his mind is full, let him empty it in the bosom of a friend."

"I thank you, Sarpent; my mind's easy enough; yes, it's tolerable easy. Idees will come uppermost that I'm not apt to think about in common, it's true, but by striving ag'in some, and lettin' other some out, all will come right in the long run. There's one thing, howsever, chief, that does seem to me to be onreasonable, and ag'in natur', though the missionaries say it's true, and bein' of my religion and colour I feel bound to believe them. They say an Injin may torment and tortur' the body to his heart's content, and scalp, and cut, and tear, and burn, and consume all his inventions and deviltries, until nothin' is left but ashes, and they shall be scattered to the four winds of heaven, yet when the trumpet of God shall sound, all will come together ag'in, and the man will stand forth in his flesh, the same creatur' as to looks, if not as to feelin's, that he was afore he was harmed!"

"The missionaries are good men—mean well," returned the Delaware courteously; "they are not great medicines. They think all they say, Deerslayer; that is no reason why warriors and orators should be all ears. When Chingachgook shall see the father of Tamenund standing in his scalp, and paint, and war lock, then will he believe the missionaries."

"Seein' is believin', of a sartainty; ahs! me—and some of us may see these things sooner than we thought. I comprehend your meanin' about Tamenund's father, Sarpent, and the idee's a close idee. Tamenund is now an elderly man, say eighty every day of it, and his father was scalped, and tormented, and burnt, when the present prophet was a youngster. Yes, if one could see that come to pass, there wouldn't be much difficulty in yieldin' faith to all that the missionaries say. Howsever, I am not ag'in the opinion now, for you must know, Sarpent, that the great principle of Christianity is to believe without seeing, and a man should always act up to his religion and principles, let them be what they may."

"That is strange for a wise nation!" said the Delaware with emphasis. "The red man looks hard, that he may see and understand."

"Yes, that's plauserble, and is agreeable to mortal pride, but it's not as deep as it seems. If we could understand all we see, Sarpent, there might be not only sense, but safety, in refusin' to give faith to any one thing that we might find oncomperhensible; but when there's so many things about which it may be said we know nothin' at all, why, there's little use, and no reason, in bein' difficult touchin' any one in partic'lar. For my part, Delaware, all my thoughts haven't been on the game, when outlyin' in the hunts and scoutin's of our youth. Many's the hour I've passed, pleasantly enough too, in what is tarmed conterplation by my people. On such occasions the mind is actyve, though the body seems lazy and listless. An open spot on a mountain side, where a wide look can be had at the heavens and the 'arth, is a most judicious place for a man to get a just idee of the power of the Manitou, and of his own littleness. At such times, there isn't any great disposition to find fault with little difficulties, in the way of comperhension, as there are so many big ones to hide them. Believin' comes easy enough to me at such times, and if the Lord made man first out of 'arth, as they tell me it is written in the Bible; then turns him into dust at death; I see no great difficulty in the way to bringin' him back in the body, though ashes be the only substance left. These things lie beyond our understandin', though they may and do lie so close to our feelin's. But, of all the doctrines, Sarpent, that which disturbs me, and disconsarts my mind the most, is the one which teaches us to think that a pale-face goes to one heaven, and a red-skin to another; it may separate in death them which lived much together, and loved each other well, in life!"

"Do the missionaries teach their white brethren to think it is so?" demanded the Indian, with serious earnestness. "The Delawares believe that good men and brave warriors will hunt together in the same pleasant woods, let them belong to whatever tribe they may; that all the unjust Indians and cowards will have to sneak in with the dogs and the wolves to get venison for their lodges."

"'Tis wonderful how many consaits mankind have consarnin' happiness and misery, here after!" exclaimed the hunter, borne away by the power of his own thoughts. "Some believe in burnin's and flames, and some think punishment is to eat with the wolves and dogs. Then, ag'in, some fancy heaven to be only the carryin' out of their own 'arthly longin's, while others fancy it all gold and shinin' lights! Well, I've an idee of my own, in that matter, which is just this, Sarpent. Whenever I've done wrong, I've ginirally found 'twas owin' to some blindness of the mind, which hid the right from view, and when sight has returned, then has come sorrow and repentance. Now, I consait that, after death, when the body is laid aside or, if used at all, is purified and without its longin's, the spirit sees all things in their ra'al lights and never becomes blind to truth and justice. Such bein' the case, all that has been done in life, is beheld as plainly as the sun is seen at noon; the good brings joy, while the evil brings sorrow. There's nothin' onreasonable in that, but it's agreeable to every man's exper'ence."

"I thought the pale-faces believed all men were wicked; who then could ever find the white man's heaven?"

"That's ingen'ous, but it falls short of the missionary teachin's. You'll be Christianized one day, I make no doubt, and then 'twill all come plain enough. You must know, Sarpent, that there's been a great deed of salvation done, that, by God's help, enables all men to find a pardon for their wickednesses, and that is the essence of the white man's religion. I can't stop to talk this matter over with you any longer, for Hetty's in the canoe, and the furlough takes me away, but the time will come I hope when you'll feel these things; for, after all, they must be felt rather than reasoned about. Ah's! me; well, Delaware, there's my hand; you know it's that of a fri'nd, and will shake it as such, though it never has done you one half the good its owner wishes it had."

The Indian took the offered hand, and returned its pressure warmly. Then falling back on his acquired stoicism of manner, which so many mistake for constitutional indifference, he drew up in reserve, and prepared to part from his friend with dignity. Deerslayer, however, was more natural, nor would he have at all cared about giving way to his feelings, had not the recent conduct and language of Judith given him some secret, though ill defined apprehensions of a scene. He was too humble to imagine the truth concerning the actual feelings of that beautiful girl, while he was too observant not to have noted the struggle she had maintained with herself, and which had so often led her to the very verge of discovery. That something extraordinary was concealed in her breast he thought obvious enough, and, through a sentiment of manly delicacy that would have done credit to the highest human refinement, he shrunk from any exposure of her secret that might subsequently cause regret to the girl, herself. He therefore determined to depart, now, and that without any further manifestations of feeling either from him, or from others.

"God bless you! Sarpent—God bless you!" cried the hunter, as the canoe left the side of the platform. "Your Manitou and my God only know when and where we shall meet ag'in; I shall count it a great blessing, and a full reward for any little good I may have done on 'arth, if we shall be permitted to know each other, and to consort together, hereafter, as we have so long done in these pleasant woods afore us!"

Chingachgook waved his hand. Drawing the light blanket he wore over his head, as a Roman would conceal his grief in his robes, he slowly withdrew into the Ark, in order to indulge his sorrow and his musings, alone. Deerslayer did not speak again until the canoe was half-way to the shore. Then he suddenly ceased paddling, at an interruption that came from the mild, musical voice of Hetty.

"Why do you go back to the Hurons, Deerslayer?" demanded the girl. "They say I am feeble-minded, and such they never harm, but you have as much sense as Hurry Harry; and more too, Judith thinks, though I don't see how that can well be."

"Ah! Hetty, afore we land I must converse a little with you child, and that too on matters touching your own welfare, principally. Stop paddling—or, rather, that the Mingos needn't think we are plotting and contriving, and so treat us accordingly, just dip your paddle lightly, and give the canoe a little motion and no more. That's just the idee and the movement; I see you're ready enough at an appearance, and might be made useful at a sarcumvention if it was lawful now to use one— that's just the idee and the movement! Ah's! me. Desait and a false tongue are evil things, and altogether onbecoming our colour, Hetty, but it is a pleasure and a satisfaction to outdo the contrivances of a red-skin in the strife of lawful warfare. My path has been short, and is like soon to have an end, but I can see that the wanderings of a warrior aren't altogether among brambles and difficulties. There's a bright side to a warpath, as well as to most other things, if we'll only have the wisdom to see it, and the ginerosity to own it."

"And why should your warpath, as you call it, come so near to an end, Deerslayer?"

"Because, my good girl, my furlough comes so near to an end. They're likely to have pretty much the same tarmination, as regards time, one following on the heels of the other, as a matter of course."

"I don't understand your meaning, Deerslayer—" returned the girl, looking a little bewildered. "Mother always said people ought to speak more plainly to me than to most other persons, because I'm feeble minded. Those that are feeble minded, don't understand as easily as those that have sense."

"Well then, Hetty, the simple truth is this. You know that I'm now a captyve to the Hurons, and captyves can't do, in all things, as they please—"

"But how can you be a captive," eagerly interrupted the girl—"when you are out here on the lake, in father's best canoe, and the Indians are in the woods with no canoe at all? That can't be true, Deerslayer!"

"I wish with all my heart and soul, Hetty, that you was right, and that I was wrong, instead of your bein' all wrong, and I bein' only too near the truth. Free as I seem to your eyes, gal, I'm bound hand and foot in ra'ality."

"Well it is a great misfortune not to have sense! Now I can't see or understand that you are a captive, or bound in any manner. If you are bound, with what are your hands and feet fastened?"

"With a furlough, gal; that's a thong that binds tighter than any chain. One may be broken, but the other can't. Ropes and chains allow of knives, and desait, and contrivances; but a furlough can be neither cut, slipped nor sarcumvented."

"What sort of a thing is a furlough, then, if it be stronger than hemp or iron? I never saw a furlough."

"I hope you may never feel one, gal; the tie is altogether in the feelin's, in these matters, and therefore is to be felt and not seen. You can understand what it is to give a promise, I dare to say, good little Hetty?"

"Certainly. A promise is to say you will do a thing, and that binds you to be as good as your word. Mother always kept her promises to me, and then she said it would be wicked if I didn't keep my promises to her, and to every body else."

"You have had a good mother, in some matters, child, whatever she may have been in other some. That is a promise, and as you say it must be kept. Now, I fell into the hands of the Mingos last night, and they let me come off to see my fri'nds and send messages in to my own colour, if any such feel consarn on my account, on condition that I shall be back when the sun is up today, and take whatever their revenge and hatred can contrive, in the way of torments, in satisfaction for the life of a warrior that fell by my rifle, as well as for that of the young woman shot by Hurry, and other disapp'intments met with on and about this lake. What is called a promise atween mother and darter, or even atween strangers in the settlements is called a furlough when given by one soldier to another, on a warpath. And now I suppose you understand my situation, Hetty."

The girl made no answer for some time, but she ceased paddling altogether, as if the novel idea distracted her mind too much to admit of other employment. Then she resumed the dialogue earnestly and with solicitude.

"Do you think the Hurons will have the heart to do what you say, Deerslayer?" she asked. "I have found them kind and harmless."

"That's true enough as consarns one like you, Hetty, but it's a very different affair when it comes to an open inimy, and he too the owner of a pretty sartain rifle. I don't say that they bear me special malice on account of any expl'ites already performed, for that would be bragging, as it might be, on the varge of the grave, but it's no vanity to believe that they know one of their bravest and cunnin'est chiefs fell by my hands. Such bein' the case, the tribe would reproach them if they failed to send the spirit of a pale-face to keep the company of the spirit of their red brother; always supposin' that he can catch it. I look for no marcy, Hetty, at their hands; and my principal sorrow is that such a calamity should befall me on my first warpath: that it would come sooner or later, every soldier counts on and expects."

"The Hurons shall not harm you, Deerslayer," cried the girl, much excited—"'Tis wicked as well as cruel; I have the Bible, here, to tell them so. Do you think I would stand by and see you tormented?"

"I hope not, my good Hetty, I hope not; and, therefore, when the moment comes, I expect you will move off, and not be a witness of what you can't help, while it would grieve you. But, I haven't stopped the paddles to talk of my own afflictions and difficulties, but to speak a little plainly to you, gal, consarnin' your own matters."

"What can you have to say to me, Deerslayer! Since mother died, few talk to me of such things."

"So much the worse, poor gal; yes, 'tis so much the worse, for one of your state of mind needs frequent talking to, in order to escape the snares and desaits of this wicked world. You haven't forgotten Hurry Harry, gal, so soon, I calculate?"

"I!—I forget Henry March!" exclaimed Hetty, starting. "Why should I forget him, Deerslayer, when he is our friend, and only left us last night. Then the large bright star that mother loved so much to gaze at was just over the top of yonder tall pine on the mountain, as Hurry got into the canoe; and when you landed him on the point, near the east bay, it wasn't more than the length of Judith's handsomest ribbon above it."

"And how can you know how long I was gone, or how far I went to land Hurry, seein' you were not with us, and the distance was so great, to say nothing of the night?"

"Oh! I know when it was, well enough," returned Hetty positively—"There's more ways than one for counting time and distance. When the mind is engaged, it is better than any clock. Mine is feeble, I know, but it goes true enough in all that touches poor Hurry Harry. Judith will never marry March, Deerslayer."

"That's the p'int, Hetty; that's the very p'int I want to come to. I suppose you know that it's nat'ral for young people to have kind feelin's for one another, more especially when one happens to be a youth and t'other a maiden. Now, one of your years and mind, gal, that has neither father nor mother, and who lives in a wilderness frequented by hunters and trappers, needs be on her guard against evils she little dreams of."

"What harm can it be to think well of a fellow creature," returned Hetty simply, though the conscious blood was stealing to her cheeks in spite of a spirit so pure that it scarce knew why it prompted the blush, "the Bible tells us to 'love them who despitefully use' us, and why shouldn't we like them that do not."

"Ah! Hetty, the love of the missionaries isn't the sort of likin' I mean. Answer me one thing, child; do you believe yourself to have mind enough to become a wife, and a mother?"

"That's not a proper question to ask a young woman, Deerslayer, and I'll not answer it," returned the girl, in a reproving manner—much as a parent rebukes a child for an act of indiscretion. "If you have any thing to say about Hurry, I'll hear that—but you must not speak evil of him; he is absent, and 'tis unkind to talk evil of the absent."

"Your mother has given you so many good lessons, Hetty, that my fears for you are not as great as they were. Nevertheless, a young woman without parents, in your state of mind, and who is not without beauty, must always be in danger in such a lawless region as this. I would say nothin' amiss of Hurry, who, in the main, is not a bad man for one of his callin', but you ought to know one thing, which it may not be altogether pleasant to tell you, but which must be said. March has a desperate likin' for your sister Judith."

"Well, what of that? Everybody admires Judith, she's so handsome, and Hurry has told me, again and again, how much he wishes to marry her. But that will never come to pass, for Judith don't like Hurry. She likes another, and talks about him in her sleep; though you need not ask me who he is, for all the gold in King George's crown, and all the jewels too, wouldn't tempt me to tell you his name. If sisters can't keep each other's secrets, who can?"

"Sartainly, I do not wish you to tell me, Hetty, nor would it be any advantage to a dyin' man to know. What the tongue says when the mind's asleep, neither head nor heart is answerable for."

"I wish I knew why Judith talks so much in her sleep, about officers, and honest hearts, and false tongues, but I suppose she don't like to tell me, as I'm feeble minded. Isn't it odd, Deerslayer, that Judith don't like Hurry—he who is the bravest looking youth that ever comes upon the lake, and is as handsome as she is herself. Father always said they would be the comeliest couple in the country, though mother didn't fancy March any more than Judith. There's no telling what will happen, they say, until things actually come to pass."

"Ahs! me—well, poor Hetty, 'tis of no great use to talk to them that can't understand you, and so I'll say no more about what I did wish to speak of, though it lay heavy on my mind. Put the paddle in motion ag'in, gal, and we'll push for the shore, for the sun is nearly up, and my furlough is almost out."

The canoe now glided ahead, holding its way towards the point where Deerslayer well knew that his enemies expected him, and where he now began to be afraid he might not arrive in season to redeem his plighted faith. Hetty, perceiving his impatience without very clearly comprehending its cause, however, seconded his efforts in a way that soon rendered their timely return no longer a matter of doubt. Then, and then only, did the young man suffer his exertions to flag, and Hetty began, again, to prattle in her simple confiding manner, though nothing farther was uttered that it may be thought necessary to relate.

CHAPTER XXVII.

"Thou hast been busy, Death, this day, and yet
But half thy work is done! The gates of hell
Are thronged, yet twice ten thousand spirits more
Who from their warm and healthful tenements
Fear no divorce; must, ere the sun go down,
Enter the world of woe!"——

Southey, Roderick, the Last of the Goths, XXIV, i–6.

One experienced in the signs of the heavens, would have seen that the sun wanted but two or three minutes of the zenith, when Deerslayer landed on the point, where the Hurons were now encamped, nearly abreast of the castle. This spot was similar to the one already described, with the exception that the surface of the land was less broken, and less crowded with trees. Owing to these two circumstances, it was all the better suited to the purpose for which it had been selected, the space beneath the branches bearing some resemblance to a densely wooded lawn. Favoured by its position and its spring, it had been much resorted to by savages and hunters, and the natural grasses had succeeded their fires, leaving an appearance of sward in places, a very unusual accompaniment of the virgin forest. Nor was the margin of water fringed with bushes, as on so much of its shore, but the eye penetrated the woods immediately on reaching the strand, commanding nearly the whole area of the projection.

If it was a point of honor with the Indian warrior to redeem his word, when pledged to return and meet his death at a given hour, so was it a point of characteristic pride to show no womanish impatience, but to reappear as nearly as possible at the appointed moment. It was well not to exceed the grace accorded by the generosity of the enemy, but it was better to meet it to a minute. Something of this dramatic effect mingles with most of the graver usages of the American aborigines, and no doubt, like the prevalence of a similar feeling among people more sophisticated and refined, may be referred to a principle of nature. We all love the wonderful, and when it comes attended by chivalrous self-devotion and a rigid regard to honor, it presents itself to our admiration in a shape doubly attractive. As respects Deerslayer, though he took a pride in showing his white blood, by often deviating from the usages of the red-men, he frequently dropped into their customs, and oftener into their feelings, unconsciously to himself, in consequence of having no other arbiters to appeal to, than their judgments and tastes. On the present occasion, he would have abstained from betraying a feverish haste by a too speedy return, since it would have contained a tacit admission that the time asked for was more than had been wanted; but, on the other hand, had the idea occurred to him, he would have quickened his movements a little, in order to avoid the dramatic appearance of returning at the precise instant set as the utmost limit of his absence. Still, accident had interfered to defeat the last intention, for when the young man put his foot on the point, and advanced with a steady tread towards the group of chiefs that was seated in grave array on a fallen tree, the oldest of their number cast his eye upward, at an opening in the trees, and pointed out to his companions the startling fact that the sun was just entering a space that was known to mark the zenith. A common, but low exclamation of surprise and admiration escaped every mouth, and the grim warriors looked at each other, some with envy and disappointment, some with astonishment at the precise accuracy of their victim, and others with a more generous and liberal feeling. The American Indian always deemed his moral victories the noblest, prizing the groans and yielding of his victim under torture, more than the trophy of his scalp; and the trophy itself more than his life. To slay, and not to bring off the proof of victory, indeed, was scarcely deemed honorable, even these rude and fierce tenants of the forest, like their more nurtured brethren of the court and the camp, having set up for themselves imaginary and arbitrary points of honor, to supplant the conclusions of the right and the decisions of reason.

The Hurons had been divided in their opinions concerning the probability of their captive's return. Most among them, indeed, had not expected it possible for a pale-face to come back voluntarily, and meet the known penalties of an Indian torture; but a few of the seniors expected better things from one who had already shown himself so singularly cool, brave and upright. The party had come to its decision, however, less in the expectation of finding the pledge redeemed, than in the hope of disgracing the Delawares by casting into their teeth the delinquency of one bred in their villages. They would have greatly preferred that Chingachgook should be their prisoner, and prove the traitor, but the pale-face scion of the hated stock was no bad substitute for their purposes, failing in their designs against the ancient stem. With a view to render their triumph as signal as possible, in the event of the hour's passing without the reappearance of the hunter, all the warriors and scouts of the party had been called in, and the whole band, men, women and children, was now assembled at this single point, to be a witness of the expected scene. As the castle was in plain view, and by no means distant, it was easily watched by daylight, and, it being thought that its inmates were now limited to Hurry, the Delaware and the two girls, no apprehensions were felt of their being able to escape unseen. A large raft having a breast-work of logs had been prepared, and was in actual readiness to be used against either Ark or castle as occasion might require, so soon as the fate of Deerslayer was determined, the seniors of the party having come to the opinion that it was getting to be hazardous to delay their departure for Canada beyond the coming night. In short the band waited merely to dispose of this single affair, ere it brought matters with those in the Castle to a crisis, and prepared to commence its retreat towards the distant waters of Ontario.

It was an imposing scene into which Deerslayer now found himself advancing. All the older warriors were seated on the trunk of the fallen tree, waiting his approach with grave decorum. On the right stood the young men, armed, while left was occupied by the women and children. In the centre was an open space of considerable extent, always canopied by trees, but from which the underbrush, dead wood, and other obstacles had been carefully removed. The more open area had probably been much used by former parties, for this was the place where the appearance of a sward was the most decided. The arches of the woods, even at high noon, cast their sombre shadows on the spot, which the brilliant rays of the sun that struggled through the leaves contributed to mellow, and, if such an expression can be used, to illuminate. It was probably from a similar scene that the mind of man first got its idea of the effects of gothic tracery and churchly hues, this temple of nature producing some such effect, so far as light and shadow were concerned, as the well-known offspring of human invention.

As was not unusual among the tribes and wandering bands of the Aborigines, two chiefs shared, in nearly equal degrees, the principal and primitive authority that was wielded over these children of the forest. There were several who might claim the distinction of being chief men, but the two in question were so much superior to all the rest in influence, that, when they agreed, no one disputed their mandates, and when they were divided the band hesitated, like men who had lost their governing principle of action. It was also in conformity with practice, perhaps we might add in conformity with nature, that one of the chiefs was indebted to his mind for his influence, whereas the other owed his distinction altogether to qualities that were physical. One was a senior, well known for eloquence in debate, wisdom in council, and prudence in measures; while his great competitor, if not his rival, was a brave distinguished in war, notorious for ferocity, and remarkable, in the way of intellect, for nothing but the cunning and expedients of the war path. The first was Rivenoak, who has already been introduced to the reader, while the last was called le Panth'ere, in the language of the Canadas, or the Panther, to resort to the vernacular of the English colonies. The appellation of the fighting chief was supposed to indicate the qualities of the warrior, agreeably to a practice of the red man's nomenclature, ferocity, cunning and treachery being, perhaps, the distinctive features of his character. The title had been received from the French, and was prized so much the more from that circumstance, the Indian submitting profoundly to the greater intelligence of his pale-face allies, in most things of this nature. How well the sobriquet was merited will be seen in the sequel.

Rivenoak and the Panther sat side by side awaiting the approach of their prisoner, as Deerslayer put his moccasined foot on the strand, nor did either move, or utter a syllable, until the young man had advanced into the centre of the area, and proclaimed his presence with his voice. This was done firmly, though in the simple manner that marked the character of the individual.

"Here I am, Mingos," he said, in the dialect of the Delawares, a language that most present understood; "here I am, and there is the sun. One is not more true to the laws of natur', than the other has proved true to his word. I am your prisoner; do with me what you please. My business with man and 'arth is settled; nothing remains now but to meet the white man's God, accordin' to a white man's duties and gifts."

A murmur of approbation escaped even the women at this address, and, for an instant there was a strong and pretty general desire to adopt into the tribe one who owned so brave a spirit. Still there were dissenters from this wish, among the principal of whom might be classed the Panther, and his sister, le Sumach, so called from the number of her children, who was the widow of le Loup Cervier, now known to have fallen by the hand of the captive. Native ferocity held one in subjection, while the corroding passion of revenge prevented the other from admitting any gentler feeling at the moment. Not so with Rivenoak. This chief arose, stretched his arm before him in a gesture of courtesy, and paid his compliments with an ease and dignity that a prince might have envied. As, in that band, his wisdom and eloquence were confessedly without rivals, he knew that on himself would properly fall the duty of first replying to the speech of the pale-face.

"Pale-face, you are honest," said the Huron orator. "My people are happy in having captured a man, and not a skulking fox. We now know you; we shall treat you like a brave. If you have slain one of our warriors, and helped to kill others, you have a life of your own ready to give away in return. Some of my young men thought that the blood of a pale-face was too thin; that it would refuse to run under the Huron knife. You will show them it is not so; your heart is stout, as well as your body. It is a pleasure to make such a prisoner; should my warriors say that the death of le Loup Cervier ought not to be forgotten, and that he cannot travel towards the land of spirits alone, that his enemy must be sent to overtake him, they will remember that he fell by the hand of a brave, and send you after him with such signs of our friendship as shall not make him ashamed to keep your company. I have spoken; you know what I have said."

"True enough, Mingo, all true as the gospel," returned the simple minded hunter, "you have spoken, and I do know not only what you have said, but, what is still more important, what you mean. I dare to say your warrior the Lynx was a stout-hearted brave, and worthy of your fri'ndship and respect, but I do not feel unworthy to keep his company, without any passport from your hands. Nevertheless, here I am, ready to receive judgment from your council, if, indeed, the matter was not determined among you afore I got back."

"My old men would not sit in council over a pale-face until they saw him among them," answered Rivenoak, looking around him a little ironically; "they said it would be like sitting in council over the winds; they go where they will, and come back as they see fit, and not otherwise. There was one voice that spoke in your favor, Deerslayer, but it was alone, like the song of the wren whose mate has been struck by the hawk."

"I thank that voice whosoever it may have been, Mingo, and will say it was as true a voice as the rest were lying voices. A furlough is as binding on a pale-face, if he be honest, as it is on a red-skin, and was it not so, I would never bring disgrace on the Delawares, among whom I may be said to have received my edication. But words are useless, and lead to braggin' feelin's; here I am; act your will on me."

Rivenoak made a sign of acquiescence, and then a short conference was privately held among the chiefs. As soon as the latter ended, three or four young men fell back from among the armed group, and disappeared. Then it was signified to the prisoner that he was at liberty to go at large on the point, until a council was held concerning his fate. There was more of seeming, than of real confidence, however, in this apparent liberality, inasmuch as the young men mentioned already formed a line of sentinels across the breadth of the point, inland, and escape from any other part was out of the question. Even the canoe was removed beyond this line of sentinels, to a spot where it was considered safe from any sudden attempt. These precautions did not proceed from a failure of confidence, but from the circumstance that the prisoner had now complied with all the required conditions of his parole, and it would have been considered a commendable and honorable exploit to escape from his foes. So nice, indeed, were the distinctions drawn by the savages in cases of this nature, that they often gave their victims a chance to evade the torture, deeming it as creditable to the captors to overtake, or to outwit a fugitive, when his exertions were supposed to be quickened by the extreme jeopardy of his situation, as it was for him to get clear from so much extraordinary vigilance.

Nor was Deerslayer unconscious of, or forgetful, of his rights and of his opportunities. Could he now have seen any probable opening for an escape, the attempt would not have been delayed a minute. But the case seem'd desperate. He was aware of the line of sentinels, and felt the difficulty of breaking through it, unharmed. The lake offered no advantages, as the canoe would have given his foes the greatest facilities for overtaking him; else would he have found it no difficult task to swim as far as the castle. As he walked about the point, he even examined the spot to ascertain if it offered no place of concealment, but its openness, its size, and the hundred watchful glances that were turned towards him, even while those who made them affected not to see him, prevented any such expedient from succeeding. The dread and disgrace of failure had no influence on Deerslayer, who deemed it even a point of honor to reason and feel like a white man, rather than as an Indian, and who felt it a sort of duty to do all he could that did not involve a dereliction from principle, in order to save his life. Still he hesitated about making the effort, for he also felt that he ought to see the chance of success before he committed himself.

In the mean time the business of the camp appeared to proceed in its regular train. The chiefs consulted apart, admitting no one but the Sumach to their councils, for she, the widow of the fallen warrior, had an exclusive right to be heard on such an occasion. The young men strolled about in indolent listlessness, awaiting the result with Indian patience, while the females prepared the feast that was to celebrate the termination of the affair, whether it proved fortunate or otherwise for our hero. No one betrayed feeling, and an indifferent observer, beyond the extreme watchfulness of the sentinels, would have detected no extraordinary movement or sensation to denote the real state of things. Two or three old women put their heads together, and it appeared unfavorably to the prospects of Deerslayer, by their scowling looks, and angry gestures; but a group of Indian girls were evidently animated by a different impulse, as was apparent by stolen glances that expressed pity and regret. In this condition of the camp, an hour soon glided away.

Suspense is perhaps the feeling of all others that is most difficult to be supported. When Deerslayer landed, he fully expected in the course of a few minutes to undergo the tortures of an Indian revenge, and he was prepared to meet his fate manfully; but, the delay proved far more trying than the nearer approach of suffering, and the intended victim began seriously to meditate some desperate effort at escape, as it might be from sheer anxiety to terminate the scene, when he was suddenly summoned, to appear once more in front of his judges, who had already arranged the band in its former order, in readiness to receive him.

"Killer of the Deer," commenced Rivenoak, as soon as his captive stood before him, "my aged men have listened to wise words; they are ready to speak. You are a man whose fathers came from beyond the rising sun; we are children of the setting sun; we turn our faces towards the Great Sweet Lakes, when we look towards our villages. It may be a wide country and full of riches towards the morning, but it is very pleasant towards the evening. We love most to look in that direction. When we gaze at the east, we feel afraid, canoe after canoe bringing more and more of your people in the track of the sun, as if their land was so full as to run over. The red men are few already; they have need of help. One of our best lodges has lately been emptied by the death of its master; it will be a long time before his son can grow big enough to sit in his place. There is his widow; she will want venison to feed her and her children, for her sons are yet like the young of the robin, before they quit the nest. By your hand has this great calamity befallen her. She has two duties; one to le Loup Cervier, and one to his children. Scalp for scalp, life for life, blood for blood, is one law; to feed her young, another. We know you, Killer of the Deer. You are honest; when you say a thing, it is so. You have but one tongue, and that is not forked, like a snake's. Your head is never hid in the grass; all can see it. What you say, that will you do. You are just. When you have done wrong, it is your wish to do right, again, as soon as you can. Here, is the Sumach; she is alone in her wigwam, with children crying around her for food—yonder is a rifle; it is loaded and ready to be fired. Take the gun, go forth and shoot a deer; bring the venison and lay it before the widow of Le Loup Cervier, feed her children; call yourself her husband. After which, your heart will no longer be Delaware, but Huron; le Sumach's ears will not hear the cries of her children; my people will count the proper number of warriors."

"I fear'd this, Rivenoak," answered Deerslayer, when the other had ceased speaking—"yes, I did dread that it would come to this. Howsever, the truth is soon told, and that will put an end to all expectations on this head. Mingo, I'm white and Christian born; 't would ill become me to take a wife, under red-skin forms, from among heathen. That which I wouldn't do, in peaceable times, and under a bright sun, still less would I do behind clouds, in order to save my life. I may never marry; most likely Providence in putting me up here in the woods, has intended I should live single, and without a lodge of my own; but should such a thing come to pass, none but a woman of my own colour and gifts shall darken the door of my wigwam. As for feeding the young of your dead warrior, I would do that cheerfully, could it be done without discredit; but it cannot, seeing that I can never live in a Huron village. Your own young men must find the Sumach in venison, and the next time she marries, let her take a husband whose legs are not long enough to overrun territory that don't belong to him. We fou't a fair battle, and he fell; in this there is nothin' but what a brave expects, and should be ready to meet. As for getting a Mingo heart, as well might you expect to see gray hairs on a boy, or the blackberry growing on the pine. No—no Huron; my gifts are white so far as wives are consarned; it is Delaware, in all things touchin' Injins."

These words were scarcely out of the mouth of Deerslayer, before a common murmur betrayed the dissatisfaction with which they had been heard. The aged women, in particular, were loud in their expressions of disgust, and the gentle Sumach, herself, a woman quite old enough to be our hero's mother, was not the least pacific in her denunciations. But all the other manifestations of disappointment and discontent were thrown into the background, by the fierce resentment of the Panther. This grim chief had thought it a degradation to permit his sister to become the wife of a pale-face of the Yengeese at all, and had only given a reluctant consent to the arrangement—one by no means unusual among the Indians, however—at the earnest solicitations of the bereaved widow; and it goaded him to the quick to find his condescension slighted, the honor he had with so much regret been persuaded to accord, condemned. The animal from which he got his name does not glare on his intended prey with more frightful ferocity than his eyes gleamed on the captive, nor was his arm backward in seconding the fierce resentment that almost consumed his breast.

"Dog of the pale-faces!" he exclaimed in Iroquois, "go yell among the curs of your own evil hunting grounds!"

The denunciation was accompanied by an appropriate action. Even while speaking his arm was lifted, and the tomahawk hurled. Luckily the loud tones of the speaker had drawn the eye of Deerslayer towards him, else would that moment have probably closed his career. So great was the dexterity with which this dangerous weapon was thrown, and so deadly the intent, that it would have riven the scull of the prisoner, had he not stretched forth an arm, and caught the handle in one of its turns, with a readiness quite as remarkable as the skill with which the missile had been hurled. The projectile force was so great, notwithstanding, that when Deerslayer's arm was arrested, his hand was raised above and behind his own head, and in the very attitude necessary to return the attack. It is not certain whether the circumstance of finding himself unexpectedly in this menacing posture and armed tempted the young man to retaliate, or whether sudden resentment overcame his forbearance and prudence. His eye kindled, however, and a small red spot appeared on each cheek, while he cast all his energy into the effort of his arm, and threw back the weapon at his assailant. The unexpectedness of this blow contributed to its success, the Panther neither raising an arm, nor bending his head to avoid it. The keen little axe struck the victim in a perpendicular line with the nose, directly between the eyes, literally braining him on the spot. Sallying forward, as the serpent darts at its enemy even while receiving its own death wound, this man of powerful frame fell his length into the open area formed by the circle, quivering in death. A common rush to his relief left the captive, in a single instant, quite without the crowd, and, willing to make one desperate effort for life, he bounded off with the activity of a deer. There was but a breathless instant, when the whole band, old and young, women and children, abandoning the lifeless body of the Panther where it lay, raised the yell of alarm and followed in pursuit.

Sudden as had been the event which induced Deerslayer to make this desperate trial of speed, his mind was not wholly unprepared for the fearful emergency. In the course of the past hour, he had pondered well on the chances of such an experiment, and had shrewdly calculated all the details of success and failure. At the first leap, therefore, his body was completely under the direction of an intelligence that turned all its efforts to the best account, and prevented everything like hesitation or indecision at the important instant of the start. To this alone was he indebted for the first great advantage, that of getting through the line of sentinels unharmed. The manner in which this was done, though sufficiently simple, merits a description.

Although the shores of the point were not fringed with bushes, as was the case with most of the others on the lake, it was owing altogether to the circumstance that the spot had been so much used by hunters and fishermen. This fringe commenced on what might be termed the main land, and was as dense as usual, extending in long lines both north and south. In the latter direction, then, Deerslayer held his way, and, as the sentinels were a little without the commencement of this thicket, before the alarm was clearly communicated to them the fugitive had gained its cover. To run among the bushes, however, was out of the question, and Deerslayer held his way, for some forty or fifty yards, in the water, which was barely knee deep, offering as great an obstacle to the speed of his pursuers as it did to his own. As soon as a favorable spot presented, he darted through the line of bushes and issued into the open woods. Several rifles were discharged at Deerslayer while in the water, and more followed as he came out into the comparative exposure of the clear forest. But the direction of his line of flight, which partially crossed that of the fire, the haste with which the weapons had been aimed, and the general confusion that prevailed in the camp prevented any harm from being done. Bullets whistled past him, and many cut twigs from the branches at his side, but not one touched even his dress. The delay caused by these fruitless attempts was of great service to the fugitive, who had gained more than a hundred yards on even the leading men of the Hurons, ere something like concert and order had entered into the chase. To think of following with rifles in hand was out of the question, and after emptying their pieces in vague hopes of wounding their captive, the best runners of the Indians threw them aside, calling out to the women and boys to recover and load them, again, as soon as possible.

Deerslayer knew too well the desperate nature of the struggle in which he was engaged to lose one of the precious moments. He also knew that his only hope was to run in a straight line, for as soon as he began to turn, or double, the greater number of his pursuers would put escape out of the question. He held his way therefore, in a diagonal direction up the acclivity, which was neither very high nor very steep in this part of the mountain, but which was sufficiently toilsome for one contending for life, to render it painfully oppressive. There, however, he slackened his speed to recover breath, proceeding even at a quick walk, or a slow trot, along the more difficult parts of the way. The Hurons were whooping and leaping behind him, but this he disregarded, well knowing they must overcome the difficulties he had surmounted ere they could reach the elevation to which he had attained. The summit of the first hill was now quite near him, and he saw, by the formation of the land, that a deep glen intervened before the base of a second hill could be reached. Walking deliberately to the summit, he glanced eagerly about him in every direction in quest of a cover. None offered in the ground, but a fallen tree lay near him, and desperate circumstances required desperate remedies. This tree lay in a line parallel to the glen, at the brow of the hill. To leap on it, and then to force his person as close as possible under its lower side, took but a moment. Previously to disappearing from his pursuers, however, Deerslayer stood on the height and gave a cry of triumph, as if exulting at the sight of the descent that lay before him. In the next instant he was stretched beneath the tree.

No sooner was this expedient adopted, than the young man ascertained how desperate had been his own efforts, by the violence of the pulsations in his frame. He could hear his heart beat, and his breathing was like the action of a bellows, in quick motion. Breath was gained, however, and the heart soon ceased to throb as if about to break through its confinement. The footsteps of those who toiled up the opposite side of the acclivity were now audible, and presently voices and treads announced the arrival of the pursuers. The foremost shouted as they reached the height; then, fearful that their enemy would escape under favor of the descent, each leaped upon the fallen tree and plunged into the ravine, trusting to get a sight of the pursued ere he reached the bottom. In this manner, Huron followed Huron until Natty began to hope the whole had passed. Others succeeded, however, until quite forty had leaped over the tree, and then he counted them, as the surest mode of ascertaining how many could be behind. Presently all were in the bottom of the glen, quite a hundred feet below him, and some had even ascended part of the opposite hill, when it became evident an inquiry was making as to the direction he had taken. This was the critical moment, and one of nerves less steady, or of a training that had been neglected, would have seized it to rise and fly. Not so with Deerslayer. He still lay quiet, watching with jealous vigilance every movement below, and fast regaining his breath.

The Hurons now resembled a pack of hounds at fault. Little was said, but each man ran about, examining the dead leaves as the hound hunts for the lost scent. The great number of moccasins that had passed made the examination difficult, though the in-toe of an Indian was easily to be distinguished from the freer and wider step of a white man. Believing that no more pursuers remained behind, and hoping to steal away unseen, Deerslayer suddenly threw himself over the tree, and fell on the upper side. This achievement appeared to be effected successfully, and hope beat high in the bosom of the fugitive.

Rising to his hands and feet, after a moment lost in listening to the sounds in the glen, in order to ascertain if he had been seen, the young man next scrambled to the top of the hill, a distance of only ten yards, in the expectation of getting its brow between him and his pursuers, and himself so far under cover. Even this was effected, and he rose to his feet, walking swiftly but steadily along the summit, in a direction opposite to that in which he had first fled. The nature of the calls in the glen, however, soon made him uneasy, and he sprang upon the summit again, in order to reconnoitre. No sooner did he reach the height than he was seen, and the chase renewed. As it was better footing on the level ground, Deerslayer now avoided the side hill, holding his flight along the ridge; while the Hurons, judging from the general formation of the land, saw that the ridge would soon melt into the hollow, and kept to the latter, as the easiest mode of heading the fugitive. A few, at the same time, turned south, with a view to prevent his escaping in that direction, while some crossed his trail towards the water, in order to prevent his retreat by the lake, running southerly.

The situation of Deerslayer was now more critical than it ever had been. He was virtually surrounded on three sides, having the lake on the fourth. But he had pondered well on all the chances, and took his measures with coolness, even while at the top of his speed. As is generally the case with the vigorous border men, he could outrun any single Indian among his pursuers, who were principally formidable to him on account of their numbers, and the advantages they possessed in position, and he would not have hesitated to break off in a straight line at any spot, could he have got the whole band again fairly behind him. But no such chance did, or indeed could now offer, and when he found that he was descending towards the glen, by the melting away of the ridge, he turned short, at right angles to his previous course, and went down the declivity with tremendous velocity, holding his way towards the shore. Some of his pursuers came panting up the hill in direct chase, while most still kept on in the ravine, intending to head him at its termination.

Deerslayer had now a different, though a desperate project in view. Abandoning all thoughts of escape by the woods, he made the best of his way towards the canoe. He knew where it lay; could it be reached, he had only to run the gauntlet of a few rifles, and success would be certain. None of the warriors had kept their weapons, which would have retarded their speed, and the risk would come either from the uncertain hands of the women, or from those of some well grown boy; though most of the latter were already out in hot pursuit. Everything seemed propitious to the execution of this plan, and the course being a continued descent, the young man went over the ground at a rate that promised a speedy termination to his toil.

As Deerslayer approached the point, several women and children were passed, but, though the former endeavoured to cast dried branches between his legs, the terror inspired by his bold retaliation on the redoubted Panther was so great, that none dared come near enough seriously to molest him. He went by all triumphantly and reached the fringe of bushes. Plunging through these, our hero found himself once more in the lake, and within fifty feet of the canoe. Here he ceased to run, for he well understood that his breath was now all important to him. He even stooped, as he advanced, and cooled his parched mouth by scooping water up in his hand to drink. Still the moments pressed, and he soon stood at the side of the canoe. The first glance told him that the paddles had been removed! This was a sore disappointment, after all his efforts, and, for a single moment, he thought of turning, and of facing his foes by walking with dignity into the centre of the camp again. But an infernal yell, such as the American savage alone can raise, proclaimed the quick approach of the nearest of his pursuers, and the instinct of life triumphed. Preparing himself duly, and giving a right direction to its bows, he ran off into the water bearing the canoe before him, threw all his strength and skill into a last effort, and cast himself forward so as to fall into the bottom of the light craft without materially impeding its way. Here he remained on his back, both to regain his breath and to cover his person from the deadly rifle. The lightness, which was such an advantage in paddling the canoe, now operated unfavorably. The material was so like a feather, that the boat had no momentum, else would the impulse in that smooth and placid sheet have impelled it to a distance from the shore that would have rendered paddling with the hands safe. Could such a point once be reached, Deerslayer thought he might get far enough out to attract the attention of Chingachgook and Judith, who would not fail to come to his relief with other canoes, a circumstance that promised everything. As the young man lay in the bottom of the canoe, he watched its movements by studying the tops of the trees on the mountainside, and judged of his distance by the time and the motions. Voices on the shore were now numerous, and he heard something said about manning the raft, which, fortunately for the fugitive, lay at a considerable distance on the other side of the point.

Perhaps the situation of Deerslayer had not been more critical that day than it was at this moment. It certainly had not been one half as tantalizing. He lay perfectly quiet for two or three minutes, trusting to the single sense of hearing, confident that the noise in the lake would reach his ears, did any one venture to approach by swimming. Once or twice he fancied that the element was stirred by the cautious movement of an arm, and then he perceived it was the wash of the water on the pebbles of the strand; for, in mimicry of the ocean, it is seldom that those little lakes are so totally tranquil as not to possess a slight heaving and setting on their shores. Suddenly all the voices ceased, and a death like stillness pervaded the spot: A quietness as profound as if all lay in the repose of inanimate life. By this time, the canoe had drifted so far as to render nothing visible to Deerslayer, as he lay on his back, except the blue void of space, and a few of those brighter rays that proceed from the effulgence of the sun, marking his proximity. It was not possible to endure this uncertainty long. The young man well knew that the profound stillness foreboded evil, the savages never being so silent as when about to strike a blow; resembling the stealthy foot of the panther ere he takes his leap. He took out a knife and was about to cut a hole through the bark, in order to get a view of the shore, when he paused from a dread of being seen in the operation, which would direct the enemy where to aim their bullets. At this instant a rifle was fired, and the ball pierced both sides of the canoe, within eighteen inches of the spot where his head lay. This was close work, but our hero had too lately gone through that which was closer to be appalled. He lay still half a minute longer, and then he saw the summit of an oak coming slowly within his narrow horizon.

Unable to account for this change, Deerslayer could restrain his impatience no longer. Hitching his body along, with the utmost caution, he got his eye at the bullet hole, and fortunately commanded a very tolerable view of the point. The canoe, by one of those imperceptible impulses that so often decide the fate of men as well as the course of things, had inclined southerly, and was slowly drifting down the lake. It was lucky that Deerslayer had given it a shove sufficiently vigorous to send it past the end of the point, ere it took this inclination, or it must have gone ashore again. As it was, it drifted so near it as to bring the tops of two or three trees within the range of the young man's view, as has been mentioned, and, indeed, to come in quite as close proximity with the extremity of the point as was at all safe. The distance could not much have exceeded a hundred feet, though fortunately a light current of air from the southwest began to set it slowly off shore.

Deerslayer now felt the urgent necessity of resorting to some expedient to get farther from his foes, and if possible to apprise his friends of his situation. The distance rendered the last difficult, while the proximity to the point rendered the first indispensable. As was usual in such craft, a large, round, smooth stone was in each end of the canoe, for the double purpose of seats and ballast; one of these was within reach of his feet. This stone he contrived to get so far between his legs as to reach it with his hands, and then he managed to roll it to the side of its fellow in the bows, where the two served to keep the trim of the light boat, while he worked his own body as far aft as possible. Before quitting the shore, and as soon as he perceived that the paddles were gone, Deerslayer had thrown a bit of dead branch into the canoe, and this was within reach of his arm. Removing the cap he wore, he put it on the end of this stick, and just let it appear over the edge of the canoe, as far as possible from his own person. This ruse was scarcely adopted before the young man had a proof how much he had underrated the intelligence of his enemies. In contempt of an artifice so shallow and common place, a bullet was fired directly through another part of the canoe, which actually raised his skin. He dropped the cap, and instantly raised it immediately over his head, as a safeguard. It would seem that this second artifice was unseen, or what was more probable, the Hurons feeling certain of recovering their captive, wished to take him alive.

Deerslayer lay passive a few minutes longer, his eye at the bullet hole, however, and much did he rejoice at seeing that he was drifting, gradually, farther and farther from the shore. When he looked upward, the treetops had disappeared, but he soon found that the canoe was slowly turning, so as to prevent his getting a view of anything at his peephole, but of the two extremities of the lake. He now bethought him of the stick, which was crooked and offered some facilities for rowing without the necessity of rising. The experiment succeeded on trial, better even than he had hoped, though his great embarrassment was to keep the canoe straight. That his present manoeuvre was seen soon became apparent by the clamor on the shore, and a bullet entering the stern of the canoe traversed its length, whistling between the arms of our hero, and passed out at the head. This satisfied the fugitive that he was getting away with tolerable speed, and induced him to increase his efforts. He was making a stronger push than common, when another messenger from the point broke the stick out-board, and at once deprived him of his oar. As the sound of voices seemed to grow more and more distant, however, Deerslayer determined to leave all to the drift, until he believed himself beyond the reach of bullets. This was nervous work, but it was the wisest of all the expedients that offered, and the young man was encouraged to persevere in it by the circumstance that he felt his face fanned by the air, a proof that there was a little more wind.

CHAPTER XXVIII.

"Nor widows' tears, nor tender orphans' cries
　Can stop th' invader's force;
Nor swelling seas, nor threatening skies,
　Prevent the pirate's course:
Their lives to selfish ends decreed
Through blood and rapine they proceed;
No anxious thoughts of ill repute,
Suspend the impetuous and unjust pursuit;
But power and wealth obtain'd, guilty and great,
Their fellow creatures' fears they raise, or urge their hate."

　Congreve, "Pindaric Ode," ii.

By this time Deerslayer had been twenty minutes in the canoe, and he began to grow a little impatient for some signs of relief from his friends. The position of the boat still prevented his seeing in any direction, unless it were up or down the lake, and, though he knew that his line of sight must pass within a hundred yards of the castle, it, in fact, passed that distance to the westward of the buildings. The profound stillness troubled him also, for he knew not whether to ascribe it to the increasing space between him and the Indians, or to some new artifice. At length, wearied with fruitless watchfulness, the young man turned himself on his back, closed his eyes, and awaited the result in determined acquiescence. If the savages could so completely control their thirst for revenge, he was resolved to be as calm as themselves, and to trust his fate to the interposition of the currents and air.

Some additional ten minutes may have passed in this quiescent manner, on both sides, when Deerslayer thought he heard a slight noise, like a low rubbing against the bottom of his canoe. He opened his eyes of course, in expectation of seeing the face or arm of an Indian rising from the water, and found that a canopy of leaves was impending directly over his head. Starting to his feet, the first object that met his eye was Rivenoak, who had so far aided the slow progress of the boat, as to draw it on the point, the grating on the strand being the sound that had first given our hero the alarm. The change in the drift of the canoe had been altogether owing to the baffling nature of the light currents of the air, aided by some eddies in the water.

"Come," said the Huron with a quiet gesture of authority, to order his prisoner to land, "my young friend has sailed about till he is tired; he will forget how to run again, unless he uses his legs."

"You've the best of it, Huron," returned Deerslayer, stepping steadily from the canoe, and passively following his leader to the open area of the point; "Providence has helped you in an onexpected manner. I'm your prisoner ag'in, and I hope you'll allow that I'm as good at breaking gaol, as I am at keeping furloughs."

"My young friend is a Moose!" exclaimed the Huron. "His legs are very long; they have given my young men trouble. But he is not a fish; he cannot find his way in the lake. We did not shoot him; fish are taken in nets, and not killed by bullets. When he turns Moose again he will be treated like a Moose."

"Ay, have your talk, Rivenoak; make the most of your advantage. 'Tis your right, I suppose, and I know it is your gift. On that p'int there'll be no words atween us, for all men must and ought to follow their gifts. Howsever, when your women begin to ta'nt and abuse me, as I suppose will soon happen, let 'em remember that if a pale-face struggles for life so long as it's lawful and manful, he knows how to loosen his hold on it, decently, when he feels that the time has come. I'm your captyve; work your will on me."

"My brother has had a long run on the hills, and a pleasant sail on the water," returned Rivenoak more mildly, smiling, at the same time, in a way that his listener knew denoted pacific intentions. "He has seen the woods; he has seen the water. Which does he like best? Perhaps he has seen enough to change his mind, and make him hear reason."

"Speak out, Huron. Something is in your thoughts, and the sooner it is said, the sooner you'll get my answer."

"That is straight! There is no turning in the talk of my pale-face friend, though he is a fox in running. I will speak to him; his ears are now open wider than before, and his eyes are not shut. The Sumach is poorer than ever. Once she had a brother and a husband. She had children, too. The time came and the husband started for the Happy Hunting Grounds, without saying farewell; he left her alone with his children. This he could not help, or he would not have done it; le Loup Cervier was a good husband. It was pleasant to see the venison, and wild ducks, and geese, and bear's meat, that hung in his lodge in winter. It is now gone; it will not keep in warm weather. Who shall bring it back again? Some thought the brother would not forget his sister, and that, next winter, he would see that the lodge should not be empty. We thought this; but the Panther yelled, and followed the husband on the path of death. They are now trying which shall first reach the Happy Hunting Grounds. Some think the Lynx can run fastest, and some think the Panther can jump the farthest. The Sumach thinks both will travel so fast and so far that neither will ever come back. Who shall feed her and her young? The man who told her husband and her brother to quit her lodge, that there might be room for him to come into it. He is a great hunter, and we know that the woman will never want."

"Ay, Huron this is soon settled, accordin' to your notions, but it goes sorely ag'in the grain of a white man's feelin's. I've heard of men's saving their lives this-a-way, and I've know'd them that would prefar death to such a sort of captivity. For my part, I do not seek my end, nor do I seek matrimony."

"The pale-face will think of this, while my people get ready for the council. He will be told what will happen. Let him remember how hard it is to lose a husband and a brother. Go; when we want him, the name of Deerslayer will be called."

This conversation had been held with no one near but the speakers. Of all the band that had so lately thronged the place, Rivenoak alone was visible. The rest seemed to have totally abandoned the spot. Even the furniture, clothes, arms, and other property of the camp had entirely disappeared, and the place bore no other proofs of the crowd that had so lately occupied it, than the traces of their fires and resting places, and the trodden earth that still showed the marks of their feet. So sudden and unexpected a change caused Deerslayer a good deal of surprise and some uneasiness, for he had never known it to occur, in the course of his experience among the Delawares. He suspected, however, and rightly, that a change of encampment was intended, and that the mystery of the movement was resorted to in order to work on his apprehensions.

Rivenoak walked up the vista of trees as soon as he ceased speaking, leaving Deerslayer by himself. The chief disappeared behind the covers of the forest, and one unpractised in such scenes might have believed the prisoner left to the dictates of his own judgment. But the young man, while he felt a little amazement at the dramatic aspect of things, knew his enemies too well to fancy himself at liberty, or a free agent. Still, he was ignorant how far the Hurons meant to carry their artifices, and he determined to bring the question, as soon as practicable, to the proof. Affecting an indifference he was far from feeling, he strolled about the area, gradually getting nearer and nearer to the spot where he had landed, when he suddenly quickened his pace, though carefully avoiding all appearance of flight, and pushing aside the bushes, he stepped upon the beach. The canoe was gone, nor could he see any traces of it, after walking to the northern and southern verges of the point, and examining the shores in both directions. It was evidently removed beyond his reach and knowledge, and under circumstances to show that such had been the intention of the savages.

Deerslayer now better understood his actual situation. He was a prisoner on the narrow tongue of land, vigilantly watched beyond a question, and with no other means of escape than that of swimming. He, again, thought of this last expedient, but the certainty that the canoe would be sent in chase, and the desperate nature of the chances of success deterred him from the undertaking. While on the strand, he came to a spot where the bushes had been cut, and thrust into a small pile. Removing a few of the upper branches, he found beneath them the dead body of the Panther. He knew that it was kept until the savages might find a place to inter it, where it would be beyond the reach of the scalping knife. He gazed wistfully towards the castle, but there all seemed to be silent and desolate, and a feeling of loneliness and desertion came over him to increase the gloom of the moment.

"God's will be done!" murmured the young man, as he walked sorrowfully away from the beach, entering again beneath the arches of the wood. "God's will be done, on 'arth as it is in heaven! I did hope that my days would not be numbered so soon, but it matters little a'ter all. A few more winters, and a few more summers, and 'twould have been over, accordin' to natur'. Ah's! me, the young and actyve seldom think death possible, till he grins in their faces, and tells 'em the hour is come!"

While this soliloquy was being pronounced, the hunter advanced into the area, where to his surprise he saw Hetty alone, evidently awaiting his return. The girl carried the Bible under her arm, and her face, over which a shadow of gentle melancholy was usually thrown, now seemed sad and downcast. Moving nearer, Deerslayer spoke.

"Poor Hetty," he said, "times have been so troublesome, of late, that I'd altogether forgotten you; we meet, as it might be to mourn over what is to happen. I wonder what has become of Chingachgook and Wah!"

"Why did you kill the Huron, Deerslayer?—" returned the girl reproachfully. "Don't you know your commandments, which say 'Thou shalt not kill!' They tell me you have now slain the woman's husband and brother!"

"It's true, my good Hetty—'tis gospel truth, and I'll not deny what has come to pass. But, you must remember, gal, that many things are lawful in war, which would be onlawful in peace. The husband was shot in open fight—or, open so far as I was consarned, while he had a better cover than common—and the brother brought his end on himself, by casting his tomahawk at an unarmed prisoner. Did you witness that deed, gal?"

"I saw it, and was sorry it happened, Deerslayer, for I hoped you wouldn't have returned blow for blow, but good for evil."

"Ah, Hetty, that may do among the Missionaries, but 'twould make an onsartain life in the woods! The Panther craved my blood, and he was foolish enough to throw arms into my hands, at the very moment he was striving a'ter it. 'Twould have been ag'in natur' not to raise a hand in such a trial, and 'twould have done discredit to my training and gifts. No—no—I'm as willing to give every man his own as another, and so I hope you'll testify to them that will be likely to question you as to what you've seen this day."

"Deerslayer, do you mean to marry Sumach, now she has neither husband nor brother to feed her?"

"Are such your ideas of matrimony, Hetty! Ought the young to wive with the old—the pale-face with the red-skin—the Christian with the heathen? It's ag'in reason and natur', and so you'll see, if you think of it a moment."

"I've always heard mother say," returned Hetty, averting her face more from a feminine instinct than from any consciousness of wrong, "that people should never marry until they loved each other better than brothers and sisters, and I suppose that is what you mean. Sumach is old, and you are young!"

"Ay and she's red, and I'm white. Beside, Hetty, suppose you was a wife, now, having married some young man of your own years, and state, and colour—Hurry Harry, for instance—" Deerslayer selected this example simply from the circumstance that he was the only young man known to both—"and that he had fallen on a war path, would you wish to take to your bosom, for a husband, the man that slew him?"

"Oh! no, no, no—" returned the girl shuddering—"That would be wicked as well as heartless! No Christian girl could, or would do that! I never shall be the wife of Hurry, I know, but were he my husband no man should ever be it, again, after his death!"

"I thought it would get to this, Hetty, when you come to understand sarcumstances. 'Tis a moral impossibility that I should ever marry Sumach, and, though Injin weddin's have no priests and not much religion, a white man who knows his gifts and duties can't profit by that, and so make his escape at the fitting time. I do think death would be more nat'ral like, and welcome, than wedlock with this woman."

"Don't say it too loud," interrupted Hetty impatiently; "I suppose she will not like to hear it. I'm sure Hurry would rather marry even me than suffer torments, though I am feeble minded; and I am sure it would kill me to think he'd prefer death to being my husband."

"Ay, gal, you ain't Sumach, but a comely young Christian, with a good heart, pleasant smile, and kind eye. Hurry might be proud to get you, and that, too, not in misery and sorrow, but in his best and happiest days. Howsever, take my advice, and never talk to Hurry about these things; he's only a borderer, at the best."

"I wouldn't tell him, for the world!" exclaimed the girl, looking about her like one affrighted, and blushing, she knew not why. "Mother always said young women shouldn't be forward, and speak their minds before they're asked; Oh! I never forget what mother told me. 'Tis a pity Hurry is so handsome, Deerslayer; I do think fewer girls would like him then, and he would sooner know his own mind."

"Poor gal, poor gal, it's plain enough how it is, but the Lord will bear in mind one of your simple heart and kind feelin's! We'll talk no more of these things; if you had reason, you'd be sorrowful at having let others so much into your secret. Tell me, Hetty, what has become of all the Hurons, and why they let you roam about the p'int as if you, too, was a prisoner?"

"I'm no prisoner, Deerslayer, but a free girl, and go when and where I please. Nobody dare hurt me! If they did, God would be angry, as I can show them in the Bible. No—no—Hetty Hutter is not afraid; she's in good hands. The Hurons are up yonder in the woods, and keep a good watch on us both, I'll answer for it, since all the women and children are on the look-out. Some are burying the body of the poor girl who was shot, so that the enemy and the wild beasts can't find it. I told 'em that father and mother lay in the lake, but I wouldn't let them know in what part of it, for Judith and I don't want any of their heathenish company in our burying ground."

"Ahs! me; Well, it is an awful despatch to be standing here, alive and angry, and with the feelin's up and ferocious, one hour, and then to be carried away at the next, and put out of sight of mankind in a hole in the 'arth! No one knows what will happen to him on a warpath, that's sartain."

Here the stirring of leaves and the cracking of dried twigs interrupted the discourse, and apprised Deerslayer of the approach of his enemies. The Hurons closed around the spot that had been prepared for the coming scene, and in the centre of which the intended victim now stood, in a circle, the armed men being so distributed among the feebler members of the band, that there was no safe opening through which the prisoner could break. But the latter no longer contemplated flight, the recent trial having satisfied him of his inability to escape when pursued so closely by numbers. On the contrary, all his energies were aroused in order to meet his expected fate, with a calmness that should do credit to his colour and his manhood; one equally removed from recreant alarm, and savage boasting.

When Rivenoak re-appeared in the circle, he occupied his old place at the head of the area. Several of the elder warriors stood near him, but, now that the brother of Sumach had fallen, there was no longer any recognised chief present whose influence and authority offered a dangerous rivalry to his own. Nevertheless, it is well known that little which could be called monarchical or despotic entered into the politics of the North American tribes, although the first colonists, bringing with them to this hemisphere the notions and opinions of their own countries, often dignified the chief men of those primitive nations with the titles of kings and princes. Hereditary influence did certainly exist, but there is much reason to believe it existed rather as a consequence of hereditary merit and acquired qualifications, than as a birthright. Rivenoak, however, had not even this claim, having risen to consideration purely by the force of talents, sagacity, and, as Bacon expresses it in relation to all distinguished statesmen, "by a union of great and mean qualities;" a truth of which the career of the profound Englishman himself furnishes so apt an illustration. Next to arms, eloquence offers the great avenue to popular favor, whether it be in civilized or savage life, and Rivenoak had succeeded, as so many have succeeded before him, quite as much by rendering fallacies acceptable to his listeners, as by any profound or learned expositions of truth, or the accuracy of his logic. Nevertheless, he had influence; and was far from being altogether without just claims to its possession. Like most men who reason more than they feel, the Huron was not addicted to the indulgence of the more ferocious passions of his people: he had been commonly found on the side of mercy, in all the scenes of vindictive torture and revenge that had occurred in his tribe since his own attainment to power. On the present occasion, he was reluctant to proceed to extremities, although the provocation was so great. Still it exceeded his ingenuity to see how that alternative could well be avoided. Sumach resented her rejection more than she did the deaths of her husband and brother, and there was little probability that the woman would pardon a man who had so unequivocally preferred death to her embraces. Without her forgiveness, there was scarce a hope that the tribe could be induced to overlook its loss, and even to Rivenoak, himself, much as he was disposed to pardon, the fate of our hero now appeared to be almost hopelessly sealed.

When the whole band was arrayed around the captive, a grave silence, so much the more threatening from its profound quiet, pervaded the place. Deerslayer perceived that the women and boys had been preparing splinters of the fat pine roots, which he well knew were to be stuck into his flesh, and set in flames, while two or three of the young men held the thongs of bark with which he was to be bound. The smoke of a distant fire announced that the burning brands were in preparation, and several of the elder warriors passed their fingers over the edges of their tomahawks, as if to prove their keenness and temper. Even the knives seemed loosened in their sheathes, impatient for the bloody and merciless work to begin.

"Killer of the Deer," recommenced Rivenoak, certainly without any signs of sympathy or pity in his manner, though with calmness and dignity, "Killer of the Deer, it is time that my people knew their minds. The sun is no longer over our heads; tired of waiting on the Hurons, he has begun to fall near the pines on this side of the valley. He is travelling fast towards the country of our French fathers; it is to warn his children that their lodges are empty, and that they ought to be at home. The roaming wolf has his den, and he goes to it when he wishes to see his young. The Iroquois are not poorer than the wolves. They have villages, and wigwams, and fields of corn; the Good Spirits will be tired of watching them alone. My people must go back and see to their own business. There will be joy in the lodges when they hear our whoop from the forest! It will be a sorrowful whoop; when it is understood, grief will come after it. There will be one scalp-whoop, but there will be only one. We have the fur of the Muskrat; his body is among the fishes. Deerslayer must say whether another scalp shall be on our pole. Two lodges are empty; a scalp, living or dead, is wanted at each door."

"Then take 'em dead, Huron," firmly, but altogether without dramatic boasting, returned the captive. "My hour is come, I do suppose, and what must be, must. If you are bent on the tortur', I'll do my indivours to bear up ag'in it, though no man can say how far his natur' will stand pain, until he's been tried."

"The pale-face cur begins to put his tail between his legs!" cried a young and garrulous savage, who bore the appropriate title of the Corbeau Rouge; a sobriquet he had gained from the French by his facility in making unseasonable noises, and an undue tendency to hear his own voice; "he is no warrior; he has killed the Loup Cervier when looking behind him not to see the flash of his own rifle. He grunts like a hog, already; when the Huron women begin to torment him, he will cry like the young of the catamount. He is a Delaware woman, dressed in the skin of a Yengeese!"

"Have your say, young man; have your say," returned Deerslayer, unmoved; "you know no better, and I can overlook it. Talking may aggravate women, but can hardly make knives sharper, fire hotter, or rifles more sartain."

Rivenoak now interposed, reproving the Red Crow for his premature interference, and then directing the proper persons to bind the captive. This expedient was adopted, not from any apprehensions that he would escape, or from any necessity that was yet apparent of his being unable to endure the torture with his limbs free, but from an ingenious design of making him feel his helplessness, and of gradually sapping his resolution by undermining it, as it might be, little by little. Deerslayer offered no resistance. He submitted his arms and legs, freely if not cheerfully, to the ligaments of bark, which were bound around them by order of the chief, in a way to produce as little pain as possible. These directions were secret, and given in the hope that the captive would finally save himself from any serious bodily suffering by consenting to take the Sumach for a wife. As soon as the body of Deerslayer was withed in bark sufficiently to create a lively sense of helplessness, he was literally carried to a young tree, and bound against it in a way that effectually prevented him from moving, as well as from falling. The hands were laid flat against the legs, and thongs were passed over all, in a way nearly to incorporate the prisoner with the tree. His cap was then removed, and he was left half-standing, half-sustained by his bonds, to face the coming scene in the best manner he could.

Previously to proceeding to any thing like extremities, it was the wish of Rivenoak to put his captive's resolution to the proof by renewing the attempt at a compromise. This could be effected only in one manner, the acquiescence of the Sumach being indispensably necessary to a compromise of her right to be revenged. With this view, then, the woman was next desired to advance, and to look to her own interests; no agent being considered as efficient as the principal, herself, in this negotiation. The Indian females, when girls, are usually mild and submissive, with musical tones, pleasant voices and merry laughs, but toil and suffering generally deprive them of most of these advantages by the time they have reached an age which the Sumach had long before passed. To render their voices harsh, it would seem to require active, malignant, passions, though, when excited, their screams can rise to a sufficiently conspicuous degree of discordancy to assert their claim to possess this distinctive peculiarity of the sex. The Sumach was not altogether without feminine attraction, however, and had so recently been deemed handsome in her tribe, as not to have yet learned the full influence that time and exposure produce on man, as well as on woman. By an arrangement of Rivenoak's, some of the women around her had been employing the time in endeavoring to persuade the bereaved widow that there was still a hope Deerslayer might be prevailed on to enter her wigwam, in preference to entering the world of spirits, and this, too, with a success that previous symptoms scarcely justified. All this was the result of a resolution on the part of the chief to leave no proper means unemployed, in order to get transferred to his own nation the greatest hunter that was then thought to exist in all that region, as well as a husband for a woman who he felt would be likely to be troublesome, were any of her claims to the attention and care of the tribe overlooked.

In conformity with this scheme, the Sumach had been secretly advised to advance into the circle, and to make her appeal to the prisoner's sense of justice, before the band had recourse to the last experiment. The woman, nothing loth, consented, for there was some such attraction in becoming the wife of a noted hunter, among the females of the tribes, as is experienced by the sex, in more refined life, when they bestow their hands on the affluent. As the duties of a mother were thought to be paramount to all other considerations, the widow felt none of that embarrassment, in preferring her claims, to which even a female fortune hunter among ourselves might be liable. When she stood forth before the whole party, therefore, the children that she led by the hands fully justified all she did.

"You see me before you, cruel pale-face," the woman commenced; "your spirit must tell you my errand. I have found you; I cannot find le Loup Cervier, nor the Panther; I have looked for them in the lake, in the woods, in the clouds. I cannot say where they have gone."

"No man knows, good Sumach, no man knows," interposed the captive. "When the spirit leaves the body, it passes into a world beyond our knowledge, and the wisest way, for them that are left behind, is to hope for the best. No doubt both your warriors have gone to the Happy Hunting Grounds, and at the proper time you will see 'em ag'in, in their improved state. The wife and sister of braves must have looked forward to some such tarmination of their 'arthly careers."

"Cruel pale-face, what had my warriors done that you should slay them! They were the best hunters, and the boldest young men of their tribe; the Great Spirit intended that they should live until they withered like the branches of the hemlock, and fell of their own weight—"

"Nay—nay—good Sumach," interrupted Deerslayer, whose love of truth was too indomitable to listen to such hyperbole with patience, even though it came from the torn breast of a widow— "Nay—nay, good Sumach, this is a little outdoing red-skin privileges. Young man was neither, any more than you can be called a young woman, and as to the Great Spirit's intending that they should fall otherwise than they did, that's a grievous mistake, inasmuch as what the Great Spirit intends is sartain to come to pass. Then, agin, it's plain enough neither of your fri'nds did me any harm; I raised my hand ag'in 'em on account of what they were striving to do, rather than what they did. This is nat'ral law, 'to do lest you should be done by.'"

"It is so. Sumach has but one tongue; she can tell but one story. The pale face struck the Hurons lest the Hurons should strike him. The Hurons are a just nation; they will forget it. The chiefs will shut their eyes and pretend not to have seen it; the young men will believe the Panther and the Lynx have gone to far off hunts, and the Sumach will take her children by the hand, and go into the lodge of the pale-face and say— 'See; these are your children; they are also mine—feed us, and we will live with you.'"

"The tarms are onadmissable, woman, and though I feel for your losses, which must be hard to bear, the tarms cannot be accepted. As to givin' you ven'son, in case we lived near enough together, that would be no great expl'ite; but as for becomin' your husband, and the father of your children, to be honest with you, I feel no callin' that-a-way."

"Look at this boy, cruel pale-face; he has no father to teach him to kill the deer, or to take scalps. See this girl; what young man will come to look for a wife in a lodge that has no head? There are more among my people in the Canadas, and the Killer of Deer will find as many mouths to feed as his heart can wish for."

"I tell you, woman," exclaimed Deerslayer, whose imagination was far from seconding the appeal of the widow, and who began to grow restive under the vivid pictures she was drawing, "all this is nothing to me. People and kindred must take care of their own fatherless, leaving them that have no children to their own loneliness. As for me, I have no offspring, and I want no wife. Now, go away Sumach; leave me in the hands of your chiefs, for my colour, and gifts, and natur' itself cry out ag'in the idee of taking you for a wife."

It is unnecessary to expatiate on the effect of this downright refusal of the woman's proposals. If there was anything like tenderness in her bosom—and no woman was probably ever entirely without that feminine quality—it all disappeared at this plain announcement. Fury, rage, mortified pride, and a volcano of wrath burst out, at one explosion, converting her into a sort of maniac, as it might beat the touch of a magician's wand. Without deigning a reply in words, she made the arches of the forest ring with screams, and then flew forward at her victim, seizing him by the hair, which she appeared resolute to draw out by the roots. It was some time before her grasp could be loosened. Fortunately for the prisoner her rage was blind; since his total helplessness left him entirely at her mercy. Had it been better directed it might have proved fatal before any relief could have been offered. As it was, she did succeed in wrenching out two or three handsful of hair, before the young men could tear her away from her victim.

The insult that had been offered to the Sumach was deemed an insult to the whole tribe; not so much, however, on account of any respect that was felt for the woman, as on account of the honor of the Huron nation. Sumach, herself, was generally considered to be as acid as the berry from which she derived her name, and now that her great supporters, her husband and brother, were both gone, few cared about concealing their aversion. Nevertheless, it had become a point of honor to punish the pale-face who disdained a Huron woman, and more particularly one who coolly preferred death to relieving the tribe from the support of a widow and her children. The young men showed an impatience to begin to torture that Rivenoak understood, and, as his older associates manifested no disposition to permit any longer delay, he was compelled to give the signal for the infernal work to proceed.

## CHAPTER XXIX.

"The ugly bear now minded not the stake,
  Nor how the cruel mastiffs do him tear,
The stag lay still unroused from the brake,
  The foamy boar feared not the hunter's spear:
All thing was still in desert, bush, and briar:"

Thomas Sackville; "The Complaint of Henry Duke of Buckingham,"
lxxxi.

'Twas one of the common expedients of the savages, on such occasions, to put the nerves of their victims to the severest proofs. On the other hand, it was a matter of Indian pride to betray no yielding to terror, or pain, but for the prisoner to provoke his enemies to such acts of violence as would soonest produce death. Many a warrior had been known to bring his own sufferings to a more speedy termination, by taunting reproaches and reviling language, when he found that his physical system was giving way under the agony of sufferings produced by a hellish ingenuity that might well eclipse all that has been said of the infernal devices of religious persecution. This happy expedient of taking refuge from the ferocity of his foes, in their passions, was denied Deerslayer however, by his peculiar notions of the duty of a white man, and he had stoutly made up his mind to endure everything, in preference to disgracing his colour.

No sooner did the young men understand that they were at liberty to commence, than some of the boldest and most forward among them sprang into the arena, tomahawk in hand. Here they prepared to throw that dangerous weapon, the object being to strike the tree as near as possible to the victim's head, without absolutely hitting him. This was so hazardous an experiment that none but those who were known to be exceedingly expert with the weapon were allowed to enter the lists at all, lest an early death might interfere with the expected entertainment. In the truest hands it was seldom that the captive escaped injury in these trials, and it often happened that death followed, even when the blow was not premeditated. In the particular case of our hero, Rivenoak and the older warriors were apprehensive that the example of the Panther's fate might prove a motive with some fiery spirit suddenly to sacrifice his conqueror, when the temptation of effecting it in precisely the same manner, and possibly with the identical weapon with which the warrior had fallen, offered. This circumstance of itself rendered the ordeal of the tomahawk doubly critical for the Deerslayer. It would seem, however, that all who now entered what we shall call the lists, were more disposed to exhibit their own dexterity, than to resent the deaths of their comrades. Each prepared himself for the trial with the feelings of rivalry, rather than with the desire for vengeance, and, for the first few minutes, the prisoner had little more connection with the result, than grew out of the interest that necessarily attached itself to a living target. The young men were eager, instead of being fierce, and Rivenoak thought he still saw signs of being able to save the life of the captive when the vanity of the young men had been gratified; always admitting that it was not sacrificed to the delicate experiments that were about to be made. The first youth who presented himself for the trial was called The Raven, having as yet had no opportunity of obtaining a more warlike sobriquet. He was remarkable for high pretension, rather than for skill or exploits, and those who knew his character thought the captive in imminent danger when he took his stand, and poised the tomahawk. Nevertheless, the young man was good natured, and no thought was uppermost in his mind other than the desire to make a better cast than any of his fellows. Deerslayer got an inkling of this warrior's want of reputation by the injunctions that he had received from the seniors, who, indeed, would have objected to his appearing in the arena, at all, but for an influence derived from his father; an aged warrior of great merit, who was then in the lodges of the tribe. Still, our hero maintained an appearance of self-possession. He had made up his mind that his hour was come, and it would have been a mercy, instead of a calamity, to fall by the unsteadiness of the first hand that was raised against him. After a suitable number of flourishes and gesticulations that promised much more than he could perform, the Raven let the tomahawk quit his hand. The weapon whirled through the air with the usual evolutions, cut a chip from the sapling to which the prisoner was bound within a few inches of his cheek, and stuck in a large oak that grew several yards behind him. This was decidedly a bad effort, and a common sneer proclaimed as much, to the great mortification of the young man. On the other hand, there was a general but suppressed murmur of admiration at the steadiness with which the captive stood the trial. The head was the only part he could move, and this had been purposely left free, that the tormentors might have the amusement, and the tormented endure the shame, of his dodging, and otherwise attempting to avoid the blows. Deerslayer disappointed these hopes by a command of nerve that rendered his whole body as immovable as the tree to which he was bound. Nor did he even adopt the natural and usual expedient of shutting his eyes, the firmest and oldest warrior of the red-men never having more disdainfully denied himself this advantage under similar circumstances.

The Raven had no sooner made his unsuccessful and puerile effort, than he was succeeded by le Daim-Mose, or the Moose; a middle aged warrior who was particularly skilful in the use of the tomahawk, and from whose attempt the spectators confidently looked for gratification. This man had none of the good nature of the Raven, but he would gladly have sacrificed the captive to his hatred of the pale-faces generally, were it not for the greater interest he felt in his own success as one particularly skilled in the use of this weapon. He took his stand quietly, but with an air of confidence, poised his little axe but a single instant, advanced a foot with a quick motion, and threw. Deerslayer saw the keen instrument whirling towards him, and believed all was over; still, he was not touched. The tomahawk had actually bound the head of the captive to the tree, by carrying before it some of his hair, having buried itself deep beneath the soft bark. A general yell expressed the delight of the spectators, and the Moose felt his heart soften a little towards the prisoner, whose steadiness of nerve alone enabled him to give this evidence of his consummate skill.

Le Daim-Mose was succeeded by the Bounding Boy, or le Garcon qui Bondi who came leaping into the circle, like a hound or a goat at play. This was one of those elastic youths whose muscles seemed always in motion, and who either affected, or who from habit was actually unable, to move in any other manner than by showing the antics just mentioned. Nevertheless, he was both brave and skilful, and had gained the respect of his people by deeds in war, as well as success in the hunts. A far nobler name would long since have fallen to his share, had not a French-man of rank inadvertently given him this sobriquet, which he religiously preserved as coming from his Great Father who lived beyond the Wide Salt Lake. The Bounding Boy skipped about in front of the captive, menacing him with his tomahawk, now on one side and now on another, and then again in front, in the vain hope of being able to extort some sign of fear by this parade of danger. At length Deerslayer's patience became exhausted by all this mummery, and he spoke for the first time since the trial had actually commenced.

"Throw away, Huron," he cried, "or your tomahawk will forget its ar'n'd. Why do you keep loping about like a fa'a'n that's showing its dam how well it can skip, when you're a warrior grown, yourself, and a warrior grown defies you and all your silly antiks. Throw, or the Huron gals will laugh in your face."

Although not intended to produce such an effect, the last words aroused the "Bounding" warrior to fury. The same nervous excitability which rendered him so active in his person, made it difficult to repress his feelings, and the words were scarcely past the lips of the speaker than the tomahawk left the hand of the Indian. Nor was it cast without ill-will, and a fierce determination to slay. Had the intention been less deadly, the danger might have been greater. The aim was uncertain, and the weapon glanced near the cheek of the captive, slightly cutting the shoulder in its evolutions. This was the first instance in which any other object than that of terrifying the prisoner, and of displaying skill had been manifested, and the Bounding Boy was immediately led from the arena, and was warmly rebuked for his intemperate haste, which had come so near defeating all the hopes of the band. To this irritable person succeeded several other young warriors, who not only hurled the tomahawk, but who cast the knife, a far more dangerous experiment, with reckless indifference; yet they always manifested a skill that prevented any injury to the captive. Several times Deerslayer was grazed, but in no instance did he receive what might be termed a wound. The unflinching firmness with which he faced his assailants, more especially in the sort of rally with which this trial terminated, excited a profound respect in the spectators, and when the chiefs announced that the prisoner had well withstood the trials of the knife and the tomahawk, there was not a single individual in the band who really felt any hostility towards him, with the exception of Sumach and the Bounding Boy. These two discontented spirits got together, it is true, feeding each other's ire, but as yet their malignant feelings were confined very much to themselves, though there existed the danger that the others, ere long, could not fail to be excited by their own efforts into that demoniacal state which usually accompanied all similar scenes among the red men.

Rivenoak now told his people that the pale-face had proved himself to be a man. He might live with the Delawares, but he had not been made woman with that tribe. He wished to know whether it was the desire of the Hurons to proceed any further. Even the gentlest of the females, however, had received too much satisfaction in the late trials to forego their expectations of a gratifying exhibition, and there was but one voice in the request to proceed. The politic chief, who had some such desire to receive so celebrated a hunter into his tribe, as a European Minister has to devise a new and available means of taxation, sought every plausible means of arresting the trial in season, for he well knew, if permitted to go far enough to arouse the more ferocious passions of the tormentors, it would be as easy to dam the waters of the great lakes of his own region, as to attempt to arrest them in their bloody career. He therefore called four or five of the best marksmen to him, and bid them put the captive to the proof of the rifle, while at the same time he cautioned them touching the necessity of their maintaining their own credit, by the closest attention to the manner of exhibiting their skill.

When Deerslayer saw the chosen warriors step into the circle, with their arms prepared for service, he felt some such relief as the miserable sufferer, who has long endured the agonies of disease, feels at the certain approach of death. Any trifling variance in the aim of this formidable weapon would prove fatal; since, the head being the target, or rather the point it was desired to graze without injuring, an inch or two of difference in the line of projection must at once determine the question of life or death.

In the torture by the rifle there was none of the latitude permitted that appeared in the case of even Gessler's apple, a hair's breadth being, in fact, the utmost limits that an expert marksman would allow himself on an occasion like this. Victims were frequently shot through the head by too eager or unskilful hands, and it often occurred that, exasperated by the fortitude and taunts of the prisoner, death was dealt intentionally in a moment of ungovernable irritation. All this Deerslayer well knew, for it was in relating the traditions of such scenes, as well as of the battles and victories of their people, that the old men beguiled the long winter evenings in their cabins. He now fully expected the end of his career, and experienced a sort of melancholy pleasure in the idea that he was to fall by a weapon as much beloved as the rifle. A slight interruption, however, took place before the business was allowed to proceed.

Hetty Hutter witnessed all that passed, and the scene at first had pressed upon her feeble mind in a way to paralyze it entirely; but, by this time she had rallied, and was growing indignant at the unmerited suffering the Indians were inflicting on her friend. Though timid, and shy as the young of the deer on so many occasions, this right-feeling girl was always intrepid in the cause of humanity; the lessons of her mother, and the impulses of her own heart—perhaps we might say the promptings of that unseen and pure spirit that seemed ever to watch over and direct her actions—uniting to keep down the apprehensions of woman, and to impel her to be bold and resolute. She now appeared in the circle, gentle, feminine, even bashful in mien, as usual, but earnest in her words and countenance, speaking like one who knew herself to be sustained by the high authority of God.

"Why do you torment Deerslayer, redmen?" she asked "What has he done that you trifle with his life; who has given you the right to be his judges? Suppose one of your knives or tomahawks had hit him; what Indian among you all could cure the wound you would make. Besides, in harming Deerslayer, you injure your own friend; when father and Hurry Harry came after your scalps, he refused to be of the party, and staid in the canoe by himself. You are tormenting a good friend, in tormenting this young man!"

The Hurons listened with grave attention, and one among them, who understood English, translated what had been said into their native tongue. As soon as Rivenoak was made acquainted with the purport of her address he answered it in his own dialect; the interpreter conveying it to the girl in English.

"My daughter is very welcome to speak," said the stern old orator, using gentle intonations and smiling as kindly as if addressing a child—"The Hurons are glad to hear her voice; they listen to what she says. The Great Spirit often speaks to men with such tongues. This time, her eyes have not been open wide enough to see all that has happened. Deerslayer did not come for our scalps, that is true; why did he not come? Here they are on our heads; the war locks are ready to be taken hold of; a bold enemy ought to stretch out his hand to seize them. The Iroquois are too great a nation to punish men that take scalps. What they do themselves, they like to see others do. Let my daughter look around her and count my warriors. Had I as many hands as four warriors, their fingers would be fewer than my people, when they came into your hunting grounds. Now, a whole hand is missing. Where are the fingers? Two have been cut off by this pale-face; my Hurons wish to see if he did this by means of a stout heart, or by treachery. Like a skulking fox, or like a leaping panther."

"You know yourself, Huron, how one of them fell. I saw it, and you all saw it, too. 'Twas too bloody to look at; but it was not Deerslayer's fault. Your warrior sought his life, and he defended himself. I don't know whether this good book says that it was right, but all men will do that. Come, if you want to know which of you can shoot best, give Deerslayer a rifle, and then you will find how much more expert he is than any of your warriors; yes, than all of them together!"

Could one have looked upon such a scene with indifference, he would have been amused at the gravity with which the savages listened to the translation of this unusual request. No taunt, no smile mingled with their surprise, for Hetty had a character and a manner too saintly to subject her infirmity to the mockings of the rude and ferocious. On the contrary, she was answered with respectful attention.

"My daughter does not always talk like a chief at a Council Fire," returned Rivenoak, "or she would not have said this. Two of my warriors have fallen by the blows of our prisoner; their grave is too small to hold a third. The Hurons do not like to crowd their dead. If there is another spirit about to set out for the far off world, it must not be the spirit of a Huron; it must be the spirit of a pale-face. Go, daughter, and sit by Sumach, who is in grief; let the Huron warriors show how well they can shoot; let the pale-face show how little he cares for their bullets."

Hetty's mind was unequal to a sustained discussion, and accustomed to defer to the directions of her seniors she did as told, seating herself passively on a log by the side of the Sumach, and averting her face from the painful scene that was occurring within the circle.

The warriors, as soon as this interruption had ceased, resumed their places, and again prepared to exhibit their skill. As there was a double object in view, that of putting the constancy of the captive to the proof, and that of showing how steady were the hands of the marksmen under circumstances of excitement, the distance was small, and, in one sense, safe. But in diminishing the distance taken by the tormentors, the trial to the nerves of the captive was essentially increased. The face of Deerslayer, indeed, was just removed sufficiently from the ends of the guns to escape the effects of the flash, and his steady eye was enabled to look directly into their muzzles, as it might be, in anticipation of the fatal messenger that was to issue from each. The cunning Hurons well knew this fact, and scarce one levelled his piece without first causing it to point as near as possible at the forehead of the prisoner, in the hope that his fortitude would fail him, and that the band would enjoy the triumph of seeing a victim quail under their ingenious cruelty. Nevertheless each of the competitors was still careful not to injure, the disgrace of striking prematurely being second only to that of failing altogether in attaining the object. Shot after shot was made; all the bullets coming in close proximity to the Deerslayer's head, without touching it. Still no one could detect even the twitching of a muscle on the part of the captive, or the slightest winking of an eye. This indomitable resolution, which so much exceeded everything of its kind that any present had before witnessed, might be referred to three distinct causes. The first was resignation to his fate, blended with natural steadiness of deportment; for our hero had calmly made up his mind that he must die, and preferred this mode to any other; the second was his great familiarity with this particular weapon, which deprived it of all the terror that is usually connected with the mere form of the danger; and the third was this familiarity carried out in practice, to a degree so nice as to enable the intended victim to tell, within an inch, the precise spot where each bullet must strike, for he calculated its range by looking in at the bore of the piece. So exact was Deerslayer's estimation of the line of fire, that his pride of feeling finally got the better of his resignation, and when five or six had discharged their bullets into the tree, he could not refrain from expressing his contempt at their want of hand and eye.

"You may call this shooting, Mingos!" he exclaimed, "but we've squaws among the Delawares, and I have known Dutch gals on the Mohawk, that could outdo your greatest indivours. Ondo these arms of mine, put a rifle into my hands, and I'll pin the thinnest warlock in your party to any tree you can show me, and this at a hundred yards—ay, or at two hundred if the objects can be seen, nineteen shots in twenty; or, for that matter twenty in twenty, if the piece is creditable and trusty!"

A low menacing murmur followed this cool taunt. The ire of the warriors kindled at listening to such a reproach from one who so far disdained their efforts as to refuse even to wink when a rifle was discharged as near his face as could be done without burning it. Rivenoak perceived that the moment was critical, and, still retaining his hope of adopting so noted a hunter into his tribe, the politic old chief interposed in time, probably to prevent an immediate resort to that portion of the torture which must necessarily have produced death through extreme bodily suffering, if in no other manner. Moving into the centre of the irritated group, he addressed them with his usual wily logic and plausible manner, at once suppressing the fierce movement that had commenced.

"I see how it is," he said. "We have been like the pale-faces when they fasten their doors at night, out of fear of the red men. They use so many bars that the fire comes and burns them before they can get out. We have bound the Deerslayer too tight: the thongs keep his limbs from shaking and his eyes from shutting. Loosen him; let us see what his own body is really made of."

It is often the case when we are thwarted in a cherished scheme, that any expedient, however unlikely to succeed, is gladly resorted to in preference to a total abandonment of the project. So it was with the Hurons. The proposal of the chief found instant favor, and several hands were immediately at work, cutting and tearing the ropes of bark from the body of our hero. In half a minute Deerslayer stood as free from bonds as when an hour before he had commenced his flight on the side of the mountain. Some little time was necessary that he should recover the use of his limbs, the circulation of the blood having been checked by the tightness of the ligatures, and this was accorded to him by the politic Rivenoak, under the pretence that his body would be more likely to submit to apprehension if its true tone were restored; though really with a view to give time to the fierce passions which had been awakened in the bosoms of his young men to subside. This ruse succeeded, and Deerslayer by rubbing his limbs, stamping his feet, and moving about, soon regained the circulation, recovering all his physical powers as effectually as if nothing had occurred to disturb them.

It is seldom men think of death in the pride of their health and strength. So it was with Deerslayer. Having been helplessly bound and, as he had every reason to suppose, so lately on the very verge of the other world, to find himself so unexpectedly liberated, in possession of his strength and with a full command of limb, acted on him like a sudden restoration to life, reanimating hopes that he had once absolutely abandoned. From that instant all his plans changed. In this, he simply obeyed a law of nature; for while we have wished to represent our hero as being resigned to his fate, it has been far from our intention to represent him as anxious to die. From the instant that his buoyancy of feeling revived, his thoughts were keenly bent on the various projects that presented themselves as modes of evading the designs of his enemies, and he again became the quick witted, ingenious and determined woodsman, alive to all his own powers and resources. The change was so great that his mind resumed its elasticity, and no longer thinking of submission, it dwelt only on the devices of the sort of warfare in which he was engaged.

As soon as Deerslayer was released, the band divided itself in a circle around him, in order to hedge him in, and the desire to break down his spirit grew in them, precisely as they saw proofs of the difficulty there would be in subduing it. The honor of the band was now involved in the issue, and even the fair sex lost all its sympathy with suffering in the desire to save the reputation of the tribe. The voices of the girls, soft and melodious as nature had made them, were heard mingling with the menaces of the men, and the wrongs of Sumach suddenly assumed the character of injuries inflicted on every Huron female. Yielding to this rising tumult, the men drew back a little, signifying to the females that they left the captive, for a time, in their hands, it being a common practice on such occasions for the women to endeavor to throw the victim into a rage by their taunts and revilings, and then to turn him suddenly over to the men in a state of mind that was little favorable to resisting the agony of bodily suffering. Nor was this party without the proper instruments for effecting such a purpose. Sumach had a notoriety as a scold, and one or two crones, like the She Bear, had come out with the party, most probably as the conservators of its decency and moral discipline; such things occurring in savage as well as in civilized life. It is unnecessary to repeat all that ferocity and ignorance could invent for such a purpose, the only difference between this outbreaking of feminine anger, and a similar scene among ourselves, consisting in the figures of speech and the epithets, the Huron women calling their prisoner by the names of the lower and least respected animals that were known to themselves.

But Deerslayer's mind was too much occupied to permit him to be disturbed by the abuse of excited hags, and their rage necessarily increasing with his indifference, as his indifference increased with their rage, the furies soon rendered themselves impotent by their own excesses. Perceiving that the attempt was a complete failure, the warriors interfered to put a stop to this scene, and this so much the more because preparations were now seriously making for the commencement of the real tortures, or that which would put the fortitude of the sufferer to the test of severe bodily pain. A sudden and unlooked for announcement, that proceeded from one of the look-outs, a boy ten or twelve years old, however, put a momentary check to the whole proceedings. As this interruption has a close connection with the dénouement of our story, it shall be given in a separate chapter.

## CHAPTER XXX.

"So deem'st thou—so each mortal deems
 Of that which is from that which seems;
 But other harvest here
 Than that which peasant's scythe demands,
 Was gather'd in by sterner hands,
 With bayonet, blade, and spear."

Scott, "The Field of Waterloo," V. 1–6.

It exceeded Deerslayer's power to ascertain what had produced the sudden pause in the movements of his enemies, until the fact was revealed in the due course of events. He perceived that much agitation prevailed among the women in particular, while the warriors rested on their arms in a sort of dignified expectation. It was plain no alarm was excited, though it was not equally apparent that a friendly occurrence produced the delay. Rivenoak was evidently apprised of all, and by a gesture of his arm he appeared to direct the circle to remain unbroken, and for each person to await the issue in the situation he or she then occupied. It required but a minute or two to bring an explanation of this singular and mysterious pause, which was soon terminated by the appearance of Judith on the exterior of the line of bodies, and her ready admission within its circle.

If Deerslayer was startled by this unexpected arrival, well knowing that the quick witted girl could claim none of that exemption from the penalties of captivity that was so cheerfully accorded to her feebler minded sister, he was equally astonished at the guise in which she came. All her ordinary forest attire, neat and becoming as this usually was, had been laid aside for the brocade that has been already mentioned, and which had once before wrought so great and magical an effect in her appearance. Nor was this all. Accustomed to see the ladies of the garrison in the formal, gala attire of the day, and familiar with the more critical niceties of these matters, the girl had managed to complete her dress in a way to leave nothing strikingly defective in its details, or even to betray an incongruity that would have been detected by one practised in the mysteries of the toilet. Head, feet, arms, hands, bust, and drapery, were all in harmony, as female attire was then deemed attractive and harmonious, and the end she aimed at, that of imposing on the uninstructed senses of the savages, by causing them to believe their guest was a woman of rank and importance, might well have succeeded with those whose habits had taught them to discriminate between persons. Judith, in addition to her rare native beauty, had a singular grace of person, and her mother had imparted enough of her own deportment to prevent any striking or offensive vulgarity of manner; so that, sooth to say, the gorgeous dress might have been worse bestowed in nearly every particular. Had it been displayed in a capital, a thousand might have worn it, before one could have been found to do more credit to its gay colours, glossy satins, and rich laces, than the beautiful creature whose person it now aided to adorn. The effect of such an apparition had not been miscalculated. The instant Judith found herself within the circle, she was, in a degree, compensated for the fearful personal risk she ran, by the unequivocal sensation of surprise and admiration produced by her appearance. The grim old warriors uttered their favorite exclamation "hugh!" The younger men were still more sensibly overcome, and even the women were not backward in letting open manifestations of pleasure escape them. It was seldom that these untutored children of the forest had ever seen any white female above the commonest sort, and, as to dress, never before had so much splendor shone before their eyes. The gayest uniforms of both French and English seemed dull compared with the lustre of the brocade, and while the rare personal beauty of the wearer added to the effect produced by its hues, the attire did not fail to adorn that beauty in a way which surpassed even the hopes of its wearer. Deerslayer himself was astounded, and this quite as much by the brilliant picture the girl presented, as at the indifference to consequences with which she had braved the danger of the step she had taken. Under such circumstances, all waited for the visitor to explain her object, which to most of the spectators seemed as inexplicable as her appearance.

"Which of these warriors is the principal chief?" demanded Judith of Deerslayer, as soon as she found it was expected that she should open the communications; "my errand is too important to be delivered to any of inferior rank. First explain to the Hurons what I say; then give an answer to the question I have put."

Deerslayer quietly complied, his auditors greedily listening to the interpretation of the first words that fell from so extraordinary a vision. The demand seemed perfectly in character for one who had every appearance of an exalted rank, herself. Rivenoak gave an appropriate reply, by presenting himself before his fair visitor in a way to leave no doubt that he was entitled to all the consideration he claimed.

"I can believe this, Huron," resumed Judith, enacting her assumed part with a steadiness and dignity that did credit to her powers of imitation, for she strove to impart to her manner the condescending courtesy she had once observed in the wife of a general officer, at a similar though a more amicable scene: "I can believe you to be the principal person of this party; I see in your countenance the marks of thought and reflection. To you, then, I must make my communication."

"Let the Flower of the Woods speak," returned the old chief courteously, as soon as her address had been translated so that all might understand it—"If her words are as pleasant as her looks, they will never quit my ears; I shall hear them long after the winter of Canada has killed all the flowers, and frozen all the speeches of summer."

This admiration was grateful to one constituted like Judith, and contributed to aid her self-possession, quite as much as it fed her vanity. Smiling involuntarily, or in spite of her wish to seem reserved, she proceeded in her plot.

"Now, Huron," she continued, "listen to my words. Your eyes tell you that I am no common woman. I will not say I am queen of this country; she is afar off, in a distant land; but under our gracious monarchs, there are many degrees of rank; one of these I fill. What that rank is precisely, it is unnecessary for me to say, since you would not understand it. For that information you must trust your eyes. You see what I am; you must feel that in listening to my words, you listen to one who can be your friend, or your enemy, as you treat her."

This was well uttered, with a due attention to manner and a steadiness of tone that was really surprising, considering all the circumstances of the case. It was well, though simply rendered into the Indian dialect too, and it was received with a respect and gravity that augured favourably for the girl's success. But Indian thought is not easily traced to its sources. Judith waited with anxiety to hear the answer, filled with hope even while she doubted. Rivenoak was a ready speaker, and he answered as promptly as comported with the notions of Indian decorum; that peculiar people seeming to think a short delay respectful, inasmuch as it manifests that the words already heard have been duly weighed.

"My daughter is handsomer than the wild roses of Ontario; her voice is pleasant to the ear as the song of the wren," answered the cautious and wily chief, who of all the band stood alone in not being fully imposed on by the magnificent and unusual appearance of Judith; but who distrusted even while he wondered: "the humming bird is not much larger than the bee; yet, its feathers are as gay as the tail of the peacock. The Great Spirit sometimes puts very bright clothes on very little animals. Still He covers the Moose with coarse hair. These things are beyond the understanding of poor Indians, who can only comprehend what they see and hear. No doubt my daughter has a very large wigwam somewhere about the lake; the Hurons have not found it, on account of their ignorance?"

"I have told you, chief, that it would be useless to state my rank and residence, in as much as you would not comprehend them. You must trust to your eyes for this knowledge; what red man is there who cannot see? This blanket that I wear is not the blanket of a common squaw; these ornaments are such as the wives and daughters of chiefs only appear in. Now, listen and hear why I have come alone among your people, and hearken to the errand that has brought me here. The Yengeese have young men, as well as the Hurons; and plenty of them, too; this you well know."

"The Yengeese are as plenty as the leaves on the trees! This every Huron knows, and feels."

"I understand you, chief. Had I brought a party with me, it might have caused trouble. My young men and your young men would have looked angrily at each other; especially had my young men seen that pale-face bound for the torture. He is a great hunter, and is much loved by all the garrisons, far and near. There would have been blows about him, and the trail of the Iroquois back to the Canadas would have been marked with blood."

"There is so much blood on it, now," returned the chief, gloomily, "that it blinds our eyes. My young men see that it is all Huron."

"No doubt; and more Huron blood would be spilt had I come surrounded with pale-faces. I have heard of Rivenoak, and have thought it would be better to send him back in peace to his village, that he might leave his women and children behind him; if he then wished to come for our scalps, we would meet him. He loves animals made of ivory, and little rifles. See; I have brought some with me to show him. I am his friend. When he has packed up these things among his goods, he will start for his village, before any of my young men can overtake him, and then he will show his people in Canada what riches they can come to seek, now that our great fathers, across the Salt Lake, have sent each other the war hatchet. I will lead back with me this great hunter, of whom I have need to keep my house in venison."

Judith, who was sufficiently familiar with Indian phraseology, endeavored to express her ideas in the sententious manner common to those people, and she succeeded even beyond her own expectations. Deerslayer did her full justice in the translation, and this so much the more readily, since the girl carefully abstained from uttering any direct untruth; a homage she paid to the young man's known aversion to falsehood, which he deemed a meanness altogether unworthy of a white man's gifts. The offering of the two remaining elephants, and of the pistols already mentioned, one of which was all the worse for the recent accident, produced a lively sensation among the Hurons, generally, though Rivenoak received it coldly, notwithstanding the delight with which he had first discovered the probable existence of a creature with two tails. In a word, this cool and sagacious savage was not so easily imposed on as his followers, and with a sentiment of honor that half the civilized world would have deemed supererogatory, he declined the acceptance of a bribe that he felt no disposition to earn by a compliance with the donor's wishes.

"Let my daughter keep her two-tailed hog, to eat when venison is scarce," he drily answered, "and the little gun, which has two muzzles. The Hurons will kill deer when they are hungry, and they have long rifles to fight with. This hunter cannot quit my young men now; they wish to know if he is as stouthearted as he boasts himself to be."

"That I deny, Huron—" interrupted Deerslayer, with warmth—"Yes, that I downright deny, as ag'in truth and reason. No man has heard me boast, and no man shall, though ye flay me alive, and then roast the quivering flesh, with your own infarnal devices and cruelties! I may be humble, and misfortunate, and your prisoner; but I'm no boaster, by my very gifts."

"My young pale-face boasts he is no boaster," returned the crafty chief: "he must be right. I hear a strange bird singing. It has very rich feathers. No Huron ever before saw such feathers! They will be ashamed to go back to their village, and tell their people that they let their prisoner go on account of the song of this strange bird and not be able to give the name of the bird. They do not know how to say whether it is a wren, or a cat bird. This would be a great disgrace; my young men would not be allowed to travel in the woods without taking their mothers with them, to tell them the names of the birds!"

"You can ask my name of your prisoner," returned the girl. "It is Judith; and there is a great deal of the history of Judith in the pale-face's best book, the Bible. If I am a bird of fine feathers, I have also my name."

"No," answered the wily Huron, betraying the artifice he had so long practised, by speaking in English with tolerable accuracy, "I not ask prisoner. He tired; he want rest. I ask my daughter, with feeble mind. She speak truth. Come here, daughter; you answer. Your name, Hetty?"

"Yes, that's what they call me," returned the girl, "though it's written Esther in the Bible."

"He write him in bible, too! All write in bible. No matter—what her name?"

"That's Judith, and it's so written in the Bible, though father sometimes called her Jude. That's my sister Judith. Thomas Hutter's daughter—Thomas Hutter, whom you called the Muskrat; though he was no muskrat, but a man like yourselves—he lived in a house on the water, and that was enough for you."

A smile of triumph gleamed on the hard wrinkled countenance of the chief, when he found how completely his appeal to the truth-loving Hetty had succeeded. As for Judith, herself, the moment her sister was questioned, she saw that all was lost; for no sign, or even intreaty could have induced the right feeling girl to utter a falsehood. To attempt to impose a daughter of the Muskrat on the savages as a princess, or a great lady, she knew would be idle, and she saw her bold and ingenious expedient for liberating the captive fail, through one of the simplest and most natural causes that could be imagined. She turned her eye on Deerslayer, therefore, as if imploring him to interfere to save them both.

"It will not do, Judith," said the young man, in answer to this appeal, which he understood, though he saw its uselessness; "it will not do. 'Twas a bold idea, and fit for a general's lady, but yonder Mingo" Rivenoak had withdrawn to a little distance, and was out of earshot—"but yonder Mingo is an oncommon man, and not to be deceived by any unnat'ral sarcumvention. Things must come afore him in their right order, to draw a cloud afore his eyes! 'Twas too much to attempt making him fancy that a queen, or a great lady, lived in these mountains, and no doubt he thinks the fine clothes you wear is some of the plunder of your own father—or, at least, of him who once passed for your father; as quite likely it was, if all they say is true."

"At all events, Deerslayer, my presence here will save you for a time. They will hardly attempt torturing you before my face!"

"Why not, Judith? Do you think they will treat a woman of the pale faces more tenderly than they treat their own? It's true that your sex will most likely save you from the torments, but it will not save your liberty, and may not save your scalp. I wish you had not come, my good Judith; it can do no good to me, while it may do great harm to yourself."

"I can share your fate," the girl answered with generous enthusiasm. "They shall not injure you while I stand by, if in my power to prevent it—besides—"

"Besides, what, Judith? What means have you to stop Injin cruelties, or to avart Injin deviltries?"

"None, perhaps, Deerslayer," answered the girl, with firmness, "but I can suffer with my friends—die with them if necessary."

"Ah! Judith—suffer you may; but die you will not, until the Lord's time shall come. It's little likely that one of your sex and beauty will meet with a harder fate than to become the wife of a chief, if, indeed your white inclinations can stoop to match with an Injin. 'Twould have been better had you staid in the Ark, or the castle, but what has been done, is done. You was about to say something, when you stopped at 'besides'?"

"It might not be safe to mention it here, Deerslayer," the girl hurriedly answered, moving past him carelessly, that she might speak in a lower tone; "half an hour is all in all to us. None of your friends are idle."

The hunter replied merely by a grateful look. Then he turned towards his enemies, as if ready again to face their torments. A short consultation had passed among the elders of the band, and by this time they also were prepared with their decision. The merciful purpose of Rivenoak had been much weakened by the artifice of Judith, which, failing of its real object, was likely to produce results the very opposite of those she had anticipated. This was natural; the feeling being aided by the resentment of an Indian who found how near he had been to becoming the dupe of an inexperienced girl. By this time, Judith's real character was fully understood, the wide spread reputation of her beauty contributing to the exposure. As for the unusual attire, it was confounded with the profound mystery of the animals with two tails, and for the moment lost its influence.

When Rivenoak, therefore, faced the captive again, it was with an altered countenance. He had abandoned the wish of saving him, and was no longer disposed to retard the more serious part of the torture. This change of sentiment was, in effect, communicated to the young men, who were already eagerly engaged in making their preparations for the contemplated scene. Fragments of dried wood were rapidly collected near the sapling, the splinters which it was intended to thrust into the flesh of the victim, previously to lighting, were all collected, and the thongs were already produced that were again to bind him to the tree. All this was done in profound silence, Judith watching every movement with breathless expectation, while Deerslayer himself stood seemingly as unmoved as one of the pines of the hills. When the warriors advanced to bind him, however, the young man glanced at Judith, as if to enquire whether resistance or submission were most advisable. By a significant gesture she counselled the last, and, in a minute, he was once more fastened to the tree, a helpless object of any insult, or wrong, that might be offered. So eagerly did every one now act, that nothing was said. The fire was immediately lighted in the pile, and the end of all was anxiously expected.

It was not the intention of the Hurons absolutely to destroy the life of their victim by means of fire. They designed merely to put his physical fortitude to the severest proofs it could endure, short of that extremity. In the end, they fully intended to carry his scalp with them into their village, but it was their wish first to break down his resolution, and to reduce him to the level of a complaining sufferer. With this view, the pile of brush and branches had been placed at a proper distance, or, one at which it was thought the heat would soon become intolerable, though it might not be immediately dangerous. As often happened, however, on these occasions, this distance had been miscalculated, and the flames began to wave their forked tongues in a proximity to the face of the victim, that would have proved fatal, in another instant, had not Hetty rushed through the crowd, armed with a stick, and scattered the blazing pile in a dozen directions. More than one hand was raised to strike this presumptuous intruder to the earth, but the chiefs prevented the blows, by reminding their irritated followers of the state of her mind. Hetty, herself, was insensible to the risk she ran, but, as soon as she had performed this bold act, she stood looking about her, in frowning resentment, as if to rebuke the crowd of attentive savages for their cruelty.

"God bless you, dearest sister, for that brave and ready act!" murmured Judith, herself unnerved so much as to be incapable of exertion—"Heaven, itself, has sent you on its holy errand."

"'Twas well meant, Judith—" rejoined the victim—"'twas excellently meant, and 'twas timely; though it may prove ontimely in the ind! What is to come to pass, must come to pass soon, or 'twill quickly be too late. Had I drawn in one mouthful of that flame in breathing, the power of man could not save my life, and you see that, this time, they've so bound my forehead, as not to leave my head the smallest chance. 'Twas well meant, but it might have been more marciful to let the flames act their part."

"Cruel, heartless Hurons!" exclaimed the still indignant Hetty—"Would you burn a man and a Christian, as you would burn a log of wood! Do you never read your Bibles? Or do you think God will forget such things?"

A gesture from Rivenoak caused the scattered brands to be collected. Fresh wood was brought, even the women and children busying themselves eagerly, in the gathering of dried sticks. The flame was just kindling a second time, when an Indian female pushed through the circle, advanced to the heap, and with her foot dashed aside the lighted twigs in time to prevent the conflagration. A yell followed this second disappointment, but when the offender turned towards the circle, and presented the countenance of Hist, it was succeeded by a common exclamation of pleasure and surprise. For a minute, all thought of pursuing the business in hand was forgotten. Young and old crowded around the girl, in haste to demand an explanation of her sudden and unlooked-for return. It was at this critical instant that Hist spoke to Judith in a low voice, placed some small object unseen in her hand, and then turned to meet the salutations of the Huron girls, with whom she was personally a great favorite. Judith recovered her self possession, and acted promptly. The small, keen edged knife that Hist had given to the other, was passed by the latter into the hands of Hetty, as the safest and least suspected medium of transferring it to Deerslayer. But the feeble intellect of the last defeated the well-grounded hopes of all three. Instead of first cutting loose the hands of the victim, and then concealing the knife in his clothes, in readiness for action at the most available instant, she went to work herself, with earnestness and simplicity, to cut the thongs that bound his head, that he might not again be in danger of inhaling flames. Of course this deliberate procedure was seen, and the hands of Hetty were arrested, ere she had more than liberated the upper portion of the captive's body, not including his arms below the elbows. This discovery at once pointed distrust towards Hist, and to Judith's surprise, when questioned on the subject, that spirited girl was not disposed to deny her agency in what had passed.

"Why should I not help the Deerslayer?" the girl demanded, in the tones of a firm minded woman. "He is the brother of a Delaware chief; my heart is all Delaware. Come forth, miserable Briarthorn, and wash the Iroquois paint from your face; stand before the Hurons the crow that you are. You would eat the carrion of your own dead, rather than starve. Put him face to face with Deerslayer, chiefs and warriors; I will show you how great a knave you have been keeping in your tribe."

This bold language, uttered in their own dialect and with a manner full of confidence, produced a deep sensation among the Hurons. Treachery is always liable to distrust, and though the recreant Briarthorn had endeavoured to serve the enemy well, his exertions and assiduities had gained for him little more than toleration. His wish to obtain Hist for a wife had first induced him to betray her, and his own people, but serious rivals to his first project had risen up among his new friends, weakening still more their sympathies with treason. In a word, Briarthorn had been barely permitted to remain in the Huron encampment, where he was as closely and as jealously watched as Hist, herself, seldom appearing before the chiefs, and sedulously keeping out of view of Deerslayer, who, until this moment, was ignorant even of his presence. Thus summoned, however, it was impossible to remain in the back ground. "Wash the Iroquois paint from his face," he did not, for when he stood in the centre of the circle, he was so disguised in these new colours, that at first, the hunter did not recognise him. He assumed an air of defiance, notwithstanding, and haughtily demanded what any could say against "Briarthorn."

"Ask yourself that," continued Hist with spirit, though her manner grew less concentrated, and there was a slight air of abstraction that became observable to Deerslayer and Judith, if to no others—"Ask that of your own heart, sneaking woodchuck of the Delawares; come not here with the face of an innocent man. Go look into the spring; see the colours of your enemies on your lying skin; then come back and boast how you run from your tribe and took the blanket of the French for your covering! Paint yourself as bright as the humming bird, you will still be black as the crow!"

Hist had been so uniformly gentle, while living with the Hurons, that they now listened to her language with surprise. As for the delinquent, his blood boiled in his veins, and it was well for the pretty speaker that it was not in his power to execute the revenge he burned to inflict on her, in spite of his pretended love.

"Who wishes Briarthorn?" he sternly asked—"If this pale-face is tired of life, if afraid of Indian torments, speak, Rivenoak; I will send him after the warriors we have lost."

"No, chiefs—no, Rivenoak—" eagerly interrupted Hist—"Deerslayer fears nothing; least of all a crow! Unbind him—cut his withes, place him face to face with this cawing bird; then let us see which is tired of life!"

Hist made a forward movement, as if to take a knife from a young man, and perform the office she had mentioned in person, but an aged warrior interposed, at a sign from Rivenoak. This chief watched all the girl did with distrust, for, even while speaking in her most boastful language, and in the steadiest manner, there was an air of uncertainty and expectation about her, that could not escape so close an observer. She acted well; but two or three of the old men were equally satisfied that it was merely acting. Her proposal to release Deerslayer, therefore, was rejected, and the disappointed Hist found herself driven back from the sapling, at the very moment she fancied herself about to be successful. At the same time, the circle, which had got to be crowded and confused, was enlarged, and brought once more into order. Rivenoak now announced the intention of the old men again to proceed, the delay having continued long enough, and leading to no result.

"Stop Huron—stay chiefs!—" exclaimed Judith, scarce knowing what she said, or why she interposed, unless to obtain time. "For God's sake, a single minute longer—"

The words were cut short, by another and a still more extraordinary interruption. A young Indian came bounding through the Huron ranks, leaping into the very centre of the circle, in a way to denote the utmost confidence, or a temerity bordering on foolhardiness. Five or six sentinels were still watching the lake at different and distant points, and it was the first impression of Rivenoak that one of these had come in, with tidings of import. Still the movements of the stranger were so rapid, and his war dress, which scarcely left him more drapery than an antique statue, had so little distinguishing about it, that, at the first moment, it was impossible to ascertain whether he were friend or foe. Three leaps carried this warrior to the side of Deerslayer, whose withes were cut in the twinkling of an eye, with a quickness and precision that left the prisoner perfect master of his limbs. Not till this was effected did the stranger bestow a glance on any other object; then he turned and showed the astonished Hurons the noble brow, fine person, and eagle eye, of a young warrior, in the paint and panoply of a Delaware. He held a rifle in each hand, the butts of both resting on the earth, while from one dangled its proper pouch and horn. This was Killdeer which, even as he looked boldly and in defiance at the crowd around him, he suffered to fall back into the hands of its proper owner. The presence of two armed men, though it was in their midst, startled the Hurons. Their rifles were scattered about against the different trees, and their only weapons were their knives and tomahawks. Still they had too much self-possession to betray fear. It was little likely that so small a force would assail so strong a band, and each man expected some extraordinary proposition to succeed so decisive a step. The stranger did not seem disposed to disappoint them; he prepared to speak.

"Hurons," he said, "this earth is very big. The Great Lakes are big, too; there is room beyond them for the Iroquois; there is room for the Delawares on this side. I am Chingachgook the Son of Uncas; the kinsman of Tamenund. This is my betrothed; that pale-face is my friend. My heart was heavy, when I missed him; I followed him to your camp, to see that no harm happened to him. All the Delaware girls are waiting for Wah; they wonder that she stays away so long. Come, let us say farewell, and go on our path."

"Hurons, this is your mortal enemy, the Great Serpent of them you hate!" cried Briarthorn. "If he escape, blood will be in your moccasin prints, from this spot to the Canadas. I am all Huron!" As the last words were uttered, the traitor cast his knife at the naked breast of the Delaware. A quick movement of the arm, on the part of Hist, who stood near, turned aside the blow, the dangerous weapon burying its point in a pine. At the next instant, a similar weapon glanced from the hand of the Serpent, and quivered in the recreant's heart. A minute had scarcely elapsed from the moment in which Chingachgook bounded into the circle, and that in which Briarthorn fell, like a log, dead in his tracks. The rapidity of events had prevented the Hurons from acting; but this catastrophe permitted no farther delay. A common exclamation followed, and the whole party was in motion. At this instant a sound unusual to the woods was heard, and every Huron, male and female, paused to listen, with ears erect and faces filled with expectation. The sound was regular and heavy, as if the earth were struck with beetles. Objects became visible among the trees of the background, and a body of troops was seen advancing with measured tread. They came upon the charge, the scarlet of the King's livery shining among the bright green foliage of the forest.

The scene that followed is not easily described. It was one in which wild confusion, despair, and frenzied efforts, were so blended as to destroy the unity and distinctness of the action. A general yell burst from the enclosed Hurons; it was succeeded by the hearty cheers of England. Still not a musket or rifle was fired, though that steady, measured tramp continued, and the bayonet was seen gleaming in advance of a line that counted nearly sixty men. The Hurons were taken at a fearful disadvantage. On three sides was the water, while their formidable and trained foes cut them off from flight on the fourth. Each warrior rushed for his arms, and then all on the point, man, woman and child, eagerly sought the covers. In this scene of confusion and dismay, however, nothing could surpass the discretion and coolness of Deerslayer. His first care was to place Judith and Hist behind trees, and he looked for Hetty; but she had been hurried away in the crowd of Huron women. This effected, he threw himself on a flank of the retiring Hurons, who were inclining off towards the southern margin of the point, in the hope of escaping through the water. Deerslayer watched his opportunity, and finding two of his recent tormentors in a range, his rifle first broke the silence of the terrific scene. The bullet brought down both at one discharge. This drew a general fire from the Hurons, and the rifle and war cry of the Serpent were heard in the clamor. Still the trained men returned no answering volley, the whoop and piece of Hurry alone being heard on their side, if we except the short, prompt word of authority, and that heavy, measured and menacing tread. Presently, however, the shrieks, groans, and denunciations that usually accompany the use of the bayonet followed. That terrible and deadly weapon was glutted in vengeance. The scene that succeeded was one of those of which so many have occurred in our own times, in which neither age nor sex forms an exemption to the lot of a savage warfare.

CHAPTER XXXI.

"The flower that smiles to-day
To-morrow dies;
All that we wish to stay,
Tempts and then flies:
What is this world's delight?
Lightning that mocks the night,
Brief even as bright."

Shelley, "Mutability," II. i-v.

The picture next presented, by the point of land that the unfortunate Hurons had selected for their last place of encampment, need scarcely be laid before the eyes of the reader. Happily for the more tender-minded and the more timid, the trunks of the trees, the leaves, and the smoke had concealed much of that which passed, and night shortly after drew its veil over the lake, and the whole of that seemingly interminable wilderness; which may be said to have then stretched, with few and immaterial interruptions, from the banks of the Hudson to the shores of the Pacific Ocean. Our business carries us into the following day, when light returned upon the earth, as sunny and as smiling as if nothing extraordinary had occurred.

When the sun rose on the following morning, every sign of hostility and alarm had vanished from the basin of the Glimmerglass. The frightful event of the preceding evening had left no impression on the placid sheet, and the untiring hours pursued their course in the placid order prescribed by the powerful hand that set them in motion. The birds were again skimming the water, or were seen poised on the wing, high above the tops of the tallest pines of the mountains, ready to make their swoops, in obedience to the irresistable law of their natures. In a word, nothing was changed, but the air of movement and life that prevailed in and around the castle. Here, indeed, was an alteration that must have struck the least observant eye. A sentinel, who wore the light infantry uniform of a royal regiment, paced the platform with measured tread, and some twenty more of the same corps lounged about the place, or were seated in the ark. Their arms were stacked under the eye of their comrade on post. Two officers stood examining the shore, with the ship's glass so often mentioned. Their looks were directed to that fatal point, where scarlet coats were still to be seen gliding among the trees, and where the magnifying power of the instrument also showed spades at work, and the sad duty of interment going on. Several of the common men bore proofs on their persons that their enemies had not been overcome entirely without resistance, and the youngest of the two officers on the platform wore an arm in a sling. His companion, who commanded the party, had been more fortunate. He it was who used the glass, in making the reconnoissances in which the two were engaged.

A sergeant approached to make a report. He addressed the senior of these officers as Capt. Warley, while the other was alluded to as Mr., which was equivalent to Ensign Thornton. The former it will at once be seen was the officer who had been named with so much feeling in the parting dialogue between Judith and Hurry. He was, in truth, the very individual with whom the scandal of the garrisons had most freely connected the name of this beautiful but indiscreet girl. He was a hard featured, red faced man of about five and thirty; but of a military carriage, and with an air of fashion that might easily impose on the imagination of one as ignorant of the world as Judith.

"Craig is covering us with benedictions," observed this person to his young ensign, with an air of indifference, as he shut the glass and handed it to his servant; "to say the truth, not without reason; it is certainly more agreeable to be here in attendance on Miss Judith Hutter, than to be burying Indians on a point of the lake, however romantic the position, or brilliant the victory. By the way, Wright—is Davis still living?"

"He died about ten minutes since, your honor," returned the sergeant to whom this question was addressed. "I knew how it would be, as soon as I found the bullet had touched the stomach. I never knew a man who could hold out long, if he had a hole in his stomach."

"No; it is rather inconvenient for carrying away any thing very nourishing," observed Warley, gaping. "This being up two nights de suite, Arthur, plays the devil with a man's faculties! I'm as stupid as one of those Dutch parsons on the Mohawk—I hope your arm is not painful, my dear boy?"

"It draws a few grimaces from me, sir, as I suppose you see," answered the youth, laughing at the very moment his countenance was a little awry with pain. "But it may be borne. I suppose Graham can spare a few minutes, soon, to look at my hurt."

"She is a lovely creature, this Judith Hutter, after all, Thornton; and it shall not be my fault if she is not seen and admired in the Parks!" resumed Warley, who thought little of his companion's wound—"your arm, eh! Quite True—Go into the ark, sergeant, and tell Dr. Graham I desire he would look at Mr. Thornton's injury, as soon as he has done with the poor fellow with the broken leg. A lovely creature! and she looked like a queen in that brocade dress in which we met her. I find all changed here; father and mother both gone, the sister dying, if not dead, and none of the family left, but the beauty! This has been a lucky expedition all round, and promises to terminate better than Indian skirmishes in general."

"Am I to suppose, sir, that you are about to desert your colours, in the great corps of bachelors, and close the campaign with matrimony?"

"I, Tom Warley, turn Benedict! Faith, my dear boy, you little know the corps you speak of, if you fancy any such thing. I do suppose there are women in the colonies that a captain of Light Infantry need not disdain; but they are not to be found up here, on a mountain lake; or even down on the Dutch river where we are posted. It is true, my uncle, the general, once did me the favor to choose a wife for me in Yorkshire; but she had no beauty—and I would not marry a princess, unless she were handsome."

"If handsome, you would marry a beggar?"

"Ay, these are the notions of an ensign! Love in a cottage—doors—and windows—the old story, for the hundredth time. The 20th—don't marry. We are not a marrying corps, my dear boy. There's the Colonel, Old Sir Edwin———, now; though a full General he has never thought of a wife; and when a man gets as high as a Lieutenant General, without matrimony, he is pretty safe. Then the Lieutenant Colonel is confirmed, as I tell my cousin the bishop. The Major is a widower, having tried matrimony for twelve months in his youth, and we look upon him, now, as one of our most certain men. Out of ten captains, but one is in the dilemma, and he, poor devil, is always kept at regimental headquarters, as a sort of memento mori, to the young men as they join. As for the subalterns, not one has ever yet had the audacity to speak of introducing a wife into the regiment. But your arm is troublesome, and we'll go ourselves and see what has become of Graham."

The surgeon who had accompanied the party was employed very differently from what the captain supposed. When the assault was over, and the dead and wounded were collected, poor Hetty had been found among the latter. A rifle bullet had passed through her body, inflicting an injury that was known at a glance to be mortal. How this wound was received, no one knew; it was probably one of those casualties that ever accompany scenes like that related in the previous chapter.

The Sumach, all the elderly women, and some of the Huron girls, had fallen by the bayonet, either in the confusion of the melee, or from the difficulty of distinguishing the sexes when the dress was so simple. Much the greater portion of the warriors suffered on the spot. A few had escaped, however, and two or three had been taken unharmed. As for the wounded, the bayonet saved the surgeon much trouble. Rivenoak had escaped with life and limb, but was injured and a prisoner. As Captain Warley and his ensign went into the Ark they passed him, seated in dignified silence in one end of the scow, his head and leg bound, but betraying no visible sign of despondency or despair. That he mourned the loss of his tribe is certain; still he did it in a manner that best became a warrior and a chief.

The two soldiers found their surgeon in the principal room of the Ark. He was just quitting the pallet of Hetty, with an expression of sorrowful regret on his hard, pock-marked Scottish features, that it was not usual to see there. All his assiduity had been useless, and he was compelled reluctantly to abandon the expectation of seeing the girl survive many hours. Dr. Graham was accustomed to death-bed scenes, and ordinarily they produced but little impression on him. In all that relates to religion, his was one of those minds which, in consequence of reasoning much on material things, logically and consecutively, and overlooking the total want of premises which such a theory must ever possess, through its want of a primary agent, had become sceptical; leaving a vague opinion concerning the origin of things, that, with high pretensions to philosophy, failed in the first of all philosophical principles, a cause. To him religious dependence appeared a weakness, but when he found one gentle and young like Hetty, with a mind beneath the level of her race, sustained at such a moment by these pious sentiments, and that, too, in a way that many a sturdy warrior and reputed hero might have looked upon with envy, he found himself affected by the sight to a degree that he would have been ashamed to confess. Edinburgh and Aberdeen, then as now, supplied no small portion of the medical men of the British service, and Dr. Graham, as indeed his name and countenance equally indicated, was, by birth a North Briton.

"Here is an extraordinary exhibition for a forest, and one but half-gifted with reason," he observed with a decided Scotch accent, as Warley and the ensign entered; "I just hope, gentlemen, that when we three shall be called on to quit the 20th, we may be found as resigned to go on the half pay of another existence, as this poor demented chiel!"

"Is there no hope that she can survive the hurt?" demanded Warley, turning his eyes towards the pallid Judith, on whose cheeks, however, two large spots of red had settled as soon as he came into the cabin.

"No more than there is for Chairlie Stuart! Approach and judge for yourselves, gentlemen; ye'll see faith exemplified in an exceeding and wonderful manner. There is a sort of arbitrium between life and death, in actual conflict in the poor girl's mind, that renders her an interesting study to a philosopher. Mr. Thornton, I'm at your service, now; we can just look at the arm in the next room, while we speculate as much as we please on the operations and sinuosities of the human mind."

The surgeon and ensign retired, and Warley had an opportunity of looking about him more at leisure, and with a better understanding of the nature and feelings of the group collected in the cabin. Poor Hetty had been placed on her own simple bed, and was reclining in a half seated attitude, with the approaches of death on her countenance, though they were singularly dimmed by the lustre of an expression in which all the intelligence of her entire being appeared to be concentrated. Judith and Hist were near her, the former seated in deep grief; the latter standing, in readiness to offer any of the gentle attentions of feminine care. Deerslayer stood at the end of the pallet, leaning on Killdeer, unharmed in person, all the fine martial ardor that had so lately glowed in his countenance having given place to the usual look of honesty and benevolence, qualities of which the expression was now softened by manly regret and pity. The Serpent was in the background of the picture, erect, and motionless as a statue; but so observant that not a look of the eye escaped his own keen glances. Hurry completed the group, being seated on a stool near the door, like one who felt himself out of place in such a scene, but who was ashamed to quit it, unbidden.

"Who is that in scarlet?" asked Hetty, as soon as the Captain's uniform caught her eye. "Tell me, Judith, is it the friend of Hurry?"

"'Tis the officer who commands the troops that have rescued us all from the hands of the Hurons," was the low answer of the sister.

"Am I rescued, too!—I thought they said I was shot, and about to die. Mother is dead; and so is father; but you are living, Judith, and so is Hurry. I was afraid Hurry would be killed, when I heard him shouting among the soldiers."

"Never mind—never mind, dear Hetty—" interrupted Judith, sensitively alive to the preservation of her sister's secret, more, perhaps, at such a moment, than at any other. "Hurry is well, and Deerslayer is well, and the Delaware is well, too."

"How came they to shoot a poor girl like me, and let so many men go unharmed? I didn't know that the Hurons were so wicked, Judith!"

"'Twas an accident, poor Hetty; a sad accident it has been! No one would willingly have injured you."

"I'm glad of that!—I thought it strange; I am feeble minded, and the redmen have never harmed me before. I should be sorry to think that they had changed their minds. I am glad too, Judith, that they haven't hurt Hurry. Deerslayer I don't think God will suffer any one to harm. It was very fortunate the soldiers came as they did though, for fire will burn!"

"It was indeed fortunate, my sister; God's holy name be forever blessed for the mercy!"

"I dare say, Judith, you know some of the officers; you used to know so many!"

Judith made no reply; she hid her face in her hands and groaned. Hetty gazed at her in wonder; but naturally supposing her own situation was the cause of this grief, she kindly offered to console her sister.

"Don't mind me, dear Judith," said the affectionate and pure-hearted creature, "I don't suffer; if I do die, why father and mother are both dead, and what happens to them may well happen to me. You know I am of less account than any of the family; therefore few will think of me after I'm in the lake."

"No, no, no—poor, dear, dear Hetty!" exclaimed Judith, in an uncontrollable burst of sorrow, "I, at least, will ever think of you; and gladly, oh! how gladly would I exchange places with you, to be the pure, excellent, sinless creature you are!"

Until now, Captain Warley had stood leaning against the door of the cabin; when this outbreak of feeling, and perchance of penitence, however, escaped the beautiful girl, he walked slowly and thoughtfully away; even passing the ensign, then suffering under the surgeon's care, without noticing him.

"I have got my Bible here, Judith," returned her sister in a voice of triumph. "It's true, I can't read any longer, there's something the matter with my eyes—you look dim and distant—and so does Hurry, now I look at him—well, I never could have believed that Henry March would have so dull a look! What can be the reason, Judith, that I see so badly, today? I, who mother always said had the best eyes in the whole family. Yes, that was it: my mind was feeble—what people call half-witted— but my eyes were so good!"

Again Judith groaned; this time no feeling of self, no retrospect of the past caused the pain. It was the pure, heartfelt sorrow of sisterly love, heightened by a sense of the meek humility and perfect truth of the being before her. At that moment, she would gladly have given up her own life to save that of Hetty. As the last, however, was beyond the reach of human power, she felt there was nothing left her but sorrow. At this moment Warley returned to the cabin, drawn by a secret impulse he could not withstand, though he felt, just then, as if he would gladly abandon the American continent forever, were it practicable. Instead of pausing at the door, he now advanced so near the pallet of the sufferer as to come more plainly within her gaze. Hetty could still distinguish large objects, and her look soon fastened on him.

"Are you the officer that came with Hurry?" she asked. "If you are, we ought all to thank you, for, though I am hurt, the rest have saved their lives. Did Harry March tell you, where to find us, and how much need there was for your services?"

"The news of the party reached us by means of a friendly runner," returned the Captain, glad to relieve his feelings by this appearance of a friendly communication, "and I was immediately sent out to cut it off. It was fortunate, certainly, that we met Hurry Harry, as you call him, for he acted as a guide, and it was not less fortunate that we heard a firing, which I now understand was merely a shooting at the mark, for it not only quickened our march, but called us to the right side of the lake. The Delaware saw us on the shore, with the glass it would seem, and he and Hist, as I find his squaw is named, did us excellent service. It was really altogether a fortunate concurrence of circumstances, Judith."

"Talk not to me of any thing fortunate, sir," returned the girl huskily, again concealing her face. "To me the world is full of misery. I wish never to hear of marks, or rifles, or soldiers, or men, again!"

"Do you know my sister?" asked Hetty, ere the rebuked soldier had time to rally for an answer. "How came you to know that her name is Judith? You are right, for that is her name; and I am Hetty; Thomas Hutter's daughters."

"For heaven's sake, dearest sister; for my sake, beloved Hetty," interposed Judith, imploringly, "say no more of this!"

Hetty looked surprised, but accustomed to comply, she ceased her awkward and painful interrogations of Warley, bending her eyes towards the Bible which she still held between her hands, as one would cling to a casket of precious stones in a shipwreck, or a conflagration. Her mind now adverted to the future, losing sight, in a great measure, of the scenes of the past.

"We shall not long be parted, Judith," she said; "when you die, you must be brought and be buried in the lake, by the side of mother, too."

"Would to God, Hetty, that I lay there at this moment!"

"No, that cannot be, Judith; people must die before they have any right to be buried. 'Twould be wicked to bury you, or for you to bury yourself, while living. Once I thought of burying myself; God kept me from that sin."

"You!—You, Hetty Hutter, think of such an act!" exclaimed Judith, looking up in uncontrollable surprise, for she well knew nothing passed the lips of her conscientious sister, that was not religiously true.

"Yes, I did, Judith, but God has forgotten—no he forgets nothing—but he has forgiven it," returned the dying girl, with the subdued manner of a repentant child. "'Twas after mother's death; I felt I had lost the best friend I had on earth, if not the only friend. 'Tis true, you and father were kind to me, Judith, but I was so feeble-minded, I knew I should only give you trouble; and then you were so often ashamed of such a sister and daughter, and 'tis hard to live in a world where all look upon you as below them. I thought then, if I could bury myself by the side of mother, I should be happier in the lake than in the hut."

"Forgive me—pardon me, dearest Hetty—on my bended knees, I beg you to pardon me, sweet sister, if any word, or act of mine drove you to so maddening and cruel a thought!"

"Get up, Judith—kneel to God; don't kneel to me. Just so I felt when mother was dying! I remembered everything I had said and done to vex her, and could have kissed her feet for forgiveness. I think it must be so with all dying people; though, now I think of it, I don't remember to have had such feelings on account of father."

Judith arose, hid her face in her apron, and wept. A long pause—one of more than two hours—succeeded, during which Warley entered and left the cabin several times; apparently uneasy when absent, and yet unable to remain. He issued various orders, which his men proceeded to execute, and there was an air of movement in the party, more especially as Mr. Craig, the lieutenant, had got through the unpleasant duty of burying the dead, and had sent for instructions from the shore, desiring to know what he was to do with his detachment. During this interval Hetty slept a little, and Deerslayer and Chingachgook left the Ark to confer together. But, at the end of the time mentioned, the Surgeon passed upon the platform, and with a degree of feeling his comrades had never before observed in one of his habits, he announced that the patient was rapidly drawing near her end. On receiving this intelligence the group collected again, curiosity to witness such a death—or a better feeling—drawing to the spot men who had so lately been actors in a scene seemingly of so much greater interest and moment. By this time Judith had got to be inactive through grief, and Hist alone was performing the little offices of feminine attention that are so appropriate to the sick bed. Hetty herself had undergone no other apparent change than the general failing that indicated the near approach of dissolution. All that she possessed of mind was as clear as ever, and, in some respects, her intellect perhaps was more than usually active.

"Don't grieve for me so much, Judith," said the gentle sufferer, after a pause in her remarks; "I shall soon see mother—I think I see her now; her face is just as sweet and smiling as it used to be! Perhaps when I'm dead, God will give me all my mind, and I shall become a more fitting companion for mother than I ever was before."

"You will be an angel in heaven, Hetty," sobbed the sister; "no spirit there will be more worthy of its holy residence!"

"I don't understand it quite; still, I know it must be all true; I've read it in the Bible. How dark it's becoming! Can it be night so soon? I can hardly see you at all—where is Hist?"

"I here, poor girl—Why you no see me?"

"I do see you; but I couldn't tell whether 'twas you, or Judith. I believe I shan't see you much longer, Hist."

"Sorry for that, poor Hetty. Never mind—pale-face got a heaven for girl as well as for warrior."

"Where's the Serpent? Let me speak to him; give me his hand; so; I feel it. Delaware, you will love and cherish this young Indian woman—I know how fond she is of you; you must be fond of her. Don't treat her as some of your people treat their wives; be a real husband to her. Now, bring Deerslayer near me; give me his hand."

This request was complied with, and the hunter stood by the side of the pallet, submitting to the wishes of the girl with the docility of a child.

"I feel, Deerslayer," she resumed, "though I couldn't tell why—but I feel that you and I are not going to part for ever. 'Tis a strange feeling! I never had it before; I wonder what it comes from!"

"'Tis God encouraging you in extremity, Hetty; as such it ought to be harbored and respected. Yes, we shall meet ag'in, though it may be a long time first, and in a far distant land."

"Do you mean to be buried in the lake, too? If so, that may account for the feeling."

"'Tis little likely, gal; 'tis little likely; but there's a region for Christian souls, where there's no lakes, nor woods, they say; though why there should be none of the last, is more than I can account for; seeing that pleasantness and peace is the object in view. My grave will be found in the forest, most likely, but I hope my spirit will not be far from your'n."

"So it must be, then. I am too weak-minded to understand these things, but I feel that you and I will meet again. Sister, where are you? I can't see, now, anything but darkness. It must be night, surely!"

"Oh! Hetty, I am here at your side; these are my arms that are around you," sobbed Judith. "Speak, dearest; is there anything you wish to say, or have done, in this awful moment."

By this time Hetty's sight had entirely failed her. Nevertheless death approached with less than usual of its horrors, as if in tenderness to one of her half-endowed faculties. She was pale as a corpse, but her breathing was easy and unbroken, while her voice, though lowered almost to a whisper, remained clear and distinct. When her sister put this question, however, a blush diffused itself over the features of the dying girl, so faint however as to be nearly imperceptible; resembling that hue of the rose which is thought to portray the tint of modesty, rather than the dye of the flower in its richer bloom. No one but Judith detected this exposure of feeling, one of the gentle expressions of womanly sensibility, even in death. On her, however, it was not lost, nor did she conceal from herself the cause.

"Hurry is here, dearest Hetty," whispered the sister, with her face so near the sufferer as to keep the words from other ears. "Shall I tell him to come and receive your good wishes?"

A gentle pressure of the hand answered in the affirmative. Then Hurry was brought to the side of the pallet. It is probable that this handsome but rude woodsman had never before found himself so awkwardly placed, though the inclination which Hetty felt for him (a sort of secret yielding to the instincts of nature, rather than any unbecoming impulse of an ill-regulated imagination), was too pure and unobtrusive to have created the slightest suspicion of the circumstance in his mind. He allowed Judith to put his hard colossal hand between those of Hetty, and stood waiting the result in awkward silence.

"This is Hurry, dearest," whispered Judith, bending over her sister, ashamed to utter the words so as to be audible to herself. "Speak to him, and let him go."

"What shall I say, Judith?"

"Nay, whatever your own pure spirit teaches, my love. Trust to that, and you need fear nothing."

"Good bye, Hurry," murmured the girl, with a gentle pressure of his hand. "I wish you would try and be more like Deerslayer."

These words were uttered with difficulty; a faint flush succeeded them for a single instant. Then the hand was relinquished, and Hetty turned her face aside, as if done with the world. The mysterious feeling that bound her to the young man, a sentiment so gentle as to be almost imperceptible to herself, and which could never have existed at all, had her reason possessed more command over her senses, was forever lost in thoughts of a more elevated, though scarcely of a purer character.

"Of what are you thinking, my sweet sister?" whispered Judith "Tell me, that I may aid you at this moment."

"Mother—I see Mother, now, and bright beings around her in the lake. Why isn't father there? It's odd that I can see Mother, when I can't see you! Farewell, Judith."

The last words were uttered after a pause, and her sister had hung over her some time, in anxious watchfulness, before she perceived that the gentle spirit had departed. Thus died Hetty Hutter, one of those mysterious links between the material and immaterial world, which, while they appear to be deprived of so much that it is esteemed and necessary for this state of being, draw so near to, and offer so beautiful an illustration of the truth, purity, and simplicity of another.

CHAPTER XXXII.

"A baron's chylde to be begylde!
  it were a cursed dede:
To be felàwe with an outlàwe!
  Almighty God forbede!
Yea, better were, the pore squy
  re alone to forest yede,
Then ye sholde say another day,
  that by my cursed dede
Ye were betrayed:
  wherefore, good mayde,
  the best rede that I can,
Is, that I to the grene wode go, alone,
  a banyshed man."

Thomas Percy, 'Nutbrowne Mayde,' 11. 265–76
from Reliques of Ancient English Poetry, Vol. II.

The day that followed proved to be melancholy, though one of much activity. The soldiers, who had so lately been employed in interring their victims, were now called on to bury their own dead. The scene of the morning had left a saddened feeling on all the gentlemen of the party, and the rest felt the influence of a similar sensation, in a variety of ways and from many causes. Hour dragged on after hour until evening arrived, and then came the last melancholy offices in honor of poor Hetty Hutter. Her body was laid in the lake, by the side of that of the mother she had so loved and reverenced, the surgeon, though actually an unbeliever, so far complying with the received decencies of life as to read the funeral service over her grave, as he had previously done over those of the other Christian slain. It mattered not; that all seeing eye which reads the heart, could not fail to discriminate between the living and the dead, and the gentle soul of the unfortunate girl was already far removed beyond the errors, or deceptions, of any human ritual. These simple rites, however, were not wholly wanting in suitable accompaniments. The tears of Judith and Hist were shed freely, and Deerslayer gazed upon the limpid water, that now flowed over one whose spirit was even purer than its own mountain springs, with glistening eyes. Even the Delaware turned aside to conceal his weakness, while the common men gazed on the ceremony with wondering eyes and chastened feelings.

The business of the day closed with this pious office. By order of the commanding officer, all retired early to rest, for it was intended to begin the march homeward with the return of light. One party, indeed, bearing the wounded, the prisoners, and the trophies, had left the castle in the middle of the day under the guidance of Hurry, intending to reach the fort by shorter marches. It had been landed on the point so often mentioned, or that described in our opening pages, and, when the sun set, was already encamped on the brow of the long, broken, and ridgy hills, that fell away towards the valley of the Mohawk. The departure of this detachment had greatly simplified the duty of the succeeding day, disencumbering its march of its baggage and wounded, and otherwise leaving him who had issued the order greater liberty of action.

Judith held no communications with any but Hist, after the death of her sister, until she retired for the night. Her sorrow had been respected, and both the females had been left with the body, unintruded on, to the last moment. The rattling of the drum broke the silence of that tranquil water, and the echoes of the tattoo were heard among the mountains, so soon after the ceremony was over as to preclude the danger of interruption. That star which had been the guide of Hist, rose on a scene as silent as if the quiet of nature had never yet been disturbed by the labors or passions of man. One solitary sentinel, with his relief, paced the platform throughout the night, and morning was ushered in, as usual, by the martial beat of the reveille.

Military precision succeeded to the desultory proceedings of border men, and when a hasty and frugal breakfast was taken, the party began its movement towards the shore with a regularity and order that prevented noise or confusion. Of all the officers, Warley alone remained. Craig headed the detachment in advance, Thornton was with the wounded, and Graham accompanied his patients as a matter of course. Even the chest of Hutter, with all the more valuable of his effects, was borne away, leaving nothing behind that was worth the labor of a removal. Judith was not sorry to see that the captain respected her feelings, and that he occupied himself entirely with the duty of his command, leaving her to her own discretion and feelings. It was understood by all that the place was to be totally abandoned; but beyond this no explanations were asked or given.

The soldiers embarked in the Ark, with the captain at their head. He had enquired of Judith in what way she chose to proceed, and understanding her wish to remain with Hist to the last moment, he neither molested her with requests, nor offended her with advice. There was but one safe and familiar trail to the Mohawk, and on that, at the proper hour, he doubted not that they should meet in amity, if not in renewed intercourse. When all were on board, the sweeps were manned, and the Ark moved in its sluggish manner towards the distant point. Deerslayer and Chingachgook now lifted two of the canoes from the water, and placed them in the castle. The windows and door were then barred, and the house was left by means of the trap, in the manner already described. On quitting the palisades, Hist was seen in the remaining canoe, where the Delaware immediately joined her, and paddled away, leaving Judith standing alone on the platform. Owing to this prompt proceeding, Deerslayer found himself alone with the beautiful and still weeping mourner. Too simple to suspect anything, the young man swept the light boat round, and received its mistress in it, when he followed the course already taken by his friend. The direction to the point led diagonally past, and at no great distance from, the graves of the dead. As the canoe glided by, Judith for the first time that morning spoke to her companion. She said but little; merely uttering a simple request to stop, for a minute or two, ere she left the place.

"I may never see this spot again, Deerslayer," she said, "and it contains the bodies of my mother and sister! Is it not possible, think you, that the innocence of one of these beings may answer in the eyes of God for the salvation of both?"

"I don't understand it so, Judith, though I'm no missionary, and am but poorly taught. Each spirit answers for its own backslidings, though a hearty repentance will satisfy God's laws."

"Then must my poor poor mother be in heaven! Bitterly, bitterly has she repented of her sins, and surely her sufferings in this life ought to count as something against her sufferings in the next!"

"All this goes beyond me, Judith. I strive to do right, here, as the surest means of keeping all right, hereafter. Hetty was oncommon, as all that know'd her must allow, and her soul was as fit to consart with angels the hour it left its body, as that of any saint in the Bible!"

"I do believe you only do her justice! Alas! Alas! that there should be so great differences between those who were nursed at the same breast, slept in the same bed, and dwelt under the same roof! But, no matter—move the canoe, a little farther east, Deerslayer—the sun so dazzles my eyes that I cannot see the graves. This is Hetty's, on the right of mother's?"

"Sartain—you ask'd that of us, and all are glad to do as you wish, Judith, when you do that which is right."

The girl gazed at him near a minute, in silent attention; then she turned her eyes backward, at the castle. "This lake will soon be entirely deserted," she said, "and this, too, at a moment when it will be a more secure dwelling place than ever. What has so lately happened will prevent the Iroquois from venturing again to visit it for a long time to come."

"That it will! Yes, that may be set down as sartain. I do not mean to pass this-a-way, ag'in, so long as the war lasts, for, to my mind no Huron moccasin will leave its print on the leaves of this forest, until their traditions have forgotten to tell their young men of their disgrace and rout."

"And do you so delight in violence and bloodshed? I had thought better of you, Deerslayer— believed you one who could find his happiness in a quiet domestic home, with an attached and loving wife ready to study your wishes, and healthy and dutiful children anxious to follow in your footsteps, and to become as honest and just as yourself."

"Lord, Judith, what a tongue you're mistress of! Speech and looks go hand in hand, like, and what one can't do, the other is pretty sartain to perform! Such a gal, in a month, might spoil the stoutest warrior in the colony."

"And am I then so mistaken? Do you really love war, Deerslayer, better than the hearth, and the affections?"

"I understand your meaning, gal; yes, I do understand what you mean, I believe, though I don't think you altogether understand me. Warrior I may now call myself, I suppose, for I've both fou't and conquered, which is sufficient for the name; neither will I deny that I've feelin's for the callin', which is both manful and honorable when carried on accordin' to nat'ral gifts, but I've no relish for blood. Youth is youth, howsever, and a Mingo is a Mingo. If the young men of this region stood by, and suffered the vagabonds to overrun the land, why, we might as well all turn Frenchers at once, and give up country and kin. I'm no fire eater, Judith, or one that likes fightin' for fightin's sake, but I can see no great difference atween givin' up territory afore a war, out of a dread of war, and givin' it up a'ter a war, because we can't help it, onless it be that the last is the most manful and honorable."

"No woman would ever wish to see her husband or brother stand by and submit to insult and wrong, Deerslayer, however she might mourn the necessity of his running into the dangers of battle. But, you've done enough already, in clearing this region of the Hurons; since to you is principally owing the credit of our late victory. Now, listen to me patiently, and answer me with that native honesty, which it is as pleasant to regard in one of your sex, as it is unusual to meet with."

Judith paused, for now that she was on the very point of explaining herself, native modesty asserted its power, notwithstanding the encouragement and confidence she derived from the great simplicity of her companion's character. Her cheeks, which had so lately been pale, flushed, and her eyes lighted with some of their former brilliancy. Feeling gave expression to her countenance and softness to her voice, rendering her who was always beautiful, trebly seductive and winning.

"Deerslayer," she said, after a considerable pause, "this is not a moment for affectation, deception, or a want of frankness of any sort. Here, over my mother's grave, and over the grave of truth-loving, truth-telling Hetty, everything like unfair dealing seems to be out of place. I will, therefore, speak to you without any reserve, and without any dread of being misunderstood. You are not an acquaintance of a week, but it appears to me as if I had known you for years. So much, and so much that is important has taken place, within that short time, that the sorrows, and dangers, and escapes of a whole life have been crowded into a few days, and they who have suffered and acted together in such scenes, ought not to feel like strangers. I know that what I am about to say might be misunderstood by most men, but I hope for a generous construction of my course from you. We are not here, dwelling among the arts and deceptions of the settlements, but young people who have no occasion to deceive each other, in any manner or form. I hope I make myself understood?"

"Sartain, Judith; few converse better than yourself, and none more agreeable, like. Your words are as pleasant as your looks."

"It is the manner in which you have so often praised those looks, that gives me courage to proceed. Still, Deerslayer, it is not easy for one of my sex and years to forget all her lessons of infancy, all her habits, and her natural diffidence, and say openly what her heart feels!"

"Why not, Judith? Why shouldn't women as well as men deal fairly and honestly by their fellow creatur's? I see no reason why you should not speak as plainly as myself, when there is any thing ra'ally important to be said."

This indomitable diffidence, which still prevented the young man from suspecting the truth, would have completely discouraged the girl, had not her whole soul, as well as her whole heart, been set upon making a desperate effort to rescue herself from a future that she dreaded with a horror as vivid as the distinctness with which she fancied she foresaw it. This motive, however, raised her above all common considerations, and she persevered even to her own surprise, if not to her great confusion.

"I will—I must deal as plainly with you, as I would with poor, dear Hetty, were that sweet child living!" she continued, turning pale instead of blushing, the high resolution by which she was prompted reversing the effect that such a procedure would ordinarily produce on one of her sex; "yes, I will smother all other feelings, in the one that is now uppermost! You love the woods and the life that we pass, here, in the wilderness, away from the dwellings and towns of the whites."

"As I loved my parents, Judith, when they was living! This very spot would be all creation to me, could this war be fairly over, once; and the settlers kept at a distance."

"Why quit it, then? It has no owner—at least none who can claim a better right than mine, and that I freely give to you. Were it a kingdom, Deerslayer, I think I should delight to say the same. Let us then return to it, after we have seen the priest at the fort, and never quit it again, until God calls us away to that world where we shall find the spirits of my poor mother and sister."

A long, thoughtful pause succeeded; Judith here covered her face with both her hands, after forcing herself to utter so plain a proposal, and Deerslayer musing equally in sorrow and surprise, on the meaning of the language he had just heard. At length the hunter broke the silence, speaking in a tone that was softened to gentleness by his desire not to offend.

"You haven't thought well of this, Judith," he said, "no, your feelin's are awakened by all that has lately happened, and believin' yourself to be without kindred in the world, you are in too great haste to find some to fill the places of them that's lost."

"Were I living in a crowd of friends, Deerslayer, I should still think as I now think—say as I now say," returned Judith, speaking with her hands still shading her lovely face.

"Thank you, gal—thank you, from the bottom of my heart. Howsever, I am not one to take advantage of a weak moment, when you're forgetful of your own great advantages, and fancy 'arth and all it holds is in this little canoe. No—no—Judith, 'twould be onginerous in me; what you've offered can never come to pass!"

"It all may be, and that without leaving cause of repentance to any," answered Judith, with an impetuosity of feeling and manner that at once unveiled her eyes. "We can cause the soldiers to leave our goods on the road, till we return, when they can easily be brought back to the house; the lake will be no more visited by the enemy, this war at least; all your skins may be readily sold at the garrison; there you can buy the few necessaries we shall want, for I wish never to see the spot, again; and Deerslayer," added the girl smiling with a sweetness and nature that the young man found it hard to resist, "as a proof how wholly I am and wish to be yours,—how completely I desire to be nothing but your wife, the very first fire that we kindle, after our return, shall be lighted with the brocade dress, and fed by every article I have that you may think unfit for the woman you wish to live with!"

"Ah's me!—you're a winning and a lovely creatur', Judith; yes, you are all that, and no one can deny it and speak truth. These pictur's are pleasant to the thoughts, but they mightn't prove so happy as you now think 'em. Forget it all, therefore, and let us paddle after the Sarpent and Hist, as if nothing had been said on the subject."

Judith was deeply mortified, and, what is more, she was profoundly grieved. Still there was a steadiness and quiet in the manner of Deerslayer that completely smothered her hopes, and told her that for once her exceeding beauty had failed to excite the admiration and homage it was wont to receive. Women are said seldom to forgive those who slight their advances, but this high spirited and impetuous girl entertained no shadow of resentment, then or ever, against the fair dealing and ingenuous hunter. At the moment, the prevailing feeling was the wish to be certain that there was no misunderstanding. After another painful pause, therefore, she brought the matter to an issue by a question too direct to admit of equivocation.

"God forbid that we lay up regrets, in after life, through my want of sincerity now," she said. "I hope we understand each other, at least. You will not accept me for a wife, Deerslayer?"

"'Tis better for both that I shouldn't take advantage of your own forgetfulness, Judith. We can never marry."

"You do not love me,—cannot find it in your heart, perhaps, to esteem me, Deerslayer!"

"Everything in the way of fri'ndship, Judith—everything, even to sarvices and life itself. Yes, I'd risk as much for you, at this moment, as I would risk in behalf of Hist, and that is sayin' as much as I can say of any darter of woman. I do not think I feel towards either—mind I say either, Judith—as if I wished to quit father and mother—if father and mother was livin', which, howsever, neither is—but if both was livin', I do not feel towards any woman as if I wish'd to quit 'em in order to cleave unto her."

"This is enough!" answered Judith, in a rebuked and smothered voice. "I understand all that you mean. Marry you cannot with loving, and that love you do not feel for me. Make no answer, if I am right, for I shall understand your silence. That will be painful enough of itself."

Deerslayer obeyed her, and he made no reply. For more than a minute, the girl riveted her bright eyes on him as if to read his soul, while he was playing with the water like a corrected school boy. Then Judith, herself, dropped the end of her paddle, and urged the canoe away from the spot, with a movement as reluctant as the feelings which controlled it. Deerslayer quietly aided the effort, however, and they were soon on the trackless line taken by the Delaware.

In their way to the point, not another syllable was exchanged between Deerslayer and his fair companion. As Judith sat in the bow of the canoe, her back was turned towards him, else it is probable the expression of her countenance might have induced him to venture some soothing terms of friendship and regard. Contrary to what would have been expected, resentment was still absent, though the colour frequently changed from the deep flush of mortification to the paleness of disappointment. Sorrow, deep, heart-felt sorrow, however, was the predominant emotion, and this was betrayed in a manner not to be mistaken.

As neither labored hard at the paddle, the ark had already arrived and the soldiers had disembarked before the canoe of the two loiterers reached the point. Chingachgook had preceded it, and was already some distance in the wood, at a spot where the two trails, that to the garrison and that to the villages of the Delawares, separated. The soldiers, too, had taken up their line of march, first setting the Ark adrift again, with a reckless disregard of its fate. All this Judith saw, but she heeded it not. The glimmerglass had no longer any charms for her, and when she put her foot on the strand, she immediately proceeded on the trail of the soldiers without casting a single glance behind her. Even Hist was passed unnoticed, that modest young creature shrinking from the averted face of Judith, as if guilty herself of some wrongdoing.

"Wait you here, Sarpent," said Deerslayer as he followed in the footsteps of the dejected beauty, while passing his friend. "I will just see Judith among her party, and come and j'ine you."

A hundred yards had hid the couple from those in front, as well as those in their rear, when Judith turned, and spoke.

"This will do, Deerslayer," she said sadly. "I understand your kindness but shall not need it. In a few minutes I shall reach the soldiers. As you cannot go with me on the journey of life, I do not wish you to go further on this. But, stop—before we part, I would ask you a single question. And I require of you, as you fear God, and reverence the truth, not to deceive me in your answer. I know you do not love another and I can see but one reason why you cannot, will not love me. Tell me then, Deerslayer," The girl paused, the words she was about to utter seeming to choke her. Then rallying all her resolution, with a face that flushed and paled at every breath she drew, she continued.

"Tell me then, Deerslayer, if anything light of me, that Henry March has said, may not have influenced your feelings?"

Truth was the Deerslayer's polar star. He ever kept it in view, and it was nearly impossible for him to avoid uttering it, even when prudence demanded silence. Judith read his answer in his countenance, and with a heart nearly broken by the consciousness of undue erring, she signed to him an adieu, and buried herself in the woods. For some time Deerslayer was irresolute as to his course; but, in the end, he retraced his steps, and joined the Delaware. That night the three camped on the head waters of their own river, and the succeeding evening they entered the village of the tribe, Chingachgook and his betrothed in triumph; their companion honored and admired, but in a sorrow that it required months of activity to remove.

The war that then had its rise was stirring and bloody. The Delaware chief rose among his people, until his name was never mentioned without eulogiums, while another Uncas, the last of his race, was added to the long line of warriors who bore that distinguishing appellation. As for the Deerslayer, under the sobriquet of Hawkeye, he made his fame spread far and near, until the crack of his rifle became as terrible to the ears of the Mingos as the thunders of the Manitou. His services were soon required by the officers of the crown, and he especially attached himself in the field to one in particular, with whose after life he had a close and important connection.

Fifteen years had passed away, ere it was in the power of the Deerslayer to revisit the Glimmerglass. A peace had intervened, and it was on the eve of another and still more important war, when he and his constant friend, Chingachgook, were hastening to the forts to join their allies. A stripling accompanied them, for Hist already slumbered beneath the pines of the Delawares, and the three survivors had now become inseparable. They reached the lake just as the sun was setting. Here all was unchanged. The river still rushed through its bower of trees; the little rock was washing away, by the slow action of the waves, in the course of centuries, the mountains stood in their native dress, dark, rich and mysterious, while the sheet glistened in its solitude, a beautiful gem of the forest.

The following morning, the youth discovered one of the canoes drifted on the shore, in a state of decay. A little labor put it in a state for service, and they all embarked, with a desire to examine the place. All the points were passed, and Chingachgook pointed out to his son the spot where the Hurons had first encamped, and the point whence he had succeeded in stealing his bride. Here they even landed, but all traces of the former visit had disappeared. Next they proceeded to the scene of the battle, and there they found a few of the signs that linger around such localities. Wild beasts had disinterred many of the bodies, and human bones were bleaching in the rains of summer. Uncas regarded all with reverence and pity, though traditions were already rousing his young mind to the ambition and sternness of a warrior.

From the point, the canoe took its way toward the shoal, where the remains of the castle were still visible, a picturesque ruin. The storms of winter had long since unroofed the house, and decay had eaten into the logs. All the fastenings were untouched, but the seasons rioted in the place, as if in mockery at the attempt to exclude them. The palisades were rotting, as were the piles, and it was evident that a few more recurrences of winter, a few more gales and tempests, would sweep all into the lake, and blot the building from the face of that magnificent solitude. The graves could not be found. Either the elements had obliterated their traces, or time had caused those who looked for them to forget their position.

The Ark was discovered stranded on the eastern shore, where it had long before been driven with the prevalent northwest winds. It lay on the sandy extremity of a long low point, that is situated about two miles from the outlet, and which is itself fast disappearing before the action of the elements. The scow was filled with water, the cabin unroofed, and the logs were decaying. Some of its coarser furniture still remained, and the heart of Deerslayer beat quick, as he found a ribbon of Judith's fluttering from a log. It recalled all her beauty, and we may add all her failings. Although the girl had never touched his heart, the Hawkeye, for so we ought now to call him, still retained a kind and sincere interest in her welfare. He tore away the ribbon, and knotted it to the stock of Killdeer, which had been the gift of the girl herself.

A few miles farther up the lake, another of the canoes was discovered, and on the point where the party finally landed, were found those which had been left there upon the shore. That in which the present navigation was made, and the one discovered on the eastern shore, had dropped through the decayed floor of the castle, drifted past the falling palisades, and had been thrown as waifs upon the beach.

From all these signs, it was probable the lake had not been visited since the occurrence of the final scene of our tale. Accident or tradition had rendered it again a spot sacred to nature, the frequent wars and the feeble population of the colonies still confining the settlements within narrow boundaries. Chingachgook and his friend left the spot with melancholy feelings. It had been the region of their First War Path, and it carried back the minds of both to scenes of tenderness, as well as to hours of triumph. They held their way towards the Mohawk in silence, however, to rush into new adventures, as stirring and as remarkable as those which had attended their opening careers on this lovely lake. At a later day they returned to the place, where the Indian found a grave.

Time and circumstances have drawn an impenetrable mystery around all else connected with the Hutters. They lived, erred, died, and are forgotten. None connected have felt sufficient interest in the disgraced and disgracing to withdraw the veil, and a century is about to erase even the recollection of their names. The history of crime is ever revolting, and it is fortunate that few love to dwell on its incidents. The sins of the family have long since been arraigned at the judgment seat of God, or are registered for the terrible settlement of the last great day.

The same fate attended Judith. When Hawkeye reached the garrison on the Mohawk he enquired anxiously after that lovely but misguided creature. None knew her—even her person was no longer remembered. Other officers had, again and again, succeeded the Warleys and Craigs and Grahams, though an old sergeant of the garrison, who had lately come from England, was enabled to tell our hero that Sir Robert Warley lived on his paternal estates, and that there was a lady of rare beauty in the Lodge who had great influence over him, though she did not bear his name. Whether this was Judith relapsed into her early failing, or some other victim of the soldier's, Hawkeye never knew, nor would it be pleasant or profitable to inquire. We live in a world of transgressions and selfishness, and no pictures that represent us otherwise can be true, though, happily, for human nature, gleamings of that pure spirit in whose likeness man has been fashioned are to be seen, relieving its deformities, and mitigating if not excusing its crimes.

# THE LAST OF THE MOHICANS: A NARRATIVE OF 1757

## INTRODUCTION.

T is believed that the scene of this tale, and most of the information necessary to understand its allusions, are rendered sufficiently obvious to the reader in the text itself, or in the accompanying notes. Still there is so much obscurity in the Indian traditions, and so much confusion in the Indian names, as to render some explanation useful.

Few men exhibit greater diversity, or, if we may so express it, greater antithesis of character, than the native warrior of North America. In war, he is daring, boastful, cunning, ruthless, self-denying, and self-devoted; in peace, just, generous, hospitable, revengeful, superstitious, modest, and commonly chaste. These are qualities, it is true, which do not distinguish all alike; but they are so far the predominating traits of these remarkable people as to be characteristic.

It is generally believed that the Aborigines of the American continent have an Asiatic origin. There are many physical as well as moral facts which corroborate this opinion, and some few that would seem to weigh against it.

The color of the Indian, the writer believes, is peculiar to himself, and while his cheek-bones have a very striking indication of a Tartar origin, his eyes have not. Climate may have had great influence on the former, but it is difficult to see how it can have produced the substantial difference which exists in the latter. The imagery of the Indian, both in his poetry and in his oratory, is oriental; chastened, and perhaps improved, by the limited range of his practical knowledge. He draws his metaphors from the clouds, the seasons, the birds, the beasts, and the vegetable world. In this, perhaps, he does no more than any other energetic and imaginative race would do, being compelled to set bounds to fancy by experience; but the North American Indian clothes his ideas in a dress which is different from that of the African, and is oriental in itself. His language has the richness and sententious fullness of the Chinese. He will express a phrase in a word, and he will qualify the meaning of an entire sentence by a syllable; he will even convey different significations by the simplest inflections of the voice.

Philologists have said that there are but two or three languages, properly speaking, among all the numerous tribes which formerly occupied the country that now composes the United States. They ascribe the known difficulty one people have to understand another to corruptions and dialects. The writer remembers to have been present at an interview between two chiefs of the Great Prairies west of the Mississippi, and when an interpreter was in attendance who spoke both their languages. The warriors appeared to be on the most friendly terms, and seemingly conversed much together; yet, according to the account of the interpreter, each was absolutely ignorant of what the other said. They were of hostile tribes, brought together by the influence of the American government; and it is worthy of remark, that a common policy led them both to adopt the same subject. They mutually exhorted each other to be of use in the event of the chances of war throwing either of the parties into the hands of his enemies. Whatever may be the truth, as respects the root and the genius of the Indian tongues, it is quite certain they are now so distinct in their words as to possess most of the disadvantages of strange languages; hence much of the embarrassment that has arisen in learning their histories, and most of the uncertainty which exists in their traditions.

Like nations of higher pretensions, the American Indian gives a very different account of his own tribe or race from that which is given by other people. He is much addicted to overestimating his own perfections, and to undervaluing those of his rival or his enemy; a trait which may possibly be thought corroborative of the Mosaic account of the creation.

The whites have assisted greatly in rendering the traditions of the Aborigines more obscure by their own manner of corrupting names. Thus, the term used in the title of this book has undergone the changes of Mahicanni, Mohicans, and Mohegans; the latter being the word commonly used by the whites. When it is remembered that the Dutch (who first settled New York), the English, and the French, all gave appellations to the tribes that dwelt within the country which is the scene of this story, and that the Indians not only gave different names to their enemies, but frequently to themselves, the cause of the confusion will be understood.

In these pages, Lenni-Lenape, Lenope, Delawares, Wapanachki, and Mohicans, all mean the same people, or tribes of the same stock. The Mengwe, the Maquas, the Mingoes, and the Iroquois, though not all strictly the same, are identified frequently by the speakers, being politically confederated and opposed to those just named. Mingo was a term of peculiar reproach, as were Mengwe and Maqua in a less degree.

The Mohicans were the possessors of the country first occupied by the Europeans in this portion of the continent. They were, consequently, the first dispossessed; and the seemingly inevitable fate of all these people, who disappear before the advances, or it might be termed the inroads, of civilization, as the verdure of their native forests falls before the nipping frosts, is represented as having already befallen them. There is sufficient historical truth in the picture to justify the use that has been made of it.

In point of fact, the country which is the scene of the following tale has undergone as little change, since the historical events alluded to had place, as almost any other district of equal extent within the whole limits of the United States. There are fashionable and well-attended watering-places at and near the spring where Hawkeye halted to drink, and roads traverse the forests where he and his friends were compelled to journey without even a path. Glen's has a large village; and while William Henry, and even a fortress of later date, are only to be traced as ruins, there is another village on the shores of the Horican. But, beyond this, the enterprise and energy of a people who have done so much in other places have done little here. The whole of that wilderness, in which the latter incidents of the legend occurred, is nearly a wilderness still, though the red man has entirely deserted this part of the state. Of all the tribes named in these pages, there exist only a few half-civilized beings of the Oneidas, on the reservations of their people in New York. The rest have disappeared, either from the regions in which their fathers dwelt, or altogether from the earth.

There is one point on which we would wish to say a word before closing this preface. Hawkeye calls the Lac du Saint Sacrement, the "Horican." As we believe this to be an appropriation of the name that has its origin with ourselves, the time has arrived, perhaps, when the fact should be frankly admitted. While writing this book, fully a quarter of a century since, it occurred to us that the French name of this lake was too complicated, the American too commonplace, and the Indian too unpronounceable, for either to be used familiarly in a work of fiction. Looking over an ancient map, it was ascertained that a tribe of Indians, called "Les Horicans" by the French, existed in the neighborhood of this beautiful sheet of water. As every word uttered by Natty Bumppo was not to be received as rigid truth, we took the liberty of putting the "Horican" into his mouth, as the substitute for "Lake George." The name has appeared to find favor, and all things considered, it may possibly be quite as well to let it stand, instead of going back to the House of Hanover for the appellation of our finest sheet of water. We relieve our conscience by the confession, at all events leaving it to exercise its authority as it may see fit.

## CHAPTER I.

> "Mine ear is open, and my heart prepared:
> The worst is wordly loss thou canst unfold:—
> Say, is my kingdom lost?"—Shakespeare

I**T** was a feature peculiar to the colonial wars of North America, that the toils and dangers of the wilderness were to be encountered before the adverse hosts could meet. A wide and apparently an impervious boundary of forests severed the possessions of the hostile provinces of France and England. The hardy colonist, and the trained European who fought at his side, frequently expended months in struggling against the rapids of the streams, or in effecting the rugged passes of the mountains, in quest of an opportunity to exhibit their courage in a more martial conflict. But, emulating the patience and self-denial of the practiced native warriors, they learned to overcome every difficulty; and it would seem that, in time, there was no recess of the woods so dark, nor any secret place so lovely, that it might claim exemption from the inroads of those who had pledged their blood to satiate their vengeance, or to uphold the cold and selfish policy of the distant monarchs of Europe.

Perhaps no district throughout the wide extent of the intermediate frontiers can furnish a livelier picture of the cruelty and fierceness of the savage warfare of those periods than the country which lies between the head waters of the Hudson and the adjacent lakes.

The facilities which nature had there offered to the march of the combatants were too obvious to be neglected. The lengthened sheet of the Champlain stretched from the frontiers of Canada, deep within the borders of the neighboring province of New York, forming a natural passage across half the distance that the French were compelled to master in order to strike their enemies. Near its southern termination, it received the contributions of another lake, whose waters were so limpid as to have been exclusively selected by the Jesuit missionaries to perform the typical purification of baptism, and to obtain for it the title of lake "du Saint Sacrement." The less zealous English thought they conferred a sufficient honor on its unsullied fountains, when they bestowed the name of their reigning prince, the second of the house of Hanover. The two united to rob the untutored possessors of its wooded scenery of their native right to perpetuate its original appellation of "Horican."*

---

* As each nation of the Indians had its language or its dialect, they usually gave different names to the same places, though nearly all of their appellations were descriptive of the object. Thus a literal translation of the name of this beautiful sheet of water, used by the tribe that dwelt on its banks, would be "The Tail of the Lake." Lake George, as it is vulgarly, and now, indeed, legally, called, forms a sort of tail to Lake Champlain, when viewed on the map. Hence, the name.

Winding its way among countless islands, and imbedded in mountains, the "holy lake" extended a dozen leagues still further to the south. With the high plain that there interposed itself to the further passage of the water, commenced a portage of as many miles, which conducted the adventurer to the banks of the Hudson, at a point where, with the usual obstructions of the rapids, or rifts, as they were then termed in the language of the country, the river became navigable to the tide.

While, in the pursuit of their daring plans of annoyance, the restless enterprise of the French even attempted the distant and difficult gorges of the Alleghany, it may easily be imagined that their proverbial acuteness would not overlook the natural advantages of the district we have just described. It became, emphatically, the bloody arena, in which most of the battles for the mastery of the colonies were contested. Forts were erected at the different points that commanded the facilities of the route, and were taken and retaken, razed and rebuilt, as victory alighted on the hostile banners. While the husbandman shrank back from the dangerous passes, within the safer boundaries of the more ancient settlements, armies larger than those that had often disposed of the scepters of the mother countries, were seen to bury themselves in these forests, whence they rarely returned but in skeleton bands, that were haggard with care or dejected by defeat. Though the arts of peace were unknown to this fatal region, its forests were alive with men; its shades and glens rang with the sounds of martial music, and the echoes of its mountains threw back the laugh, or repeated the wanton cry, of many a gallant and reckless youth, as he hurried by them, in the noontide of his spirits, to slumber in a long night of forgetfulness.

It was in this scene of strife and bloodshed that the incidents we shall attempt to relate occurred, during the third year of the war which England and France last waged for the possession of a country that neither was destined to retain.

The imbecility of her military leaders abroad, and the fatal want of energy in her councils at home, had lowered the character of Great Britain from the proud elevation on which it had been placed by the talents and enterprise of her former warriors and statesmen. No longer dreaded by her enemies, her servants were fast losing the confidence of self-respect. In this mortifying abasement, the colonists, though innocent of her imbecility, and too humble to be the agents of her blunders, were but the natural participators. They had recently seen a chosen army from that country, which, reverencing as a mother, they had blindly believed invincible—an army led by a chief who had been selected from a crowd of trained warriors, for his rare military endowments, disgracefully routed by a handful of French and Indians, and only saved from annihilation by the coolness and spirit of a Virginian boy, whose riper fame has since diffused itself, with the steady influence of moral truth, to the uttermost confines of Christendom.[*] A wide frontier had been laid naked by this unexpected disaster, and more substantial evils were preceded by a thousand fanciful and imaginary dangers. The alarmed colonists believed that the yells of the savages mingled with every fitful gust of wind that

---

[*] Washington, who, after uselessly admonishing the European general of the danger into which he was heedlessly running, saved the remnants of the British army, on this occasion, by his decision and courage. The reputation earned by Washington in this battle was the principal cause of his being selected to command the American armies at a later day. It is a circumstance worthy of observation, that while all America rang with his well-merited reputation, his name does not occur in any European account of the battle; at least the author has searched for it without success. In this manner does the mother country absorb even the fame, under that system of rule.

issued from the interminable forests of the west. The terrific character of their merciless enemies increased immeasurably the natural horrors of warfare. Numberless recent massacres were still vivid in their recollections; nor was there any ear in the provinces so deaf as not to have drunk in with avidity the narrative of some fearful tale of midnight murder, in which the natives of the forests were the principal and barbarous actors. As the credulous and excited traveler related the hazardous chances of the wilderness, the blood of the timid curdled with terror, and mothers cast anxious glances even at those children which slumbered within the security of the largest towns. In short, the magnifying influence of fear began to set at naught the calculations of reason, and to render those who should have remembered their manhood, the slaves of the basest passions. Even the most confident and the stoutest hearts began to think the issue of the contest was becoming doubtful; and that abject class was hourly increasing in numbers, who thought they foresaw all the possessions of the English crown in America subdued by their Christian foes, or laid waste by the inroads of their relentless allies.

When, therefore, intelligence was received at the fort which covered the southern termination of the portage between the Hudson and the lakes, that Montcalm had been seen moving up the Champlain, with an army "numerous as the leaves on the trees," its truth was admitted with more of the craven reluctance of fear than with the stern joy that a warrior should feel, in finding an enemy within reach of his blow. The news had been brought, toward the decline of a day in midsummer, by an Indian runner, who also bore an urgent request from Munro, the commander of a work on the shore of the "holy lake," for a speedy and powerful reinforcement. It has already been mentioned that the distance between these two posts was less than five leagues. The rude path, which originally formed their line of communication, had been widened for the passage of wagons; so that the distance which had been traveled by the son of the forest in two hours, might easily be effected by a detachment of troops, with their necessary baggage, between the rising and setting of a summer sun. The loyal servants of the British crown had given to one of these forest-fastnesses the name of William Henry, and to the other that of Fort Edward, calling each after a favorite prince of the reigning family. The veteran Scotchman just named held the first, with a regiment of regulars and a few provincials; a force really by far too small to make head against the formidable power that Montcalm was leading to the foot of his earthen mounds. At the latter, however, lay General Webb, who commanded the armies of the king in the northern provinces, with a body of more than five thousand men. By uniting the several detachments of his command, this officer might have arrayed nearly double that number of combatants against the enterprising Frenchman, who had ventured so far from his reinforcements, with an army but little superior in numbers.

But under the influence of their degraded fortunes, both officers and men appeared better disposed to await the approach of their formidable antagonists, within their works, than to resist the progress of their march, by emulating the successful example of the French at Fort du Quesne, and striking a blow on their advance.

After the first surprise of the intelligence had a little abated, a rumor was spread through the entrenched camp, which stretched along the margin of the Hudson, forming a chain of outworks to the body of the fort itself, that a chosen detachment of fifteen hundred men was to depart, with the dawn, for William Henry, the post at the northern extremity of the portage. That which at first was only rumor, soon became certainty, as orders passed from the quarters of the commander-in-chief to the several corps he had selected for this service, to prepare for their speedy departure. All doubts as to the intention of Webb now vanished, and an hour or two of hurried footsteps and anxious faces succeeded. The novice in the military art flew from point to point, retarding his own preparations by the excess of his violent and somewhat distempered zeal; while the more practiced veteran made his arrangements with a deliberation that scorned every appearance of haste; though his sober lineaments and anxious eye sufficiently betrayed that he had no very strong professional relish for the, as yet, untried and dreaded warfare of the wilderness. At length the sun set in a flood of glory, behind the distant western hills, and as darkness drew its veil around the secluded spot the sounds of preparation diminished; the last light finally disappeared from the log cabin of some officer; the trees cast their deeper shadows over the mounds and the rippling stream, and a silence soon pervaded the camp, as deep as that which reigned in the vast forest by which it was environed.

According to the orders of the preceding night, the heavy sleep of the army was broken by the rolling of the warning drums, whose rattling echoes were heard issuing, on the damp morning air, out of every vista of the woods, just as day began to draw the shaggy outlines of some tall pines of the vicinity, on the opening brightness of a soft and cloudless eastern sky. In an instant the whole camp was in motion; the meanest soldier arousing from his lair to witness the departure of his comrades, and to share in the excitement and incidents of the hour. The simple array of the chosen band was soon completed. While the regular and trained hirelings of the king marched with haughtiness to the right of the line, the less pretending colonists took their humbler position on its left, with a docility that long practice had rendered easy. The scouts departed; strong guards preceded and followed the lumbering vehicles that bore the baggage; and before the gray light of the morning was mellowed by the rays of the sun, the main body of the combatants wheeled into column, and left the encampment with a show of high military bearing, that served to drown the slumbering apprehensions of many a novice, who was now about to make his first essay in arms. While in view of their admiring comrades, the same proud front and ordered array was observed, until the notes of their fifes growing fainter in distance, the forest at length appeared to swallow up the living mass which had slowly entered its bosom.

The deepest sounds of the retiring and invisible column had ceased to be borne on the breeze to the listeners, and the latest straggler had already disappeared in pursuit; but there still remained the signs of another departure, before a log cabin of unusual size and accommodations, in front of which those sentinels paced their rounds, who were known to guard the person of the English general. At this spot were gathered some half dozen horses, caparisoned in a manner which showed that two, at least, were destined to bear the persons of females, of a rank that it was not usual to meet so far in the wilds of the country. A third wore trappings and arms of an officer of the staff; while the rest, from the plainness of the housings, and the traveling mails with which they were encumbered, were evidently fitted for the reception of as many menials, who were, seemingly, already waiting the pleasure of those they served. At a respectful distance from this unusual show, were gathered divers groups of curious idlers; some admiring the blood and bone of the high-mettled military charger, and others gazing at the preparations, with the dull wonder of vulgar curiosity. There was one man, however, who, by his countenance and actions, formed a marked exception to those who composed the latter class of spectators, being neither idle, nor seemingly very ignorant.

The person of this individual was to the last degree ungainly, without being in any particular manner deformed. He had all the bones and joints of other men, without any of their proportions. Erect, his stature surpassed that of his fellows; though seated, he appeared reduced within the ordinary limits of the race. The same contrariety in his members seemed to exist throughout the whole man. His head was large; his shoulders narrow; his arms long and dangling; while his hands were small, if not delicate. His legs and thighs were thin, nearly to emaciation, but of extraordinary length; and his knees would have been considered tremendous, had they not been outdone by the broader foundations on which this false superstructure of blended human orders was so profanely reared. The ill-assorted and injudicious attire of the individual only served to render his awkwardness more conspicuous. A sky-blue coat, with short and broad skirts and low cape, exposed a long, thin neck, and longer and thinner legs, to the worst animadversions of the evil-disposed. His nether garment was a yellow nankeen, closely fitted to the shape, and tied at his bunches of knees by large knots of white ribbon, a good deal sullied by use. Clouded cotton stockings, and shoes, on one of the latter of which was a plated spur, completed the costume of the lower extremity of this figure, no curve or angle of which was concealed, but, on the other hand, studiously exhibited, through the vanity or simplicity of its owner.

From beneath the flap of an enormous pocket of a soiled vest of embossed silk, heavily ornamented with tarnished silver lace, projected an instrument, which, from being seen in such martial company, might have been easily mistaken for some mischievous and unknown implement of war. Small as it was, this uncommon engine had excited the curiosity of most of the Europeans in the camp, though several of the provincials were seen to handle it, not only without fear, but with the utmost familiarity. A large, civil cocked hat, like those worn by clergymen within the last thirty years, surmounted the whole, furnishing dignity to a good-natured and somewhat vacant countenance, that apparently needed such artificial aid, to support the gravity of some high and extraordinary trust.

While the common herd stood aloof, in deference to the quarters of Webb, the figure we have described stalked into the center of the domestics, freely expressing his censures or commendations on the merits of the horses, as by chance they displeased or satisfied his judgment.

"This beast, I rather conclude, friend, is not of home raising, but is from foreign lands, or perhaps from the little island itself over the blue water?" he said, in a voice as remarkable for the softness and sweetness of its tones, as was his person for its rare proportions; "I may speak of these things, and be no braggart; for I have been down at both havens; that which is situate at the mouth of Thames, and is named after the capital of Old England, and that which is called 'Haven', with the addition of the word 'New'; and have seen the scows and brigantines collecting their droves, like the gathering to the ark, being outward bound to the Island of Jamaica, for the purpose of barter and traffic in four-footed animals; but never before have I beheld a beast which verified the true scripture war-horse like this: 'He paweth in the valley, and rejoiceth in his strength; he goeth on to meet the armed men. He saith among the trumpets, Ha, ha; and he smelleth the battle afar off, the thunder of the captains, and the shouting' It would seem that the stock of the horse of Israel had descended to our own time; would it not, friend?"

Receiving no reply to this extraordinary appeal, which in truth, as it was delivered with the vigor of full and sonorous tones, merited some sort of notice, he who had thus sung forth the language of the holy book turned to the silent figure to whom he had unwittingly addressed himself, and found a new and more powerful subject of admiration in the object that encountered his gaze. His eyes fell on the still, upright, and rigid form of the "Indian runner," who had borne to the camp the unwelcome tidings of the preceding evening. Although in a state of perfect repose, and apparently disregarding, with characteristic stoicism, the excitement and bustle around him, there was a sullen fierceness mingled with the quiet of the savage, that was likely to arrest the attention of much more experienced eyes than those which now scanned him, in unconcealed amazement. The native bore both the tomahawk and knife of his tribe; and yet his appearance was not altogether that of a warrior. On the contrary, there was an air of neglect about his person, like that which might have proceeded from great and recent exertion, which he had not yet found leisure to repair. The colors of the war-paint had blended in dark confusion about his fierce countenance, and rendered his swarthy lineaments still more savage and repulsive than if art had attempted an effect which had been thus produced by chance. His eye, alone, which glistened like a fiery star amid lowering clouds, was to be seen in its state of native wildness. For a single instant his searching and yet wary glance met the wondering look of the other, and then changing its direction, partly in cunning, and partly in disdain, it remained fixed, as if penetrating the distant air.

It is impossible to say what unlooked-for remark this short and silent communication, between two such singular men, might have elicited from the white man, had not his active curiosity been again drawn to other objects. A general movement among the domestics, and a low sound of gentle voices, announced the approach of those whose presence alone was wanted to enable the cavalcade to move. The simple admirer of the war-horse instantly fell back to a low, gaunt, switch-tailed mare, that was unconsciously gleaning the faded herbage of the camp nigh by; where, leaning with one elbow on the blanket that concealed an apology for a saddle, he became a spectator of the departure, while a foal was quietly making its morning repast, on the opposite side of the same animal.

A young man, in the dress of an officer, conducted to their steeds two females, who, as it was apparent by their dresses, were prepared to encounter the fatigues of a journey in the woods. One, and she was the more juvenile in her appearance, though both were young, permitted glimpses of her dazzling complexion, fair golden hair, and bright blue eyes, to be caught, as she artlessly suffered the morning air to blow aside the green veil which descended low from her beaver.

The flush which still lingered above the pines in the western sky was not more bright nor delicate than the bloom on her cheek; nor was the opening day more cheering than the animated smile which she bestowed on the youth, as he assisted her into the saddle. The other, who appeared to share equally in the attention of the young officer, concealed her charms from the gaze of the soldiery with a care that seemed better fitted to the experience of four or five additional years. It could be seen, however, that her person, though molded with the same exquisite proportions, of which none of the graces were lost by the traveling dress she wore, was rather fuller and more mature than that of her companion.

No sooner were these females seated, than their attendant sprang lightly into the saddle of the war-horse, when the whole three bowed to Webb, who in courtesy, awaited their parting on the threshold of his cabin and turning their horses' heads, they proceeded at a slow amble, followed by their train, toward the northern entrance of the encampment. As they traversed that short distance, not a voice was heard among them; but a slight exclamation proceeded from the younger of the females, as the Indian runner glided by her, unexpectedly, and led the way along the military road in her front. Though this sudden and startling movement of the Indian produced no sound from the other, in the surprise her veil also was allowed to open its folds, and betrayed an indescribable look of pity, admiration, and horror, as her dark eye followed the easy motions of the savage. The tresses of this lady were shining and black, like the plumage of the raven. Her complexion was not brown, but it rather appeared charged with the color of the rich blood, that seemed ready to burst its bounds. And yet there was neither coarseness nor want of shadowing in a countenance that was exquisitely regular, and dignified and surpassingly beautiful. She smiled, as if in pity at her own momentary forgetfulness, discovering by the act a row of teeth that would have shamed the purest ivory; when, replacing the veil, she bowed her face, and rode in silence, like one whose thoughts were abstracted from the scene around her.

CHAPTER II.

"Sola, sola, wo ha, ho, sola!"
—Shakespeare

While one of the lovely beings we have so cursorily presented to the reader was thus lost in thought, the other quickly recovered from the alarm which induced the exclamation, and, laughing at her own weakness, she inquired of the youth who rode by her side:

"Are such specters frequent in the woods, Heyward, or is this sight an especial entertainment ordered on our behalf? If the latter, gratitude must close our mouths; but if the former, both Cora and I shall have need to draw largely on that stock of hereditary courage which we boast, even before we are made to encounter the redoubtable Montcalm."

"Yon Indian is a 'runner' of the army; and, after the fashion of his people, he may be accounted a hero," returned the officer. "He has volunteered to guide us to the lake, by a path but little known, sooner than if we followed the tardy movements of the column; and, by consequence, more agreeably."

"I like him not," said the lady, shuddering, partly in assumed, yet more in real terror. "You know him, Duncan, or you would not trust yourself so freely to his keeping?"

"Say, rather, Alice, that I would not trust you. I do know him, or he would not have my confidence, and least of all at this moment. He is said to be a Canadian too; and yet he served with our friends the Mohawks, who, as you know, are one of the six allied nations. He was brought among us, as I have heard, by some strange accident in which your father was interested, and in which the savage was rigidly dealt by; but I forget the idle tale, it is enough, that he is now our friend."

"If he has been my father's enemy, I like him still less!" exclaimed the now really anxious girl. "Will you not speak to him, Major Heyward, that I may hear his tones? Foolish though it may be, you have often heard me avow my faith in the tones of the human voice!"

"It would be in vain; and answered, most probably, by an ejaculation. Though he may understand it, he affects, like most of his people, to be ignorant of the English; and least of all will he condescend to speak it, now that the war demands the utmost exercise of his dignity. But he stops; the private path by which we are to journey is, doubtless, at hand."

The conjecture of Major Heyward was true. When they reached the spot where the Indian stood, pointing into the thicket that fringed the military road; a narrow and blind path, which might, with some little inconvenience, receive one person at a time, became visible.

"Here, then, lies our way," said the young man, in a low voice. "Manifest no distrust, or you may invite the danger you appear to apprehend."

"Cora, what think you?" asked the reluctant fair one. "If we journey with the troops, though we may find their presence irksome, shall we not feel better assurance of our safety?"

"Being little accustomed to the practices of the savages, Alice, you mistake the place of real danger," said Heyward. "If enemies have reached the portage at all, a thing by no means probable, as our scouts are abroad, they will surely be found skirting the column, where scalps abound the most. The route of the detachment is known, while ours, having been determined within the hour, must still be secret."

"Should we distrust the man because his manners are not our manners, and that his skin is dark?" coldly asked Cora.

Alice hesitated no longer; but giving her Narrangansett* a smart cut of the whip, she was the first to dash aside the slight branches of the bushes, and to follow the runner along the dark and tangled pathway. The young man regarded the last speaker in open admiration, and even permitted her fairer, though certainly not more beautiful companion, to proceed unattended, while he sedulously opened the way himself for the passage of her who has been called Cora. It would seem that the domestics had been previously instructed; for, instead of penetrating the thicket, they followed the route of the column; a measure which Heyward stated had been dictated by the sagacity of their guide, in order to diminish the marks of their trail, if, haply, the Canadian savages should be lurking so far in advance of their army. For many minutes the intricacy of the route admitted of no further dialogue; after which they emerged from the broad border of underbrush which grew along the line of the highway, and entered under the high but dark arches of the forest. Here their progress was less interrupted; and the instant the guide perceived that the females could command their steeds, he moved on, at a pace between a trot and a walk, and at a rate which kept the sure-footed and peculiar animals they rode at a fast yet easy amble. The youth had turned to speak to the dark-eyed Cora, when the distant sound of horses hoofs, clattering over the roots of the broken way in his rear, caused him to check his charger; and, as his companions drew their reins at the same instant, the whole party came to a halt, in order to obtain an explanation of the unlooked-for interruption.

In a few moments a colt was seen gliding, like a fallow deer, among the straight trunks of the pines; and, in another instant, the person of the ungainly man, described in the preceding chapter, came into view, with as much rapidity as he could excite his meager beast to endure without coming to an open rupture. Until now this personage had escaped the observation of the travelers. If he possessed the power to arrest any wandering eye when exhibiting the glories of his altitude on foot, his equestrian graces were still more likely to attract attention.

Notwithstanding a constant application of his one armed heel to the flanks of the mare, the most confirmed gait that he could establish was a Canterbury gallop with the hind legs, in which those more forward assisted for doubtful moments, though generally content to maintain a loping trot. Perhaps the rapidity of the changes from one of these paces to the other created an optical illusion, which might thus magnify the powers of the beast; for it is certain that Heyward, who possessed a true eye for the merits of a horse, was unable, with his utmost ingenuity, to decide by what sort of movement his pursuer worked his sinuous way on his footsteps with such persevering hardihood.

The industry and movements of the rider were not less remarkable than those of the ridden. At each change in the evolutions of the latter, the former raised his tall person in the stirrups; producing, in this manner, by the undue elongation of his legs, such sudden growths and diminishings of the stature, as baffled every conjecture that might be made as to his dimensions. If to this be added the fact that, in consequence of the ex parte application of the spur, one side of the mare appeared to

---

* In the state of Rhode Island there is a bay called Narragansett, so named after a powerful tribe of Indians, which formerly dwelt on its banks. Accident, or one of those unaccountable freaks which nature sometimes plays in the animal world, gave rise to a breed of horses which were once well known in America, and distinguished by their habit of pacing. Horses of this race were, and are still, in much request as saddle horses, on account of their hardiness and the ease of their movements. As they were also sure of foot, the Narragansetts were greatly sought for by females who were obliged to travel over the roots and holes in the "new countries."

journey faster than the other; and that the aggrieved flank was resolutely indicated by unremitted flourishes of a bushy tail, we finish the picture of both horse and man.

The frown which had gathered around the handsome, open, and manly brow of Heyward, gradually relaxed, and his lips curled into a slight smile, as he regarded the stranger. Alice made no very powerful effort to control her merriment; and even the dark, thoughtful eye of Cora lighted with a humor that it would seem, the habit, rather than the nature, of its mistress repressed.

"Seek you any here?" demanded Heyward, when the other had arrived sufficiently nigh to abate his speed; "I trust you are no messenger of evil tidings?"

"Even so," replied the stranger, making diligent use of his triangular castor, to produce a circulation in the close air of the woods, and leaving his hearers in doubt to which of the young man's questions he responded; when, however, he had cooled his face, and recovered his breath, he continued, "I hear you are riding to William Henry; as I am journeying thitherward myself, I concluded good company would seem consistent to the wishes of both parties."

"You appear to possess the privilege of a casting vote," returned Heyward; "we are three, while you have consulted no one but yourself."

"Even so. The first point to be obtained is to know one's own mind. Once sure of that, and where women are concerned it is not easy, the next is, to act up to the decision. I have endeavored to do both, and here I am."

"If you journey to the lake, you have mistaken your route," said Heyward, haughtily; "the highway thither is at least half a mile behind you."

"Even so," returned the stranger, nothing daunted by this cold reception; "I have tarried at 'Edward' a week, and I should be dumb not to have inquired the road I was to journey; and if dumb there would be an end to my calling." After simpering in a small way, like one whose modesty prohibited a more open expression of his admiration of a witticism that was perfectly unintelligible to his hearers, he continued, "It is not prudent for any one of my profession to be too familiar with those he has to instruct; for which reason I follow not the line of the army; besides which, I conclude that a gentleman of your character has the best judgment in matters of wayfaring; I have, therefore, decided to join company, in order that the ride may be made agreable, and partake of social communion."

"A most arbitrary, if not a hasty decision!" exclaimed Heyward, undecided whether to give vent to his growing anger, or to laugh in the other's face. "But you speak of instruction, and of a profession; are you an adjunct to the provincial corps, as a master of the noble science of defense and offense; or, perhaps, you are one who draws lines and angles, under the pretense of expounding the mathematics?"

The stranger regarded his interrogator a moment in wonder; and then, losing every mark of self-satisfaction in an expression of solemn humility, he answered:

"Of offense, I hope there is none, to either party: of defense, I make none—by God's good mercy, having committed no palpable sin since last entreating his pardoning grace. I understand not your allusions about lines and angles; and I leave expounding to those who have been called and set apart for that holy office. I lay claim to no higher gift than a small insight into the glorious art of petitioning and thanksgiving, as practiced in psalmody."

"The man is, most manifestly, a disciple of Apollo," cried the amused Alice, "and I take him under my own especial protection. Nay, throw aside that frown, Heyward, and in pity to my longing ears, suffer him to journey in our train. Besides," she added, in a low and hurried voice, casting a glance at the distant Cora, who slowly followed the footsteps of their silent, but sullen guide, "it may be a friend added to our strength, in time of need."

"Think you, Alice, that I would trust those I love by this secret path, did I imagine such need could happen?"

"Nay, nay, I think not of it now; but this strange man amuses me; and if he 'hath music in his soul', let us not churlishly reject his company." She pointed persuasively along the path with her riding whip, while their eyes met in a look which the young man lingered a moment to prolong; then, yielding to her gentle influence, he clapped his spurs into his charger, and in a few bounds was again at the side of Cora.

"I am glad to encounter thee, friend," continued the maiden, waving her hand to the stranger to proceed, as she urged her Narragansett to renew its amble. "Partial relatives have almost persuaded me that I am not entirely worthless in a duet myself; and we may enliven our wayfaring by indulging in our favorite pursuit. It might be of signal advantage to one, ignorant as I, to hear the opinions and experience of a master in the art."

"It is refreshing both to the spirits and to the body to indulge in psalmody, in befitting seasons," returned the master of song, unhesitatingly complying with her intimation to follow; "and nothing would relieve the mind more than such a consoling communion. But four parts are altogether necessary to the perfection of melody. You have all the manifestations of a soft and rich treble; I can, by especial aid, carry a full tenor to the highest letter; but we lack counter and bass! Yon officer of the king, who hesitated to admit me to his company, might fill the latter, if one may judge from the intonations of his voice in common dialogue."

"Judge not too rashly from hasty and deceptive appearances," said the lady, smiling; "though Major Heyward can assume such deep notes on occasion, believe me, his natural tones are better fitted for a mellow tenor than the bass you heard."

"Is he, then, much practiced in the art of psalmody?" demanded her simple companion.

Alice felt disposed to laugh, though she succeeded in suppressing her merriment, ere she answered:

"I apprehend that he is rather addicted to profane song. The chances of a soldier's life are but little fitted for the encouragement of more sober inclinations."

"Man's voice is given to him, like his other talents, to be used, and not to be abused. None can say they have ever known me to neglect my gifts! I am thankful that, though my boyhood may be said to have been set apart, like the youth of the royal David, for the purposes of music, no syllable of rude verse has ever profaned my lips."

"You have, then, limited your efforts to sacred song?"

"Even so. As the psalms of David exceed all other language, so does the psalmody that has been fitted to them by the divines and sages of the land, surpass all vain poetry. Happily, I may say that I utter nothing but the thoughts and the wishes of the King of Israel himself; for though the times may call for some slight changes, yet does this version which we use in the colonies of New England so much exceed all other versions, that, by its richness, its exactness, and its spiritual simplicity, it approacheth, as near as may be, to the great work of the inspired writer. I never abide in any place, sleeping or waking, without an example of this gifted work. 'Tis the six-and-twentieth edition, promulgated at Boston, Anno Domini 1744; and is entitled, 'The Psalms, Hymns, and Spiritual Songs of the Old and New Testaments; faithfully translated into English Metre, for the Use, Edification, and Comfort of the Saints, in Public and Private, especially in New England'."

During this eulogium on the rare production of his native poets, the stranger had drawn the book from his pocket, and fitting a pair of iron-rimmed spectacles to his nose, opened the volume with a care and veneration suited to its sacred purposes. Then, without circumlocution or apology, first pronounced the word "Standish," and placing the unknown engine, already described, to his mouth, from which he drew a high, shrill sound, that was followed by an octave below, from his own voice, he commenced singing the following words, in full, sweet, and melodious tones, that set the music, the poetry, and even the uneasy motion of his ill-trained beast at defiance; "How good it is, O see, And how it pleaseth well, Together e'en in unity, For brethren so to dwell. It's like the choice ointment, From the head to the beard did go; Down Aaron's head, that downward went His garment's skirts unto."

The delivery of these skillful rhymes was accompanied, on the part of the stranger, by a regular rise and fall of his right hand, which terminated at the descent, by suffering the fingers to dwell a moment on the leaves of the little volume; and on the ascent, by such a flourish of the member as none but the initiated may ever hope to imitate. It would seem long practice had rendered this manual accompaniment necessary; for it did not cease until the preposition which the poet had selected for the close of his verse had been duly delivered like a word of two syllables.

Such an innovation on the silence and retirement of the forest could not fail to enlist the ears of those who journeyed at so short a distance in advance. The Indian muttered a few words in broken English to Heyward, who, in his turn, spoke to the stranger; at once interrupting, and, for the time, closing his musical efforts.

"Though we are not in danger, common prudence would teach us to journey through this wilderness in as quiet a manner as possible. You will then, pardon me, Alice, should I diminish your enjoyments, by requesting this gentleman to postpone his chant until a safer opportunity."

"You will diminish them, indeed," returned the arch girl; "for never did I hear a more unworthy conjunction of execution and language than that to which I have been listening; and I was far gone in a learned inquiry into the causes of such an unfitness between sound and sense, when you broke the charm of my musings by that bass of yours, Duncan!"

"I know not what you call my bass," said Heyward, piqued at her remark, "but I know that your safety, and that of Cora, is far dearer to me than could be any orchestra of Handel's music." He paused and turned his head quickly toward a thicket, and then bent his eyes suspiciously on their guide, who continued his steady pace, in undisturbed gravity. The young man smiled to himself, for he believed he had mistaken some shining berry of the woods for the glistening eyeballs of a prowling savage, and he rode forward, continuing the conversation which had been interrupted by the passing thought.

Major Heyward was mistaken only in suffering his youthful and generous pride to suppress his active watchfulness. The cavalcade had not long passed, before the branches of the bushes that formed the thicket were cautiously moved asunder, and a human visage, as fiercely wild as savage art and unbridled passions could make it, peered out on the retiring footsteps of the travelers. A gleam of exultation shot across the darkly-painted lineaments of the inhabitant of the forest, as he traced the route of his intended victims, who rode unconsciously onward, the light and graceful forms of the females waving among the trees, in the curvatures of their path, followed at each bend by the manly figure of Heyward, until, finally, the shapeless person of the singing master was concealed behind the numberless trunks of trees, that rose, in dark lines, in the intermediate space.

CHAPTER III.

"Before these fields were shorn and till'd,
Full to the brim our rivers flow'd;
The melody of waters fill'd
The fresh and boundless wood;
And torrents dash'd, and rivulets play'd,
And fountains spouted in the shade."—Bryant

Leaving the unsuspecting Heyward and his confiding companions to penetrate still deeper into a forest that contained such treacherous inmates, we must use an author's privilege, and shift the scene a few miles to the westward of the place where we have last seen them.

On that day, two men were lingering on the banks of a small but rapid stream, within an hour's journey of the encampment of Webb, like those who awaited the appearance of an absent person, or the approach of some expected event. The vast canopy of woods spread itself to the margin of the river, overhanging the water, and shadowing its dark current with a deeper hue. The rays of the sun were beginning to grow less fierce, and the intense heat of the day was lessened, as the cooler vapors of the springs and fountains rose above their leafy beds, and rested in the atmosphere. Still that breathing silence, which marks the drowsy sultriness of an American landscape in July, pervaded the secluded spot, interrupted only by the low voices of the men, the occasional and lazy tap of a woodpecker, the discordant cry of some gaudy jay, or a swelling on the ear, from the dull roar of a distant waterfall. These feeble and broken sounds were, however, too familiar to the foresters to draw their attention from the more interesting matter of their dialogue. While one of these loiterers showed the red skin and wild accouterments of a native of the woods, the other exhibited, through the mask of his rude and nearly savage equipments, the brighter, though sun-burned and long-faced complexion of one who might claim descent from a European parentage. The former was seated on the end of a mossy log, in a posture that permitted him to heighten the effect of his earnest language, by the calm but expressive gestures of an Indian engaged in debate. His body, which was nearly naked, presented a terrific emblem of death, drawn in intermingled colors of white and black. His closely-shaved head, on which no other hair than the well-known and chivalrous scalping tuft* was preserved, was without ornament of any kind, with the exception of a solitary eagle's plume, that crossed his crown, and depended over the left shoulder. A tomahawk and scalping knife, of English manufacture, were in his girdle; while a short military rifle, of that sort with which the policy of the whites armed their savage allies, lay carelessly across his bare and sinewy knee. The expanded chest, full formed limbs, and grave countenance of this warrior, would denote that he had reached the vigor of his days, though no symptoms of decay appeared to have yet weakened his manhood.

---

* The North American warrior caused the hair to be plucked from his whole body; a small tuft was left on the crown of his head, in order that his enemy might avail himself of it, in wrenching off the scalp in the event of his fall. The scalp was the only admissible trophy of victory. Thus, it was deemed more important to obtain the scalp than to kill the man. Some tribes lay great stress on the honor of striking a dead body. These practices have nearly disappeared among the Indians of the Atlantic states.

The frame of the white man, judging by such parts as were not concealed by his clothes, was like that of one who had known hardships and exertion from his earliest youth. His person, though muscular, was rather attenuated than full; but every nerve and muscle appeared strung and indurated by unremitted exposure and toil. He wore a hunting shirt of forest-green, fringed with faded yellow,* and a summer cap of skins which had been shorn of their fur. He also bore a knife in a girdle of wampum, like that which confined the scanty garments of the Indian, but no tomahawk. His moccasins were ornamented after the gay fashion of the natives, while the only part of his under dress which appeared below the hunting-frock was a pair of buckskin leggings, that laced at the sides, and which were gartered above the knees, with the sinews of a deer. A pouch and horn completed his personal accouterments, though a rifle of great length,† which the theory of the more ingenious whites had taught them was the most dangerous of all firearms, leaned against a neighboring sapling. The eye of the hunter, or scout, whichever he might be, was small, quick, keen, and restless, roving while he spoke, on every side of him, as if in quest of game, or distrusting the sudden approach of some lurking enemy. Notwithstanding the symptoms of habitual suspicion, his countenance was not only without guile, but at the moment at which he is introduced, it was charged with an expression of sturdy honesty.

"Even your traditions make the case in my favor, Chingachgook," he said, speaking in the tongue which was known to all the natives who formerly inhabited the country between the Hudson and the Potomac, and of which we shall give a free translation for the benefit of the reader; endeavoring, at the same time, to preserve some of the peculiarities, both of the individual and of the language. "Your fathers came from the setting sun, crossed the big river,‡ fought the people of the country, and took the land; and mine came from the red sky of the morning, over the salt lake, and did their work much after the fashion that had been set them by yours; then let God judge the matter between us, and friends spare their words!"

"My fathers fought with the naked red man!" returned the Indian, sternly, in the same language. "Is there no difference, Hawkeye, between the stone-headed arrow of the warrior, and the leaden bullet with which you kill?"

"There is reason in an Indian, though nature has made him with a red skin!" said the white man, shaking his head like one on whom such an appeal to his justice was not thrown away. For a moment he appeared to be conscious of having the worst of the argument, then, rallying again, he answered the objection of his antagonist in the best manner his limited information would allow:

"I am no scholar, and I care not who knows it; but, judging from what I have seen, at deer chases and squirrel hunts, of the sparks below, I should think a rifle in the hands of their grandfathers was

---

* The hunting-shirt is a picturesque smock-frock, being shorter, and ornamented with fringes and tassels. The colors are intended to imitate the hues of the wood, with a view to concealment. Many corps of American riflemen have been thus attired, and the dress is one of the most striking of modern times. The hunting-shirt is frequently white.
† The rifle of the army is short; that of the hunter is always long.
‡ The Mississippi. The scout alludes to a tradition which is very popular among the tribes of the Atlantic states. Evidence of their Asiatic origin is deduced from the circumstances, though great uncertainty hangs over the whole history of the Indians.

not so dangerous as a hickory bow and a good flint-head might be, if drawn with Indian judgment, and sent by an Indian eye."

"You have the story told by your fathers," returned the other, coldly waving his hand. "What say your old men? Do they tell the young warriors that the pale faces met the red men, painted for war and armed with the stone hatchet and wooden gun?"

"I am not a prejudiced man, nor one who vaunts himself on his natural privileges, though the worst enemy I have on earth, and he is an Iroquois, daren't deny that I am genuine white," the scout replied, surveying, with secret satisfaction, the faded color of his bony and sinewy hand, "and I am willing to own that my people have many ways, of which, as an honest man, I can't approve. It is one of their customs to write in books what they have done and seen, instead of telling them in their villages, where the lie can be given to the face of a cowardly boaster, and the brave soldier can call on his comrades to witness for the truth of his words. In consequence of this bad fashion, a man, who is too conscientious to misspend his days among the women, in learning the names of black marks, may never hear of the deeds of his fathers, nor feel a pride in striving to outdo them. For myself, I conclude the Bumppos could shoot, for I have a natural turn with a rifle, which must have been handed down from generation to generation, as, our holy commandments tell us, all good and evil gifts are bestowed; though I should be loath to answer for other people in such a matter. But every story has its two sides; so I ask you, Chingachgook, what passed, according to the traditions of the red men, when our fathers first met?"

A silence of a minute succeeded, during which the Indian sat mute; then, full of the dignity of his office, he commenced his brief tale, with a solemnity that served to heighten its appearance of truth.

"Listen, Hawkeye, and your ear shall drink no lie. 'Tis what my fathers have said, and what the Mohicans have done." He hesitated a single instant, and bending a cautious glance toward his companion, he continued, in a manner that was divided between interrogation and assertion. "Does not this stream at our feet run toward the summer, until its waters grow salt, and the current flows upward?"

"It can't be denied that your traditions tell you true in both these matters," said the white man; "for I have been there, and have seen them, though why water, which is so sweet in the shade, should become bitter in the sun, is an alteration for which I have never been able to account."

"And the current!" demanded the Indian, who expected his reply with that sort of interest that a man feels in the confirmation of testimony, at which he marvels even while he respects it; "the fathers of Chingachgook have not lied!"

"The holy Bible is not more true, and that is the truest thing in nature. They call this up-stream current the tide, which is a thing soon explained, and clear enough. Six hours the waters run in, and six hours they run out, and the reason is this: when there is higher water in the sea than in the river, they run in until the river gets to be highest, and then it runs out again."

"The waters in the woods, and on the great lakes, run downward until they lie like my hand," said the Indian, stretching the limb horizontally before him, "and then they run no more."

"No honest man will deny it," said the scout, a little nettled at the implied distrust of his explanation of the mystery of the tides; "and I grant that it is true on the small scale, and where the land is level. But everything depends on what scale you look at things. Now, on the small scale, the 'arth is level; but on the large scale it is round. In this manner, pools and ponds, and even the great fresh-water lakes, may be stagnant, as you and I both know they are, having seen them; but when you come to spread water over a great tract, like the sea, where the earth is round, how in reason can the water be quiet? You might as well expect the river to lie still on the brink of those black rocks a mile above us, though your own ears tell you that it is tumbling over them at this very moment."

If unsatisfied by the philosophy of his companion, the Indian was far too dignified to betray his unbelief. He listened like one who was convinced, and resumed his narrative in his former solemn manner.

"We came from the place where the sun is hid at night, over great plains where the buffaloes live, until we reached the big river. There we fought the Alligewi, till the ground was red with their blood. From the banks of the big river to the shores of the salt lake, there was none to meet us. The Maquas followed at a distance. We said the country should be ours from the place where the water runs up no longer on this stream, to a river twenty sun's journey toward the summer. We drove the Maquas into the woods with the bears. They only tasted salt at the licks; they drew no fish from the great lake; we threw them the bones."

"All this I have heard and believe," said the white man, observing that the Indian paused; "but it was long before the English came into the country."

"A pine grew then where this chestnut now stands. The first pale faces who came among us spoke no English. They came in a large canoe, when my fathers had buried the tomahawk with the red men around them. Then, Hawkeye," he continued, betraying his deep emotion, only by permitting his voice to fall to those low, guttural tones, which render his language, as spoken at times, so very musical; "then, Hawkeye, we were one people, and we were happy. The salt lake gave us its fish, the wood its deer, and the air its birds. We took wives who bore us children; we worshipped the Great Spirit; and we kept the Maquas beyond the sound of our songs of triumph."

"Know you anything of your own family at that time?" demanded the white. "But you are just a man, for an Indian; and as I suppose you hold their gifts, your fathers must have been brave warriors, and wise men at the council-fire."

"My tribe is the grandfather of nations, but I am an unmixed man. The blood of chiefs is in my veins, where it must stay forever. The Dutch landed, and gave my people the fire-water; they drank until the heavens and the earth seemed to meet, and they foolishly thought they had found the Great Spirit. Then they parted with their land. Foot by foot, they were driven back from the shores, until I, that am a chief and a Sagamore, have never seen the sun shine but through the trees, and have never visited the graves of my fathers."

"Graves bring solemn feelings over the mind," returned the scout, a good deal touched at the calm suffering of his companion; "and they often aid a man in his good intentions; though, for myself, I expect to leave my own bones unburied, to bleach in the woods, or to be torn asunder by the wolves. But where are to be found those of your race who came to their kin in the Delaware country, so many summers since?"

"Where are the blossoms of those summers!—fallen, one by one; so all of my family departed, each in his turn, to the land of spirits. I am on the hilltop and must go down into the valley; and when Uncas follows in my footsteps there will no longer be any of the blood of the Sagamores, for my boy is the last of the Mohicans."

"Uncas is here," said another voice, in the same soft, guttural tones, near his elbow; "who speaks to Uncas?"

The white man loosened his knife in his leathern sheath, and made an involuntary movement of the hand toward his rifle, at this sudden interruption; but the Indian sat composed, and without turning his head at the unexpected sounds.

At the next instant, a youthful warrior passed between them, with a noiseless step, and seated himself on the bank of the rapid stream. No exclamation of surprise escaped the father, nor was any question asked, or reply given, for several minutes; each appearing to await the moment when he might speak, without betraying womanish curiosity or childish impatience. The white man seemed to take counsel from their customs, and, relinquishing his grasp of the rifle, he also remained silent and reserved. At length Chingachgook turned his eyes slowly toward his son, and demanded:

"Do the Maquas dare to leave the print of their moccasins in these woods?"

"I have been on their trail," replied the young Indian, "and know that they number as many as the fingers of my two hands; but they lie hid like cowards."

"The thieves are outlying for scalps and plunder," said the white man, whom we shall call Hawkeye, after the manner of his companions. "That busy Frenchman, Montcalm, will send his spies into our very camp, but he will know what road we travel!"

"'Tis enough," returned the father, glancing his eye toward the setting sun; "they shall be driven like deer from their bushes. Hawkeye, let us eat to-night, and show the Maquas that we are men to-morrow."

"I am as ready to do the one as the other; but to fight the Iroquois 'tis necessary to find the skulkers; and to eat, 'tis necessary to get the game—talk of the devil and he will come; there is a pair of the biggest antlers I have seen this season, moving the bushes below the hill! Now, Uncas," he continued, in a half whisper, and laughing with a kind of inward sound, like one who had learned to be watchful, "I will bet my charger three times full of powder, against a foot of wampum, that I take him atwixt the eyes, and nearer to the right than to the left."

"It cannot be!" said the young Indian, springing to his feet with youthful eagerness; "all but the tips of his horns are hid!"

"He's a boy!" said the white man, shaking his head while he spoke, and addressing the father. "Does he think when a hunter sees a part of the creature', he can't tell where the rest of him should be!"

Adjusting his rifle, he was about to make an exhibition of that skill on which he so much valued himself, when the warrior struck up the piece with his hand, saying:

"Hawkeye! will you fight the Maquas?"

"These Indians know the nature of the woods, as it might be by instinct!" returned the scout, dropping his rifle, and turning away like a man who was convinced of his error. "I must leave the buck to your arrow, Uncas, or we may kill a deer for them thieves, the Iroquois, to eat."

The instant the father seconded this intimation by an expressive gesture of the hand, Uncas threw himself on the ground, and approached the animal with wary movements. When within a few yards of the cover, he fitted an arrow to his bow with the utmost care, while the antlers moved, as if their owner snuffed an enemy in the tainted air. In another moment the twang of the cord was heard, a white streak was seen glancing into the bushes, and the wounded buck plunged from the cover, to the very feet of his hidden enemy. Avoiding the horns of the infuriated animal, Uncas darted to his side, and passed his knife across the throat, when bounding to the edge of the river it fell, dyeing the waters with its blood.

"'Twas done with Indian skill," said the scout laughing inwardly, but with vast satisfaction; "and 'twas a pretty sight to behold! Though an arrow is a near shot, and needs a knife to finish the work."

"Hugh!" ejaculated his companion, turning quickly, like a hound who scented game.

"By the Lord, there is a drove of them!" exclaimed the scout, whose eyes began to glisten with the ardor of his usual occupation; "if they come within range of a bullet I will drop one, though the whole Six Nations should be lurking within sound! What do you hear, Chingachgook? for to my ears the woods are dumb."

"There is but one deer, and he is dead," said the Indian, bending his body till his ear nearly touched the earth. "I hear the sounds of feet!"

"Perhaps the wolves have driven the buck to shelter, and are following on his trail."

"No. The horses of white men are coming!" returned the other, raising himself with dignity, and resuming his seat on the log with his former composure. "Hawkeye, they are your brothers; speak to them."

"That I will, and in English that the king needn't be ashamed to answer," returned the hunter, speaking in the language of which he boasted; "but I see nothing, nor do I hear the sounds of man or beast; 'tis strange that an Indian should understand white sounds better than a man who, his very enemies will own, has no cross in his blood, although he may have lived with the red skins long enough to be suspected! Ha! there goes something like the cracking of a dry stick, too—now I hear the bushes move—yes, yes, there is a trampling that I mistook for the falls—and—but here they come themselves; God keep them from the Iroquois!"

CHAPTER IV.

"Well go thy way: thou shalt not from this grove
Till I torment thee for this injury."—Midsummer Night's Dream.

The words were still in the mouth of the scout, when the leader of the party, whose approaching footsteps had caught the vigilant ear of the Indian, came openly into view. A beaten path, such as those made by the periodical passage of the deer, wound through a little glen at no great distance, and struck the river at the point where the white man and his red companions had posted themselves. Along this track the travelers, who had produced a surprise so unusual in the depths of the forest, advanced slowly toward the hunter, who was in front of his associates, in readiness to receive them.

"Who comes?" demanded the scout, throwing his rifle carelessly across his left arm, and keeping the forefinger of his right hand on the trigger, though he avoided all appearance of menace in the act. "Who comes hither, among the beasts and dangers of the wilderness?"

"Believers in religion, and friends to the law and to the king," returned he who rode foremost. "Men who have journeyed since the rising sun, in the shades of this forest, without nourishment, and are sadly tired of their wayfaring."

"You are, then, lost," interrupted the hunter, "and have found how helpless 'tis not to know whether to take the right hand or the left?"

"Even so; sucking babes are not more dependent on those who guide them than we who are of larger growth, and who may now be said to possess the stature without the knowledge of men. Know you the distance to a post of the crown called William Henry?"

"Hoot!" shouted the scout, who did not spare his open laughter, though instantly checking the dangerous sounds he indulged his merriment at less risk of being overheard by any lurking enemies. "You are as much off the scent as a hound would be, with Horican atwixt him and the deer! William Henry, man! if you are friends to the king and have business with the army, your way would be to follow the river down to Edward, and lay the matter before Webb, who tarries there, instead of pushing into the defiles, and driving this saucy Frenchman back across Champlain, into his den again."

Before the stranger could make any reply to this unexpected proposition, another horseman dashed the bushes aside, and leaped his charger into the pathway, in front of his companion.

"What, then, may be our distance from Fort Edward?" demanded a new speaker; "the place you advise us to seek we left this morning, and our destination is the head of the lake."

"Then you must have lost your eyesight afore losing your way, for the road across the portage is cut to a good two rods, and is as grand a path, I calculate, as any that runs into London, or even before the palace of the king himself."

"We will not dispute concerning the excellence of the passage," returned Heyward, smiling; for, as the reader has anticipated, it was he. "It is enough, for the present, that we trusted to an Indian guide to take us by a nearer, though blinder path, and that we are deceived in his knowledge. In plain words, we know not where we are."

"An Indian lost in the woods!" said the scout, shaking his head doubtingly; "When the sun is scorching the tree tops, and the water courses are full; when the moss on every beech he sees will tell him in what quarter the north star will shine at night. The woods are full of deer-paths which run to the streams and licks, places well known to everybody; nor have the geese done their flight to the Canada waters altogether! 'Tis strange that an Indian should be lost atwixt Horican and the bend in the river! Is he a Mohawk?"

"Not by birth, though adopted in that tribe; I think his birthplace was farther north, and he is one of those you call a Huron."

"Hugh!" exclaimed the two companions of the scout, who had continued until this part of the dialogue, seated immovable, and apparently indifferent to what passed, but who now sprang to their feet with an activity and interest that had evidently got the better of their reserve by surprise.

"A Huron!" repeated the sturdy scout, once more shaking his head in open distrust; "they are a thievish race, nor do I care by whom they are adopted; you can never make anything of them but skulks and vagabonds. Since you trusted yourself to the care of one of that nation, I only wonder that you have not fallen in with more."

"Of that there is little danger, since William Henry is so many miles in our front. You forget that I have told you our guide is now a Mohawk, and that he serves with our forces as a friend."

"And I tell you that he who is born a Mingo will die a Mingo," returned the other positively. "A Mohawk! No, give me a Delaware or a Mohican for honesty; and when they will fight, which they won't all do, having suffered their cunning enemies, the Maquas, to make them women—but when they will fight at all, look to a Delaware, or a Mohican, for a warrior!"

"Enough of this," said Heyward, impatiently; "I wish not to inquire into the character of a man that I know, and to whom you must be a stranger. You have not yet answered my question; what is our distance from the main army at Edward?"

"It seems that may depend on who is your guide. One would think such a horse as that might get over a good deal of ground atwixt sun-up and sun-down."

"I wish no contention of idle words with you, friend," said Heyward, curbing his dissatisfied manner, and speaking in a more gentle voice; "if you will tell me the distance to Fort Edward, and conduct me thither, your labor shall not go without its reward."

"And in so doing, how know I that I don't guide an enemy and a spy of Montcalm, to the works of the army? It is not every man who can speak the English tongue that is an honest subject."

"If you serve with the troops, of whom I judge you to be a scout, you should know of such a regiment of the king as the Sixtieth."

"The Sixtieth! you can tell me little of the Royal Americans that I don't know, though I do wear a hunting-shirt instead of a scarlet jacket."

"Well, then, among other things, you may know the name of its major?"

"Its major!" interrupted the hunter, elevating his body like one who was proud of his trust. "If there is a man in the country who knows Major Effingham, he stands before you."

"It is a corps which has many majors; the gentleman you name is the senior, but I speak of the junior of them all; he who commands the companies in garrison at William Henry."

"Yes, yes, I have heard that a young gentleman of vast riches, from one of the provinces far south, has got the place. He is over young, too, to hold such rank, and to be put above men whose heads are beginning to bleach; and yet they say he is a soldier in his knowledge, and a gallant gentleman!"

"Whatever he may be, or however he may be qualified for his rank, he now speaks to you and, of course, can be no enemy to dread."

The scout regarded Heyward in surprise, and then lifting his cap, he answered, in a tone less confident than before—though still expressing doubt.

"I have heard a party was to leave the encampment this morning for the lake shore?"

"You have heard the truth; but I preferred a nearer route, trusting to the knowledge of the Indian I mentioned."

"And he deceived you, and then deserted?"

"Neither, as I believe; certainly not the latter, for he is to be found in the rear."

"I should like to look at the creature; if it is a true Iroquois I can tell him by his knavish look, and by his paint," said the scout; stepping past the charger of Heyward, and entering the path behind the mare of the singing master, whose foal had taken advantage of the halt to exact the maternal contribution. After shoving aside the bushes, and proceeding a few paces, he encountered the females, who awaited the result of the conference with anxiety, and not entirely without apprehension. Behind these, the runner leaned against a tree, where he stood the close examination of the scout with an air unmoved, though with a look so dark and savage, that it might in itself excite fear. Satisfied with his scrutiny, the hunter soon left him. As he repassed the females, he paused a moment to gaze upon their beauty, answering to the smile and nod of Alice with a look of open pleasure. Thence he went to the side of the motherly animal, and spending a minute in a fruitless inquiry into the character of her rider, he shook his head and returned to Heyward.

"A Mingo is a Mingo, and God having made him so, neither the Mohawks nor any other tribe can alter him," he said, when he had regained his former position. "If we were alone, and you would leave that noble horse at the mercy of the wolves to-night, I could show you the way to Edward myself, within an hour, for it lies only about an hour's journey hence; but with such ladies in your company 'tis impossible!"

"And why? They are fatigued, but they are quite equal to a ride of a few more miles."

"'Tis a natural impossibility!" repeated the scout; "I wouldn't walk a mile in these woods after night gets into them, in company with that runner, for the best rifle in the colonies. They are full of outlying Iroquois, and your mongrel Mohawk knows where to find them too well to be my companion."

"Think you so?" said Heyward, leaning forward in the saddle, and dropping his voice nearly to a whisper; "I confess I have not been without my own suspicions, though I have endeavored to conceal them, and affected a confidence I have not always felt, on account of my companions. It was because I suspected him that I would follow no longer; making him, as you see, follow me."

"I knew he was one of the cheats as soon as I laid eyes on him!" returned the scout, placing a finger on his nose, in sign of caution.

"The thief is leaning against the foot of the sugar sapling, that you can see over them bushes; his right leg is in a line with the bark of the tree, and," tapping his rifle, "I can take him from where I stand, between the angle and the knee, with a single shot, putting an end to his tramping through the woods, for at least a month to come. If I should go back to him, the cunning varmint would suspect something, and be dodging through the trees like a frightened deer."

"It will not do. He may be innocent, and I dislike the act. Though, if I felt confident of his treachery…"

"'Tis a safe thing to calculate on the knavery of an Iroquois," said the scout, throwing his rifle forward, by a sort of instinctive movement.

"Hold!" interrupted Heyward, "it will not do—we must think of some other scheme—and yet, I have much reason to believe the rascal has deceived me."

The hunter, who had already abandoned his intention of maiming the runner, mused a moment, and then made a gesture, which instantly brought his two red companions to his side. They spoke together earnestly in the Delaware language, though in an undertone; and by the gestures of the white man, which were frequently directed towards the top of the sapling, it was evident he pointed out the situation of their hidden enemy. His companions were not long in comprehending his wishes, and laying aside their firearms, they parted, taking opposite sides of the path, and burying themselves in the thicket, with such cautious movements, that their steps were inaudible.

"Now, go you back," said the hunter, speaking again to Heyward, "and hold the imp in talk; these Mohicans here will take him without breaking his paint."

"Nay," said Heyward, proudly, "I will seize him myself."

"Hist! what could you do, mounted, against an Indian in the bushes!"

"I will dismount."

"And, think you, when he saw one of your feet out of the stirrup, he would wait for the other to be free? Whoever comes into the woods to deal with the natives, must use Indian fashions, if he would wish to prosper in his undertakings. Go, then; talk openly to the miscreant, and seem to believe him the truest friend you have on 'arth."

Heyward prepared to comply, though with strong disgust at the nature of the office he was compelled to execute. Each moment, however, pressed upon him a conviction of the critical situation in which he had suffered his invaluable trust to be involved through his own confidence. The sun had already disappeared, and the woods, suddenly deprived of his light,* were assuming a dusky hue, which keenly reminded him that the hour the savage usually chose for his most barbarous and remorseless acts of vengeance or hostility, was speedily drawing near. Stimulated by apprehension, he left the scout, who immediately entered into a loud conversation with the stranger that had so unceremoniously enlisted himself in the party of travelers that morning. In passing his gentler companions Heyward uttered a few words of encouragement, and was pleased to find that, though fatigued with the exercise of the day, they appeared to entertain no suspicion that their present

---

*The scene of this tale was in the 42d degree of latitude, where the twilight is never of long continuation.

embarrassment was other than the result of accident. Giving them reason to believe he was merely employed in a consultation concerning the future route, he spurred his charger, and drew the reins again when the animal had carried him within a few yards of the place where the sullen runner still stood, leaning against the tree.

"You may see, Magua," he said, endeavoring to assume an air of freedom and confidence, "that the night is closing around us, and yet we are no nearer to William Henry than when we left the encampment of Webb with the rising sun.

"You have missed the way, nor have I been more fortunate. But, happily, we have fallen in with a hunter, he whom you hear talking to the singer, that is acquainted with the deerpaths and by-ways of the woods, and who promises to lead us to a place where we may rest securely till the morning."

The Indian riveted his glowing eyes on Heyward as he asked, in his imperfect English, "Is he alone?"

"Alone!" hesitatingly answered Heyward, to whom deception was too new to be assumed without embarrassment. "Oh! not alone, surely, Magua, for you know that we are with him."

"Then Le Renard Subtil will go," returned the runner, coolly raising his little wallet from the place where it had lain at his feet; "and the pale faces will see none but their own color."

"Go! Whom call you Le Renard?"

"'Tis the name his Canada fathers have given to Magua," returned the runner, with an air that manifested his pride at the distinction. "Night is the same as day to Le Subtil, when Munro waits for him."

"And what account will Le Renard give the chief of William Henry concerning his daughters? Will he dare to tell the hot-blooded Scotsman that his children are left without a guide, though Magua promised to be one?"

"Though the gray head has a loud voice, and a long arm, Le Renard will not hear him, nor feel him, in the woods."

"But what will the Mohawks say? They will make him petticoats, and bid him stay in the wigwam with the women, for he is no longer to be trusted with the business of a man."

"Le Subtil knows the path to the great lakes, and he can find the bones of his fathers," was the answer of the unmoved runner.

"Enough, Magua," said Heyward; "are we not friends? Why should there be bitter words between us? Munro has promised you a gift for your services when performed, and I shall be your debtor for another. Rest your weary limbs, then, and open your wallet to eat. We have a few moments to spare; let us not waste them in talk like wrangling women. When the ladies are refreshed we will proceed."

"The pale faces make themselves dogs to their women," muttered the Indian, in his native language, "and when they want to eat, their warriors must lay aside the tomahawk to feed their laziness."

"What say you, Renard?"

"Le Subtil says it is good."

The Indian then fastened his eyes keenly on the open countenance of Heyward, but meeting his glance, he turned them quickly away, and seating himself deliberately on the ground, he drew forth the remnant of some former repast, and began to eat, though not without first bending his looks slowly and cautiously around him.

"This is well," continued Heyward; "and Le Renard will have strength and sight to find the path in the morning"; he paused, for sounds like the snapping of a dried stick, and the rustling of leaves, rose from the adjacent bushes, but recollecting himself instantly, he continued, "we must be moving before the sun is seen, or Montcalm may lie in our path, and shut us out from the fortress."

The hand of Magua dropped from his mouth to his side, and though his eyes were fastened on the ground, his head was turned aside, his nostrils expanded, and his ears seemed even to stand more erect than usual, giving to him the appearance of a statue that was made to represent intense attention.

Heyward, who watched his movements with a vigilant eye, carelessly extricated one of his feet from the stirrup, while he passed a hand toward the bear-skin covering of his holsters.

Every effort to detect the point most regarded by the runner was completely frustrated by the tremulous glances of his organs, which seemed not to rest a single instant on any particular object, and which, at the same time, could be hardly said to move. While he hesitated how to proceed, Le Subtil cautiously raised himself to his feet, though with a motion so slow and guarded, that not the slightest noise was produced by the change. Heyward felt it had now become incumbent on him to act. Throwing his leg over the saddle, he dismounted, with a determination to advance and seize his treacherous companion, trusting the result to his own manhood. In order, however, to prevent unnecessary alarm, he still preserved an air of calmness and friendship.

"Le Renard Subtil does not eat," he said, using the appellation he had found most flattering to the vanity of the Indian. "His corn is not well parched, and it seems dry. Let me examine; perhaps something may be found among my own provisions that will help his appetite."

Magua held out the wallet to the proffer of the other. He even suffered their hands to meet, without betraying the least emotion, or varying his riveted attitude of attention. But when he felt the fingers of Heyward moving gently along his own naked arm, he struck up the limb of the young man, and, uttering a piercing cry, he darted beneath it, and plunged, at a single bound, into the opposite thicket. At the next instant the form of Chingachgook appeared from the bushes, looking like a specter in its paint, and glided across the path in swift pursuit. Next followed the shout of Uncas, when the woods were lighted by a sudden flash, that was accompanied by the sharp report of the hunter's rifle.

CHAPTER V.

> ..."In such a night
> Did This be fearfully o'ertrip the dew;
> And saw the lion's shadow ere himself."—Merchant of Venice

The suddenness of the flight of his guide, and the wild cries of the pursuers, caused Heyward to remain fixed, for a few moments, in inactive surprise. Then recollecting the importance of securing the fugitive, he dashed aside the surrounding bushes, and pressed eagerly forward to lend his aid in the chase. Before he had, however, proceeded a hundred yards, he met the three foresters already returning from their unsuccessful pursuit.

"Why so soon disheartened!" he exclaimed; "the scoundrel must be concealed behind some of these trees, and may yet be secured. We are not safe while he goes at large."

"Would you set a cloud to chase the wind?" returned the disappointed scout; "I heard the imp brushing over the dry leaves, like a black snake, and blinking a glimpse of him, just over ag'in yon big pine, I pulled as it might be on the scent; but 'twouldn't do! and yet for a reasoning aim, if anybody but myself had touched the trigger, I should call it a quick sight; and I may be accounted to have experience in these matters, and one who ought to know. Look at this sumach; its leaves are red, though everybody knows the fruit is in the yellow blossom in the month of July!"

"'Tis the blood of Le Subtil! he is hurt, and may yet fall!"

"No, no," returned the scout, in decided disapprobation of this opinion, "I rubbed the bark off a limb, perhaps, but the creature leaped the longer for it. A rifle bullet acts on a running animal, when it barks him, much the same as one of your spurs on a horse; that is, it quickens motion, and puts life into the flesh, instead of taking it away. But when it cuts the ragged hole, after a bound or two, there is, commonly, a stagnation of further leaping, be it Indian or be it deer!"

"We are four able bodies, to one wounded man!"

"Is life grievous to you?" interrupted the scout. "Yonder red devil would draw you within swing of the tomahawks of his comrades, before you were heated in the chase. It was an unthoughtful act in a man who has so often slept with the war-whoop ringing in the air, to let off his piece within sound of an ambushment! But then it was a natural temptation! 'twas very natural! Come, friends, let us move our station, and in such fashion, too, as will throw the cunning of a Mingo on a wrong scent, or our scalps will be drying in the wind in front of Montcalm's marquee, ag'in this hour to-morrow."

This appalling declaration, which the scout uttered with the cool assurance of a man who fully comprehended, while he did not fear to face the danger, served to remind Heyward of the importance of the charge with which he himself had been intrusted. Glancing his eyes around, with a vain effort to pierce the gloom that was thickening beneath the leafy arches of the forest, he felt as if, cut off from human aid, his unresisting companions would soon lie at the entire mercy of those barbarous enemies, who, like beasts of prey, only waited till the gathering darkness might render their blows more fatally certain. His awakened imagination, deluded by the deceptive light, converted each waving bush, or the fragment of some fallen tree, into human forms, and twenty times he fancied he could distinguish the horrid visages of his lurking foes, peering from their hiding places, in never ceasing watchfulness of the movements of his party. Looking upward, he found that the thin fleecy clouds, which evening had painted on the blue sky, were already losing their faintest tints of rose-color, while the imbedded stream, which glided past the spot where he stood, was to be traced only by the dark boundary of its wooded banks.

"What is to be done!" he said, feeling the utter helplessness of doubt in such a pressing strait; "desert me not, for God's sake! remain to defend those I escort, and freely name your own reward!"

His companions, who conversed apart in the language of their tribe, heeded not this sudden and earnest appeal. Though their dialogue was maintained in low and cautious sounds, but little above a whisper, Heyward, who now approached, could easily distinguish the earnest tones of the younger warrior from the more deliberate speeches of his seniors. It was evident that they debated on the propriety of some measure, that nearly concerned the welfare of the travelers. Yielding to his powerful interest in the subject, and impatient of a delay that seemed fraught with so much additional danger, Heyward drew still nigher to the dusky group, with an intention of making his offers of compensation more definite, when the white man, motioning with his hand, as if he conceded the disputed point, turned away, saying in a sort of soliloquy, and in the English tongue:

"Uncas is right! it would not be the act of men to leave such harmless things to their fate, even though it breaks up the harboring place forever. If you would save these tender blossoms from the fangs of the worst of serpents, gentleman, you have neither time to lose nor resolution to throw away!"

"How can such a wish be doubted! Have I not already offered—"

"Offer your prayers to Him who can give us wisdom to circumvent the cunning of the devils who fill these woods," calmly interrupted the scout, "but spare your offers of money, which neither you may live to realize, nor I to profit by. These Mohicans and I will do what man's thoughts can invent, to keep such flowers, which, though so sweet, were never made for the wilderness, from harm, and that without hope of any other recompense but such as God always gives to upright dealings. First, you must promise two things, both in your own name and for your friends, or without serving you we shall only injure ourselves!"

"Name them."

"The one is, to be still as these sleeping woods, let what will happen and the other is, to keep the place where we shall take you, forever a secret from all mortal men."

"I will do my utmost to see both these conditions fulfilled."

"Then follow, for we are losing moments that are as precious as the heart's blood to a stricken deer!"

Heyward could distinguish the impatient gesture of the scout, through the increasing shadows of the evening, and he moved in his footsteps, swiftly, toward the place where he had left the remainder of the party. When they rejoined the expecting and anxious females, he briefly acquainted them with the conditions of their new guide, and with the necessity that existed for their hushing every apprehension in instant and serious exertions. Although his alarming communication was not received without much secret terror by the listeners, his earnest and impressive manner, aided perhaps by the nature of the danger, succeeded in bracing their nerves to undergo some unlooked-for and unusual trial. Silently, and without a moment's delay, they permitted him to assist them from their saddles, and when they descended quickly to the water's edge, where the scout had collected the rest of the party, more by the agency of expressive gestures than by any use of words.

"What to do with these dumb creatures!" muttered the white man, on whom the sole control of their future movements appeared to devolve; "it would be time lost to cut their throats, and cast them into the river; and to leave them here would be to tell the Mingoes that they have not far to seek to find their owners!"

"Then give them their bridles, and let them range the woods," Heyward ventured to suggest.

"No; it would be better to mislead the imps, and make them believe they must equal a horse's speed to run down their chase. Ay, ay, that will blind their fireballs of eyes! Chingach—Hist! what stirs the bush?"

"The colt."

"That colt, at least, must die," muttered the scout, grasping at the mane of the nimble beast, which easily eluded his hand; "Uncas, your arrows!"

"Hold!" exclaimed the proprietor of the condemned animal, aloud, without regard to the whispering tones used by the others; "spare the foal of Miriam! it is the comely offspring of a faithful dam, and would willingly injure naught."

"When men struggle for the single life God has given them," said the scout, sternly, "even their own kind seem no more than the beasts of the wood. If you speak again, I shall leave you to the mercy of the Maquas! Draw to your arrow's head, Uncas; we have no time for second blows."

The low, muttering sounds of his threatening voice were still audible, when the wounded foal, first rearing on its hinder legs, plunged forward to its knees. It was met by Chingachgook, whose knife passed across its throat quicker than thought, and then precipitating the motions of the struggling victim, he dashed into the river, down whose stream it glided away, gasping audibly for breath with its ebbing life. This deed of apparent cruelty, but of real necessity, fell upon the spirits of the travelers like a terrific warning of the peril in which they stood, heightened as it was by the calm though steady resolution of the actors in the scene. The sisters shuddered and clung closer to each other, while Heyward instinctively laid his hand on one of the pistols he had just drawn from their holsters, as he placed himself between his charge and those dense shadows that seemed to draw an impenetrable veil before the bosom of the forest.

The Indians, however, hesitated not a moment, but taking the bridles, they led the frightened and reluctant horses into the bed of the river.

At a short distance from the shore they turned, and were soon concealed by the projection of the bank, under the brow of which they moved, in a direction opposite to the course of the waters. In the meantime, the scout drew a canoe of bark from its place of concealment beneath some low bushes, whose branches were waving with the eddies of the current, into which he silently motioned for the females to enter. They complied without hesitation, though many a fearful and anxious glance was thrown behind them, toward the thickening gloom, which now lay like a dark barrier along the margin of the stream.

So soon as Cora and Alice were seated, the scout, without regarding the element, directed Heyward to support one side of the frail vessel, and posting himself at the other, they bore it up against the stream, followed by the dejected owner of the dead foal. In this manner they proceeded, for many rods, in a silence that was only interrupted by the rippling of the water, as its eddies played around them, or the low dash made by their own cautious footsteps. Heyward yielded the guidance of the canoe implicitly to the scout, who approached or receded from the shore, to avoid the fragments of rocks, or deeper parts of the river, with a readiness that showed his knowledge of the route they held. Occasionally he would stop; and in the midst of a breathing stillness, that the dull but increasing roar of the waterfall only served to render more impressive, he would listen with painful intenseness, to catch any sounds that might arise from the slumbering forest. When assured that all was still, and unable to detect, even by the aid of his practiced senses, any sign of his approaching foes, he would deliberately resume his slow and guarded progress. At length they reached a point in the river where the roving eye of Heyward became riveted on a cluster of black objects, collected at a spot where the high bank threw a deeper shadow than usual on the dark waters. Hesitating to advance, he pointed out the place to the attention of his companion.

"Ay," returned the composed scout, "the Indians have hid the beasts with the judgment of natives! Water leaves no trail, and an owl's eyes would be blinded by the darkness of such a hole."

The whole party was soon reunited, and another consultation was held between the scout and his new comrades, during which, they, whose fates depended on the faith and ingenuity of these unknown foresters, had a little leisure to observe their situation more minutely.

The river was confined between high and cragged rocks, one of which impended above the spot where the canoe rested. As these, again, were surmounted by tall trees, which appeared to totter on the brows of the precipice, it gave the stream the appearance of running through a deep and narrow dell. All beneath the fantastic limbs and ragged tree tops, which were, here and there, dimly painted against the starry zenith, lay alike in shadowed obscurity. Behind them, the curvature of the banks soon bounded the view by the same dark and wooded outline; but in front, and apparently at no great distance, the water seemed piled against the heavens, whence it tumbled into caverns, out of which issued those sullen sounds that had loaded the evening atmosphere. It seemed, in truth, to be a spot devoted to seclusion, and the sisters imbibed a soothing impression of security, as they gazed upon its romantic though not unappalling beauties. A general movement among their conductors, however, soon recalled them from a contemplation of the wild charms that night had assisted to lend the place to a painful sense of their real peril.

The horses had been secured to some scattering shrubs that grew in the fissures of the rocks, where, standing in the water, they were left to pass the night. The scout directed Heyward and his disconsolate fellow travelers to seat themselves in the forward end of the canoe, and took possession of the other himself, as erect and steady as if he floated in a vessel of much firmer materials. The Indians warily retraced their steps toward the place they had left, when the scout, placing his pole against a rock, by a powerful shove, sent his frail bark directly into the turbulent stream. For many minutes the struggle between the light bubble in which they floated and the swift current was severe and doubtful. Forbidden to stir even a hand, and almost afraid to breath, lest they should expose the frail fabric to the fury of the stream, the passengers watched the glancing waters in feverish suspense. Twenty times they thought the whirling eddies were sweeping them to destruction, when the master-hand of their pilot would bring the bows of the canoe to stem the rapid. A long, a vigorous, and, as it appeared to the females, a desperate effort, closed the struggle. Just as Alice veiled her eyes in horror, under the impression that they were about to be swept within the vortex at the foot of the cataract, the canoe floated, stationary, at the side of a flat rock, that lay on a level with the water.

"Where are we, and what is next to be done!" demanded Heyward, perceiving that the exertions of the scout had ceased.

"You are at the foot of Glenn's," returned the other, speaking aloud, without fear of consequences within the roar of the cataract; "and the next thing is to make a steady landing, lest the canoe upset, and you should go down again the hard road we have traveled faster than you came up; 'tis a hard rift to stem, when the river is a little swelled; and five is an unnatural number to keep dry, in a hurry-skurry, with a little birchen bark and gum. There, go you all on the rock, and I will bring up the Mohicans with the venison. A man had better sleep without his scalp, than famish in the midst of plenty."

His passengers gladly complied with these directions. As the last foot touched the rock, the canoe whirled from its station, when the tall form of the scout was seen, for an instant, gliding above the waters, before it disappeared in the impenetrable darkness that rested on the bed of the river. Left by their guide, the travelers remained a few minutes in helpless ignorance, afraid even to move along the broken rocks, lest a false step should precipitate them down some one of the many deep and roaring caverns, into which the water seemed to tumble, on every side of them. Their suspense, however, was soon relieved; for, aided by the skill of the natives, the canoe shot back into the eddy, and floated again at the side of the low rock, before they thought the scout had even time to rejoin his companions.

"We are now fortified, garrisoned, and provisioned," cried Heyward cheerfully, "and may set Montcalm and his allies at defiance. How, now, my vigilant sentinel, can see anything of those you call the Iroquois, on the main land!"

"I call them Iroquois, because to me every native, who speaks a foreign tongue, is accounted an enemy, though he may pretend to serve the king! If Webb wants faith and honesty in an Indian, let him bring out the tribes of the Delawares, and send these greedy and lying Mohawks and Oneidas, with their six nations of varlets, where in nature they belong, among the French!"

"We should then exchange a warlike for a useless friend! I have heard that the Delawares have laid aside the hatchet, and are content to be called women!"

"Aye, shame on the Hollanders and Iroquois, who circumvented them by their deviltries, into such a treaty! But I have known them for twenty years, and I call him liar that says cowardly blood runs in the veins of a Delaware. You have driven their tribes from the seashore, and would now believe what their enemies say, that you may sleep at night upon an easy pillow. No, no; to me, every Indian who speaks a foreign tongue is an Iroquois, whether the castle* of his tribe be in Canada, or be in York."

Heyward, perceiving that the stubborn adherence of the scout to the cause of his friends the Delawares, or Mohicans, for they were branches of the same numerous people, was likely to prolong a useless discussion, changed the subject.

"Treaty or no treaty, I know full well that your two companions are brave and cautious warriors! have they heard or seen anything of our enemies!"

"An Indian is a mortal to be felt afore he is seen," returned the scout, ascending the rock, and throwing the deer carelessly down. "I trust to other signs than such as come in at the eye, when I am outlying on the trail of the Mingoes."

"Do your ears tell you that they have traced our retreat?"

"I should be sorry to think they had, though this is a spot that stout courage might hold for a smart scrimmage. I will not deny, however, but the horses cowered when I passed them, as though they scented the wolves; and a wolf is a beast that is apt to hover about an Indian ambushment, craving the offals of the deer the savages kill."

"You forget the buck at your feet! or, may we not owe their visit to the dead colt? Ha! what noise is that?"

"Poor Miriam!" murmured the stranger; "thy foal was foreordained to become a prey to ravenous beasts!" Then, suddenly lifting up his voice, amid the eternal din of the waters, he sang aloud: "First born of Egypt, smite did he, Of mankind, and of beast also: O, Egypt! wonders sent 'midst thee, On Pharaoh and his servants too!"

"The death of the colt sits heavy on the heart of its owner," said the scout; "but it's a good sign to see a man account upon his dumb friends. He has the religion of the matter, in believing what is to happen will happen; and with such a consolation, it won't be long afore he submits to the rationality of killing a four-footed beast to save the lives of human men. It may be as you say," he continued, reverting to the purport of Heyward's last remark; "and the greater the reason why we should cut our steaks, and let the carcass drive down the stream, or we shall have the pack howling along the cliffs, begrudging every mouthful we swallow. Besides, though the Delaware tongue is the same as a book to the Iroquois, the cunning varlets are quick enough at understanding the reason of a wolf's howl."

The scout, while making his remarks, was busied in collecting certain necessary implements; as he concluded, he moved silently by the group of travelers, accompanied by the Mohicans, who seemed to comprehend his intentions with instinctive readiness, when the whole three disappeared in succession, seeming to vanish against the dark face of a perpendicular rock that rose to the height of a few yards, within as many feet of the water's edge.

---

* The principal villages of the Indians are still called "castles" by the whites of New York. "Oneida castle" is no more than a scattered hamlet; but the name is in general use.

CHAPTER VI.

"Those strains that once did sweet in Zion glide;
He wales a portion with judicious care;
And 'Let us worship God', he says, with solemn air."—Burns

Heyward and his female companions witnessed this mysterious movement with secret uneasiness; for, though the conduct of the white man had hitherto been above reproach, his rude equipments, blunt address, and strong antipathies, together with the character of his silent associates, were all causes for exciting distrust in minds that had been so recently alarmed by Indian treachery.

The stranger alone disregarded the passing incidents. He seated himself on a projection of the rocks, whence he gave no other signs of consciousness than by the struggles of his spirit, as manifested in frequent and heavy sighs. Smothered voices were next heard, as though men called to each other in the bowels of the earth, when a sudden light flashed upon those without, and laid bare the much-prized secret of the place.

At the further extremity of a narrow, deep cavern in the rock, whose length appeared much extended by the perspective and the nature of the light by which it was seen, was seated the scout, holding a blazing knot of pine. The strong glare of the fire fell full upon his sturdy, weather-beaten countenance and forest attire, lending an air of romantic wildness to the aspect of an individual, who, seen by the sober light of day, would have exhibited the peculiarities of a man remarkable for the strangeness of his dress, the iron-like inflexibility of his frame, and the singular compound of quick, vigilant sagacity, and of exquisite simplicity, that by turns usurped the possession of his muscular features. At a little distance in advance stood Uncas, his whole person thrown powerfully into view. The travelers anxiously regarded the upright, flexible figure of the young Mohican, graceful and unrestrained in the attitudes and movements of nature. Though his person was more than usually screened by a green and fringed hunting-shirt, like that of the white man, there was no concealment to his dark, glancing, fearless eye, alike terrible and calm; the bold outline of his high, haughty features, pure in their native red; or to the dignified elevation of his receding forehead, together with all the finest proportions of a noble head, bared to the generous scalping tuft. It was the first opportunity possessed by Duncan and his companions to view the marked lineaments of either of their Indian attendants, and each individual of the party felt relieved from a burden of doubt, as the proud and determined, though wild expression of the features of the young warrior forced itself on their notice. They felt it might be a being partially benighted in the vale of ignorance, but it could not be one who would willingly devote his rich natural gifts to the purposes of wanton treachery. The ingenuous Alice gazed at his free air and proud carriage, as she would have looked upon some precious relic of the Grecian chisel, to which life had been imparted by the intervention of a miracle; while Heyward, though accustomed to see the perfection of form which abounds among the uncorrupted natives, openly expressed his admiration at such an unblemished specimen of the noblest proportions of man.

"I could sleep in peace," whispered Alice, in reply, "with such a fearless and generous-looking youth for my sentinel. Surely, Duncan, those cruel murders, those terrific scenes of torture, of which we read and hear so much, are never acted in the presence of such as he!"

"This certainly is a rare and brilliant instance of those natural qualities in which these peculiar people are said to excel," he answered. "I agree with you, Alice, in thinking that such a front and eye were formed rather to intimidate than to deceive; but let us not practice a deception upon ourselves, by expecting any other exhibition of what we esteem virtue than according to the fashion of the savage. As bright examples of great qualities are but too uncommon among Christians, so are they singular and solitary with the Indians; though, for the honor of our common nature, neither are incapable of producing them. Let us then hope that this Mohican may not disappoint our wishes, but prove what his looks assert him to be, a brave and constant friend."

"Now Major Heyward speaks as Major Heyward should," said Cora; "who that looks at this creature of nature, remembers the shade of his skin?"

A short and apparently an embarrassed silence succeeded this remark, which was interrupted by the scout calling to them, aloud, to enter.

"This fire begins to show too bright a flame," he continued, as they complied, "and might light the Mingoes to our undoing. Uncas, drop the blanket, and show the knaves its dark side. This is not such a supper as a major of the Royal Americans has a right to expect, but I've known stout detachments of the corps glad to eat their venison raw, and without a relish, too.* Here, you see, we have plenty of salt, and can make a quick broil. There's fresh sassafras boughs for the ladies to sit on, which may not be as proud as their my-hog-guinea chairs, but which sends up a sweeter flavor, than the skin of any hog can do, be it of Guinea, or be it of any other land. Come, friend, don't be mournful for the colt; 'twas an innocent thing, and had not seen much hardship. Its death will save the creature many a sore back and weary foot!"

Uncas did as the other had directed, and when the voice of Hawkeye ceased, the roar of the cataract sounded like the rumbling of distant thunder.

"Are we quite safe in this cavern?" demanded Heyward. "Is there no danger of surprise? A single armed man, at its entrance, would hold us at his mercy."

A spectral-looking figure stalked from out of the darkness behind the scout, and seizing a blazing brand, held it toward the further extremity of their place of retreat. Alice uttered a faint shriek, and even Cora rose to her feet, as this appalling object moved into the light; but a single word from Heyward calmed them, with the assurance it was only their attendant, Chingachgook, who, lifting another blanket, discovered that the cavern had two outlets. Then, holding the brand, he crossed a deep, narrow chasm in the rocks which ran at right angles with the passage they were in, but which, unlike that, was open to the heavens, and entered another cave, answering to the description of the first, in every essential particular.

"Such old foxes as Chingachgook and myself are not often caught in a barrow with one hole," said Hawkeye, laughing; "you can easily see the cunning of the place—the rock is black limestone, which everybody knows is soft; it makes no uncomfortable pillow, where brush and pine wood is scarce; well, the fall was once a few yards below us, and I dare to say was, in its time, as regular and as handsome a sheet of water as any along the Hudson. But old age is a great injury to good looks, as these sweet young ladies have yet to l'arn! The place is sadly changed! These rocks are full of cracks,

---

* In vulgar parlance the condiments of a repast are called by the American "a relish," substituting the thing for its effect. These provincial terms are frequently put in the mouths of the speakers, according to their several conditions in life. Most of them are of local use, and others quite peculiar to the particular class of men to which the character belongs. In the present instance, the scout uses the word with immediate reference to the "salt," with which his own party was so fortunate as to be provided.

and in some places they are softer than at othersome, and the water has worked out deep hollows for itself, until it has fallen back, ay, some hundred feet, breaking here and wearing there, until the falls have neither shape nor consistency."

"In what part of them are we?" asked Heyward.

"Why, we are nigh the spot that Providence first placed them at, but where, it seems, they were too rebellious to stay. The rock proved softer on each side of us, and so they left the center of the river bare and dry, first working out these two little holes for us to hide in."

"We are then on an island!"

"Ay! there are the falls on two sides of us, and the river above and below. If you had daylight, it would be worth the trouble to step up on the height of this rock, and look at the perversity of the water. It falls by no rule at all; sometimes it leaps, sometimes it tumbles; there it skips; here it shoots; in one place 'tis white as snow, and in another 'tis green as grass; hereabouts, it pitches into deep hollows, that rumble and crush the 'arth; and thereaways, it ripples and sings like a brook, fashioning whirlpools and gullies in the old stone, as if 'twas no harder than trodden clay. The whole design of the river seems disconcerted. First it runs smoothly, as if meaning to go down the descent as things were ordered; then it angles about and faces the shores; nor are there places wanting where it looks backward, as if unwilling to leave the wilderness, to mingle with the salt. Ay, lady, the fine cobweb-looking cloth you wear at your throat is coarse, and like a fishnet, to little spots I can show you, where the river fabricates all sorts of images, as if having broke loose from order, it would try its hand at everything. And yet what does it amount to! After the water has been suffered so to have its will, for a time, like a headstrong man, it is gathered together by the hand that made it, and a few rods below you may see it all, flowing on steadily toward the sea, as was foreordained from the first foundation of the 'arth!"

While his auditors received a cheering assurance of the security of their place of concealment from this untutored description of Glenn's,* they were much inclined to judge differently from Hawkeye, of its wild beauties. But they were not in a situation to suffer their thoughts to dwell on the charms of natural objects; and, as the scout had not found it necessary to cease his culinary labors while he spoke, unless to point out, with a broken fork, the direction of some particularly obnoxious point in the rebellious stream, they now suffered their attention to be drawn to the necessary though more vulgar consideration of their supper.

The repast, which was greatly aided by the addition of a few delicacies that Heyward had the precaution to bring with him when they left their horses, was exceedingly refreshing to the weary party. Uncas acted as attendant to the females, performing all the little offices within his power, with

---

* Glenn's Falls are on the Hudson, some forty or fifty miles above the head of tide, or that place where the river becomes navigable for sloops. The description of this picturesque and remarkable little cataract, as given by the scout, is sufficiently correct, though the application of the water to uses of civilized life has materially injured its beauties. The rocky island and the two caverns are known to every traveler, since the former sustains the pier of a bridge, which is now thrown across the river, immediately above the fall. In explanation of the taste of Hawkeye, it should be remembered that men always prize that most which is least enjoyed. Thus, in a new country, the woods and other objects, which in an old country would be maintained at great cost, are got rid of, simply with a view of "improving" as it is called.

a mixture of dignity and anxious grace, that served to amuse Heyward, who well knew that it was an utter innovation on the Indian customs, which forbid their warriors to descend to any menial employment, especially in favor of their women. As the rights of hospitality were, however, considered sacred among them, this little departure from the dignity of manhood excited no audible comment. Had there been one there sufficiently disengaged to become a close observer, he might have fancied that the services of the young chief were not entirely impartial. That while he tendered to Alice the gourd of sweet water, and the venison in a trencher, neatly carved from the knot of the pepperidge, with sufficient courtesy, in performing the same offices to her sister, his dark eye lingered on her rich, speaking countenance. Once or twice he was compelled to speak, to command her attention of those he served. In such cases he made use of English, broken and imperfect, but sufficiently intelligible, and which he rendered so mild and musical, by his deep, guttural voice, that it never failed to cause both ladies to look up in admiration and astonishment. In the course of these civilities, a few sentences were exchanged, that served to establish the appearance of an amicable intercourse between the parties.

In the meanwhile, the gravity of Chingcachgook remained immovable. He had seated himself more within the circle of light, where the frequent, uneasy glances of his guests were better enabled to separate the natural expression of his face from the artificial terrors of the war paint. They found a strong resemblance between father and son, with the difference that might be expected from age and hardships. The fierceness of his countenance now seemed to slumber, and in its place was to be seen the quiet, vacant composure which distinguishes an Indian warrior, when his faculties are not required for any of the greater purposes of his existence. It was, however, easy to be seen, by the occasional gleams that shot across his swarthy visage, that it was only necessary to arouse his passions, in order to give full effect to the terrific device which he had adopted to intimidate his enemies. On the other hand, the quick, roving eye of the scout seldom rested. He ate and drank with an appetite that no sense of danger could disturb, but his vigilance seemed never to desert him. Twenty times the gourd or the venison was suspended before his lips, while his head was turned aside, as though he listened to some distant and distrusted sounds—a movement that never failed to recall his guests from regarding the novelties of their situation, to a recollection of the alarming reasons that had driven them to seek it. As these frequent pauses were never followed by any remark, the momentary uneasiness they created quickly passed away, and for a time was forgotten.

"Come, friend," said Hawkeye, drawing out a keg from beneath a cover of leaves, toward the close of the repast, and addressing the stranger who sat at his elbow, doing great justice to his culinary skill, "try a little spruce; 'twill wash away all thoughts of the colt, and quicken the life in your bosom. I drink to our better friendship, hoping that a little horse-flesh may leave no heart-burnings atween us. How do you name yourself?"

"Gamut—David Gamut," returned the singing master, preparing to wash down his sorrows in a powerful draught of the woodsman's high-flavored and well-laced compound.

"A very good name, and, I dare say, handed down from honest forefathers. I'm an admirer of names, though the Christian fashions fall far below savage customs in this particular. The biggest coward I ever knew as called Lyon; and his wife, Patience, would scold you out of hearing in less time than a hunted deer would run a rod. With an Indian 'tis a matter of conscience; what he calls himself, he generally is—not that Chingachgook, which signifies Big Sarpent, is really a snake, big or little; but that he understands the windings and turnings of human natur', and is silent, and strikes his enemies when they least expect him. What may be your calling?"

"I am an unworthy instructor in the art of psalmody."

"Anan!"

"I teach singing to the youths of the Connecticut levy."

"You might be better employed. The young hounds go laughing and singing too much already through the woods, when they ought not to breathe louder than a fox in his cover. Can you use the smoothbore, or handle the rifle?"

"Praised be God, I have never had occasion to meddle with murderous implements!"

"Perhaps you understand the compass, and lay down the watercourses and mountains of the wilderness on paper, in order that they who follow may find places by their given names?"

"I practice no such employment."

"You have a pair of legs that might make a long path seem short! you journey sometimes, I fancy, with tidings for the general."

"Never; I follow no other than my own high vocation, which is instruction in sacred music!"

"'Tis a strange calling!" muttered Hawkeye, with an inward laugh, "to go through life, like a catbird, mocking all the ups and downs that may happen to come out of other men's throats. Well, friend, I suppose it is your gift, and mustn't be denied any more than if 'twas shooting, or some other better inclination. Let us hear what you can do in that way; 'twill be a friendly manner of saying good-night, for 'tis time that these ladies should be getting strength for a hard and a long push, in the pride of the morning, afore the Maquas are stirring."

"With joyful pleasure do I consent", said David, adjusting his iron-rimmed spectacles, and producing his beloved little volume, which he immediately tendered to Alice. "What can be more fitting and consolatory, than to offer up evening praise, after a day of such exceeding jeopardy!"

Alice smiled; but, regarding Heyward, she blushed and hesitated.

"Indulge yourself," he whispered; "ought not the suggestion of the worthy namesake of the Psalmist to have its weight at such a moment?"

Encouraged by his opinion, Alice did what her pious inclinations, and her keen relish for gentle sounds, had before so strongly urged. The book was open at a hymn not ill adapted to their situation, and in which the poet, no longer goaded by his desire to excel the inspired King of Israel, had discovered some chastened and respectable powers. Cora betrayed a disposition to support her sister, and the sacred song proceeded, after the indispensable preliminaries of the pitchpipe, and the tune had been duly attended to by the methodical David.

The air was solemn and slow. At times it rose to the fullest compass of the rich voices of the females, who hung over their little book in holy excitement, and again it sank so low, that the rushing of the waters ran through their melody, like a hollow accompaniment. The natural taste and true ear of David governed and modified the sounds to suit the confined cavern, every crevice and cranny of which was filled with the thrilling notes of their flexible voices. The Indians riveted their eyes on the rocks, and listened with an attention that seemed to turn them into stone. But the scout, who had placed his chin in his hand, with an expression of cold indifference, gradually suffered his rigid features to relax, until, as verse succeeded verse, he felt his iron nature subdued, while his recollection was carried back to boyhood, when his ears had been accustomed to listen to similar sounds of praise, in the settlements of the colony. His roving eyes began to moisten, and before the hymn was ended scalding tears rolled out of fountains that had long seemed dry, and followed each other down those cheeks, that had oftener felt the storms of heaven than any testimonials of weakness. The singers were dwelling on one of those low, dying chords, which the ear devours with such greedy rapture, as if conscious that it is about to lose them, when a cry, that seemed neither human nor earthly, rose in the outward air, penetrating not only the recesses of the cavern, but to the inmost hearts of all who heard it. It was followed by a stillness apparently as deep as if the waters had been checked in their furious progress, at such a horrid and unusual interruption.

"What is it?" murmured Alice, after a few moments of terrible suspense.

"What is it?" repeated Hewyard aloud.

Neither Hawkeye nor the Indians made any reply. They listened, as if expecting the sound would be repeated, with a manner that expressed their own astonishment. At length they spoke together, earnestly, in the Delaware language, when Uncas, passing by the inner and most concealed aperture, cautiously left the cavern. When he had gone, the scout first spoke in English.

"What it is, or what it is not, none here can tell, though two of us have ranged the woods for more than thirty years. I did believe there was no cry that Indian or beast could make, that my ears had not heard; but this has proved that I was only a vain and conceited mortal."

"Was it not, then, the shout the warriors make when they wish to intimidate their enemies?" asked Cora who stood drawing her veil about her person, with a calmness to which her agitated sister was a stranger.

"No, no; this was bad, and shocking, and had a sort of unhuman sound; but when you once hear the war-whoop, you will never mistake it for anything else. Well, Uncas!" speaking in Delaware to the young chief as he re-entered, "what see you? do our lights shine through the blankets?"

The answer was short, and apparently decided, being given in the same tongue.

"There is nothing to be seen without," continued Hawkeye, shaking his head in discontent; "and our hiding-place is still in darkness. Pass into the other cave, you that need it, and seek for sleep; we must be afoot long before the sun, and make the most of our time to get to Edward, while the Mingoes are taking their morning nap."

Cora set the example of compliance, with a steadiness that taught the more timid Alice the necessity of obedience. Before leaving the place, however, she whispered a request to Duncan, that he would follow. Uncas raised the blanket for their passage, and as the sisters turned to thank him for this act of attention, they saw the scout seated again before the dying embers, with his face resting on his hands, in a manner which showed how deeply he brooded on the unaccountable interruption which had broken up their evening devotions.

Heyward took with him a blazing knot, which threw a dim light through the narrow vista of their new apartment. Placing it in a favorable position, he joined the females, who now found themselves alone with him for the first time since they had left the friendly ramparts of Fort Edward.

"Leave us not, Duncan," said Alice: "we cannot sleep in such a place as this, with that horrid cry still ringing in our ears."

"First let us examine into the security of your fortress," he answered, "and then we will speak of rest."

He approached the further end of the cavern, to an outlet, which, like the others, was concealed by blankets; and removing the thick screen, breathed the fresh and reviving air from the cataract. One arm of the river flowed through a deep, narrow ravine, which its current had worn in the soft rock, directly beneath his feet, forming an effectual defense, as he believed, against any danger from that quarter; the water, a few rods above them, plunging, glancing, and sweeping along in its most violent and broken manner.

"Nature has made an impenetrable barrier on this side," he continued, pointing down the perpendicular declivity into the dark current before he dropped the blanket; "and as you know that good men and true are on guard in front I see no reason why the advice of our honest host should be disregarded. I am certain Cora will join me in saying that sleep is necessary to you both."

"Cora may submit to the justice of your opinion though she cannot put it in practice," returned the elder sister, who had placed herself by the side of Alice, on a couch of sassafras; "there would be other causes to chase away sleep, though we had been spared the shock of this mysterious noise. Ask yourself, Heyward, can daughters forget the anxiety a father must endure, whose children lodge he knows not where or how, in such a wilderness, and in the midst of so many perils?"

"He is a soldier, and knows how to estimate the chances of the woods."

"He is a father, and cannot deny his nature."

"How kind has he ever been to all my follies, how tender and indulgent to all my wishes!" sobbed Alice. "We have been selfish, sister, in urging our visit at such hazard."

"I may have been rash in pressing his consent in a moment of much embarrassment, but I would have proved to him, that however others might neglect him in his strait his children at least were faithful."

"When he heard of your arrival at Edward," said Heyward, kindly, "there was a powerful struggle in his bosom between fear and love; though the latter, heightened, if possible, by so long a separation, quickly prevailed. 'It is the spirit of my noble-minded Cora that leads them, Duncan', he said, 'and I will not balk it. Would to God, that he who holds the honor of our royal master in his guardianship, would show but half her firmness!'"

"And did he not speak of me, Heyward?" demanded Alice, with jealous affection; "surely, he forgot not altogether his little Elsie?"

"That were impossible," returned the young man; "he called you by a thousand endearing epithets, that I may not presume to use, but to the justice of which, I can warmly testify. Once, indeed, he said—"

Duncan ceased speaking; for while his eyes were riveted on those of Alice, who had turned toward him with the eagerness of filial affection, to catch his words, the same strong, horrid cry, as before, filled the air, and rendered him mute. A long, breathless silence succeeded, during which each looked at the others in fearful expectation of hearing the sound repeated. At length, the blanket was slowly raised, and the scout stood in the aperture with a countenance whose firmness evidently began to give way before a mystery that seemed to threaten some danger, against which all his cunning and experience might prove of no avail.

<br>

CHAPTER VII.

> "They do not sleep,
> On yonder cliffs, a grizzly band,
> I see them sit."—Gray

"'Twould be neglecting a warning that is given for our good to lie hid any longer," said Hawkeye "when such sounds are raised in the forest. These gentle ones may keep close, but the Mohicans and I will watch upon the rock, where I suppose a major of the Sixtieth would wish to keep us company."

"Is, then, our danger so pressing?" asked Cora.

"He who makes strange sounds, and gives them out for man's information, alone knows our danger. I should think myself wicked, unto rebellion against His will, was I to burrow with such warnings in the air! Even the weak soul who passes his days in singing is stirred by the cry, and, as he says, is 'ready to go forth to the battle' If 'twere only a battle, it would be a thing understood by us all, and easily managed; but I have heard that when such shrieks are atween heaven and 'arth, it betokens another sort of warfare!"

"If all our reasons for fear, my friend, are confined to such as proceed from supernatural causes, we have but little occasion to be alarmed," continued the undisturbed Cora, "are you certain that our enemies have not invented some new and ingenious method to strike us with terror, that their conquest may become more easy?"

"Lady," returned the scout, solemnly, "I have listened to all the sounds of the woods for thirty years, as a man will listen whose life and death depend on the quickness of his ears. There is no whine of the panther, no whistle of the catbird, nor any invention of the devilish Mingoes, that can cheat me! I have heard the forest moan like mortal men in their affliction; often, and again, have I listened to the wind playing its music in the branches of the girdled trees; and I have heard the lightning cracking in the air like the snapping of blazing brush as it spitted forth sparks and forked flames; but never have I thought that I heard more than the pleasure of him who sported with the things of his hand. But neither the Mohicans, nor I, who am a white man without a cross, can explain the cry just heard. We, therefore, believe it a sign given for our good."

"It is extraordinary!" said Heyward, taking his pistols from the place where he had laid them on entering; "be it a sign of peace or a signal of war, it must be looked to. Lead the way, my friend; I follow."

On issuing from their place of confinement, the whole party instantly experienced a grateful renovation of spirits, by exchanging the pent air of the hiding-place for the cool and invigorating atmosphere which played around the whirlpools and pitches of the cataract. A heavy evening breeze swept along the surface of the river, and seemed to drive the roar of the falls into the recesses of their own cavern, whence it issued heavily and constant, like thunder rumbling beyond the distant hills. The moon had risen, and its light was already glancing here and there on the waters above them; but the extremity of the rock where they stood still lay in shadow. With the exception of the sounds produced by the rushing waters, and an occasional breathing of the air, as it murmured past them in fitful currents, the scene was as still as night and solitude could make it. In vain were the eyes of each individual bent along the opposite shores, in quest of some signs of life, that might explain the nature of the interruption they had heard. Their anxious and eager looks were baffled by the deceptive light, or rested only on naked rocks, and straight and immovable trees.

"Here is nothing to be seen but the gloom and quiet of a lovely evening," whispered Duncan; "how much should we prize such a scene, and all this breathing solitude, at any other moment, Cora! Fancy yourselves in security, and what now, perhaps, increases your terror, may be made conducive to enjoyment—"

"Listen!" interrupted Alice.

The caution was unnecessary. Once more the same sound arose, as if from the bed of the river, and having broken out of the narrow bounds of the cliffs, was heard undulating through the forest, in distant and dying cadences.

"Can any here give a name to such a cry?" demanded Hawkeye, when the last echo was lost in the woods; "if so, let him speak; for myself, I judge it not to belong to 'arth!"

"Here, then, is one who can undeceive you," said Duncan; "I know the sound full well, for often have I heard it on the field of battle, and in situations which are frequent in a soldier's life. 'Tis the horrid shriek that a horse will give in his agony; oftener drawn from him in pain, though sometimes in terror. My charger is either a prey to the beasts of the forest, or he sees his danger, without the power to avoid it. The sound might deceive me in the cavern, but in the open air I know it too well to be wrong."

The scout and his companions listened to this simple explanation with the interest of men who imbibe new ideas, at the same time that they get rid of old ones, which had proved disagreeable inmates. The two latter uttered their usual expressive exclamation, "hugh!" as the truth first glanced upon their minds, while the former, after a short, musing pause, took upon himself to reply.

"I cannot deny your words," he said, "for I am little skilled in horses, though born where they abound. The wolves must be hovering above their heads on the bank, and the timorsome creatures are calling on man for help, in the best manner they are able. Uncas"—he spoke in Delaware—"Uncas, drop down in the canoe, and whirl a brand among the pack; or fear may do what the wolves can't get at to perform, and leave us without horses in the morning, when we shall have so much need to journey swiftly!"

The young native had already descended to the water to comply, when a long howl was raised on the edge of the river, and was borne swiftly off into the depths of the forest, as though the beasts, of their own accord, were abandoning their prey in sudden terror. Uncas, with instinctive quickness, receded, and the three foresters held another of their low, earnest conferences.

"We have been like hunters who have lost the points of the heavens, and from whom the sun has been hid for days," said Hawkeye, turning away from his companions; "now we begin again to know the signs of our course, and the paths are cleared from briers! Seat yourselves in the shade which the moon throws from yonder beech—'tis thicker than that of the pines—and let us wait for that which the Lord may choose to send next. Let all your conversation be in whispers; though it would be better, and, perhaps, in the end, wiser, if each one held discourse with his own thoughts, for a time."

The manner of the scout was seriously impressive, though no longer distinguished by any signs of unmanly apprehension. It was evident that his momentary weakness had vanished with the explanation of a mystery which his own experience had not served to fathom; and though he now felt all the realities of their actual condition, that he was prepared to meet them with the energy of his hardy nature. This feeling seemed also common to the natives, who placed themselves in positions which commanded a full view of both shores, while their own persons were effectually concealed from observation. In such circumstances, common prudence dictated that Heyward and his companions should imitate a caution that proceeded from so intelligent a source. The young man drew a pile of the sassafras from the cave, and placing it in the chasm which separated the two caverns, it was occupied by the sisters, who were thus protected by the rocks from any missiles, while their anxiety was relieved by the assurance that no danger could approach without a warning. Heyward himself was posted at hand, so near that he might communicate with his companions without raising his voice to a dangerous elevation; while David, in imitation of the woodsmen, bestowed his person in such a manner among the fissures of the rocks, that his ungainly limbs were no longer offensive to the eye.

In this manner hours passed without further interruption. The moon reached the zenith, and shed its mild light perpendicularly on the lovely sight of the sisters slumbering peacefully in each other's arms. Duncan cast the wide shawl of Cora before a spectacle he so much loved to contemplate, and then suffered his own head to seek a pillow on the rock. David began to utter sounds that would have shocked his delicate organs in more wakeful moments; in short, all but Hawkeye and the Mohicans lost every idea of consciousness, in uncontrollable drowsiness. But the watchfulness of these vigilant protectors neither tired nor slumbered. Immovable as that rock, of which each appeared to form a part, they lay, with their eyes roving, without intermission, along the dark margin of trees, that bounded the adjacent shores of the narrow stream. Not a sound escaped them; the most subtle examination could not have told they breathed. It was evident that this excess of caution proceeded from an experience that no subtlety on the part of their enemies could deceive. It was, however, continued without any apparent consequences, until the moon had set, and a pale streak above the treetops, at the bend of the river a little below, announced the approach of day.

Then, for the first time, Hawkeye was seen to stir. He crawled along the rock and shook Duncan from his heavy slumbers.

"Now is the time to journey," he whispered; "awake the gentle ones, and be ready to get into the canoe when I bring it to the landing-place."

"Have you had a quiet night?" said Heyward; "for myself, I believe sleep has got the better of my vigilance."

"All is yet still as midnight. Be silent, but be quick."

By this time Duncan was thoroughly awake, and he immediately lifted the shawl from the sleeping females. The motion caused Cora to raise her hand as if to repulse him, while Alice murmured, in her soft, gentle voice, "No, no, dear father, we were not deserted; Duncan was with us!"

"Yes, sweet innocence," whispered the youth; "Duncan is here, and while life continues or danger remains, he will never quit thee. Cora! Alice! awake! The hour has come to move!"

A loud shriek from the younger of the sisters, and the form of the other standing upright before him, in bewildered horror, was the unexpected answer he received.

While the words were still on the lips of Heyward, there had arisen such a tumult of yells and cries as served to drive the swift currents of his own blood back from its bounding course into the fountains of his heart. It seemed, for near a minute, as if the demons of hell had possessed themselves of the air about them, and were venting their savage humors in barbarous sounds. The cries came from no particular direction, though it was evident they filled the woods, and, as the appalled listeners easily imagined, the caverns of the falls, the rocks, the bed of the river, and the upper air. David raised his tall person in the midst of the infernal din, with a hand on either ear, exclaiming:

"Whence comes this discord! Has hell broke loose, that man should utter sounds like these!"

The bright flashes and the quick reports of a dozen rifles, from the opposite banks of the stream, followed this incautious exposure of his person, and left the unfortunate singing master senseless on that rock where he had been so long slumbering. The Mohicans boldly sent back the intimidating yell of their enemies, who raised a shout of savage triumph at the fall of Gamut. The flash of rifles was then quick and close between them, but either party was too well skilled to leave even a limb exposed to the hostile aim. Duncan listened with intense anxiety for the strokes of the paddle, believing that flight was now their only refuge. The river glanced by with its ordinary velocity, but the canoe was nowhere to be seen on its dark waters. He had just fancied they were cruelly deserted by their scout, as a stream of flame issued from the rock beneath them, and a fierce yell, blended with a shriek of agony, announced that the messenger of death sent from the fatal weapon of Hawkeye, had found a victim. At this slight repulse the assailants instantly withdrew, and gradually the place became as still as before the sudden tumult.

Duncan seized the favorable moment to spring to the body of Gamut, which he bore within the shelter of the narrow chasm that protected the sisters. In another minute the whole party was collected in this spot of comparative safety.

"The poor fellow has saved his scalp," said Hawkeye, coolly passing his hand over the head of David; "but he is a proof that a man may be born with too long a tongue! 'Twas downright madness to show six feet of flesh and blood, on a naked rock, to the raging savages. I only wonder he has escaped with life."

"Is he not dead?" demanded Cora, in a voice whose husky tones showed how powerfully natural horror struggled with her assumed firmness. "Can we do aught to assist the wretched man?"

"No, no! the life is in his heart yet, and after he has slept awhile he will come to himself, and be a wiser man for it, till the hour of his real time shall come," returned Hawkeye, casting another oblique glance at the insensible body, while he filled his charger with admirable nicety. "Carry him in, Uncas, and lay him on the sassafras. The longer his nap lasts the better it will be for him, as I doubt whether he can find a proper cover for such a shape on these rocks; and singing won't do any good with the Iroquois."

"You believe, then, the attack will be renewed?" asked Heyward.

"Do I expect a hungry wolf will satisfy his craving with a mouthful! They have lost a man, and 'tis their fashion, when they meet a loss, and fail in the surprise, to fall back; but we shall have them on again, with new expedients to circumvent us, and master our scalps. Our main hope," he continued, raising his rugged countenance, across which a shade of anxiety just then passed like a darkening cloud, "will be to keep the rock until Munro can send a party to our help! God send it may be soon and under a leader that knows the Indian customs!"

"You hear our probable fortunes, Cora," said Duncan, "and you know we have everything to hope from the anxiety and experience of your father. Come, then, with Alice, into this cavern, where you, at least, will be safe from the murderous rifles of our enemies, and where you may bestow a care suited to your gentle natures on our unfortunate comrade."

The sisters followed him into the outer cave, where David was beginning, by his sighs, to give symptoms of returning consciousness, and then commending the wounded man to their attention, he immediately prepared to leave them.

"Duncan!" said the tremulous voice of Cora, when he had reached the mouth of the cavern. He turned and beheld the speaker, whose color had changed to a deadly paleness, and whose lips quivered, gazing after him, with an expression of interest which immediately recalled him to her side. "Remember, Duncan, how necessary your safety is to our own—how you bear a father's sacred trust—how much depends on your discretion and care—in short," she added, while the telltale blood stole over her features, crimsoning her very temples, "how very deservedly dear you are to all of the name of Munro."

"If anything could add to my own base love of life," said Heyward, suffering his unconscious eyes to wander to the youthful form of the silent Alice, "it would be so kind an assurance. As major of the Sixtieth, our honest host will tell you I must take my share of the fray; but our task will be easy; it is merely to keep these blood-hounds at bay for a few hours."

Without waiting for a reply, he tore himself from the presence of the sisters, and joined the scout and his companions, who still lay within the protection of the little chasm between the two caves.

"I tell you, Uncas," said the former, as Heyward joined them, "you are wasteful of your powder, and the kick of the rifle disconcerts your aim! Little powder, light lead, and a long arm, seldom fail of bringing the death screech from a Mingo! At least, such has been my experience with the creatur's. Come, friends: let us to our covers, for no man can tell when or where a Maqua* will strike his blow."

The Indians silently repaired to their appointed stations, which were fissures in the rocks, whence they could command the approaches to the foot of the falls. In the center of the little island, a few short and stunted pines had found root, forming a thicket, into which Hawkeye darted with the swiftness of a deer, followed by the active Duncan. Here they secured themselves, as well as circumstances would permit, among the shrubs and fragments of stone that were scattered about the place. Above them was a bare, rounded rock, on each side of which the water played its gambols, and plunged into the abysses beneath, in the manner already described. As the day had now dawned, the opposite shores no longer presented a confused outline, but they were able to look into the woods, and distinguish objects beneath a canopy of gloomy pines.

A long and anxious watch succeeded, but without any further evidences of a renewed attack; and Duncan began to hope that their fire had proved more fatal than was supposed, and that their enemies had been effectually repulsed. When he ventured to utter this impression to his companions, it was met by Hawkeye with an incredulous shake of the head.

"You know not the nature of a Maqua, if you think he is so easily beaten back without a scalp!" he answered. "If there was one of the imps yelling this morning, there were forty! and they know our number and quality too well to give up the chase so soon. Hist! look into the water above, just where it breaks over the rocks. I am no mortal, if the risky devils haven't swam down upon the very pitch, and, as bad luck would have it, they have hit the head of the island. Hist! man, keep close! or the hair will be off your crown in the turning of a knife!"

Heyward lifted his head from the cover, and beheld what he justly considered a prodigy of rashness and skill. The river had worn away the edge of the soft rock in such a manner as to render its first pitch less abrupt and perpendicular than is usual at waterfalls. With no other guide than the ripple of the stream where it met the head of the island, a party of their insatiable foes had ventured into the current, and swam down upon this point, knowing the ready access it would give, if successful, to their intended victims.

As Hawkeye ceased speaking, four human heads could be seen peering above a few logs of drift-wood that had lodged on these naked rocks, and which had probably suggested the idea of the practicability of the hazardous undertaking. At the next moment, a fifth form was seen floating over the green edge of the fall, a little from the line of the island. The savage struggled powerfully to gain the point of safety, and, favored by the glancing water, he was already stretching forth an arm to meet the grasp of his companions, when he shot away again with the shirling current, appeared to rise into the air, with uplifted arms and starting eyeballs, and fell, with a sudden plunge, into that deep and yawning abyss over which he hovered. A single, wild, despairing shriek rose from the cavern, and all was hushed again as the grave.

The first generous impulse of Duncan was to rush to the rescue of the hapless wretch; but he felt himself bound to the spot by the iron grasp of the immovable scout.

---

* Mingo was the Delaware term of the Five Nations. Maquas was the name given them by the Dutch. The French, from their first intercourse with them, called them Iroquois.

"Would ye bring certain death upon us, by telling the Mingoes where we lie?" demanded Hawkeye, sternly; "'Tis a charge of powder saved, and ammunition is as precious now as breath to a worried deer! Freshen the priming of your pistols—the midst of the falls is apt to dampen the brimstone—and stand firm for a close struggle, while I fire on their rush."

He placed a finger in his mouth, and drew a long, shrill whistle, which was answered from the rocks that were guarded by the Mohicans. Duncan caught glimpses of heads above the scattered driftwood, as this signal rose on the air, but they disappeared again as suddenly as they had glanced upon his sight. A low, rustling sound next drew his attention behind him, and turning his head, he beheld Uncas within a few feet, creeping to his side. Hawkeye spoke to him in Delaware, when the young chief took his position with singular caution and undisturbed coolness. To Heyward this was a moment of feverish and impatient suspense; though the scout saw fit to select it as a fit occasion to read a lecture to his more youthful associates on the art of using firearms with discretion.

"Of all we'pons," he commenced, "the long barreled, true-grooved, soft-metaled rifle is the most dangerous in skillful hands, though it wants a strong arm, a quick eye, and great judgment in charging, to put forth all its beauties. The gunsmiths can have but little insight into their trade when they make their fowling-pieces and short horsemen's—"

He was interrupted by the low but expressive "hugh" of Uncas.

"I see them, boy, I see them!" continued Hawkeye; "they are gathering for the rush, or they would keep their dingy backs below the logs. Well, let them," he added, examining his flint; "the leading man certainly comes on to his death, though it should be Montcalm himself!"

At that moment the woods were filled with another burst of cries, and at the signal four savages sprang from the cover of the driftwood. Heyward felt a burning desire to rush forward to meet them, so intense was the delirious anxiety of the moment; but he was restrained by the deliberate examples of the scout and Uncas.

When their foes, who had leaped over the black rocks that divided them, with long bounds, uttering the wildest yells, were within a few rods, the rifle of Hawkeye slowly rose among the shrubs, and poured out its fatal contents. The foremost Indian bounded like a stricken deer, and fell headlong among the clefts of the island.

"Now, Uncas!" cried the scout, drawing his long knife, while his quick eyes began to flash with ardor, "take the last of the screeching imps; of the other two we are sartain!"

He was obeyed; and but two enemies remained to be overcome. Heyward had given one of his pistols to Hawkeye, and together they rushed down a little declivity toward their foes; they discharged their weapons at the same instant, and equally without success.

"I know'd it! and I said it!" muttered the scout, whirling the despised little implement over the falls with bitter disdain. "Come on, ye bloody minded hell-hounds! ye meet a man without a cross!"

The words were barely uttered, when he encountered a savage of gigantic stature, of the fiercest mien. At the same moment, Duncan found himself engaged with the other, in a similar contest of hand to hand. With ready skill, Hawkeye and his antagonist each grasped that uplifted arm of the other which held the dangerous knife. For near a minute they stood looking one another in the eye, and gradually exerting the power of their muscles for the mastery.

At length, the toughened sinews of the white man prevailed over the less practiced limbs of the native. The arm of the latter slowly gave way before the increasing force of the scout, who, suddenly wresting his armed hand from the grasp of the foe, drove the sharp weapon through his naked bosom to the heart. In the meantime, Heyward had been pressed in a more deadly struggle. His slight sword was snapped in the first encounter. As he was destitute of any other means of defense, his safety now depended entirely on bodily strength and resolution. Though deficient in neither of these qualities, he had met an enemy every way his equal. Happily, he soon succeeded in disarming his adversary, whose knife fell on the rock at their feet; and from this moment it became a fierce struggle who should cast the other over the dizzy height into a neighboring cavern of the falls. Every successive struggle brought them nearer to the verge, where Duncan perceived the final and conquering effort must be made. Each of the combatants threw all his energies into that effort, and the result was, that both tottered on the brink of the precipice. Heyward felt the grasp of the other at his throat, and saw the grim smile the savage gave, under the revengeful hope that he hurried his enemy to a fate similar to his own, as he felt his body slowly yielding to a resistless power, and the young man experienced the passing agony of such a moment in all its horrors. At that instant of extreme danger, a dark hand and glancing knife appeared before him; the Indian released his hold, as the blood flowed freely from around the severed tendons of the wrist; and while Duncan was drawn backward by the saving hand of Uncas, his charmed eyes still were riveted on the fierce and disappointed countenance of his foe, who fell sullenly and disappointed down the irrecoverable precipice.

"To cover! to cover!" cried Hawkeye, who just then had despatched the enemy; "to cover, for your lives! the work is but half ended!"

The young Mohican gave a shout of triumph, and followed by Duncan, he glided up the acclivity they had descended to the combat, and sought the friendly shelter of the rocks and shrubs.


## CHAPTER VIII.

> "They linger yet,
> Avengers of their native land."—Gray

The warning call of the scout was not uttered without occasion. During the occurrence of the deadly encounter just related, the roar of the falls was unbroken by any human sound whatever. It would seem that interest in the result had kept the natives on the opposite shores in breathless suspense, while the quick evolutions and swift changes in the positions of the combatants effectually prevented a fire that might prove dangerous alike to friend and enemy. But the moment the struggle was decided, a yell arose as fierce and savage as wild and revengeful passions could throw into the air. It was followed by the swift flashes of the rifles, which sent their leaden messengers across the rock in volleys, as though the assailants would pour out their impotent fury on the insensible scene of the fatal contest.

A steady, though deliberate return was made from the rifle of Chingachgook, who had maintained his post throughout the fray with unmoved resolution. When the triumphant shout of Uncas was borne to his ears, the gratified father raised his voice in a single responsive cry, after which his busy piece alone proved that he still guarded his pass with unwearied diligence. In this manner many minutes flew by with the swiftness of thought; the rifles of the assailants speaking, at times, in rattling volleys, and at others in occasional, scattering shots. Though the rock, the trees, and the shrubs, were cut and torn in a hundred places around the besieged, their cover was so close, and so rigidly maintained, that, as yet, David had been the only sufferer in their little band.

"Let them burn their powder," said the deliberate scout, while bullet after bullet whizzed by the place where he securely lay; "there will be a fine gathering of lead when it is over, and I fancy the imps will tire of the sport afore these old stones cry out for mercy! Uncas, boy, you waste the kernels by overcharging; and a kicking rifle never carries a true bullet. I told you to take that loping miscreant under the line of white point; now, if your bullet went a hair's breadth it went two inches above it. The life lies low in a Mingo, and humanity teaches us to make a quick end to the sarpents."

A quiet smile lighted the haughty features of the young Mohican, betraying his knowledge of the English language as well as of the other's meaning; but he suffered it to pass away without vindication of reply.

"I cannot permit you to accuse Uncas of want of judgment or of skill," said Duncan; "he saved my life in the coolest and readiest manner, and he has made a friend who never will require to be reminded of the debt he owes."

Uncas partly raised his body, and offered his hand to the grasp of Heyward. During this act of friendship, the two young men exchanged looks of intelligence which caused Duncan to forget the character and condition of his wild associate. In the meanwhile, Hawkeye, who looked on this burst of youthful feeling with a cool but kind regard made the following reply:

"Life is an obligation which friends often owe each other in the wilderness. I dare say I may have served Uncas some such turn myself before now; and I very well remember that he has stood between me and death five different times; three times from the Mingoes, once in crossing Horican, and—"

"That bullet was better aimed than common!" exclaimed Duncan, involuntarily shrinking from a shot which struck the rock at his side with a smart rebound.

Hawkeye laid his hand on the shapeless metal, and shook his head, as he examined it, saying, "Falling lead is never flattened, had it come from the clouds this might have happened."

But the rifle of Uncas was deliberately raised toward the heavens, directing the eyes of his companions to a point, where the mystery was immediately explained. A ragged oak grew on the right bank of the river, nearly opposite to their position, which, seeking the freedom of the open space, had inclined so far forward that its upper branches overhung that arm of the stream which flowed nearest to its own shore. Among the topmost leaves, which scantily concealed the gnarled and stunted limbs, a savage was nestled, partly concealed by the trunk of the tree, and partly exposed, as though looking down upon them to ascertain the effect produced by his treacherous aim.

"These devils will scale heaven to circumvent us to our ruin," said Hawkeye; "keep him in play, boy, until I can bring 'killdeer' to bear, when we will try his metal on each side of the tree at once."

Uncas delayed his fire until the scout uttered the word.

The rifles flashed, the leaves and bark of the oak flew into the air, and were scattered by the wind, but the Indian answered their assault by a taunting laugh, sending down upon them another bullet in return, that struck the cap of Hawkeye from his head. Once more the savage yells burst out of the woods, and the leaden hail whistled above the heads of the besieged, as if to confine them to a place where they might become easy victims to the enterprise of the warrior who had mounted the tree.

"This must be looked to," said the scout, glancing about him with an anxious eye. "Uncas, call up your father; we have need of all our we'pons to bring the cunning varmint from his roost."

The signal was instantly given; and, before Hawkeye had reloaded his rifle, they were joined by Chingachgook. When his son pointed out to the experienced warrior the situation of their dangerous enemy, the usual exclamatory "hugh" burst from his lips; after which, no further expression of surprise or alarm was suffered to escape him. Hawkeye and the Mohicans conversed earnestly together in Delaware for a few moments, when each quietly took his post, in order to execute the plan they had speedily devised.

The warrior in the oak had maintained a quick, though ineffectual fire, from the moment of his discovery. But his aim was interrupted by the vigilance of his enemies, whose rifles instantaneously bore on any part of his person that was left exposed. Still his bullets fell in the center of the crouching party. The clothes of Heyward, which rendered him peculiarly conspicuous, were repeatedly cut, and once blood was drawn from a slight wound in his arm.

At length, emboldened by the long and patient watchfulness of his enemies, the Huron attempted a better and more fatal aim. The quick eyes of the Mohicans caught the dark line of his lower limbs incautiously exposed through the thin foliage, a few inches from the trunk of the tree. Their rifles made a common report, when, sinking on his wounded limb, part of the body of the savage came into view. Swift as thought, Hawkeye seized the advantage, and discharged his fatal weapon into the top of the oak. The leaves were unusually agitated; the dangerous rifle fell from its commanding elevation, and after a few moments of vain struggling, the form of the savage was seen swinging in the wind, while he still grasped a ragged and naked branch of the tree with hands clenched in desperation.

"Give him, in pity, give him the contents of another rifle," cried Duncan, turning away his eyes in horror from the spectacle of a fellow creature in such awful jeopardy.

"Not a karnel!" exclaimed the obdurate Hawkeye; "his death is certain, and we have no powder to spare, for Indian fights sometimes last for days; 'tis their scalps or ours! and God, who made us, has put into our natures the craving to keep the skin on the head."

Against this stern and unyielding morality, supported as it was by such visible policy, there was no appeal. From that moment the yells in the forest once more ceased, the fire was suffered to decline, and all eyes, those of friends as well as enemies, became fixed on the hopeless condition of the wretch who was dangling between heaven and earth. The body yielded to the currents of air, and though no murmur or groan escaped the victim, there were instants when he grimly faced his foes, and the anguish of cold despair might be traced, through the intervening distance, in possession of his swarthy lineaments. Three several times the scout raised his piece in mercy, and as often, prudence getting the better of his intention, it was again silently lowered. At length one hand of the Huron lost its hold, and dropped exhausted to his side. A desperate and fruitless struggle to recover the branch succeeded, and then the savage was seen for a fleeting instant, grasping wildly at the empty air. The lightning is not quicker than was the flame from the rifle of Hawkeye; the limbs of the victim trembled and contracted, the head fell to the bosom, and the body parted the foaming waters like lead, when the element closed above it, in its ceaseless velocity, and every vestige of the unhappy Huron was lost forever.

No shout of triumph succeeded this important advantage, but even the Mohicans gazed at each other in silent horror. A single yell burst from the woods, and all was again still. Hawkeye, who alone appeared to reason on the occasion, shook his head at his own momentary weakness, even uttering his self-disapprobation aloud.

"'Twas the last charge in my horn and the last bullet in my pouch, and 'twas the act of a boy!" he said; "what mattered it whether he struck the rock living or dead! feeling would soon be over. Uncas, lad, go down to the canoe, and bring up the big horn; it is all the powder we have left, and we shall need it to the last grain, or I am ignorant of the Mingo nature."

The young Mohican complied, leaving the scout turning over the useless contents of his pouch, and shaking the empty horn with renewed discontent. From this unsatisfactory examination, however, he was soon called by a loud and piercing exclamation from Uncas, that sounded, even to the unpracticed ears of Duncan, as the signal of some new and unexpected calamity. Every thought filled with apprehension for the previous treasure he had concealed in the cavern, the young man started to his feet, totally regardless of the hazard he incurred by such an exposure. As if actuated by a common impulse, his movement was imitated by his companions, and, together they rushed down the pass to the friendly chasm, with a rapidity that rendered the scattering fire of their enemies perfectly harmless. The unwonted cry had brought the sisters, together with the wounded David, from their place of refuge; and the whole party, at a single glance, was made acquainted with the nature of the disaster that had disturbed even the practiced stoicism of their youthful Indian protector.

At a short distance from the rock, their little bark was to be seen floating across the eddy, toward the swift current of the river, in a manner which proved that its course was directed by some hidden agent. The instant this unwelcome sight caught the eye of the scout, his rifle was leveled as by instinct, but the barrel gave no answer to the bright sparks of the flint.

"'Tis too late, 'tis too late!" Hawkeye exclaimed, dropping the useless piece in bitter disappointment; "the miscreant has struck the rapid; and had we powder, it could hardly send the lead swifter than he now goes!"

The adventurous Huron raised his head above the shelter of the canoe, and, while it glided swiftly down the stream, he waved his hand, and gave forth the shout, which was the known signal of success. His cry was answered by a yell and a laugh from the woods, as tauntingly exulting as if fifty demons were uttering their blasphemies at the fall of some Christian soul.

"Well may you laugh, ye children of the devil!" said the scout, seating himself on a projection of the rock, and suffering his gun to fall neglected at his feet, "for the three quickest and truest rifles in these woods are no better than so many stalks of mullein, or the last year's horns of a buck!"

"What is to be done?" demanded Duncan, losing the first feeling of disappointment in a more manly desire for exertion; "what will become of us?"

Hawkeye made no other reply than by passing his finger around the crown of his head, in a manner so significant, that none who witnessed the action could mistake its meaning.

"Surely, surely, our case is not so desperate!" exclaimed the youth; "the Hurons are not here; we may make good the caverns, we may oppose their landing."

"With what?" coolly demanded the scout. "The arrows of Uncas, or such tears as women shed! No, no; you are young, and rich, and have friends, and at such an age I know it is hard to die! But," glancing his eyes at the Mohicans, "let us remember we are men without a cross, and let us teach these natives of the forest that white blood can run as freely as red, when the appointed hour is come."

Duncan turned quickly in the direction indicated by the other's eyes, and read a confirmation of his worst apprehensions in the conduct of the Indians. Chingachgook, placing himself in a dignified posture on another fragment of the rock, had already laid aside his knife and tomahawk, and was in the act of taking the eagle's plume from his head, and smoothing the solitary tuft of hair in readiness to perform its last and revolting office. His countenance was composed, though thoughtful, while his dark, gleaming eyes were gradually losing the fierceness of the combat in an expression better suited to the change he expected momentarily to undergo.

"Our case is not, cannot be so hopeless!" said Duncan; "even at this very moment succor may be at hand. I see no enemies! They have sickened of a struggle in which they risk so much with so little prospect of gain!"

"It may be a minute, or it may be an hour, afore the wily sarpents steal upon us, and it is quite in natur' for them to be lying within hearing at this very moment," said Hawkeye; "but come they will, and in such a fashion as will leave us nothing to hope! Chingachgook"—he spoke in Delaware—"my brother, we have fought our last battle together, and the Maquas will triumph in the death of the sage man of the Mohicans, and of the pale face, whose eyes can make night as day, and level the clouds to the mists of the springs!"

"Let the Mingo women go weep over the slain!" returned the Indian, with characteristic pride and unmoved firmness; "the Great Snake of the Mohicans has coiled himself in their wigwams, and has poisoned their triumph with the wailings of children, whose fathers have not returned! Eleven warriors lie hid from the graves of their tribes since the snows have melted, and none will tell where to find them when the tongue of Chingachgook shall be silent! Let them draw the sharpest knife, and whirl the swiftest tomahawk, for their bitterest enemy is in their hands. Uncas, topmost branch of a noble trunk, call on the cowards to hasten, or their hearts will soften, and they will change to women!"

"They look among the fishes for their dead!" returned the low, soft voice of the youthful chieftain; "the Hurons float with the slimy eels! They drop from the oaks like fruit that is ready to be eaten! and the Delawares laugh!"

"Ay, ay," muttered the scout, who had listened to this peculiar burst of the natives with deep attention; "they have warmed their Indian feelings, and they'll soon provoke the Maquas to give them a speedy end. As for me, who am of the whole blood of the whites, it is befitting that I should die as becomes my color, with no words of scoffing in my mouth, and without bitterness at the heart!"

"Why die at all!" said Cora, advancing from the place where natural horror had, until this moment, held her riveted to the rock; "the path is open on every side; fly, then, to the woods, and call on God for succor. Go, brave men, we owe you too much already; let us no longer involve you in our hapless fortunes!"

"You but little know the craft of the Iroquois, lady, if you judge they have left the path open to the woods!" returned Hawkeye, who, however, immediately added in his simplicity, "the down stream current, it is certain, might soon sweep us beyond the reach of their rifles or the sound of their voices."

"Then try the river. Why linger to add to the number of the victims of our merciless enemies?"

"Why," repeated the scout, looking about him proudly; "because it is better for a man to die at peace with himself than to live haunted by an evil conscience! What answer could we give Munro, when he asked us where and how we left his children?"

"Go to him, and say that you left them with a message to hasten to their aid," returned Cora, advancing nigher to the scout in her generous ardor; "that the Hurons bear them into the northern wilds, but that by vigilance and speed they may yet be rescued; and if, after all, it should please heaven that his assistance come too late, bear to him," she continued, her voice gradually lowering, until it seemed nearly choked, "the love, the blessings, the final prayers of his daughters, and bid him not mourn their early fate, but to look forward with humble confidence to the Christian's goal to meet his children." The hard, weather-beaten features of the scout began to work, and when she had ended, he dropped his chin to his hand, like a man musing profoundly on the nature of the proposal.

"There is reason in her words!" at length broke from his compressed and trembling lips; "ay, and they bear the spirit of Christianity; what might be right and proper in a red-skin, may be sinful in a man who has not even a cross in blood to plead for his ignorance. Chingachgook! Uncas! hear you the talk of the dark-eyed woman?"

He now spoke in Delaware to his companions, and his address, though calm and deliberate, seemed very decided. The elder Mohican heard with deep gravity, and appeared to ponder on his words, as though he felt the importance of their import. After a moment of hesitation, he waved his hand in assent, and uttered the English word "Good!" with the peculiar emphasis of his people. Then, replacing his knife and tomahawk in his girdle, the warrior moved silently to the edge of the rock which was most concealed from the banks of the river. Here he paused a moment, pointed significantly to the woods below, and saying a few words in his own language, as if indicating his intended route, he dropped into the water, and sank from before the eyes of the witnesses of his movements.

The scout delayed his departure to speak to the generous girl, whose breathing became lighter as she saw the success of her remonstrance.

"Wisdom is sometimes given to the young, as well as to the old," he said; "and what you have spoken is wise, not to call it by a better word. If you are led into the woods, that is such of you as may be spared for awhile, break the twigs on the bushes as you pass, and make the marks of your trail as broad as you can, when, if mortal eyes can see them, depend on having a friend who will follow to the ends of the 'arth afore he desarts you."

He gave Cora an affectionate shake of the hand, lifted his rifle, and after regarding it a moment with melancholy solicitude, laid it carefully aside, and descended to the place where Chingachgook had just disappeared. For an instant he hung suspended by the rock, and looking about him, with a countenance of peculiar care, he added bitterly, "Had the powder held out, this disgrace could never have befallen!" then, loosening his hold, the water closed above his head, and he also became lost to view.

All eyes now were turned on Uncas, who stood leaning against the ragged rock, in immovable composure. After waiting a short time, Cora pointed down the river, and said:

"Your friends have not been seen, and are now, most probably, in safety. Is it not time for you to follow?"

"Uncas will stay," the young Mohican calmly answered in English.

"To increase the horror of our capture, and to diminish the chances of our release! Go, generous young man," Cora continued, lowering her eyes under the gaze of the Mohican, and perhaps, with an intuitive consciousness of her power; "go to my father, as I have said, and be the most confidential of my messengers. Tell him to trust you with the means to buy the freedom of his daughters. Go! 'tis my wish, 'tis my prayer, that you will go!"

The settled, calm look of the young chief changed to an expression of gloom, but he no longer hesitated. With a noiseless step he crossed the rock, and dropped into the troubled stream. Hardly a breath was drawn by those he left behind, until they caught a glimpse of his head emerging for air, far down the current, when he again sank, and was seen no more.

These sudden and apparently successful experiments had all taken place in a few minutes of that time which had now become so precious. After a last look at Uncas, Cora turned and with a quivering lip, addressed herself to Heyward:

"I have heard of your boasted skill in the water, too, Duncan," she said; "follow, then, the wise example set you by these simple and faithful beings."

"Is such the faith that Cora Munro would exact from her protector?" said the young man, smiling mournfully, but with bitterness.

"This is not a time for idle subtleties and false opinions," she answered; "but a moment when every duty should be equally considered. To us you can be of no further service here, but your precious life may be saved for other and nearer friends."

He made no reply, though his eye fell wistfully on the beautiful form of Alice, who was clinging to his arm with the dependency of an infant.

"Consider," continued Cora, after a pause, during which she seemed to struggle with a pang even more acute than any that her fears had excited, "that the worst to us can be but death; a tribute that all must pay at the good time of God's appointment."

"There are evils worse than death," said Duncan, speaking hoarsely, and as if fretful at her importunity, "but which the presence of one who would die in your behalf may avert."

Cora ceased her entreaties; and veiling her face in her shawl, drew the nearly insensible Alice after her into the deepest recess of the inner cavern.

## CHAPTER IX.

> "Be gay securely;
> Dispel, my fair, with smiles, the tim'rous clouds,
> That hang on thy clear brow."—Death of Agrippina

The sudden and almost magical change, from the stirring incidents of the combat to the stillness that now reigned around him, acted on the heated imagination of Heyward like some exciting dream. While all the images and events he had witnessed remained deeply impressed on his memory, he felt a difficulty in persuading him of their truth. Still ignorant of the fate of those who had trusted to the aid of the swift current, he at first listened intently to any signal or sounds of alarm, which might announce the good or evil fortune of their hazardous undertaking. His attention was, however, bestowed in vain; for with the disappearance of Uncas, every sign of the adventurers had been lost, leaving him in total uncertainty of their fate.

In a moment of such painful doubt, Duncan did not hesitate to look around him, without consulting that protection from the rocks which just before had been so necessary to his safety. Every effort, however, to detect the least evidence of the approach of their hidden enemies was as fruitless as the inquiry after his late companions. The wooded banks of the river seemed again deserted by everything possessing animal life. The uproar which had so lately echoed through the vaults of the forest was gone, leaving the rush of the waters to swell and sink on the currents of the air, in the unmingled sweetness of nature. A fish-hawk, which, secure on the topmost branches of a dead pine, had been a distant spectator of the fray, now swooped from his high and ragged perch, and soared, in wide sweeps, above his prey; while a jay, whose noisy voice had been stilled by the hoarser cries of the savages, ventured again to open his discordant throat, as though once more in undisturbed possession of his wild domains. Duncan caught from these natural accompaniments of the solitary scene a glimmering of hope; and he began to rally his faculties to renewed exertions, with something like a reviving confidence of success.

"The Hurons are not to be seen," he said, addressing David, who had by no means recovered from the effects of the stunning blow he had received; "let us conceal ourselves in the cavern, and trust the rest to Providence."

"I remember to have united with two comely maidens, in lifting up our voices in praise and thanksgiving," returned the bewildered singing-master; "since which time I have been visited by a heavy judgment for my sins. I have been mocked with the likeness of sleep, while sounds of discord have rent my ears, such as might manifest the fullness of time, and that nature had forgotten her harmony."

"Poor fellow! thine own period was, in truth, near its accomplishment! But arouse, and come with me; I will lead you where all other sounds but those of your own psalmody shall be excluded."

"There is melody in the fall of the cataract, and the rushing of many waters is sweet to the senses!" said David, pressing his hand confusedly on his brow. "Is not the air yet filled with shrieks and cries, as though the departed spirits of the damned—"

"Not now, not now," interrupted the impatient Heyward, "they have ceased, and they who raised them, I trust in God, they are gone, too! everything but the water is still and at peace; in, then, where you may create those sounds you love so well to hear."

David smiled sadly, though not without a momentary gleam of pleasure, at this allusion to his beloved vocation. He no longer hesitated to be led to a spot which promised such unalloyed gratification to his wearied senses; and leaning on the arm of his companion, he entered the narrow mouth of the cave. Duncan seized a pile of the sassafras, which he drew before the passage, studiously concealing every appearance of an aperture. Within this fragile barrier he arranged the blankets abandoned by the foresters, darkening the inner extremity of the cavern, while its outer received a chastened light from the narrow ravine, through which one arm of the river rushed to form the junction with its sister branch a few rods below.

"I like not the principle of the natives, which teaches them to submit without a struggle, in emergencies that appear desperate," he said, while busied in this employment; "our own maxim, which says, 'while life remains there is hope', is more consoling, and better suited to a soldier's temperament. To you, Cora, I will urge no words of idle encouragement; your own fortitude and undisturbed reason will teach you all that may become your sex; but cannot we dry the tears of that trembling weeper on your bosom?"

"I am calmer, Duncan," said Alice, raising herself from the arms of her sister, and forcing an appearance of composure through her tears; "much calmer, now. Surely, in this hidden spot we are safe, we are secret, free from injury; we will hope everything from those generous men who have risked so much already in our behalf."

"Now does our gentle Alice speak like a daughter of Munro!" said Heyward, pausing to press her hand as he passed toward the outer entrance of the cavern. "With two such examples of courage before him, a man would be ashamed to prove other than a hero." He then seated himself in the center of the cavern, grasping his remaining pistol with a hand convulsively clenched, while his contracted and frowning eye announced the sullen desperation of his purpose. "The Hurons, if they come, may not gain our position so easily as they think," he slowly muttered; and propping his head back against the rock, he seemed to await the result in patience, though his gaze was unceasingly bent on the open avenue to their place of retreat.

With the last sound of his voice, a deep, a long, and almost breathless silence succeeded. The fresh air of the morning had penetrated the recess, and its influence was gradually felt on the spirits of its inmates. As minute after minute passed by, leaving them in undisturbed security, the insinuating feeling of hope was gradually gaining possession of every bosom, though each one felt reluctant to give utterance to expectations that the next moment might so fearfully destroy.

David alone formed an exception to these varying emotions. A gleam of light from the opening crossed his wan countenance, and fell upon the pages of the little volume, whose leaves he was again occupied in turning, as if searching for some song more fitted to their condition than any that had yet met their eye. He was, most probably, acting all this time under a confused recollection of the promised consolation of Duncan. At length, it would seem, his patient industry found its reward; for, without explanation or apology, he pronounced aloud the words "Isle of Wight," drew a long, sweet sound from his pitch-pipe, and then ran through the preliminary modulations of the air whose name he had just mentioned, with the sweeter tones of his own musical voice.

"May not this prove dangerous?" asked Cora, glancing her dark eye at Major Heyward.

"Poor fellow! his voice is too feeble to be heard above the din of the falls," was the answer; "beside, the cavern will prove his friend. Let him indulge his passions since it may be done without hazard."

"Isle of Wight!" repeated David, looking about him with that dignity with which he had long been wont to silence the whispering echoes of his school; "'tis a brave tune, and set to solemn words! let it be sung with meet respect!"

After allowing a moment of stillness to enforce his discipline, the voice of the singer was heard, in low, murmuring syllables, gradually stealing on the ear, until it filled the narrow vault with sounds rendered trebly thrilling by the feeble and tremulous utterance produced by his debility. The melody, which no weakness could destroy, gradually wrought its sweet influence on the senses of those who heard it. It even prevailed over the miserable travesty of the song of David which the singer had selected from a volume of similar effusions, and caused the sense to be forgotten in the insinuating harmony of the sounds. Alice unconsciously dried her tears, and bent her melting eyes on the pallid features of Gamut, with an expression of chastened delight that she neither affected or wished to conceal. Cora bestowed an approving smile on the pious efforts of the namesake of the Jewish prince, and Heyward soon turned his steady, stern look from the outlet of the cavern, to fasten it, with a milder character, on the face of David, or to meet the wandering beams which at moments strayed from the humid eyes of Alice. The open sympathy of the listeners stirred the spirit of the votary of music, whose voice regained its richness and volume, without losing that touching softness which proved its secret charm. Exerting his renovated powers to their utmost, he was yet filling the arches of the cave with long and full tones, when a yell burst into the air without, that instantly stilled his pious strains, choking his voice suddenly, as though his heart had literally bounded into the passage of his throat.

"We are lost!" exclaimed Alice, throwing herself into the arms of Cora.

"Not yet, not yet," returned the agitated but undaunted Heyward: "the sound came from the center of the island, and it has been produced by the sight of their dead companions. We are not yet discovered, and there is still hope."

Faint and almost despairing as was the prospect of escape, the words of Duncan were not thrown away, for it awakened the powers of the sisters in such a manner that they awaited the results in silence. A second yell soon followed the first, when a rush of voices was heard pouring down the island, from its upper to its lower extremity, until they reached the naked rock above the caverns, where, after a shout of savage triumph, the air continued full of horrible cries and screams, such as man alone can utter, and he only when in a state of the fiercest barbarity.

The sounds quickly spread around them in every direction. Some called to their fellows from the water's edge, and were answered from the heights above. Cries were heard in the startling vicinity of the chasm between the two caves, which mingled with hoarser yells that arose out of the abyss of the deep ravine. In short, so rapidly had the savage sounds diffused themselves over the barren rock, that it was not difficult for the anxious listeners to imagine they could be heard beneath, as in truth they were above on every side of them.

In the midst of this tumult, a triumphant yell was raised within a few yards of the hidden entrance to the cave. Heyward abandoned every hope, with the belief it was the signal that they were discovered. Again the impression passed away, as he heard the voices collect near the spot where the white man had so reluctantly abandoned his rifle. Amid the jargon of Indian dialects that he now plainly heard, it was easy to distinguish not only words, but sentences, in the patois of the Canadas. A burst of voices had shouted simultaneously, "La Longue Carabine!" causing the opposite woods to re-echo with a name which, Heyward well remembered, had been given by his enemies to a celebrated hunter and scout of the English camp, and who, he now learned for the first time, had been his late companion.

"La Longue Carabine! La Longue Carabine!" passed from mouth to mouth, until the whole band appeared to be collected around a trophy which would seem to announce the death of its formidable owner. After a vociferous consultation, which was, at times, deafened by bursts of savage joy, they again separated, filling the air with the name of a foe, whose body, Heywood could collect from their expressions, they hoped to find concealed in some crevice of the island.

"Now," he whispered to the trembling sisters, "now is the moment of uncertainty! if our place of retreat escape this scrutiny, we are still safe! In every event, we are assured, by what has fallen from our enemies, that our friends have escaped, and in two short hours we may look for succor from Webb."

There were now a few minutes of fearful stillness, during which Heyward well knew that the savages conducted their search with greater vigilance and method. More than once he could distinguish their footsteps, as they brushed the sassafras, causing the faded leaves to rustle, and the branches to snap. At length, the pile yielded a little, a corner of a blanket fell, and a faint ray of light gleamed into the inner part of the cave. Cora folded Alice to her bosom in agony, and Duncan sprang to his feet. A shout was at that moment heard, as if issuing from the center of the rock, announcing that the neighboring cavern had at length been entered. In a minute, the number and loudness of the voices indicated that the whole party was collected in and around that secret place.

As the inner passages to the two caves were so close to each other, Duncan, believing that escape was no longer possible, passed David and the sisters, to place himself between the latter and the first onset of the terrible meeting. Grown desperate by his situation, he drew nigh the slight barrier which separated him only by a few feet from his relentless pursuers, and placing his face to the casual opening, he even looked out with a sort of desperate indifference, on their movements.

Within reach of his arm was the brawny shoulder of a gigantic Indian, whose deep and authoritative voice appeared to give directions to the proceedings of his fellows. Beyond him again, Duncan could look into the vault opposite, which was filled with savages, upturning and rifling the humble furniture of the scout. The wound of David had dyed the leaves of sassafras with a color that the native well knew as anticipating the season. Over this sign of their success, they sent up a howl, like an opening from so many hounds who had recovered a lost trail. After this yell of victory, they tore up the fragrant bed of the cavern, and bore the branches into the chasm, scattering the boughs, as if they suspected them of concealing the person of the man they had so long hated and feared. One fierce and wild-looking warrior approached the chief, bearing a load of the brush, and pointing exultingly to the deep red stains with which it was sprinkled, uttered his joy in Indian yells, whose meaning Heyward was only enabled to comprehend by the frequent repetition of the name "La Longue Carabine!" When his triumph had ceased, he cast the brush on the slight heap Duncan had made before the entrance of the second cavern, and closed the view. His example was followed by others, who, as they drew the branches from the cave of the scout, threw them into one pile, adding, unconsciously, to the security of those they sought. The very slightness of the defense was its chief merit, for no one thought of disturbing a mass of brush, which all of them believed, in that moment of hurry and confusion, had been accidentally raised by the hands of their own party.

As the blankets yielded before the outward pressure, and the branches settled in the fissure of the rock by their own weight, forming a compact body, Duncan once more breathed freely. With a light step and lighter heart, he returned to the center of the cave, and took the place he had left, where he could command a view of the opening next the river. While he was in the act of making this movement, the Indians, as if changing their purpose by a common impulse, broke away from the chasm in a body, and were heard rushing up the island again, toward the point whence they had originally descended. Here another wailing cry betrayed that they were again collected around the bodies of their dead comrades.

Duncan now ventured to look at his companions; for, during the most critical moments of their danger, he had been apprehensive that the anxiety of his countenance might communicate some additional alarm to those who were so little able to sustain it.

"They are gone, Cora!" he whispered; "Alice, they are returned whence they came, and we are saved! To Heaven, that has alone delivered us from the grasp of so merciless an enemy, be all the praise!"

"Then to Heaven will I return my thanks!" exclaimed the younger sister, rising from the encircling arm of Cora, and casting herself with enthusiastic gratitude on the naked rock; "to that Heaven who has spared the tears of a gray-headed father; has saved the lives of those I so much love."

Both Heyward and the more temperate Cora witnessed the act of involuntary emotion with powerful sympathy, the former secretly believing that piety had never worn a form so lovely as it had now assumed in the youthful person of Alice. Her eyes were radiant with the glow of grateful feelings; the flush of her beauty was again seated on her cheeks, and her whole soul seemed ready and anxious to pour out its thanksgivings through the medium of her eloquent features. But when her lips moved, the words they should have uttered appeared frozen by some new and sudden chill. Her bloom gave place to the paleness of death; her soft and melting eyes grew hard, and seemed contracting with horror; while those hands, which she had raised, clasped in each other, toward heaven, dropped in horizontal lines before her, the fingers pointed forward in convulsed motion. Heyward turned the instant she gave a direction to his suspicions, and peering just above the ledge which formed the threshold of the open outlet of the cavern, he beheld the malignant, fierce and savage features of Le Renard Subtil.

In that moment of surprise, the self-possession of Heyward did not desert him. He observed by the vacant expression of the Indian's countenance, that his eye, accustomed to the open air had not yet been able to penetrate the dusky light which pervaded the depth of the cavern. He had even thought of retreating beyond a curvature in the natural wall, which might still conceal him and his companions, when by the sudden gleam of intelligence that shot across the features of the savage, he saw it was too late, and that they were betrayed.

The look of exultation and brutal triumph which announced this terrible truth was irresistibly irritating. Forgetful of everything but the impulses of his hot blood, Duncan leveled his pistol and fired. The report of the weapon made the cavern bellow like an eruption from a volcano; and when the smoke it vomited had been driven away before the current of air which issued from the ravine the place so lately occupied by the features of his treacherous guide was vacant. Rushing to the outlet, Heyward caught a glimpse of his dark figure stealing around a low and narrow ledge, which soon hid him entirely from sight.

Among the savages a frightful stillness succeeded the explosion, which had just been heard bursting from the bowels of the rock. But when Le Renard raised his voice in a long and intelligible whoop, it was answered by a spontaneous yell from the mouth of every Indian within hearing of the sound.

The clamorous noises again rushed down the island; and before Duncan had time to recover from the shock, his feeble barrier of brush was scattered to the winds, the cavern was entered at both its extremities, and he and his companions were dragged from their shelter and borne into the day, where they stood surrounded by the whole band of the triumphant Hurons.

CHAPTER X.

"I fear we shall outsleep the coming morn
As much as we this night have overwatched!"
—Midsummer Night's Dream

The instant the shock of this sudden misfortune had abated, Duncan began to make his observations on the appearance and proceedings of their captors. Contrary to the usages of the natives in the wantonness of their success they had respected, not only the persons of the trembling sisters, but his own. The rich ornaments of his military attire had indeed been repeatedly handled by different individuals of the tribes with eyes expressing a savage longing to possess the baubles; but before the customary violence could be resorted to, a mandate in the authoritative voice of the large warrior, already mentioned, stayed the uplifted hand, and convinced Heyward that they were to be reserved for some object of particular moment.

While, however, these manifestations of weakness were exhibited by the young and vain of the party, the more experienced warriors continued their search throughout both caverns, with an activity that denoted they were far from being satisfied with those fruits of their conquest which had already been brought to light. Unable to discover any new victim, these diligent workers of vengeance soon approached their male prisoners, pronouncing the name "La Longue Carabine," with a fierceness that could not be easily mistaken. Duncan affected not to comprehend the meaning of their repeated and violent interrogatories, while his companion was spared the effort of a similar deception by his ignorance of French. Wearied at length by their importunities, and apprehensive of irritating his captors by too stubborn a silence, the former looked about him in quest of Magua, who might interpret his answers to questions which were at each moment becoming more earnest and threatening.

The conduct of this savage had formed a solitary exception to that of all his fellows. While the others were busily occupied in seeking to gratify their childish passion for finery, by plundering even the miserable effects of the scout, or had been searching with such bloodthirsty vengeance in their looks for their absent owner, Le Renard had stood at a little distance from the prisoners, with a demeanor so quiet and satisfied, as to betray that he had already effected the grand purpose of his treachery. When the eyes of Heyward first met those of his recent guide, he turned them away in horror at the sinister though calm look he encountered. Conquering his disgust, however, he was able, with an averted face, to address his successful enemy.

"Le Renard Subtil is too much of a warrior," said the reluctant Heyward, "to refuse telling an unarmed man what his conquerors say."

"They ask for the hunter who knows the paths through the woods," returned Magua, in his broken English, laying his hand, at the same time, with a ferocious smile, on the bundle of leaves with which a wound on his own shoulder was bandaged. "'La Longue Carabine'! His rifle is good, and his eye never shut; but, like the short gun of the white chief, it is nothing against the life of Le Subtil."

"Le Renard is too brave to remember the hurts received in war, or the hands that gave them."

"Was it war, when the tired Indian rested at the sugartree to taste his corn! who filled the bushes with creeping enemies! who drew the knife, whose tongue was peace, while his heart was colored with blood! Did Magua say that the hatchet was out of the ground, and that his hand had dug it up?"

As Duncan dared not retort upon his accuser by reminding him of his own premeditated treachery, and disdained to deprecate his resentment by any words of apology, he remained silent. Magua seemed also content to rest the controversy as well as all further communication there, for he resumed the leaning attitude against the rock from which, in momentary energy, he had arisen. But the cry of "La Longue Carabine" was renewed the instant the impatient savages perceived that the short dialogue was ended.

"You hear," said Magua, with stubborn indifference: "the red Hurons call for the life of 'The Long Rifle', or they will have the blood of him that keep him hid!"

"He is gone—escaped; he is far beyond their reach."

Renard smiled with cold contempt, as he answered:

"When the white man dies, he thinks he is at peace; but the red men know how to torture even the ghosts of their enemies. Where is his body? Let the Hurons see his scalp."

"He is not dead, but escaped."

Magua shook his head incredulously.

"Is he a bird, to spread his wings; or is he a fish, to swim without air! The white chief read in his books, and he believes the Hurons are fools!"

"Though no fish, 'The Long Rifle' can swim. He floated down the stream when the powder was all burned, and when the eyes of the Hurons were behind a cloud."

"And why did the white chief stay?" demanded the still incredulous Indian. "Is he a stone that goes to the bottom, or does the scalp burn his head?"

"That I am not stone, your dead comrade, who fell into the falls, might answer, were the life still in him," said the provoked young man, using, in his anger, that boastful language which was most likely to excite the admiration of an Indian. "The white man thinks none but cowards desert their women."

Magua muttered a few words, inaudibly, between his teeth, before he continued, aloud:

"Can the Delawares swim, too, as well as crawl in the bushes? Where is 'Le Gros Serpent'?"

Duncan, who perceived by the use of these Canadian appellations, that his late companions were much better known to his enemies than to himself, answered, reluctantly: "He also is gone down with the water."

"'Le Cerf Agile' is not here?"

"I know not whom you call 'The Nimble Deer'," said Duncan gladly profiting by any excuse to create delay.

"Uncas," returned Magua, pronouncing the Delaware name with even greater difficulty than he spoke his English words. "'Bounding Elk' is what the white man says, when he calls to the young Mohican."

"Here is some confusion in names between us, Le Renard," said Duncan, hoping to provoke a discussion. "Daim is the French for deer, and cerf for stag; elan is the true term, when one would speak of an elk."

"Yes," muttered the Indian, in his native tongue; "the pale faces are prattling women! they have two words for each thing, while a red-skin will make the sound of his voice speak to him." Then, changing his language, he continued, adhering to the imperfect nomenclature of his provincial instructors. "The deer is swift, but weak; the elk is swift, but strong; and the son of 'Le Serpent' is 'Le Cerf Agile.' Has he leaped the river to the woods?"

"If you mean the younger Delaware, he, too, has gone down with the water."

As there was nothing improbable to an Indian in the manner of the escape, Magua admitted the truth of what he had heard, with a readiness that afforded additional evidence how little he would prize such worthless captives. With his companions, however, the feeling was manifestly different.

The Hurons had awaited the result of this short dialogue with characteristic patience, and with a silence that increased until there was a general stillness in the band. When Heyward ceased to speak, they turned their eyes, as one man, on Magua, demanding, in this expressive manner, an explanation of what had been said. Their interpreter pointed to the river, and made them acquainted with the result, as much by the action as by the few words he uttered. When the fact was generally understood, the savages raised a frightful yell, which declared the extent of their disappointment. Some ran furiously to the water's edge, beating the air with frantic gestures, while others spat upon the element, to resent the supposed treason it had committed against their acknowledged rights as conquerors. A few, and they not the least powerful and terrific of the band, threw lowering looks, in which the fiercest passion was only tempered by habitual self-command, at those captives who still remained in their power, while one or two even gave vent to their malignant feelings by the most menacing gestures, against which neither the sex nor the beauty of the sisters was any protection. The young soldier made a desperate but fruitless effort to spring to the side of Alice, when he saw the dark hand of a savage twisted in the rich tresses which were flowing in volumes over her shoulders, while a knife was passed around the head from which they fell, as if to denote the horrid manner in which it was about to be robbed of its beautiful ornament. But his hands were bound; and at the first movement he made, he felt the grasp of the powerful Indian who directed the band, pressing his shoulder like a vise. Immediately conscious how unavailing any struggle against such an overwhelming force must prove, he submitted to his fate, encouraging his gentle companions by a few low and tender assurances, that the natives seldom failed to threaten more than they performed.

But while Duncan resorted to these words of consolation to quiet the apprehensions of the sisters, he was not so weak as to deceive himself. He well knew that the authority of an Indian chief was so little conventional, that it was oftener maintained by physical superiority than by any moral supremacy he might possess. The danger was, therefore, magnified exactly in proportion to the number of the savage spirits by which they were surrounded. The most positive mandate from him who seemed the acknowledged leader, was liable to be violated at each moment by any rash hand that might choose to sacrifice a victim to the manes of some dead friend or relative. While, therefore, he sustained an outward appearance of calmness and fortitude, his heart leaped into his throat, whenever any of their fierce captors drew nearer than common to the helpless sisters, or fastened one of their sullen, wandering looks on those fragile forms which were so little able to resist the slightest assault.

His apprehensions were, however, greatly relieved, when he saw that the leader had summoned his warriors to himself in counsel. Their deliberations were short, and it would seem, by the silence of most of the party, the decision unanimous. By the frequency with which the few speakers pointed in the direction of the encampment of Webb, it was apparent they dreaded the approach of danger from that quarter. This consideration probably hastened their determination, and quickened the subsequent movements.

During his short conference, Heyward, finding a respite from his gravest fears, had leisure to admire the cautious manner in which the Hurons had made their approaches, even after hostilities had ceased.

It has already been stated that the upper half of the island was a naked rock, and destitute of any other defenses than a few scattered logs of driftwood. They had selected this point to make their descent, having borne the canoe through the wood around the cataract for that purpose. Placing their arms in the little vessel a dozen men clinging to its sides had trusted themselves to the direction of the canoe, which was controlled by two of the most skillful warriors, in attitudes that enabled them to command a view of the dangerous passage. Favored by this arrangement, they touched the head of the island at that point which had proved so fatal to their first adventurers, but with the advantages of superior numbers, and the possession of firearms. That such had been the manner of their descent was rendered quite apparent to Duncan; for they now bore the light bark from the upper end of the rock, and placed it in the water, near the mouth of the outer cavern. As soon as this change was made, the leader made signs to the prisoners to descend and enter.

As resistance was impossible, and remonstrance useless, Heyward set the example of submission, by leading the way into the canoe, where he was soon seated with the sisters and the still wondering David. Notwithstanding the Hurons were necessarily ignorant of the little channels among the eddies and rapids of the stream, they knew the common signs of such a navigation too well to commit any material blunder. When the pilot chosen for the task of guiding the canoe had taken his station, the whole band plunged again into the river, the vessel glided down the current, and in a few moments the captives found themselves on the south bank of the stream, nearly opposite to the point where they had struck it the preceding evening.

Here was held another short but earnest consultation, during which the horses, to whose panic their owners ascribed their heaviest misfortune, were led from the cover of the woods, and brought to the sheltered spot. The band now divided. The great chief, so often mentioned, mounting the charger of Heyward, led the way directly across the river, followed by most of his people, and disappeared in the woods, leaving the prisoners in charge of six savages, at whose head was Le Renard Subtil. Duncan witnessed all their movements with renewed uneasiness.

He had been fond of believing, from the uncommon forbearance of the savages, that he was reserved as a prisoner to be delivered to Montcalm. As the thoughts of those who are in misery seldom slumber, and the invention is never more lively than when it is stimulated by hope, however feeble and remote, he had even imagined that the parental feelings of Munro were to be made instrumental in seducing him from his duty to the king. For though the French commander bore a high character for courage and enterprise, he was also thought to be expert in those political practises which do not always respect the nicer obligations of morality, and which so generally disgraced the European diplomacy of that period.

All those busy and ingenious speculations were now annihilated by the conduct of his captors. That portion of the band who had followed the huge warrior took the route toward the foot of the Horican, and no other expectation was left for himself and companions, than that they were to be retained as hopeless captives by their savage conquerors. Anxious to know the worst, and willing, in such an emergency, to try the potency of gold he overcame his reluctance to speak to Magua. Addressing himself to his former guide, who had now assumed the authority and manner of one who was to direct the future movements of the party, he said, in tones as friendly and confiding as he could assume:

"I would speak to Magua, what is fit only for so great a chief to hear."

The Indian turned his eyes on the young soldier scornfully, as he answered:

"Speak; trees have no ears."

"But the red Hurons are not deaf; and counsel that is fit for the great men of a nation would make the young warriors drunk. If Magua will not listen, the officer of the king knows how to be silent."

The savage spoke carelessly to his comrades, who were busied, after their awkward manner, in preparing the horses for the reception of the sisters, and moved a little to one side, whither by a cautious gesture he induced Heyward to follow.

"Now, speak," he said; "if the words are such as Magua should hear."

"Le Renard Subtil has proved himself worthy of the honorable name given to him by his Canada fathers," commenced Heyward; "I see his wisdom, and all that he has done for us, and shall remember it when the hour to reward him arrives. Yes! Renard has proved that he is not only a great chief in council, but one who knows how to deceive his enemies!"

"What has Renard done?" coldly demanded the Indian.

"What! has he not seen that the woods were filled with outlying parties of the enemies, and that the serpent could not steal through them without being seen? Then, did he not lose his path to blind the eyes of the Hurons? Did he not pretend to go back to his tribe, who had treated him ill, and driven him from their wigwams like a dog? And when he saw what he wished to do, did we not aid him, by making a false face, that the Hurons might think the white man believed that his friend was his enemy? Is not all this true? And when Le Subtil had shut the eyes and stopped the ears of his nation by his wisdom, did they not forget that they had once done him wrong, and forced him to flee to the Mohawks? And did they not leave him on the south side of the river, with their prisoners, while they have gone foolishly on the north? Does not Renard mean to turn like a fox on his footsteps, and to carry to the rich and gray-headed Scotchman his daughters? Yes, Magua, I see it all, and I have already been thinking how so much wisdom and honesty should be repaid. First, the chief of William Henry will give as a great chief should for such a service. The medal* of Magua will no longer be of tin, but of beaten gold; his horn will run over with powder; dollars will be as plenty in his pouch as pebbles on the shore of Horican; and the deer will lick his hand, for they will know it to be vain to fly from the rifle he will carry! As for myself, I know not how to exceed the gratitude of the Scotchman, but I—yes, I will—"

"What will the young chief, who comes from toward the sun, give?" demanded the Huron, observing that Heyward hesitated in his desire to end the enumeration of benefits with that which might form the climax of an Indian's wishes.

"He will make the fire-water from the islands in the salt lake flow before the wigwam of Magua, until the heart of the Indian shall be lighter than the feathers of the humming-bird, and his breath sweeter than the wild honeysuckle."

Le Renard had listened gravely as Heyward slowly proceeded in this subtle speech. When the young man mentioned the artifice he supposed the Indian to have practised on his own nation, the countenance of the listener was veiled in an expression of cautious gravity. At the allusion to the injury which Duncan affected to believe had driven the Huron from his native tribe, a gleam of such ungovernable ferocity flashed from the other's eyes, as induced the adventurous speaker to believe he

---

* It has long been a practice with the whites to conciliate the important men of the Indians by presenting medals, which are worn in the place of their own rude ornaments. Those given by the English generally bear the impression of the reigning king, and those given by the Americans that of the president.

had struck the proper chord. And by the time he reached the part where he so artfully blended the thirst of vengeance with the desire of gain, he had, at least, obtained a command of the deepest attention of the savage. The question put by Le Renard had been calm, and with all the dignity of an Indian; but it was quite apparent, by the thoughtful expression of the listener's countenance, that the answer was most cunningly devised. The Huron mused a few moments, and then laying his hand on the rude bandages of his wounded shoulder, he said, with some energy:

"Do friends make such marks?"

"Would 'La Longue Carbine' cut one so slight on an enemy?"

"Do the Delawares crawl upon those they love like snakes, twisting themselves to strike?"

"Would 'Le Gros Serpent' have been heard by the ears of one he wished to be deaf?"

"Does the white chief burn his powder in the faces of his brothers?"

"Does he ever miss his aim, when seriously bent to kill?" returned Duncan, smiling with well acted sincerity.

Another long and deliberate pause succeeded these sententious questions and ready replies. Duncan saw that the Indian hesitated. In order to complete his victory, he was in the act of recommencing the enumeration of the rewards, when Magua made an expressive gesture and said:

"Enough; Le Renard is a wise chief, and what he does will be seen. Go, and keep the mouth shut. When Magua speaks, it will be the time to answer."

Heyward, perceiving that the eyes of his companion were warily fastened on the rest of the band, fell back immediately, in order to avoid the appearance of any suspicious confederacy with their leader. Magua approached the horses, and affected to be well pleased with the diligence and ingenuity of his comrades. He then signed to Heyward to assist the sisters into the saddles, for he seldom deigned to use the English tongue, unless urged by some motive of more than usual moment.

There was no longer any plausible pretext for delay; and Duncan was obliged, however reluctantly, to comply. As he performed this office, he whispered his reviving hopes in the ears of the trembling females, who, through dread of encountering the savage countenances of their captors, seldom raised their eyes from the ground. The mare of David had been taken with the followers of the large chief; in consequence, its owner, as well as Duncan, was compelled to journey on foot. The latter did not, however, so much regret this circumstance, as it might enable him to retard the speed of the party; for he still turned his longing looks in the direction of Fort Edward, in the vain expectation of catching some sound from that quarter of the forest, which might denote the approach of succor. When all were prepared, Magua made the signal to proceed, advancing in front to lead the party in person. Next followed David, who was gradually coming to a true sense of his condition, as the effects of the wound became less and less apparent. The sisters rode in his rear, with Heyward at their side, while the Indians flanked the party, and brought up the close of the march, with a caution that seemed never to tire.

In this manner they proceeded in uninterrupted silence, except when Heyward addressed some solitary word of comfort to the females, or David gave vent to the moanings of his spirit, in piteous exclamations, which he intended should express the humility of resignation. Their direction lay toward the south, and in a course nearly opposite to the road to William Henry. Notwithstanding this apparent adherence in Magua to the original determination of his conquerors, Heyward could not believe his tempting bait was so soon forgotten; and he knew the windings of an Indian's path too well to suppose that its apparent course led directly to its object, when artifice was at all necessary. Mile after mile was, however, passed through the boundless woods, in this painful manner, without any prospect of a termination to their journey. Heyward watched the sun, as he darted his meridian rays through the branches of the trees, and pined for the moment when the policy of Magua should change their route to one more favorable to his hopes. Sometimes he fancied the wary savage, despairing of passing the army of Montcalm in safety, was holding his way toward a well-known border settlement, where a distinguished officer of the crown, and a favored friend of the Six Nations, held his large possessions, as well as his usual residence. To be delivered into the hands of Sir William Johnson was far preferable to being led into the wilds of Canada; but in order to effect even the former, it would be necessary to traverse the forest for many weary leagues, each step of which was carrying him further from the scene of the war, and, consequently, from the post, not only of honor, but of duty.

Cora alone remembered the parting injunctions of the scout, and whenever an opportunity offered, she stretched forth her arm to bend aside the twigs that met her hands. But the vigilance of the Indians rendered this act of precaution both difficult and dangerous. She was often defeated in her purpose, by encountering their watchful eyes, when it became necessary to feign an alarm she did not feel, and occupy the limb by some gesture of feminine apprehension. Once, and once only, was she completely successful; when she broke down the bough of a large sumach, and by a sudden thought, let her glove fall at the same instant. This sign, intended for those that might follow, was observed by one of her conductors, who restored the glove, broke the remaining branches of the bush in such a manner that it appeared to proceed from the struggling of some beast in its branches, and then laid his hand on his tomahawk, with a look so significant, that it put an effectual end to these stolen memorials of their passage.

As there were horses, to leave the prints of their footsteps, in both bands of the Indians, this interruption cut off any probable hopes of assistance being conveyed through the means of their trail.

Heyward would have ventured a remonstrance had there been anything encouraging in the gloomy reserve of Magua. But the savage, during all this time, seldom turned to look at his followers, and never spoke. With the sun for his only guide, or aided by such blind marks as are only known to the sagacity of a native, he held his way along the barrens of pine, through occasional little fertile vales, across brooks and rivulets, and over undulating hills, with the accuracy of instinct, and nearly with the directness of a bird. He never seemed to hesitate. Whether the path was hardly distinguishable, whether it disappeared, or whether it lay beaten and plain before him, made no sensible difference in his speed or certainty. It seemed as if fatigue could not affect him. Whenever the eyes of the wearied travelers rose from the decayed leaves over which they trod, his dark form was to be seen glancing among the stems of the trees in front, his head immovably fastened in a forward position, with the light plume on his crest fluttering in a current of air, made solely by the swiftness of his own motion.

But all this diligence and speed were not without an object. After crossing a low vale, through which a gushing brook meandered, he suddenly ascended a hill, so steep and difficult of ascent, that the sisters were compelled to alight in order to follow. When the summit was gained, they found themselves on a level spot, but thinly covered with trees, under one of which Magua had thrown his dark form, as if willing and ready to seek that rest which was so much needed by the whole party.

CHAPTER XI.

"Cursed be my tribe If I forgive him."
—Shylock

The Indian had selected for this desirable purpose one of those steep, pyramidal hills, which bear a strong resemblance to artificial mounds, and which so frequently occur in the valleys of America. The one in question was high and precipitous; its top flattened, as usual; but with one of its sides more than ordinarily irregular. It possessed no other apparent advantage for a resting place, than in its elevation and form, which might render defense easy, and surprise nearly impossible. As Heyward, however, no longer expected that rescue which time and distance now rendered so improbable, he regarded these little peculiarities with an eye devoid of interest, devoting himself entirely to the comfort and condolence of his feebler companions. The Narragansetts were suffered to browse on the branches of the trees and shrubs that were thinly scattered over the summit of the hill, while the remains of their provisions were spread under the shade of a beech, that stretched its horizontal limbs like a canopy above them.

Notwithstanding the swiftness of their flight, one of the Indians had found an opportunity to strike a straggling fawn with an arrow, and had borne the more preferable fragments of the victim, patiently on his shoulders, to the stopping place. Without any aid from the science of cookery, he was immediately employed, in common with his fellows, in gorging himself with this digestible sustenance. Magua alone sat apart, without participating in the revolting meal, and apparently buried in the deepest thought.

This abstinence, so remarkable in an Indian, when he possessed the means of satisfying hunger, at length attracted the notice of Heyward. The young man willingly believed that the Huron deliberated on the most eligible manner of eluding the vigilance of his associates. With a view to assist his plans by any suggestion of his own, and to strengthen the temptation, he left the beech, and straggled, as if without an object, to the spot where Le Renard was seated.

"Has not Magua kept the sun in his face long enough to escape all danger from the Canadians?" he asked, as though no longer doubtful of the good intelligence established between them; "and will not the chief of William Henry be better pleased to see his daughters before another night may have hardened his heart to their loss, to make him less liberal in his reward?"

"Do the pale faces love their children less in the morning than at night?" asked the Indian, coldly.

"By no means," returned Heyward, anxious to recall his error, if he had made one; "the white man may, and does often, forget the burial place of his fathers; he sometimes ceases to remember those he should love, and has promised to cherish; but the affection of a parent for his child is never permitted to die."

"And is the heart of the white-headed chief soft, and will he think of the babes that his squaws have given him? He is hard on his warriors and his eyes are made of stone?"

"He is severe to the idle and wicked, but to the sober and deserving he is a leader, both just and humane. I have known many fond and tender parents, but never have I seen a man whose heart was softer toward his child. You have seen the gray-head in front of his warriors, Magua; but I have seen his eyes swimming in water, when he spoke of those children who are now in your power!"

Heyward paused, for he knew not how to construe the remarkable expression that gleamed across the swarthy features of the attentive Indian. At first it seemed as if the remembrance of the promised reward grew vivid in his mind, while he listened to the sources of parental feeling which were to assure its possession; but, as Duncan proceeded, the expression of joy became so fiercely malignant that it was impossible not to apprehend it proceeded from some passion more sinister than avarice.

"Go," said the Huron, suppressing the alarming exhibition in an instant, in a death-like calmness of countenance; "go to the dark-haired daughter, and say, 'Magua waits to speak' The father will remember what the child promises."

Duncan, who interpreted this speech to express a wish for some additional pledge that the promised gifts should not be withheld, slowly and reluctantly repaired to the place where the sisters were now resting from their fatigue, to communicate its purport to Cora.

"You understand the nature of an Indian's wishes," he concluded, as he led her toward the place where she was expected, "and must be prodigal of your offers of powder and blankets. Ardent spirits are, however, the most prized by such as he; nor would it be amiss to add some boon from your own hand, with that grace you so well know how to practise. Remember, Cora, that on your presence of mind and ingenuity, even your life, as well as that of Alice, may in some measure depend."

"Heyward, and yours!"

"Mine is of little moment; it is already sold to my king, and is a prize to be seized by any enemy who may possess the power. I have no father to expect me, and but few friends to lament a fate which I have courted with the insatiable longings of youth after distinction. But hush! we approach the Indian. Magua, the lady with whom you wish to speak, is here."

The Indian rose slowly from his seat, and stood for near a minute silent and motionless. He then signed with his hand for Heyward to retire, saying, coldly:

"When the Huron talks to the women, his tribe shut their ears."

Duncan, still lingering, as if refusing to comply, Cora said, with a calm smile:

"You hear, Heyward, and delicacy at least should urge you to retire. Go to Alice, and comfort her with our reviving prospects."

She waited until he had departed, and then turning to the native, with the dignity of her sex in her voice and manner, she added: "What would Le Renard say to the daughter of Munro?"

"Listen," said the Indian, laying his hand firmly upon her arm, as if willing to draw her utmost attention to his words; a movement that Cora as firmly but quietly repulsed, by extricating the limb from his grasp: "Magua was born a chief and a warrior among the red Hurons of the lakes; he saw the suns of twenty summers make the snows of twenty winters run off in the streams before he saw a pale face; and he was happy! Then his Canada fathers came into the woods, and taught him to drink the fire-water, and he became a rascal. The Hurons drove him from the graves of his fathers, as they would chase the hunted buffalo. He ran down the shores of the lakes, and followed their outlet to the 'city of cannon' There he hunted and fished, till the people chased him again through the woods into the arms of his enemies. The chief, who was born a Huron, was at last a warrior among the Mohawks!"

"Something like this I had heard before," said Cora, observing that he paused to suppress those passions which began to burn with too bright a flame, as he recalled the recollection of his supposed injuries.

"Was it the fault of Le Renard that his head was not made of rock? Who gave him the fire-water? who made him a villain? 'Twas the pale faces, the people of your own color."

"And am I answerable that thoughtless and unprincipled men exist, whose shades of countenance may resemble mine?" Cora calmly demanded of the excited savage.

"No; Magua is a man, and not a fool; such as you never open their lips to the burning stream: the Great Spirit has given you wisdom!"

"What, then, have I do to, or say, in the matter of your misfortunes, not to say of your errors?"

"Listen," repeated the Indian, resuming his earnest attitude; "when his English and French fathers dug up the hatchet, Le Renard struck the war-post of the Mohawks, and went out against his own nation. The pale faces have driven the red-skins from their hunting grounds, and now when they fight, a white man leads the way. The old chief at Horican, your father, was the great captain of our war-party. He said to the Mohawks do this, and do that, and he was minded. He made a law, that if an Indian swallowed the fire-water, and came into the cloth wigwams of his warriors, it should not be forgotten. Magua foolishly opened his mouth, and the hot liquor led him into the cabin of Munro. What did the gray-head? let his daughter say."

"He forgot not his words, and did justice, by punishing the offender," said the undaunted daughter.

"Justice!" repeated the Indian, casting an oblique glance of the most ferocious expression at her unyielding countenance; "is it justice to make evil and then punish for it? Magua was not himself; it was the fire-water that spoke and acted for him! but Munro did believe it. The Huron chief was tied up before all the pale-faced warriors, and whipped like a dog."

Cora remained silent, for she knew not how to palliate this imprudent severity on the part of her father in a manner to suit the comprehension of an Indian.

"See!" continued Magua, tearing aside the slight calico that very imperfectly concealed his painted breast; "here are scars given by knives and bullets—of these a warrior may boast before his nation; but the gray-head has left marks on the back of the Huron chief that he must hide like a squaw, under this painted cloth of the whites."

"I had thought," resumed Cora, "that an Indian warrior was patient, and that his spirit felt not and knew not the pain his body suffered."

"When the Chippewas tied Magua to the stake, and cut this gash," said the other, laying his finger on a deep scar, "the Huron laughed in their faces, and told them, Women struck so light! His spirit was then in the clouds! But when he felt the blows of Munro, his spirit lay under the birch. The spirit of a Huron is never drunk; it remembers forever!"

"But it may be appeased. If my father has done you this injustice, show him how an Indian can forgive an injury, and take back his daughters. You have heard from Major Heyward—"

Magua shook his head, forbidding the repetition of offers he so much despised.

"What would you have?" continued Cora, after a most painful pause, while the conviction forced itself on her mind that the too sanguine and generous Duncan had been cruelly deceived by the cunning of the savage.

"What a Huron loves—good for good; bad for bad!"

"You would, then, revenge the injury inflicted by Munro on his helpless daughters. Would it not be more like a man to go before his face, and take the satisfaction of a warrior?"

"The arms of the pale faces are long, and their knives sharp!" returned the savage, with a malignant laugh: "why should Le Renard go among the muskets of his warriors, when he holds the spirit of the gray-head in his hand?"

"Name your intention, Magua," said Cora, struggling with herself to speak with steady calmness. "Is it to lead us prisoners to the woods, or do you contemplate even some greater evil? Is there no reward, no means of palliating the injury, and of softening your heart? At least, release my gentle sister, and pour out all your malice on me. Purchase wealth by her safety and satisfy your revenge with a single victim. The loss of both his daughters might bring the aged man to his grave, and where would then be the satisfaction of Le Renard?"

"Listen," said the Indian again. "The light eyes can go back to the Horican, and tell the old chief what has been done, if the dark-haired woman will swear by the Great Spirit of her fathers to tell no lie."

"What must I promise?" demanded Cora, still maintaining a secret ascendancy over the fierce native by the collected and feminine dignity of her presence.

"When Magua left his people his wife was given to another chief; he has now made friends with the Hurons, and will go back to the graves of his tribe, on the shores of the great lake. Let the daughter of the English chief follow, and live in his wigwam forever."

However revolting a proposal of such a character might prove to Cora, she retained, notwithstanding her powerful disgust, sufficient self-command to reply, without betraying the weakness.

"And what pleasure would Magua find in sharing his cabin with a wife he did not love; one who would be of a nation and color different from his own? It would be better to take the gold of Munro, and buy the heart of some Huron maid with his gifts."

The Indian made no reply for near a minute, but bent his fierce looks on the countenance of Cora, in such wavering glances, that her eyes sank with shame, under an impression that for the first time they had encountered an expression that no chaste female might endure. While she was shrinking within herself, in dread of having her ears wounded by some proposal still more shocking than the last, the voice of Magua answered, in its tones of deepest malignancy:

"When the blows scorched the back of the Huron, he would know where to find a woman to feel the smart. The daughter of Munro would draw his water, hoe his corn, and cook his venison. The body of the gray-head would sleep among his cannon, but his heart would lie within reach of the knife of Le Subtil."

"Monster! well dost thou deserve thy treacherous name," cried Cora, in an ungovernable burst of filial indignation. "None but a fiend could meditate such a vengeance. But thou overratest thy power! You shall find it is, in truth, the heart of Munro you hold, and that it will defy your utmost malice!"

The Indian answered this bold defiance by a ghastly smile, that showed an unaltered purpose, while he motioned her away, as if to close the conference forever. Cora, already regretting her precipitation, was obliged to comply, for Magua instantly left the spot, and approached his gluttonous comrades. Heyward flew to the side of the agitated female, and demanded the result of a dialogue that he had watched at a distance with so much interest. But, unwilling to alarm the fears of Alice, she evaded a direct reply, betraying only by her anxious looks fastened on the slightest movements of her captors. To the reiterated and earnest questions of her sister concerning their probable destination, she made no other answer than by pointing toward the dark group, with an agitation she could not control, and murmuring as she folded Alice to her bosom.

"There, there; read our fortunes in their faces; we shall see; we shall see!"

The action, and the choked utterance of Cora, spoke more impressively than any words, and quickly drew the attention of her companions on that spot where her own was riveted with an intenseness that nothing but the importance of the stake could create.

When Magua reached the cluster of lolling savages, who, gorged with their disgusting meal, lay stretched on the earth in brutal indulgence, he commenced speaking with the dignity of an Indian chief. The first syllables he uttered had the effect to cause his listeners to raise themselves in attitudes of respectful attention. As the Huron used his native language, the prisoners, notwithstanding the caution of the natives had kept them within the swing of their tomahawks, could only conjecture the substance of his harangue from the nature of those significant gestures with which an Indian always illustrates his eloquence.

At first, the language, as well as the action of Magua, appeared calm and deliberative. When he had succeeded in sufficiently awakening the attention of his comrades, Heyward fancied, by his pointing so frequently toward the direction of the great lakes, that he spoke of the land of their fathers, and of their distant tribe. Frequent indications of applause escaped the listeners, who, as they uttered the expressive "Hugh!" looked at each other in commendation of the speaker. Le Renard was too skillful to neglect his advantage. He now spoke of the long and painful route by which they had left those spacious grounds and happy villages, to come and battle against the enemies of their Canadian fathers. He enumerated the warriors of the party; their several merits; their frequent services to the nation; their wounds, and the number of the scalps they had taken. Whenever he alluded to any present (and the subtle Indian neglected none), the dark countenance of the flattered individual gleamed with exultation, nor did he even hesitate to assert the truth of the words, by gestures of applause and confirmation. Then the voice of the speaker fell, and lost the loud, animated tones of triumph with which he had enumerated their deeds of success and victory. He described the cataract of Glenn's; the impregnable position of its rocky island, with its caverns and its numerous rapids and whirlpools; he named the name of "La Longue Carabine," and paused until the forest beneath them had sent up the last echo of a loud and long yell, with which the hated appellation was received. He pointed toward the youthful military captive, and described the death of a favorite warrior, who had been precipitated into the deep ravine by his hand. He not only mentioned the fate of him who, hanging between heaven and earth, had presented such a spectacle of horror to the whole band, but he acted anew the terrors of his situation, his resolution and his death, on the branches of a sapling; and, finally, he rapidly recounted the manner in which each of their friends had fallen, never failing to touch upon their courage, and their most acknowledged virtues. When this recital of events was ended, his voice once more changed, and became plaintive and even musical, in its low guttural sounds. He now spoke of the wives and children of the slain; their destitution; their misery, both physical and moral; their distance; and, at last, of their unavenged wrongs. Then suddenly lifting his voice to a pitch of terrific energy, he concluded by demanding:

"Are the Hurons dogs to bear this? Who shall say to the wife of Menowgua that the fishes have his scalp, and that his nation have not taken revenge! Who will dare meet the mother of Wassawattimie, that scornful woman, with his hands clean! What shall be said to the old men when they ask us for scalps, and we have not a hair from a white head to give them! The women will point their fingers at us. There is a dark spot on the names of the Hurons, and it must be hid in blood!" His voice was no longer audible in the burst of rage which now broke into the air, as if the wood, instead of containing so small a band, was filled with the nation. During the foregoing address the progress of the speaker was too plainly read by those most interested in his success through the medium of the countenances of the men he addressed. They had answered his melancholy and mourning by sympathy and sorrow; his assertions, by gestures of confirmation; and his boasting, with the exultation of savages. When he spoke of courage, their looks were firm and responsive; when he alluded to their injuries, their eyes kindled with fury; when he mentioned the taunts of the women, they dropped their heads in shame; but when he pointed out their means of vengeance, he struck a chord which never failed to thrill in the breast of an Indian. With the first intimation that it was within their reach, the whole band sprang upon their feet as one man; giving utterance to their rage in the most frantic cries, they rushed upon their prisoners in a body with drawn knives and uplifted tomahawks. Heyward threw himself between the sisters and the foremost, whom he grappled with a desperate strength that for a moment checked his violence. This unexpected resistance gave Magua time to interpose, and with rapid enunciation and animated gesture, he drew the attention of the band again to himself. In that language he knew so well how to assume, he diverted his comrades from their instant purpose, and invited them to prolong the misery of their victims. His proposal was received with acclamations, and executed with the swiftness of thought.

Two powerful warriors cast themselves on Heyward, while another was occupied in securing the less active singing-master. Neither of the captives, however, submitted without a desperate, though fruitless, struggle. Even David hurled his assailant to the earth; nor was Heyward secured until the victory over his companion enabled the Indians to direct their united force to that object. He was then bound and fastened to the body of the sapling, on whose branches Magua had acted the pantomime of the falling Huron. When the young soldier regained his recollection, he had the painful certainty before his eyes that a common fate was intended for the whole party. On his right was Cora in a durance similar to his own, pale and agitated, but with an eye whose steady look still read the proceedings of their enemies. On his left, the withes which bound her to a pine, performed that office for Alice which her trembling limbs refused, and alone kept her fragile form from sinking. Her hands were clasped before her in prayer, but instead of looking upward toward that power which alone could rescue them, her unconscious looks wandered to the countenance of Duncan with infantile dependency. David had contended, and the novelty of the circumstance held him silent, in deliberation on the propriety of the unusual occurrence.

The vengeance of the Hurons had now taken a new direction, and they prepared to execute it with that barbarous ingenuity with which they were familiarized by the practise of centuries. Some sought knots, to raise the blazing pile; one was riving the splinters of pine, in order to pierce the flesh of their captives with the burning fragments; and others bent the tops of two saplings to the earth, in order to suspend Heyward by the arms between the recoiling branches. But the vengeance of Magua sought a deeper and more malignant enjoyment.

While the less refined monsters of the band prepared, before the eyes of those who were to suffer, these well-known and vulgar means of torture, he approached Cora, and pointed out, with the most malign expression of countenance, the speedy fate that awaited her:

"Ha!" he added, "what says the daughter of Munro? Her head is too good to find a pillow in the wigwam of Le Renard; will she like it better when it rolls about this hill a plaything for the wolves? Her bosom cannot nurse the children of a Huron; she will see it spit upon by Indians!"

"What means the monster!" demanded the astonished Heyward.

"Nothing!" was the firm reply. "He is a savage, a barbarous and ignorant savage, and knows not what he does. Let us find leisure, with our dying breath, to ask for him penitence and pardon."

"Pardon!" echoed the fierce Huron, mistaking in his anger, the meaning of her words; "the memory of an Indian is no longer than the arm of the pale faces; his mercy shorter than their justice! Say; shall I send the yellow hair to her father, and will you follow Magua to the great lakes, to carry his water, and feed him with corn?"

Cora beckoned him away, with an emotion of disgust she could not control.

"Leave me," she said, with a solemnity that for a moment checked the barbarity of the Indian; "you mingle bitterness in my prayers; you stand between me and my God!"

The slight impression produced on the savage was, however, soon forgotten, and he continued pointing, with taunting irony, toward Alice.

"Look! the child weeps! She is too young to die! Send her to Munro, to comb his gray hairs, and keep life in the heart of the old man."

Cora could not resist the desire to look upon her youthful sister, in whose eyes she met an imploring glance, that betrayed the longings of nature.

"What says he, dearest Cora?" asked the trembling voice of Alice. "Did he speak of sending me to our father?"

For many moments the elder sister looked upon the younger, with a countenance that wavered with powerful and contending emotions. At length she spoke, though her tones had lost their rich and calm fullness, in an expression of tenderness that seemed maternal.

"Alice," she said, "the Huron offers us both life, nay, more than both; he offers to restore Duncan, our invaluable Duncan, as well as you, to our friends—to our father—to our heart-stricken, childless father, if I will bow down this rebellious, stubborn pride of mine, and consent—"

Her voice became choked, and clasping her hands, she looked upward, as if seeking, in her agony, intelligence from a wisdom that was infinite.

"Say on," cried Alice; "to what, dearest Cora? Oh! that the proffer were made to me! to save you, to cheer our aged father, to restore Duncan, how cheerfully could I die!"

"Die!" repeated Cora, with a calmer and firmer voice, "that were easy! Perhaps the alternative may not be less so. He would have me," she continued, her accents sinking under a deep consciousness of the degradation of the proposal, "follow him to the wilderness; go to the habitations of the Hurons; to remain there; in short, to become his wife! Speak, then, Alice; child of my affections! sister of my love! And you, too, Major Heyward, aid my weak reason with your counsel. Is life to be purchased by such a sacrifice? Will you, Alice, receive it at my hands at such a price? And you, Duncan, guide me; control me between you; for I am wholly yours!"

"Would I!" echoed the indignant and astonished youth. "Cora! Cora! you jest with our misery! Name not the horrid alternative again; the thought itself is worse than a thousand deaths."

"That such would be your answer, I well knew!" exclaimed Cora, her cheeks flushing, and her dark eyes once more sparkling with the lingering emotions of a woman. "What says my Alice? for her will I submit without another murmur."

Although both Heyward and Cora listened with painful suspense and the deepest attention, no sounds were heard in reply. It appeared as if the delicate and sensitive form of Alice would shrink into itself, as she listened to this proposal. Her arms had fallen lengthwise before her, the fingers moving in slight convulsions; her head dropped upon her bosom, and her whole person seemed suspended against the tree, looking like some beautiful emblem of the wounded delicacy of her sex, devoid of animation and yet keenly conscious. In a few moments, however, her head began to move slowly, in a sign of deep, unconquerable disapprobation.

"No, no, no; better that we die as we have lived, together!"

"Then die!" shouted Magua, hurling his tomahawk with violence at the unresisting speaker, and gnashing his teeth with a rage that could no longer be bridled at this sudden exhibition of firmness in the one he believed the weakest of the party. The axe cleaved the air in front of Heyward, and cutting some of the flowing ringlets of Alice, quivered in the tree above her head. The sight maddened Duncan to desperation. Collecting all his energies in one effort he snapped the twigs which bound him and rushed upon another savage, who was preparing, with loud yells and a more deliberate aim, to repeat the blow. They encountered, grappled, and fell to the earth together. The naked body of his antagonist afforded Heyward no means of holding his adversary, who glided from his grasp, and rose again with one knee on his chest, pressing him down with the weight of a giant. Duncan already saw the knife gleaming in the air, when a whistling sound swept past him, and was rather accompanied than followed by the sharp crack of a rifle. He felt his breast relieved from the load it had endured; he saw the savage expression of his adversary's countenance change to a look of vacant wildness, when the Indian fell dead on the faded leaves by his side.

CHAPTER XII.

> "Clo.—I am gone, sire,
>     And anon, sire, I'll be with you again."
> —Twelfth Night

The Hurons stood aghast at this sudden visitation of death on one of their band. But as they regarded the fatal accuracy of an aim which had dared to immolate an enemy at so much hazard to a friend, the name of "La Longue Carabine" burst simultaneously from every lip, and was succeeded by a wild and a sort of plaintive howl. The cry was answered by a loud shout from a little thicket, where the incautious party had piled their arms; and at the next moment, Hawkeye, too eager to load the rifle he had regained, was seen advancing upon them, brandishing the clubbed weapon, and cutting the air with wide and powerful sweeps. Bold and rapid as was the progress of the scout, it was exceeded by that of a light and vigorous form which, bounding past him, leaped, with incredible activity and daring, into the very center of the Hurons, where it stood, whirling a tomahawk, and flourishing a glittering knife, with fearful menaces, in front of Cora. Quicker than the thoughts could follow those unexpected and audacious movements, an image, armed in the emblematic panoply of death, glided before their eyes, and assumed a threatening attitude at the other's side. The savage tormentors recoiled before these warlike intruders, and uttered, as they appeared in such quick succession, the often repeated and peculiar exclamations of surprise, followed by the well-known and dreaded appellations of:

"Le Cerf Agile! Le Gros Serpent!"

But the wary and vigilant leader of the Hurons was not so easily disconcerted. Casting his keen eyes around the little plain, he comprehended the nature of the assault at a glance, and encouraging his followers by his voice as well as by his example, he unsheathed his long and dangerous knife, and rushed with a loud whoop upon the expected Chingachgook. It was the signal for a general combat. Neither party had firearms, and the contest was to be decided in the deadliest manner, hand to hand, with weapons of offense, and none of defense.

Uncas answered the whoop, and leaping on an enemy, with a single, well-directed blow of his tomahawk, cleft him to the brain. Heyward tore the weapon of Magua from the sapling, and rushed eagerly toward the fray. As the combatants were now equal in number, each singled an opponent from the adverse band. The rush and blows passed with the fury of a whirlwind, and the swiftness of lightning. Hawkeye soon got another enemy within reach of his arm, and with one sweep of his formidable weapon he beat down the slight and inartificial defenses of his antagonist, crushing him to the earth with the blow. Heyward ventured to hurl the tomahawk he had seized, too ardent to await the moment of closing. It struck the Indian he had selected on the forehead, and checked for an instant his onward rush. Encouraged by this slight advantage, the impetuous young man continued his onset, and sprang upon his enemy with naked hands. A single instant was enough to assure him of the rashness of the measure, for he immediately found himself fully engaged, with all his activity and courage, in endeavoring to ward the desperate thrusts made with the knife of the Huron. Unable longer to foil an enemy so alert and vigilant, he threw his arms about him, and succeeded in pinning the limbs of the other to his side, with an iron grasp, but one that was far too exhausting to himself to continue long. In this extremity he heard a voice near him, shouting:

"Extarminate the varlets! no quarter to an accursed Mingo!"

At the next moment, the breech of Hawkeye's rifle fell on the naked head of his adversary, whose muscles appeared to wither under the shock, as he sank from the arms of Duncan, flexible and motionless.

When Uncas had brained his first antagonist, he turned, like a hungry lion, to seek another. The fifth and only Huron disengaged at the first onset had paused a moment, and then seeing that all around him were employed in the deadly strife, he had sought, with hellish vengeance, to complete the baffled work of revenge. Raising a shout of triumph, he sprang toward the defenseless Cora, sending his keen axe as the dreadful precursor of his approach. The tomahawk grazed her shoulder, and cutting the withes which bound her to the tree, left the maiden at liberty to fly. She eluded the grasp of the savage, and reckless of her own safety, threw herself on the bosom of Alice, striving with convulsed and ill-directed fingers, to tear asunder the twigs which confined the person of her sister. Any other than a monster would have relented at such an act of generous devotion to the best and purest affection; but the breast of the Huron was a stranger to sympathy. Seizing Cora by the rich tresses which fell in confusion about her form, he tore her from her frantic hold, and bowed her down with brutal violence to her knees. The savage drew the flowing curls through his hand, and raising them on high with an outstretched arm, he passed the knife around the exquisitely molded head of his victim, with a taunting and exulting laugh. But he purchased this moment of fierce gratification with the loss of the fatal opportunity. It was just then the sight caught the eye of Uncas. Bounding from his footsteps he appeared for an instant darting through the air and descending in a ball he fell on the chest of his enemy, driving him many yards from the spot, headlong and prostrate. The violence of the exertion cast the young Mohican at his side. They arose together, fought, and bled, each in his turn. But the conflict was soon decided; the tomahawk of Heyward and the rifle of Hawkeye descended on the skull of the Huron, at the same moment that the knife of Uncas reached his heart.

The battle was now entirely terminated with the exception of the protracted struggle between "Le Renard Subtil" and "Le Gros Serpent." Well did these barbarous warriors prove that they deserved those significant names which had been bestowed for deeds in former wars. When they engaged, some little time was lost in eluding the quick and vigorous thrusts which had been aimed at their lives. Suddenly darting on each other, they closed, and came to the earth, twisted together like twining serpents, in pliant and subtle folds. At the moment when the victors found themselves unoccupied, the spot where these experienced and desperate combatants lay could only be distinguished by a cloud of dust and leaves, which moved from the center of the little plain toward its boundary, as if raised by the passage of a whirlwind. Urged by the different motives of filial affection, friendship and gratitude, Heyward and his companions rushed with one accord to the place, encircling the little canopy of dust which hung above the warriors. In vain did Uncas dart around the cloud, with a wish to strike his knife into the heart of his father's foe; the threatening rifle of Hawkeye was raised and suspended in vain, while Duncan endeavored to seize the limbs of the Huron with hands that appeared to have lost their power. Covered as they were with dust and blood, the swift evolutions of the combatants seemed to incorporate their bodies into one. The death-like looking figure of the Mohican, and the dark form of the Huron, gleamed before their eyes in such quick and confused succession, that the friends of the former knew not where to plant the succoring blow. It is true there were short and fleeting moments, when the fiery eyes of Magua were seen glittering, like the fabled organs of the basilisk through the dusty wreath by which he was enveloped, and he read by those short and deadly glances the fate of the combat in the presence of his enemies; ere, however, any hostile hand could descend on his devoted head, its place was filled by the scowling visage of Chingachgook. In this manner the scene of the combat was removed from the center of the little plain to its verge. The Mohican now found an opportunity to make a powerful thrust with his knife; Magua suddenly relinquished his grasp, and fell backward without motion, and seemingly without life. His adversary leaped on his feet, making the arches of the forest ring with the sounds of triumph.

"Well done for the Delawares! victory to the Mohicans!" cried Hawkeye, once more elevating the butt of the long and fatal rifle; "a finishing blow from a man without a cross will never tell against his honor, nor rob him of his right to the scalp."

But at the very moment when the dangerous weapon was in the act of descending, the subtle Huron rolled swiftly from beneath the danger, over the edge of the precipice, and falling on his feet, was seen leaping, with a single bound, into the center of a thicket of low bushes, which clung along its sides. The Delawares, who had believed their enemy dead, uttered their exclamation of surprise, and were following with speed and clamor, like hounds in open view of the deer, when a shrill and peculiar cry from the scout instantly changed their purpose, and recalled them to the summit of the hill.

"'Twas like himself!" cried the inveterate forester, whose prejudices contributed so largely to veil his natural sense of justice in all matters which concerned the Mingoes; "a lying and deceitful varlet as he is. An honest Delaware now, being fairly vanquished, would have lain still, and been knocked on the head, but these knavish Maquas cling to life like so many cats-o'-the-mountain. Let him go—let him go; 'tis but one man, and he without rifle or bow, many a long mile from his French commerades; and like a rattler that lost his fangs, he can do no further mischief, until such time as he, and we too, may leave the prints of our moccasins over a long reach of sandy plain. See, Uncas," he added, in Delaware, "your father is flaying the scalps already. It may be well to go round and feel the vagabonds that are left, or we may have another of them loping through the woods, and screeching like a jay that has been winged."

So saying the honest but implacable scout made the circuit of the dead, into whose senseless bosoms he thrust his long knife, with as much coolness as though they had been so many brute carcasses. He had, however, been anticipated by the elder Mohican, who had already torn the emblems of victory from the unresisting heads of the slain.

But Uncas, denying his habits, we had almost said his nature, flew with instinctive delicacy, accompanied by Heyward, to the assistance of the females, and quickly releasing Alice, placed her in the arms of Cora. We shall not attempt to describe the gratitude to the Almighty Disposer of Events which glowed in the bosoms of the sisters, who were thus unexpectedly restored to life and to each other. Their thanksgivings were deep and silent; the offerings of their gentle spirits burning brightest and purest on the secret altars of their hearts; and their renovated and more earthly feelings exhibiting themselves in long and fervent though speechless caresses. As Alice rose from her knees, where she had sunk by the side of Cora, she threw herself on the bosom of the latter, and sobbed aloud the name of their aged father, while her soft, dove-like eyes, sparkled with the rays of hope.

"We are saved! we are saved!" she murmured; "to return to the arms of our dear, dear father, and his heart will not be broken with grief. And you, too, Cora, my sister, my more than sister, my mother; you, too, are spared. And Duncan," she added, looking round upon the youth with a smile of ineffable innocence, "even our own brave and noble Duncan has escaped without a hurt."

To these ardent and nearly innocent words Cora made no other answer than by straining the youthful speaker to her heart, as she bent over her in melting tenderness. The manhood of Heyward felt no shame in dropping tears over this spectacle of affectionate rapture; and Uncas stood, fresh and blood-stained from the combat, a calm, and, apparently, an unmoved looker-on, it is true, but with eyes that had already lost their fierceness, and were beaming with a sympathy that elevated him far above the intelligence, and advanced him probably centuries before, the practises of his nation.

During this display of emotions so natural in their situation, Hawkeye, whose vigilant distrust had satisfied itself that the Hurons, who disfigured the heavenly scene, no longer possessed the power to interrupt its harmony, approached David, and liberated him from the bonds he had, until that moment, endured with the most exemplary patience.

"There," exclaimed the scout, casting the last withe behind him, "you are once more master of your own limbs, though you seem not to use them with much greater judgment than that in which they were first fashioned. If advice from one who is not older than yourself, but who, having lived most of his time in the wilderness, may be said to have experience beyond his years, will give no offense, you are welcome to my thoughts; and these are, to part with the little tooting instrument in your jacket to the first fool you meet with, and buy some we'pon with the money, if it be only the barrel of a horseman's pistol. By industry and care, you might thus come to some prefarment; for by this time, I should think, your eyes would plainly tell you that a carrion crow is a better bird than a mocking-thresher. The one will, at least, remove foul sights from before the face of man, while the other is only good to brew disturbances in the woods, by cheating the ears of all that hear them."

"Arms and the clarion for the battle, but the song of thanksgiving to the victory!" answered the liberated David. "Friend," he added, thrusting forth his lean, delicate hand toward Hawkeye, in kindness, while his eyes twinkled and grew moist, "I thank thee that the hairs of my head still grow where they were first rooted by Providence; for, though those of other men may be more glossy and curling, I have ever found mine own well suited to the brain they shelter. That I did not join myself to the battle, was less owing to disinclination, than to the bonds of the heathen. Valiant and skillful hast thou proved thyself in the conflict, and I hereby thank thee, before proceeding to discharge other and more important duties, because thou hast proved thyself well worthy of a Christian's praise."

"The thing is but a trifle, and what you may often see if you tarry long among us," returned the scout, a good deal softened toward the man of song, by this unequivocal expression of gratitude. "I have got back my old companion, 'killdeer'," he added, striking his hand on the breech of his rifle; "and that in itself is a victory. These Iroquois are cunning, but they outwitted themselves when they placed their firearms out of reach; and had Uncas or his father been gifted with only their common Indian patience, we should have come in upon the knaves with three bullets instead of one, and that would have made a finish of the whole pack; yon loping varlet, as well as his commerades. But 'twas all fore-ordered, and for the best."

"Thou sayest well," returned David, "and hast caught the true spirit of Christianity. He that is to be saved will be saved, and he that is predestined to be damned will be damned. This is the doctrine of truth, and most consoling and refreshing it is to the true believer."

The scout, who by this time was seated, examining into the state of his rifle with a species of parental assiduity, now looked up at the other in a displeasure that he did not affect to conceal, roughly interrupting further speech.

"Doctrine or no doctrine," said the sturdy woodsman, "'tis the belief of knaves, and the curse of an honest man. I can credit that yonder Huron was to fall by my hand, for with my own eyes I have seen it; but nothing short of being a witness will cause me to think he has met with any reward, or that Chingachgook there will be condemned at the final day."

"You have no warranty for such an audacious doctrine, nor any covenant to support it," cried David who was deeply tinctured with the subtle distinctions which, in his time, and more especially in his province, had been drawn around the beautiful simplicity of revelation, by endeavoring to penetrate the awful mystery of the divine nature, supplying faith by self-sufficiency, and by consequence, involving those who reasoned from such human dogmas in absurdities and doubt; "your temple is reared on the sands, and the first tempest will wash away its foundation. I demand your authorities for such an uncharitable assertion (like other advocates of a system, David was not always accurate in his use of terms). Name chapter and verse; in which of the holy books do you find language to support you?"

"Book!" repeated Hawkeye, with singular and ill-concealed disdain; "do you take me for a whimpering boy at the apronstring of one of your old gals; and this good rifle on my knee for the feather of a goose's wing, my ox's horn for a bottle of ink, and my leathern pouch for a cross-barred handkercher to carry my dinner? Book! what have such as I, who am a warrior of the wilderness, though a man without a cross, to do with books? I never read but in one, and the words that are written there are too simple and too plain to need much schooling; though I may boast that of forty long and hard-working years."

"What call you the volume?" said David, misconceiving the other's meaning.

"'Tis open before your eyes," returned the scout; "and he who owns it is not a niggard of its use. I have heard it said that there are men who read in books to convince themselves there is a God. I know not but man may so deform his works in the settlement, as to leave that which is so clear in the wilderness a matter of doubt among traders and priests. If any such there be, and he will follow me from sun to sun, through the windings of the forest, he shall see enough to teach him that he is a fool, and that the greatest of his folly lies in striving to rise to the level of One he can never equal, be it in goodness, or be it in power."

The instant David discovered that he battled with a disputant who imbibed his faith from the lights of nature, eschewing all subtleties of doctrine, he willingly abandoned a controversy from which he believed neither profit nor credit was to be derived. While the scout was speaking, he had also seated himself, and producing the ready little volume and the iron-rimmed spectacles, he prepared to discharge a duty, which nothing but the unexpected assault he had received in his orthodoxy could have so long suspended. He was, in truth, a minstrel of the western continent—of a much later day, certainly, than those gifted bards, who formerly sang the profane renown of baron and prince, but after the spirit of his own age and country; and he was now prepared to exercise the cunning of his craft, in celebration of, or rather in thanksgiving for, the recent victory. He waited patiently for Hawkeye to cease, then lifting his eyes, together with his voice, he said, aloud:

"I invite you, friends, to join in praise for this signal deliverance from the hands of barbarians and infidels, to the comfortable and solemn tones of the tune called 'Northampton'."

He next named the page and verse where the rhymes selected were to be found, and applied the pitch-pipe to his lips, with the decent gravity that he had been wont to use in the temple. This time he was, however, without any accompaniment, for the sisters were just then pouring out those tender effusions of affection which have been already alluded to. Nothing deterred by the smallness of his audience, which, in truth, consisted only of the discontented scout, he raised his voice, commencing and ending the sacred song without accident or interruption of any kind.

Hawkeye listened while he coolly adjusted his flint and reloaded his rifle; but the sounds, wanting the extraneous assistance of scene and sympathy, failed to awaken his slumbering emotions. Never minstrel, or by whatever more suitable name David should be known, drew upon his talents in the presence of more insensible auditors; though considering the singleness and sincerity of his motive, it is probable that no bard of profane song ever uttered notes that ascended so near to that throne where all homage and praise is due. The scout shook his head, and muttering some unintelligible words, among which "throat" and "Iroquois" were alone audible, he walked away, to collect and to examine into the state of the captured arsenal of the Hurons. In this office he was now joined by Chingachgook, who found his own, as well as the rifle of his son, among the arms. Even Heyward and David were furnished with weapons; nor was ammunition wanting to render them all effectual.

When the foresters had made their selection, and distributed their prizes, the scout announced that the hour had arrived when it was necessary to move. By this time the song of Gamut had ceased, and the sisters had learned to still the exhibition of their emotions. Aided by Duncan and the younger Mohican, the two latter descended the precipitous sides of that hill which they had so lately ascended under so very different auspices, and whose summit had so nearly proved the scene of their massacre. At the foot they found the Narragansetts browsing the herbage of the bushes, and having mounted, they followed the movements of a guide, who, in the most deadly straits, had so often proved himself their friend. The journey was, however, short. Hawkeye, leaving the blind path that the Hurons had followed, turned short to his right, and entering the thicket, he crossed a babbling brook, and halted in a narrow dell, under the shade of a few water elms. Their distance from the base of the fatal hill was but a few rods, and the steeds had been serviceable only in crossing the shallow stream.

The scout and the Indians appeared to be familiar with the sequestered place where they now were; for, leaning their rifle against the trees, they commenced throwing aside the dried leaves, and opening the blue clay, out of which a clear and sparkling spring of bright, glancing water, quickly bubbled. The white man then looked about him, as though seeking for some object, which was not to be found as readily as he expected.

"Them careless imps, the Mohawks, with their Tuscarora and Onondaga brethren, have been here slaking their thirst," he muttered, "and the vagabonds have thrown away the gourd! This is the way with benefits, when they are bestowed on such disremembering hounds! Here has the Lord laid his hand, in the midst of the howling wilderness, for their good, and raised a fountain of water from the bowels of the 'arth, that might laugh at the richest shop of apothecary's ware in all the colonies; and see! the knaves have trodden in the clay, and deformed the cleanliness of the place, as though they were brute beasts, instead of human men."

Uncas silently extended toward him the desired gourd, which the spleen of Hawkeye had hitherto prevented him from observing on a branch of an elm. Filling it with water, he retired a short distance, to a place where the ground was more firm and dry; here he coolly seated himself, and after taking a long, and, apparently, a grateful draught, he commenced a very strict examination of the fragments of food left by the Hurons, which had hung in a wallet on his arm.

"Thank you, lad!" he continued, returning the empty gourd to Uncas; "now we will see how these rampaging Hurons lived, when outlying in ambushments. Look at this! The varlets know the better pieces of the deer; and one would think they might carve and roast a saddle, equal to the best cook in the land! But everything is raw, for the Iroquois are thorough savages. Uncas, take my steel and kindle a fire; a mouthful of a tender broil will give natur' a helping hand, after so long a trail."

Heyward, perceiving that their guides now set about their repast in sober earnest, assisted the ladies to alight, and placed himself at their side, not unwilling to enjoy a few moments of grateful rest, after the bloody scene he had just gone through. While the culinary process was in hand, curiosity induced him to inquire into the circumstances which had led to their timely and unexpected rescue:

"How is it that we see you so soon, my generous friend," he asked, "and without aid from the garrison of Edward?"

"Had we gone to the bend in the river, we might have been in time to rake the leaves over your bodies, but too late to have saved your scalps," coolly answered the scout. "No, no; instead of throwing away strength and opportunity by crossing to the fort, we lay by, under the bank of the Hudson, waiting to watch the movements of the Hurons."

"You were, then, witnesses of all that passed?"

"Not of all; for Indian sight is too keen to be easily cheated, and we kept close. A difficult matter it was, too, to keep this Mohican boy snug in the ambushment. Ah! Uncas, Uncas, your behavior was more like that of a curious woman than of a warrior on his scent."

Uncas permitted his eyes to turn for an instant on the sturdy countenance of the speaker, but he neither spoke nor gave any indication of repentance. On the contrary, Heyward thought the manner of the young Mohican was disdainful, if not a little fierce, and that he suppressed passions that were ready to explode, as much in compliment to the listeners, as from the deference he usually paid to his white associate.

"You saw our capture?" Heyward next demanded.

"We heard it," was the significant answer. "An Indian yell is plain language to men who have passed their days in the woods. But when you landed, we were driven to crawl like sarpents, beneath the leaves; and then we lost sight of you entirely, until we placed eyes on you again trussed to the trees, and ready bound for an Indian massacre."

"Our rescue was the deed of Providence. It was nearly a miracle that you did not mistake the path, for the Hurons divided, and each band had its horses."

"Ay! there we were thrown off the scent, and might, indeed, have lost the trail, had it not been for Uncas; we took the path, however, that led into the wilderness; for we judged, and judged rightly, that the savages would hold that course with their prisoners. But when we had followed it for many miles, without finding a single twig broken, as I had advised, my mind misgave me; especially as all the footsteps had the prints of moccasins."

"Our captors had the precaution to see us shod like themselves," said Duncan, raising a foot, and exhibiting the buckskin he wore.

"Aye, 'twas judgmatical and like themselves; though we were too expart to be thrown from a trail by so common an invention."

"To what, then, are we indebted for our safety?"

"To what, as a white man who has no taint of Indian blood, I should be ashamed to own; to the judgment of the young Mohican, in matters which I should know better than he, but which I can now hardly believe to be true, though my own eyes tell me it is so."

"'Tis extraordinary! will you not name the reason?"

"Uncas was bold enough to say, that the beasts ridden by the gentle ones," continued Hawkeye, glancing his eyes, not without curious interest, on the fillies of the ladies, "planted the legs of one side on the ground at the same time, which is contrary to the movements of all trotting four-footed animals of my knowledge, except the bear. And yet here are horses that always journey in this manner, as my own eyes have seen, and as their trail has shown for twenty long miles."

"'Tis the merit of the animal! They come from the shores of Narrangansett Bay, in the small province of Providence Plantations, and are celebrated for their hardihood, and the ease of this peculiar movement; though other horses are not unfrequently trained to the same."

"It may be—it may be," said Hawkeye, who had listened with singular attention to this explanation; "though I am a man who has the full blood of the whites, my judgment in deer and beaver is greater than in beasts of burden. Major Effingham has many noble chargers, but I have never seen one travel after such a sidling gait."

"True; for he would value the animals for very different properties. Still is this a breed highly esteemed and, as you witness, much honored with the burdens it is often destined to bear."

The Mohicans had suspended their operations about the glimmering fire to listen; and, when Duncan had done, they looked at each other significantly, the father uttering the never-failing exclamation of surprise. The scout ruminated, like a man digesting his newly-acquired knowledge, and once more stole a glance at the horses.

"I dare to say there are even stranger sights to be seen in the settlements!" he said, at length. "Natur' is sadly abused by man, when he once gets the mastery. But, go sidling or go straight, Uncas had seen the movement, and their trail led us on to the broken bush. The outer branch, near the prints of one of the horses, was bent upward, as a lady breaks a flower from its stem, but all the rest were ragged and broken down, as if the strong hand of a man had been tearing them! So I concluded that the cunning varments had seen the twig bent, and had torn the rest, to make us believe a buck had been feeling the boughs with his antlers."

"I do believe your sagacity did not deceive you; for some such thing occurred!"

"That was easy to see," added the scout, in no degree conscious of having exhibited any extraordinary sagacity; "and a very different matter it was from a waddling horse! It then struck me the Mingoes would push for this spring, for the knaves well know the vartue of its waters!"

"Is it, then, so famous?" demanded Heyward, examining, with a more curious eye, the secluded dell, with its bubbling fountain, surrounded, as it was, by earth of a deep, dingy brown.

"Few red-skins, who travel south and east of the great lakes but have heard of its qualities. Will you taste for yourself?"

Heyward took the gourd, and after swallowing a little of the water, threw it aside with grimaces of discontent. The scout laughed in his silent but heartfelt manner, and shook his head with vast satisfaction.

"Ah! you want the flavor that one gets by habit; the time was when I liked it as little as yourself; but I have come to my taste, and I now crave it, as a deer does the licks.* Your high-spiced wines are not better liked than a red-skin relishes this water; especially when his natur' is ailing. But Uncas has made his fire, and it is time we think of eating, for our journey is long, and all before us."

---

* Many of the animals of the American forests resort to those spots where salt springs are found. These are called "licks" or "salt licks," in the language of the country, from the circumstance that the quadruped is often obliged to lick the earth, in order to obtain the saline particles. These licks are great places of resort with the hunters, who waylay their game near the paths that lead to them.

Interrupting the dialogue by this abrupt transition, the scout had instant recourse to the fragments of food which had escaped the voracity of the Hurons. A very summary process completed the simple cookery, when he and the Mohicans commenced their humble meal, with the silence and characteristic diligence of men who ate in order to enable themselves to endure great and unremitting toil.

When this necessary, and, happily, grateful duty had been performed, each of the foresters stooped and took a long and parting draught at that solitary and silent spring,* around which and its sister fountains, within fifty years, the wealth, beauty and talents of a hemisphere were to assemble in throngs, in pursuit of health and pleasure. Then Hawkeye announced his determination to proceed. The sisters resumed their saddles; Duncan and David grapsed their rifles, and followed on footsteps; the scout leading the advance, and the Mohicans bringing up the rear. The whole party moved swiftly through the narrow path, toward the north, leaving the healing waters to mingle unheeded with the adjacent brooks and the bodies of the dead to fester on the neighboring mount, without the rites of sepulture; a fate but too common to the warriors of the woods to excite either commiseration or comment.

CHAPTER XIII.

"I'll seek a readier path."
—Parnell

The route taken by Hawkeye lay across those sandy plains, relived by occasional valleys and swells of land, which had been traversed by their party on the morning of the same day, with the baffled Magua for their guide. The sun had now fallen low toward the distant mountains; and as their journey lay through the interminable forest, the heat was no longer oppressive. Their progress, in consequence, was proportionate; and long before the twilight gathered about them, they had made good many toilsome miles on their return.

The hunter, like the savage whose place he filled, seemed to select among the blind signs of their wild route, with a species of instinct, seldom abating his speed, and never pausing to deliberate. A rapid and oblique glance at the moss on the trees, with an occasional upward gaze toward the setting sun, or a steady but passing look at the direction of the numerous water courses, through which he waded, were sufficient to determine his path, and remove his greatest difficulties. In the meantime, the forest began to change its hues, losing that lively green which had embellished its arches, in the graver light which is the usual precursor of the close of day.

While the eyes of the sisters were endeavoring to catch glimpses through the trees, of the flood of golden glory which formed a glittering halo around the sun, tinging here and there with ruby streaks, or bordering with narrow edgings of shining yellow, a mass of clouds that lay piled at no great

---

* The scene of the foregoing incidents is on the spot where the village of Ballston now stands; one of the two principal watering places of America.

distance above the western hills, Hawkeye turned suddenly and pointing upward toward the gorgeous heavens, he spoke:

"Yonder is the signal given to man to seek his food and natural rest," he said; "better and wiser would it be, if he could understand the signs of nature, and take a lesson from the fowls of the air and the beasts of the field! Our night, however, will soon be over, for with the moon we must be up and moving again. I remember to have fou't the Maquas, hereaways, in the first war in which I ever drew blood from man; and we threw up a work of blocks, to keep the ravenous varmints from handling our scalps. If my marks do not fail me, we shall find the place a few rods further to our left."

Without waiting for an assent, or, indeed, for any reply, the sturdy hunter moved boldly into a dense thicket of young chestnuts, shoving aside the branches of the exuberant shoots which nearly covered the ground, like a man who expected, at each step, to discover some object he had formerly known. The recollection of the scout did not deceive him. After penetrating through the brush, matted as it was with briars, for a few hundred feet, he entered an open space, that surrounded a low, green hillock, which was crowned by the decayed blockhouse in question. This rude and neglected building was one of those deserted works, which, having been thrown up on an emergency, had been abandoned with the disappearance of danger, and was now quietly crumbling in the solitude of the forest, neglected and nearly forgotten, like the circumstances which had caused it to be reared. Such memorials of the passage and struggles of man are yet frequent throughout the broad barrier of wilderness which once separated the hostile provinces, and form a species of ruins that are intimately associated with the recollections of colonial history, and which are in appropriate keeping with the gloomy character of the surrounding scenery. The roof of bark had long since fallen, and mingled with the soil, but the huge logs of pine, which had been hastily thrown together, still preserved their relative positions, though one angle of the work had given way under the pressure, and threatened a speedy downfall to the remainder of the rustic edifice. While Heyward and his companions hesitated to approach a building so decayed, Hawkeye and the Indians entered within the low walls, not only without fear, but with obvious interest. While the former surveyed the ruins, both internally and externally, with the curiosity of one whose recollections were reviving at each moment, Chingachgook related to his son, in the language of the Delawares, and with the pride of a conqueror, the brief history of the skirmish which had been fought, in his youth, in that secluded spot. A strain of melancholy, however, blended with his triumph, rendering his voice, as usual, soft and musical.

In the meantime, the sisters gladly dismounted, and prepared to enjoy their halt in the coolness of the evening, and in a security which they believed nothing but the beasts of the forest could invade.

"Would not our resting-place have been more retired, my worthy friend," demanded the more vigilant Duncan, perceiving that the scout had already finished his short survey, "had we chosen a spot less known, and one more rarely visited than this?"

"Few live who know the blockhouse was ever raised," was the slow and musing answer; "'tis not often that books are made, and narratives written of such a scrimmage as was here fou't atween the Mohicans and the Mohawks, in a war of their own waging. I was then a younker, and went out with the Delawares, because I know'd they were a scandalized and wronged race. Forty days and forty nights did the imps crave our blood around this pile of logs, which I designed and partly reared, being, as you'll remember, no Indian myself, but a man without a cross. The Delawares lent themselves to the work, and we made it good, ten to twenty, until our numbers were nearly equal, and then we sallied out upon the hounds, and not a man of them ever got back to tell the fate of his party. Yes, yes; I was then young, and new to the sight of blood; and not relishing the thought that creatures who had spirits like myself should lay on the naked ground, to be torn asunder by beasts, or to bleach in the rains, I buried the dead with my own hands, under that very little hillock where you have placed yourselves; and no bad seat does it make neither, though it be raised by the bones of mortal men."

Heyward and the sisters arose, on the instant, from the grassy sepulcher; nor could the two latter, notwithstanding the terrific scenes they had so recently passed through, entirely suppress an emotion of natural horror, when they found themselves in such familiar contact with the grave of the dead Mohawks. The gray light, the gloomy little area of dark grass, surrounded by its border of brush, beyond which the pines rose, in breathing silence, apparently into the very clouds, and the deathlike stillness of the vast forest, were all in unison to deepen such a sensation. "They are gone, and they are harmless," continued Hawkeye, waving his hand, with a melancholy smile at their manifest alarm; "they'll never shout the war-whoop nor strike a blow with the tomahawk again! And of all those who aided in placing them where they lie, Chingachgook and I only are living! The brothers and family of the Mohican formed our war party; and you see before you all that are now left of his race."

The eyes of the listeners involuntarily sought the forms of the Indians, with a compassionate interest in their desolate fortune. Their dark persons were still to be seen within the shadows of the blockhouse, the son listening to the relation of his father with that sort of intenseness which would be created by a narrative that redounded so much to the honor of those whose names he had long revered for their courage and savage virtues.

"I had thought the Delawares a pacific people," said Duncan, "and that they never waged war in person; trusting the defense of their hands to those very Mohawks that you slew!"

"'Tis true in part," returned the scout, "and yet, at the bottom, 'tis a wicked lie. Such a treaty was made in ages gone by, through the deviltries of the Dutchers, who wished to disarm the natives that had the best right to the country, where they had settled themselves. The Mohicans, though a part of the same nation, having to deal with the English, never entered into the silly bargain, but kept to their manhood; as in truth did the Delawares, when their eyes were open to their folly. You see before you a chief of the great Mohican Sagamores! Once his family could chase their deer over tracts of country wider than that which belongs to the Albany Patteroon, without crossing brook or hill that was not their own; but what is left of their descendant? He may find his six feet of earth when God chooses, and keep it in peace, perhaps, if he has a friend who will take the pains to sink his head so low that the plowshares cannot reach it!"

"Enough!" said Heyward, apprehensive that the subject might lead to a discussion that would interrupt the harmony so necessary to the preservation of his fair companions; "we have journeyed far, and few among us are blessed with forms like that of yours, which seems to know neither fatigue nor weakness."

"The sinews and bones of a man carry me through it all," said the hunter, surveying his muscular limbs with a simplicity that betrayed the honest pleasure the compliment afforded him; "there are larger and heavier men to be found in the settlements, but you might travel many days in a city before you could meet one able to walk fifty miles without stopping to take breath, or who has kept the hounds within hearing during a chase of hours. However, as flesh and blood are not always the same, it is quite reasonable to suppose that the gentle ones are willing to rest, after all they have seen and done this day. Uncas, clear out the spring, while your father and I make a cover for their tender heads of these chestnut shoots, and a bed of grass and leaves."

The dialogue ceased, while the hunter and his companions busied themselves in preparations for the comfort and protection of those they guided. A spring, which many long years before had induced the natives to select the place for their temporary fortification, was soon cleared of leaves, and a fountain of crystal gushed from the bed, diffusing its waters over the verdant hillock. A corner of the building was then roofed in such a manner as to exclude the heavy dew of the climate, and piles of sweet shrubs and dried leaves were laid beneath it for the sisters to repose on.

While the diligent woodsmen were employed in this manner, Cora and Alice partook of that refreshment which duty required much more than inclination prompted them to accept. They then retired within the walls, and first offering up their thanksgivings for past mercies, and petitioning for a continuance of the Divine favor throughout the coming night, they laid their tender forms on the fragrant couch, and in spite of recollections and forebodings, soon sank into those slumbers which nature so imperiously demanded, and which were sweetened by hopes for the morrow. Duncan had prepared himself to pass the night in watchfulness near them, just without the ruin, but the scout, perceiving his intention, pointed toward Chingachgook, as he coolly disposed his own person on the grass, and said:

"The eyes of a white man are too heavy and too blind for such a watch as this! The Mohican will be our sentinel, therefore let us sleep."

"I proved myself a sluggard on my post during the past night," said Heyward, "and have less need of repose than you, who did more credit to the character of a soldier. Let all the party seek their rest, then, while I hold the guard."

"If we lay among the white tents of the Sixtieth, and in front of an enemy like the French, I could not ask for a better watchman," returned the scout; "but in the darkness and among the signs of the wilderness your judgment would be like the folly of a child, and your vigilance thrown away. Do then, like Uncas and myself, sleep, and sleep in safety."

Heyward perceived, in truth, that the younger Indian had thrown his form on the side of the hillock while they were talking, like one who sought to make the most of the time allotted to rest, and that his example had been followed by David, whose voice literally "clove to his jaws," with the fever of his wound, heightened, as it was, by their toilsome march. Unwilling to prolong a useless discussion, the young man affected to comply, by posting his back against the logs of the blockhouse, in a half recumbent posture, though resolutely determined, in his own mind, not to close an eye until he had delivered his precious charge into the arms of Munro himself. Hawkeye, believing he had prevailed, soon fell asleep, and a silence as deep as the solitude in which they had found it, pervaded the retired spot.

For many minutes Duncan succeeded in keeping his senses on the alert, and alive to every moaning sound that arose from the forest. His vision became more acute as the shades of evening settled on the place; and even after the stars were glimmering above his head, he was able to distinguish the recumbent forms of his companions, as they lay stretched on the grass, and to note the person of Chingachgook, who sat upright and motionless as one of the trees which formed the dark barrier on every side. He still heard the gentle breathings of the sisters, who lay within a few feet of him, and not a leaf was ruffled by the passing air of which his ear did not detect the whispering sound. At length, however, the mournful notes of a whip-poor-will became blended with the moanings of an owl; his heavy eyes occasionally sought the bright rays of the stars, and he then fancied he saw them through the fallen lids. At instants of momentary wakefulness he mistook a bush for his associate sentinel; his head next sank upon his shoulder, which, in its turn, sought the support of the ground; and, finally, his whole person became relaxed and pliant, and the young man sank into a deep sleep, dreaming that he was a knight of ancient chivalry, holding his midnight vigils before the tent of a recaptured princess, whose favor he did not despair of gaining, by such a proof of devotion and watchfulness.

How long the tired Duncan lay in this insensible state he never knew himself, but his slumbering visions had been long lost in total forgetfulness, when he was awakened by a light tap on the shoulder. Aroused by this signal, slight as it was, he sprang upon his feet with a confused recollection of the self-imposed duty he had assumed with the commencement of the night.

"Who comes?" he demanded, feeling for his sword, at the place where it was usually suspended. "Speak! friend or enemy?"

"Friend," replied the low voice of Chingachgook; who, pointing upward at the luminary which was shedding its mild light through the opening in the trees, directly in their bivouac, immediately added, in his rude English: "Moon comes and white man's fort far—far off; time to move, when sleep shuts both eyes of the Frenchman!"

"You say true! Call up your friends, and bridle the horses while I prepare my own companions for the march!"

"We are awake, Duncan," said the soft, silvery tones of Alice within the building, "and ready to travel very fast after so refreshing a sleep; but you have watched through the tedious night in our behalf, after having endured so much fatigue the livelong day!"

"Say, rather, I would have watched, but my treacherous eyes betrayed me; twice have I proved myself unfit for the trust I bear."

"Nay, Duncan, deny it not," interrupted the smiling Alice, issuing from the shadows of the building into the light of the moon, in all the loveliness of her freshened beauty; "I know you to be a heedless one, when self is the object of your care, and but too vigilant in favor of others. Can we not tarry here a little longer while you find the rest you need? Cheerfully, most cheerfully, will Cora and I keep the vigils, while you and all these brave men endeavor to snatch a little sleep!"

"If shame could cure me of my drowsiness, I should never close an eye again," said the uneasy youth, gazing at the ingenuous countance of Alice, where, however, in its sweet solicitude, he read nothing to confirm his half-awakened suspicion. "It is but too true, that after leading you into danger by my heedlessness, I have not even the merit of guarding your pillows as should become a soldier."

"No one but Duncan himself should accuse Duncan of such a weakness. Go, then, and sleep; believe me, neither of us, weak girls as we are, will betray our watch."

The young man was relieved from the awkwardness of making any further protestations of his own demerits, by an exclamation from Chingachgook, and the attitude of riveted attention assumed by his son.

"The Mohicans hear an enemy!" whispered Hawkeye, who, by this time, in common with the whole party, was awake and stirring. "They scent danger in the wind!"

"God forbid!" exclaimed Heyward. "Surely we have had enough of bloodshed!"

While he spoke, however, the young soldier seized his rifle, and advancing toward the front, prepared to atone for his venial remissness, by freely exposing his life in defense of those he attended.

"'Tis some creature of the forest prowling around us in quest of food," he said, in a whisper, as soon as the low, and apparently distant sounds, which had startled the Mohicans, reached his own ears.

"Hist!" returned the attentive scout; "'tis man; even I can now tell his tread, poor as my senses are when compared to an Indian's! That Scampering Huron has fallen in with one of Montcalm's outlying parties, and they have struck upon our trail. I shouldn't like, myself, to spill more human blood in this spot," he added, looking around with anxiety in his features, at the dim objects by which he was surrounded; "but what must be, must! Lead the horses into the blockhouse, Uncas; and, friends, do you follow to the same shelter. Poor and old as it is, it offers a cover, and has rung with the crack of a rifle afore to-night!"

He was instantly obeyed, the Mohicans leading the Narrangansetts within the ruin, whither the whole party repaired with the most guarded silence.

The sound of approaching footsteps were now too distinctly audible to leave any doubts as to the nature of the interruption. They were soon mingled with voices calling to each other in an Indian dialect, which the hunter, in a whisper, affirmed to Heyward was the language of the Hurons. When the party reached the point where the horses had entered the thicket which surrounded the blockhouse, they were evidently at fault, having lost those marks which, until that moment, had directed their pursuit.

It would seem by the voices that twenty men were soon collected at that one spot, mingling their different opinions and advice in noisy clamor.

"The knaves know our weakness," whispered Hawkeye, who stood by the side of Heyward, in deep shade, looking through an opening in the logs, "or they wouldn't indulge their idleness in such a squaw's march. Listen to the reptiles! each man among them seems to have two tongues, and but a single leg."

Duncan, brave as he was in the combat, could not, in such a moment of painful suspense, make any reply to the cool and characteristic remark of the scout. He only grasped his rifle more firmly, and fastened his eyes upon the narrow opening, through which he gazed upon the moonlight view with increasing anxiety. The deeper tones of one who spoke as having authority were next heard, amid a silence that denoted the respect with which his orders, or rather advice, was received. After which, by the rustling of leaves, and crackling of dried twigs, it was apparent the savages were separating in pursuit of the lost trail. Fortunately for the pursued, the light of the moon, while it shed a flood of mild luster upon the little area around the ruin, was not sufficiently strong to penetrate the deep arches of the forest, where the objects still lay in deceptive shadow. The search proved fruitless; for so short and sudden had been the passage from the faint path the travelers had journeyed into the thicket, that every trace of their footsteps was lost in the obscurity of the woods.

It was not long, however, before the restless savages were heard beating the brush, and gradually approaching the inner edge of that dense border of young chestnuts which encircled the little area.

"They are coming," muttered Heyward, endeavoring to thrust his rifle through the chink in the logs; "let us fire on their approach."

"Keep everything in the shade," returned the scout; "the snapping of a flint, or even the smell of a single karnel of the brimstone, would bring the hungry varlets upon us in a body. Should it please God that we must give battle for the scalps, trust to the experience of men who know the ways of the savages, and who are not often backward when the war-whoop is howled."

Duncan cast his eyes behind him, and saw that the trembling sisters were cowering in the far corner of the building, while the Mohicans stood in the shadow, like two upright posts, ready, and apparently willing, to strike when the blow should be needed. Curbing his impatience, he again looked out upon the area, and awaited the result in silence. At that instant the thicket opened, and a tall and armed Huron advanced a few paces into the open space. As he gazed upon the silent blockhouse, the moon fell upon his swarthy countenance, and betrayed its surprise and curiosity. He made the exclamation which usually accompanies the former emotion in an Indian, and, calling in a low voice, soon drew a companion to his side.

These children of the woods stood together for several moments pointing at the crumbling edifice, and conversing in the unintelligible language of their tribe. They then approached, though with slow and cautious steps, pausing every instant to look at the building, like startled deer whose curiosity struggled powerfully with their awakened apprehensions for the mastery. The foot of one of them suddenly rested on the mound, and he stopped to examine its nature. At this moment, Heyward observed that the scout loosened his knife in its sheath, and lowered the muzzle of his rifle. Imitating these movements, the young man prepared himself for the struggle which now seemed inevitable.

The savages were so near, that the least motion in one of the horses, or even a breath louder than common, would have betrayed the fugitives. But in discovering the character of the mound, the attention of the Hurons appeared directed to a different object. They spoke together, and the sounds of their voices were low and solemn, as if influenced by a reverence that was deeply blended with awe. Then they drew warily back, keeping their eyes riveted on the ruin, as if they expected to see the apparitions of the dead issue from its silent walls, until, having reached the boundary of the area, they moved slowly into the thicket and disappeared.

Hawkeye dropped the breech of his rifle to the earth, and drawing a long, free breath, exclaimed, in an audible whisper:

"Ay! they respect the dead, and it has this time saved their own lives, and, it may be, the lives of better men too."

Heyward lent his attention for a single moment to his companion, but without replying, he again turned toward those who just then interested him more. He heard the two Hurons leave the bushes, and it was soon plain that all the pursuers were gathered about them, in deep attention to their report. After a few minutes of earnest and solemn dialogue, altogether different from the noisy clamor with which they had first collected about the spot, the sounds grew fainter and more distant, and finally were lost in the depths of the forest.

Hawkeye waited until a signal from the listening Chingachgook assured him that every sound from the retiring party was completely swallowed by the distance, when he motioned to Heyward to lead forth the horses, and to assist the sisters into their saddles. The instant this was done they issued through the broken gateway, and stealing out by a direction opposite to the one by which they entered, they quitted the spot, the sisters casting furtive glances at the silent, grave and crumbling ruin, as they left the soft light of the moon, to bury themselves in the gloom of the woods.

CHAPTER XIV.

"Guard.—Qui est la?
Puc.  —Paisans, pauvres gens de France."
—King Henry VI

During the rapid movement from the blockhouse, and until the party was deeply buried in the forest, each individual was too much interested in the escape to hazard a word even in whispers. The scout resumed his post in advance, though his steps, after he had thrown a safe distance between himself and his enemies, were more deliberate than in their previous march, in consequence of his utter ignorance of the localities of the surrounding woods. More than once he halted to consult with his confederates, the Mohicans, pointing upward at the moon, and examining the barks of the trees with care. In these brief pauses, Heyward and the sisters listened, with senses rendered doubly acute by the danger, to detect any symptoms which might announce the proximity of their foes. At such moments, it seemed as if a vast range of country lay buried in eternal sleep; not the least sound arising from the forest, unless it was the distant and scarcely audible rippling of a water-course. Birds, beasts, and man, appeared to slumber alike, if, indeed, any of the latter were to be found in that wide tract of wilderness. But the sounds of the rivulet, feeble and murmuring as they were, relieved the guides at once from no trifling embarrassment, and toward it they immediately held their way.

When the banks of the little stream were gained, Hawkeye made another halt; and taking the moccasins from his feet, he invited Heyward and Gamut to follow his example. He then entered the water, and for near an hour they traveled in the bed of the brook, leaving no trail. The moon had already sunk into an immense pile of black clouds, which lay impending above the western horizon, when they issued from the low and devious water-course to rise again to the light and level of the sandy but wooded plain. Here the scout seemed to be once more at home, for he held on this way with the certainty and diligence of a man who moved in the security of his own knowledge. The path soon became more uneven, and the travelers could plainly perceive that the mountains drew nigher to them on each hand, and that they were, in truth, about entering one of their gorges. Suddenly, Hawkeye made a pause, and, waiting until he was joined by the whole party, he spoke, though in tones so low and cautious, that they added to the solemnity of his words, in the quiet and darkness of the place.

"It is easy to know the pathways, and to find the licks and water-courses of the wilderness," he said; "but who that saw this spot could venture to say, that a mighty army was at rest among yonder silent trees and barren mountains?"

"We are, then, at no great distance from William Henry?" said Heyward, advancing nigher to the scout.

"It is yet a long and weary path, and when and where to strike it is now our greatest difficulty. See," he said, pointing through the trees toward a spot where a little basin of water reflected the stars from its placid bosom, "here is the 'bloody pond'; and I am on ground that I have not only often traveled, but over which I have fou't the enemy, from the rising to the setting sun."

"Ha! that sheet of dull and dreary water, then, is the sepulcher of the brave men who fell in the contest. I have heard it named, but never have I stood on its banks before."

"Three battles did we make with the Dutch-Frenchman* in a day," continued Hawkeye, pursuing the train of his own thoughts, rather than replying to the remark of Duncan. "He met us hard by, in our outward march to ambush his advance, and scattered us, like driven deer, through the defile, to the shores of Horican. Then we rallied behind our fallen trees, and made head against him, under Sir William—who was made Sir William for that very deed; and well did we pay him for the disgrace of the morning! Hundreds of Frenchmen saw the sun that day for the last time; and even their leader, Dieskau himself, fell into our hands, so cut and torn with the lead, that he has gone back to his own country, unfit for further acts in war."

"'Twas a noble repulse!" exclaimed Heyward, in the heat of his youthful ardor; "the fame of it reached us early, in our southern army."

"Ay! but it did not end there. I was sent by Major Effingham, at Sir William's own bidding, to outflank the French, and carry the tidings of their disaster across the portage, to the fort on the Hudson. Just hereaway, where you see the trees rise into a mountain swell, I met a party coming

---

* Baron Dieskau, a German, in the service of France. A few years previously to the period of the tale, this officer was defeated by Sir William Johnson, of Johnstown, New York, on the shores of Lake George.

down to our aid, and I led them where the enemy were taking their meal, little dreaming that they had not finished the bloody work of the day."

"And you surprised them?"

"If death can be a surprise to men who are thinking only of the cravings of their appetites. We gave them but little breathing time, for they had borne hard upon us in the fight of the morning, and there were few in our party who had not lost friend or relative by their hands."

"When all was over, the dead, and some say the dying, were cast into that little pond. These eyes have seen its waters colored with blood, as natural water never yet flowed from the bowels of the 'arth."

"It was a convenient, and, I trust, will prove a peaceful grave for a soldier. You have then seen much service on this frontier?"

"Ay!" said the scout, erecting his tall person with an air of military pride; "there are not many echoes among these hills that haven't rung with the crack of my rifle, nor is there the space of a square mile atwixt Horican and the river, that 'killdeer' hasn't dropped a living body on, be it an enemy or be it a brute beast. As for the grave there being as quiet as you mention, it is another matter. There are them in the camp who say and think, man, to lie still, should not be buried while the breath is in the body; and certain it is that in the hurry of that evening, the doctors had but little time to say who was living and who was dead. Hist! see you nothing walking on the shore of the pond?"

"'Tis not probable that any are as houseless as ourselves in this dreary forest."

"Such as he may care but little for house or shelter, and night dew can never wet a body that passes its days in the water," returned the scout, grasping the shoulder of Heyward with such convulsive strength as to make the young soldier painfully sensible how much superstitious terror had got the mastery of a man usually so dauntless.

"By heaven, there is a human form, and it approaches! Stand to your arms, my friends; for we know not whom we encounter."

"Qui vive?" demanded a stern, quick voice, which sounded like a challenge from another world, issuing out of that solitary and solemn place.

"What says it?" whispered the scout; "it speaks neither Indian nor English."

"Qui vive?" repeated the same voice, which was quickly followed by the rattling of arms, and a menacing attitude.

"France!" cried Heyward, advancing from the shadow of the trees to the shore of the pond, within a few yards of the sentinel.

"D'ou venez-vous—ou allez-vous, d'aussi bonne heure?" demanded the grenadier, in the language and with the accent of a man from old France.

"Je viens de la decouverte, et je vais me coucher."

"Etes-vous officier du roi?"

"Sans doute, mon camarade; me prends-tu pour un provincial! Je suis capitaine de chasseurs (Heyward well knew that the other was of a regiment in the line); j'ai ici, avec moi, les filles du commandant de la fortification. Aha! tu en as entendu parler! je les ai fait prisonnieres pres de l'autre fort, et je les conduis au general."

"Ma foi! mesdames; j'en suis fâche pour vous," exclaimed the young soldier, touching his cap with grace; "mais—fortune de guerre! vous trouverez notre general un brave homme, et bien poli avec les dames."

"C'est le caractere des gens de guerre," said Cora, with admirable self-possession. "Adieu, mon ami; je vous souhaiterais un devoir plus agreable a remplir."

The soldier made a low and humble acknowledgment for her civility; and Heyward adding a "Bonne nuit, mon camarade," they moved deliberately forward, leaving the sentinel pacing the banks of the silent pond, little suspecting an enemy of so much effrontery, and humming to himself those words which were recalled to his mind by the sight of women, and, perhaps, by recollections of his own distant and beautiful France: "Vive le vin, vive l'amour," etc., etc.

"'Tis well you understood the knave!" whispered the scout, when they had gained a little distance from the place, and letting his rifle fall into the hollow of his arm again; "I soon saw that he was one of them uneasy Frenchers; and well for him it was that his speech was friendly and his wishes kind, or a place might have been found for his bones among those of his countrymen."

He was interrupted by a long and heavy groan which arose from the little basin, as though, in truth, the spirits of the departed lingered about their watery sepulcher.

"Surely it was of flesh," continued the scout; "no spirit could handle its arms so steadily."

"It was of flesh; but whether the poor fellow still belongs to this world may well be doubted," said Heyward, glancing his eyes around him, and missing Chingachgook from their little band. Another groan more faint than the former was succeeded by a heavy and sullen plunge into the water, and all was still again as if the borders of the dreary pool had never been awakened from the silence of creation. While they yet hesitated in uncertainty, the form of the Indian was seen gliding out of the thicket. As the chief rejoined them, with one hand he attached the reeking scalp of the unfortunate young Frenchman to his girdle, and with the other he replaced the knife and tomahawk that had drunk his blood. He then took his wonted station, with the air of a man who believed he had done a deed of merit.

The scout dropped one end of his rifle to the earth, and leaning his hands on the other, he stood musing in profound silence. Then, shaking his head in a mournful manner, he muttered:

"'Twould have been a cruel and an unhuman act for a white-skin; but 'tis the gift and natur' of an Indian, and I suppose it should not be denied. I could wish, though, it had befallen an accursed Mingo, rather than that gay young boy from the old countries."

"Enough!" said Heyward, apprehensive the unconscious sisters might comprehend the nature of the detention, and conquering his disgust by a train of reflections very much like that of the hunter; "'tis done; and though better it were left undone, cannot be amended. You see, we are, too obviously within the sentinels of the enemy; what course do you propose to follow?"

"Yes," said Hawkeye, rousing himself again; "'tis as you say, too late to harbor further thoughts about it. Ay, the French have gathered around the fort in good earnest and we have a delicate needle to thread in passing them."

"And but little time to do it in," added Heyward, glancing his eyes upwards, toward the bank of vapor that concealed the setting moon.

"And little time to do it in!" repeated the scout. "The thing may be done in two fashions, by the help of Providence, without which it may not be done at all."

"Name them quickly for time presses."

"One would be to dismount the gentle ones, and let their beasts range the plain, by sending the Mohicans in front, we might then cut a lane through their sentries, and enter the fort over the dead bodies."

"It will not do—it will not do!" interrupted the generous Heyward; "a soldier might force his way in this manner, but never with such a convoy."

"'Twould be, indeed, a bloody path for such tender feet to wade in," returned the equally reluctant scout; "but I thought it befitting my manhood to name it. We must, then, turn in our trail and get without the line of their lookouts, when we will bend short to the west, and enter the mountains; where I can hide you, so that all the devil's hounds in Montcalm's pay would be thrown off the scent for months to come."

"Let it be done, and that instantly."

Further words were unnecessary; for Hawkeye, merely uttering the mandate to "follow," moved along the route by which they had just entered their present critical and even dangerous situation. Their progress, like their late dialogue, was guarded, and without noise; for none knew at what moment a passing patrol, or a crouching picket of the enemy, might rise upon their path. As they held their silent way along the margin of the pond, again Heyward and the scout stole furtive glances at its appalling dreariness. They looked in vain for the form they had so recently seen stalking along in silent shores, while a low and regular wash of the little waves, by announcing that the waters were not yet subsided, furnished a frightful memorial of the deed of blood they had just witnessed. Like all that passing and gloomy scene, the low basin, however, quickly melted in the darkness, and became blended with the mass of black objects in the rear of the travelers.

Hawkeye soon deviated from the line of their retreat, and striking off towards the mountains which form the western boundary of the narrow plain, he led his followers, with swift steps, deep within the shadows that were cast from their high and broken summits. The route was now painful; lying over ground ragged with rocks, and intersected with ravines, and their progress proportionately slow. Bleak and black hills lay on every side of them, compensating in some degree for the additional toil of the march by the sense of security they imparted. At length the party began slowly to rise a steep and rugged ascent, by a path that curiously wound among rocks and trees, avoiding the one and supported by the other, in a manner that showed it had been devised by men long practised in the arts of the wilderness. As they gradually rose from the level of the valleys, the thick darkness which usually precedes the approach of day began to disperse, and objects were seen in the plain and palpable colors with which they had been gifted by nature. When they issued from the stunted woods which clung to the barren sides of the mountain, upon a flat and mossy rock that formed its summit, they met the morning, as it came blushing above the green pines of a hill that lay on the opposite side of the valley of the Horican.

The scout now told the sisters to dismount; and taking the bridles from the mouths, and the saddles off the backs of the jaded beasts, he turned them loose, to glean a scanty subsistence among the shrubs and meager herbage of that elevated region.

"Go," he said, "and seek your food where natur' gives it to you; and beware that you become not food to ravenous wolves yourselves, among these hills."

"Have we no further need of them?" demanded Heyward.

"See, and judge with your own eyes," said the scout, advancing toward the eastern brow of the mountain, whither he beckoned for the whole party to follow; "if it was as easy to look into the heart of man as it is to spy out the nakedness of Montcalm's camp from this spot, hypocrites would grow scarce, and the cunning of a Mingo might prove a losing game, compared to the honesty of a Delaware."

When the travelers reached the verge of the precipices they saw, at a glance, the truth of the scout's declaration, and the admirable foresight with which he had led them to their commanding station.

The mountain on which they stood, elevated perhaps a thousand feet in the air, was a high cone that rose a little in advance of that range which stretches for miles along the western shores of the lake, until meeting its sisters miles beyond the water, it ran off toward the Canadas, in confused and broken masses of rock, thinly sprinkled with evergreens. Immediately at the feet of the party, the southern shore of the Horican swept in a broad semicircle from mountain to mountain, marking a wide strand, that soon rose into an uneven and somewhat elevated plain. To the north stretched the limpid, and, as it appeared from that dizzy height, the narrow sheet of the "holy lake," indented with numberless bays, embellished by fantastic headlands, and dotted with countless islands. At the distance of a few leagues, the bed of the water became lost among mountains, or was wrapped in the masses of vapor that came slowly rolling along their bosom, before a light morning air. But a narrow opening between the crests of the hills pointed out the passage by which they found their way still further north, to spread their pure and ample sheets again, before pouring out their tribute into the distant Champlain. To the south stretched the defile, or rather broken plain, so often mentioned. For several miles in this direction, the mountains appeared reluctant to yield their dominion, but within reach of the eye they diverged, and finally melted into the level and sandy lands, across which we have accompanied our adventurers in their double journey. Along both ranges of hills, which bounded the opposite sides of the lake and valley, clouds of light vapor were rising in spiral wreaths from the uninhabited woods, looking like the smoke of hidden cottages; or rolled lazily down the declivities, to mingle with the fogs of the lower land. A single, solitary, snow-white cloud floated above the valley, and marked the spot beneath which lay the silent pool of the "bloody pond."

Directly on the shore of the lake, and nearer to its western than to its eastern margin, lay the extensive earthen ramparts and low buildings of William Henry. Two of the sweeping bastions appeared to rest on the water which washed their bases, while a deep ditch and extensive morasses guarded its other sides and angles. The land had been cleared of wood for a reasonable distance around the work, but every other part of the scene lay in the green livery of nature, except where the limpid water mellowed the view, or the bold rocks thrust their black and naked heads above the undulating outline of the mountain ranges. In its front might be seen the scattered sentinels, who held a weary watch against their numerous foes; and within the walls themselves, the travelers looked down upon men still drowsy with a night of vigilance. Toward the southeast, but in immediate contact with the fort, was an entrenched camp, posted on a rocky eminence, that would have been far more eligible for the work itself, in which Hawkeye pointed out the presence of those auxiliary regiments that had so recently left the Hudson in their company. From the woods, a little further to the south, rose numerous dark and lurid smokes, that were easily to be distinguished from the purer exhalations of the springs, and which the scout also showed to Heyward, as evidences that the enemy lay in force in that direction.

But the spectacle which most concerned the young soldier was on the western bank of the lake, though quite near to its southern termination. On a strip of land, which appeared from his stand too narrow to contain such an army, but which, in truth, extended many hundreds of yards from the shores of the Horican to the base of the mountain, were to be seen the white tents and military engines of an encampment of ten thousand men. Batteries were already thrown up in their front, and even while the spectators above them were looking down, with such different emotions, on a scene which lay like a map beneath their feet, the roar of artillery rose from the valley, and passed off in thundering echoes along the eastern hills.

"Morning is just touching them below," said the deliberate and musing scout, "and the watchers have a mind to wake up the sleepers by the sound of cannon. We are a few hours too late! Montcalm has already filled the woods with his accursed Iroquois."

"The place is, indeed, invested," returned Duncan; "but is there no expedient by which we may enter? capture in the works would be far preferable to falling again into the hands of roving Indians."

"See!" exclaimed the scout, unconsciously directing the attention of Cora to the quarters of her own father, "how that shot has made the stones fly from the side of the commandant's house! Ay! these Frenchers will pull it to pieces faster than it was put together, solid and thick though it be!"

"Heyward, I sicken at the sight of danger that I cannot share," said the undaunted but anxious daughter. "Let us go to Montcalm, and demand admission: he dare not deny a child the boon."

"You would scarce find the tent of the Frenchman with the hair on your head"; said the blunt scout. "If I had but one of the thousand boats which lie empty along that shore, it might be done! Ha! here will soon be an end of the firing, for yonder comes a fog that will turn day to night, and make an Indian arrow more dangerous than a molded cannon. Now, if you are equal to the work, and will follow, I will make a push; for I long to get down into that camp, if it be only to scatter some Mingo dogs that I see lurking in the skirts of yonder thicket of birch."

"We are equal," said Cora, firmly; "on such an errand we will follow to any danger."

The scout turned to her with a smile of honest and cordial approbation, as he answered:

"I would I had a thousand men, of brawny limbs and quick eyes, that feared death as little as you! I'd send them jabbering Frenchers back into their den again, afore the week was ended, howling like so many fettered hounds or hungry wolves. But, sir," he added, turning from her to the rest of the party, "the fog comes rolling down so fast, we shall have but just the time to meet it on the plain, and use it as a cover. Remember, if any accident should befall me, to keep the air blowing on your left cheeks—or, rather, follow the Mohicans; they'd scent their way, be it in day or be it at night."

He then waved his hand for them to follow, and threw himself down the steep declivity, with free, but careful footsteps. Heyward assisted the sisters to descend, and in a few minutes they were all far down a mountain whose sides they had climbed with so much toil and pain.

The direction taken by Hawkeye soon brought the travelers to the level of the plain, nearly opposite to a sally-port in the western curtain of the fort, which lay itself at the distance of about half a mile from the point where he halted to allow Duncan to come up with his charge. In their eagerness, and favored by the nature of the ground, they had anticipated the fog, which was rolling heavily down the lake, and it became necessary to pause, until the mists had wrapped the camp of the enemy in their fleecy mantle. The Mohicans profited by the delay, to steal out of the woods, and to make a survey of surrounding objects. They were followed at a little distance by the scout, with a view to profit early by their report, and to obtain some faint knowledge for himself of the more immediate localities.

In a very few moments he returned, his face reddened with vexation, while he muttered his disappointment in words of no very gentle import.

"Here has the cunning Frenchman been posting a picket directly in our path," he said; "red-skins and whites; and we shall be as likely to fall into their midst as to pass them in the fog!"

"Cannot we make a circuit to avoid the danger," asked Heyward, "and come into our path again when it is passed?"

"Who that once bends from the line of his march in a fog can tell when or how to find it again! The mists of Horican are not like the curls from a peace-pipe, or the smoke which settles above a mosquito fire."

He was yet speaking, when a crashing sound was heard, and a cannon-ball entered the thicket, striking the body of a sapling, and rebounding to the earth, its force being much expended by previous resistance. The Indians followed instantly like busy attendants on the terrible messenger, and Uncas commenced speaking earnestly and with much action, in the Delaware tongue.

"It may be so, lad," muttered the scout, when he had ended; "for desperate fevers are not to be treated like a toothache. Come, then, the fog is shutting in."

"Stop!" cried Heyward; "first explain your expectations."

"'Tis soon done, and a small hope it is; but it is better than nothing. This shot that you see," added the scout, kicking the harmless iron with his foot, "has plowed the 'arth in its road from the fort, and we shall hunt for the furrow it has made, when all other signs may fail. No more words, but follow, or the fog may leave us in the middle of our path, a mark for both armies to shoot at."

Heyward perceiving that, in fact, a crisis had arrived, when acts were more required than words, placed himself between the sisters, and drew them swiftly forward, keeping the dim figure of their leader in his eye. It was soon apparent that Hawkeye had not magnified the power of the fog, for before they had proceeded twenty yards, it was difficult for the different individuals of the party to distinguish each other in the vapor.

They had made their little circuit to the left, and were already inclining again toward the right, having, as Heyward thought, got over nearly half the distance to the friendly works, when his ears were saluted with the fierce summons, apparently within twenty feet of them, of:

"Qui va la?"

"Push on!" whispered the scout, once more bending to the left.

"Push on!" repeated Heyward; when the summons was renewed by a dozen voices, each of which seemed charged with menace.

"C'est moi," cried Duncan, dragging rather than leading those he supported swiftly onward.

"Bete!—qui?—moi!"

"Ami de la France."

"Tu m'as plus l'air d'un ennemi de la France; arrete ou pardieu je te ferai ami du diable. Non! feu, camarades, feu!"

The order was instantly obeyed, and the fog was stirred by the explosion of fifty muskets. Happily, the aim was bad, and the bullets cut the air in a direction a little different from that taken by the fugitives; though still so nigh them, that to the unpractised ears of David and the two females, it appeared as if they whistled within a few inches of the organs. The outcry was renewed, and the order, not only to fire again, but to pursue, was too plainly audible. When Heyward briefly explained the meaning of the words they heard, Hawkeye halted and spoke with quick decision and great firmness.

"Let us deliver our fire," he said; "they will believe it a sortie, and give way, or they will wait for reinforcements."

The scheme was well conceived, but failed in its effects. The instant the French heard the pieces, it seemed as if the plain was alive with men, muskets rattling along its whole extent, from the shores of the lake to the furthest boundary of the woods.

"We shall draw their entire army upon us, and bring on a general assault," said Duncan: "lead on, my friend, for your own life and ours."

The scout seemed willing to comply; but, in the hurry of the moment, and in the change of position, he had lost the direction. In vain he turned either cheek toward the light air; they felt equally cool. In this dilemma, Uncas lighted on the furrow of the cannon ball, where it had cut the ground in three adjacent ant-hills.

"Give me the range!" said Hawkeye, bending to catch a glimpse of the direction, and then instantly moving onward.

Cries, oaths, voices calling to each other, and the reports of muskets, were now quick and incessant, and, apparently, on every side of them. Suddenly a strong glare of light flashed across the scene, the fog rolled upward in thick wreaths, and several cannons belched across the plain, and the roar was thrown heavily back from the bellowing echoes of the mountain.

"'Tis from the fort!" exclaimed Hawkeye, turning short on his tracks; "and we, like stricken fools, were rushing to the woods, under the very knives of the Maquas."

The instant their mistake was rectified, the whole party retraced the error with the utmost diligence. Duncan willingly relinquished the support of Cora to the arm of Uncas and Cora as readily accepted the welcome assistance. Men, hot and angry in pursuit, were evidently on their footsteps, and each instant threatened their capture, if not their destruction.

"Point de quartier aux coquins!" cried an eager pursuer, who seemed to direct the operations of the enemy.

"Stand firm, and be ready, my gallant Sixtieths!" suddenly exclaimed a voice above them; "wait to see the enemy, fire low and sweep the glacis."

"Father! father!" exclaimed a piercing cry from out the mist: "it is I! Alice! thy own Elsie! Spare, oh! save your daughters!"

"Hold!" shouted the former speaker, in the awful tones of parental agony, the sound reaching even to the woods, and rolling back in solemn echo. "'Tis she! God has restored me to my children! Throw open the sally-port; to the field, Sixtieths, to the field; pull not a trigger, lest ye kill my lambs! Drive off these dogs of France with your steel."

Duncan heard the grating of the rusty hinges, and darting to the spot, directed by the sound, he met a long line of dark red warriors, passing swiftly toward the glacis. He knew them for his own battalion of the Royal Americans, and flying to their head, soon swept every trace of his pursuers from before the works.

For an instant, Cora and Alice had stood trembling and bewildered by this unexpected desertion; but before either had leisure for speech, or even thought, an officer of gigantic frame, whose locks were bleached with years and service, but whose air of military grandeur had been rather softened than destroyed by time, rushed out of the body of mist, and folded them to his bosom, while large scalding tears rolled down his pale and wrinkled cheeks, and he exclaimed, in the peculiar accent of Scotland:

"For this I thank thee, Lord! Let danger come as it will, thy servant is now prepared!"


CHAPTER XV.

"Then go we in, to know his embassy;
Which I could, with ready guess, declare,
Before the Frenchmen speak a word of it."
—King Henry V


A few succeeding days were passed amid the privations, the uproar, and the dangers of the siege, which was vigorously pressed by a power, against whose approaches Munro possessed no competent means of resistance. It appeared as if Webb, with his army, which lay slumbering on the banks of the Hudson, had utterly forgotten the strait to which his countrymen were reduced. Montcalm had filled the woods of the portage with his savages, every yell and whoop from whom rang through the British encampment, chilling the hearts of men who were already but too much disposed to magnify the danger.

Not so, however, with the besieged. Animated by the words, and stimulated by the examples of their leaders, they had found their courage, and maintained their ancient reputation, with a zeal that did justice to the stern character of their commander. As if satisfied with the toil of marching through the wilderness to encounter his enemy, the French general, though of approved skill, had neglected to seize the adjacent mountains; whence the besieged might have been exterminated with impunity, and which, in the more modern warfare of the country, would not have been neglected for a single hour. This sort of contempt for eminences, or rather dread of the labor of ascending them, might have been termed the besetting weakness of the warfare of the period. It originated in the simplicity of the Indian contests, in which, from the nature of the combats, and the density of the forests, fortresses were rare, and artillery next to useless. The carelessness engendered by these usages descended even to the war of the Revolution and lost the States the important fortress of Ticonderoga opening a way for the army of Burgoyne into what was then the bosom of the country. We look back at this ignorance, or infatuation, whichever it may be called, with wonder, knowing that the neglect of an eminence, whose difficulties, like those of Mount Defiance, have been so greatly exaggerated, would, at the present time, prove fatal to the reputation of the engineer who had planned the works at their base, or to that of the general whose lot it was to defend them.

The tourist, the valetudinarian, or the amateur of the beauties of nature, who, in the train of his four-in-hand, now rolls through the scenes we have attempted to describe, in quest of information, health, or pleasure, or floats steadily toward his object on those artificial waters which have sprung up under the administration of a statesman[*] who has dared to stake his political character on the hazardous issue, is not to suppose that his ancestors traversed those hills, or struggled with the same currents with equal facility. The transportation of a single heavy gun was often considered equal to a victory gained; if happily, the difficulties of the passage had not so far separated it from its necessary concomitant, the ammunition, as to render it no more than a useless tube of unwieldy iron.

The evils of this state of things pressed heavily on the fortunes of the resolute Scotsman who now defended William Henry. Though his adversary neglected the hills, he had planted his batteries with judgment on the plain, and caused them to be served with vigor and skill. Against this assault, the besieged could only oppose the imperfect and hasty preparations of a fortress in the wilderness.

It was in the afternoon of the fifth day of the siege, and the fourth of his own service in it, that Major Heyward profited by a parley that had just been beaten, by repairing to the ramparts of one of the water bastions, to breathe the cool air from the lake, and to take a survey of the progress of the siege. He was alone, if the solitary sentinel who paced the mound be excepted; for the artillerists had hastened also to profit by the temporary suspension of their arduous duties. The evening was delightfully calm, and the light air from the limpid water fresh and soothing. It seemed as if, with the

---

[*] Evidently the late De Witt Clinton, who died governor of New York in 1828.

termination of the roar of artillery and the plunging of shot, nature had also seized the moment to assume her mildest and most captivating form. The sun poured down his parting glory on the scene, without the oppression of those fierce rays that belong to the climate and the season. The mountains looked green, and fresh, and lovely, tempered with the milder light, or softened in shadow, as thin vapors floated between them and the sun. The numerous islands rested on the bosom of the Horican, some low and sunken, as if embedded in the waters, and others appearing to hover about the element, in little hillocks of green velvet; among which the fishermen of the beleaguering army peacefully rowed their skiffs, or floated at rest on the glassy mirror in quiet pursuit of their employment.

The scene was at once animated and still. All that pertained to nature was sweet, or simply grand; while those parts which depended on the temper and movements of man were lively and playful.

Two little spotless flags were abroad, the one on a salient angle of the fort, and the other on the advanced battery of the besiegers; emblems of the truth which existed, not only to the acts, but it would seem, also, to the enmity of the combatants.

Behind these again swung, heavily opening and closing in silken folds, the rival standards of England and France.

A hundred gay and thoughtless young Frenchmen were drawing a net to the pebbly beach, within dangerous proximity to the sullen but silent cannon of the fort, while the eastern mountain was sending back the loud shouts and gay merriment that attended their sport. Some were rushing eagerly to enjoy the aquatic games of the lake, and others were already toiling their way up the neighboring hills, with the restless curiosity of their nation. To all these sports and pursuits, those of the enemy who watched the besieged, and the besieged themselves, were, however, merely the idle though sympathizing spectators. Here and there a picket had, indeed, raised a song, or mingled in a dance, which had drawn the dusky savages around them, from their lairs in the forest. In short, everything wore rather the appearance of a day of pleasure, than of an hour stolen from the dangers and toil of a bloody and vindictive warfare.

Duncan had stood in a musing attitude, contemplating this scene a few minutes, when his eyes were directed to the glacis in front of the sally-port already mentioned, by the sounds of approaching footsteps. He walked to an angle of the bastion, and beheld the scout advancing, under the custody of a French officer, to the body of the fort. The countenance of Hawkeye was haggard and careworn, and his air dejected, as though he felt the deepest degradation at having fallen into the power of his enemies. He was without his favorite weapon, and his arms were even bound behind him with thongs, made of the skin of a deer. The arrival of flags to cover the messengers of summons, had occurred so often of late, that when Heyward first threw his careless glance on this group, he expected to see another of the officers of the enemy, charged with a similar office but the instant he recognized the tall person and still sturdy though downcast features of his friend, the woodsman, he started with surprise, and turned to descend from the bastion into the bosom of the work.

The sounds of other voices, however, caught his attention, and for a moment caused him to forget his purpose. At the inner angle of the mound he met the sisters, walking along the parapet, in search, like himself, of air and relief from confinement. They had not met from that painful moment when he deserted them on the plain, only to assure their safety. He had parted from them worn with care, and jaded with fatigue; he now saw them refreshed and blooming, though timid and anxious. Under such an inducement it will cause no surprise that the young man lost sight for a time, of other objects in order to address them. He was, however, anticipated by the voice of the ingenuous and youthful Alice.

"Ah! thou tyrant! thou recreant knight! he who abandons his damsels in the very lists," she cried; "here have we been days, nay, ages, expecting you at our feet, imploring mercy and forgetfulness of your craven backsliding, or I should rather say, backrunning—for verily you fled in the manner that no stricken deer, as our worthy friend the scout would say, could equal!"

"You know that Alice means our thanks and our blessings," added the graver and more thoughtful Cora. "In truth, we have a little wonder why you should so rigidly absent yourself from a place where the gratitude of the daughters might receive the support of a parent's thanks."

"Your father himself could tell you, that, though absent from your presence, I have not been altogether forgetful of your safety," returned the young man; "the mastery of yonder village of huts," pointing to the neighboring entrenched camp, "has been keenly disputed; and he who holds it is sure to be possessed of this fort, and that which it contains. My days and nights have all been passed there since we separated, because I thought that duty called me thither. But," he added, with an air of chagrin, which he endeavored, though unsuccessfully, to conceal, "had I been aware that what I then believed a soldier's conduct could be so construed, shame would have been added to the list of reasons."

"Heyward! Duncan!" exclaimed Alice, bending forward to read his half-averted countenance, until a lock of her golden hair rested on her flushed cheek, and nearly concealed the tear that had started to her eye; "did I think this idle tongue of mine had pained you, I would silence it forever. Cora can say, if Cora would, how justly we have prized your services, and how deep—I had almost said, how fervent—is our gratitude."

"And will Cora attest the truth of this?" cried Duncan, suffering the cloud to be chased from his countenance by a smile of open pleasure. "What says our graver sister? Will she find an excuse for the neglect of the knight in the duty of a soldier?"

Cora made no immediate answer, but turned her face toward the water, as if looking on the sheet of the Horican. When she did bend her dark eyes on the young man, they were yet filled with an expression of anguish that at once drove every thought but that of kind solicitude from his mind.

"You are not well, dearest Miss Munro!" he exclaimed; "we have trifled while you are in suffering!"

"'Tis nothing," she answered, refusing his support with feminine reserve. "That I cannot see the sunny side of the picture of life, like this artless but ardent enthusiast," she added, laying her hand lightly, but affectionately, on the arm of her sister, "is the penalty of experience, and, perhaps, the misfortune of my nature. See," she continued, as if determined to shake off infirmity, in a sense of duty; "look around you, Major Heyward, and tell me what a prospect is this for the daughter of a soldier whose greatest happiness is his honor and his military renown."

"Neither ought nor shall be tarnished by circumstances over which he has had no control," Duncan warmly replied. "But your words recall me to my own duty. I go now to your gallant father, to hear his determination in matters of the last moment to the defense. God bless you in every fortune, noble—Cora—I may and must call you." She frankly gave him her hand, though her lip quivered, and her cheeks gradually became of ashly paleness. "In every fortune, I know you will be an ornament and honor to your sex. Alice, adieu"—his voice changed from admiration to tenderness— "adieu, Alice; we shall soon meet again; as conquerors, I trust, and amid rejoicings!"

Without waiting for an answer from either, the young man threw himself down the grassy steps of the bastion, and moving rapidly across the parade, he was quickly in the presence of their father. Munro was pacing his narrow apartment with a disturbed air and gigantic strides as Duncan entered.

"You have anticipated my wishes, Major Heyward," he said; "I was about to request this favor."

"I am sorry to see, sir, that the messenger I so warmly recommended has returned in custody of the French! I hope there is no reason to distrust his fidelity?"

"The fidelity of 'The Long Rifle' is well known to me," returned Munro, "and is above suspicion; though his usual good fortune seems, at last, to have failed. Montcalm has got him, and with the accursed politeness of his nation, he has sent him in with a doleful tale, of 'knowing how I valued the fellow, he could not think of retaining him.' A Jesuitical way that, Major Duncan Heyward, of telling a man of his misfortunes!"

"But the general and his succor?"

"Did ye look to the south as ye entered, and could ye not see them?" said the old soldier, laughing bitterly.

"Hoot! hoot! you're an impatient boy, sir, and cannot give the gentlemen leisure for their march!"

"They are coming, then? The scout has said as much?"

"When? and by what path? for the dunce has omitted to tell me this. There is a letter, it would seem, too; and that is the only agreeable part of the matter. For the customary attentions of your Marquis of Montcalm—I warrant me, Duncan, that he of Lothian would buy a dozen such marquisates—but if the news of the letter were bad, the gentility of this French monsieur would certainly compel him to let us know it."

"He keeps the letter, then, while he releases the messenger?"

"Ay, that does he, and all for the sake of what you call your 'bonhommie' I would venture, if the truth was known, the fellow's grandfather taught the noble science of dancing."

"But what says the scout? he has eyes and ears, and a tongue. What verbal report does he make?"

"Oh! sir, he is not wanting in natural organs, and he is free to tell all that he has seen and heard. The whole amount is this; there is a fort of his majesty's on the banks of the Hudson, called Edward, in honor of his gracious highness of York, you'll know; and it is well filled with armed men, as such a work should be."

"But was there no movement, no signs of any intention to advance to our relief?"

"There were the morning and evening parades; and when one of the provincial loons—you'll know, Duncan, you're half a Scotsman yourself—when one of them dropped his powder over his porretch, if it touched the coals, it just burned!" Then, suddenly changing his bitter, ironical manner, to one more grave and thoughtful, he continued: "and yet there might, and must be, something in that letter which it would be well to know!"

"Our decision should be speedy," said Duncan, gladly availing himself of this change of humor, to press the more important objects of their interview; "I cannot conceal from you, sir, that the camp will not be much longer tenable; and I am sorry to add, that things appear no better in the fort; more than half the guns are bursted."

"And how should it be otherwise? Some were fished from the bottom of the lake; some have been rusting in woods since the discovery of the country; and some were never guns at all—mere privateersmen's playthings! Do you think, sir, you can have Woolwich Warren in the midst of a wilderness, three thousand miles from Great Britain?"

"The walls are crumbling about our ears, and provisions begin to fail us," continued Heyward, without regarding the new burst of indignation; "even the men show signs of discontent and alarm."

"Major Heyward," said Munro, turning to his youthful associate with the dignity of his years and superior rank; "I should have served his majesty for half a century, and earned these gray hairs in vain, were I ignorant of all you say, and of the pressing nature of our circumstances; still, there is everything due to the honor of the king's arms, and something to ourselves. While there is hope of succor, this fortress will I defend, though it be to be done with pebbles gathered on the lake shore. It is a sight of the letter, therefore, that we want, that we may know the intentions of the man the earl of Loudon has left among us as his substitute."

"And can I be of service in the matter?"

"Sir, you can; the marquis of Montcalm has, in addition to his other civilities, invited me to a personal interview between the works and his own camp; in order, as he says, to impart some additional information. Now, I think it would not be wise to show any undue solicitude to meet him, and I would employ you, an officer of rank, as my substitute; for it would but ill comport with the honor of Scotland to let it be said one of her gentlemen was outdone in civility by a native of any other country on earth."

Without assuming the supererogatory task of entering into a discussion of the comparative merits of national courtesy, Duncan cheerfully assented to supply the place of the veteran in the approaching interview. A long and confidential communication now succeeded, during which the young man received some additional insight into his duty, from the experience and native acuteness of his commander, and then the former took his leave.

As Duncan could only act as the representative of the commandant of the fort, the ceremonies which should have accompanied a meeting between the heads of the adverse forces were, of course, dispensed with. The truce still existed, and with a roll and beat of the drum, and covered by a little white flag, Duncan left the sally-port, within ten minutes after his instructions were ended. He was received by the French officer in advance with the usual formalities, and immediately accompanied to a distant marquee of the renowned soldier who led the forces of France.

The general of the enemy received the youthful messenger, surrounded by his principal officers, and by a swarthy band of the native chiefs, who had followed him to the field, with the warriors of their several tribes. Heyward paused short, when, in glancing his eyes rapidly over the dark group of the latter, he beheld the malignant countenance of Magua, regarding him with the calm but sullen attention which marked the expression of that subtle savage. A slight exclamation of surprise even burst from the lips of the young man, but instantly, recollecting his errand, and the presence in which he stood, he suppressed every appearance of emotion, and turned to the hostile leader, who had already advanced a step to receive him.

The marquis of Montcalm was, at the period of which we write, in the flower of his age, and, it may be added, in the zenith of his fortunes. But even in that enviable situation, he was affable, and distinguished as much for his attention to the forms of courtesy, as for that chivalrous courage which, only two short years afterward, induced him to throw away his life on the plains of Abraham. Duncan, in turning his eyes from the malign expression of Magua, suffered them to rest with pleasure on the smiling and polished features, and the noble military air, of the French general.

"Monsieur," said the latter, "j'ai beaucoup de plaisir a—bah!—ou est cet interprete?"

"Je crois, monsieur, qu'il ne sear pas necessaire," Heyward modestly replied; "je parle un peu francais."

"Ah! j'en suis bien aise," said Montcalm, taking Duncan familiarly by the arm, and leading him deep into the marquee, a little out of earshot; "je deteste ces fripons-la; on ne sait jamais sur quel pie on est avec eux. Eh, bien! monsieur," he continued still speaking in French; "though I should have been proud of receiving your commandant, I am very happy that he has seen proper to employ an officer so distinguished, and who, I am sure, is so amiable, as yourself."

Duncan bowed low, pleased with the compliment, in spite of a most heroic determination to suffer no artifice to allure him into forgetfulness of the interest of his prince; and Montcalm, after a pause of a moment, as if to collect his thoughts, proceeded:

"Your commandant is a brave man, and well qualified to repel my assault. Mais, monsieur, is it not time to begin to take more counsel of humanity, and less of your courage? The one as strongly characterizes the hero as the other."

"We consider the qualities as inseparable," returned Duncan, smiling; "but while we find in the vigor of your excellency every motive to stimulate the one, we can, as yet, see no particular call for the exercise of the other."

Montcalm, in his turn, slightly bowed, but it was with the air of a man too practised to remember the language of flattery. After musing a moment, he added:

"It is possible my glasses have deceived me, and that your works resist our cannon better than I had supposed. You know our force?"

"Our accounts vary," said Duncan, carelessly; "the highest, however, has not exceeded twenty thousand men."

The Frenchman bit his lip, and fastened his eyes keenly on the other as if to read his thoughts; then, with a readiness peculiar to himself, he continued, as if assenting to the truth of an enumeration which quite doubled his army:

"It is a poor compliment to the vigilance of us soldiers, monsieur, that, do what we will, we never can conceal our numbers. If it were to be done at all, one would believe it might succeed in these woods. Though you think it too soon to listen to the calls of humanity," he added, smiling archly, "I may be permitted to believe that gallantry is not forgotten by one so young as yourself. The daughters of the commandant, I learn, have passed into the fort since it was invested?"

"It is true, monsieur; but, so far from weakening our efforts, they set us an example of courage in their own fortitude. Were nothing but resolution necessary to repel so accomplished a soldier as M. de Montcalm, I would gladly trust the defense of William Henry to the elder of those ladies."

"We have a wise ordinance in our Salique laws, which says, 'The crown of France shall never degrade the lance to the distaff'," said Montcalm, dryly, and with a little hauteur; but instantly adding, with his former frank and easy air: "as all the nobler qualities are hereditary, I can easily credit you; though, as I said before, courage has its limits, and humanity must not be forgotten. I trust, monsieur, you come authorized to treat for the surrender of the place?"

"Has your excellency found our defense so feeble as to believe the measure necessary?"

"I should be sorry to have the defense protracted in such a manner as to irritate my red friends there," continued Montcalm, glancing his eyes at the group of grave and attentive Indians, without attending to the other's questions; "I find it difficult, even now, to limit them to the usages of war."

Heyward was silent; for a painful recollection of the dangers he had so recently escaped came over his mind, and recalled the images of those defenseless beings who had shared in all his sufferings.

"Ces messieurs-la," said Montcalm, following up the advantage which he conceived he had gained, "are most formidable when baffled; and it is unnecessary to tell you with what difficulty they are restrained in their anger. Eh bien, monsieur! shall we speak of the terms?"

"I fear your excellency has been deceived as to the strength of William Henry, and the resources of its garrison!"

"I have not sat down before Quebec, but an earthen work, that is defended by twenty-three hundred gallant men," was the laconic reply.

"Our mounds are earthen, certainly—nor are they seated on the rocks of Cape Diamond; but they stand on that shore which proved so destructive to Dieskau and his army. There is also a powerful force within a few hours' march of us, which we account upon as a part of our means."

"Some six or eight thousand men," returned Montcalm, with much apparent indifference, "whom their leader wisely judges to be safer in their works than in the field."

It was now Heyward's turn to bite his lip with vexation as the other so coolly alluded to a force which the young man knew to be overrated. Both mused a little while in silence, when Montcalm renewed the conversation, in a way that showed he believed the visit of his guest was solely to propose terms of capitulation. On the other hand, Heyward began to throw sundry inducements in the way of the French general, to betray the discoveries he had made through the intercepted letter. The artifice of neither, however, succeeded; and after a protracted and fruitless interview, Duncan took his leave, favorably impressed with an opinion of the courtesy and talents of the enemy's captain, but as ignorant of what he came to learn as when he arrived. Montcalm followed him as far as the entrance of the marquee, renewing his invitations to the commandant of the fort to give him an immediate meeting in the open ground between the two armies.

There they separated, and Duncan returned to the advanced post of the French, accompanied as before; whence he instantly proceeded to the fort, and to the quarters of his own commander.

CHAPTER XVI.

"EDG.—Before you fight the battle ope this letter."
—Lear

Major Heyward found Munro attended only by his daughters. Alice sat upon his knee, parting the gray hairs on the forehead of the old man with her delicate fingers; and whenever he affected to frown on her trifling, appeasing his assumed anger by pressing her ruby lips fondly on his wrinkled brow. Cora was seated nigh them, a calm and amused looker-on; regarding the wayward movements of her more youthful sister with that species of maternal fondness which characterized her love for Alice. Not only the dangers through which they had passed, but those which still impended above them, appeared to be momentarily forgotten, in the soothing indulgence of such a family meeting. It seemed as if they had profited by the short truce, to devote an instant to the purest and best affection; the daughters forgetting their fears, and the veteran his cares, in the security of the moment. Of this scene, Duncan, who, in his eagerness to report his arrival, had entered unannounced, stood many moments an unobserved and a delighted spectator. But the quick and dancing eyes of Alice soon caught a glimpse of his figure reflected from a glass, and she sprang blushing from her father's knee, exclaiming aloud:

"Major Heyward!"

"What of the lad?" demanded her father; "I have sent him to crack a little with the Frenchman. Ha, sir, you are young, and you're nimble! Away with you, ye baggage; as if there were not troubles enough for a soldier, without having his camp filled with such prattling hussies as yourself!"

Alice laughingly followed her sister, who instantly led the way from an apartment where she perceived their presence was no longer desirable. Munro, instead of demanding the result of the young man's mission, paced the room for a few moments, with his hands behind his back, and his head inclined toward the floor, like a man lost in thought. At length he raised his eyes, glistening with a father's fondness, and exclaimed:

"They are a pair of excellent girls, Heyward, and such as any one may boast of."

"You are not now to learn my opinion of your daughters, Colonel Munro."

"True, lad, true," interrupted the impatient old man; "you were about opening your mind more fully on that matter the day you got in, but I did not think it becoming in an old soldier to be talking of nuptial blessings and wedding jokes when the enemies of his king were likely to be unbidden guests at the feast. But I was wrong, Duncan, boy, I was wrong there; and I am now ready to hear what you have to say."

"Notwithstanding the pleasure your assurance gives me, dear sir, I have just now, a message from Montcalm—"

"Let the Frenchman and all his host go to the devil, sir!" exclaimed the hasty veteran. "He is not yet master of William Henry, nor shall he ever be, provided Webb proves himself the man he should. No, sir, thank Heaven we are not yet in such a strait that it can be said Munro is too much pressed to discharge the little domestic duties of his own family. Your mother was the only child of my bosom friend, Duncan; and I'll just give you a hearing, though all the knights of St. Louis were in a body at the sally-port, with the French saint at their head, crying to speak a word under favor. A pretty degree of knighthood, sir, is that which can be bought with sugar hogsheads! and then your twopenny marquisates. The thistle is the order for dignity and antiquity; the veritable 'nemo me impune lacessit' of chivalry. Ye had ancestors in that degree, Duncan, and they were an ornament to the nobles of Scotland."

Heyward, who perceived that his superior took a malicious pleasure in exhibiting his contempt for the message of the French general, was fain to humor a spleen that he knew would be short-lived; he therefore, replied with as much indifference as he could assume on such a subject:

"My request, as you know, sir, went so far as to presume to the honor of being your son."

"Ay, boy, you found words to make yourself very plainly comprehended. But, let me ask ye, sir, have you been as intelligible to the girl?"

"On my honor, no," exclaimed Duncan, warmly; "there would have been an abuse of a confided trust, had I taken advantage of my situation for such a purpose."

"Your notions are those of a gentleman, Major Heyward, and well enough in their place. But Cora Munro is a maiden too discreet, and of a mind too elevated and improved, to need the guardianship even of a father."

"Cora!"

"Ay—Cora! we are talking of your pretensions to Miss Munro, are we not, sir?"

"I—I—I was not conscious of having mentioned her name," said Duncan, stammering.

"And to marry whom, then, did you wish my consent, Major Heyward?" demanded the old soldier, erecting himself in the dignity of offended feeling.

"You have another, and not less lovely child."

"Alice!" exclaimed the father, in an astonishment equal to that with which Duncan had just repeated the name of her sister.

"Such was the direction of my wishes, sir."

The young man awaited in silence the result of the extraordinary effect produced by a communication, which, as it now appeared, was so unexpected. For several minutes Munro paced the chamber with long and rapid strides, his rigid features working convulsively, and every faculty seemingly absorbed in the musings of his own mind. At length, he paused directly in front of Heyward, and riveting his eyes upon those of the other, he said, with a lip that quivered violently:

"Duncan Heyward, I have loved you for the sake of him whose blood is in your veins; I have loved you for your own good qualities; and I have loved you, because I thought you would contribute to the happiness of my child. But all this love would turn to hatred, were I assured that what I so much apprehend is true."

"God forbid that any act or thought of mine should lead to such a change!" exclaimed the young man, whose eye never quailed under the penetrating look it encountered. Without adverting to the impossibility of the other's comprehending those feelings which were hid in his own bosom, Munro suffered himself to be appeased by the unaltered countenance he met, and with a voice sensibly softened, he continued:

"You would be my son, Duncan, and you're ignorant of the history of the man you wish to call your father. Sit ye down, young man, and I will open to you the wounds of a seared heart, in as few words as may be suitable."

By this time, the message of Montcalm was as much forgotten by him who bore it as by the man for whose ears it was intended. Each drew a chair, and while the veteran communed a few moments with his own thoughts, apparently in sadness, the youth suppressed his impatience in a look and attitude of respectful attention. At length, the former spoke:

"You'll know, already, Major Heyward, that my family was both ancient and honorable," commenced the Scotsman; "though it might not altogether be endowed with that amount of wealth that should correspond with its degree. I was, maybe, such an one as yourself when I plighted my faith to Alice Graham, the only child of a neighboring laird of some estate. But the connection was disagreeable to her father, on more accounts than my poverty. I did, therefore, what an honest man should—restored the maiden her troth, and departed the country in the service of my king. I had seen many regions, and had shed much blood in different lands, before duty called me to the islands of the West Indies. There it was my lot to form a connection with one who in time became my wife, and the mother of Cora. She was the daughter of a gentleman of those isles, by a lady whose misfortune it was, if you will," said the old man, proudly, "to be descended, remotely, from that unfortunate class who are so basely enslaved to administer to the wants of a luxurious people. Ay, sir, that is a curse, entailed on Scotland by her unnatural union with a foreign and trading people. But could I find a man among them who would dare to reflect on my child, he should feel the weight of a father's anger! Ha! Major Heyward, you are yourself born at the south, where these unfortunate beings are considered of a race inferior to your own."

"'Tis most unfortunately true, sir," said Duncan, unable any longer to prevent his eyes from sinking to the floor in embarrassment.

"And you cast it on my child as a reproach! You scorn to mingle the blood of the Heywards with one so degraded—lovely and virtuous though she be?" fiercely demanded the jealous parent.

"Heaven protect me from a prejudice so unworthy of my reason!" returned Duncan, at the same time conscious of such a feeling, and that as deeply rooted as if it had been ingrafted in his nature. "The sweetness, the beauty, the witchery of your younger daughter, Colonel Munro, might explain my motives without imputing to me this injustice."

"Ye are right, sir," returned the old man, again changing his tones to those of gentleness, or rather softness; "the girl is the image of what her mother was at her years, and before she had become acquainted with grief. When death deprived me of my wife I returned to Scotland, enriched by the marriage; and, would you think it, Duncan! the suffering angel had remained in the heartless state of celibacy twenty long years, and that for the sake of a man who could forget her! She did more, sir;

she overlooked my want of faith, and, all difficulties being now removed, she took me for her husband."

"And became the mother of Alice?" exclaimed Duncan, with an eagerness that might have proved dangerous at a moment when the thoughts of Munro were less occupied that at present.

"She did, indeed," said the old man, "and dearly did she pay for the blessing she bestowed. But she is a saint in heaven, sir; and it ill becomes one whose foot rests on the grave to mourn a lot so blessed. I had her but a single year, though; a short term of happiness for one who had seen her youth fade in hopeless pining."

There was something so commanding in the distress of the old man, that Heyward did not dare to venture a syllable of consolation. Munro sat utterly unconscious of the other's presence, his features exposed and working with the anguish of his regrets, while heavy tears fell from his eyes, and rolled unheeded from his cheeks to the floor. At length he moved, and as if suddenly recovering his recollection; when he arose, and taking a single turn across the room, he approached his companion with an air of military grandeur, and demanded:

"Have you not, Major Heyward, some communication that I should hear from the marquis de Montcalm?"

Duncan started in his turn, and immediately commenced in an embarrassed voice, the half-forgotten message. It is unnecessary to dwell upon the evasive though polite manner with which the French general had eluded every attempt of Heyward to worm from him the purport of the communication he had proposed making, or on the decided, though still polished message, by which he now gave his enemy to understand, that, unless he chose to receive it in person, he should not receive it at all. As Munro listened to the detail of Duncan, the excited feelings of the father gradually gave way before the obligations of his station, and when the other was done, he saw before him nothing but the veteran, swelling with the wounded feelings of a soldier.

"You have said enough, Major Heyward," exclaimed the angry old man; "enough to make a volume of commentary on French civility. Here has this gentleman invited me to a conference, and when I send him a capable substitute, for ye're all that, Duncan, though your years are but few, he answers me with a riddle."

"He may have thought less favorably of the substitute, my dear sir; and you will remember that the invitation, which he now repeats, was to the commandant of the works, and not to his second."

"Well, sir, is not a substitute clothed with all the power and dignity of him who grants the commission? He wishes to confer with Munro! Faith, sir, I have much inclination to indulge the man, if it should only be to let him behold the firm countenance we maintain in spite of his numbers and his summons. There might be not bad policy in such a stroke, young man."

Duncan, who believed it of the last importance that they should speedily come to the contents of the letter borne by the scout, gladly encouraged this idea.

"Without doubt, he could gather no confidence by witnessing our indifference," he said.

"You never said truer word. I could wish, sir, that he would visit the works in open day, and in the form of a storming party; that is the least failing method of proving the countenance of an enemy, and would be far preferable to the battering system he has chosen. The beauty and manliness of warfare has been much deformed, Major Heyward, by the arts of your Monsieur Vauban. Our ancestors were far above such scientific cowardice!"

"It may be very true, sir; but we are now obliged to repel art by art. What is your pleasure in the matter of the interview?"

"I will meet the Frenchman, and that without fear or delay; promptly, sir, as becomes a servant of my royal master. Go, Major Heyward, and give them a flourish of the music; and send out a messenger to let them know who is coming. We will follow with a small guard, for such respect is due to one who holds the honor of his king in keeping; and hark'ee, Duncan," he added, in a half whisper, though they were alone, "it may be prudent to have some aid at hand, in case there should be treachery at the bottom of it all."

The young man availed himself of this order to quit the apartment; and, as the day was fast coming to a close, he hastened without delay, to make the necessary arrangements. A very few minutes only were necessary to parade a few files, and to dispatch an orderly with a flag to announce the approach of the commandant of the fort. When Duncan had done both these, he led the guard to the sally-port, near which he found his superior ready, waiting his appearance. As soon as the usual ceremonials of a military departure were observed, the veteran and his more youthful companion left the fortress, attended by the escort.

They had proceeded only a hundred yards from the works, when the little array which attended the French general to the conference was seen issuing from the hollow way which formed the bed of a brook that ran between the batteries of the besiegers and the fort. From the moment that Munro left his own works to appear in front of his enemy's, his air had been grand, and his step and countenance highly military. The instant he caught a glimpse of the white plume that waved in the hat of Montcalm, his eye lighted, and age no longer appeared to possess any influence over his vast and still muscular person.

"Speak to the boys to be watchful, sir," he said, in an undertone, to Duncan; "and to look well to their flints and steel, for one is never safe with a servant of these Louis's; at the same time, we shall show them the front of men in deep security. Ye'll understand me, Major Heyward!"

He was interrupted by the clamor of a drum from the approaching Frenchmen, which was immediately answered, when each party pushed an orderly in advance, bearing a white flag, and the wary Scotsman halted with his guard close at his back. As soon as this slight salutation had passed, Montcalm moved toward them with a quick but graceful step, baring his head to the veteran, and dropping his spotless plume nearly to the earth in courtesy. If the air of Munro was more commanding and manly, it wanted both the ease and insinuating polish of that of the Frenchman. Neither spoke for a few moments, each regarding the other with curious and interested eyes. Then, as became his superior rank and the nature of the interview, Montcalm broke the silence. After uttering the usual words of greeting, he turned to Duncan, and continued, with a smile of recognition, speaking always in French:

"I am rejoiced, monsieur, that you have given us the pleasure of your company on this occasion. There will be no necessity to employ an ordinary interpreter; for, in your hands, I feel the same security as if I spoke your language myself."

Duncan acknowledged the compliment, when Montcalm, turning to his guard, which in imitation of that of their enemies, pressed close upon him, continued:

"En arriere, mes enfants—il fait chaud—-retirez-vous un peu."

Before Major Heyward would imitate this proof of confidence, he glanced his eyes around the plain, and beheld with uneasiness the numerous dusky groups of savages, who looked out from the margin of the surrounding woods, curious spectators of the interview.

"Monsieur de Montcalm will readily acknowledge the difference in our situation," he said, with some embarrassment, pointing at the same time toward those dangerous foes, who were to be seen in almost every direction. "Were we to dismiss our guard, we should stand here at the mercy of our enemies."

"Monsieur, you have the plighted faith of 'un gentilhomme Francais', for your safety," returned Montcalm, laying his hand impressively on his heart; "it should suffice."

"It shall. Fall back," Duncan added to the officer who led the escort; "fall back, sir, beyond hearing, and wait for orders."

Munro witnessed this movement with manifest uneasiness; nor did he fail to demand an instant explanation.

"Is it not our interest, sir, to betray distrust?" retorted Duncan. "Monsieur de Montcalm pledges his word for our safety, and I have ordered the men to withdraw a little, in order to prove how much we depend on his assurance."

"It may be all right, sir, but I have no overweening reliance on the faith of these marquesses, or marquis, as they call themselves. Their patents of nobility are too common to be certain that they bear the seal of true honor."

"You forget, dear sir, that we confer with an officer, distinguished alike in Europe and America for his deeds. From a soldier of his reputation we can have nothing to apprehend."

The old man made a gesture of resignation, though his rigid features still betrayed his obstinate adherence to a distrust, which he derived from a sort of hereditary contempt of his enemy, rather than from any present signs which might warrant so uncharitable a feeling. Montcalm waited patiently until this little dialogue in demi-voice was ended, when he drew nigher, and opened the subject of their conference.

"I have solicited this interview from your superior, monsieur," he said, "because I believe he will allow himself to be persuaded that he has already done everything which is necessary for the honor of his prince, and will now listen to the admonitions of humanity. I will forever bear testimony that his resistance has been gallant, and was continued as long as there was hope."

When this opening was translated to Munro, he answered with dignity, but with sufficient courtesy:

"However I may prize such testimony from Monsieur Montcalm, it will be more valuable when it shall be better merited."

The French general smiled, as Duncan gave him the purport of this reply, and observed:

"What is now so freely accorded to approved courage, may be refused to useless obstinacy. Monsieur would wish to see my camp, and witness for himself our numbers, and the impossibility of his resisting them with success?"

"I know that the king of France is well served," returned the unmoved Scotsman, as soon as Duncan ended his translation; "but my own royal master has as many and as faithful troops."

"Though not at hand, fortunately for us," said Montcalm, without waiting, in his ardor, for the interpreter. "There is a destiny in war, to which a brave man knows how to submit with the same courage that he faces his foes."

"Had I been conscious that Monsieur Montcalm was master of the English, I should have spared myself the trouble of so awkward a translation," said the vexed Duncan, dryly; remembering instantly his recent by-play with Munro.

"Your pardon, monsieur," rejoined the Frenchman, suffering a slight color to appear on his dark cheek. "There is a vast difference between understanding and speaking a foreign tongue; you will, therefore, please to assist me still." Then, after a short pause, he added: "These hills afford us every opportunity of reconnoitering your works, messieurs, and I am possibly as well acquainted with their weak condition as you can be yourselves."

"Ask the French general if his glasses can reach to the Hudson," said Munro, proudly; "and if he knows when and where to expect the army of Webb."

"Let General Webb be his own interpreter," returned the politic Montcalm, suddenly extending an open letter toward Munro as he spoke; "you will there learn, monsieur, that his movements are not likely to prove embarrassing to my army."

The veteran seized the offered paper, without waiting for Duncan to translate the speech, and with an eagerness that betrayed how important he deemed its contents. As his eye passed hastily over the words, his countenance changed from its look of military pride to one of deep chagrin; his lip began to quiver; and suffering the paper to fall from his hand, his head dropped upon his chest, like that of a man whose hopes were withered at a single blow. Duncan caught the letter from the ground, and without apology for the liberty he took, he read at a glance its cruel purport. Their common superior, so far from encouraging them to resist, advised a speedy surrender, urging in the plainest language, as a reason, the utter impossibility of his sending a single man to their rescue.

"Here is no deception!" exclaimed Duncan, examining the billet both inside and out; "this is the signature of Webb, and must be the captured letter."

"The man has betrayed me!" Munro at length bitterly exclaimed; "he has brought dishonor to the door of one where disgrace was never before known to dwell, and shame has he heaped heavily on my gray hairs."

"Say not so," cried Duncan; "we are yet masters of the fort, and of our honor. Let us, then, sell our lives at such a rate as shall make our enemies believe the purchase too dear."

"Boy, I thank thee," exclaimed the old man, rousing himself from his stupor; "you have, for once, reminded Munro of his duty. We will go back, and dig our graves behind those ramparts."

"Messieurs," said Montcalm, advancing toward them a step, in generous interest, "you little know Louis de St. Veran if you believe him capable of profiting by this letter to humble brave men, or to build up a dishonest reputation for himself. Listen to my terms before you leave me."

"What says the Frenchman?" demanded the veteran, sternly; "does he make a merit of having captured a scout, with a note from headquarters? Sir, he had better raise this siege, to go and sit down before Edward if he wishes to frighten his enemy with words."

Duncan explained the other's meaning.

"Monsieur de Montcalm, we will hear you," the veteran added, more calmly, as Duncan ended.

"To retain the fort is now impossible," said his liberal enemy; "it is necessary to the interests of my master that it should be destroyed; but as for yourselves and your brave comrades, there is no privilege dear to a soldier that shall be denied."

"Our colors?" demanded Heyward.

"Carry them to England, and show them to your king."

"Our arms?"

"Keep them; none can use them better."

"Our march; the surrender of the place?"

"Shall all be done in a way most honorable to yourselves."

Duncan now turned to explain these proposals to his commander, who heard him with amazement, and a sensibility that was deeply touched by so unusual and unexpected generosity.

"Go you, Duncan," he said; "go with this marquess, as, indeed, marquess he should be; go to his marquee and arrange it all. I have lived to see two things in my old age that never did I expect to behold. An Englishman afraid to support a friend, and a Frenchman too honest to profit by his advantage."

So saying, the veteran again dropped his head to his chest, and returned slowly toward the fort, exhibiting, by the dejection of his air, to the anxious garrison, a harbinger of evil tidings.

From the shock of this unexpected blow the haughty feelings of Munro never recovered; but from that moment there commenced a change in his determined character, which accompanied him to a speedy grave. Duncan remained to settle the terms of the capitulation. He was seen to re-enter the works during the first watches of the night, and immediately after a private conference with the commandant, to leave them again. It was then openly announced that hostilities must cease—Munro having signed a treaty by which the place was to be yielded to the enemy, with the morning; the garrison to retain their arms, the colors and their baggage, and, consequently, according to military opinion, their honor.

CHAPTER XVII.

> "Weave we the woof.
> The thread is spun.
> The web is wove.
> The work is done."—Gray

The hostile armies, which lay in the wilds of the Horican, passed the night of the ninth of August, 1757, much in the manner they would, had they encountered on the fairest field of Europe. While the conquered were still, sullen, and dejected, the victors triumphed. But there are limits alike to grief and joy; and long before the watches of the morning came the stillness of those boundless woods was only broken by a gay call from some exulting young Frenchman of the advanced pickets, or a menacing challenge from the fort, which sternly forbade the approach of any hostile footsteps before the stipulated moment. Even these occasional threatening sounds ceased to be heard in that dull hour which precedes the day, at which period a listener might have sought in vain any evidence of the presence of those armed powers that then slumbered on the shores of the "holy lake."

It was during these moments of deep silence that the canvas which concealed the entrance to a spacious marquee in the French encampment was shoved aside, and a man issued from beneath the drapery into the open air. He was enveloped in a cloak that might have been intended as a protection from the chilling damps of the woods, but which served equally well as a mantle to conceal his person. He was permitted to pass the grenadier, who watched over the slumbers of the French commander, without interruption, the man making the usual salute which betokens military deference, as the other passed swiftly through the little city of tents, in the direction of William Henry. Whenever this unknown individual encountered one of the numberless sentinels who crossed his path, his answer was prompt, and, as it appeared, satisfactory; for he was uniformly allowed to proceed without further interrogation.

With the exception of such repeated but brief interruptions, he had moved silently from the center of the camp to its most advanced outposts, when he drew nigh the soldier who held his watch nearest to the works of the enemy. As he approached he was received with the usual challenge:

"Qui vive?"

"France," was the reply.

"Le mot d'ordre?"

"La victorie," said the other, drawing so nigh as to be heard in a loud whisper.

"C'est bien," returned the sentinel, throwing his musket from the charge to his shoulder; "vous promenez bien matin, monsieur!"

"Il est nécessaire d'être vigilant, mon enfant," the other observed, dropping a fold of his cloak, and looking the soldier close in the face as he passed him, still continuing his way toward the British fortification. The man started; his arms rattled heavily as he threw them forward in the lowest and most respectful salute; and when he had again recovered his piece, he turned to walk his post, muttering between his teeth:

"Il faut être vigilant, en vérité! je crois que nous avons la, un caporal qui ne dort jamais!"

The officer proceeded, without affecting to hear the words which escaped the sentinel in his surprise; nor did he again pause until he had reached the low strand, and in a somewhat dangerous vicinity to the western water bastion of the fort. The light of an obscure moon was just sufficient to render objects, though dim, perceptible in their outlines. He, therefore, took the precaution to place himself against the trunk of a tree, where he leaned for many minutes, and seemed to contemplate the dark and silent mounds of the English works in profound attention. His gaze at the ramparts was not that of a curious or idle spectator; but his looks wandered from point to point, denoting his knowledge of military usages, and betraying that his search was not unaccompanied by distrust. At length he appeared satisfied; and having cast his eyes impatiently upward toward the summit of the eastern mountain, as if anticipating the approach of the morning, he was in the act of turning on his footsteps, when a light sound on the nearest angle of the bastion caught his ear, and induced him to remain.

Just then a figure was seen to approach the edge of the rampart, where it stood, apparently contemplating in its turn the distant tents of the French encampment. Its head was then turned toward the east, as though equally anxious for the appearance of light, when the form leaned against the mound, and seemed to gaze upon the glassy expanse of the waters, which, like a submarine firmament, glittered with its thousand mimic stars. The melancholy air, the hour, together with the vast frame of the man who thus leaned, musing, against the English ramparts, left no doubt as to his person in the mind of the observant spectator. Delicacy, no less than prudence, now urged him to retire; and he had moved cautiously round the body of the tree for that purpose, when another sound drew his attention, and once more arrested his footsteps. It was a low and almost inaudible movement of the water, and was succeeded by a grating of pebbles one against the other. In a moment he saw a dark form rise, as it were, out of the lake, and steal without further noise to the land, within a few feet of the place where he himself stood. A rifle next slowly rose between his eyes and the watery mirror; but before it could be discharged his own hand was on the lock.

"Hugh!" exclaimed the savage, whose treacherous aim was so singularly and so unexpectedly interrupted.

Without making any reply, the French officer laid his hand on the shoulder of the Indian, and led him in profound silence to a distance from the spot, where their subsequent dialogue might have proved dangerous, and where it seemed that one of them, at least, sought a victim. Then throwing open his cloak, so as to expose his uniform and the cross of St. Louis which was suspended at his breast, Montcalm sternly demanded:

"What means this? Does not my son know that the hatchet is buried between the English and his Canadian Father?"

"What can the Hurons do?" returned the savage, speaking also, though imperfectly, in the French language.

"Not a warrior has a scalp, and the pale faces make friends!"

"Ha, Le Renard Subtil! Methinks this is an excess of zeal for a friend who was so late an enemy! How many suns have set since Le Renard struck the war-post of the English?"

"Where is that sun?" demanded the sullen savage. "Behind the hill; and it is dark and cold. But when he comes again, it will be bright and warm. Le Subtil is the sun of his tribe. There have been clouds, and many mountains between him and his nation; but now he shines and it is a clear sky!"

"That Le Renard has power with his people, I well know," said Montcalm; "for yesterday he hunted for their scalps, and to-day they hear him at the council-fire."

"Magua is a great chief."

"Let him prove it, by teaching his nation how to conduct themselves toward our new friends."

"Why did the chief of the Canadas bring his young men into the woods, and fire his cannon at the earthen house?" demanded the subtle Indian.

"To subdue it. My master owns the land, and your father was ordered to drive off these English squatters. They have consented to go, and now he calls them enemies no longer."

"'Tis well. Magua took the hatchet to color it with blood. It is now bright; when it is red, it shall be buried."

"But Magua is pledged not to sully the lilies of France. The enemies of the great king across the salt lake are his enemies; his friends, the friends of the Hurons."

"Friends!" repeated the Indian in scorn. "Let his father give Magua a hand."

Montcalm, who felt that his influence over the warlike tribes he had gathered was to be maintained by concession rather than by power, complied reluctantly with the other's request. The savage placed the fingers of the French commander on a deep scar in his bosom, and then exultingly demanded:

"Does my father know that?"

"What warrior does not? 'Tis where a leaden bullet has cut."

"And this?" continued the Indian, who had turned his naked back to the other, his body being without its usual calico mantle.

"This!—my son has been sadly injured here; who has done this?"

"Magua slept hard in the English wigwams, and the sticks have left their mark," returned the savage, with a hollow laugh, which did not conceal the fierce temper that nearly choked him. Then, recollecting himself, with sudden and native dignity, he added: "Go; teach your young men it is peace. Le Renard Subtil knows how to speak to a Huron warrior."

Without deigning to bestow further words, or to wait for any answer, the savage cast his rifle into the hollow of his arm, and moved silently through the encampment toward the woods where his own tribe was known to lie. Every few yards as he proceeded he was challenged by the sentinels; but he stalked sullenly onward, utterly disregarding the summons of the soldiers, who only spared his life because they knew the air and tread no less than the obstinate daring of an Indian.

Montcalm lingered long and melancholy on the strand where he had been left by his companion, brooding deeply on the temper which his ungovernable ally had just discovered. Already had his fair fame been tarnished by one horrid scene, and in circumstances fearfully resembling those under which he now found himself. As he mused he became keenly sensible of the deep responsibility they assume who disregard the means to attain the end, and of all the danger of setting in motion an engine which it exceeds human power to control. Then shaking off a train of reflections that he accounted a weakness in such a moment of triumph, he retraced his steps toward his tent, giving the order as he passed to make the signal that should arouse the army from its slumbers.

The first tap of the French drums was echoed from the bosom of the fort, and presently the valley was filled with the strains of martial music, rising long, thrilling and lively above the rattling accompaniment. The horns of the victors sounded merry and cheerful flourishes, until the last laggard of the camp was at his post; but the instant the British fifes had blown their shrill signal, they became mute. In the meantime the day had dawned, and when the line of the French army was ready to receive its general, the rays of a brilliant sun were glancing along the glittering array. Then that success, which was already so well known, was officially announced; the favored band who were selected to guard the gates of the fort were detailed, and defiled before their chief; the signal of their approach was given, and all the usual preparations for a change of masters were ordered and executed directly under the guns of the contested works.

A very different scene presented itself within the lines of the Anglo-American army. As soon as the warning signal was given, it exhibited all the signs of a hurried and forced departure. The sullen soldiers shouldered their empty tubes and fell into their places, like men whose blood had been heated by the past contest, and who only desired the opportunity to revenge an indignity which was still wounding to their pride, concealed as it was under the observances of military etiquette.

Women and children ran from place to place, some bearing the scanty remnants of their baggage, and others searching in the ranks for those countenances they looked up to for protection.

Munro appeared among his silent troops firm but dejected. It was evident that the unexpected blow had struck deep into his heart, though he struggled to sustain his misfortune with the port of a man.

Duncan was touched at the quiet and impressive exhibition of his grief. He had discharged his own duty, and he now pressed to the side of the old man, to know in what particular he might serve him.

"My daughters," was the brief but expressive reply.

"Good heavens! are not arrangements already made for their convenience?"

"To-day I am only a soldier, Major Heyward," said the veteran. "All that you see here, claim alike to be my children."

Duncan had heard enough. Without losing one of those moments which had now become so precious, he flew toward the quarters of Munro, in quest of the sisters. He found them on the threshold of the low edifice, already prepared to depart, and surrounded by a clamorous and weeping assemblage of their own sex, that had gathered about the place, with a sort of instinctive consciousness that it was the point most likely to be protected. Though the cheeks of Cora were pale and her countenance anxious, she had lost none of her firmness; but the eyes of Alice were inflamed, and betrayed how long and bitterly she had wept. They both, however, received the young man with undisguised pleasure; the former, for a novelty, being the first to speak.

"The fort is lost," she said, with a melancholy smile; "though our good name, I trust, remains."

"'Tis brighter than ever. But, dearest Miss Munro, it is time to think less of others, and to make some provision for yourself. Military usage—pride—that pride on which you so much value yourself, demands that your father and I should for a little while continue with the troops. Then where to seek a proper protector for you against the confusion and chances of such a scene?"

"None is necessary," returned Cora; "who will dare to injure or insult the daughter of such a father, at a time like this?"

"I would not leave you alone," continued the youth, looking about him in a hurried manner, "for the command of the best regiment in the pay of the king. Remember, our Alice is not gifted with all your firmness, and God only knows the terror she might endure."

"You may be right," Cora replied, smiling again, but far more sadly than before. "Listen! chance has already sent us a friend when he is most needed."

Duncan did listen, and on the instant comprehended her meaning. The low and serious sounds of the sacred music, so well known to the eastern provinces, caught his ear, and instantly drew him to an apartment in an adjacent building, which had already been deserted by its customary tenants. There he found David, pouring out his pious feelings through the only medium in which he ever indulged. Duncan waited, until, by the cessation of the movement of the hand, he believed the strain was ended, when, by touching his shoulder, he drew the attention of the other to himself, and in a few words explained his wishes.

"Even so," replied the single-minded disciple of the King of Israel, when the young man had ended; "I have found much that is comely and melodious in the maidens, and it is fitting that we who have consorted in so much peril, should abide together in peace. I will attend them, when I have completed my morning praise, to which nothing is now wanting but the doxology. Wilt thou bear a part, friend? The meter is common, and the tune 'Southwell'."

Then, extending the little volume, and giving the pitch of the air anew with considerate attention, David recommenced and finished his strains, with a fixedness of manner that it was not easy to interrupt. Heyward was fain to wait until the verse was ended; when, seeing David relieving himself from the spectacles, and replacing the book, he continued.

"It will be your duty to see that none dare to approach the ladies with any rude intention, or to offer insult or taunt at the misfortune of their brave father. In this task you will be seconded by the domestics of their household."

"Even so."

"It is possible that the Indians and stragglers of the enemy may intrude, in which case you will remind them of the terms of the capitulation, and threaten to report their conduct to Montcalm. A word will suffice."

"If not, I have that here which shall," returned David, exhibiting his book, with an air in which meekness and confidence were singularly blended. Here are words which, uttered, or rather thundered, with proper emphasis, and in measured time, shall quiet the most unruly temper:

"'Why rage the heathen furiously'?"

"Enough," said Heyward, interrupting the burst of his musical invocation; "we understand each other; it is time that we should now assume our respective duties."

Gamut cheerfully assented, and together they sought the females. Cora received her new and somewhat extraordinary protector courteously, at least; and even the pallid features of Alice lighted again with some of their native archness as she thanked Heyward for his care. Duncan took occasion to assure them he had done the best that circumstances permitted, and, as he believed, quite enough for the security of their feelings; of danger there was none. He then spoke gladly of his intention to rejoin them the moment he had led the advance a few miles toward the Hudson, and immediately took his leave.

By this time the signal for departure had been given, and the head of the English column was in motion. The sisters started at the sound, and glancing their eyes around, they saw the white uniforms of the French grenadiers, who had already taken possession of the gates of the fort. At that moment an enormous cloud seemed to pass suddenly above their heads, and, looking upward, they discovered that they stood beneath the wide folds of the standard of France.

"Let us go," said Cora; "this is no longer a fit place for the children of an English officer."

Alice clung to the arm of her sister, and together they left the parade, accompanied by the moving throng that surrounded them.

As they passed the gates, the French officers, who had learned their rank, bowed often and low, forbearing, however, to intrude those attentions which they saw, with peculiar tact, might not be agreeable. As every vehicle and each beast of burden was occupied by the sick and wounded, Cora had decided to endure the fatigues of a foot march, rather than interfere with their comforts. Indeed, many a maimed and feeble soldier was compelled to drag his exhausted limbs in the rear of the columns, for the want of the necessary means of conveyance in that wilderness. The whole, however, was in motion; the weak and wounded, groaning and in suffering; their comrades silent and sullen; and the women and children in terror, they knew not of what.

As the confused and timid throng left the protecting mounds of the fort, and issued on the open plain, the whole scene was at once presented to their eyes. At a little distance on the right, and somewhat in the rear, the French army stood to their arms, Montcalm having collected his parties, so soon as his guards had possession of the works. They were attentive but silent observers of the proceedings of the vanquished, failing in none of the stipulated military honors, and offering no taunt or insult, in their success, to their less fortunate foes. Living masses of the English, to the amount, in the whole, of near three thousand, were moving slowly across the plain, toward the common center, and gradually approached each other, as they converged to the point of their march, a vista cut through the lofty trees, where the road to the Hudson entered the forest. Along the sweeping borders of the woods hung a dark cloud of savages, eyeing the passage of their enemies, and hovering at a distance, like vultures who were only kept from swooping on their prey by the presence and restraint of a superior army. A few had straggled among the conquered columns, where they stalked in sullen discontent; attentive, though, as yet, passive observers of the moving multitude.

The advance, with Heyward at its head, had already reached the defile, and was slowly disappearing, when the attention of Cora was drawn to a collection of stragglers by the sounds of contention. A truant provincial was paying the forfeit of his disobedience, by being plundered of those very effects which had caused him to desert his place in the ranks. The man was of powerful frame, and too avaricious to part with his goods without a struggle. Individuals from either party interfered; the one side to prevent and the other to aid in the robbery. Voices grew loud and angry, and a hundred savages appeared, as it were, by magic, where a dozen only had been seen a minute before. It was then that Cora saw the form of Magua gliding among his countrymen, and speaking with his fatal and artful eloquence. The mass of women and children stopped, and hovered together like alarmed and fluttering birds. But the cupidity of the Indian was soon gratified, and the different bodies again moved slowly onward.

The savages now fell back, and seemed content to let their enemies advance without further molestation. But, as the female crowd approached them, the gaudy colors of a shawl attracted the eyes of a wild and untutored Huron. He advanced to seize it without the least hesitation. The woman, more in terror than through love of the ornament, wrapped her child in the coveted article, and folded both more closely to her bosom. Cora was in the act of speaking, with an intent to advise the woman to abandon the trifle, when the savage relinquished his hold of the shawl, and tore the screaming infant from her arms. Abandoning everything to the greedy grasp of those around her, the mother darted, with distraction in her mien, to reclaim her child. The Indian smiled grimly, and extended one hand, in sign of a willingness to exchange, while, with the other, he flourished the babe over his head, holding it by the feet as if to enhance the value of the ransom.

"Here—here—there—all—any—everything!" exclaimed the breathless woman, tearing the lighter articles of dress from her person with ill-directed and trembling fingers; "take all, but give me my babe!"

The savage spurned the worthless rags, and perceiving that the shawl had already become a prize to another, his bantering but sullen smile changing to a gleam of ferocity, he dashed the head of the infant against a rock, and cast its quivering remains to her very feet. For an instant the mother stood, like a statue of despair, looking wildly down at the unseemly object, which had so lately nestled in her bosom and smiled in her face; and then she raised her eyes and countenance toward heaven, as if calling on God to curse the perpetrator of the foul deed. She was spared the sin of such a prayer for, maddened at his disappointment, and excited at the sight of blood, the Huron mercifully drove his tomahawk into her own brain. The mother sank under the blow, and fell, grasping at her child, in death, with the same engrossing love that had caused her to cherish it when living.

At that dangerous moment, Magua placed his hands to his mouth, and raised the fatal and appalling whoop. The scattered Indians started at the well-known cry, as coursers bound at the signal to quit the goal; and directly there arose such a yell along the plain, and through the arches of the wood, as seldom burst from human lips before. They who heard it listened with a curdling horror at the heart, little inferior to that dread which may be expected to attend the blasts of the final summons.

More than two thousand raving savages broke from the forest at the signal, and threw themselves across the fatal plain with instinctive alacrity. We shall not dwell on the revolting horrors that succeeded. Death was everywhere, and in his most terrific and disgusting aspects. Resistance only served to inflame the murderers, who inflicted their furious blows long after their victims were beyond the power of their resentment. The flow of blood might be likened to the outbreaking of a torrent; and as the natives became heated and maddened by the sight, many among them even kneeled to the earth, and drank freely, exultingly, hellishly, of the crimson tide.

The trained bodies of the troops threw themselves quickly into solid masses, endeavoring to awe their assailants by the imposing appearance of a military front. The experiment in some measure succeeded, though far too many suffered their unloaded muskets to be torn from their hands, in the vain hope of appeasing the savages.

In such a scene none had leisure to note the fleeting moments. It might have been ten minutes (it seemed an age) that the sisters had stood riveted to one spot, horror-stricken and nearly helpless. When the first blow was struck, their screaming companions had pressed upon them in a body, rendering flight impossible; and now that fear or death had scattered most, if not all, from around them, they saw no avenue open, but such as conducted to the tomahawks of their foes. On every side arose shrieks, groans, exhortations and curses. At this moment, Alice caught a glimpse of the vast form of her father, moving rapidly across the plain, in the direction of the French army. He was, in truth, proceeding to Montcalm, fearless of every danger, to claim the tardy escort for which he had before conditioned. Fifty glittering axes and barbed spears were offered unheeded at his life, but the savages respected his rank and calmness, even in their fury. The dangerous weapons were brushed aside by the still nervous arm of the veteran, or fell of themselves, after menacing an act that it would seem no one had courage to perform. Fortunately, the vindictive Magua was searching for his victim in the very band the veteran had just quitted.

"Father—father—we are here!" shrieked Alice, as he passed, at no great distance, without appearing to heed them. "Come to us, father, or we die!"

The cry was repeated, and in terms and tones that might have melted a heart of stone, but it was unanswered. Once, indeed, the old man appeared to catch the sound, for he paused and listened; but Alice had dropped senseless on the earth, and Cora had sunk at her side, hovering in untiring tenderness over her lifeless form. Munro shook his head in disappointment, and proceeded, bent on the high duty of his station.

"Lady," said Gamut, who, helpless and useless as he was, had not yet dreamed of deserting his trust, "it is the jubilee of the devils, and this is not a meet place for Christians to tarry in. Let us up and fly."

"Go," said Cora, still gazing at her unconscious sister; "save thyself. To me thou canst not be of further use."

David comprehended the unyielding character of her resolution, by the simple but expressive gesture that accompanied her words. He gazed for a moment at the dusky forms that were acting their hellish rites on every side of him, and his tall person grew more erect while his chest heaved, and every feature swelled, and seemed to speak with the power of the feelings by which he was governed.

"If the Jewish boy might tame the great spirit of Saul by the sound of his harp, and the words of sacred song, it may not be amiss," he said, "to try the potency of music here."

Then raising his voice to its highest tone, he poured out a strain so powerful as to be heard even amid the din of that bloody field. More than one savage rushed toward them, thinking to rifle the unprotected sisters of their attire, and bear away their scalps; but when they found this strange and unmoved figure riveted to his post, they paused to listen. Astonishment soon changed to admiration, and they passed on to other and less courageous victims, openly expressing their satisfaction at the firmness with which the white warrior sang his death song. Encouraged and deluded by his success, David exerted all his powers to extend what he believed so holy an influence. The unwonted sounds caught the ears of a distant savage, who flew raging from group to group, like one who, scorning to touch the vulgar herd, hunted for some victim more worthy of his renown. It was Magua, who uttered a yell of pleasure when he beheld his ancient prisoners again at his mercy.

"Come," he said, laying his soiled hands on the dress of Cora, "the wigwam of the Huron is still open. Is it not better than this place?"

"Away!" cried Cora, veiling her eyes from his revolting aspect.

The Indian laughed tauntingly, as he held up his reeking hand, and answered: "It is red, but it comes from white veins!"

"Monster! there is blood, oceans of blood, upon thy soul; thy spirit has moved this scene."

"Magua is a great chief!" returned the exulting savage, "will the dark-hair go to his tribe?"

"Never! strike if thou wilt, and complete thy revenge." He hesitated a moment, and then catching the light and senseless form of Alice in his arms, the subtle Indian moved swiftly across the plain toward the woods.

"Hold!" shrieked Cora, following wildly on his footsteps; "release the child! wretch! what is't you do?"

But Magua was deaf to her voice; or, rather, he knew his power, and was determined to maintain it.

"Stay—lady—stay," called Gamut, after the unconscious Cora. "The holy charm is beginning to be felt, and soon shalt thou see this horrid tumult stilled."

Perceiving that, in his turn, he was unheeded, the faithful David followed the distracted sister, raising his voice again in sacred song, and sweeping the air to the measure, with his long arm, in diligent accompaniment. In this manner they traversed the plain, through the flying, the wounded and the dead. The fierce Huron was, at any time, sufficient for himself and the victim that he bore; though Cora would have fallen more than once under the blows of her savage enemies, but for the extraordinary being who stalked in her rear, and who now appeared to the astonished natives gifted with the protecting spirit of madness.

Magua, who knew how to avoid the more pressing dangers, and also to elude pursuit, entered the woods through a low ravine, where he quickly found the Narragansetts, which the travelers had abandoned so shortly before, awaiting his appearance, in custody of a savage as fierce and malign in his expression as himself. Laying Alice on one of the horses, he made a sign to Cora to mount the other.

Notwithstanding the horror excited by the presence of her captor, there was a present relief in escaping from the bloody scene enacting on the plain, to which Cora could not be altogether insensible. She took her seat, and held forth her arms for her sister, with an air of entreaty and love that even the Huron could not deny. Placing Alice, then, on the same animal with Cora, he seized the bridle, and commenced his route by plunging deeper into the forest. David, perceiving that he was left alone, utterly disregarded as a subject too worthless even to destroy, threw his long limb across the saddle of the beast they had deserted, and made such progress in the pursuit as the difficulties of the path permitted.

They soon began to ascend; but as the motion had a tendency to revive the dormant faculties of her sister, the attention of Cora was too much divided between the tenderest solicitude in her behalf, and in listening to the cries which were still too audible on the plain, to note the direction in which they journeyed. When, however, they gained the flattened surface of the mountain-top, and approached the eastern precipice, she recognized the spot to which she had once before been led under the more friendly auspices of the scout. Here Magua suffered them to dismount; and notwithstanding their own captivity, the curiosity which seems inseparable from horror, induced them to gaze at the sickening sight below.

The cruel work was still unchecked. On every side the captured were flying before their relentless persecutors, while the armed columns of the Christian king stood fast in an apathy which has never been explained, and which has left an immovable blot on the otherwise fair escutcheon of their leader. Nor was the sword of death stayed until cupidity got the mastery of revenge. Then, indeed, the shrieks of the wounded, and the yells of their murderers grew less frequent, until, finally, the cries of horror were lost to their ear, or were drowned in the loud, long and piercing whoops of the triumphant savages.

CHAPTER XVIII.

"Why, anything;
An honorable murderer, if you will;
For naught I did in hate, but all in honor."
—Othello

The bloody and inhuman scene rather incidentally mentioned than described in the preceding chapter, is conspicuous in the pages of colonial history by the merited title of "The Massacre of William Henry." It so far deepened the stain which a previous and very similar event had left upon the reputation of the French commander that it was not entirely erased by his early and glorious death. It is now becoming obscured by time; and thousands, who know that Montcalm died like a hero on the plains of Abraham, have yet to learn how much he was deficient in that moral courage without which no man can be truly great. Pages might yet be written to prove, from this illustrious example, the defects of human excellence; to show how easy it is for generous sentiments, high courtesy, and chivalrous courage to lose their influence beneath the chilling blight of selfishness, and to exhibit to the world a man who was great in all the minor attributes of character, but who was found wanting when it became necessary to prove how much principle is superior to policy. But the task would exceed our prerogatives; and, as history, like love, is so apt to surround her heroes with an atmosphere of imaginary brightness, it is probable that Louis de Saint Veran will be viewed by posterity only as the gallant defender of his country, while his cruel apathy on the shores of the Oswego and of the Horican will be forgotten. Deeply regretting this weakness on the part of a sister muse, we shall at once retire from her sacred precincts, within the proper limits of our own humble vocation.

The third day from the capture of the fort was drawing to a close, but the business of the narrative must still detain the reader on the shores of the "holy lake." When last seen, the environs of the works were filled with violence and uproar. They were now possessed by stillness and death. The blood-stained conquerors had departed; and their camp, which had so lately rung with the merry rejoicings of a victorious army, lay a silent and deserted city of huts. The fortress was a smoldering ruin; charred rafters, fragments of exploded artillery, and rent mason-work covering its earthen mounds in confused disorder.

A frightful change had also occurred in the season. The sun had hid its warmth behind an impenetrable mass of vapor, and hundreds of human forms, which had blackened beneath the fierce heats of August, were stiffening in their deformity before the blasts of a premature November. The curling and spotless mists, which had been seen sailing above the hills toward the north, were now returning in an interminable dusky sheet, that was urged along by the fury of a tempest. The crowded mirror of the Horican was gone; and, in its place, the green and angry waters lashed the shores, as if indignantly casting back its impurities to the polluted strand. Still the clear fountain retained a portion of its charmed influence, but it reflected only the somber gloom that fell from the impending heavens. That humid and congenial atmosphere which commonly adorned the view, veiling its harshness, and softening its asperities, had disappeared, the northern air poured across the waste of water so harsh and unmingled, that nothing was left to be conjectured by the eye, or fashioned by the fancy.

The fiercer element had cropped the verdure of the plain, which looked as though it were scathed by the consuming lightning. But, here and there, a dark green tuft rose in the midst of the desolation; the earliest fruits of a soil that had been fattened with human blood. The whole landscape, which, seen by a favoring light, and in a genial temperature, had been found so lovely, appeared now like some pictured allegory of life, in which objects were arrayed in their harshest but truest colors, and without the relief of any shadowing.

The solitary and arid blades of grass arose from the passing gusts fearfully perceptible; the bold and rocky mountains were too distinct in their barrenness, and the eye even sought relief, in vain, by attempting to pierce the illimitable void of heaven, which was shut to its gaze by the dusky sheet of ragged and driving vapor.

The wind blew unequally; sometimes sweeping heavily along the ground, seeming to whisper its moanings in the cold ears of the dead, then rising in a shrill and mournful whistling, it entered the forest with a rush that filled the air with the leaves and branches it scattered in its path. Amid the unnatural shower, a few hungry ravens struggled with the gale; but no sooner was the green ocean of woods which stretched beneath them, passed, than they gladly stopped, at random, to their hideous banquet.

In short, it was a scene of wildness and desolation; and it appeared as if all who had profanely entered it had been stricken, at a blow, by the relentless arm of death. But the prohibition had ceased; and for the first time since the perpetrators of those foul deeds which had assisted to disfigure the scene were gone, living human beings had now presumed to approach the place.

About an hour before the setting of the sun, on the day already mentioned, the forms of five men might have been seen issuing from the narrow vista of trees, where the path to the Hudson entered the forest, and advancing in the direction of the ruined works. At first their progress was slow and guarded, as though they entered with reluctance amid the horrors of the post, or dreaded the renewal of its frightful incidents. A light figure preceded the rest of the party, with the caution and activity of a native; ascending every hillock to reconnoiter, and indicating by gestures, to his companions, the route he deemed it most prudent to pursue. Nor were those in the rear wanting in every caution and foresight known to forest warfare. One among them, he also was an Indian, moved a little on one flank, and watched the margin of the woods, with eyes long accustomed to read the smallest sign of danger. The remaining three were white, though clad in vestments adapted, both in quality and color, to their present hazardous pursuit—that of hanging on the skirts of a retiring army in the wilderness.

The effects produced by the appalling sights that constantly arose in their path to the lake shore, were as different as the characters of the respective individuals who composed the party. The youth in front threw serious but furtive glances at the mangled victims, as he stepped lightly across the plain, afraid to exhibit his feelings, and yet too inexperienced to quell entirely their sudden and powerful influence. His red associate, however, was superior to such a weakness. He passed the groups of dead with a steadiness of purpose, and an eye so calm, that nothing but long and inveterate practise could enable him to maintain. The sensations produced in the minds of even the white men were different, though uniformly sorrowful. One, whose gray locks and furrowed lineaments, blending with a martial air and tread, betrayed, in spite of the disguise of a woodsman's dress, a man long experienced in scenes of war, was not ashamed to groan aloud, whenever a spectacle of more than usual horror came under his view. The young man at his elbow shuddered, but seemed to suppress his feelings in tenderness to his companion. Of them all, the straggler who brought up the rear appeared alone to betray his real thoughts, without fear of observation or dread of consequences. He gazed at the most appalling sight with eyes and muscles that knew not how to waver, but with execrations so bitter and deep as to denote how much he denounced the crime of his enemies.

The reader will perceive at once, in these respective characters, the Mohicans, and their white friend, the scout; together with Munro and Heyward. It was, in truth, the father in quest of his children, attended by the youth who felt so deep a stake in their happiness, and those brave and trusty foresters, who had already proved their skill and fidelity through the trying scenes related.

When Uncas, who moved in front, had reached the center of the plain, he raised a cry that drew his companions in a body to the spot. The young warrior had halted over a group of females who lay in a cluster, a confused mass of dead. Notwithstanding the revolting horror of the exhibition, Munro and Heyward flew toward the festering heap, endeavoring, with a love that no unseemliness could extinguish, to discover whether any vestiges of those they sought were to be seen among the tattered and many-colored garments. The father and the lover found instant relief in the search; though each was condemned again to experience the misery of an uncertainty that was hardly less insupportable than the most revolting truth. They were standing, silent and thoughtful, around the melancholy pile, when the scout approached. Eyeing the sad spectacle with an angry countenance, the sturdy woodsman, for the first time since his entering the plain, spoke intelligibly and aloud:

"I have been on many a shocking field, and have followed a trail of blood for weary miles," he said, "but never have I found the hand of the devil so plain as it is here to be seen! Revenge is an Indian feeling, and all who know me know that there is no cross in my veins; but this much will I say—here, in the face of heaven, and with the power of the Lord so manifest in this howling wilderness—that should these Frenchers ever trust themselves again within the range of a ragged bullet, there is one rifle which shall play its part so long as flint will fire or powder burn! I leave the tomahawk and knife to such as have a natural gift to use them. What say you, Chingachgook," he added, in Delaware; "shall the Hurons boast of this to their women when the deep snows come?"

A gleam of resentment flashed across the dark lineaments of the Mohican chief; he loosened his knife in his sheath; and then turning calmly from the sight, his countenance settled into a repose as deep as if he knew the instigation of passion.

"Montcalm! Montcalm!" continued the deeply resentful and less self-restrained scout; "they say a time must come when all the deeds done in the flesh will be seen at a single look; and that by eyes cleared from mortal infirmities. Woe betide the wretch who is born to behold this plain, with the judgment hanging about his soul! Ha—as I am a man of white blood, yonder lies a red-skin, without the hair of his head where nature rooted it! Look to him, Delaware; it may be one of your missing people; and he should have burial like a stout warrior. I see it in your eye, Sagamore; a Huron pays for this, afore the fall winds have blown away the scent of the blood!"

Chingachgook approached the mutilated form, and, turning it over, he found the distinguishing marks of one of those six allied tribes, or nations, as they were called, who, while they fought in the English ranks, were so deadly hostile to his own people. Spurning the loathsome object with his foot, he turned from it with the same indifference he would have quitted a brute carcass. The scout comprehended the action, and very deliberately pursued his own way, continuing, however, his denunciations against the French commander in the same resentful strain.

"Nothing but vast wisdom and unlimited power should dare to sweep off men in multitudes," he added; "for it is only the one that can know the necessity of the judgment; and what is there, short of the other, that can replace the creatures of the Lord? I hold it a sin to kill the second buck afore the first is eaten, unless a march in front, or an ambushment, be contemplated. It is a different matter with a few warriors in open and rugged fight, for 'tis their gift to die with the rifle or the tomahawk in hand; according as their natures may happen to be, white or red. Uncas, come this way, lad, and let the ravens settle upon the Mingo. I know, from often seeing it, that they have a craving for the flesh of an Oneida; and it is as well to let the bird follow the gift of its natural appetite."

"Hugh!" exclaimed the young Mohican, rising on the extremities of his feet, and gazing intently in his front, frightening the ravens to some other prey by the sound and the action.

"What is it, boy?" whispered the scout, lowering his tall form into a crouching attitude, like a panther about to take his leap; "God send it be a tardy Frencher, skulking for plunder. I do believe 'killdeer' would take an uncommon range today!"

Uncas, without making any reply, bounded away from the spot, and in the next instant he was seen tearing from a bush, and waving in triumph, a fragment of the green riding-veil of Cora. The movement, the exhibition, and the cry which again burst from the lips of the young Mohican, instantly drew the whole party about him.

"My child!" said Munro, speaking quickly and wildly; "give me my child!"

"Uncas will try," was the short and touching answer.

The simple but meaning assurance was lost on the father, who seized the piece of gauze, and crushed it in his hand, while his eyes roamed fearfully among the bushes, as if he equally dreaded and hoped for the secrets they might reveal.

"Here are no dead," said Heyward; "the storm seems not to have passed this way."

"That's manifest; and clearer than the heavens above our heads," returned the undisturbed scout; "but either she, or they that have robbed her, have passed the bush; for I remember the rag she wore to hide a face that all did love to look upon. Uncas, you are right; the dark-hair has been here, and she has fled like a frightened fawn, to the wood; none who could fly would remain to be murdered. Let us search for the marks she left; for, to Indian eyes, I sometimes think a humming-bird leaves his trail in the air."

The young Mohican darted away at the suggestion, and the scout had hardly done speaking, before the former raised a cry of success from the margin of the forest. On reaching the spot, the anxious party perceived another portion of the veil fluttering on the lower branch of a beech.

"Softly, softly," said the scout, extending his long rifle in front of the eager Heyward; "we now know our work, but the beauty of the trail must not be deformed. A step too soon may give us hours of trouble. We have them, though; that much is beyond denial."

"Bless ye, bless ye, worthy man!" exclaimed Munro; "whither then, have they fled, and where are my babes?"

"The path they have taken depends on many chances. If they have gone alone, they are quite as likely to move in a circle as straight, and they may be within a dozen miles of us; but if the Hurons, or any of the French Indians, have laid hands on them, 'tis probably they are now near the borders of the Canadas. But what matters that?" continued the deliberate scout, observing the powerful anxiety and disappointment the listeners exhibited; "here are the Mohicans and I on one end of the trail, and, rely on it, we find the other, though they should be a hundred leagues asunder! Gently, gently, Uncas, you are as impatient as a man in the settlements; you forget that light feet leave but faint marks!"

"Hugh!" exclaimed Chingachgook, who had been occupied in examining an opening that had been evidently made through the low underbrush which skirted the forest; and who now stood erect, as he pointed downward, in the attitude and with the air of a man who beheld a disgusting serpent.

"Here is the palpable impression of the footstep of a man," cried Heyward, bending over the indicated spot; "he has trod in the margin of this pool, and the mark cannot be mistaken. They are captives."

"Better so than left to starve in the wilderness," returned the scout; "and they will leave a wider trail. I would wager fifty beaver skins against as many flints, that the Mohicans and I enter their wigwams within the month! Stoop to it, Uncas, and try what you can make of the moccasin; for moccasin it plainly is, and no shoe."

The young Mohican bent over the track, and removing the scattered leaves from around the place, he examined it with much of that sort of scrutiny that a money dealer, in these days of pecuniary doubts, would bestow on a suspected due-bill. At length he arose from his knees, satisfied with the result of the examination.

"Well, boy," demanded the attentive scout; "what does it say? Can you make anything of the tell-tale?"

"Le Renard Subtil!"

"Ha! that rampaging devil again! there will never be an end of his loping till 'killdeer' has said a friendly word to him."

Heyward reluctantly admitted the truth of this intelligence, and now expressed rather his hopes than his doubts by saying:

"One moccasin is so much like another, it is probable there is some mistake."

"One moccasin like another! you may as well say that one foot is like another; though we all know that some are long, and others short; some broad and others narrow; some with high, and some with low insteps; some intoed, and some out. One moccasin is no more like another than one book is like another: though they who can read in one are seldom able to tell the marks of the other. Which is all ordered for the best, giving to every man his natural advantages. Let me get down to it, Uncas; neither book nor moccasin is the worse for having two opinions, instead of one." The scout stooped to the task, and instantly added:

"You are right, boy; here is the patch we saw so often in the other chase. And the fellow will drink when he can get an opportunity; your drinking Indian always learns to walk with a wider toe than the natural savage, it being the gift of a drunkard to straddle, whether of white or red skin. 'Tis just the length and breadth, too! look at it, Sagamore; you measured the prints more than once, when we hunted the varmints from Glenn's to the health springs."

Chingachgook complied; and after finishing his short examination, he arose, and with a quiet demeanor, he merely pronounced the word:

"Magua!"

"Ay, 'tis a settled thing; here, then, have passed the dark-hair and Magua."

"And not Alice?" demanded Heyward.

"Of her we have not yet seen the signs," returned the scout, looking closely around at the trees, the bushes and the ground. "What have we there? Uncas, bring hither the thing you see dangling from yonder thorn-bush."

When the Indian had complied, the scout received the prize, and holding it on high, he laughed in his silent but heartfelt manner.

"'Tis the tooting we'pon of the singer! now we shall have a trail a priest might travel," he said. "Uncas, look for the marks of a shoe that is long enough to uphold six feet two of tottering human flesh. I begin to have some hopes of the fellow, since he has given up squalling to follow some better trade."

"At least he has been faithful to his trust," said Heyward. "And Cora and Alice are not without a friend."

"Yes," said Hawkeye, dropping his rifle, and leaning on it with an air of visible contempt, "he will do their singing. Can he slay a buck for their dinner; journey by the moss on the beeches, or cut the throat of a Huron? If not, the first catbird* he meets is the cleverer of the two. Well, boy, any signs of such a foundation?"

"Here is something like the footstep of one who has worn a shoe; can it be that of our friend?"

---

* The powers of the American mocking-bird are generally known. But the true mocking-bird is not found so far north as the state of New York, where it has, however, two substitutes of inferior excellence, the catbird, so often named by the scout, and the bird vulgarly called ground-thresher. Either of these last two birds is superior to the nightingale or the lark, though, in general, the American birds are less musical than those of Europe.

"Touch the leaves lightly or you'll disconsart the formation. That! that is the print of a foot, but 'tis the dark-hair's; and small it is, too, for one of such a noble height and grand appearance. The singer would cover it with his heel."

"Where! let me look on the footsteps of my child," said Munro, shoving the bushes aside, and bending fondly over the nearly obliterated impression. Though the tread which had left the mark had been light and rapid, it was still plainly visible. The aged soldier examined it with eyes that grew dim as he gazed; nor did he rise from this stooping posture until Heyward saw that he had watered the trace of his daughter's passage with a scalding tear. Willing to divert a distress which threatened each moment to break through the restraint of appearances, by giving the veteran something to do, the young man said to the scout:

"As we now possess these infallible signs, let us commence our march. A moment, at such a time, will appear an age to the captives."

"It is not the swiftest leaping deer that gives the longest chase," returned Hawkeye, without moving his eyes from the different marks that had come under his view; "we know that the rampaging Huron has passed, and the dark-hair, and the singer, but where is she of the yellow locks and blue eyes? Though little, and far from being as bold as her sister, she is fair to the view, and pleasant in discourse. Has she no friend, that none care for her?"

"God forbid she should ever want hundreds! Are we not now in her pursuit? For one, I will never cease the search till she be found."

"In that case we may have to journey by different paths; for here she has not passed, light and little as her footsteps would be."

Heyward drew back, all his ardor to proceed seeming to vanish on the instant. Without attending to this sudden change in the other's humor, the scout after musing a moment continued:

"There is no woman in this wilderness could leave such a print as that, but the dark-hair or her sister. We know that the first has been here, but where are the signs of the other? Let us push deeper on the trail, and if nothing offers, we must go back to the plain and strike another scent. Move on, Uncas, and keep your eyes on the dried leaves. I will watch the bushes, while your father shall run with a low nose to the ground. Move on, friends; the sun is getting behind the hills."

"Is there nothing that I can do?" demanded the anxious Heyward.

"You?" repeated the scout, who, with his red friends, was already advancing in the order he had prescribed; "yes, you can keep in our rear and be careful not to cross the trail."

Before they had proceeded many rods, the Indians stopped, and appeared to gaze at some signs on the earth with more than their usual keenness. Both father and son spoke quick and loud, now looking at the object of their mutual admiration, and now regarding each other with the most unequivocal pleasure.

"They have found the little foot!" exclaimed the scout, moving forward, without attending further to his own portion of the duty. "What have we here? An ambushment has been planted in the spot! No, by the truest rifle on the frontiers, here have been them one-sided horses again! Now the whole secret is out, and all is plain as the north star at midnight. Yes, here they have mounted. There the beasts have been bound to a sapling, in waiting; and yonder runs the broad path away to the north, in full sweep for the Canadas."

"But still there are no signs of Alice, of the younger Miss Munro," said Duncan.

"Unless the shining bauble Uncas has just lifted from the ground should prove one. Pass it this way, lad, that we may look at it."

Heyward instantly knew it for a trinket that Alice was fond of wearing, and which he recollected, with the tenacious memory of a lover, to have seen, on the fatal morning of the massacre, dangling from the fair neck of his mistress. He seized the highly prized jewel; and as he proclaimed the fact, it vanished from the eyes of the wondering scout, who in vain looked for it on the ground, long after it was warmly pressed against the beating heart of Duncan.

"Pshaw!" said the disappointed Hawkeye, ceasing to rake the leaves with the breech of his rifle; "'tis a certain sign of age, when the sight begins to weaken. Such a glittering gewgaw, and not to be seen! Well, well, I can squint along a clouded barrel yet, and that is enough to settle all disputes between me and the Mingoes. I should like to find the thing, too, if it were only to carry it to the right owner, and that would be bringing the two ends of what I call a long trail together, for by this time the broad St. Lawrence, or perhaps, the Great Lakes themselves, are between us."

"So much the more reason why we should not delay our march," returned Heyward; "let us proceed."

"Young blood and hot blood, they say, are much the same thing. We are not about to start on a squirrel hunt, or to drive a deer into the Horican, but to outlie for days and nights, and to stretch across a wilderness where the feet of men seldom go, and where no bookish knowledge would carry you through harmless. An Indian never starts on such an expedition without smoking over his council-fire; and, though a man of white blood, I honor their customs in this particular, seeing that they are deliberate and wise. We will, therefore, go back, and light our fire to-night in the ruins of the old fort, and in the morning we shall be fresh, and ready to undertake our work like men, and not like babbling women or eager boys."

Heyward saw, by the manner of the scout, that altercation would be useless. Munro had again sunk into that sort of apathy which had beset him since his late overwhelming misfortunes, and from which he was apparently to be roused only by some new and powerful excitement. Making a merit of necessity, the young man took the veteran by the arm, and followed in the footsteps of the Indians and the scout, who had already begun to retrace the path which conducted them to the plain.

## CHAPTER XIX.

> "Salar.—Why, I am sure, if he forfeit, thou wilt not take
> his flesh; what's that good for?
> Shy.—To bait fish withal; if it will feed nothing else, it
> will feed my revenge."
> —Merchant of Venice

The shades of evening had come to increase the dreariness of the place, when the party entered the ruins of William Henry. The scout and his companions immediately made their preparations to pass the night there; but with an earnestness and sobriety of demeanor that betrayed how much the unusual horrors they had just witnessed worked on even their practised feelings. A few fragments of rafters were reared against a blackened wall; and when Uncas had covered them slightly with brush, the temporary accommodations were deemed sufficient. The young Indian pointed toward his rude hut when his labor was ended; and Heyward, who understood the meaning of the silent gestures, gently urged Munro to enter. Leaving the bereaved old man alone with his sorrows, Duncan immediately returned into the open air, too much excited himself to seek the repose he had recommended to his veteran friend.

While Hawkeye and the Indians lighted their fire and took their evening's repast, a frugal meal of dried bear's meat, the young man paid a visit to that curtain of the dilapidated fort which looked out on the sheet of the Horican. The wind had fallen, and the waves were already rolling on the sandy beach beneath him, in a more regular and tempered succession. The clouds, as if tired of their furious chase, were breaking asunder; the heavier volumes, gathering in black masses about the horizon, while the lighter scud still hurried above the water, or eddied among the tops of the mountains, like broken flights of birds, hovering around their roosts. Here and there, a red and fiery star struggled through the drifting vapor, furnishing a lurid gleam of brightness to the dull aspect of the heavens. Within the bosom of the encircling hills, an impenetrable darkness had already settled; and the plain lay like a vast and deserted charnel-house, without omen or whisper to disturb the slumbers of its numerous and hapless tenants.

Of this scene, so chillingly in accordance with the past, Duncan stood for many minutes a rapt observer. His eyes wandered from the bosom of the mound, where the foresters were seated around their glimmering fire, to the fainter light which still lingered in the skies, and then rested long and anxiously on the embodied gloom, which lay like a dreary void on that side of him where the dead reposed. He soon fancied that inexplicable sounds arose from the place, though so indistinct and stolen, as to render not only their nature but even their existence uncertain. Ashamed of his apprehensions, the young man turned toward the water, and strove to divert his attention to the mimic stars that dimly glimmered on its moving surface. Still, his too-conscious ears performed their ungrateful duty, as if to warn him of some lurking danger. At length, a swift trampling seemed, quite audibly, to rush athwart the darkness. Unable any longer to quiet his uneasiness, Duncan spoke in a low voice to the scout, requesting him to ascend the mound to the place where he stood. Hawkeye threw his rifle across an arm and complied, but with an air so unmoved and calm, as to prove how much he counted on the security of their position.

"Listen!" said Duncan, when the other placed himself deliberately at his elbow; "there are suppressed noises on the plain which may show Montcalm has not yet entirely deserted his conquest."

"Then ears are better than eyes," said the undisturbed scout, who, having just deposited a portion of a bear between his grinders, spoke thick and slow, like one whose mouth was doubly occupied. "I myself saw him caged in Ty, with all his host; for your Frenchers, when they have done a clever thing, like to get back, and have a dance, or a merry-making, with the women over their success."

"I know not. An Indian seldom sleeps in war, and plunder may keep a Huron here after his tribe has departed. It would be well to extinguish the fire, and have a watch—listen! you hear the noise I mean!"

"An Indian more rarely lurks about the graves. Though ready to slay, and not over regardful of the means, he is commonly content with the scalp, unless when blood is hot, and temper up; but after spirit is once fairly gone, he forgets his enmity, and is willing to let the dead find their natural rest. Speaking of spirits, major, are you of opinion that the heaven of a red-skin and of us whites will be of one and the same?"

"No doubt—no doubt. I thought I heard it again! or was it the rustling of the leaves in the top of the beech?"

"For my own part," continued Hawkeye, turning his face for a moment in the direction indicated by Heyward, but with a vacant and careless manner, "I believe that paradise is ordained for happiness; and that men will be indulged in it according to their dispositions and gifts. I, therefore, judge that a red-skin is not far from the truth when he believes he is to find them glorious hunting grounds of which his traditions tell; nor, for that matter, do I think it would be any disparagement to a man without a cross to pass his time—"

"You hear it again?" interrupted Duncan.

"Ay, ay; when food is scarce, and when food is plenty, a wolf grows bold," said the unmoved scout. "There would be picking, too, among the skins of the devils, if there was light and time for the sport. But, concerning the life that is to come, major; I have heard preachers say, in the settlements, that heaven was a place of rest. Now, men's minds differ as to their ideas of enjoyment. For myself, and I say it with reverence to the ordering of Providence, it would be no great indulgence to be kept shut up in those mansions of which they preach, having a natural longing for motion and the chase."

Duncan, who was now made to understand the nature of the noise he had heard, answered, with more attention to the subject which the humor of the scout had chosen for discussion, by saying:

"It is difficult to account for the feelings that may attend the last great change."

"It would be a change, indeed, for a man who has passed his days in the open air," returned the single-minded scout; "and who has so often broken his fast on the head waters of the Hudson, to sleep within sound of the roaring Mohawk. But it is a comfort to know we serve a merciful Master, though we do it each after his fashion, and with great tracts of wilderness atween us—what goes there?"

"Is it not the rushing of the wolves you have mentioned?"

Hawkeye slowly shook his head, and beckoned for Duncan to follow him to a spot to which the glare from the fire did not extend. When he had taken this precaution, the scout placed himself in an attitude of intense attention and listened long and keenly for a repetition of the low sound that had so unexpectedly startled him. His vigilance, however, seemed exercised in vain; for after a fruitless pause, he whispered to Duncan:

"We must give a call to Uncas. The boy has Indian senses, and he may hear what is hid from us; for, being a white-skin, I will not deny my nature."

The young Mohican, who was conversing in a low voice with his father, started as he heard the moaning of an owl, and, springing on his feet, he looked toward the black mounds, as if seeking the place whence the sounds proceeded. The scout repeated the call, and in a few moments, Duncan saw the figure of Uncas stealing cautiously along the rampart, to the spot where they stood.

Hawkeye explained his wishes in a very few words, which were spoken in the Delaware tongue. So soon as Uncas was in possession of the reason why he was summoned, he threw himself flat on the turf; where, to the eyes of Duncan, he appeared to lie quiet and motionless. Surprised at the immovable attitude of the young warrior, and curious to observe the manner in which he employed his faculties to obtain the desired information, Heyward advanced a few steps, and bent over the dark object on which he had kept his eye riveted. Then it was he discovered that the form of Uncas vanished, and that he beheld only the dark outline of an inequality in the embankment.

"What has become of the Mohican?" he demanded of the scout, stepping back in amazement; "it was here that I saw him fall, and could have sworn that here he yet remained."

"Hist! speak lower; for we know not what ears are open, and the Mingoes are a quick-witted breed. As for Uncas, he is out on the plain, and the Maquas, if any such are about us, will find their equal."

"You think that Montcalm has not called off all his Indians? Let us give the alarm to our companions, that we may stand to our arms. Here are five of us, who are not unused to meet an enemy."

"Not a word to either, as you value your life. Look at the Sagamore, how like a grand Indian chief he sits by the fire. If there are any skulkers out in the darkness, they will never discover, by his countenance, that we suspect danger at hand."

"But they may discover him, and it will prove his death. His person can be too plainly seen by the light of that fire, and he will become the first and most certain victim."

"It is undeniable that now you speak the truth," returned the scout, betraying more anxiety than was usual; "yet what can be done? A single suspicious look might bring on an attack before we are ready to receive it. He knows, by the call I gave to Uncas, that we have struck a scent; I will tell him that we are on the trail of the Mingoes; his Indian nature will teach him how to act."

The scout applied his fingers to his mouth, and raised a low hissing sound, that caused Duncan at first to start aside, believing that he heard a serpent. The head of Chingachgook was resting on a hand, as he sat musing by himself but the moment he had heard the warning of the animal whose name he bore, he arose to an upright position, and his dark eyes glanced swiftly and keenly on every side of him. With his sudden and, perhaps, involuntary movement, every appearance of surprise or alarm ended. His rifle lay untouched, and apparently unnoticed, within reach of his hand. The tomahawk that he had loosened in his belt for the sake of ease, was even suffered to fall from its usual situation to the ground, and his form seemed to sink, like that of a man whose nerves and sinews were suffered to relax for the purpose of rest. Cunningly resuming his former position, though with a change of hands, as if the movement had been made merely to relieve the limb, the native awaited the result with a calmness and fortitude that none but an Indian warrior would have known how to exercise.

But Heyward saw that while to a less instructed eye the Mohican chief appeared to slumber, his nostrils were expanded, his head was turned a little to one side, as if to assist the organs of hearing, and that his quick and rapid glances ran incessantly over every object within the power of his vision.

"See the noble fellow!" whispered Hawkeye, pressing the arm of Heyward; "he knows that a look or a motion might disconsart our schemes, and put us at the mercy of them imps—"

He was interrupted by the flash and report of a rifle. The air was filled with sparks of fire, around that spot where the eyes of Heyward were still fastened, with admiration and wonder. A second look told him that Chingachgook had disappeared in the confusion. In the meantime, the scout had thrown forward his rifle, like one prepared for service, and awaited impatiently the moment when an enemy might rise to view. But with the solitary and fruitless attempt made on the life of Chingachgook, the attack appeared to have terminated. Once or twice the listeners thought they could distinguish the distant rustling of bushes, as bodies of some unknown description rushed through them; nor was it long before Hawkeye pointed out the "scampering of the wolves," as they fled precipitately before the passage of some intruder on their proper domains. After an impatient and breathless pause, a plunge was heard in the water, and it was immediately followed by the report of another rifle.

"There goes Uncas!" said the scout; "the boy bears a smart piece! I know its crack, as well as a father knows the language of his child, for I carried the gun myself until a better offered."

"What can this mean?" demanded Duncan, "we are watched, and, as it would seem, marked for destruction."

"Yonder scattered brand can witness that no good was intended, and this Indian will testify that no harm has been done," returned the scout, dropping his rifle across his arm again, and following Chingachgook, who just then reappeared within the circle of light, into the bosom of the work. "How is it, Sagamore? Are the Mingoes upon us in earnest, or is it only one of those reptiles who hang upon the skirts of a war-party, to scalp the dead, go in, and make their boast among the squaws of the valiant deeds done on the pale faces?"

Chingachgook very quietly resumed his seat; nor did he make any reply, until after he had examined the firebrand which had been struck by the bullet that had nearly proved fatal to himself. After which he was content to reply, holding a single finger up to view, with the English monosyllable:

"One."

"I thought as much," returned Hawkeye, seating himself; "and as he had got the cover of the lake afore Uncas pulled upon him, it is more than probable the knave will sing his lies about some great ambushment, in which he was outlying on the trail of two Mohicans and a white hunter—for the officers can be considered as little better than idlers in such a scrimmage. Well, let him—let him. There are always some honest men in every nation, though heaven knows, too, that they are scarce among the Maquas, to look down an upstart when he brags ag'in the face of reason. The varlet sent his lead within whistle of your ears, Sagamore."

Chingachgook turned a calm and incurious eye toward the place where the ball had struck, and then resumed his former attitude, with a composure that could not be disturbed by so trifling an incident. Just then Uncas glided into the circle, and seated himself at the fire, with the same appearance of indifference as was maintained by his father.

Of these several moments Heyward was a deeply interested and wondering observer. It appeared to him as though the foresters had some secret means of intelligence, which had escaped the vigilance of his own faculties. In place of that eager and garrulous narration with which a white youth would have endeavored to communicate, and perhaps exaggerate, that which had passed out in the darkness of the plain, the young warrior was seemingly content to let his deeds speak for themselves. It was, in fact, neither the moment nor the occasion for an Indian to boast of his exploits; and it is probably that, had Heyward neglected to inquire, not another syllable would, just then, have been uttered on the subject.

"What has become of our enemy, Uncas?" demanded Duncan; "we heard your rifle, and hoped you had not fired in vain."

The young chief removed a fold of his hunting skirt, and quietly exposed the fatal tuft of hair, which he bore as the symbol of victory. Chingachgook laid his hand on the scalp, and considered it for a moment with deep attention. Then dropping it, with disgust depicted in his strong features, he ejaculated:

"Oneida!"

"Oneida!" repeated the scout, who was fast losing his interest in the scene, in an apathy nearly assimilated to that of his red associates, but who now advanced in uncommon earnestness to regard the bloody badge. "By the Lord, if the Oneidas are outlying upon the trail, we shall by flanked by devils on every side of us! Now, to white eyes there is no difference between this bit of skin and that of any other Indian, and yet the Sagamore declares it came from the poll of a Mingo; nay, he even names the tribe of the poor devil, with as much ease as if the scalp was the leaf of a book, and each hair a letter. What right have Christian whites to boast of their learning, when a savage can read a language that would prove too much for the wisest of them all! What say you, lad, of what people was the knave?"

Uncas raised his eyes to the face of the scout, and answered, in his soft voice:

"Oneida."

"Oneida, again! when one Indian makes a declaration it is commonly true; but when he is supported by his people, set it down as gospel!"

"The poor fellow has mistaken us for French," said Heyward; "or he would not have attempted the life of a friend."

"He mistake a Mohican in his paint for a Huron! You would be as likely to mistake the white-coated grenadiers of Montcalm for the scarlet jackets of the Royal Americans," returned the scout. "No, no, the sarpent knew his errand; nor was there any great mistake in the matter, for there is but little love atween a Delaware and a Mingo, let their tribes go out to fight for whom they may, in a white quarrel. For that matter, though the Oneidas do serve his sacred majesty, who is my sovereign lord and master, I should not have deliberated long about letting off 'killdeer' at the imp myself, had luck thrown him in my way."

"That would have been an abuse of our treaties, and unworthy of your character."

"When a man consort much with a people," continued Hawkeye, "if they were honest and he no knave, love will grow up atwixt them. It is true that white cunning has managed to throw the tribes into great confusion, as respects friends and enemies; so that the Hurons and the Oneidas, who speak the same tongue, or what may be called the same, take each other's scalps, and the Delawares are divided among themselves; a few hanging about their great council-fire on their own river, and fighting on the same side with the Mingoes while the greater part are in the Canadas, out of natural enmity to the Maquas—thus throwing everything into disorder, and destroying all the harmony of warfare. Yet a red natur' is not likely to alter with every shift of policy; so that the love atwixt a Mohican and a Mingo is much like the regard between a white man and a sarpent."

"I regret to hear it; for I had believed those natives who dwelt within our boundaries had found us too just and liberal, not to identify themselves fully with our quarrels."

"Why, I believe it is natur' to give a preference to one's own quarrels before those of strangers. Now, for myself, I do love justice; and, therefore, I will not say I hate a Mingo, for that may be unsuitable to my color and my religion, though I will just repeat, it may have been owing to the night that 'killdeer' had no hand in the death of this skulking Oneida."

Then, as if satisfied with the force of his own reasons, whatever might be their effect on the opinions of the other disputant, the honest but implacable woodsman turned from the fire, content to let the controversy slumber. Heyward withdrew to the rampart, too uneasy and too little accustomed to the warfare of the woods to remain at ease under the possibility of such insidious attacks. Not so, however, with the scout and the Mohicans. Those acute and long-practised senses, whose powers so often exceed the limits of all ordinary credulity, after having detected the danger, had enabled them to ascertain its magnitude and duration. Not one of the three appeared in the least to doubt their perfect security, as was indicated by the preparations that were soon made to sit in council over their future proceedings.

The confusion of nations, and even of tribes, to which Hawkeye alluded, existed at that period in the fullest force. The great tie of language, and, of course, of a common origin, was severed in many places; and it was one of its consequences, that the Delaware and the Mingo (as the people of the Six Nations were called) were found fighting in the same ranks, while the latter sought the scalp of the Huron, though believed to be the root of his own stock. The Delawares were even divided among themselves. Though love for the soil which had belonged to his ancestors kept the Sagamore of the Mohicans with a small band of followers who were serving at Edward, under the banners of the English king, by far the largest portion of his nation were known to be in the field as allies of Montcalm. The reader probably knows, if enough has not already been gleaned form this narrative, that the Delaware, or Lenape, claimed to be the progenitors of that numerous people, who once were masters of most of the eastern and northern states of America, of whom the community of the Mohicans was an ancient and highly honored member.

It was, of course, with a perfect understanding of the minute and intricate interests which had armed friend against friend, and brought natural enemies to combat by each other's side, that the scout and his companions now disposed themselves to deliberate on the measures that were to govern their future movements, amid so many jarring and savage races of men. Duncan knew enough of Indian customs to understand the reason that the fire was replenished, and why the warriors, not excepting Hawkeye, took their seats within the curl of its smoke with so much gravity and decorum. Placing himself at an angle of the works, where he might be a spectator of the scene without, he awaited the result with as much patience as he could summon.

After a short and impressive pause, Chingachgook lighted a pipe whose bowl was curiously carved in one of the soft stones of the country, and whose stem was a tube of wood, and commenced smoking. When he had inhaled enough of the fragrance of the soothing weed, he passed the instrument into the hands of the scout. In this manner the pipe had made its rounds three several times, amid the most profound silence, before either of the party opened his lips. Then the Sagamore, as the oldest and highest in rank, in a few calm and dignified words, proposed the subject for deliberation. He was answered by the scout; and Chingachgook rejoined, when the other objected to his opinions. But the youthful Uncas continued a silent and respectful listener, until Hawkeye, in complaisance, demanded his opinion. Heyward gathered from the manners of the different speakers, that the father and son espoused one side of a disputed question, while the white man maintained the other. The contest gradually grew warmer, until it was quite evident the feelings of the speakers began to be somewhat enlisted in the debate.

Notwithstanding the increasing warmth of the amicable contest, the most decorous Christian assembly, not even excepting those in which its reverend ministers are collected, might have learned a wholesome lesson of moderation from the forbearance and courtesy of the disputants. The words of Uncas were received with the same deep attention as those which fell from the maturer wisdom of his father; and so far from manifesting any impatience, neither spoke in reply, until a few moments of silent meditation were, seemingly, bestowed in deliberating on what had already been said.

The language of the Mohicans was accompanied by gestures so direct and natural that Heyward had but little difficulty in following the thread of their argument. On the other hand, the scout was obscure; because from the lingering pride of color, he rather affected the cold and artificial manner which characterizes all classes of Anglo-Americans when unexcited. By the frequency with which the Indians described the marks of a forest trial, it was evident they urged a pursuit by land, while the repeated sweep of Hawkeye's arm toward the Horican denoted that he was for a passage across its waters.

The latter was to every appearance fast losing ground, and the point was about to be decided against him, when he arose to his feet, and shaking off his apathy, he suddenly assumed the manner of an Indian, and adopted all the arts of native eloquence. Elevating an arm, he pointed out the track of the sun, repeating the gesture for every day that was necessary to accomplish their objects. Then he delineated a long and painful path, amid rocks and water-courses. The age and weakness of the slumbering and unconscious Munro were indicated by signs too palpable to be mistaken. Duncan perceived that even his own powers were spoken lightly of, as the scout extended his palm, and mentioned him by the appellation of the "Open Hand"—a name his liberality had purchased of all the friendly tribes. Then came a representation of the light and graceful movements of a canoe, set in forcible contrast to the tottering steps of one enfeebled and tired. He concluded by pointing to the scalp of the Oneida, and apparently urging the necessity of their departing speedily, and in a manner that should leave no trail.

The Mohicans listened gravely, and with countenances that reflected the sentiments of the speaker. Conviction gradually wrought its influence, and toward the close of Hawkeye's speech, his sentences were accompanied by the customary exclamation of commendation. In short, Uncas and his father became converts to his way of thinking, abandoning their own previously expressed opinions with a liberality and candor that, had they been the representatives of some great and civilized people, would have infallibly worked their political ruin, by destroying forever their reputation for consistency.

The instant the matter in discussion was decided, the debate, and everything connected with it, except the result appeared to be forgotten. Hawkeye, without looking round to read his triumph in applauding eyes, very composedly stretched his tall frame before the dying embers, and closed his own organs in sleep.

Left now in a measure to themselves, the Mohicans, whose time had been so much devoted to the interests of others, seized the moment to devote some attention to themselves. Casting off at once the grave and austere demeanor of an Indian chief, Chingachgook commenced speaking to his son in the soft and playful tones of affection. Uncas gladly met the familiar air of his father; and before the hard breathing of the scout announced that he slept, a complete change was effected in the manner of his two associates.

It is impossible to describe the music of their language, while thus engaged in laughter and endearments, in such a way as to render it intelligible to those whose ears have never listened to its melody. The compass of their voices, particularly that of the youth, was wonderful—extending from the deepest bass to tones that were even feminine in softness. The eyes of the father followed the plastic and ingenious movements of the son with open delight, and he never failed to smile in reply to the other's contagious but low laughter. While under the influence of these gentle and natural feelings, no trace of ferocity was to be seen in the softened features of the Sagamore. His figured panoply of death looked more like a disguise assumed in mockery than a fierce annunciation of a desire to carry destruction in his footsteps.

After an hour had passed in the indulgence of their better feelings, Chingachgook abruptly announced his desire to sleep, by wrapping his head in his blanket and stretching his form on the naked earth. The merriment of Uncas instantly ceased; and carefully raking the coals in such a manner that they should impart their warmth to his father's feet, the youth sought his own pillow among the ruins of the place.

Imbibing renewed confidence from the security of these experienced foresters, Heyward soon imitated their example; and long before the night had turned, they who lay in the bosom of the ruined work, seemed to slumber as heavily as the unconscious multitude whose bones were already beginning to bleach on the surrounding plain.

CHAPTER XX.

"Land of Albania! let me bend mine eyes
  On thee; thou rugged nurse of savage men!"
  —Childe Harold

The heavens were still studded with stars, when Hawkeye came to arouse the sleepers. Casting aside their cloaks Munro and Heyward were on their feet while the woodsman was still making his low calls, at the entrance of the rude shelter where they had passed the night. When they issued from beneath its concealment, they found the scout awaiting their appearance nigh by, and the only salutation between them was the significant gesture for silence, made by their sagacious leader.

"Think over your prayers," he whispered, as they approached him; "for He to whom you make them, knows all tongues; that of the heart, as well as those of the mouth. But speak not a syllable; it is rare for a white voice to pitch itself properly in the woods, as we have seen by the example of that miserable devil, the singer. Come," he continued, turning toward a curtain of the works; "let us get into the ditch on this side, and be regardful to step on the stones and fragments of wood as you go."

His companions complied, though to two of them the reasons of this extraordinary precaution were yet a mystery. When they were in the low cavity that surrounded the earthen fort on three sides, they found that passage nearly choked by the ruins. With care and patience, however, they succeeded in clambering after the scout, until they reached the sandy shore of the Horican.

"That's a trail that nothing but a nose can follow," said the satisfied scout, looking back along their difficult way; "grass is a treacherous carpet for a flying party to tread on, but wood and stone take no print from a moccasin. Had you worn your armed boots, there might, indeed, have been something to fear; but with the deer-skin suitably prepared, a man may trust himself, generally, on rocks with safety. Shove in the canoe nigher to the land, Uncas; this sand will take a stamp as easily as the butter of the Jarmans on the Mohawk. Softly, lad, softly; it must not touch the beach, or the knaves will know by what road we have left the place."

The young man observed the precaution; and the scout, laying a board from the ruins to the canoe, made a sign for the two officers to enter. When this was done, everything was studiously restored to its former disorder; and then Hawkeye succeeded in reaching his little birchen vessel, without leaving behind him any of those marks which he appeared so much to dread. Heyward was silent until the Indians had cautiously paddled the canoe some distance from the fort, and within the broad and dark shadows that fell from the eastern mountain on the glassy surface of the lake; then he demanded:

"What need have we for this stolen and hurried departure?"

"If the blood of an Oneida could stain such a sheet of pure water as this we float on," returned the scout, "your two eyes would answer your own question. Have you forgotten the skulking reptile Uncas slew?"

"By no means. But he was said to be alone, and dead men give no cause for fear."

"Ay, he was alone in his deviltry! but an Indian whose tribe counts so many warriors, need seldom fear his blood will run without the death shriek coming speedily from some of his enemies."

"But our presence—the authority of Colonel Munro—would prove sufficient protection against the anger of our allies, especially in a case where the wretch so well merited his fate. I trust in Heaven you have not deviated a single foot from the direct line of our course with so slight a reason!"

"Do you think the bullet of that varlet's rifle would have turned aside, though his sacred majesty the king had stood in its path?" returned the stubborn scout. "Why did not the grand Frencher, he who is captain-general of the Canadas, bury the tomahawks of the Hurons, if a word from a white can work so strongly on the natur' of an Indian?"

The reply of Heyward was interrupted by a groan from Munro; but after he had paused a moment, in deference to the sorrow of his aged friend he resumed the subject.

"The marquis of Montcalm can only settle that error with his God," said the young man solemnly.

"Ay, ay, now there is reason in your words, for they are bottomed on religion and honesty. There is a vast difference between throwing a regiment of white coats atwixt the tribes and the prisoners, and coaxing an angry savage to forget he carries a knife and rifle, with words that must begin with calling him your son. No, no," continued the scout, looking back at the dim shore of William Henry, which was now fast receding, and laughing in his own silent but heartfelt manner; "I have put a trail of water atween us; and unless the imps can make friends with the fishes, and hear who has paddled across their basin this fine morning, we shall throw the length of the Horican behind us before they have made up their minds which path to take."

"With foes in front, and foes in our rear, our journey is like to be one of danger."

"Danger!" repeated Hawkeye, calmly; "no, not absolutely of danger; for, with vigilant ears and quick eyes, we can manage to keep a few hours ahead of the knaves; or, if we must try the rifle, there are three of us who understand its gifts as well as any you can name on the borders. No, not of danger; but that we shall have what you may call a brisk push of it, is probable; and it may happen, a brush, a scrimmage, or some such divarsion, but always where covers are good, and ammunition abundant."

It is possible that Heyward's estimate of danger differed in some degree from that of the scout, for, instead of replying, he now sat in silence, while the canoe glided over several miles of water. Just as the day dawned, they entered the narrows of the lake,[*] and stole swiftly and cautiously among their numberless little islands. It was by this road that Montcalm had retired with his army, and the adventurers knew not but he had left some of his Indians in ambush, to protect the rear of his forces, and collect the stragglers. They, therefore, approached the passage with the customary silence of their guarded habits.

Chingachgook laid aside his paddle; while Uncas and the scout urged the light vessel through crooked and intricate channels, where every foot that they advanced exposed them to the danger of some sudden rising on their progress. The eyes of the Sagamore moved warily from islet to islet, and copse to copse, as the canoe proceeded; and, when a clearer sheet of water permitted, his keen vision was bent along the bald rocks and impending forests that frowned upon the narrow strait.

---

[*] The beauties of Lake George are well known to every American tourist. In the height of the mountains which surround it, and in artificial accessories, it is inferior to the finest of the Swiss and Italian lakes, while in outline and purity of water it is fully their equal; and in the number and disposition of its isles and islets much superior to them all together. There are said to be some hundreds of islands in a sheet of water less than thirty miles long. The narrows, which connect what may be called, in truth, two lakes, are crowded with islands to such a degree as to leave passages between them frequently of only a few feet in width. The lake itself varies in breadth from one to three miles.

Heyward, who was a doubly interested spectator, as well from the beauties of the place as from the apprehension natural to his situation, was just believing that he had permitted the latter to be excited without sufficient reason, when the paddle ceased moving, in obedience to a signal from Chingachgook.

"Hugh!" exclaimed Uncas, nearly at the moment that the light tap his father had made on the side of the canoe notified them of the vicinity of danger.

"What now?" asked the scout; "the lake is as smooth as if the winds had never blown, and I can see along its sheet for miles; there is not so much as the black head of a loon dotting the water."

The Indian gravely raised his paddle, and pointed in the direction in which his own steady look was riveted. Duncan's eyes followed the motion. A few rods in their front lay another of the wooded islets, but it appeared as calm and peaceful as if its solitude had never been disturbed by the foot of man.

"I see nothing," he said, "but land and water; and a lovely scene it is."

"Hist!" interrupted the scout. "Ay, Sagamore, there is always a reason for what you do. 'Tis but a shade, and yet it is not natural. You see the mist, major, that is rising above the island; you can't call it a fog, for it is more like a streak of thin cloud—"

"It is vapor from the water."

"That a child could tell. But what is the edging of blacker smoke that hangs along its lower side, and which you may trace down into the thicket of hazel? 'Tis from a fire; but one that, in my judgment, has been suffered to burn low."

"Let us, then, push for the place, and relieve our doubts," said the impatient Duncan; "the party must be small that can lie on such a bit of land."

"If you judge of Indian cunning by the rules you find in books, or by white sagacity, they will lead you astray, if not to your death," returned Hawkeye, examining the signs of the place with that acuteness which distinguished him. "If I may be permitted to speak in this matter, it will be to say, that we have but two things to choose between: the one is, to return, and give up all thoughts of following the Hurons—"

"Never!" exclaimed Heyward, in a voice far too loud for their circumstances.

"Well, well," continued Hawkeye, making a hasty sign to repress his impatience; "I am much of your mind myself; though I thought it becoming my experience to tell the whole. We must, then, make a push, and if the Indians or Frenchers are in the narrows, run the gauntlet through these toppling mountains. Is there reason in my words, Sagamore?"

The Indian made no other answer than by dropping his paddle into the water, and urging forward the canoe. As he held the office of directing its course, his resolution was sufficiently indicated by the movement. The whole party now plied their paddles vigorously, and in a very few moments they had reached a point whence they might command an entire view of the northern shore of the island, the side that had hitherto been concealed.

"There they are, by all the truth of signs," whispered the scout, "two canoes and a smoke. The knaves haven't yet got their eyes out of the mist, or we should hear the accursed whoop. Together, friends! we are leaving them, and are already nearly out of whistle of a bullet."

The well-known crack of a rifle, whose ball came skipping along the placid surface of the strait, and a shrill yell from the island, interrupted his speech, and announced that their passage was discovered. In another instant several savages were seen rushing into canoes, which were soon dancing over the water in pursuit. These fearful precursors of a coming struggle produced no change in the countenances and movements of his three guides, so far as Duncan could discover, except that the strokes of their paddles were longer and more in unison, and caused the little bark to spring forward like a creature possessing life and volition.

"Hold them there, Sagamore," said Hawkeye, looking coolly backward over this left shoulder, while he still plied his paddle; "keep them just there. Them Hurons have never a piece in their nation that will execute at this distance; but 'killdeer' has a barrel on which a man may calculate."

The scout having ascertained that the Mohicans were sufficient of themselves to maintain the requisite distance, deliberately laid aside his paddle, and raised the fatal rifle. Three several times he brought the piece to his shoulder, and when his companions were expecting its report, he as often lowered it to request the Indians would permit their enemies to approach a little nigher. At length his accurate and fastidious eye seemed satisfied, and, throwing out his left arm on the barrel, he was slowly elevating the muzzle, when an exclamation from Uncas, who sat in the bow, once more caused him to suspend the shot.

"What, now, lad?" demanded Hawkeye; "you save a Huron from the death-shriek by that word; have you reason for what you do?"

Uncas pointed toward a rocky shore a little in their front, whence another war canoe was darting directly across their course. It was too obvious now that their situation was imminently perilous to need the aid of language to confirm it. The scout laid aside his rifle, and resumed the paddle, while Chingachgook inclined the bows of the canoe a little toward the western shore, in order to increase the distance between them and this new enemy. In the meantime they were reminded of the presence of those who pressed upon their rear, by wild and exulting shouts. The stirring scene awakened even Munro from his apathy.

"Let us make for the rocks on the main," he said, with the mien of a tired soldier, "and give battle to the savages. God forbid that I, or those attached to me and mine, should ever trust again to the faith of any servant of the Louis's!"

"He who wishes to prosper in Indian warfare," returned the scout, "must not be too proud to learn from the wit of a native. Lay her more along the land, Sagamore; we are doubling on the varlets, and perhaps they may try to strike our trail on the long calculation."

Hawkeye was not mistaken; for when the Hurons found their course was likely to throw them behind their chase they rendered it less direct, until, by gradually bearing more and more obliquely, the two canoes were, ere long, gliding on parallel lines, within two hundred yards of each other. It now became entirely a trial of speed. So rapid was the progress of the light vessels, that the lake curled in their front, in miniature waves, and their motion became undulating by its own velocity. It was, perhaps, owing to this circumstance, in addition to the necessity of keeping every hand employed at the paddles, that the Hurons had not immediate recourse to their firearms. The exertions of the fugitives were too severe to continue long, and the pursuers had the advantage of numbers. Duncan observed with uneasiness, that the scout began to look anxiously about him, as if searching for some further means of assisting their flight.

"Edge her a little more from the sun, Sagamore," said the stubborn woodsman; "I see the knaves are sparing a man to the rifle. A single broken bone might lose us our scalps. Edge more from the sun and we will put the island between us."

The expedient was not without its use. A long, low island lay at a little distance before them, and, as they closed with it, the chasing canoe was compelled to take a side opposite to that on which the pursued passed. The scout and his companions did not neglect this advantage, but the instant they were hid from observation by the bushes, they redoubled efforts that before had seemed prodigious. The two canoes came round the last low point, like two coursers at the top of their speed, the fugitives taking the lead. This change had brought them nigher to each other, however, while it altered their relative positions.

"You showed knowledge in the shaping of a birchen bark, Uncas, when you chose this from among the Huron canoes," said the scout, smiling, apparently more in satisfaction at their superiority in the race than from that prospect of final escape which now began to open a little upon them. "The imps have put all their strength again at the paddles, and we are to struggle for our scalps with bits of flattened wood, instead of clouded barrels and true eyes. A long stroke, and together, friends."

"They are preparing for a shot," said Heyward; "and as we are in a line with them, it can scarcely fail."

"Get you, then, into the bottom of the canoe," returned the scout; "you and the colonel; it will be so much taken from the size of the mark."

Heyward smiled, as he answered:

"It would be but an ill example for the highest in rank to dodge, while the warriors were under fire."

"Lord! Lord! That is now a white man's courage!" exclaimed the scout; "and like to many of his notions, not to be maintained by reason. Do you think the Sagamore, or Uncas, or even I, who am a man without a cross, would deliberate about finding a cover in the scrimmage, when an open body would do no good? For what have the Frenchers reared up their Quebec, if fighting is always to be done in the clearings?"

"All that you say is very true, my friend," replied Heyward; "still, our customs must prevent us from doing as you wish."

A volley from the Hurons interrupted the discourse, and as the bullets whistled about them, Duncan saw the head of Uncas turned, looking back at himself and Munro. Notwithstanding the nearness of the enemy, and his own great personal danger, the countenance of the young warrior expressed no other emotion, as the former was compelled to think, than amazement at finding men willing to encounter so useless an exposure. Chingachgook was probably better acquainted with the notions of white men, for he did not even cast a glance aside from the riveted look his eye maintained on the object by which he governed their course. A ball soon struck the light and polished paddle from the hands of the chief, and drove it through the air, far in the advance. A shout arose from the Hurons, who seized the opportunity to fire another volley. Uncas described an arc in the water with his own blade, and as the canoe passed swiftly on, Chingachgook recovered his paddle, and flourishing it on high, he gave the war-whoop of the Mohicans, and then lent his strength and skill again to the important task.

The clamorous sounds of "Le Gros Serpent!" "La Longue Carabine!" "Le Cerf Agile!" burst at once from the canoes behind, and seemed to give new zeal to the pursuers. The scout seized "killdeer" in his left hand, and elevating it about his head, he shook it in triumph at his enemies. The savages answered the insult with a yell, and immediately another volley succeeded. The bullets pattered along the lake, and one even pierced the bark of their little vessel. No perceptible emotion could be discovered in the Mohicans during this critical moment, their rigid features expressing neither hope nor alarm; but the scout again turned his head, and, laughing in his own silent manner, he said to Heyward:

"The knaves love to hear the sounds of their pieces; but the eye is not to be found among the Mingoes that can calculate a true range in a dancing canoe! You see the dumb devils have taken off a man to charge, and by the smallest measurement that can be allowed, we move three feet to their two!"

Duncan, who was not altogether as easy under this nice estimate of distances as his companions, was glad to find, however, that owing to their superior dexterity, and the diversion among their enemies, they were very sensibly obtaining the advantage. The Hurons soon fired again, and a bullet struck the blade of Hawkeye's paddle without injury.

"That will do," said the scout, examining the slight indentation with a curious eye; "it would not have cut the skin of an infant, much less of men, who, like us, have been blown upon by the heavens in their anger. Now, major, if you will try to use this piece of flattened wood, I'll let 'killdeer' take a part in the conversation."

Heyward seized the paddle, and applied himself to the work with an eagerness that supplied the place of skill, while Hawkeye was engaged in inspecting the priming of his rifle. The latter then took a swift aim and fired. The Huron in the bows of the leading canoe had risen with a similar object, and he now fell backward, suffering his gun to escape from his hands into the water. In an instant, however, he recovered his feet, though his gestures were wild and bewildered. At the same moment his companions suspended their efforts, and the chasing canoes clustered together, and became stationary. Chingachgook and Uncas profited by the interval to regain their wind, though Duncan continued to work with the most persevering industry. The father and son now cast calm but inquiring glances at each other, to learn if either had sustained any injury by the fire; for both well knew that no cry or exclamation would, in such a moment of necessity have been permitted to betray the accident. A few large drops of blood were trickling down the shoulder of the Sagamore, who, when he perceived that the eyes of Uncas dwelt too long on the sight, raised some water in the hollow of his hand, and washing off the stain, was content to manifest, in this simple manner, the slightness of the injury.

"Softly, softly, major," said the scout, who by this time had reloaded his rifle; "we are a little too far already for a rifle to put forth its beauties, and you see yonder imps are holding a council. Let them come up within striking distance—my eye may well be trusted in such a matter—and I will trail the varlets the length of the Horican, guaranteeing that not a shot of theirs shall, at the worst, more than break the skin, while 'killdeer' shall touch the life twice in three times."

"We forget our errand," returned the diligent Duncan. "For God's sake let us profit by this advantage, and increase our distance from the enemy."

"Give me my children," said Munro, hoarsely; "trifle no longer with a father's agony, but restore me my babes."

Long and habitual deference to the mandates of his superiors had taught the scout the virtue of obedience. Throwing a last and lingering glance at the distant canoes, he laid aside his rifle, and, relieving the wearied Duncan, resumed the paddle, which he wielded with sinews that never tired. His efforts were seconded by those of the Mohicans and a very few minutes served to place such a sheet of water between them and their enemies, that Heyward once more breathed freely.

The lake now began to expand, and their route lay along a wide reach, that was lined, as before, by high and ragged mountains. But the islands were few, and easily avoided. The strokes of the paddles grew more measured and regular, while they who plied them continued their labor, after the close and deadly chase from which they had just relieved themselves, with as much coolness as though their speed had been tried in sport, rather than under such pressing, nay, almost desperate, circumstances.

Instead of following the western shore, whither their errand led them, the wary Mohican inclined his course more toward those hills behind which Montcalm was known to have led his army into the formidable fortress of Ticonderoga. As the Hurons, to every appearance, had abandoned the pursuit, there was no apparent reason for this excess of caution. It was, however, maintained for hours, until they had reached a bay, nigh the northern termination of the lake. Here the canoe was driven upon the beach, and the whole party landed. Hawkeye and Heyward ascended an adjacent bluff, where the former, after considering the expanse of water beneath him, pointed out to the latter a small black object, hovering under a headland, at the distance of several miles.

"Do you see it?" demanded the scout. "Now, what would you account that spot, were you left alone to white experience to find your way through this wilderness?"

"But for its distance and its magnitude, I should suppose it a bird. Can it be a living object?"

"'Tis a canoe of good birchen bark, and paddled by fierce and crafty Mingoes. Though Providence has lent to those who inhabit the woods eyes that would be needless to men in the settlements, where there are inventions to assist the sight, yet no human organs can see all the dangers which at this moment circumvent us. These varlets pretend to be bent chiefly on their sun-down meal, but the moment it is dark they will be on our trail, as true as hounds on the scent. We must throw them off, or our pursuit of Le Renard Subtil may be given up. These lakes are useful at times, especially when the game take the water," continued the scout, gazing about him with a countenance of concern; "but they give no cover, except it be to the fishes. God knows what the country would be, if the settlements should ever spread far from the two rivers. Both hunting and war would lose their beauty."

"Let us not delay a moment, without some good and obvious cause."

"I little like that smoke, which you may see worming up along the rock above the canoe," interrupted the abstracted scout. "My life on it, other eyes than ours see it, and know its meaning. Well, words will not mend the matter, and it is time that we were doing."

Hawkeye moved away from the lookout, and descended, musing profoundly, to the shore. He communicated the result of his observations to his companions, in Delaware, and a short and earnest consultation succeeded. When it terminated, the three instantly set about executing their new resolutions.

The canoe was lifted from the water, and borne on the shoulders of the party, they proceeded into the wood, making as broad and obvious a trail as possible. They soon reached the water-course, which they crossed, and, continuing onward, until they came to an extensive and naked rock. At this point, where their footsteps might be expected to be no longer visible, they retraced their route to the brook, walking backward, with the utmost care. They now followed the bed of the little stream to the lake, into which they immediately launched their canoe again. A low point concealed them from the headland, and the margin of the lake was fringed for some distance with dense and overhanging bushes. Under the cover of these natural advantages, they toiled their way, with patient industry, until the scout pronounced that he believed it would be safe once more to land.

The halt continued until evening rendered objects indistinct and uncertain to the eye. Then they resumed their route, and, favored by the darkness, pushed silently and vigorously toward the western shore. Although the rugged outline of mountain, to which they were steering, presented no distinctive marks to the eyes of Duncan, the Mohican entered the little haven he had selected with the confidence and accuracy of an experienced pilot.

The boat was again lifted and borne into the woods, where it was carefully concealed under a pile of brush. The adventurers assumed their arms and packs, and the scout announced to Munro and Heyward that he and the Indians were at last in readiness to proceed.

CHAPTER XXI.

"If you find a man there, he shall die a flea's death."
—Merry Wives of Windsor.

The party had landed on the border of a region that is, even to this day, less known to the inhabitants of the States than the deserts of Arabia, or the steppes of Tartary. It was the sterile and rugged district which separates the tributaries of Champlain from those of the Hudson, the Mohawk, and the St. Lawrence. Since the period of our tale the active spirit of the country has surrounded it with a belt of rich and thriving settlements, though none but the hunter or the savage is ever known even now to penetrate its wild recesses.

As Hawkeye and the Mohicans had, however, often traversed the mountains and valleys of this vast wilderness, they did not hesitate to plunge into its depth, with the freedom of men accustomed to its privations and difficulties. For many hours the travelers toiled on their laborious way, guided by a star, or following the direction of some water-course, until the scout called a halt, and holding a short consultation with the Indians, they lighted their fire, and made the usual preparations to pass the remainder of the night where they then were.

Imitating the example, and emulating the confidence of their more experienced associates, Munro and Duncan slept without fear, if not without uneasiness. The dews were suffered to exhale, and the sun had dispersed the mists, and was shedding a strong and clear light in the forest, when the travelers resumed their journey.

After proceeding a few miles, the progress of Hawkeye, who led the advance, became more deliberate and watchful. He often stopped to examine the trees; nor did he cross a rivulet without attentively considering the quantity, the velocity, and the color of its waters. Distrusting his own judgment, his appeals to the opinion of Chingachgook were frequent and earnest. During one of these conferences Heyward observed that Uncas stood a patient and silent, though, as he imagined, an interested listener. He was strongly tempted to address the young chief, and demand his opinion of their progress; but the calm and dignified demeanor of the native induced him to believe, that, like himself, the other was wholly dependent on the sagacity and intelligence of the seniors of the party. At last the scout spoke in English, and at once explained the embarrassment of their situation.

"When I found that the home path of the Hurons run north," he said, "it did not need the judgment of many long years to tell that they would follow the valleys, and keep atween the waters of the Hudson and the Horican, until they might strike the springs of the Canada streams, which would lead them into the heart of the country of the Frenchers. Yet here are we, within a short range of the Scaroons, and not a sign of a trail have we crossed! Human natur' is weak, and it is possible we may not have taken the proper scent."

"Heaven protect us from such an error!" exclaimed Duncan. "Let us retrace our steps, and examine as we go, with keener eyes. Has Uncas no counsel to offer in such a strait?"

The young Mohican cast a glance at his father, but, maintaining his quiet and reserved mien, he continued silent. Chingachgook had caught the look, and motioning with his hand, he bade him speak. The moment this permission was accorded, the countenance of Uncas changed from its grave composure to a gleam of intelligence and joy. Bounding forward like a deer, he sprang up the side of a little acclivity, a few rods in advance, and stood, exultingly, over a spot of fresh earth, that looked as though it had been recently upturned by the passage of some heavy animal. The eyes of the whole party followed the unexpected movement, and read their success in the air of triumph that the youth assumed.

"'Tis the trail!" exclaimed the scout, advancing to the spot; "the lad is quick of sight and keen of wit for his years."

"'Tis extraordinary that he should have withheld his knowledge so long," muttered Duncan, at his elbow.

"It would have been more wonderful had he spoken without a bidding. No, no; your young white, who gathers his learning from books and can measure what he knows by the page, may conceit that his knowledge, like his legs, outruns that of his fathers', but, where experience is the master, the scholar is made to know the value of years, and respects them accordingly."

"See!" said Uncas, pointing north and south, at the evident marks of the broad trail on either side of him, "the dark-hair has gone toward the forest."

"Hound never ran on a more beautiful scent," responded the scout, dashing forward, at once, on the indicated route; "we are favored, greatly favored, and can follow with high noses. Ay, here are both your waddling beasts: this Huron travels like a white general. The fellow is stricken with a judgment, and is mad! Look sharp for wheels, Sagamore," he continued, looking back, and laughing in his newly awakened satisfaction; "we shall soon have the fool journeying in a coach, and that with three of the best pair of eyes on the borders in his rear."

The spirits of the scout, and the astonishing success of the chase, in which a circuitous distance of more than forty miles had been passed, did not fail to impart a portion of hope to the whole party. Their advance was rapid; and made with as much confidence as a traveler would proceed along a wide highway. If a rock, or a rivulet, or a bit of earth harder than common, severed the links of the clew they followed, the true eye of the scout recovered them at a distance, and seldom rendered the delay of a single moment necessary. Their progress was much facilitated by the certainty that Magua had found it necessary to journey through the valleys; a circumstance which rendered the general direction of the route sure. Nor had the Huron entirely neglected the arts uniformly practised by the natives when retiring in front of an enemy. False trails and sudden turnings were frequent, wherever a brook or the formation of the ground rendered them feasible; but his pursuers were rarely deceived, and never failed to detect their error, before they had lost either time or distance on the deceptive track.

By the middle of the afternoon they had passed the Scaroons, and were following the route of the declining sun. After descending an eminence to a low bottom, through which a swift stream glided, they suddenly came to a place where the party of Le Renard had made a halt. Extinguished brands were lying around a spring, the offals of a deer were scattered about the place, and the trees bore evident marks of having been browsed by the horses. At a little distance, Heyward discovered, and contemplated with tender emotion, the small bower under which he was fain to believe that Cora and Alice had reposed. But while the earth was trodden, and the footsteps of both men and beasts were so plainly visible around the place, the trail appeared to have suddenly ended.

It was easy to follow the tracks of the Narragansetts, but they seemed only to have wandered without guides, or any other object than the pursuit of food. At length Uncas, who, with his father, had endeavored to trace the route of the horses, came upon a sign of their presence that was quite recent. Before following the clew, he communicated his success to his companions; and while the latter were consulting on the circumstance, the youth reappeared, leading the two fillies, with their saddles broken, and the housings soiled, as though they had been permitted to run at will for several days.

"What should this prove?" said Duncan, turning pale, and glancing his eyes around him, as if he feared the brush and leaves were about to give up some horrid secret.

"That our march is come to a quick end, and that we are in an enemy's country," returned the scout. "Had the knave been pressed, and the gentle ones wanted horses to keep up with the party, he might have taken their scalps; but without an enemy at his heels, and with such rugged beasts as these, he would not hurt a hair of their heads. I know your thoughts, and shame be it to our color that you have reason for them; but he who thinks that even a Mingo would ill-treat a woman, unless it be to tomahawk her, knows nothing of Indian natur', or the laws of the woods. No, no; I have heard that the French Indians had come into these hills to hunt the moose, and we are getting within scent of their camp. Why should they not? The morning and evening guns of Ty may be heard any day among these mountains; for the Frenchers are running a new line atween the provinces of the king and the Canadas. It is true that the horses are here, but the Hurons are gone; let us, then, hunt for the path by which they parted."

Hawkeye and the Mohicans now applied themselves to their task in good earnest. A circle of a few hundred feet in circumference was drawn, and each of the party took a segment for his portion. The examination, however, resulted in no discovery. The impressions of footsteps were numerous, but they all appeared like those of men who had wandered about the spot, without any design to quit it. Again the scout and his companions made the circuit of the halting place, each slowly following the other, until they assembled in the center once more, no wiser than when they started.

"Such cunning is not without its deviltry," exclaimed Hawkeye, when he met the disappointed looks of his assistants.

"We must get down to it, Sagamore, beginning at the spring, and going over the ground by inches. The Huron shall never brag in his tribe that he has a foot which leaves no print."

Setting the example himself, the scout engaged in the scrutiny with renewed zeal. Not a leaf was left unturned. The sticks were removed, and the stones lifted; for Indian cunning was known frequently to adopt these objects as covers, laboring with the utmost patience and industry, to conceal each footstep as they proceeded. Still no discovery was made. At length Uncas, whose activity had enabled him to achieve his portion of the task the soonest, raked the earth across the turbid little rill which ran from the spring, and diverted its course into another channel. So soon as its narrow bed below the dam was dry, he stooped over it with keen and curious eyes. A cry of exultation immediately announced the success of the young warrior. The whole party crowded to the spot where Uncas pointed out the impression of a moccasin in the moist alluvion.

"This lad will be an honor to his people," said Hawkeye, regarding the trail with as much admiration as a naturalist would expend on the tusk of a mammoth or the rib of a mastodon; "ay, and a thorn in the sides of the Hurons. Yet that is not the footstep of an Indian! the weight is too much on the heel, and the toes are squared, as though one of the French dancers had been in, pigeon-winging his tribe! Run back, Uncas, and bring me the size of the singer's foot. You will find a beautiful print of it just opposite yon rock, agin the hillside."

While the youth was engaged in this commission, the scout and Chingachgook were attentively considering the impressions. The measurements agreed, and the former unhesitatingly pronounced that the footstep was that of David, who had once more been made to exchange his shoes for moccasins.

"I can now read the whole of it, as plainly as if I had seen the arts of Le Subtil," he added; "the singer being a man whose gifts lay chiefly in his throat and feet, was made to go first, and the others have trod in his steps, imitating their formation."

"But," cried Duncan, "I see no signs of——"

"The gentle ones," interrupted the scout; "the varlet has found a way to carry them, until he supposed he had thrown any followers off the scent. My life on it, we see their pretty little feet again, before many rods go by."

The whole party now proceeded, following the course of the rill, keeping anxious eyes on the regular impressions. The water soon flowed into its bed again, but watching the ground on either side, the foresters pursued their way content with knowing that the trail lay beneath. More than half a mile was passed, before the rill rippled close around the base of an extensive and dry rock. Here they paused to make sure that the Hurons had not quitted the water.

It was fortunate they did so. For the quick and active Uncas soon found the impression of a foot on a bunch of moss, where it would seem an Indian had inadvertently trodden. Pursuing the direction given by this discovery, he entered the neighboring thicket, and struck the trail, as fresh and obvious as it had been before they reached the spring. Another shout announced the good fortune of the youth to his companions, and at once terminated the search.

"Ay, it has been planned with Indian judgment," said the scout, when the party was assembled around the place, "and would have blinded white eyes."

"Shall we proceed?" demanded Heyward.

"Softly, softly, we know our path; but it is good to examine the formation of things. This is my schooling, major; and if one neglects the book, there is little chance of learning from the open land of Providence. All is plain but one thing, which is the manner that the knave contrived to get the gentle ones along the blind trail. Even a Huron would be too proud to let their tender feet touch the water."

"Will this assist in explaining the difficulty?" said Heyward, pointing toward the fragments of a sort of handbarrow, that had been rudely constructed of boughs, and bound together with withes, and which now seemed carelessly cast aside as useless.

"'Tis explained!" cried the delighted Hawkeye. "If them varlets have passed a minute, they have spent hours in striving to fabricate a lying end to their trail! Well, I've known them to waste a day in the same manner to as little purpose. Here we have three pair of moccasins, and two of little feet. It is amazing that any mortal beings can journey on limbs so small! Pass me the thong of buckskin, Uncas, and let me take the length of this foot. By the Lord, it is no longer than a child's and yet the maidens are tall and comely. That Providence is partial in its gifts, for its own wise reasons, the best and most contented of us must allow."

"The tender limbs of my daughters are unequal to these hardships," said Munro, looking at the light footsteps of his children, with a parent's love; "we shall find their fainting forms in this desert."

"Of that there is little cause of fear," returned the scout, slowly shaking his head; "this is a firm and straight, though a light step, and not over long. See, the heel has hardly touched the ground; and there the dark-hair has made a little jump, from root to root. No, no; my knowledge for it, neither of them was nigh fainting, hereaway. Now, the singer was beginning to be footsore and leg-weary, as is plain by his trail. There, you see, he slipped; here he has traveled wide and tottered; and there again it looks as though he journeyed on snowshoes. Ay, ay, a man who uses his throat altogether, can hardly give his legs a proper training."

From such undeniable testimony did the practised woodsman arrive at the truth, with nearly as much certainty and precision as if he had been a witness of all those events which his ingenuity so easily elucidated. Cheered by these assurances, and satisfied by a reasoning that was so obvious, while it was so simple, the party resumed its course, after making a short halt, to take a hurried repast.

When the meal was ended, the scout cast a glance upward at the setting sun, and pushed forward with a rapidity which compelled Heyward and the still vigorous Munro to exert all their muscles to equal. Their route now lay along the bottom which has already been mentioned. As the Hurons had made no further efforts to conceal their footsteps, the progress of the pursuers was no longer delayed by uncertainty. Before an hour had elapsed, however, the speed of Hawkeye sensibly abated, and his head, instead of maintaining its former direct and forward look, began to turn suspiciously from side to side, as if he were conscious of approaching danger. He soon stopped again, and waited for the whole party to come up.

"I scent the Hurons," he said, speaking to the Mohicans; "yonder is open sky, through the treetops, and we are getting too nigh their encampment. Sagamore, you will take the hillside, to the right; Uncas will bend along the brook to the left, while I will try the trail. If anything should happen, the call will be three croaks of a crow. I saw one of the birds fanning himself in the air, just beyond the dead oak—another sign that we are approaching an encampment."

The Indians departed their several ways without reply, while Hawkeye cautiously proceeded with the two gentlemen. Heyward soon pressed to the side of their guide, eager to catch an early glimpse of those enemies he had pursued with so much toil and anxiety. His companion told him to steal to the edge of the wood, which, as usual, was fringed with a thicket, and wait his coming, for he wished to examine certain suspicious signs a little on one side. Duncan obeyed, and soon found himself in a situation to command a view which he found as extraordinary as it was novel.

The trees of many acres had been felled, and the glow of a mild summer's evening had fallen on the clearing, in beautiful contrast to the gray light of the forest. A short distance from the place where Duncan stood, the stream had seemingly expanded into a little lake, covering most of the low land, from mountain to mountain. The water fell out of this wide basin, in a cataract so regular and gentle, that it appeared rather to be the work of human hands than fashioned by nature. A hundred earthen dwellings stood on the margin of the lake, and even in its waters, as though the latter had overflowed its usual banks. Their rounded roofs, admirably molded for defense against the weather, denoted more of industry and foresight than the natives were wont to bestow on their regular habitations, much less on those they occupied for the temporary purposes of hunting and war. In short, the whole village or town, whichever it might be termed, possessed more of method and neatness of execution, than the white men had been accustomed to believe belonged, ordinarily, to the Indian habits. It appeared, however, to be deserted. At least, so thought Duncan for many minutes; but, at length, he fancied he discovered several human forms advancing toward him on all fours, and apparently dragging in the train some heavy, and as he was quick to apprehend, some formidable engine. Just then a few dark-looking heads gleamed out of the dwellings, and the place seemed suddenly alive with beings, which, however, glided from cover to cover so swiftly, as to allow no opportunity of examining their humors or pursuits. Alarmed at these suspicious and inexplicable movements, he was about to attempt the signal of the crows, when the rustling of leaves at hand drew his eyes in another direction.

The young man started, and recoiled a few paces instinctively, when he found himself within a hundred yards of a stranger Indian. Recovering his recollection on the instant, instead of sounding an alarm, which might prove fatal to himself, he remained stationary, an attentive observer of the other's motions.

An instant of calm observation served to assure Duncan that he was undiscovered. The native, like himself, seemed occupied in considering the low dwellings of the village, and the stolen movements of its inhabitants. It was impossible to discover the expression of his features through the grotesque mask of paint under which they were concealed, though Duncan fancied it was rather melancholy than savage. His head was shaved, as usual, with the exception of the crown, from whose tuft three or four faded feathers from a hawk's wing were loosely dangling. A ragged calico mantle half encircled his body, while his nether garment was composed of an ordinary shirt, the sleeves of which were made to perform the office that is usually executed by a much more commodious arrangement. His legs were, however, covered with a pair of good deer-skin moccasins. Altogether, the appearance of the individual was forlorn and miserable.

Duncan was still curiously observing the person of his neighbor when the scout stole silently and cautiously to his side.

"You see we have reached their settlement or encampment," whispered the young man; "and here is one of the savages himself, in a very embarrassing position for our further movements."

Hawkeye started, and dropped his rifle, when, directed by the finger of his companion, the stranger came under his view. Then lowering the dangerous muzzle he stretched forward his long neck, as if to assist a scrutiny that was already intensely keen.

"The imp is not a Huron," he said, "nor of any of the Canada tribes; and yet you see, by his clothes, the knave has been plundering a white. Ay, Montcalm has raked the woods for his inroad, and a whooping, murdering set of varlets has he gathered together. Can you see where he has put his rifle or his bow?"

"He appears to have no arms; nor does he seem to be viciously inclined. Unless he communicate the alarm to his fellows, who, as you see, are dodging about the water, we have but little to fear from him."

The scout turned to Heyward, and regarded him a moment with unconcealed amazement. Then opening wide his mouth, he indulged in unrestrained and heartfelt laughter, though in that silent and peculiar manner which danger had so long taught him to practise.

Repeating the words, "Fellows who are dodging about the water!" he added, "so much for schooling and passing a boyhood in the settlements! The knave has long legs, though, and shall not be trusted. Do you keep him under your rifle while I creep in behind, through the bush, and take him alive. Fire on no account."

Heyward had already permitted his companion to bury part of his person in the thicket, when, stretching forth his arm, he arrested him, in order to ask:

"If I see you in danger, may I not risk a shot?"

Hawkeye regarded him a moment, like one who knew not how to take the question; then, nodding his head, he answered, still laughing, though inaudibly:

"Fire a whole platoon, major."

In the next moment he was concealed by the leaves. Duncan waited several minutes in feverish impatience, before he caught another glimpse of the scout. Then he reappeared, creeping along the earth, from which his dress was hardly distinguishable, directly in the rear of his intended captive. Having reached within a few yards of the latter, he arose to his feet, silently and slowly. At that instant, several loud blows were struck on the water, and Duncan turned his eyes just in time to perceive that a hundred dark forms were plunging, in a body, into the troubled little sheet. Grasping his rifle his looks were again bent on the Indian near him. Instead of taking the alarm, the unconscious savage stretched forward his neck, as if he also watched the movements about the gloomy lake, with a sort of silly curiosity. In the meantime, the uplifted hand of Hawkeye was above him. But, without any apparent reason, it was withdrawn, and its owner indulged in another long, though still silent, fit of merriment. When the peculiar and hearty laughter of Hawkeye was ended, instead of grasping his victim by the throat, he tapped him lightly on the shoulder, and exclaimed aloud:

"How now, friend! have you a mind to teach the beavers to sing?"

"Even so," was the ready answer. "It would seem that the Being that gave them power to improve His gifts so well, would not deny them voices to proclaim His praise."

CHAPTER XXII.

"Bot.—Abibl we all met?
Qui.—Pat—pat; and here's a marvelous convenient place
for our rehearsal."
—Midsummer Night's Dream

The reader may better imagine, than we describe the surprise of Heyward. His lurking Indians were suddenly converted into four-footed beasts; his lake into a beaver pond; his cataract into a dam, constructed by those industrious and ingenious quadrupeds; and a suspected enemy into his tried friend, David Gamut, the master of psalmody. The presence of the latter created so many unexpected hopes relative to the sisters that, without a moment's hesitation, the young man broke out of his ambush, and sprang forward to join the two principal actors in the scene.

The merriment of Hawkeye was not easily appeased. Without ceremony, and with a rough hand, he twirled the supple Gamut around on his heel, and more than once affirmed that the Hurons had done themselves great credit in the fashion of his costume. Then, seizing the hand of the other, he squeezed it with a grip that brought tears into the eyes of the placid David, and wished him joy of his new condition.

"You were about opening your throat-practisings among the beavers, were ye?" he said. "The cunning devils know half the trade already, for they beat the time with their tails, as you heard just now; and in good time it was, too, or 'killdeer' might have sounded the first note among them. I have known greater fools, who could read and write, than an experienced old beaver; but as for squalling, the animals are born dumb! What think you of such a song as this?"

David shut his sensitive ears, and even Heyward apprised as he was of the nature of the cry, looked upward in quest of the bird, as the cawing of a crow rang in the air about them.

"See!" continued the laughing scout, as he pointed toward the remainder of the party, who, in obedience to the signal, were already approaching; "this is music which has its natural virtues; it brings two good rifles to my elbow, to say nothing of the knives and tomahawks. But we see that you are safe; now tell us what has become of the maidens."

"They are captives to the heathen," said David; "and, though greatly troubled in spirit, enjoying comfort and safety in the body."

"Both!" demanded the breathless Heyward.

"Even so. Though our wayfaring has been sore and our sustenance scanty, we have had little other cause for complaint, except the violence done our feelings, by being thus led in captivity into a far land."

"Bless ye for these very words!" exclaimed the trembling Munro; "I shall then receive my babes, spotless and angel-like, as I lost them!"

"I know not that their delivery is at hand," returned the doubting David; "the leader of these savages is possessed of an evil spirit that no power short of Omnipotence can tame. I have tried him sleeping and waking, but neither sounds nor language seem to touch his soul."

"Where is the knave?" bluntly interrupted the scout.

"He hunts the moose to-day, with his young men; and tomorrow, as I hear, they pass further into the forests, and nigher to the borders of Canada. The elder maiden is conveyed to a neighboring people, whose lodges are situate beyond yonder black pinnacle of rock; while the younger is detained among the women of the Hurons, whose dwellings are but two short miles hence, on a table-land, where the fire had done the office of the axe, and prepared the place for their reception."

"Alice, my gentle Alice!" murmured Heyward; "she has lost the consolation of her sister's presence!"

"Even so. But so far as praise and thanksgiving in psalmody can temper the spirit in affliction, she has not suffered."

"Has she then a heart for music?"

"Of the graver and more solemn character; though it must be acknowledged that, in spite of all my endeavors, the maiden weeps oftener than she smiles. At such moments I forbear to press the holy songs; but there are many sweet and comfortable periods of satisfactory communication, when the ears of the savages are astounded with the upliftings of our voices."

"And why are you permitted to go at large, unwatched?"

David composed his features into what he intended should express an air of modest humility, before he meekly replied:

"Little be the praise to such a worm as I. But, though the power of psalmody was suspended in the terrible business of that field of blood through which we have passed, it has recovered its influence even over the souls of the heathen, and I am suffered to go and come at will."

The scout laughed, and, tapping his own forehead significantly, he perhaps explained the singular indulgence more satisfactorily when he said:

"The Indians never harm a non-composser. But why, when the path lay open before your eyes, did you not strike back on your own trail (it is not so blind as that which a squirrel would make), and bring in the tidings to Edward?"

The scout, remembering only his own sturdy and iron nature, had probably exacted a task that David, under no circumstances, could have performed. But, without entirely losing the meekness of his air, the latter was content to answer:

"Though my soul would rejoice to visit the habitations of Christendom once more, my feet would rather follow the tender spirits intrusted to my keeping, even into the idolatrous province of the Jesuits, than take one step backward, while they pined in captivity and sorrow."

Though the figurative language of David was not very intelligible, the sincere and steady expression of his eye, and the glow of his honest countenance, were not easily mistaken. Uncas pressed closer to his side, and regarded the speaker with a look of commendation, while his father expressed his satisfaction by the ordinary pithy exclamation of approbation. The scout shook his head as he rejoined:

"The Lord never intended that the man should place all his endeavors in his throat, to the neglect of other and better gifts! But he has fallen into the hands of some silly woman, when he should have been gathering his education under a blue sky, among the beauties of the forest. Here, friend; I did intend to kindle a fire with this tooting-whistle of thine; but, as you value the thing, take it, and blow your best on it."

Gamut received his pitch-pipe with as strong an expression of pleasure as he believed compatible with the grave functions he exercised. After essaying its virtues repeatedly, in contrast with his own voice, and, satisfying himself that none of its melody was lost, he made a very serious demonstration toward achieving a few stanzas of one of the longest effusions in the little volume so often mentioned.

Heyward, however, hastily interrupted his pious purpose by continuing questions concerning the past and present condition of his fellow captives, and in a manner more methodical than had been permitted by his feelings in the opening of their interview. David, though he regarded his treasure with longing eyes, was constrained to answer, especially as the venerable father took a part in the interrogatories, with an interest too imposing to be denied. Nor did the scout fail to throw in a pertinent inquiry, whenever a fitting occasion presented. In this manner, though with frequent interruptions which were filled with certain threatening sounds from the recovered instrument, the pursuers were put in possession of such leading circumstances as were likely to prove useful in accomplishing their great and engrossing object—the recovery of the sisters. The narrative of David was simple, and the facts but few.

Magua had waited on the mountain until a safe moment to retire presented itself, when he had descended, and taken the route along the western side of the Horican in direction of the Canadas. As the subtle Huron was familiar with the paths, and well knew there was no immediate danger of pursuit, their progress had been moderate, and far from fatiguing. It appeared from the unembellished statement of David, that his own presence had been rather endured than desired; though even Magua had not been entirely exempt from that veneration with which the Indians regard those whom the Great Spirit had visited in their intellects. At night, the utmost care had been taken of the captives, both to prevent injury from the damps of the woods and to guard against an escape. At the spring, the horses were turned loose, as has been seen; and, notwithstanding the remoteness and length of their trail, the artifices already named were resorted to, in order to cut off every clue to their place of retreat. On their arrival at the encampment of his people, Magua, in obedience to a policy seldom departed from, separated his prisoners. Cora had been sent to a tribe that temporarily occupied an adjacent valley, though David was far too ignorant of the customs and history of the natives, to be able to declare anything satisfactory concerning their name or character. He only knew that they had not engaged in the late expedition against William Henry; that, like the Hurons themselves they were allies of Montcalm; and that they maintained an amicable, though a watchful intercourse with the warlike and savage people whom chance had, for a time, brought in such close and disagreeable contact with themselves.

The Mohicans and the scout listened to his interrupted and imperfect narrative, with an interest that obviously increased as he proceeded; and it was while attempting to explain the pursuits of the community in which Cora was detained, that the latter abruptly demanded:

"Did you see the fashion of their knives? were they of English or French formation?"

"My thoughts were bent on no such vanities, but rather mingled in consolation with those of the maidens."

"The time may come when you will not consider the knife of a savage such a despicable vanity," returned the scout, with a strong expression of contempt for the other's dullness. "Had they held their corn feast—or can you say anything of the totems of the tribe?"

"Of corn, we had many and plentiful feasts; for the grain, being in the milk is both sweet to the mouth and comfortable to the stomach. Of totem, I know not the meaning; but if it appertaineth in any wise to the art of Indian music, it need not be inquired after at their hands. They never join their voices in praise, and it would seem that they are among the profanest of the idolatrous."

"Therein you belie the natur' of an Indian. Even the Mingo adores but the true and loving God. 'Tis wicked fabrication of the whites, and I say it to the shame of my color that would make the warrior bow down before images of his own creation. It is true, they endeavor to make truces to the wicked one—as who would not with an enemy he cannot conquer! but they look up for favor and assistance to the Great and Good Spirit only."

"It may be so," said David; "but I have seen strange and fantastic images drawn in their paint, of which their admiration and care savored of spiritual pride; especially one, and that, too, a foul and loathsome object."

"Was it a sarpent?" quickly demanded the scout.

"Much the same. It was in the likeness of an abject and creeping tortoise."

"Hugh!" exclaimed both the attentive Mohicans in a breath; while the scout shook his head with the air of one who had made an important but by no means a pleasing discovery. Then the father spoke, in the language of the Delawares, and with a calmness and dignity that instantly arrested the attention even of those to whom his words were unintelligible. His gestures were impressive, and at times energetic. Once he lifted his arm on high; and, as it descended, the action threw aside the folds of his light mantle, a finger resting on his breast, as if he would enforce his meaning by the attitude. Duncan's eyes followed the movement, and he perceived that the animal just mentioned was beautifully, though faintly, worked in blue tint, on the swarthy breast of the chief. All that he had ever heard of the violent separation of the vast tribes of the Delawares rushed across his mind, and he awaited the proper moment to speak, with a suspense that was rendered nearly intolerable by his interest in the stake. His wish, however, was anticipated by the scout who turned from his red friend, saying:

"We have found that which may be good or evil to us, as heaven disposes. The Sagamore is of the high blood of the Delawares, and is the great chief of their Tortoises! That some of this stock are among the people of whom the singer tells us, is plain by his words; and, had he but spent half the breath in prudent questions that he has blown away in making a trumpet of his throat, we might have known how many warriors they numbered. It is, altogether, a dangerous path we move in; for a friend whose face is turned from you often bears a bloodier mind than the enemy who seeks your scalp."

"Explain," said Duncan.

"'Tis a long and melancholy tradition, and one I little like to think of; for it is not to be denied that the evil has been mainly done by men with white skins. But it has ended in turning the tomahawk of brother against brother, and brought the Mingo and the Delaware to travel in the same path."

"You, then, suspect it is a portion of that people among whom Cora resides?"

The scout nodded his head in assent, though he seemed anxious to waive the further discussion of a subject that appeared painful. The impatient Duncan now made several hasty and desperate propositions to attempt the release of the sisters. Munro seemed to shake off his apathy, and listened to the wild schemes of the young man with a deference that his gray hairs and reverend years should have denied. But the scout, after suffering the ardor of the lover to expend itself a little, found means to convince him of the folly of precipitation, in a manner that would require their coolest judgment and utmost fortitude.

"It would be well," he added, "to let this man go in again, as usual, and for him to tarry in the lodges, giving notice to the gentle ones of our approach, until we call him out, by signal, to consult. You know the cry of a crow, friend, from the whistle of the whip-poor-will?"

"'Tis a pleasing bird," returned David, "and has a soft and melancholy note! though the time is rather quick and ill-measured."

"He speaks of the wish-ton-wish," said the scout; "well, since you like his whistle, it shall be your signal. Remember, then, when you hear the whip-poor-will's call three times repeated, you are to come into the bushes where the bird might be supposed—"

"Stop," interrupted Heyward; "I will accompany him."

"You!" exclaimed the astonished Hawkeye; "are you tired of seeing the sun rise and set?"

"David is a living proof that the Hurons can be merciful."

"Ay, but David can use his throat, as no man in his senses would pervart the gift."

"I too can play the madman, the fool, the hero; in short, any or everything to rescue her I love. Name your objections no longer: I am resolved."

Hawkeye regarded the young man a moment in speechless amazement. But Duncan, who, in deference to the other's skill and services, had hitherto submitted somewhat implicitly to his dictation, now assumed the superior, with a manner that was not easily resisted. He waved his hand, in sign of his dislike to all remonstrance, and then, in more tempered language, he continued:

"You have the means of disguise; change me; paint me, too, if you will; in short, alter me to anything—a fool."

"It is not for one like me to say that he who is already formed by so powerful a hand as Providence, stands in need of a change," muttered the discontented scout. "When you send your parties abroad in war, you find it prudent, at least, to arrange the marks and places of encampment, in order that they who fight on your side may know when and where to expect a friend."

"Listen," interrupted Duncan; "you have heard from this faithful follower of the captives, that the Indians are of two tribes, if not of different nations. With one, whom you think to be a branch of the Delawares, is she you call the 'dark-hair'; the other, and younger, of the ladies, is undeniably with our declared enemies, the Hurons. It becomes my youth and rank to attempt the latter adventure. While you, therefore, are negotiating with your friends for the release of one of the sisters, I will effect that of the other, or die."

The awakened spirit of the young soldier gleamed in his eyes, and his form became imposing under its influence. Hawkeye, though too much accustomed to Indian artifices not to foresee the danger of the experiment, knew not well how to combat this sudden resolution.

Perhaps there was something in the proposal that suited his own hardy nature, and that secret love of desperate adventure, which had increased with his experience, until hazard and danger had become, in some measure, necessary to the enjoyment of his existence. Instead of continuing to oppose the scheme of Duncan, his humor suddenly altered, and he lent himself to its execution.

"Come," he said, with a good-humored smile; "the buck that will take to the water must be headed, and not followed. Chingachgook has as many different paints as the engineer officer's wife, who takes down natur' on scraps of paper, making the mountains look like cocks of rusty hay, and placing the blue sky in reach of your hand. The Sagamore can use them, too. Seat yourself on the log; and my life on it, he can soon make a natural fool of you, and that well to your liking."

Duncan complied; and the Mohican, who had been an attentive listener to the discourse, readily undertook the office. Long practised in all the subtle arts of his race, he drew, with great dexterity and quickness, the fantastic shadow that the natives were accustomed to consider as the evidence of a friendly and jocular disposition. Every line that could possibly be interpreted into a secret inclination for war, was carefully avoided; while, on the other hand, he studied those conceits that might be construed into amity.

In short, he entirely sacrificed every appearance of the warrior to the masquerade of a buffoon. Such exhibitions were not uncommon among the Indians, and as Duncan was already sufficiently disguised in his dress, there certainly did exist some reason for believing that, with his knowledge of French, he might pass for a juggler from Ticonderoga, straggling among the allied and friendly tribes.

When he was thought to be sufficiently painted, the scout gave him much friendly advice; concerted signals, and appointed the place where they should meet, in the event of mutual success. The parting between Munro and his young friend was more melancholy; still, the former submitted to the separation with an indifference that his warm and honest nature would never have permitted in a more healthful state of mind. The scout led Heyward aside, and acquainted him with his intention to leave the veteran in some safe encampment, in charge of Chingachgook, while he and Uncas pursued their inquires among the people they had reason to believe were Delawares. Then, renewing his cautions and advice, he concluded by saying, with a solemnity and warmth of feeling, with which Duncan was deeply touched:

"And, now, God bless you! You have shown a spirit that I like; for it is the gift of youth, more especially one of warm blood and a stout heart. But believe the warning of a man who has reason to know all he says to be true. You will have occasion for your best manhood, and for a sharper wit than what is to be gathered in books, afore you outdo the cunning or get the better of the courage of a Mingo. God bless you! if the Hurons master your scalp, rely on the promise of one who has two stout warriors to back him. They shall pay for their victory, with a life for every hair it holds. I say, young gentleman, may Providence bless your undertaking, which is altogether for good; and, remember, that to outwit the knaves it is lawful to practise things that may not be naturally the gift of a white-skin."

Duncan shook his worthy and reluctant associate warmly by the hand, once more recommended his aged friend to his care, and returning his good wishes, he motioned to David to proceed. Hawkeye gazed after the high-spirited and adventurous young man for several moments, in open admiration; then, shaking his head doubtingly, he turned, and led his own division of the party into the concealment of the forest.

The route taken by Duncan and David lay directly across the clearing of the beavers, and along the margin of their pond.

When the former found himself alone with one so simple, and so little qualified to render any assistance in desperate emergencies, he first began to be sensible of the difficulties of the task he had undertaken. The fading light increased the gloominess of the bleak and savage wilderness that stretched so far on every side of him, and there was even a fearful character in the stillness of those little huts, that he knew were so abundantly peopled. It struck him, as he gazed at the admirable structures and the wonderful precautions of their sagacious inmates, that even the brutes of these vast wilds were possessed of an instinct nearly commensurate with his own reason; and he could not reflect, without anxiety, on the unequal contest that he had so rashly courted. Then came the glowing image of Alice; her distress; her actual danger; and all the peril of his situation was forgotten. Cheering David, he moved on with the light and vigorous step of youth and enterprise.

After making nearly a semicircle around the pond, they diverged from the water-course, and began to ascend to the level of a slight elevation in that bottom land, over which they journeyed. Within half an hour they gained the margin of another opening that bore all the signs of having been also made by the beavers, and which those sagacious animals had probably been induced, by some accident, to abandon, for the more eligible position they now occupied. A very natural sensation caused Duncan to hesitate a moment, unwilling to leave the cover of their bushy path, as a man pauses to collect his energies before he essays any hazardous experiment, in which he is secretly conscious they will all be needed. He profited by the halt, to gather such information as might be obtained from his short and hasty glances.

On the opposite side of the clearing, and near the point where the brook tumbled over some rocks, from a still higher level, some fifty or sixty lodges, rudely fabricated of logs brush, and earth intermingled, were to be discovered. They were arranged without any order, and seemed to be constructed with very little attention to neatness or beauty. Indeed, so very inferior were they in the two latter particulars to the village Duncan had just seen, that he began to expect a second surprise, no less astonishing that the former. This expectation was in no degree diminished, when, by the doubtful twilight, he beheld twenty or thirty forms rising alternately from the cover of the tall, coarse grass, in front of the lodges, and then sinking again from the sight, as it were to burrow in the earth. By the sudden and hasty glimpses that he caught of these figures, they seemed more like dark, glancing specters, or some other unearthly beings, than creatures fashioned with the ordinary and vulgar materials of flesh and blood. A gaunt, naked form was seen, for a single instant, tossing its arms wildly in the air, and then the spot it had filled was vacant; the figure appearing suddenly in some other and distant place, or being succeeded by another, possessing the same mysterious character. David, observing that his companion lingered, pursued the direction of his gaze, and in some measure recalled the recollection of Heyward, by speaking.

"There is much fruitful soil uncultivated here," he said; "and, I may add, without the sinful leaven of self-commendation, that, since my short sojourn in these heathenish abodes, much good seed has been scattered by the wayside."

"The tribes are fonder of the chase than of the arts of men of labor," returned the unconscious Duncan, still gazing at the objects of his wonder.

"It is rather joy than labor to the spirit, to lift up the voice in praise; but sadly do these boys abuse their gifts. Rarely have I found any of their age, on whom nature has so freely bestowed the elements of psalmody; and surely, surely, there are none who neglect them more. Three nights have I now tarried here, and three several times have I assembled the urchins to join in sacred song; and as often have they responded to my efforts with whoopings and howlings that have chilled my soul!"

"Of whom speak you?"

"Of those children of the devil, who waste the precious moments in yonder idle antics. Ah! the wholesome restraint of discipline is but little known among this self-abandoned people. In a country of birches, a rod is never seen, and it ought not to appear a marvel in my eyes, that the choicest blessings of Providence are wasted in such cries as these."

David closed his ears against the juvenile pack, whose yell just then rang shrilly through the forest; and Duncan, suffering his lip to curl, as in mockery of his own superstition, said firmly:

"We will proceed."

Without removing the safeguards form his ears, the master of song complied, and together they pursued their way toward what David was sometimes wont to call the "tents of the Philistines."

CHAPTER XXIII.

"But though the beast of game
The privilege of chase may claim;
Though space and law the stag we lend
Ere hound we slip, or bow we bend;
Whoever recked, where, how, or when
The prowling fox was trapped or slain?"
——Lady of the Lake.

It is unusual to find an encampment of the natives, like those of the more instructed whites, guarded by the presence of armed men. Well informed of the approach of every danger, while it is yet at a distance, the Indian generally rests secure under his knowledge of the signs of the forest, and the long and difficult paths that separate him from those he has most reason to dread. But the enemy who, by any lucky concurrence of accidents, has found means to elude the vigilance of the scouts, will seldom meet with sentinels nearer home to sound the alarm. In addition to this general usage, the tribes friendly to the French knew too well the weight of the blow that had just been struck, to apprehend any immediate danger from the hostile nations that were tributary to the crown of Britain.

When Duncan and David, therefore, found themselves in the center of the children, who played the antics already mentioned, it was without the least previous intimation of their approach. But so soon as they were observed the whole of the juvenile pack raised, by common consent, a shrill and warning whoop; and then sank, as it were, by magic, from before the sight of their visitors. The naked, tawny bodies of the crouching urchins blended so nicely at that hour, with the withered herbage, that at first it seemed as if the earth had, in truth, swallowed up their forms; though when surprise permitted Duncan to bend his look more curiously about the spot, he found it everywhere met by dark, quick, and rolling eyeballs.

Gathering no encouragement from this startling presage of the nature of the scrutiny he was likely to undergo from the more mature judgments of the men, there was an instant when the young soldier would have retreated. It was, however, too late to appear to hesitate. The cry of the children had drawn a dozen warriors to the door of the nearest lodge, where they stood clustered in a dark and savage group, gravely awaiting the nearer approach of those who had unexpectedly come among them.

David, in some measure familiarized to the scene, led the way with a steadiness that no slight obstacle was likely to disconcert, into this very building. It was the principal edifice of the village, though roughly constructed of the bark and branches of trees; being the lodge in which the tribe held its councils and public meetings during their temporary residence on the borders of the English province. Duncan found it difficult to assume the necessary appearance of unconcern, as he brushed the dark and powerful frames of the savages who thronged its threshold; but, conscious that his existence depended on his presence of mind, he trusted to the discretion of his companion, whose footsteps he closely followed, endeavoring, as he proceeded, to rally his thoughts for the occasion. His blood curdled when he found himself in absolute contact with such fierce and implacable enemies; but he so far mastered his feelings as to pursue his way into the center of the lodge, with an exterior that did not betray the weakness. Imitating the example of the deliberate Gamut, he drew a bundle of fragrant brush from beneath a pile that filled the corner of the hut, and seated himself in silence.

So soon as their visitor had passed, the observant warriors fell back from the entrance, and arranging themselves about him, they seemed patiently to await the moment when it might comport with the dignity of the stranger to speak. By far the greater number stood leaning, in lazy, lounging attitudes, against the upright posts that supported the crazy building, while three or four of the oldest and most distinguished of the chiefs placed themselves on the earth a little more in advance.

A flaring torch was burning in the place, and set its red glare from face to face and figure to figure, as it waved in the currents of air. Duncan profited by its light to read the probable character of his reception, in the countenances of his hosts. But his ingenuity availed him little, against the cold artifices of the people he had encountered. The chiefs in front scarce cast a glance at his person, keeping their eyes on the ground, with an air that might have been intended for respect, but which it was quite easy to construe into distrust. The men in the shadow were less reserved. Duncan soon detected their searching, but stolen, looks which, in truth, scanned his person and attire inch by inch; leaving no emotion of the countenance, no gesture, no line of the paint, nor even the fashion of a garment, unheeded, and without comment.

At length one whose hair was beginning to be sprinkled with gray, but whose sinewy limbs and firm tread announced that he was still equal to the duties of manhood, advanced out of the gloom of a corner, whither he had probably posted himself to make his observations unseen, and spoke. He used the language of the Wyandots, or Hurons; his words were, consequently, unintelligible to Heyward, though they seemed, by the gestures that accompanied them, to be uttered more in courtesy than anger. The latter shook his head, and made a gesture indicative of his inability to reply.

"Do none of my brothers speak the French or the English?" he said, in the former language, looking about him from countenance to countenance, in hopes of finding a nod of assent.

Though more than one had turned, as if to catch the meaning of his words, they remained unanswered.

"I should be grieved to think," continued Duncan, speaking slowly, and using the simplest French of which he was the master, "to believe that none of this wise and brave nation understand the language that the 'Grand Monarque' uses when he talks to his children. His heart would be heavy did he believe his red warriors paid him so little respect!"

A long and grave pause succeeded, during which no movement of a limb, nor any expression of an eye, betrayed the expression produced by his remark. Duncan, who knew that silence was a virtue among his hosts, gladly had recourse to the custom, in order to arrange his ideas. At length the same warrior who had before addressed him replied, by dryly demanding, in the language of the Canadas:

"When our Great Father speaks to his people, is it with the tongue of a Huron?"

"He knows no difference in his children, whether the color of the skin be red, or black, or white," returned Duncan, evasively; "though chiefly is he satisfied with the brave Hurons."

"In what manner will he speak," demanded the wary chief, "when the runners count to him the scalps which five nights ago grew on the heads of the Yengeese?"

"They were his enemies," said Duncan, shuddering involuntarily; "and doubtless, he will say, it is good; my Hurons are very gallant."

"Our Canada father does not think it. Instead of looking forward to reward his Indians, his eyes are turned backward. He sees the dead Yengeese, but no Huron. What can this mean?"

"A great chief, like him, has more thoughts than tongues. He looks to see that no enemies are on his trail."

"The canoe of a dead warrior will not float on the Horican," returned the savage, gloomily. "His ears are open to the Delawares, who are not our friends, and they fill them with lies."

"It cannot be. See; he has bid me, who am a man that knows the art of healing, to go to his children, the red Hurons of the great lakes, and ask if any are sick!"

Another silence succeeded this annunciation of the character Duncan had assumed. Every eye was simultaneously bent on his person, as if to inquire into the truth or falsehood of the declaration, with an intelligence and keenness that caused the subject of their scrutiny to tremble for the result. He was, however, relieved again by the former speaker.

"Do the cunning men of the Canadas paint their skins?" the Huron coldly continued; "we have heard them boast that their faces were pale."

"When an Indian chief comes among his white fathers," returned Duncan, with great steadiness, "he lays aside his buffalo robe, to carry the shirt that is offered him. My brothers have given me paint and I wear it."

A low murmur of applause announced that the compliment of the tribe was favorably received. The elderly chief made a gesture of commendation, which was answered by most of his companions, who each threw forth a hand and uttered a brief exclamation of pleasure. Duncan began to breathe more freely, believing that the weight of his examination was past; and, as he had already prepared a simple and probable tale to support his pretended occupation, his hopes of ultimate success grew brighter.

After a silence of a few moments, as if adjusting his thoughts, in order to make a suitable answer to the declaration their guests had just given, another warrior arose, and placed himself in an attitude to speak. While his lips were yet in the act of parting, a low but fearful sound arose from the forest, and was immediately succeeded by a high, shrill yell, that was drawn out, until it equaled the longest and most plaintive howl of the wolf. The sudden and terrible interruption caused Duncan to start from his seat, unconscious of everything but the effect produced by so frightful a cry. At the same moment, the warriors glided in a body from the lodge, and the outer air was filled with loud shouts, that nearly drowned those awful sounds, which were still ringing beneath the arches of the woods. Unable to command himself any longer, the youth broke from the place, and presently stood in the center of a disorderly throng, that included nearly everything having life, within the limits of the encampment. Men, women, and children; the aged, the inform, the active, and the strong, were alike abroad, some exclaiming aloud, others clapping their hands with a joy that seemed frantic, and all expressing their savage pleasure in some unexpected event. Though astounded, at first, by the uproar, Heyward was soon enabled to find its solution by the scene that followed.

There yet lingered sufficient light in the heavens to exhibit those bright openings among the tree-tops, where different paths left the clearing to enter the depths of the wilderness. Beneath one of them, a line of warriors issued from the woods, and advanced slowly toward the dwellings. One in front bore a short pole, on which, as it afterwards appeared, were suspended several human scalps. The startling sounds that Duncan had heard were what the whites have not inappropriately called the "death-hallo"; and each repetition of the cry was intended to announce to the tribe the fate of an enemy. Thus far the knowledge of Heyward assisted him in the explanation; and as he now knew that the interruption was caused by the unlooked-for return of a successful war-party, every disagreeable sensation was quieted in inward congratulation, for the opportune relief and insignificance it conferred on himself.

When at the distance of a few hundred feet from the lodges the newly arrived warriors halted. Their plaintive and terrific cry, which was intended to represent equally the wailings of the dead and the triumph to the victors, had entirely ceased. One of their number now called aloud, in words that were far from appalling, though not more intelligible to those for whose ears they were intended, than their expressive yells. It would be difficult to convey a suitable idea of the savage ecstasy with which the news thus imparted was received. The whole encampment, in a moment, became a scene of the most violent bustle and commotion. The warriors drew their knives, and flourishing them, they arranged themselves in two lines, forming a lane that extended from the war-party to the lodges. The squaws seized clubs, axes, or whatever weapon of offense first offered itself to their hands, and rushed eagerly to act their part in the cruel game that was at hand. Even the children would not be excluded; but boys, little able to wield the instruments, tore the tomahawks from the belts of their fathers, and stole into the ranks, apt imitators of the savage traits exhibited by their parents.

Large piles of brush lay scattered about the clearing, and a wary and aged squaw was occupied in firing as many as might serve to light the coming exhibition. As the flame arose, its power exceeded that of the parting day, and assisted to render objects at the same time more distinct and more hideous. The whole scene formed a striking picture, whose frame was composed of the dark and tall border of pines. The warriors just arrived were the most distant figures. A little in advance stood two men, who were apparently selected from the rest, as the principal actors in what was to follow. The light was not strong enough to render their features distinct, though it was quite evident that they were governed by very different emotions. While one stood erect and firm, prepared to meet his fate like a hero, the other bowed his head, as if palsied by terror or stricken with shame. The high-spirited Duncan felt a powerful impulse of admiration and pity toward the former, though no opportunity could offer to exhibit his generous emotions. He watched his slightest movement, however, with eager eyes; and, as he traced the fine outline of his admirably proportioned and active frame, he endeavored to persuade himself, that, if the powers of man, seconded by such noble resolution, could bear one harmless through so severe a trial, the youthful captive before him might hope for success in the hazardous race he was about to run. Insensibly the young man drew nigher to the swarthy lines of the Hurons, and scarcely breathed, so intense became his interest in the spectacle. Just then the signal yell was given, and the momentary quiet which had preceded it was broken by a burst of cries, that far exceeded any before heard. The more abject of the two victims continued motionless; but the other bounded from the place at the cry, with the activity and swiftness of a deer. Instead of rushing through the hostile lines, as had been expected, he just entered the dangerous defile, and before time was given for a single blow, turned short, and leaping the heads of a row of children, he gained at once the exterior and safer side of the formidable array. The artifice was answered by a hundred voices raised in imprecations; and the whole of the excited multitude broke from their order, and spread themselves about the place in wild confusion.

A dozen blazing piles now shed their lurid brightness on the place, which resembled some unhallowed and supernatural arena, in which malicious demons had assembled to act their bloody and lawless rites. The forms in the background looked like unearthly beings, gliding before the eye, and cleaving the air with frantic and unmeaning gestures; while the savage passions of such as passed the flames were rendered fearfully distinct by the gleams that shot athwart their inflamed visages.

It will easily be understood that, amid such a concourse of vindictive enemies, no breathing time was allowed the fugitive. There was a single moment when it seemed as if he would have reached the forest, but the whole body of his captors threw themselves before him, and drove him back into the center of his relentless persecutors. Turning like a headed deer, he shot, with the swiftness of an arrow, through a pillar of forked flame, and passing the whole multitude harmless, he appeared on the opposite side of the clearing. Here, too, he was met and turned by a few of the older and more subtle of the Hurons. Once more he tried the throng, as if seeking safety in its blindness, and then several moments succeeded, during which Duncan believed the active and courageous young stranger was lost.

Nothing could be distinguished but a dark mass of human forms tossed and involved in inexplicable confusion. Arms, gleaming knives, and formidable clubs, appeared above them, but the blows were evidently given at random. The awful effect was heightened by the piercing shrieks of the women and the fierce yells of the warriors. Now and then Duncan caught a glimpse of a light form cleaving the air in some desperate bound, and he rather hoped than believed that the captive yet retained the command of his astonishing powers of activity. Suddenly the multitude rolled backward, and approached the spot where he himself stood. The heavy body in the rear pressed upon the women and children in front, and bore them to the earth. The stranger reappeared in the confusion. Human power could not, however, much longer endure so severe a trial. Of this the captive seemed conscious. Profiting by the momentary opening, he darted from among the warriors, and made a desperate, and what seemed to Duncan a final effort to gain the wood. As if aware that no danger was to be apprehended from the young soldier, the fugitive nearly brushed his person in his flight. A tall and powerful Huron, who had husbanded his forces, pressed close upon his heels, and with an uplifted arm menaced a fatal blow. Duncan thrust forth a foot, and the shock precipitated the eager savage headlong, many feet in advance of his intended victim. Thought itself is not quicker than was the motion with which the latter profited by the advantage; he turned, gleamed like a meteor again before the eyes of Duncan, and, at the next moment, when the latter recovered his recollection, and gazed around in quest of the captive, he saw him quietly leaning against a small painted post, which stood before the door of the principal lodge.

Apprehensive that the part he had taken in the escape might prove fatal to himself, Duncan left the place without delay. He followed the crowd, which drew nigh the lodges, gloomy and sullen, like any other multitude that had been disappointed in an execution. Curiosity, or perhaps a better feeling, induced him to approach the stranger. He found him, standing with one arm cast about the protecting post, and breathing thick and hard, after his exertions, but disdaining to permit a single sign of suffering to escape. His person was now protected by immemorial and sacred usage, until the tribe in council had deliberated and determined on his fate. It was not difficult, however, to foretell the result, if any presage could be drawn from the feelings of those who crowded the place.

There was no term of abuse known to the Huron vocabulary that the disappointed women did not lavishly expend on the successful stranger. They flouted at his efforts, and told him, with bitter scoffs, that his feet were better than his hands; and that he merited wings, while he knew not the use of an arrow or a knife. To all this the captive made no reply; but was content to preserve an attitude in which dignity was singularly blended with disdain. Exasperated as much by his composure as by his good-fortune, their words became unintelligible, and were succeeded by shrill, piercing yells. Just then the crafty squaw, who had taken the necessary precaution to fire the piles, made her way through the throng, and cleared a place for herself in front of the captive. The squalid and withered person of this hag might well have obtained for her the character of possessing more than human cunning. Throwing back her light vestment, she stretched forth her long, skinny arm, in derision, and using the language of the Lenape, as more intelligible to the subject of her gibes, she commenced aloud:

"Look you, Delaware," she said, snapping her fingers in his face; "your nation is a race of women, and the hoe is better fitted to your hands than the gun. Your squaws are the mothers of deer; but if a bear, or a wildcat, or a serpent were born among you, ye would flee. The Huron girls shall make you petticoats, and we will find you a husband."

A burst of savage laughter succeeded this attack, during which the soft and musical merriment of the younger females strangely chimed with the cracked voice of their older and more malignant companion. But the stranger was superior to all their efforts. His head was immovable; nor did he betray the slightest consciousness that any were present, except when his haughty eye rolled toward the dusky forms of the warriors, who stalked in the background silent and sullen observers of the scene.

Infuriated at the self-command of the captive, the woman placed her arms akimbo; and, throwing herself into a posture of defiance, she broke out anew, in a torrent of words that no art of ours could commit successfully to paper. Her breath was, however, expended in vain; for, although distinguished in her nation as a proficient in the art of abuse, she was permitted to work herself into such a fury as actually to foam at the mouth, without causing a muscle to vibrate in the motionless figure of the stranger. The effect of his indifference began to extend itself to the other spectators; and a youngster, who was just quitting the condition of a boy to enter the state of manhood, attempted to assist the termagant, by flourishing his tomahawk before their victim, and adding his empty boasts to the taunts of the women. Then, indeed, the captive turned his face toward the light, and looked down on the stripling with an expression that was superior to contempt. At the next moment he resumed his quiet and reclining attitude against the post. But the change of posture had permitted Duncan to exchange glances with the firm and piercing eyes of Uncas.

Breathless with amazement, and heavily oppressed with the critical situation of his friend, Heyward recoiled before the look, trembling lest its meaning might, in some unknown manner, hasten the prisoner's fate. There was not, however, any instant cause for such an apprehension. Just then a warrior forced his way into the exasperated crowd. Motioning the women and children aside with a stern gesture, he took Uncas by the arm, and led him toward the door of the council-lodge. Thither all the chiefs, and most of the distinguished warriors, followed; among whom the anxious Heyward found means to enter without attracting any dangerous attention to himself.

A few minutes were consumed in disposing of those present in a manner suitable to their rank and influence in the tribe. An order very similar to that adopted in the preceding interview was observed; the aged and superior chiefs occupying the area of the spacious apartment, within the powerful light of a glaring torch, while their juniors and inferiors were arranged in the background, presenting a dark outline of swarthy and marked visages. In the very center of the lodge, immediately under an opening that admitted the twinkling light of one or two stars, stood Uncas, calm, elevated, and collected. His high and haughty carriage was not lost on his captors, who often bent their looks on his person, with eyes which, while they lost none of their inflexibility of purpose, plainly betrayed their admiration of the stranger's daring.

The case was different with the individual whom Duncan had observed to stand forth with his friend, previously to the desperate trial of speed; and who, instead of joining in the chase, had remained, throughout its turbulent uproar, like a cringing statue, expressive of shame and disgrace. Though not a hand had been extended to greet him, nor yet an eye had condescended to watch his movements, he had also entered the lodge, as though impelled by a fate to whose decrees he submitted, seemingly, without a struggle. Heyward profited by the first opportunity to gaze in his face, secretly apprehensive he might find the features of another acquaintance; but they proved to be those of a stranger, and, what was still more inexplicable, of one who bore all the distinctive marks of a Huron warrior. Instead of mingling with his tribe, however, he sat apart, a solitary being in a multitude, his form shrinking into a crouching and abject attitude, as if anxious to fill as little space as possible. When each individual had taken his proper station, and silence reigned in the place, the gray-haired chief already introduced to the reader, spoke aloud, in the language of the Lenni Lenape.

"Delaware," he said, "though one of a nation of women, you have proved yourself a man. I would give you food; but he who eats with a Huron should become his friend. Rest in peace till the morning sun, when our last words shall be spoken."

"Seven nights, and as many summer days, have I fasted on the trail of the Hurons," Uncas coldly replied; "the children of the Lenape know how to travel the path of the just without lingering to eat."

"Two of my young men are in pursuit of your companion," resumed the other, without appearing to regard the boast of his captive; "when they get back, then will our wise man say to you 'live' or 'die'."

"Has a Huron no ears?" scornfully exclaimed Uncas; "twice, since he has been your prisoner, has the Delaware heard a gun that he knows. Your young men will never come back!"

A short and sullen pause succeeded this bold assertion. Duncan, who understood the Mohican to allude to the fatal rifle of the scout, bent forward in earnest observation of the effect it might produce on the conquerors; but the chief was content with simply retorting:

"If the Lenape are so skillful, why is one of their bravest warriors here?"

"He followed in the steps of a flying coward, and fell into a snare. The cunning beaver may be caught."

As Uncas thus replied, he pointed with his finger toward the solitary Huron, but without deigning to bestow any other notice on so unworthy an object. The words of the answer and the air of the speaker produced a strong sensation among his auditors. Every eye rolled sullenly toward the individual indicated by the simple gesture, and a low, threatening murmur passed through the crowd. The ominous sounds reached the outer door, and the women and children pressing into the throng, no gap had been left, between shoulder and shoulder, that was not now filled with the dark lineaments of some eager and curious human countenance.

In the meantime, the more aged chiefs, in the center, communed with each other in short and broken sentences. Not a word was uttered that did not convey the meaning of the speaker, in the simplest and most energetic form. Again, a long and deeply solemn pause took place. It was known, by all present, to be the brave precursor of a weighty and important judgment. They who composed the outer circle of faces were on tiptoe to gaze; and even the culprit for an instant forgot his shame in a deeper emotion, and exposed his abject features, in order to cast an anxious and troubled glance at the dark assemblage of chiefs. The silence was finally broken by the aged warrior so often named. He arose from the earth, and moving past the immovable form of Uncas, placed himself in a dignified attitude before the offender. At that moment, the withered squaw already mentioned moved into the circle, in a slow, sidling sort of a dance, holding the torch, and muttering the indistinct words of what might have been a species of incantation. Though her presence was altogether an intrusion, it was unheeded.

Approaching Uncas, she held the blazing brand in such a manner as to cast its red glare on his person, and to expose the slightest emotion of his countenance. The Mohican maintained his firm and haughty attitude; and his eyes, so far from deigning to meet her inquisitive look, dwelt steadily on the distance, as though it penetrated the obstacles which impeded the view and looked into futurity. Satisfied with her examination, she left him, with a slight expression of pleasure, and proceeded to practise the same trying experiment on her delinquent countryman.

The young Huron was in his war paint, and very little of a finely molded form was concealed by his attire. The light rendered every limb and joint discernible, and Duncan turned away in horror when he saw they were writhing in irrepressible agony. The woman was commencing a low and plaintive howl at the sad and shameful spectacle, when the chief put forth his hand and gently pushed her aside.

"Reed-that-bends," he said, addressing the young culprit by name, and in his proper language, "though the Great Spirit has made you pleasant to the eyes, it would have been better that you had not been born. Your tongue is loud in the village, but in battle it is still. None of my young men strike the tomahawk deeper into the war-post—none of them so lightly on the Yengeese. The enemy know the shape of your back, but they have never seen the color of your eyes. Three times have they called on you to come, and as often did you forget to answer. Your name will never be mentioned again in your tribe—it is already forgotten."

As the chief slowly uttered these words, pausing impressively between each sentence, the culprit raised his face, in deference to the other's rank and years. Shame, horror, and pride struggled in its lineaments. His eye, which was contracted with inward anguish, gleamed on the persons of those whose breath was his fame; and the latter emotion for an instant predominated. He arose to his feet, and baring his bosom, looked steadily on the keen, glittering knife, that was already upheld by his inexorable judge. As the weapon passed slowly into his heart he even smiled, as if in joy at having found death less dreadful than he had anticipated, and fell heavily on his face, at the feet of the rigid and unyielding form of Uncas.

The squaw gave a loud and plaintive yell, dashed the torch to the earth, and buried everything in darkness. The whole shuddering group of spectators glided from the lodge like troubled sprites; and Duncan thought that he and the yet throbbing body of the victim of an Indian judgment had now become its only tenants.

CHAPTER XXIV.

"Thus spoke the sage: the kings without delay
Dissolve the council, and their chief obey."
—Pope's Iliad

A single moment served to convince the youth that he was mistaken. A hand was laid, with a powerful pressure, on his arm, and the low voice of Uncas muttered in his ear:

"The Hurons are dogs. The sight of a coward's blood can never make a warrior tremble. The 'Gray Head' and the Sagamore are safe, and the rifle of Hawkeye is not asleep. Go—Uncas and the 'Open Hand' are now strangers. It is enough."

Heyward would gladly have heard more, but a gentle push from his friend urged him toward the door, and admonished him of the danger that might attend the discovery of their intercourse. Slowly and reluctantly yielding to the necessity, he quitted the place, and mingled with the throng that hovered nigh. The dying fires in the clearing cast a dim and uncertain light on the dusky figures that were silently stalking to and fro; and occasionally a brighter gleam than common glanced into the lodge, and exhibited the figure of Uncas still maintaining its upright attitude near the dead body of the Huron.

A knot of warriors soon entered the place again, and reissuing, they bore the senseless remains into the adjacent woods. After this termination of the scene, Duncan wandered among the lodges, unquestioned and unnoticed, endeavoring to find some trace of her in whose behalf he incurred the risk he ran. In the present temper of the tribe it would have been easy to have fled and rejoined his companions, had such a wish crossed his mind. But, in addition to the never-ceasing anxiety on account of Alice, a fresher though feebler interest in the fate of Uncas assisted to chain him to the spot. He continued, therefore, to stray from hut to hut, looking into each only to encounter additional disappointment, until he had made the entire circuit of the village. Abandoning a species of inquiry that proved so fruitless, he retraced his steps to the council-lodge, resolved to seek and question David, in order to put an end to his doubts.

On reaching the building, which had proved alike the seat of judgment and the place of execution, the young man found that the excitement had already subsided. The warriors had reassembled, and were now calmly smoking, while they conversed gravely on the chief incidents of their recent expedition to the head of the Horican. Though the return of Duncan was likely to remind them of his character, and the suspicious circumstances of his visit, it produced no visible sensation. So far, the terrible scene that had just occurred proved favorable to his views, and he required no other prompter than his own feelings to convince him of the expediency of profiting by so unexpected an advantage.

Without seeming to hesitate, he walked into the lodge, and took his seat with a gravity that accorded admirably with the deportment of his hosts. A hasty but searching glance sufficed to tell him that, though Uncas still remained where he had left him, David had not reappeared. No other restraint was imposed on the former than the watchful looks of a young Huron, who had placed himself at hand; though an armed warrior leaned against the post that formed one side of the narrow doorway. In every other respect, the captive seemed at liberty; still he was excluded from all participation in the discourse, and possessed much more of the air of some finely molded statue than a man having life and volition.

Heyward had too recently witnessed a frightful instance of the prompt punishments of the people into whose hands he had fallen to hazard an exposure by any officious boldness. He would greatly have preferred silence and meditation to speech, when a discovery of his real condition might prove so instantly fatal. Unfortunately for this prudent resolution, his entertainers appeared otherwise disposed. He had not long occupied the seat wisely taken a little in the shade, when another of the elder warriors, who spoke the French language, addressed him:

"My Canada father does not forget his children," said the chief; "I thank him. An evil spirit lives in the wife of one of my young men. Can the cunning stranger frighten him away?"

Heyward possessed some knowledge of the mummery practised among the Indians, in the cases of such supposed visitations. He saw, at a glance, that the circumstance might possibly be improved to further his own ends. It would, therefore, have been difficult, just then to have uttered a proposal that would have given him more satisfaction. Aware of the necessity of preserving the dignity of his imaginary character, however, he repressed his feelings, and answered with suitable mystery:

"Spirits differ; some yield to the power of wisdom, while others are too strong."

"My brother is a great medicine," said the cunning savage; "he will try?"

A gesture of assent was the answer. The Huron was content with the assurance, and, resuming his pipe, he awaited the proper moment to move. The impatient Heyward, inwardly execrating the cold customs of the savages, which required such sacrifices to appearance, was fain to assume an air of indifference, equal to that maintained by the chief, who was, in truth, a near relative of the afflicted woman. The minutes lingered, and the delay had seemed an hour to the adventurer in empiricism, when the Huron laid aside his pipe and drew his robe across his breast, as if about to lead the way to the lodge of the invalid. Just then, a warrior of powerful frame, darkened the door, and stalking d may you never commit an act, that shall cause Him to darken His face. I know not whether we shall sustained Duncan. The latter cast an impatient look at his neighbor, and felt his flesh creep with uncontrollable horror when he found himself in actual contact with Magua.

The sudden return of this artful and dreaded chief caused a delay in the departure of the Huron. Several pipes, that had been extinguished, were lighted again; while the newcomer, without speaking a word, drew his tomahawk from his girdle, and filling the bowl on its head began to inhale the vapors of the weed through the hollow handle, with as much indifference as if he had not been absent two weary days on a long and toilsome hunt. Ten minutes, which appeared so many ages to Duncan, might have passed in this manner; and the warriors were fairly enveloped in a cloud of white smoke before any of them spoke.

"Welcome!" one at length uttered; "has my friend found the moose?"

"The young men stagger under their burdens," returned Magua. "Let 'Reed-that-bends' go on the hunting path; he will meet them."

A deep and awful silence succeeded the utterance of the forbidden name. Each pipe dropped from the lips of its owner as though all had inhaled an impurity at the same instant. The smoke wreathed above their heads in little eddies, and curling in a spiral form it ascended swiftly through the opening in the roof of the lodge, leaving the place beneath clear of its fumes, and each dark visage distinctly visible. The looks of most of the warriors were riveted on the earth; though a few of the younger and less gifted of the party suffered their wild and glaring eyeballs to roll in the direction of a white-headed savage, who sat between two of the most venerated chiefs of the tribe. There was nothing in the air or attire of this Indian that would seem to entitle him to such a distinction. The former was rather depressed, than remarkable for the bearing of the natives; and the latter was such as was commonly worn by the ordinary men of the nation. Like most around him for more than a minute his look, too, was on the ground; but, trusting his eyes at length to steal a glance aside, he perceived that he was becoming an object of general attention. Then he arose and lifted his voice in the general silence.

"It was a lie," he said; "I had no son. He who was called by that name is forgotten; his blood was pale, and it came not from the veins of a Huron; the wicked Chippewas cheated my squaw. The Great Spirit has said, that the family of Wiss-entush should end; he is happy who knows that the evil of his race dies with himself. I have done."

The speaker, who was the father of the recreant young Indian, looked round and about him, as if seeking commendation of his stoicism in the eyes of the auditors. But the stern customs of his people had made too severe an exaction of the feeble old man. The expression of his eye contradicted his figurative and boastful language, while every muscle in his wrinkled visage was working with anguish. Standing a single minute to enjoy his bitter triumph, he turned away, as if sickening at the gaze of men, and, veiling his face in his blanket, he walked from the lodge with the noiseless step of an Indian seeking, in the privacy of his own abode, the sympathy of one like himself, aged, forlorn and childless.

The Indians, who believe in the hereditary transmission of virtues and defects in character, suffered him to depart in silence. Then, with an elevation of breeding that many in a more cultivated state of society might profitably emulate, one of the chiefs drew the attention of the young men from the weakness they had just witnessed, by saying, in a cheerful voice, addressing himself in courtesy to Magua, as the newest comer:

"The Delawares have been like bears after the honey pots, prowling around my village. But who has ever found a Huron asleep?"

The darkness of the impending cloud which precedes a burst of thunder was not blacker than the brow of Magua as he exclaimed:

"The Delawares of the Lakes!"

"Not so. They who wear the petticoats of squaws, on their own river. One of them has been passing the tribe."

"Did my young men take his scalp?"

"His legs were good, though his arm is better for the hoe than the tomahawk," returned the other, pointing to the immovable form of Uncas.

Instead of manifesting any womanish curiosity to feast his eyes with the sight of a captive from a people he was known to have so much reason to hate, Magua continued to smoke, with the meditative air that he usually maintained, when there was no immediate call on his cunning or his eloquence. Although secretly amazed at the facts communicated by the speech of the aged father, he permitted himself to ask no questions, reserving his inquiries for a more suitable moment. It was only after a sufficient interval that he shook the ashes from his pipe, replaced the tomahawk, tightened his girdle, and arose, casting for the first time a glance in the direction of the prisoner, who stood a little behind him. The wary, though seemingly abstracted Uncas, caught a glimpse of the movement, and turning suddenly to the light, their looks met. Near a minute these two bold and untamed spirits stood regarding one another steadily in the eye, neither quailing in the least before the fierce gaze he encountered. The form of Uncas dilated, and his nostrils opened like those of a tiger at bay; but so rigid and unyielding was his posture, that he might easily have been converted by the imagination into an exquisite and faultless representation of the warlike deity of his tribe. The lineaments of the quivering features of Magua proved more ductile; his countenance gradually lost its character of defiance in an expression of ferocious joy, and heaving a breath from the very bottom of his chest, he pronounced aloud the formidable name of:

"Le Cerf Agile!"

Each warrior sprang upon his feet at the utterance of the well-known appellation, and there was a short period during which the stoical constancy of the natives was completely conquered by surprise. The hated and yet respected name was repeated as by one voice, carrying the sound even beyond the limits of the lodge. The women and children, who lingered around the entrance, took up the words in an echo, which was succeeded by another shrill and plaintive howl. The latter was not yet ended, when the sensation among the men had entirely abated. Each one in presence seated himself, as though ashamed of his precipitation; but it was many minutes before their meaning eyes ceased to roll toward their captive, in curious examination of a warrior who had so often proved his prowess on the best and proudest of their nation. Uncas enjoyed his victory, but was content with merely exhibiting his triumph by a quiet smile—an emblem of scorn which belongs to all time and every nation.

Magua caught the expression, and raising his arm, he shook it at the captive, the light silver ornaments attached to his bracelet rattling with the trembling agitation of the limb, as, in a tone of vengeance, he exclaimed, in English:

"Mohican, you die!"

"The healing waters will never bring the dead Hurons to life," returned Uncas, in the music of the Delawares; "the tumbling river washes their bones; their men are squaws: their women owls. Go! call together the Huron dogs, that they may look upon a warrior, My nostrils are offended; they scent the blood of a coward."

The latter allusion struck deep, and the injury rankled. Many of the Hurons understood the strange tongue in which the captive spoke, among which number was Magua. This cunning savage beheld, and instantly profited by his advantage. Dropping the light robe of skin from his shoulder, he stretched forth his arm, and commenced a burst of his dangerous and artful eloquence. However much his influence among his people had been impaired by his occasional and besetting weakness, as well as by his desertion of the tribe, his courage and his fame as an orator were undeniable. He never spoke without auditors, and rarely without making converts to his opinions. On the present occasion, his native powers were stimulated by the thirst of revenge.

He again recounted the events of the attack on the island at Glenn's, the death of his associates and the escape of their most formidable enemies. Then he described the nature and position of the mount whither he had led such captives as had fallen into their hands. Of his own bloody intentions toward the maidens, and of his baffled malice he made no mention, but passed rapidly on to the surprise of the party by "La Longue Carabine," and its fatal termination. Here he paused, and looked about him, in affected veneration for the departed, but, in truth, to note the effect of his opening narrative. As usual, every eye was riveted on his face. Each dusky figure seemed a breathing statue, so motionless was the posture, so intense the attention of the individual.

Then Magua dropped his voice which had hitherto been clear, strong and elevated, and touched upon the merits of the dead. No quality that was likely to command the sympathy of an Indian escaped his notice. One had never been known to follow the chase in vain; another had been indefatigable on the trail of their enemies. This was brave, that generous. In short, he so managed his allusions, that in a nation which was composed of so few families, he contrived to strike every chord that might find, in its turn, some breast in which to vibrate.

"Are the bones of my young men," he concluded, "in the burial-place of the Hurons? You know they are not. Their spirits are gone toward the setting sun, and are already crossing the great waters, to the happy hunting-grounds. But they departed without food, without guns or knives, without moccasins, naked and poor as they were born. Shall this be? Are their souls to enter the land of the just like hungry Iroquois or unmanly Delawares, or shall they meet their friends with arms in their hands and robes on their backs? What will our fathers think the tribes of the Wyandots have become? They will look on their children with a dark eye, and say, 'Go! a Chippewa has come hither with the name of a Huron.' Brothers, we must not forget the dead; a red-skin never ceases to remember. We will load the back of this Mohican until he staggers under our bounty, and dispatch him after my young men. They call to us for aid, though our ears are not open; they say, 'Forget us not.' When they see the spirit of this Mohican toiling after them with his burden, they will know we are of that mind. Then will they go on happy; and our children will say, 'So did our fathers to their friends, so must we do to them.' What is a Yengee? we have slain many, but the earth is still pale. A stain on the name of Huron can only be hid by blood that comes from the veins of an Indian. Let this Delaware die."

The effect of such an harangue, delivered in the nervous language and with the emphatic manner of a Huron orator, could scarcely be mistaken. Magua had so artfully blended the natural sympathies with the religious superstition of his auditors, that their minds, already prepared by custom to sacrifice a victim to the manes of their countrymen, lost every vestige of humanity in a wish for revenge. One warrior in particular, a man of wild and ferocious mien, had been conspicuous for the attention he had given to the words of the speaker. His countenance had changed with each passing emotion, until it settled into a look of deadly malice. As Magua ended he arose and, uttering the yell of a demon, his polished little axe was seen glancing in the torchlight as he whirled it above his head. The motion and the cry were too sudden for words to interrupt his bloody intention. It appeared as if a bright gleam shot from his hand, which was crossed at the same moment by a dark and powerful line. The former was the tomahawk in its passage; the latter the arm that Magua darted forward to divert its aim. The quick and ready motion of the chief was not entirely too late. The keen weapon cut the war plume from the scalping tuft of Uncas, and passed through the frail wall of the lodge as though it were hurled from some formidable engine.

Duncan had seen the threatening action, and sprang upon his feet, with a heart which, while it leaped into his throat, swelled with the most generous resolution in behalf of his friend. A glance told him that the blow had failed, and terror changed to admiration. Uncas stood still, looking his enemy in the eye with features that seemed superior to emotion. Marble could not be colder, calmer, or steadier than the countenance he put upon this sudden and vindictive attack. Then, as if pitying a want of skill which had proved so fortunate to himself, he smiled, and muttered a few words of contempt in his own tongue.

"No!" said Magua, after satisfying himself of the safety of the captive; "the sun must shine on his shame; the squaws must see his flesh tremble, or our revenge will be like the play of boys. Go! take him where there is silence; let us see if a Delaware can sleep at night, and in the morning die."

The young men whose duty it was to guard the prisoner instantly passed their ligaments of bark across his arms, and led him from the lodge, amid a profound and ominous silence. It was only as the figure of Uncas stood in the opening of the door that his firm step hesitated. There he turned, and, in the sweeping and haughty glance that he threw around the circle of his enemies, Duncan caught a look which he was glad to construe into an expression that he was not entirely deserted by hope.

Magua was content with his success, or too much occupied with his secret purposes to push his inquiries any further. Shaking his mantle, and folding it on his bosom, he also quitted the place, without pursuing a subject which might have proved so fatal to the individual at his elbow. Notwithstanding his rising resentment, his natural firmness, and his anxiety on behalf of Uncas, Heyward felt sensibly relieved by the absence of so dangerous and so subtle a foe. The excitement produced by the speech gradually subsided. The warriors resumed their seats and clouds of smoke once more filled the lodge. For near half an hour, not a syllable was uttered, or scarcely a look cast aside; a grave and meditative silence being the ordinary succession to every scene of violence and commotion among these beings, who were alike so impetuous and yet so self-restrained.

When the chief, who had solicited the aid of Duncan, finished his pipe, he made a final and successful movement toward departing. A motion of a finger was the intimation he gave the supposed physician to follow; and passing through the clouds of smoke, Duncad was glad, on more accounts than one, to be able at last to breathe the pure air of a cool and refreshing summer evening.

Instead of pursuing his way among those lodges where Heyward had already made his unsuccessful search, his companion turned aside, and proceeded directly toward the base of an adjacent mountain, which overhung the temporary village. A thicket of brush skirted its foot, and it became necessary to proceed through a crooked and narrow path. The boys had resumed their sports in the clearing, and were enacting a mimic chase to the post among themselves. In order to render their games as like the reality as possible, one of the boldest of their number had conveyed a few brands into some piles of tree-tops that had hitherto escaped the burning. The blaze of one of these fires lighted the way of the chief and Duncan, and gave a character of additional wildness to the rude scenery. At a little distance from a bald rock, and directly in its front, they entered a grassy opening, which they prepared to cross. Just then fresh fuel was added to the fire, and a powerful light penetrated even to that distant spot. It fell upon the white surface of the mountain, and was reflected downward upon a dark and mysterious-looking being that arose, unexpectedly, in their path. The

Indian paused, as if doubtful whether to proceed, and permitted his companion to approach his side. A large black ball, which at first seemed stationary, now began to move in a manner that to the latter was inexplicable. Again the fire brightened and its glare fell more distinctly on the object. Then even Duncan knew it, by its restless and sidling attitudes, which kept the upper part of its form in constant motion, while the animal itself appeared seated, to be a bear. Though it growled loudly and fiercely, and there were instants when its glistening eyeballs might be seen, it gave no other indications of hostility. The Huron, at least, seemed assured that the intentions of this singular intruder were peaceable, for after giving it an attentive examination, he quietly pursued his course.

Duncan, who knew that the animal was often domesticated among the Indians, followed the example of his companion, believing that some favorite of the tribe had found its way into the thicket, in search of food. They passed it unmolested. Though obliged to come nearly in contact with the monster, the Huron, who had at first so warily determined the character of his strange visitor, was now content with proceeding without wasting a moment in further examination; but Heyward was unable to prevent his eyes from looking backward, in salutary watchfulness against attacks in the rear. His uneasiness was in no degree diminished when he perceived the beast rolling along their path, and following their footsteps. He would have spoken, but the Indian at that moment shoved aside a door of bark, and entered a cavern in the bosom of the mountain.

Profiting by so easy a method of retreat, Duncan stepped after him, and was gladly closing the slight cover to the opening, when he felt it drawn from his hand by the beast, whose shaggy form immediately darkened the passage. They were now in a straight and long gallery, in a chasm of the rocks, where retreat without encountering the animal was impossible. Making the best of the circumstances, the young man pressed forward, keeping as close as possible to his conductor. The bear growled frequently at his heels, and once or twice its enormous paws were laid on his person, as if disposed to prevent his further passage into the den.

How long the nerves of Heyward would have sustained him in this extraordinary situation, it might be difficult to decide, for, happily, he soon found relief. A glimmer of light had constantly been in their front, and they now arrived at the place whence it proceeded.

A large cavity in the rock had been rudely fitted to answer the purposes of many apartments. The subdivisions were simple but ingenious, being composed of stone, sticks, and bark, intermingled. Openings above admitted the light by day, and at night fires and torches supplied the place of the sun. Hither the Hurons had brought most of their valuables, especially those which more particularly pertained to the nation; and hither, as it now appeared, the sick woman, who was believed to be the victim of supernatural power, had been transported also, under an impression that her tormentor would find more difficulty in making his assaults through walls of stone than through the leafy coverings of the lodges. The apartment into which Duncan and his guide first entered, had been exclusively devoted to her accommodation. The latter approached her bedside, which was surrounded by females, in the center of whom Heyward was surprised to find his missing friend David.

A single look was sufficient to apprise the pretended leech that the invalid was far beyond his powers of healing. She lay in a sort of paralysis, indifferent to the objects which crowded before her sight, and happily unconscious of suffering. Heyward was far from regretting that his mummeries were to be performed on one who was much too ill to take an interest in their failure or success. The slight qualm of conscience which had been excited by the intended deception was instantly appeased, and he began to collect his thoughts, in order to enact his part with suitable spirit, when he found he was about to be anticipated in his skill by an attempt to prove the power of music.

Gamut, who had stood prepared to pour forth his spirit in song when the visitors entered, after delaying a moment, drew a strain from his pipe, and commenced a hymn that might have worked a miracle, had faith in its efficacy been of much avail. He was allowed to proceed to the close, the Indians respecting his imaginary infirmity, and Duncan too glad of the delay to hazard the slightest interruption. As the dying cadence of his strains was falling on the ears of the latter, he started aside at hearing them repeated behind him, in a voice half human and half sepulchral. Looking around, he beheld the shaggy monster seated on end in a shadow of the cavern, where, while his restless body swung in the uneasy manner of the animal, it repeated, in a sort of low growl, sounds, if not words, which bore some slight resemblance to the melody of the singer.

The effect of so strange an echo on David may better be imagined than described. His eyes opened as if he doubted their truth; and his voice became instantly mute in excess of wonder. A deep-laid scheme, of communicating some important intelligence to Heyward, was driven from his recollection by an emotion which very nearly resembled fear, but which he was fain to believe was admiration. Under its influence, he exclaimed aloud: "She expects you, and is at hand"; and precipitately left the cavern.

## CHAPTER XXV.

"Snug.—Have you the lion's part written? Pray you, if it
be, give it to me, for I am slow of study.

Quince.—You may do it extempore, for it is nothing but
roaring."
—Midsummer Night's Dream.

There was a strange blending of the ridiculous with that which was solemn in this scene. The beast still continued its rolling, and apparently untiring movements, though its ludicrous attempt to imitate the melody of David ceased the instant the latter abandoned the field. The words of Gamut were, as has been seen, in his native tongue; and to Duncan they seem pregnant with some hidden meaning, though nothing present assisted him in discovering the object of their allusion. A speedy end was, however, put to every conjecture on the subject, by the manner of the chief, who advanced to the bedside of the invalid, and beckoned away the whole group of female attendants that had clustered there to witness the skill of the stranger. He was implicitly, though reluctantly, obeyed; and when the low echo which rang along the hollow, natural gallery, from the distant closing door, had ceased, pointing toward his insensible daughter, he said:

"Now let my brother show his power."

Thus unequivocally called on to exercise the functions of his assumed character, Heyward was apprehensive that the smallest delay might prove dangerous. Endeavoring, then, to collect his ideas, he prepared to perform that species of incantation, and those uncouth rites, under which the Indian conjurers are accustomed to conceal their ignorance and impotency. It is more than probable that, in the disordered state of his thoughts, he would soon have fallen into some suspicious, if not fatal, error had not his incipient attempts been interrupted by a fierce growl from the quadruped. Three several times did he renew his efforts to proceed, and as often was he met by the same unaccountable opposition, each interruption seeming more savage and threatening than the preceding.

"The cunning ones are jealous," said the Huron; "I go. Brother, the woman is the wife of one of my bravest young men; deal justly by her. Peace!" he added, beckoning to the discontented beast to be quiet; "I go."

The chief was as good as his word, and Duncan now found himself alone in that wild and desolate abode with the helpless invalid and the fierce and dangerous brute. The latter listened to the movements of the Indian with that air of sagacity that a bear is known to possess, until another echo announced that he had also left the cavern, when it turned and came waddling up to Duncan before whom it seated itself in its natural attitude, erect like a man. The youth looked anxiously about him for some weapon, with which he might make a resistance against the attack he now seriously expected.

It seemed, however, as if the humor of the animal had suddenly changed. Instead of continuing its discontented growls, or manifesting any further signs of anger, the whole of its shaggy body shook violently, as if agitated by some strange internal convulsion. The huge and unwieldy talons pawed stupidly about the grinning muzzle, and while Heyward kept his eyes riveted on its movements with jealous watchfulness, the grim head fell on one side and in its place appeared the honest sturdy countenance of the scout, who was indulging from the bottom of his soul in his own peculiar expression of merriment.

"Hist!" said the wary woodsman, interrupting Heyward's exclamation of surprise; "the varlets are about the place, and any sounds that are not natural to witchcraft would bring them back upon us in a body."

"Tell me the meaning of this masquerade; and why you have attempted so desperate an adventure?"

"Ah, reason and calculation are often outdone by accident," returned the scout. "But, as a story should always commence at the beginning, I will tell you the whole in order. After we parted I placed the commandant and the Sagamore in an old beaver lodge, where they are safer from the Hurons than they would be in the garrison of Edward; for your high north-west Indians, not having as yet got the traders among them, continued to venerate the beaver. After which Uncas and I pushed for the other encampment as was agreed. Have you seen the lad?"

"To my great grief! He is captive, and condemned to die at the rising of the sun."

"I had misgivings that such would be his fate," resumed the scout, in a less confident and joyous tone. But soon regaining his naturally firm voice, he continued: "His bad fortune is the true reason of my being here, for it would never do to abandon such a boy to the Hurons. A rare time the knaves would have of it, could they tie 'The Bounding Elk' and 'The Long Carabine', as they call me, to the same stake! Though why they have given me such a name I never knew, there being as little likeness between the gifts of 'killdeer' and the performance of one of your real Canada carabynes, as there is between the natur' of a pipe-stone and a flint."

"Keep to your tale," said the impatient Heyward; "we know not at what moment the Hurons may return."

"No fear of them. A conjurer must have his time, like a straggling priest in the settlements. We are as safe from interruption as a missionary would be at the beginning of a two hours' discourse. Well, Uncas and I fell in with a return party of the varlets; the lad was much too forward for a scout; nay, for that matter, being of hot blood, he was not so much to blame; and, after all, one of the Hurons proved a coward, and in fleeing led him into an ambushment."

"And dearly has he paid for the weakness."

The scout significantly passed his hand across his own throat, and nodded, as if he said, "I comprehend your meaning." After which he continued, in a more audible though scarcely more intelligible language:

"After the loss of the boy I turned upon the Hurons, as you may judge. There have been scrimmages atween one or two of their outlyers and myself; but that is neither here nor there. So, after I had shot the imps, I got in pretty nigh to the lodges without further commotion. Then what should luck do in my favor but lead me to the very spot where one of the most famous conjurers of the tribe was dressing himself, as I well knew, for some great battle with Satan—though why should I call that luck, which it now seems was an especial ordering of Providence. So a judgmatical rap over the head stiffened the lying impostor for a time, and leaving him a bit of walnut for his supper, to prevent an uproar, and stringing him up atween two saplings, I made free with his finery, and took the part of the bear on myself, in order that the operations might proceed."

"And admirably did you enact the character; the animal itself might have been shamed by the representation."

"Lord, major," returned the flattered woodsman, "I should be but a poor scholar for one who has studied so long in the wilderness, did I not know how to set forth the movements or natur' of such a beast. Had it been now a catamount, or even a full-size panther, I would have embellished a performance for you worth regarding. But it is no such marvelous feat to exhibit the feats of so dull a beast; though, for that matter, too, a bear may be overacted. Yes, yes; it is not every imitator that knows natur' may be outdone easier than she is equaled. But all our work is yet before us. Where is the gentle one?"

"Heaven knows. I have examined every lodge in the village, without discovering the slightest trace of her presence in the tribe."

"You heard what the singer said, as he left us: 'She is at hand, and expects you'?"

"I have been compelled to believe he alluded to this unhappy woman."

"The simpleton was frightened, and blundered through his message; but he had a deeper meaning. Here are walls enough to separate the whole settlement. A bear ought to climb; therefore will I take a look above them. There may be honey-pots hid in these rocks, and I am a beast, you know, that has a hankering for the sweets."

The scout looked behind him, laughing at his own conceit, while he clambered up the partition, imitating, as he went, the clumsy motions of the beast he represented; but the instant the summit was gained he made a gesture for silence, and slid down with the utmost precipitation.

"She is here," he whispered, "and by that door you will find her. I would have spoken a word of comfort to the afflicted soul; but the sight of such a monster might upset her reason. Though for that matter, major, you are none of the most inviting yourself in your paint."

Duncan, who had already swung eagerly forward, drew instantly back on hearing these discouraging words.

"Am I, then, so very revolting?" he demanded, with an air of chagrin.

"You might not startle a wolf, or turn the Royal Americans from a discharge; but I have seen the time when you had a better favored look; your streaked countenances are not ill-judged of by the squaws, but young women of white blood give the preference to their own color. See," he added, pointing to a place where the water trickled from a rock, forming a little crystal spring, before it found an issue through the adjacent crevices; "you may easily get rid of the Sagamore's daub, and when you come back I will try my hand at a new embellishment. It's as common for a conjurer to alter his paint as for a buck in the settlements to change his finery."

The deliberate woodsman had little occasion to hunt for arguments to enforce his advice. He was yet speaking when Duncan availed himself of the water. In a moment every frightful or offensive mark was obliterated, and the youth appeared again in the lineaments with which he had been gifted by nature. Thus prepared for an interview with his mistress, he took a hasty leave of his companion, and disappeared through the indicated passage. The scout witnessed his departure with complacency, nodding his head after him, and muttering his good wishes; after which he very coolly set about an examination of the state of the larder, among the Hurons, the cavern, among other purposes, being used as a receptacle for the fruits of their hunts.

Duncan had no other guide than a distant glimmering light, which served, however, the office of a polar star to the lover. By its aid he was enabled to enter the haven of his hopes, which was merely another apartment of the cavern, that had been solely appropriated to the safekeeping of so important a prisoner as a daughter of the commandant of William Henry. It was profusely strewed with the plunder of that unlucky fortress. In the midst of this confusion he found her he sought, pale, anxious and terrified, but lovely. David had prepared her for such a visit.

"Duncan!" she exclaimed, in a voice that seemed to tremble at the sounds created by itself.

"Alice!" he answered, leaping carelessly among trunks, boxes, arms, and furniture, until he stood at her side.

"I knew that you would never desert me," she said, looking up with a momentary glow on her otherwise dejected countenance. "But you are alone! Grateful as it is to be thus remembered, I could wish to think you are not entirely alone."

Duncan, observing that she trembled in a manner which betrayed her inability to stand, gently induced her to be seated, while he recounted those leading incidents which it has been our task to accord. Alice listened with breathless interest; and though the young man touched lightly on the sorrows of the stricken father; taking care, however, not to wound the self-love of his auditor, the tears ran as freely down the cheeks of the daughter as though she had never wept before. The soothing tenderness of Duncan, however, soon quieted the first burst of her emotions, and she then heard him to the close with undivided attention, if not with composure.

"And now, Alice," he added, "you will see how much is still expected of you. By the assistance of our experienced and invaluable friend, the scout, we may find our way from this savage people, but you will have to exert your utmost fortitude. Remember that you fly to the arms of your venerable parent, and how much his happiness, as well as your own, depends on those exertions."

"Can I do otherwise for a father who has done so much for me?"

"And for me, too," continued the youth, gently pressing the hand he held in both his own.

The look of innocence and surprise which he received in return convinced Duncan of the necessity of being more explicit.

"This is neither the place nor the occasion to detain you with selfish wishes," he added; "but what heart loaded like mine would not wish to cast its burden? They say misery is the closest of all ties; our common suffering in your behalf left but little to be explained between your father and myself."

"And, dearest Cora, Duncan; surely Cora was not forgotten?"

"Not forgotten! no; regretted, as woman was seldom mourned before. Your venerable father knew no difference between his children; but I—Alice, you will not be offended when I say, that to me her worth was in a degree obscured—"

"Then you knew not the merit of my sister," said Alice, withdrawing her hand; "of you she ever speaks as of one who is her dearest friend."

"I would gladly believe her such," returned Duncan, hastily; "I could wish her to be even more; but with you, Alice, I have the permission of your father to aspire to a still nearer and dearer tie."

Alice trembled violently, and there was an instant during which she bent her face aside, yielding to the emotions common to her sex; but they quickly passed away, leaving her mistress of her deportment, if not of her affections.

"Heyward," she said, looking him full in the face with a touching expression of innocence and dependency, "give me the sacred presence and the holy sanction of that parent before you urge me further."

"Though more I should not, less I could not say," the youth was about to answer, when he was interrupted by a light tap on his shoulder. Starting to his feet, he turned, and, confronting the intruder, his looks fell on the dark form and malignant visage of Magua. The deep guttural laugh of the savage sounded, at such a moment, to Duncan, like the hellish taunt of a demon. Had he pursued the sudden and fierce impulse of the instant, he would have cast himself on the Huron, and committed their fortunes to the issue of a deadly struggle. But, without arms of any description, ignorant of what succor his subtle enemy could command, and charged with the safety of one who was just then dearer than ever to his heart, he no sooner entertained than he abandoned the desperate intention.

"What is your purpose?" said Alice, meekly folding her arms on her bosom, and struggling to conceal an agony of apprehension in behalf of Heyward, in the usual cold and distant manner with which she received the visits of her captor.

The exulting Indian had resumed his austere countenance, though he drew warily back before the menacing glance of the young man's fiery eye. He regarded both his captives for a moment with a steady look, and then, stepping aside, he dropped a log of wood across a door different from that by which Duncan had entered. The latter now comprehended the manner of his surprise, and, believing himself irretrievably lost, he drew Alice to his bosom, and stood prepared to meet a fate which he hardly regretted, since it was to be suffered in such company. But Magua meditated no immediate violence. His first measures were very evidently taken to secure his new captive; nor did he even bestow a second glance at the motionless forms in the center of the cavern, until he had completely cut off every hope of retreat through the private outlet he had himself used. He was watched in all his movements by Heyward, who, however, remained firm, still folding the fragile form of Alice to his heart, at once too proud and too hopeless to ask favor of an enemy so often foiled. When Magua had effected his object he approached his prisoners, and said in English:

"The pale faces trap the cunning beavers; but the red-skins know how to take the Yengeese."

"Huron, do your worst!" exclaimed the excited Heyward, forgetful that a double stake was involved in his life; "you and your vengeance are alike despised."

"Will the white man speak these words at the stake?" asked Magua; manifesting, at the same time, how little faith he had in the other's resolution by the sneer that accompanied his words.

"Here; singly to your face, or in the presence of your nation."

"Le Renard Subtil is a great chief!" returned the Indian; "he will go and bring his young men, to see how bravely a pale face can laugh at tortures."

He turned away while speaking, and was about to leave the place through the avenue by which Duncan had approached, when a growl caught his ear, and caused him to hesitate. The figure of the bear appeared in the door, where it sat, rolling from side to side in its customary restlessness. Magua, like the father of the sick woman, eyed it keenly for a moment, as if to ascertain its character. He was far above the more vulgar superstitions of his tribe, and so soon as he recognized the well-known attire of the conjurer, he prepared to pass it in cool contempt. But a louder and more threatening growl caused him again to pause. Then he seemed as if suddenly resolved to trifle no longer, and moved resolutely forward.

The mimic animal, which had advanced a little, retired slowly in his front, until it arrived again at the pass, when, rearing on his hinder legs, it beat the air with its paws, in the manner practised by its brutal prototype.

"Fool!" exclaimed the chief, in Huron, "go play with the children and squaws; leave men to their wisdom."

He once more endeavored to pass the supposed empiric, scorning even the parade of threatening to use the knife, or tomahawk, that was pendent from his belt. Suddenly the beast extended its arms, or rather legs, and inclosed him in a grasp that might have vied with the far-famed power of the "bear's hug" itself. Heyward had watched the whole procedure, on the part of Hawkeye, with breathless interest. At first he relinquished his hold of Alice; then he caught up a thong of buckskin, which had been used around some bundle, and when he beheld his enemy with his two arms pinned to his side by the iron muscles of the scout, he rushed upon him, and effectually secured them there. Arms, legs, and feet were encircled in twenty folds of the thong, in less time than we have taken to record the circumstance. When the formidable Huron was completely pinioned, the scout released his hold, and Duncan laid his enemy on his back, utterly helpless.

Throughout the whole of this sudden and extraordinary operation, Magua, though he had struggled violently, until assured he was in the hands of one whose nerves were far better strung than his own, had not uttered the slightest exclamation. But when Hawkeye, by way of making a summary explanation of his conduct, removed the shaggy jaws of the beast, and exposed his own rugged and earnest countenance to the gaze of the Huron, the philosophy of the latter was so far mastered as to permit him to utter the never failing:

"Hugh!"

"Ay, you've found your tongue," said his undisturbed conqueror; "now, in order that you shall not use it to our ruin, I must make free to stop your mouth."

As there was no time to be lost, the scout immediately set about effecting so necessary a precaution; and when he had gagged the Indian, his enemy might safely have been considered as "hors de combat."

"By what place did the imp enter?" asked the industrious scout, when his work was ended. "Not a soul has passed my way since you left me."

Duncan pointed out the door by which Magua had come, and which now presented too many obstacles to a quick retreat.

"Bring on the gentle one, then," continued his friend; "we must make a push for the woods by the other outlet."

"'Tis impossible!" said Duncan; "fear has overcome her, and she is helpless. Alice! my sweet, my own Alice, arouse yourself; now is the moment to fly. 'Tis in vain! she hears, but is unable to follow. Go, noble and worthy friend; save yourself, and leave me to my fate."

"Every trail has its end, and every calamity brings its lesson!" returned the scout. "There, wrap her in them Indian cloths. Conceal all of her little form. Nay, that foot has no fellow in the wilderness; it will betray her. All, every part. Now take her in your arms, and follow. Leave the rest to me."

Duncan, as may be gathered from the words of his companion, was eagerly obeying; and, as the other finished speaking, he took the light person of Alice in his arms, and followed in the footsteps of the scout. They found the sick woman as they had left her, still alone, and passed swiftly on, by the natural gallery, to the place of entrance. As they approached the little door of bark, a murmur of voices without announced that the friends and relatives of the invalid were gathered about the place, patiently awaiting a summons to re-enter.

"If I open my lips to speak," Hawkeye whispered, "my English, which is the genuine tongue of a white-skin, will tell the varlets that an enemy is among them. You must give 'em your jargon, major; and say that we have shut the evil spirit in the cave, and are taking the woman to the woods in order to find strengthening roots. Practise all your cunning, for it is a lawful undertaking."

The door opened a little, as if one without was listening to the proceedings within, and compelled the scout to cease his directions. A fierce growl repelled the eavesdropper, and then the scout boldly threw open the covering of bark, and left the place, enacting the character of a bear as he proceeded. Duncan kept close at his heels, and soon found himself in the center of a cluster of twenty anxious relatives and friends.

The crowd fell back a little, and permitted the father, and one who appeared to be the husband of the woman, to approach.

"Has my brother driven away the evil spirit?" demanded the former. "What has he in his arms?"

"Thy child," returned Duncan, gravely; "the disease has gone out of her; it is shut up in the rocks. I take the woman to a distance, where I will strengthen her against any further attacks. She will be in the wigwam of the young man when the sun comes again."

When the father had translated the meaning of the stranger's words into the Huron language, a suppressed murmur announced the satisfaction with which this intelligence was received. The chief himself waved his hand for Duncan to proceed, saying aloud, in a firm voice, and with a lofty manner:

"Go; I am a man, and I will enter the rock and fight the wicked one."

Heyward had gladly obeyed, and was already past the little group, when these startling words arrested him.

"Is my brother mad?" he exclaimed; "is he cruel? He will meet the disease, and it will enter him; or he will drive out the disease, and it will chase his daughter into the woods. No; let my children wait without, and if the spirit appears beat him down with clubs. He is cunning, and will bury himself in the mountain, when he sees how many are ready to fight him."

This singular warning had the desired effect. Instead of entering the cavern, the father and husband drew their tomahawks, and posted themselves in readiness to deal their vengeance on the imaginary tormentor of their sick relative, while the women and children broke branches from the bushes, or seized fragments of the rock, with a similar intention. At this favorable moment the counterfeit conjurers disappeared.

Hawkeye, at the same time that he had presumed so far on the nature of the Indian superstitions, was not ignorant that they were rather tolerated than relied on by the wisest of the chiefs. He well knew the value of time in the present emergency. Whatever might be the extent of the self-delusion of his enemies, and however it had tended to assist his schemes, the slightest cause of suspicion, acting on the subtle nature of an Indian, would be likely to prove fatal. Taking the path, therefore, that was most likely to avoid observation, he rather skirted than entered the village. The warriors were still to be seen in the distance, by the fading light of the fires, stalking from lodge to lodge. But the children had abandoned their sports for their beds of skins, and the quiet of night was already beginning to prevail over the turbulence and excitement of so busy and important an evening.

Alice revived under the renovating influence of the open air, and, as her physical rather than her mental powers had been the subject of weakness, she stood in no need of any explanation of that which had occurred.

"Now let me make an effort to walk," she said, when they had entered the forest, blushing, though unseen, that she had not been sooner able to quit the arms of Duncan; "I am indeed restored."

"Nay, Alice, you are yet too weak."

The maiden struggled gently to release herself, and Heyward was compelled to part with his precious burden. The representative of the bear had certainly been an entire stranger to the delicious emotions of the lover while his arms encircled his mistress; and he was, perhaps, a stranger also to the nature of that feeling of ingenuous shame that oppressed the trembling Alice. But when he found himself at a suitable distance from the lodges he made a halt, and spoke on a subject of which he was thoroughly the master.

"This path will lead you to the brook," he said; "follow its northern bank until you come to a fall; mount the hill on your right, and you will see the fires of the other people. There you must go and demand protection; if they are true Delawares you will be safe. A distant flight with that gentle one, just now, is impossible. The Hurons would follow up our trail, and master our scalps before we had got a dozen miles. Go, and Providence be with you."

"And you!" demanded Heyward, in surprise; "surely we part not here?"

"The Hurons hold the pride of the Delawares; the last of the high blood of the Mohicans is in their power," returned the scout; "I go to see what can be done in his favor. Had they mastered your scalp, major, a knave should have fallen for every hair it held, as I promised; but if the young Sagamore is to be led to the stake, the Indians shall see also how a man without a cross can die."

Not in the least offended with the decided preference that the sturdy woodsman gave to one who might, in some degree, be called the child of his adoption, Duncan still continued to urge such reasons against so desperate an effort as presented themselves. He was aided by Alice, who mingled her entreaties with those of Heyward that he would abandon a resolution that promised so much danger, with so little hope of success. Their eloquence and ingenuity were expended in vain. The scout heard them attentively, but impatiently, and finally closed the discussion, by answering, in a tone that instantly silenced Alice, while it told Heyward how fruitless any further remonstrances would be.

"I have heard," he said, "that there is a feeling in youth which binds man to woman closer than the father is tied to the son. It may be so. I have seldom been where women of my color dwell; but such may be the gifts of nature in the settlements. You have risked life, and all that is dear to you, to bring off this gentle one, and I suppose that some such disposition is at the bottom of it all. As for me, I taught the lad the real character of a rifle; and well has he paid me for it. I have fou't at his side in many a bloody scrimmage; and so long as I could hear the crack of his piece in one ear, and that of the Sagamore in the other, I knew no enemy was on my back. Winters and summer, nights and days, have we roved the wilderness in company, eating of the same dish, one sleeping while the other watched; and afore it shall be said that Uncas was taken to the torment, and I at hand—There is but a single Ruler of us all, whatever may the color of the skin; and Him I call to witness, that before the Mohican boy shall perish for the want of a friend, good faith shall depart the 'arth, and 'killdeer' become as harmless as the tooting we'pon of the singer!"

Duncan released his hold on the arm of the scout, who turned, and steadily retraced his steps toward the lodges. After pausing a moment to gaze at his retiring form, the successful and yet sorrowful Heyward and Alice took their way together toward the distant village of the Delawares.

CHAPTER XXVI.

"Bot.—Let me play the lion too."
—Midsummer Night's Dream

Notwithstanding the high resolution of Hawkeye he fully comprehended all the difficulties and danger he was about to incur. In his return to the camp, his acute and practised intellects were intently engaged in devising means to counteract a watchfulness and suspicion on the part of his enemies, that he knew were, in no degree, inferior to his own. Nothing but the color of his skin had saved the lives of Magua and the conjurer, who would have been the first victims sacrificed to his own security, had not the scout believed such an act, however congenial it might be to the nature of an Indian, utterly unworthy of one who boasted a descent from men that knew no cross of blood. Accordingly, he trusted to the withes and ligaments with which he had bound his captives, and pursued his way directly toward the center of the lodges. As he approached the buildings, his steps become more deliberate, and his vigilant eye suffered no sign, whether friendly or hostile, to escape him. A neglected hut was a little in advance of the others, and appeared as if it had been deserted when half completed—most probably on account of failing in some of the more important requisites; such as wood or water. A faint light glimmered through its cracks, however, and announced that, notwithstanding its imperfect structure, it was not without a tenant. Thither, then, the scout proceeded, like a prudent general, who was about to feel the advanced positions of his enemy, before he hazarded the main attack.

Throwing himself into a suitable posture for the beast he represented, Hawkeye crawled to a little opening, where he might command a view of the interior. It proved to be the abiding place of David Gamut. Hither the faithful singing-master had now brought himself, together with all his sorrows, his apprehensions, and his meek dependence on the protection of Providence. At the precise moment when his ungainly person came under the observation of the scout, in the manner just mentioned, the woodsman himself, though in his assumed character, was the subject of the solitary being's profounded reflections.

However implicit the faith of David was in the performance of ancient miracles, he eschewed the belief of any direct supernatural agency in the management of modern morality. In other words, while he had implicit faith in the ability of Balaam's ass to speak, he was somewhat skeptical on the subject of a bear's singing; and yet he had been assured of the latter, on the testimony of his own exquisite organs. There was something in his air and manner that betrayed to the scout the utter confusion of the state of his mind. He was seated on a pile of brush, a few twigs from which occasionally fed his low fire, with his head leaning on his arm, in a posture of melancholy musing. The costume of the votary of music had undergone no other alteration from that so lately described, except that he had covered his bald head with the triangular beaver, which had not proved sufficiently alluring to excite the cupidity of any of his captors.

The ingenious Hawkeye, who recalled the hasty manner in which the other had abandoned his post at the bedside of the sick woman, was not without his suspicions concerning the subject of so much solemn deliberation. First making the circuit of the hut, and ascertaining that it stood quite alone, and that the character of its inmate was likely to protect it from visitors, he ventured through its low door, into the very presence of Gamut. The position of the latter brought the fire between them; and when Hawkeye had seated himself on end, near a minute elapsed, during which the two remained regarding each other without speaking. The suddenness and the nature of the surprise had nearly proved too much for—we will not say the philosophy—but for the pitch and resolution of David. He fumbled for his pitch-pipe, and arose with a confused intention of attempting a musical exorcism.

"Dark and mysterious monster!" he exclaimed, while with trembling hands he disposed of his auxiliary eyes, and sought his never-failing resource in trouble, the gifted version of the psalms; "I know not your nature nor intents; but if aught you meditate against the person and rights of one of the humblest servants of the temple, listen to the inspired language of the youth of Israel, and repent."

The bear shook his shaggy sides, and then a well-known voice replied:

"Put up the tooting we'pon, and teach your throat modesty. Five words of plain and comprehendible English are worth just now an hour of squalling."

"What art thou?" demanded David, utterly disqualified to pursue his original intention, and nearly gasping for breath.

"A man like yourself; and one whose blood is as little tainted by the cross of a bear, or an Indian, as your own. Have you so soon forgotten from whom you received the foolish instrument you hold in your hand?"

"Can these things be?" returned David, breathing more freely, as the truth began to dawn upon him. "I have found many marvels during my sojourn with the heathen, but surely nothing to excel this."

"Come, come," returned Hawkeye, uncasing his honest countenance, the better to assure the wavering confidence of his companion; "you may see a skin, which, if it be not as white as one of the gentle ones, has no tinge of red to it that the winds of the heaven and the sun have not bestowed. Now let us to business."

"First tell me of the maiden, and of the youth who so bravely sought her," interrupted David.

"Ay, they are happily freed from the tomahawks of these varlets. But can you put me on the scent of Uncas?"

"The young man is in bondage, and much I fear his death is decreed. I greatly mourn that one so well disposed should die in his ignorance, and I have sought a goodly hymn—"

"Can you lead me to him?"

"The task will not be difficult," returned David, hesitating; "though I greatly fear your presence would rather increase than mitigate his unhappy fortunes."

"No more words, but lead on," returned Hawkeye, concealing his face again, and setting the example in his own person, by instantly quitting the lodge.

As they proceeded, the scout ascertained that his companion found access to Uncas, under privilege of his imaginary infirmity, aided by the favor he had acquired with one of the guards, who, in consequence of speaking a little English, had been selected by David as the subject of a religious conversion. How far the Huron comprehended the intentions of his new friend may well be doubted; but as exclusive attention is as flattering to a savage as to a more civilized individual, it had produced the effect we have mentioned. It is unnecessary to repeat the shrewd manner with which the scout extracted these particulars from the simple David; neither shall we dwell in this place on the nature of the instruction he delivered, when completely master of all the necessary facts; as the whole will be sufficiently explained to the reader in the course of the narrative.

The lodge in which Uncas was confined was in the very center of the village, and in a situation, perhaps, more difficult than any other to approach, or leave, without observation. But it was not the policy of Hawkeye to affect the least concealment. Presuming on his disguise, and his ability to sustain the character he had assumed, he took the most plain and direct route to the place. The hour, however, afforded him some little of that protection which he appeared so much to despise. The boys were already buried in sleep, and all the women, and most of the warriors, had retired to their lodges for the night. Four or five of the latter only lingered about the door of the prison of Uncas, wary but close observers of the manner of their captive.

At the sight of Gamut, accompanied by one in the well-known masquerade of their most distinguished conjurer, they readily made way for them both. Still they betrayed no intention to depart. On the other hand, they were evidently disposed to remain bound to the place by an additional interest in the mysterious mummeries that they of course expected from such a visit.

From the total inability of the scout to address the Hurons in their own language, he was compelled to trust the conversation entirely to David. Notwithstanding the simplicity of the latter, he did ample justice to the instructions he had received, more than fulfilling the strongest hopes of his teacher.

"The Delawares are women!" he exclaimed, addressing himself to the savage who had a slight understanding of the language in which he spoke; "the Yengeese, my foolish countrymen, have told them to take up the tomahawk, and strike their fathers in the Canadas, and they have forgotten their sex. Does my brother wish to hear 'Le Cerf Agile' ask for his petticoats, and see him weep before the Hurons, at the stake?"

The exclamation "Hugh!" delivered in a strong tone of assent, announced the gratification the savage would receive in witnessing such an exhibition of weakness in an enemy so long hated and so much feared.

"Then let him step aside, and the cunning man will blow upon the dog. Tell it to my brothers."

The Huron explained the meaning of David to his fellows, who, in their turn, listened to the project with that sort of satisfaction that their untamed spirits might be expected to find in such a refinement in cruelty. They drew back a little from the entrance and motioned to the supposed conjurer to enter. But the bear, instead of obeying, maintained the seat it had taken, and growled:

"The cunning man is afraid that his breath will blow upon his brothers, and take away their courage too," continued David, improving the hint he received; "they must stand further off."

The Hurons, who would have deemed such a misfortune the heaviest calamity that could befall them, fell back in a body, taking a position where they were out of earshot, though at the same time they could command a view of the entrance to the lodge. Then, as if satisfied of their safety, the scout left his position, and slowly entered the place. It was silent and gloomy, being tenanted solely by the captive, and lighted by the dying embers of a fire, which had been used for the purposed of cookery.

Uncas occupied a distant corner, in a reclining attitude, being rigidly bound, both hands and feet, by strong and painful withes. When the frightful object first presented itself to the young Mohican, he did not deign to bestow a single glance on the animal. The scout, who had left David at the door, to ascertain they were not observed, thought it prudent to preserve his disguise until assured of their privacy. Instead of speaking, therefore, he exerted himself to enact one of the antics of the animal he represented. The young Mohican, who at first believed his enemies had sent in a real beast to torment him, and try his nerves, detected in those performances that to Heyward had appeared so accurate, certain blemishes, that at once betrayed the counterfeit. Had Hawkeye been aware of the low estimation in which the skillful Uncas held his representations, he would probably have prolonged the entertainment a little in pique. But the scornful expression of the young man's eye admitted of so many constructions, that the worthy scout was spared the mortification of such a discovery. As soon, therefore, as David gave the preconcerted signal, a low hissing sound was heard in the lodge in place of the fierce growlings of the bear.

Uncas had cast his body back against the wall of the hut and closed his eyes, as if willing to exclude so contemptible and disagreeable an object from his sight. But the moment the noise of the serpent was heard, he arose, and cast his looks on each side of him, bending his head low, and turning it inquiringly in every direction, until his keen eye rested on the shaggy monster, where it remained riveted, as though fixed by the power of a charm. Again the same sounds were repeated, evidently proceeding from the mouth of the beast. Once more the eyes of the youth roamed over the interior of the lodge, and returning to the former resting place, he uttered, in a deep, suppressed voice:

"Hawkeye!"

"Cut his bands," said Hawkeye to David, who just then approached them.

The singer did as he was ordered, and Uncas found his limbs released. At the same moment the dried skin of the animal rattled, and presently the scout arose to his feet, in proper person. The Mohican appeared to comprehend the nature of the attempt his friend had made, intuitively, neither tongue nor feature betraying another symptom of surprise. When Hawkeye had cast his shaggy vestment, which was done by simply loosing certain thongs of skin, he drew a long, glittering knife, and put it in the hands of Uncas.

"The red Hurons are without," he said; "let us be ready." At the same time he laid his finger significantly on another similar weapon, both being the fruits of his prowess among their enemies during the evening.

"We will go," said Uncas.

"Whither?"

"To the Tortoises; they are the children of my grandfathers."

"Ay, lad," said the scout in English—a language he was apt to use when a little abstracted in mind; "the same blood runs in your veins, I believe; but time and distance has a little changed its color. What shall we do with the Mingoes at the door? They count six, and this singer is as good as nothing."

"The Hurons are boasters," said Uncas, scornfully; "their 'totem' is a moose, and they run like snails. The Delawares are children of the tortoise, and they outstrip the deer."

"Ay, lad, there is truth in what you say; and I doubt not, on a rush, you would pass the whole nation; and, in a straight race of two miles, would be in, and get your breath again, afore a knave of them all was within hearing of the other village. But the gift of a white man lies more in his arms than in his legs. As for myself, I can brain a Huron as well as a better man; but when it comes to a race the knaves would prove too much for me."

Uncas, who had already approached the door, in readiness to lead the way, now recoiled, and placed himself, once more, in the bottom of the lodge. But Hawkeye, who was too much occupied with his own thoughts to note the movement, continued speaking more to himself than to his companion.

"After all," he said, "it is unreasonable to keep one man in bondage to the gifts of another. So, Uncas, you had better take the lead, while I will put on the skin again, and trust to cunning for want of speed."

The young Mohican made no reply, but quietly folded his arms, and leaned his body against one of the upright posts that supported the wall of the hut.

"Well," said the scout looking up at him, "why do you tarry? There will be time enough for me, as the knaves will give chase to you at first."

"Uncas will stay," was the calm reply.

"For what?"

"To fight with his father's brother, and die with the friend of the Delawares."

"Ay, lad," returned Hawkeye, squeezing the hand of Uncas between his own iron fingers; "'twould have been more like a Mingo than a Mohican had you left me. But I thought I would make the offer, seeing that youth commonly loves life. Well, what can't be done by main courage, in war, must be done by circumvention. Put on the skin; I doubt not you can play the bear nearly as well as myself."

Whatever might have been the private opinion of Uncas of their respective abilities in this particular, his grave countenance manifested no opinion of his superiority. He silently and expeditiously encased himself in the covering of the beast, and then awaited such other movements as his more aged companion saw fit to dictate.

"Now, friend," said Hawkeye, addressing David, "an exchange of garments will be a great convenience to you, inasmuch as you are but little accustomed to the make-shifts of the wilderness. Here, take my hunting shirt and cap, and give me your blanket and hat. You must trust me with the book and spectacles, as well as the tooter, too; if we ever meet again, in better times, you shall have all back again, with many thanks into the bargain."

David parted with the several articles named with a readiness that would have done great credit to his liberality, had he not certainly profited, in many particulars, by the exchange. Hawkeye was not long in assuming his borrowed garments; and when his restless eyes were hid behind the glasses, and his head was surmounted by the triangular beaver, as their statures were not dissimilar, he might readily have passed for the singer, by starlight. As soon as these dispositions were made, the scout turned to David, and gave him his parting instructions.

"Are you much given to cowardice?" he bluntly asked, by way of obtaining a suitable understanding of the whole case before he ventured a prescription.

"My pursuits are peaceful, and my temper, I humbly trust, is greatly given to mercy and love," returned David, a little nettled at so direct an attack on his manhood; "but there are none who can say that I have ever forgotten my faith in the Lord, even in the greatest straits."

"Your chiefest danger will be at the moment when the savages find out that they have been deceived. If you are not then knocked on the head, your being a non-composser will protect you; and you'll then have a good reason to expect to die in your bed. If you stay, it must be to sit down here in the shadow, and take the part of Uncas, until such times as the cunning of the Indians discover the cheat, when, as I have already said, your times of trial will come. So choose for yourself—to make a rush or tarry here."

"Even so," said David, firmly; "I will abide in the place of the Delaware. Bravely and generously has he battled in my behalf, and this, and more, will I dare in his service."

"You have spoken as a man, and like one who, under wiser schooling, would have been brought to better things. Hold your head down, and draw in your legs; their formation might tell the truth too early. Keep silent as long as may be; and it would be wise, when you do speak, to break out suddenly in one of your shoutings, which will serve to remind the Indians that you are not altogether as responsible as men should be. If however, they take your scalp, as I trust and believe they will not, depend on it, Uncas and I will not forget the deed, but revenge it as becomes true warriors and trusty friends."

"Hold!" said David, perceiving that with this assurance they were about to leave him; "I am an unworthy and humble follower of one who taught not the damnable principle of revenge. Should I fall, therefore, seek no victims to my manes, but rather forgive my destroyers; and if you remember them at all, let it be in prayers for the enlightening of their minds, and for their eternal welfare."

The scout hesitated, and appeared to muse.

"There is a principle in that," he said, "different from the law of the woods; and yet it is fair and noble to reflect upon." Then heaving a heavy sigh, probably among the last he ever drew in pining for a condition he had so long abandoned, he added: "it is what I would wish to practise myself, as one without a cross of blood, though it is not always easy to deal with an Indian as you would with a fellow Christian. God bless you, friend; I do believe your scent is not greatly wrong, when the matter is duly considered, and keeping eternity before the eyes, though much depends on the natural gifts, and the force of temptation."

So saying, the scout returned and shook David cordially by the hand; after which act of friendship he immediately left the lodge, attended by the new representative of the beast.

The instant Hawkeye found himself under the observation of the Hurons, he drew up his tall form in the rigid manner of David, threw out his arm in the act of keeping time, and commenced what he intended for an imitation of his psalmody. Happily for the success of this delicate adventure, he had to deal with ears but little practised in the concord of sweet sounds, or the miserable effort would infallibly have been detected. It was necessary to pass within a dangerous proximity of the dark group of the savages, and the voice of the scout grew louder as they drew nigher. When at the nearest point the Huron who spoke the English thrust out an arm, and stopped the supposed singing-master.

"The Delaware dog!" he said, leaning forward, and peering through the dim light to catch the expression of the other's features; "is he afraid? Will the Hurons hear his groans?"

A growl, so exceedingly fierce and natural, proceeded from the beast, that the young Indian released his hold and started aside, as if to assure himself that it was not a veritable bear, and no counterfeit, that was rolling before him. Hawkeye, who feared his voice would betray him to his subtle enemies, gladly profited by the interruption, to break out anew in such a burst of musical expression as would, probably, in a more refined state of society have been termed "a grand crash." Among his actual auditors, however, it merely gave him an additional claim to that respect which they never withhold from such as are believed to be the subjects of mental alienation. The little knot of Indians drew back in a body, and suffered, as they thought, the conjurer and his inspired assistant to proceed.

It required no common exercise of fortitude in Uncas and the scout to continue the dignified and deliberate pace they had assumed in passing the lodge; especially as they immediately perceived that curiosity had so far mastered fear, as to induce the watchers to approach the hut, in order to witness the effect of the incantations. The least injudicious or impatient movement on the part of David might betray them, and time was absolutely necessary to insure the safety of the scout. The loud noise the latter conceived it politic to continue, drew many curious gazers to the doors of the different huts as thy passed; and once or twice a dark-looking warrior stepped across their path, led to the act by superstition and watchfulness. They were not, however, interrupted, the darkness of the hour, and the boldness of the attempt, proving their principal friends.

The adventurers had got clear of the village, and were now swiftly approaching the shelter of the woods, when a loud and long cry arose from the lodge where Uncas had been confined. The Mohican started on his feet, and shook his shaggy covering, as though the animal he counterfeited was about to make some desperate effort.

"Hold!" said the scout, grasping his friend by the shoulder, "let them yell again! 'Twas nothing but wonderment."

He had no occasion to delay, for at the next instant a burst of cries filled the outer air, and ran along the whole extent of the village. Uncas cast his skin, and stepped forth in his own beautiful proportions. Hawkeye tapped him lightly on the shoulder, and glided ahead.

"Now let the devils strike our scent!" said the scout, tearing two rifles, with all their attendant accouterments, from beneath a bush, and flourishing "killdeer" as he handed Uncas his weapon; "two, at least, will find it to their deaths."

Then, throwing their pieces to a low trail, like sportsmen in readiness for their game, they dashed forward, and were soon buried in the somber darkness of the forest.

## CHAPTER XXVII.

"Ant. I shall remember: When C'sar says
Do this, it is performed."
—Julius Caesar

The impatience of the savages who lingered about the prison of Uncas, as has been seen, had overcome their dread of the conjurer's breath. They stole cautiously, and with beating hearts, to a crevice, through which the faint light of the fire was glimmering. For several minutes they mistook the form of David for that of the prisoner; but the very accident which Hawkeye had foreseen occurred. Tired of keeping the extremities of his long person so near together, the singer gradually suffered the lower limbs to extend themselves, until one of his misshapen feet actually came in contact with and shoved aside the embers of the fire. At first the Hurons believed the Delaware had been thus deformed by witchcraft. But when David, unconscious of being observed, turned his head, and exposed his simple, mild countenance, in place of the haughty lineaments of their prisoner, it would have exceeded the credulity of even a native to have doubted any longer. They rushed together into the lodge, and, laying their hands, with but little ceremony, on their captive, immediately detected the imposition. Then arose the cry first heard by the fugitives. It was succeeded by the most frantic and angry demonstrations of vengeance. David, however, firm in his determination to cover the retreat of his friends, was compelled to believe that his own final hour had come. Deprived of his book and his pipe, he was fain to trust to a memory that rarely failed him on such subjects; and breaking forth in a loud and impassioned strain, he endeavored to smooth his passage into the other world by singing the opening verse of a funeral anthem. The Indians were seasonably reminded of his infirmity, and, rushing into the open air, they aroused the village in the manner described.

A native warrior fights as he sleeps, without the protection of anything defensive. The sounds of the alarm were, therefore, hardly uttered before two hundred men were afoot, and ready for the battle or the chase, as either might be required. The escape was soon known; and the whole tribe crowded, in a body, around the council-lodge, impatiently awaiting the instruction of their chiefs. In such a sudden demand on their wisdom, the presence of the cunning Magua could scarcely fail of being needed. His name was mentioned, and all looked round in wonder that he did not appear. Messengers were then despatched to his lodge requiring his presence.

In the meantime, some of the swiftest and most discreet of the young men were ordered to make the circuit of the clearing, under cover of the woods, in order to ascertain that their suspected neighbors, the Delawares, designed no mischief. Women and children ran to and fro; and, in short, the whole encampment exhibited another scene of wild and savage confusion. Gradually, however, these symptoms of disorder diminished; and in a few minutes the oldest and most distinguished chiefs were assembled in the lodge, in grave consultation.

The clamor of many voices soon announced that a party approached, who might be expected to communicate some intelligence that would explain the mystery of the novel surprise. The crowd without gave way, and several warriors entered the place, bringing with them the hapless conjurer, who had been left so long by the scout in duress.

Notwithstanding this man was held in very unequal estimation among the Hurons, some believing implicitly in his power, and others deeming him an impostor, he was now listened to by all with the deepest attention. When his brief story was ended, the father of the sick woman stepped forth, and, in a few pithy expression, related, in his turn, what he knew. These two narratives gave a proper direction to the subsequent inquiries, which were now made with the characteristic cunning of savages.

Instead of rushing in a confused and disorderly throng to the cavern, ten of the wisest and firmest among the chiefs were selected to prosecute the investigation. As no time was to be lost, the instant the choice was made the individuals appointed rose in a body and left the place without speaking. On reaching the entrance, the younger men in advance made way for their seniors; and the whole proceeded along the low, dark gallery, with the firmness of warriors ready to devote themselves to the public good, though, at the same time, secretly doubting the nature of the power with which they were about to contend.

The outer apartment of the cavern was silent and gloomy. The woman lay in her usual place and posture, though there were those present who affirmed they had seen her borne to the woods by the supposed "medicine of the white men." Such a direct and palpable contradiction of the tale related by the father caused all eyes to be turned on him. Chafed by the silent imputation, and inwardly troubled by so unaccountable a circumstance, the chief advanced to the side of the bed, and, stooping, cast an incredulous look at the features, as if distrusting their reality. His daughter was dead.

The unerring feeling of nature for a moment prevailed and the old warrior hid his eyes in sorrow. Then, recovering his self-possession, he faced his companions, and, pointing toward the corpse, he said, in the language of his people:

"The wife of my young man has left us! The Great Spirit is angry with his children."

The mournful intelligence was received in solemn silence. After a short pause, one of the elder Indians was about to speak, when a dark-looking object was seen rolling out of an adjoining apartment, into the very center of the room where they stood. Ignorant of the nature of the beings they had to deal with, the whole party drew back a little, and, rising on end, exhibited the distorted but still fierce and sullen features of Magua. The discovery was succeeded by a general exclamation of amazement.

As soon, however, as the true situation of the chief was understood, several knives appeared, and his limbs and tongue were quickly released. The Huron arose, and shook himself like a lion quitting his lair. Not a word escaped him, though his hand played convulsively with the handle of his knife, while his lowering eyes scanned the whole party, as if they sought an object suited to the first burst of his vengeance.

It was happy for Uncas and the scout, and even David, that they were all beyond the reach of his arm at such a moment; for, assuredly, no refinement in cruelty would then have deferred their deaths, in opposition to the promptings of the fierce temper that nearly choked him. Meeting everywhere faces that he knew as friends, the savage grated his teeth together like rasps of iron, and swallowed his passion for want of a victim on whom to vent it. This exhibition of anger was noted by all present; and from an apprehension of exasperating a temper that was already chafed nearly to madness, several minutes were suffered to pass before another word was uttered. When, however, suitable time had elapsed, the oldest of the party spoke.

"My friend has found an enemy," he said. "Is he nigh that the Hurons might take revenge?"

"Let the Delaware die!" exclaimed Magua, in a voice of thunder.

Another longer and expressive silence was observed, and was broken, as before, with due precaution, by the same individual.

"The Mohican is swift of foot, and leaps far," he said; "but my young men are on his trail."

"Is he gone?" demanded Magua, in tones so deep and guttural, that they seemed to proceed from his inmost chest.

"An evil spirit has been among us, and the Delaware has blinded our eyes."

"An evil spirit!" repeated the other, mockingly; "'tis the spirit that has taken the lives of so many Hurons; the spirit that slew my young men at 'the tumbling river'; that took their scalps at the 'healing spring'; and who has, now, bound the arms of Le Renard Subtil!"

"Of whom does my friend speak?"

"Of the dog who carries the heart and cunning of a Huron under a pale skin—La Longue Carabine."

The pronunciation of so terrible a name produced the usual effect among his auditors. But when time was given for reflection, and the warriors remembered that their formidable and daring enemy had even been in the bosom of their encampment, working injury, fearful rage took the place of wonder, and all those fierce passions with which the bosom of Magua had just been struggling were suddenly transferred to his companions. Some among them gnashed their teeth in anger, others vented their feelings in yells, and some, again, beat the air as frantically as if the object of their resentment were suffering under their blows. But this sudden outbreaking of temper as quickly subsided in the still and sullen restraint they most affected in their moments of inaction.

Magua, who had in his turn found leisure for reflection, now changed his manner, and assumed the air of one who knew how to think and act with a dignity worthy of so grave a subject.

"Let us go to my people," he said; "they wait for us."

His companions consented in silence, and the whole of the savage party left the cavern and returned to the council-lodge. When they were seated, all eyes turned on Magua, who understood, from such an indication, that, by common consent, they had devolved the duty of relating what had passed on him. He arose, and told his tale without duplicity or reservation. The whole deception practised by both Duncan and Hawkeye was, of course, laid naked, and no room was found, even for the most superstitious of the tribe, any longer to affix a doubt on the character of the occurrences. It was but too apparent that they had been insultingly, shamefully, disgracefully deceived. When he had ended, and resumed his seat, the collected tribe—for his auditors, in substance, included all the fighting men of the party—sat regarding each other like men astonished equally at the audacity and the success of their enemies. The next consideration, however, was the means and opportunities for revenge.

Additional pursuers were sent on the trail of the fugitives; and then the chiefs applied themselves, in earnest, to the business of consultation. Many different expedients were proposed by the elder warriors, in succession, to all of which Magua was a silent and respectful listener. That subtle savage had recovered his artifice and self-command, and now proceeded toward his object with his customary caution and skill. It was only when each one disposed to speak had uttered his sentiments, that he prepared to advance his own opinions. They were given with additional weight from the circumstance that some of the runners had already returned, and reported that their enemies had been traced so far as to leave no doubt of their having sought safety in the neighboring camp of their suspected allies, the Delawares. With the advantage of possessing this important intelligence, the chief warily laid his plans before his fellows, and, as might have been anticipated from his eloquence and cunning, they were adopted without a dissenting voice. They were, briefly, as follows, both in opinions and in motives.

It has been already stated that, in obedience to a policy rarely departed from, the sisters were separated so soon as they reached the Huron village. Magua had early discovered that in retaining the person of Alice, he possessed the most effectual check on Cora. When they parted, therefore, he kept the former within reach of his hand, consigning the one he most valued to the keeping of their allies. The arrangement was understood to be merely temporary, and was made as much with a view to flatter his neighbors as in obedience to the invariable rule of Indian policy.

While goaded incessantly by these revengeful impulses that in a savage seldom slumber, the chief was still attentive to his more permanent personal interests. The follies and disloyalty committed in his youth were to be expiated by a long and painful penance, ere he could be restored to the full enjoyment of the confidence of his ancient people; and without confidence there could be no authority in an Indian tribe. In this delicate and arduous situation, the crafty native had neglected no means of increasing his influence; and one of the happiest of his expedients had been the success with which he had cultivated the favor of their powerful and dangerous neighbors. The result of his experiment had answered all the expectations of his policy; for the Hurons were in no degree exempt from that governing principle of nature, which induces man to value his gifts precisely in the degree that they are appreciated by others.

But, while he was making this ostensible sacrifice to general considerations, Magua never lost sight of his individual motives. The latter had been frustrated by the unlooked-for events which had placed all his prisoners beyond his control; and he now found himself reduced to the necessity of suing for favors to those whom it had so lately been his policy to oblige.

Several of the chiefs had proposed deep and treacherous schemes to surprise the Delawares and, by gaining possession of their camp, to recover their prisoners by the same blow; for all agreed that their honor, their interests, and the peace and happiness of their dead countrymen, imperiously required them speedily to immolate some victims to their revenge. But plans so dangerous to attempt, and of such doubtful issue, Magua found little difficulty in defeating. He exposed their risk and fallacy with his usual skill; and it was only after he had removed every impediment, in the shape of opposing advice, that he ventured to propose his own projects.

He commenced by flattering the self-love of his auditors; a never-failing method of commanding attention. When he had enumerated the many different occasions on which the Hurons had exhibited their courage and prowess, in the punishment of insults, he digressed in a high encomium on the virtue of wisdom. He painted the quality as forming the great point of difference between the beaver and other brutes; between the brutes and men; and, finally, between the Hurons, in particular, and the rest of the human race. After he had sufficiently extolled the property of discretion, he undertook to exhibit in what manner its use was applicable to the present situation of their tribe. On the one hand, he said, was their great pale father, the governor of the Canadas, who had looked upon his children with a hard eye since their tomahawks had been so red; on the other, a people as numerous as themselves, who spoke a different language, possessed different interests, and loved them not, and who would be glad of any pretense to bring them in disgrace with the great white chief. Then he spoke of their necessities; of the gifts they had a right to expect for their past services; of their distance from their proper hunting-grounds and native villages; and of the necessity of consulting prudence more, and inclination less, in so critical circumstances. When he perceived that, while the old men applauded his moderation, many of the fiercest and most distinguished of the warriors listened to these politic plans with lowering looks, he cunningly led them back to the subject which they most loved. He spoke openly of the fruits of their wisdom, which he boldly pronounced would be a complete and final triumph over their enemies. He even darkly hinted that their success might be extended, with proper caution, in such a manner as to include the destruction of all whom they had reason to hate. In short, he so blended the warlike with the artful, the obvious with the obscure, as to flatter the propensities of both parties, and to leave to each subject of hope, while neither could say it clearly comprehended his intentions.

The orator, or the politician, who can produce such a state of things, is commonly popular with his contemporaries, however he may be treated by posterity. All perceived that more was meant than was uttered, and each one believed that the hidden meaning was precisely such as his own faculties enabled him to understand, or his own wishes led him to anticipate.

In this happy state of things, it is not surprising that the management of Magua prevailed. The tribe consented to act with deliberation, and with one voice they committed the direction of the whole affair to the government of the chief who had suggested such wise and intelligible expedients.

Magua had now attained one great object of all his cunning and enterprise. The ground he had lost in the favor of his people was completely regained, and he found himself even placed at the head of affairs. He was, in truth, their ruler; and, so long as he could maintain his popularity, no monarch could be more despotic, especially while the tribe continued in a hostile country. Throwing off, therefore, the appearance of consultation, he assumed the grave air of authority necessary to support the dignity of his office.

Runners were despatched for intelligence in different directions; spies were ordered to approach and feel the encampment of the Delawares; the warriors were dismissed to their lodges, with an intimation that their services would soon be needed; and the women and children were ordered to retire, with a warning that it was their province to be silent. When these several arrangements were made, Magua passed through the village, stopping here and there to pay a visit where he thought his presence might be flattering to the individual. He confirmed his friends in their confidence, fixed the wavering, and gratified all. Then he sought his own lodge. The wife the Huron chief had abandoned, when he was chased from among his people, was dead. Children he had none; and he now occupied a hut, without companion of any sort. It was, in fact, the dilapidated and solitary structure in which David had been discovered, and whom he had tolerated in his presence, on those few occasions when they met, with the contemptuous indifference of a haughty superiority.

Hither, then, Magua retired, when his labors of policy were ended. While others slept, however, he neither knew or sought repose. Had there been one sufficiently curious to have watched the movements of the newly elected chief, he would have seen him seated in a corner of his lodge, musing on the subject of his future plans, from the hour of his retirement to the time he had appointed for the warriors to assemble again. Occasionally the air breathed through the crevices of the hut, and the low flame that fluttered about the embers of the fire threw their wavering light on the person of the sullen recluse. At such moments it would not have been difficult to have fancied the dusky savage the Prince of Darkness brooding on his own fancied wrongs, and plotting evil.

Long before the day dawned, however, warrior after warrior entered the solitary hut of Magua, until they had collected to the number of twenty. Each bore his rifle, and all the other accouterments of war, though the paint was uniformly peaceful. The entrance of these fierce-looking beings was unnoticed: some seating themselves in the shadows of the place, and others standing like motionless statues, until the whole of the designated band was collected.

Then Magua arose and gave the signal to proceed, marching himself in advance. They followed their leader singly, and in that well-known order which has obtained the distinguishing appellation of

"Indian file." Unlike other men engaged in the spirit-stirring business of war, they stole from their camp unostentatiously and unobserved resembling a band of gliding specters, more than warriors seeking the bubble reputation by deeds of desperate daring.

Instead of taking the path which led directly toward the camp of the Delawares, Magua led his party for some distance down the windings of the stream, and along the little artificial lake of the beavers. The day began to dawn as they entered the clearing which had been formed by those sagacious and industrious animals. Though Magua, who had resumed his ancient garb, bore the outline of a fox on the dressed skin which formed his robe, there was one chief of his party who carried the beaver as his peculiar symbol, or "totem." There would have been a species of profanity in the omission, had this man passed so powerful a community of his fancied kindred, without bestowing some evidence of his regard. Accordingly, he paused, and spoke in words as kind and friendly as if he were addressing more intelligent beings. He called the animals his cousins, and reminded them that his protecting influence was the reason they remained unharmed, while many avaricious traders were prompting the Indians to take their lives. He promised a continuance of his favors, and admonished them to be grateful. After which, he spoke of the expedition in which he was himself engaged, and intimated, though with sufficient delicacy and circumlocution, the expediency of bestowing on their relative a portion of that wisdom for which they were so renowned.*

During the utterance of this extraordinary address, the companions of the speaker were as grave and as attentive to his language as though they were all equally impressed with its propriety. Once or twice black objects were seen rising to the surface of the water, and the Huron expressed pleasure, conceiving that his words were not bestowed in vain. Just as he ended his address, the head of a large beaver was thrust from the door of a lodge, whose earthen walls had been much injured, and which the party had believed, from its situation, to be uninhabited. Such an extraordinary sign of confidence was received by the orator as a highly favorable omen; and though the animal retreated a little precipitately, he was lavish of his thanks and commendations.

When Magua thought sufficient time had been lost in gratifying the family affection of the warrior, he again made the signal to proceed. As the Indians moved away in a body, and with a step that would have been inaudible to the ears of any common man, the same venerable-looking beaver once more ventured his head from its cover. Had any of the Hurons turned to look behind them, they would have seen the animal watching their movements with an interest and sagacity that might easily have been mistaken for reason. Indeed, so very distinct and intelligible were the devices of the quadruped, that even the most experienced observer would have been at a loss to account for its actions, until the moment when the party entered the forest, when the whole would have been explained, by seeing the entire animal issue from the lodge, uncasing, by the act, the grave features of Chingachgook from his mask of fur.

---

* These harangues of the beasts were frequent among the Indians. They often address their victims in this way, reproaching them for cowardice or commending their resolution, as they may happen to exhibit fortitude or the reverse, in suffering.

CHAPTER XXVIII.

"Brief, I pray for you; for you see, 'tis a busy time with me."
—Much Ado About Nothing.

The tribe, or rather half tribe, of Delawares, which has been so often mentioned, and whose present place of encampment was so nigh the temporary village of the Hurons, could assemble about an equal number of warriors with the latter people. Like their neighbors, they had followed Montcalm into the territories of the English crown, and were making heavy and serious inroads on the hunting-grounds of the Mohawks; though they had seen fit, with the mysterious reserve so common among the natives, to withhold their assistance at the moment when it was most required. The French had accounted for this unexpected defection on the part of their ally in various ways. It was the prevalent opinion, however, that they had been influenced by veneration for the ancient treaty, that had once made them dependent on the Six Nations for military protection, and now rendered them reluctant to encounter their former masters. As for the tribe itself, it had been content to announce to Montcalm, through his emissaries, with Indian brevity, that their hatchets were dull, and time was necessary to sharpen them. The politic captain of the Canadas had deemed it wiser to submit to entertain a passive friend, than by any acts of ill-judged severity to convert him into an open enemy.

On that morning when Magua led his silent party from the settlement of the beavers into the forests, in the manner described, the sun rose upon the Delaware encampment as if it had suddenly burst upon a busy people, actively employed in all the customary avocations of high noon. The women ran from lodge to lodge, some engaged in preparing their morning's meal, a few earnestly bent on seeking the comforts necessary to their habits, but more pausing to exchange hasty and whispered sentences with their friends. The warriors were lounging in groups, musing more than they conversed and when a few words were uttered, speaking like men who deeply weighed their opinions. The instruments of the chase were to be seen in abundance among the lodges; but none departed. Here and there a warrior was examining his arms, with an attention that is rarely bestowed on the implements, when no other enemy than the beasts of the forest is expected to be encountered. And occasionally, the eyes of a whole group were turned simultaneously toward a large and silent lodge in the center of the village, as if it contained the subject of their common thoughts.

During the existence of this scene, a man suddenly appeared at the furthest extremity of a platform of rock which formed the level of the village. He was without arms, and his paint tended rather to soften than increase the natural sternness of his austere countenance. When in full view of the Delawares he stopped, and made a gesture of amity, by throwing his arm upward toward heaven, and then letting it fall impressively on his breast. The inhabitants of the village answered his salute by a low murmur of welcome, and encouraged him to advance by similar indications of friendship. Fortified by these assurances, the dark figure left the brow of the natural rocky terrace, where it had stood a moment, drawn in a strong outline against the blushing morning sky, and moved with dignity into the very center of the huts. As he approached, nothing was audible but the rattling of the light silver ornaments that loaded his arms and neck, and the tinkling of the little bells that fringed his deerskin moccasins. He made, as he advanced, many courteous signs of greeting to the men he passed, neglecting to notice the women, however, like one who deemed their favor, in the present enterprise, of no importance. When he had reached the group in which it was evident, by the haughtiness of their common mien, that the principal chiefs were collected, the stranger paused, and then the Delawares saw that the active and erect form that stood before them was that of the well-known Huron chief, Le Renard Subtil.

His reception was grave, silent, and wary. The warriors in front stepped aside, opening the way to their most approved orator by the action; one who spoke all those languages that were cultivated among the northern aborigines.

"The wise Huron is welcome," said the Delaware, in the language of the Maquas; "he is come to eat his 'succotash',[*] with his brothers of the lakes."

"He is come," repeated Magua, bending his head with the dignity of an eastern prince.

The chief extended his arm and taking the other by the wrist, they once more exchanged friendly salutations. Then the Delaware invited his guest to enter his own lodge, and share his morning meal. The invitation was accepted; and the two warriors, attended by three or four of the old men, walked calmly away, leaving the rest of the tribe devoured by a desire to understand the reasons of so unusual a visit, and yet not betraying the least impatience by sign or word.

During the short and frugal repast that followed, the conversation was extremely circumspect, and related entirely to the events of the hunt, in which Magua had so lately been engaged. It would have been impossible for the most finished breeding to wear more of the appearance of considering the visit as a thing of course, than did his hosts, notwithstanding every individual present was perfectly aware that it must be connected with some secret object and that probably of importance to themselves. When the appetites of the whole were appeased, the squaws removed the trenchers and gourds, and the two parties began to prepare themselves for a subtle trial of their wits.

"Is the face of my great Canada father turned again toward his Huron children?" demanded the orator of the Delawares.

"When was it ever otherwise?" returned Magua. "He calls my people 'most beloved'."

The Delaware gravely bowed his acquiescence to what he knew to be false, and continued:

"The tomahawks of your young men have been very red."

"It is so; but they are now bright and dull; for the Yengeese are dead, and the Delawares are our neighbors."

The other acknowledged the pacific compliment by a gesture of the hand, and remained silent. Then Magua, as if recalled to such a recollection, by the allusion to the massacre, demanded:

"Does my prisoner give trouble to my brothers?"

"She is welcome."

"The path between the Hurons and the Delawares is short and it is open; let her be sent to my squaws, if she gives trouble to my brother."

"She is welcome," returned the chief of the latter nation, still more emphatically.

The baffled Magua continued silent several minutes, apparently indifferent, however, to the repulse he had received in this his opening effort to regain possession of Cora.

"Do my young men leave the Delawares room on the mountains for their hunts?" he at length continued.

"The Lenape are rulers of their own hills," returned the other a little haughtily.

---

[*] A dish composed of cracked corn and beans. It is much used also by the whites. By corn is meant maise.

"It is well. Justice is the master of a red-skin. Why should they brighten their tomahawks and sharpen their knives against each other? Are not the pale faces thicker than the swallows in the season of flowers?"

"Good!" exclaimed two or three of his auditors at the same time.

Magua waited a little, to permit his words to soften the feelings of the Delawares, before he added:

"Have there not been strange moccasins in the woods? Have not my brothers scented the feet of white men?"

"Let my Canada father come," returned the other, evasively; "his children are ready to see him."

"When the great chief comes, it is to smoke with the Indians in their wigwams. The Hurons say, too, he is welcome. But the Yengeese have long arms, and legs that never tire! My young men dreamed they had seen the trail of the Yengeese nigh the village of the Delawares!"

"They will not find the Lenape asleep."

"It is well. The warrior whose eye is open can see his enemy," said Magua, once more shifting his ground, when he found himself unable to penetrate the caution of his companion. "I have brought gifts to my brother. His nation would not go on the warpath, because they did not think it well, but their friends have remembered where they lived."

When he had thus announced his liberal intention, the crafty chief arose, and gravely spread his presents before the dazzled eyes of his hosts. They consisted principally of trinkets of little value, plundered from the slaughtered females of William Henry. In the division of the baubles the cunning Huron discovered no less art than in their selection. While he bestowed those of greater value on the two most distinguished warriors, one of whom was his host, he seasoned his offerings to their inferiors with such well-timed and apposite compliments, as left them no ground of complaint. In short, the whole ceremony contained such a happy blending of the profitable with the flattering, that it was not difficult for the donor immediately to read the effect of a generosity so aptly mingled with praise, in the eyes of those he addressed.

This well-judged and politic stroke on the part of Magua was not without instantaneous results. The Delawares lost their gravity in a much more cordial expression; and the host, in particular, after contemplating his own liberal share of the spoil for some moments with peculiar gratification, repeated with strong emphasis, the words:

"My brother is a wise chief. He is welcome."

"The Hurons love their friends the Delawares," returned Magua. "Why should they not? they are colored by the same sun, and their just men will hunt in the same grounds after death. The red-skins should be friends, and look with open eyes on the white men. Has not my brother scented spies in the woods?"

The Delaware, whose name in English signified "Hard Heart," an appellation that the French had translated into "le Coeur-dur," forgot that obduracy of purpose, which had probably obtained him so significant a title. His countenance grew very sensibly less stern and he now deigned to answer more directly.

"There have been strange moccasins about my camp. They have been tracked into my lodges."

"Did my brother beat out the dogs?" asked Magua, without adverting in any manner to the former equivocation of the chief.

"It would not do. The stranger is always welcome to the children of the Lenape."

"The stranger, but not the spy."

"Would the Yengeese send their women as spies? Did not the Huron chief say he took women in the battle?"

"He told no lie. The Yengeese have sent out their scouts. They have been in my wigwams, but they found there no one to say welcome. Then they fled to the Delawares—for, say they, the Delawares are our friends; their minds are turned from their Canada father!"

This insinuation was a home thrust, and one that in a more advanced state of society would have entitled Magua to the reputation of a skillful diplomatist. The recent defection of the tribe had, as they well knew themselves, subjected the Delawares to much reproach among their French allies; and they were now made to feel that their future actions were to be regarded with jealousy and distrust. There was no deep insight into causes and effects necessary to foresee that such a situation of things was likely to prove highly prejudicial to their future movements. Their distant villages, their hunting-grounds and hundreds of their women and children, together with a material part of their physical force, were actually within the limits of the French territory. Accordingly, this alarming annunciation was received, as Magua intended, with manifest disapprobation, if not with alarm.

"Let my father look in my face," said Le Coeur-dur; "he will see no change. It is true, my young men did not go out on the war-path; they had dreams for not doing so. But they love and venerate the great white chief."

"Will he think so when he hears that his greatest enemy is fed in the camp of his children? When he is told a bloody Yengee smokes at your fire? That the pale face who has slain so many of his friends goes in and out among the Delawares? Go! my great Canada father is not a fool!"

"Where is the Yengee that the Delawares fear?" returned the other; "who has slain my young men? Who is the mortal enemy of my Great Father?"

"La Longue Carabine!"

The Delaware warriors started at the well-known name, betraying by their amazement, that they now learned, for the first time, one so famous among the Indian allies of France was within their power.

"What does my brother mean?" demanded Le Coeur-dur, in a tone that, by its wonder, far exceeded the usual apathy of his race.

"A Huron never lies!" returned Magua, coldly, leaning his head against the side of the lodge, and drawing his slight robe across his tawny breast. "Let the Delawares count their prisoners; they will find one whose skin is neither red nor pale."

A long and musing pause succeeded. The chief consulted apart with his companions, and messengers despatched to collect certain others of the most distinguished men of the tribe.

As warrior after warrior dropped in, they were each made acquainted, in turn, with the important intelligence that Magua had just communicated. The air of surprise, and the usual low, deep, guttural exclamation, were common to them all. The news spread from mouth to mouth, until the whole encampment became powerfully agitated. The women suspended their labors, to catch such syllables as unguardedly fell from the lips of the consulting warriors. The boys deserted their sports, and walking fearlessly among their fathers, looked up in curious admiration, as they heard the brief exclamations of wonder they so freely expressed the temerity of their hated foe. In short, every occupation was abandoned for the time, and all other pursuits seemed discarded in order that the tribe might freely indulge, after their own peculiar manner, in an open expression of feeling.

When the excitement had a little abated, the old men disposed themselves seriously to consider that which it became the honor and safety of their tribe to perform, under circumstances of so much delicacy and embarrassment. During all these movements, and in the midst of the general commotion, Magua had not only maintained his seat, but the very attitude he had originally taken, against the side of the lodge, where he continued as immovable, and, apparently, as unconcerned, as if he had no interest in the result. Not a single indication of the future intentions of his hosts, however, escaped his vigilant eyes. With his consummate knowledge of the nature of the people with whom he had to deal, he anticipated every measure on which they decided; and it might almost be said, that, in many instances, he knew their intentions, even before they became known to themselves.

The council of the Delawares was short. When it was ended, a general bustle announced that it was to be immediately succeeded by a solemn and formal assemblage of the nation. As such meetings were rare, and only called on occasions of the last importance, the subtle Huron, who still sat apart, a wily and dark observer of the proceedings, now knew that all his projects must be brought to their final issue. He, therefore, left the lodge and walked silently forth to the place, in front of the encampment, whither the warriors were already beginning to collect.

It might have been half an hour before each individual, including even the women and children, was in his place. The delay had been created by the grave preparations that were deemed necessary to so solemn and unusual a conference. But when the sun was seen climbing above the tops of that mountain, against whose bosom the Delawares had constructed their encampment, most were seated; and as his bright rays darted from behind the outline of trees that fringed the eminence, they fell upon as grave, as attentive, and as deeply interested a multitude, as was probably ever before lighted by his morning beams. Its number somewhat exceeded a thousand souls.

In a collection of so serious savages, there is never to be found any impatient aspirant after premature distinction, standing ready to move his auditors to some hasty, and, perhaps, injudicious discussion, in order that his own reputation may be the gainer. An act of so much precipitancy and presumption would seal the downfall of precocious intellect forever. It rested solely with the oldest and most experienced of the men to lay the subject of the conference before the people. Until such a one chose to make some movement, no deeds in arms, no natural gifts, nor any renown as an orator, would have justified the slightest interruption. On the present occasion, the aged warrior whose privilege it was to speak, was silent, seemingly oppressed with the magnitude of his subject. The delay had already continued long beyond the usual deliberative pause that always preceded a conference; but no sign of impatience or surprise escaped even the youngest boy. Occasionally an eye was raised from the earth, where the looks of most were riveted, and strayed toward a particular lodge, that was, however, in no manner distinguished from those around it, except in the peculiar care that had been taken to protect it against the assaults of the weather.

At length one of those low murmurs, that are so apt to disturb a multitude, was heard, and the whole nation arose to their feet by a common impulse. At that instant the door of the lodge in question opened, and three men, issuing from it, slowly approached the place of consultation. They were all aged, even beyond that period to which the oldest present had reached; but one in the center, who leaned on his companions for support, had numbered an amount of years to which the human race is seldom permitted to attain. His frame, which had once been tall and erect, like the cedar, was now bending under the pressure of more than a century. The elastic, light step of an Indian was gone, and in its place he was compelled to toil his tardy way over the ground, inch by inch. His dark, wrinkled countenance was in singular and wild contrast with the long white locks which floated on his shoulders, in such thickness, as to announce that generations had probably passed away since they had last been shorn.

The dress of this patriarch—for such, considering his vast age, in conjunction with his affinity and influence with his people, he might very properly be termed—was rich and imposing, though strictly after the simple fashions of the tribe. His robe was of the finest skins, which had been deprived of their fur, in order to admit of a hieroglyphical representation of various deeds in arms, done in former ages. His bosom was loaded with medals, some in massive silver, and one or two even in gold, the gifts of various Christian potentates during the long period of his life. He also wore armlets, and cinctures above the ankles, of the latter precious metal. His head, on the whole of which the hair had been permitted to grow, the pursuits of war having so long been abandoned, was encircled by a sort of plated diadem, which, in its turn, bore lesser and more glittering ornaments, that sparkled amid the glossy hues of three drooping ostrich feathers, dyed a deep black, in touching contrast to the color of his snow-white locks. His tomahawk was nearly hid in silver, and the handle of his knife shone like a horn of solid gold.

So soon as the first hum of emotion and pleasure, which the sudden appearance of this venerated individual created, had a little subsided, the name of "Tamenund" was whispered from mouth to mouth. Magua had often heard the fame of this wise and just Delaware; a reputation that even proceeded so far as to bestow on him the rare gift of holding secret communion with the Great Spirit, and which has since transmitted his name, with some slight alteration, to the white usurpers of his ancient territory, as the imaginary tutelar saint* of a vast empire. The Huron chief, therefore, stepped eagerly out a little from the throng, to a spot whence he might catch a nearer glimpse of the features of the man, whose decision was likely to produce so deep an influence on his own fortunes.

The eyes of the old man were closed, as though the organs were wearied with having so long witnessed the selfish workings of the human passions. The color of his skin differed from that of most around him, being richer and darker, the latter having been produced by certain delicate and mazy lines of complicated and yet beautiful figures, which had been traced over most of his person by the operation of tattooing. Notwithstanding the position of the Huron, he passed the observant and silent Magua without notice, and leaning on his two venerable supporters proceeded to the high place of the multitude, where he seated himself in the center of his nation, with the dignity of a monarch and the air of a father.

Nothing could surpass the reverence and affection with which this unexpected visit from one who belongs rather to another world than to this, was received by his people. After a suitable and decent pause, the principal chiefs arose, and, approaching the patriarch, they placed his hands reverently on their heads, seeming to entreat a blessing. The younger men were content with touching his robe, or even drawing nigh his person, in order to breathe in the atmosphere of one so aged, so just, and so valiant. None but the most distinguished among the youthful warriors even presumed so far as to perform the latter ceremony, the great mass of the multitude deeming it a sufficient happiness to look upon a form so deeply venerated, and so well beloved. When these acts of affection and respect were performed, the chiefs drew back again to their several places, and silence reigned in the whole encampment.

After a short delay, a few of the young men, to whom instructions had been whispered by one of the aged attendants of Tamenund, arose, left the crowd, and entered the lodge which has already been noted as the object of so much attention throughout that morning. In a few minutes they reappeared,

---

*The Americans sometimes called their tutelar saint Tamenay, a corruption of the name of the renowned chief here introduced. There are many traditions which speak of the character and power of Tamenund.

escorting the individuals who had caused all these solemn preparations toward the seat of judgment. The crowd opened in a lane; and when the party had re-entered, it closed in again, forming a large and dense belt of human bodies, arranged in an open circle.

CHAPTER XXIX.

> "The assembly seated, rising o'er the rest,
> Achilles thus the king of men addressed."
> —Pope's Illiad

Cora stood foremost among the prisoners, entwining her arms in those of Alice, in the tenderness of sisterly love. Notwithstanding the fearful and menacing array of savages on every side of her, no apprehension on her own account could prevent the nobler-minded maiden from keeping her eyes fastened on the pale and anxious features of the trembling Alice. Close at their side stood Heyward, with an interest in both, that, at such a moment of intense uncertainty, scarcely knew a preponderance in favor of her whom he most loved. Hawkeye had placed himself a little in the rear, with a deference to the superior rank of his companions, that no similarity in the state of their present fortunes could induce him to forget. Uncas was not there.

When perfect silence was again restored, and after the usual long, impressive pause, one of the two aged chiefs who sat at the side of the patriarch arose, and demanded aloud, in very intelligible English:

"Which of my prisoners is La Longue Carabine?"

Neither Duncan nor the scout answered. The former, however, glanced his eyes around the dark and silent assembly, and recoiled a pace, when they fell on the malignant visage of Magua. He saw, at once, that this wily savage had some secret agency in their present arraignment before the nation, and determined to throw every possible impediment in the way of the execution of his sinister plans. He had witnessed one instance of the summary punishments of the Indians, and now dreaded that his companion was to be selected for a second. In this dilemma, with little or no time for reflection, he suddenly determined to cloak his invaluable friend, at any or every hazard to himself. Before he had time, however, to speak, the question was repeated in a louder voice, and with a clearer utterance.

"Give us arms," the young man haughtily replied, "and place us in yonder woods. Our deeds shall speak for us!"

"This is the warrior whose name has filled our ears!" returned the chief, regarding Heyward with that sort of curious interest which seems inseparable from man, when first beholding one of his fellows to whom merit or accident, virtue or crime, has given notoriety. "What has brought the white man into the camp of the Delawares?"

"My necessities. I come for food, shelter, and friends."

"It cannot be. The woods are full of game. The head of a warrior needs no other shelter than a sky without clouds; and the Delawares are the enemies, and not the friends of the Yengeese. Go, the mouth has spoken, while the heart said nothing."

Duncan, a little at a loss in what manner to proceed, remained silent; but the scout, who had listened attentively to all that passed, now advanced steadily to the front.

"That I did not answer to the call for La Longue Carabine, was not owing either to shame or fear," he said, "for neither one nor the other is the gift of an honest man. But I do not admit the right of the Mingoes to bestow a name on one whose friends have been mindful of his gifts, in this particular;

especially as their title is a lie, 'killdeer' being a grooved barrel and no carabyne. I am the man, however, that got the name of Nathaniel from my kin; the compliment of Hawkeye from the Delawares, who live on their own river; and whom the Iroquois have presumed to style the 'Long Rifle', without any warranty from him who is most concerned in the matter."

The eyes of all present, which had hitherto been gravely scanning the person of Duncan, were now turned, on the instant, toward the upright iron frame of this new pretender to the distinguished appellation. It was in no degree remarkable that there should be found two who were willing to claim so great an honor, for impostors, though rare, were not unknown among the natives; but it was altogether material to the just and severe intentions of the Delawares, that there should be no mistake in the matter. Some of their old men consulted together in private, and then, as it would seem, they determined to interrogate their visitor on the subject.

"My brother has said that a snake crept into my camp," said the chief to Magua; "which is he?"

The Huron pointed to the scout.

"Will a wise Delaware believe the barking of a wolf?" exclaimed Duncan, still more confirmed in the evil intentions of his ancient enemy: "a dog never lies, but when was a wolf known to speak the truth?"

The eyes of Magua flashed fire; but suddenly recollecting the necessity of maintaining his presence of mind, he turned away in silent disdain, well assured that the sagacity of the Indians would not fail to extract the real merits of the point in controversy. He was not deceived; for, after another short consultation, the wary Delaware turned to him again, and expressed the determination of the chiefs, though in the most considerate language.

"My brother has been called a liar," he said, "and his friends are angry. They will show that he has spoken the truth. Give my prisoners guns, and let them prove which is the man."

Magua affected to consider the expedient, which he well knew proceeded from distrust of himself, as a compliment, and made a gesture of acquiescence, well content that his veracity should be supported by so skillful a marksman as the scout. The weapons were instantly placed in the hands of the friendly opponents, and they were bid to fire, over the heads of the seated multitude, at an earthen vessel, which lay, by accident, on a stump, some fifty yards from the place where they stood.

Heyward smiled to himself at the idea of a competition with the scout, though he determined to persevere in the deception, until apprised of the real designs of Magua.

Raising his rifle with the utmost care, and renewing his aim three several times, he fired. The bullet cut the wood within a few inches of the vessel; and a general exclamation of satisfaction announced that the shot was considered a proof of great skill in the use of a weapon. Even Hawkeye nodded his head, as if he would say, it was better than he expected. But, instead of manifesting an intention to contend with the successful marksman, he stood leaning on his rifle for more than a minute, like a man who was completely buried in thought. From this reverie, he was, however, awakened by one of the young Indians who had furnished the arms, and who now touched his shoulder, saying in exceedingly broken English:

"Can the pale face beat it?"

"Yes, Huron!" exclaimed the scout, raising the short rifle in his right hand, and shaking it at Magua, with as much apparent ease as if it were a reed; "yes, Huron, I could strike you now, and no power on earth could prevent the deed! The soaring hawk is not more certain of the dove than I am this moment of you, did I choose to send a bullet to your heart! Why should I not? Why!—because the gifts of my color forbid it, and I might draw down evil on tender and innocent heads. If you know such a being as God, thank Him, therefore, in your inward soul; for you have reason!"

The flushed countenance, angry eye and swelling figure of the scout, produced a sensation of secret awe in all that heard him. The Delawares held their breath in expectation; but Magua himself, even while he distrusted the forbearance of his enemy, remained immovable and calm, where he stood wedged in by the crowd, as one who grew to the spot.

"Beat it," repeated the young Delaware at the elbow of the scout.

"Beat what, fool!—what?" exclaimed Hawkeye, still flourishing the weapon angrily above his head, though his eye no longer sought the person of Magua.

"If the white man is the warrior he pretends," said the aged chief, "let him strike nigher to the mark."

The scout laughed aloud—a noise that produced the startling effect of an unnatural sound on Heyward; then dropping the piece, heavily, into his extended left hand, it was discharged, apparently by the shock, driving the fragments of the vessel into the air, and scattering them on every side. Almost at the same instant, the rattling sound of the rifle was heard, as he suffered it to fall, contemptuously, to the earth.

The first impression of so strange a scene was engrossing admiration. Then a low, but increasing murmur, ran through the multitude, and finally swelled into sounds that denoted a lively opposition in the sentiments of the spectators. While some openly testified their satisfaction at so unexampled dexterity, by far the larger portion of the tribe were inclined to believe the success of the shot was the result of accident. Heyward was not slow to confirm an opinion that was so favorable to his own pretensions.

"It was chance!" he exclaimed; "none can shoot without an aim!"

"Chance!" echoed the excited woodsman, who was now stubbornly bent on maintaining his identity at every hazard, and on whom the secret hints of Heyward to acquiesce in the deception were entirely lost. "Does yonder lying Huron, too, think it chance? Give him another gun, and place us face to face, without cover or dodge, and let Providence, and our own eyes, decide the matter atween us! I do not make the offer, to you, major; for our blood is of a color, and we serve the same master."

"That the Huron is a liar, is very evident," returned Heyward, coolly; "you have yourself heard him assert you to be La Longue Carabine."

It were impossible to say what violent assertion the stubborn Hawkeye would have next made, in his headlong wish to vindicate his identity, had not the aged Delaware once more interposed.

"The hawk which comes from the clouds can return when he will," he said; "give them the guns."

This time the scout seized the rifle with avidity; nor had Magua, though he watched the movements of the marksman with jealous eyes, any further cause for apprehension.

"Now let it be proved, in the face of this tribe of Delawares, which is the better man," cried the scout, tapping the butt of his piece with that finger which had pulled so many fatal triggers.

"You see that gourd hanging against yonder tree, major; if you are a marksman fit for the borders, let me see you break its shell!"

Duncan noted the object, and prepared himself to renew the trial. The gourd was one of the usual little vessels used by the Indians, and it was suspended from a dead branch of a small pine, by a thong of deerskin, at the full distance of a hundred yards. So strangely compounded is the feeling of self-love, that the young soldier, while he knew the utter worthlessness of the suffrages of his savage umpires, forgot the sudden motives of the contest in a wish to excel. It had been seen, already, that his skill was far from being contemptible, and he now resolved to put forth its nicest qualities. Had his life depended on the issue, the aim of Duncan could not have been more deliberate or guarded.

He fired; and three or four young Indians, who sprang forward at the report, announced with a shout, that the ball was in the tree, a very little on one side of the proper object. The warriors uttered a common ejaculation of pleasure, and then turned their eyes, inquiringly, on the movements of his rival.

"It may do for the Royal Americans!" said Hawkeye, laughing once more in his own silent, heartfelt manner; "but had my gun often turned so much from the true line, many a marten, whose skin is now in a lady's muff, would still be in the woods; ay, and many a bloody Mingo, who has departed to his final account, would be acting his deviltries at this very day, atween the provinces. I hope the squaw who owns the gourd has more of them in her wigwam, for this will never hold water again!"

The scout had shook his priming, and cocked his piece, while speaking; and, as he ended, he threw back a foot, and slowly raised the muzzle from the earth: the motion was steady, uniform, and in one direction. When on a perfect level, it remained for a single moment, without tremor or variation, as though both man and rifle were carved in stone. During that stationary instant, it poured forth its contents, in a bright, glancing sheet of flame. Again the young Indians bounded forward; but their hurried search and disappointed looks announced that no traces of the bullet were to be seen.

"Go!" said the old chief to the scout, in a tone of strong disgust; "thou art a wolf in the skin of a dog. I will talk to the 'Long Rifle' of the Yengeese."

"Ah! had I that piece which furnished the name you use, I would obligate myself to cut the thong, and drop the gourd without breaking it!" returned Hawkeye, perfectly undisturbed by the other's manner. "Fools, if you would find the bullet of a sharpshooter in these woods, you must look in the object, and not around it!"

The Indian youths instantly comprehended his meaning—for this time he spoke in the Delaware tongue—and tearing the gourd from the tree, they held it on high with an exulting shout, displaying a hole in its bottom, which had been cut by the bullet, after passing through the usual orifice in the center of its upper side. At this unexpected exhibition, a loud and vehement expression of pleasure burst from the mouth of every warrior present. It decided the question, and effectually established Hawkeye in the possession of his dangerous reputation. Those curious and admiring eyes which had been turned again on Heyward, were finally directed to the weather-beaten form of the scout, who immediately became the principal object of attention to the simple and unsophisticated beings by whom he was surrounded. When the sudden and noisy commotion had a little subsided, the aged chief resumed his examination.

"Why did you wish to stop my ears?" he said, addressing Duncan; "are the Delawares fools that they could not know the young panther from the cat?"

"They will yet find the Huron a singing-bird," said Duncan, endeavoring to adopt the figurative language of the natives.

"It is good. We will know who can shut the ears of men. Brother," added the chief turning his eyes on Magua, "the Delawares listen."

Thus singled, and directly called on to declare his object, the Huron arose; and advancing with great deliberation and dignity into the very center of the circle, where he stood confronted by the prisoners, he placed himself in an attitude to speak. Before opening his mouth, however, he bent his eyes slowly along the whole living boundary of earnest faces, as if to temper his expressions to the capacities of his audience. On Hawkeye he cast a glance of respectful enmity; on Duncan, a look of inextinguishable hatred; the shrinking figure of Alice he scarcely deigned to notice; but when his glance met the firm, commanding, and yet lovely form of Cora, his eye lingered a moment, with an expression that it might have been difficult to define. Then, filled with his own dark intentions, he spoke in the language of the Canadas, a tongue that he well knew was comprehended by most of his auditors.

"The Spirit that made men colored them differently," commenced the subtle Huron. "Some are blacker than the sluggish bear. These He said should be slaves; and He ordered them to work forever, like the beaver. You may hear them groan, when the south wind blows, louder than the lowing buffaloes, along the shores of the great salt lake, where the big canoes come and go with them in droves. Some He made with faces paler than the ermine of the forests; and these He ordered to be traders; dogs to their women, and wolves to their slaves. He gave this people the nature of the pigeon; wings that never tire; young, more plentiful than the leaves on the trees, and appetites to devour the earth. He gave them tongues like the false call of the wildcat; hearts like rabbits; the cunning of the hog (but none of the fox), and arms longer than the legs of the moose. With his tongue he stops the ears of the Indians; his heart teaches him to pay warriors to fight his battles; his cunning tells him how to get together the goods of the earth; and his arms inclose the land from the shores of the salt-water to the islands of the great lake. His gluttony makes him sick. God gave him enough, and yet he wants all. Such are the pale faces.

"Some the Great Spirit made with skins brighter and redder than yonder sun," continued Magua, pointing impressively upward to the lurid luminary, which was struggling through the misty atmosphere of the horizon; "and these did He fashion to His own mind. He gave them this island as He had made it, covered with trees, and filled with game. The wind made their clearings; the sun and rain ripened their fruits; and the snows came to tell them to be thankful. What need had they of roads to journey by! They saw through the hills! When the beavers worked, they lay in the shade, and looked on. The winds cooled them in summer; in winter, skins kept them warm. If they fought among themselves, it was to prove that they were men. They were brave; they were just; they were happy."

Here the speaker paused, and again looked around him to discover if his legend had touched the sympathies of his listeners. He met everywhere, with eyes riveted on his own, heads erect and nostrils expanded, as if each individual present felt himself able and willing, singly, to redress the wrongs of his race.

"If the Great Spirit gave different tongues to his red children," he continued, in a low, still melancholy voice, "it was that all animals might understand them. Some He placed among the snows, with their cousin, the bear. Some he placed near the setting sun, on the road to the happy hunting grounds. Some on the lands around the great fresh waters; but to His greatest, and most beloved, He gave the sands of the salt lake. Do my brothers know the name of this favored people?"

"It was the Lenape!" exclaimed twenty eager voices in a breath.

"It was the Lenni Lenape," returned Magua, affecting to bend his head in reverence to their former greatness. "It was the tribes of the Lenape! The sun rose from water that was salt, and set in water that was sweet, and never hid himself from their eyes. But why should I, a Huron of the woods, tell a wise people their own traditions? Why remind them of their injuries; their ancient greatness; their deeds; their glory; their happiness; their losses; their defeats; their misery? Is there not one among them who has seen it all, and who knows it to be true? I have done. My tongue is still for my heart is of lead. I listen."

As the voice of the speaker suddenly ceased, every face and all eyes turned, by a common movement, toward the venerable Tamenund. From the moment that he took his seat, until the present instant, the lips of the patriarch had not severed, and scarcely a sign of life had escaped him.

He sat bent in feebleness, and apparently unconscious of the presence he was in, during the whole of that opening scene, in which the skill of the scout had been so clearly established. At the nicely graduated sound of Magua's voice, however, he betrayed some evidence of consciousness, and once or twice he even raised his head, as if to listen. But when the crafty Huron spoke of his nation by name, the eyelids of the old man raised themselves, and he looked out upon the multitude with that sort of dull, unmeaning expression which might be supposed to belong to the countenance of a specter. Then he made an effort to rise, and being upheld by his supporters, he gained his feet, in a posture commanding by its dignity, while he tottered with weakness.

"Who calls upon the children of the Lenape?" he said, in a deep, guttural voice, that was rendered awfully audible by the breathless silence of the multitude; "who speaks of things gone? Does not the egg become a worm—the worm a fly, and perish? Why tell the Delawares of good that is past? Better thank the Manitou for that which remains."

"It is a Wyandot," said Magua, stepping nigher to the rude platform on which the other stood; "a friend of Tamenund."

"A friend!" repeated the sage, on whose brow a dark frown settled, imparting a portion of that severity which had rendered his eye so terrible in middle age. "Are the Mingoes rulers of the earth? What brings a Huron in here?"

"Justice. His prisoners are with his brothers, and he comes for his own."

Tamenund turned his head toward one of his supporters, and listened to the short explanation the man gave.

Then, facing the applicant, he regarded him a moment with deep attention; after which he said, in a low and reluctant voice:

"Justice is the law of the great Manitou. My children, give the stranger food. Then, Huron, take thine own and depart."

On the delivery of this solemn judgment, the patriarch seated himself, and closed his eyes again, as if better pleased with the images of his own ripened experience than with the visible objects of the world. Against such a decree there was no Delaware sufficiently hardy to murmur, much less oppose himself. The words were barely uttered when four or five of the younger warriors, stepping behind Heyward and the scout, passed thongs so dexterously and rapidly around their arms, as to hold them both in instant bondage. The former was too much engrossed with his precious and nearly insensible burden, to be aware of their intentions before they were executed; and the latter, who considered even the hostile tribes of the Delawares a superior race of beings, submitted without resistance. Perhaps, however, the manner of the scout would not have been so passive, had he fully comprehended the language in which the preceding dialogue had been conducted.

Magua cast a look of triumph around the whole assembly before he proceeded to the execution of his purpose. Perceiving that the men were unable to offer any resistance, he turned his looks on her he valued most. Cora met his gaze with an eye so calm and firm, that his resolution wavered. Then, recollecting his former artifice, he raised Alice from the arms of the warrior against whom she leaned, and beckoning Heyward to follow, he motioned for the encircling crowd to open. But Cora, instead of obeying the impulse he had expected, rushed to the feet of the patriarch, and, raising her voice, exclaimed aloud:

"Just and venerable Delaware, on thy wisdom and power we lean for mercy! Be deaf to yonder artful and remorseless monster, who poisons thy ears with falsehoods to feed his thirst for blood. Thou that hast lived long, and that hast seen the evil of the world, should know how to temper its calamities to the miserable."

The eyes of the old man opened heavily, and he once more looked upward at the multitude. As the piercing tones of the suppliant swelled on his ears, they moved slowly in the direction of her person, and finally settled there in a steady gaze. Cora had cast herself to her knees; and, with hands clenched in each other and pressed upon her bosom, she remained like a beauteous and breathing model of her sex, looking up in his faded but majestic countenance, with a species of holy reverence. Gradually the expression of Tamenund's features changed, and losing their vacancy in admiration, they lighted with a portion of that intelligence which a century before had been wont to communicate his youthful fire to the extensive bands of the Delawares. Rising without assistance, and seemingly without an effort, he demanded, in a voice that startled its auditors by its firmness:

"What art thou?"

"A woman. One of a hated race, if thou wilt—a Yengee. But one who has never harmed thee, and who cannot harm thy people, if she would; who asks for succor."

"Tell me, my children," continued the patriarch, hoarsely, motioning to those around him, though his eyes still dwelt upon the kneeling form of Cora, "where have the Delawares camped?"

"In the mountains of the Iroquois, beyond the clear springs of the Horican."

"Many parching summers are come and gone," continued the sage, "since I drank of the water of my own rivers. The children of Minquon* are the justest white men, but they were thirsty and they took it to themselves. Do they follow us so far?"

"We follow none, we covet nothing," answered Cora. "Captives against our wills, have we been brought amongst you; and we ask but permission to depart to our own in peace. Art thou not Tamenund—the father, the judge, I had almost said, the prophet—of this people?"

"I am Tamenund of many days."

"'Tis now some seven years that one of thy people was at the mercy of a white chief on the borders of this province. He claimed to be of the blood of the good and just Tamenund. 'Go', said the white man, 'for thy parent's sake thou art free.' Dost thou remember the name of that English warrior?"

"I remember, that when a laughing boy," returned the patriarch, with the peculiar recollection of vast age, "I stood upon the sands of the sea shore, and saw a big canoe, with wings whiter than the swan's, and wider than many eagles, come from the rising sun."

"Nay, nay; I speak not of a time so very distant, but of favor shown to thy kindred by one of mine, within the memory of thy youngest warrior."

"Was it when the Yengeese and the Dutchmanne fought for the hunting-grounds of the Delawares? Then Tamenund was a chief, and first laid aside the bow for the lightning of the pale faces—"

"Not yet then," interrupted Cora, "by many ages; I speak of a thing of yesterday. Surely, surely, you forget it not."

---

* William Penn was termed Minquon by the Delawares, and, as he never used violence or injustice in his dealings with them, his reputation for probity passed into a proverb. The American is justly proud of the origin of his nation, which is perhaps unequaled in the history of the world; but the Pennsylvanian and Jerseyman have more reason to value themselves in their ancestors than the natives of any other state, since no wrong was done the original owners of the soil.

"It was but yesterday," rejoined the aged man, with touching pathos, "that the children of the Lenape were masters of the world. The fishes of the salt lake, the birds, the beasts, and the Mengee of the woods, owned them for Sagamores."

Cora bowed her head in disappointment, and, for a bitter moment struggled with her chagrin. Then, elevating her rich features and beaming eyes, she continued, in tones scarcely less penetrating than the unearthly voice of the patriarch himself:

"Tell me, is Tamenund a father?"

The old man looked down upon her from his elevated stand, with a benignant smile on his wasted countenance, and then casting his eyes slowly over the whole assemblage, he answered:

"Of a nation."

"For myself I ask nothing. Like thee and thine, venerable chief," she continued, pressing her hands convulsively on her heart, and suffering her head to droop until her burning cheeks were nearly concealed in the maze of dark, glossy tresses that fell in disorder upon her shoulders, "the curse of my ancestors has fallen heavily on their child. But yonder is one who has never known the weight of Heaven's displeasure until now. She is the daughter of an old and failing man, whose days are near their close. She has many, very many, to love her, and delight in her; and she is too good, much too precious, to become the victim of that villain."

"I know that the pale faces are a proud and hungry race. I know that they claim not only to have the earth, but that the meanest of their color is better than the Sachems of the red man. The dogs and crows of their tribes," continued the earnest old chieftain, without heeding the wounded spirit of his listener, whose head was nearly crushed to the earth in shame, as he proceeded, "would bark and caw before they would take a woman to their wigwams whose blood was not of the color of snow. But let them not boast before the face of the Manitou too loud. They entered the land at the rising, and may yet go off at the setting sun. I have often seen the locusts strip the leaves from the trees, but the season of blossoms has always come again."

"It is so," said Cora, drawing a long breath, as if reviving from a trance, raising her face, and shaking back her shining veil, with a kindling eye, that contradicted the death-like paleness of her countenance; "but why—it is not permitted us to inquire. There is yet one of thine own people who has not been brought before thee; before thou lettest the Huron depart in triumph, hear him speak."

Observing Tamenund to look about him doubtingly, one of his companions said:

"It is a snake—a red-skin in the pay of the Yengeese. We keep him for the torture."

"Let him come," returned the sage.

Then Tamenund once more sank into his seat, and a silence so deep prevailed while the young man prepared to obey his simple mandate, that the leaves, which fluttered in the draught of the light morning air, were distinctly heard rustling in the surrounding forest.

CHAPTER XXX.

> "If you deny me, fie upon your law!
> There is no force in the decrees of Venice:
> I stand for judgment: answer, shall I have it?"
> —Merchant of Venice

The silence continued unbroken by human sounds for many anxious minutes. Then the waving multitude opened and shut again, and Uncas stood in the living circle. All those eyes, which had been curiously studying the lineaments of the sage, as the source of their own intelligence, turned on the instant, and were now bent in secret admiration on the erect, agile, and faultless person of the captive. But neither the presence in which he found himself, nor the exclusive attention that he attracted, in any manner disturbed the self-possession of the young Mohican. He cast a deliberate and observing look on every side of him, meeting the settled expression of hostility that lowered in the visages of the chiefs with the same calmness as the curious gaze of the attentive children. But when, last in this haughty scrutiny, the person of Tamenund came under his glance, his eye became fixed, as though all other objects were already forgotten. Then, advancing with a slow and noiseless step up the area, he placed himself immediately before the footstool of the sage. Here he stood unnoted, though keenly observant himself, until one of the chiefs apprised the latter of his presence.

"With what tongue does the prisoner speak to the Manitou?" demanded the patriarch, without unclosing his eyes.

"Like his fathers," Uncas replied; "with the tongue of a Delaware."

At this sudden and unexpected annunciation, a low, fierce yell ran through the multitude, that might not inaptly be compared to the growl of the lion, as his choler is first awakened—a fearful omen of the weight of his future anger. The effect was equally strong on the sage, though differently exhibited. He passed a hand before his eyes, as if to exclude the least evidence of so shameful a spectacle, while he repeated, in his low, guttural tones, the words he had just heard.

"A Delaware! I have lived to see the tribes of the Lenape driven from their council-fires, and scattered, like broken herds of deer, among the hills of the Iroquois! I have seen the hatchets of a strong people sweep woods from the valleys, that the winds of heaven have spared! The beasts that run on the mountains, and the birds that fly above the trees, have I seen living in the wigwams of men; but never before have I found a Delaware so base as to creep, like a poisonous serpent, into the camps of his nation."

"The singing-birds have opened their bills," returned Uncas, in the softest notes of his own musical voice; "and Tamenund has heard their song."

The sage started, and bent his head aside, as if to catch the fleeting sounds of some passing melody.

"Does Tamenund dream!" he exclaimed. "What voice is at his ear! Have the winters gone backward! Will summer come again to the children of the Lenape!"

A solemn and respectful silence succeeded this incoherent burst from the lips of the Delaware prophet. His people readily constructed his unintelligible language into one of those mysterious conferences he was believed to hold so frequently with a superior intelligence and they awaited the issue of the revelation in awe. After a patient pause, however, one of the aged men, perceiving that the sage had lost the recollection of the subject before them, ventured to remind him again of the presence of the prisoner.

"The false Delaware trembles lest he should hear the words of Tamenund," he said. "'Tis a hound that howls, when the Yengeese show him a trail."

"And ye," returned Uncas, looking sternly around him, "are dogs that whine, when the Frenchman casts ye the offals of his deer!"

Twenty knives gleamed in the air, and as many warriors sprang to their feet, at this biting, and perhaps merited retort; but a motion from one of the chiefs suppressed the outbreaking of their tempers, and restored the appearance of quiet. The task might probably have been more difficult, had not a movement made by Tamenund indicated that he was again about to speak.

"Delaware!" resumed the sage, "little art thou worthy of thy name. My people have not seen a bright sun in many winters; and the warrior who deserts his tribe when hid in clouds is doubly a traitor. The law of the Manitou is just. It is so; while the rivers run and the mountains stand, while the blossoms come and go on the trees, it must be so. He is thine, my children; deal justly by him."

Not a limb was moved, nor was a breath drawn louder and longer than common, until the closing syllable of this final decree had passed the lips of Tamenund. Then a cry of vengeance burst at once, as it might be, from the united lips of the nation; a frightful augury of their ruthless intentions. In the midst of these prolonged and savage yells, a chief proclaimed, in a high voice, that the captive was condemned to endure the dreadful trial of torture by fire. The circle broke its order, and screams of delight mingled with the bustle and tumult of preparation. Heyward struggled madly with his captors; the anxious eye of Hawkeye began to look around him, with an expression of peculiar earnestness; and Cora again threw herself at the feet of the patriarch, once more a suppliant for mercy.

Throughout the whole of these trying moments, Uncas had alone preserved his serenity. He looked on the preparations with a steady eye, and when the tormentors came to seize him, he met them with a firm and upright attitude. One among them, if possible more fierce and savage than his fellows, seized the hunting-shirt of the young warrior, and at a single effort tore it from his body. Then, with a yell of frantic pleasure, he leaped toward his unresisting victim and prepared to lead him to the stake. But, at that moment, when he appeared most a stranger to the feelings of humanity, the purpose of the savage was arrested as suddenly as if a supernatural agency had interposed in the behalf of Uncas. The eyeballs of the Delaware seemed to start from their sockets; his mouth opened and his whole form became frozen in an attitude of amazement. Raising his hand with a slow and regulated motion, he pointed with a finger to the bosom of the captive. His companions crowded about him in wonder and every eye was like his own, fastened intently on the figure of a small tortoise, beautifully tattooed on the breast of the prisoner, in a bright blue tint.

For a single instant Uncas enjoyed his triumph, smiling calmly on the scene. Then motioning the crowd away with a high and haughty sweep of his arm, he advanced in front of the nation with the air of a king, and spoke in a voice louder than the murmur of admiration that ran through the multitude.

"Men of the Lenni Lenape!" he said, "my race upholds the earth! Your feeble tribe stands on my shell! What fire that a Delaware can light would burn the child of my fathers," he added, pointing proudly to the simple blazonry on his skin; "the blood that came from such a stock would smother your flames! My race is the grandfather of nations!"

"Who art thou?" demanded Tamenund, rising at the startling tones he heard, more than at any meaning conveyed by the language of the prisoner.

"Uncas, the son of Chingachgook," answered the captive modestly, turning from the nation, and bending his head in reverence to the other's character and years; "a son of the great Unamis."*

"The hour of Tamenund is nigh!" exclaimed the sage; "the day is come, at last, to the night! I thank the Manitou, that one is here to fill my place at the council-fire. Uncas, the child of Uncas, is found! Let the eyes of a dying eagle gaze on the rising sun."

---

*Turtle.

The youth stepped lightly, but proudly on the platform, where he became visible to the whole agitated and wondering multitude. Tamenund held him long at the length of his arm and read every turn in the fine lineaments of his countenance, with the untiring gaze of one who recalled days of happiness.

"Is Tamenund a boy?" at length the bewildered prophet exclaimed. "Have I dreamed of so many snows—that my people were scattered like floating sands—of Yengeese, more plenty than the leaves on the trees! The arrow of Tamenund would not frighten the fawn; his arm is withered like the branch of a dead oak; the snail would be swifter in the race; yet is Uncas before him as they went to battle against the pale faces! Uncas, the panther of his tribe, the eldest son of the Lenape, the wisest Sagamore of the Mohicans! Tell me, ye Delawares, has Tamenund been a sleeper for a hundred winters?"

The calm and deep silence which succeeded these words sufficiently announced the awful reverence with which his people received the communication of the patriarch. None dared to answer, though all listened in breathless expectation of what might follow. Uncas, however, looking in his face with the fondness and veneration of a favored child, presumed on his own high and acknowledged rank, to reply.

"Four warriors of his race have lived and died," he said, "since the friend of Tamenund led his people in battle. The blood of the turtle has been in many chiefs, but all have gone back into the earth from whence they came, except Chingachgook and his son."

"It is true—it is true," returned the sage, a flash of recollection destroying all his pleasing fancies, and restoring him at once to a consciousness of the true history of his nation. "Our wise men have often said that two warriors of the unchanged race were in the hills of the Yengeese; why have their seats at the council-fires of the Delawares been so long empty?"

At these words the young man raised his head, which he had still kept bowed a little, in reverence; and lifting his voice so as to be heard by the multitude, as if to explain at once and forever the policy of his family, he said aloud:

"Once we slept where we could hear the salt lake speak in its anger. Then we were rulers and Sagamores over the land. But when a pale face was seen on every brook, we followed the deer back to the river of our nation. The Delawares were gone. Few warriors of them all stayed to drink of the stream they loved. Then said my fathers, 'Here will we hunt. The waters of the river go into the salt lake. If we go toward the setting sun, we shall find streams that run into the great lakes of sweet water; there would a Mohican die, like fishes of the sea, in the clear springs. When the Manitou is ready and shall say "Come," we will follow the river to the sea, and take our own again.' Such, Delawares, is the belief of the children of the Turtle. Our eyes are on the rising and not toward the setting sun. We know whence he comes, but we know not whither he goes. It is enough."

The men of the Lenape listened to his words with all the respect that superstition could lend, finding a secret charm even in the figurative language with which the young Sagamore imparted his ideas. Uncas himself watched the effect of his brief explanation with intelligent eyes, and gradually dropped the air of authority he had assumed, as he perceived that his auditors were content. Then, permitting his looks to wander over the silent throng that crowded around the elevated seat of Tamenund, he first perceived Hawkeye in his bonds. Stepping eagerly from his stand, he made way for himself to the side of his friend; and cutting his thongs with a quick and angry stroke of his own knife, he motioned to the crowd to divide. The Indians silently obeyed, and once more they stood ranged in their circle, as before his appearance among them. Uncas took the scout by the hand, and led him to the feet of the patriarch.

"Father," he said, "look at this pale face; a just man, and the friend of the Delawares."

"Is he a son of Minquon?"

"Not so; a warrior known to the Yengeese, and feared by the Maquas."

"What name has he gained by his deeds?"

"We call him Hawkeye," Uncas replied, using the Delaware phrase; "for his sight never fails. The Mingoes know him better by the death he gives their warriors; with them he is 'The Long Rifle'."

"La Longue Carabine!" exclaimed Tamenund, opening his eyes, and regarding the scout sternly. "My son has not done well to call him friend."

"I call him so who proves himself such," returned the young chief, with great calmness, but with a steady mien. "If Uncas is welcome among the Delawares, then is Hawkeye with his friends."

"The pale face has slain my young men; his name is great for the blows he has struck the Lenape."

"If a Mingo has whispered that much in the ear of the Delaware, he has only shown that he is a singing-bird," said the scout, who now believed that it was time to vindicate himself from such offensive charges, and who spoke as the man he addressed, modifying his Indian figures, however, with his own peculiar notions. "That I have slain the Maquas I am not the man to deny, even at their own council-fires; but that, knowingly, my hand has never harmed a Delaware, is opposed to the reason of my gifts, which is friendly to them, and all that belongs to their nation."

A low exclamation of applause passed among the warriors who exchanged looks with each other like men that first began to perceive their error.

"Where is the Huron?" demanded Tamenund. "Has he stopped my ears?"

Magua, whose feelings during that scene in which Uncas had triumphed may be much better imagined than described, answered to the call by stepping boldly in front of the patriarch.

"The just Tamenund," he said, "will not keep what a Huron has lent."

"Tell me, son of my brother," returned the sage, avoiding the dark countenance of Le Subtil, and turning gladly to the more ingenuous features of Uncas, "has the stranger a conqueror's right over you?"

"He has none. The panther may get into snares set by the women; but he is strong, and knows how to leap through them."

"La Longue Carabine?"

"Laughs at the Mingoes. Go, Huron, ask your squaws the color of a bear."

"The stranger and white maiden that come into my camp together?"

"Should journey on an open path."

"And the woman that Huron left with my warriors?"

Uncas made no reply.

"And the woman that the Mingo has brought into my camp?" repeated Tamenund, gravely.

"She is mine," cried Magua, shaking his hand in triumph at Uncas. "Mohican, you know that she is mine."

"My son is silent," said Tamenund, endeavoring to read the expression of the face that the youth turned from him in sorrow.

"It is so," was the low answer.

A short and impressive pause succeeded, during which it was very apparent with what reluctance the multitude admitted the justice of the Mingo's claim. At length the sage, on whom alone the decision depended, said, in a firm voice:

"Huron, depart."

"As he came, just Tamenund," demanded the wily Magua, "or with hands filled with the faith of the Delawares? The wigwam of Le Renard Subtil is empty. Make him strong with his own."

The aged man mused with himself for a time; and then, bending his head toward one of his venerable companions, he asked:

"Are my ears open?"

"It is true."

"Is this Mingo a chief?"

"The first in his nation."

"Girl, what wouldst thou? A great warrior takes thee to wife. Go! thy race will not end."

"Better, a thousand times, it should," exclaimed the horror-struck Cora, "than meet with such a degradation!"

"Huron, her mind is in the tents of her fathers. An unwilling maiden makes an unhappy wigwam."

"She speaks with the tongue of her people," returned Magua, regarding his victim with a look of bitter irony.

"She is of a race of traders, and will bargain for a bright look. Let Tamenund speak the words."

"Take you the wampum, and our love."

"Nothing hence but what Magua brought hither."

"Then depart with thine own. The Great Manitou forbids that a Delaware should be unjust."

Magua advanced, and seized his captive strongly by the arm; the Delawares fell back, in silence; and Cora, as if conscious that remonstrance would be useless, prepared to submit to her fate without resistance.

"Hold, hold!" cried Duncan, springing forward; "Huron, have mercy! her ransom shall make thee richer than any of thy people were ever yet known to be."

"Magua is a red-skin; he wants not the beads of the pale faces."

"Gold, silver, powder, lead—all that a warrior needs shall be in thy wigwam; all that becomes the greatest chief."

"Le Subtil is very strong," cried Magua, violently shaking the hand which grasped the unresisting arm of Cora; "he has his revenge!"

"Mighty ruler of Providence!" exclaimed Heyward, clasping his hands together in agony, "can this be suffered! To you, just Tamenund, I appeal for mercy."

"The words of the Delaware are said," returned the sage, closing his eyes, and dropping back into his seat, alike wearied with his mental and his bodily exertion. "Men speak not twice."

"That a chief should not misspend his time in unsaying what has once been spoken is wise and reasonable," said Hawkeye, motioning to Duncan to be silent; "but it is also prudent in every warrior to consider well before he strikes his tomahawk into the head of his prisoner. Huron, I love you not; nor can I say that any Mingo has ever received much favor at my hands. It is fair to conclude that, if this war does not soon end, many more of your warriors will meet me in the woods. Put it to your judgment, then, whether you would prefer taking such a prisoner as that into your encampment, or one like myself, who am a man that it would greatly rejoice your nation to see with naked hands."

"Will 'The Long Rifle' give his life for the woman?" demanded Magua, hesitatingly; for he had already made a motion toward quitting the place with his victim.

"No, no; I have not said so much as that," returned Hawkeye, drawing back with suitable discretion, when he noted the eagerness with which Magua listened to his proposal. "It would be an unequal exchange, to give a warrior, in the prime of his age and usefulness, for the best woman on the frontiers. I might consent to go into winter quarters, now —at least six weeks afore the leaves will turn—on condition you will release the maiden."

Magua shook his head, and made an impatient sign for the crowd to open.

"Well, then," added the scout, with the musing air of a man who had not half made up his mind; "I will throw 'killdeer' into the bargain. Take the word of an experienced hunter, the piece has not its equal atween the provinces."

Magua still disdained to reply, continuing his efforts to disperse the crowd.

"Perhaps," added the scout, losing his dissembled coolness exactly in proportion as the other manifested an indifference to the exchange, "if I should condition to teach your young men the real virtue of the we'pon, it would smoothe the little differences in our judgments."

Le Renard fiercely ordered the Delawares, who still lingered in an impenetrable belt around him, in hopes he would listen to the amicable proposal, to open his path, threatening, by the glance of his eye, another appeal to the infallible justice of their "prophet."

"What is ordered must sooner or later arrive," continued Hawkeye, turning with a sad and humbled look to Uncas. "The varlet knows his advantage and will keep it! God bless you, boy; you have found friends among your natural kin, and I hope they will prove as true as some you have met who had no Indian cross. As for me, sooner or later, I must die; it is, therefore, fortunate there are but few to make my death-howl. After all, it is likely the imps would have managed to master my scalp, so a day or two will make no great difference in the everlasting reckoning of time. God bless you," added the rugged woodsman, bending his head aside, and then instantly changing its direction again, with a wistful look toward the youth; "I loved both you and your father, Uncas, though our skins are not altogether of a color, and our gifts are somewhat different. Tell the Sagamore I never lost sight of him in my greatest trouble; and, as for you, think of me sometimes when on a lucky trail, and depend on it, boy, whether there be one heaven or two, there is a path in the other world by which honest men may come together again. You'll find the rifle in the place we hid it; take it, and keep it for my sake; and, harkee, lad, as your natural gifts don't deny you the use of vengeance, use it a little freely on the Mingoes; it may unburden griefs at my loss, and ease your mind. Huron, I accept your offer; release the woman. I am your prisoner!"

A suppressed, but still distinct murmur of approbation ran through the crowd at this generous proposition; even the fiercest among the Delaware warriors manifesting pleasure at the manliness of the intended sacrifice. Magua paused, and for an anxious moment, it might be said, he doubted; then, casting his eyes on Cora, with an expression in which ferocity and admiration were strangely mingled, his purpose became fixed forever.

He intimated his contempt of the offer with a backward motion of his head, and said, in a steady and settled voice:

"Le Renard Subtil is a great chief; he has but one mind. Come," he added, laying his hand too familiarly on the shoulder of his captive to urge her onward; "a Huron is no tattler; we will go."

The maiden drew back in lofty womanly reserve, and her dark eye kindled, while the rich blood shot, like the passing brightness of the sun, into her very temples, at the indignity.

"I am your prisoner, and, at a fitting time shall be ready to follow, even to my death. But violence is unnecessary," she coldly said; and immediately turning to Hawkeye, added: "Generous hunter! from my soul I thank you. Your offer is vain, neither could it be accepted; but still you may serve me, even more than in your own noble intention. Look at that drooping humbled child! Abandon her not until you leave her in the habitations of civilized men. I will not say," wringing the hard hand of the scout, "that her father will reward you—for such as you are above the rewards of men—but he will thank you and bless you. And, believe me, the blessing of a just and aged man has virtue in the sight of Heaven. Would to God I could hear one word from his lips at this awful moment!" Her voice became choked, and, for an instant, she was silent; then, advancing a step nigher to Duncan, who was supporting her unconscious sister, she continued, in more subdued tones, but in which feeling and the habits of her sex maintained a fearful struggle: "I need not tell you to cherish the treasure you will possess. You love her, Heyward; that would conceal a thousand faults, though she had them. She is kind, gentle, sweet, good, as mortal may be. There is not a blemish in mind or person at which the proudest of you all would sicken. She is fair—oh! how surpassingly fair!" laying her own beautiful, but less brilliant, hand in melancholy affection on the alabaster forehead of Alice, and parting the golden hair which clustered about her brows; "and yet her soul is pure and spotless as her skin! I could say much—more, perhaps, than cooler reason would approve; but I will spare you and myself—" Her voice became inaudible, and her face was bent over the form of her sister. After a long and burning kiss, she arose, and with features of the hue of death, but without even a tear in her feverish eye, she turned away, and added, to the savage, with all her former elevation of manner: "Now, sir, if it be your pleasure, I will follow."

"Ay, go," cried Duncan, placing Alice in the arms of an Indian girl; "go, Magua, go. These Delawares have their laws, which forbid them to detain you; but I—I have no such obligation. Go, malignant monster—why do you delay?"

It would be difficult to describe the expression with which Magua listened to this threat to follow. There was at first a fierce and manifest display of joy, and then it was instantly subdued in a look of cunning coldness.

"The words are open," he was content with answering, "'The Open Hand' can come."

"Hold," cried Hawkeye, seizing Duncan by the arm, and detaining him by violence; "you know not the craft of the imp. He would lead you to an ambushment, and your death—"

"Huron," interrupted Uncas, who submissive to the stern customs of his people, had been an attentive and grave listener to all that passed; "Huron, the justice of the Delawares comes from the Manitou. Look at the sun. He is now in the upper branches of the hemlock. Your path is short and open. When he is seen above the trees, there will be men on your trail."

"I hear a crow!" exclaimed Magua, with a taunting laugh. "Go!" he added, shaking his hand at the crowd, which had slowly opened to admit his passage. "Where are the petticoats of the Delawares! Let them send their arrows and their guns to the Wyandots; they shall have venison to eat, and corn to hoe. Dogs, rabbits, thieves—I spit on you!"

His parting gibes were listened to in a dead, boding silence, and, with these biting words in his mouth, the triumphant Magua passed unmolested into the forest, followed by his passive captive, and protected by the inviolable laws of Indian hospitality.

CHAPTER XXXI.

"Flue.—Kill the poys and the luggage! 'Tis expressly
against the law of arms; 'tis as arrant a piece of knavery,
mark you now, as can be offered in the 'orld."
—King Henry V.

So long as their enemy and his victim continued in sight, the multitude remained motionless as beings charmed to the place by some power that was friendly to the Huron; but, the instant he disappeared, it became tossed and agitated by fierce and powerful passion. Uncas maintained his elevated stand, keeping his eyes on the form of Cora, until the colors of her dress were blended with the foliage of the forest; when he descended, and, moving silently through the throng, he disappeared in that lodge from which he had so recently issued. A few of the graver and more attentive warriors, who caught the gleams of anger that shot from the eyes of the young chief in passing, followed him to the place he had selected for his meditations. After which, Tamenund and Alice were removed, and the women and children were ordered to disperse. During the momentous hour that succeeded, the encampment resembled a hive of troubled bees, who only awaited the appearance and example of their leader to take some distant and momentous flight.

A young warrior at length issued from the lodge of Uncas; and, moving deliberately, with a sort of grave march, toward a dwarf pine that grew in the crevices of the rocky terrace, he tore the bark from its body, and then turned whence he came without speaking. He was soon followed by another, who stripped the sapling of its branches, leaving it a naked and blazed* trunk. A third colored the post with stripes of a dark red paint; all which indications of a hostile design in the leaders of the nation were received by the men without in a gloomy and ominous silence. Finally, the Mohican himself reappeared, divested of all his attire, except his girdle and leggings, and with one-half of his fine features hid under a cloud of threatening black.

Uncas moved with a slow and dignified tread toward the post, which he immediately commenced encircling with a measured step, not unlike an ancient dance, raising his voice, at the same time, in the wild and irregular chant of his war song. The notes were in the extremes of human sounds; being sometimes melancholy and exquisitely plaintive, even rivaling the melody of birds—and then, by sudden and startling transitions, causing the auditors to tremble by their depth and energy. The words were few and often repeated, proceeding gradually from a sort of invocation, or hymn, to the Deity, to an intimation of the warrior's object, and terminating as they commenced with an acknowledgment of his own dependence on the Great Spirit. If it were possible to translate the comprehensive and melodious language in which he spoke, the ode might read something like the following: "Manitou! Manitou! Manitou! Thou art great, thou art good, thou art wise: Manitou! Manitou! Thou art just. In the heavens, in the clouds, oh, I see many spots—many dark, many red: In the heavens, oh, I see many clouds."

"In the woods, in the air, oh, I hear the whoop, the long yell, and the cry: In the woods, oh, I hear the loud whoop!"

"Manitou! Manitou! Manitou! I am weak—thou art strong; I am slow; Manitou! Manitou! Give me aid."

At the end of what might be called each verse he made a pause, by raising a note louder and longer than common, that was peculiarly suited to the sentiment just expressed. The first close was solemn, and intended to convey the idea of veneration; the second descriptive, bordering on the alarming; and the third was the well-known and terrific war-whoop, which burst from the lips of the young warrior, like a combination of all the frightful sounds of battle. The last was like the first,

---

* A tree which has been partially or entirely stripped of its bark is said, in the language of the country, to be "blazed." The term is strictly English, for a horse is said to be blazed when it has a white mark.

humble and imploring. Three times did he repeat this song, and as often did he encircle the post in his dance.

At the close of the first turn, a grave and highly esteemed chief of the Lenape followed his example, singing words of his own, however, to music of a similar character. Warrior after warrior enlisted in the dance, until all of any renown and authority were numbered in its mazes. The spectacle now became wildly terrific; the fierce-looking and menacing visages of the chiefs receiving additional power from the appalling strains in which they mingled their guttural tones. Just then Uncas struck his tomahawk deep into the post, and raised his voice in a shout, which might be termed his own battle cry. The act announced that he had assumed the chief authority in the intended expedition.

It was a signal that awakened all the slumbering passions of the nation. A hundred youths, who had hitherto been restrained by the diffidence of their years, rushed in a frantic body on the fancied emblem of their enemy, and severed it asunder, splinter by splinter, until nothing remained of the trunk but its roots in the earth. During this moment of tumult, the most ruthless deeds of war were performed on the fragments of the tree, with as much apparent ferocity as if they were the living victims of their cruelty. Some were scalped; some received the keen and trembling axe; and others suffered by thrusts from the fatal knife. In short, the manifestations of zeal and fierce delight were so great and unequivocal, that the expedition was declared to be a war of the nation.

The instant Uncas had struck the blow, he moved out of the circle, and cast his eyes up to the sun, which was just gaining the point, when the truce with Magua was to end. The fact was soon announced by a significant gesture, accompanied by a corresponding cry; and the whole of the excited multitude abandoned their mimic warfare, with shrill yells of pleasure, to prepare for the more hazardous experiment of the reality.

The whole face of the encampment was instantly changed. The warriors, who were already armed and painted, became as still as if they were incapable of any uncommon burst of emotion. On the other hand, the women broke out of the lodges, with the songs of joy and those of lamentation so strangely mixed that it might have been difficult to have said which passion preponderated. None, however, was idle. Some bore their choicest articles, others their young, and some their aged and infirm, into the forest, which spread itself like a verdant carpet of bright green against the side of the mountain. Thither Tamenund also retired, with calm composure, after a short and touching interview with Uncas; from whom the sage separated with the reluctance that a parent would quit a long lost and just recovered child. In the meantime, Duncan saw Alice to a place of safety, and then sought the scout, with a countenance that denoted how eagerly he also panted for the approaching contest.

But Hawkeye was too much accustomed to the war song and the enlistments of the natives, to betray any interest in the passing scene. He merely cast an occasional look at the number and quality of the warriors, who, from time to time, signified their readiness to accompany Uncas to the field. In this particular he was soon satisfied; for, as has been already seen, the power of the young chief quickly embraced every fighting man in the nation. After this material point was so satisfactorily decided, he despatched an Indian boy in quest of "killdeer" and the rifle of Uncas, to the place where they had deposited their weapons on approaching the camp of the Delawares; a measure of double policy, inasmuch as it protected the arms from their own fate, if detained as prisoners, and gave them the advantage of appearing among the strangers rather as sufferers than as men provided with means of defense and subsistence. In selecting another to perform the office of reclaiming his highly prized rifle, the scout had lost sight of none of his habitual caution. He knew that Magua had not come unattended, and he also knew that Huron spies watched the movements of their new enemies, along the whole boundary of the woods. It would, therefore, have been fatal to himself to have attempted the experiment; a warrior would have fared no better; but the danger of a boy would not be likely to commence until after his object was discovered. When Heyward joined him, the scout was coolly awaiting the result of this experiment.

The boy, who had been well instructed, and was sufficiently crafty, proceeded, with a bosom that was swelling with the pride of such a confidence, and all the hopes of young ambition, carelessly across the clearing to the wood, which he entered at a point at some little distance from the place where the guns were secreted. The instant, however, he was concealed by the foliage of the bushes, his dusky form was to be seen gliding, like that of a serpent, toward the desired treasure. He was successful; and in another moment he appeared flying across the narrow opening that skirted the base of the terrace on which the village stood, with the velocity of an arrow, and bearing a prize in each hand. He had actually gained the crags, and was leaping up their sides with incredible activity, when a shot from the woods showed how accurate had been the judgment of the scout. The boy answered it with a feeble but contemptuous shout; and immediately a second bullet was sent after him from another part of the cover. At the next instant he appeared on the level above, elevating his guns in triumph, while he moved with the air of a conqueror toward the renowned hunter who had honored him by so glorious a commission.

Notwithstanding the lively interest Hawkeye had taken in the fate of his messenger, he received "killdeer" with a satisfaction that, momentarily, drove all other recollections from his mind. After examining the piece with an intelligent eye, and opening and shutting the pan some ten or fifteen times, and trying sundry other equally important experiments on the lock, he turned to the boy and demanded with great manifestations of kindness, if he was hurt. The urchin looked proudly up in his face, but made no reply.

"Ah! I see, lad, the knaves have barked your arm!" added the scout, taking up the limb of the patient sufferer, across which a deep flesh wound had been made by one of the bullets; "but a little bruised alder will act like a charm. In the meantime I will wrap it in a badge of wampum! You have commenced the business of a warrior early, my brave boy, and are likely to bear a plenty of honorable scars to your grave. I know many young men that have taken scalps who cannot show such a mark as this. Go!" having bound up the arm; "you will be a chief!"

The lad departed, prouder of his flowing blood than the vainest courtier could be of his blushing ribbon; and stalked among the fellows of his age, an object of general admiration and envy.

But, in a moment of so many serious and important duties, this single act of juvenile fortitude did not attract the general notice and commendation it would have received under milder auspices. It had, however, served to apprise the Delawares of the position and the intentions of their enemies. Accordingly a party of adventurers, better suited to the task than the weak though spirited boy, was ordered to dislodge the skulkers. The duty was soon performed; for most of the Hurons retired of themselves when they found they had been discovered. The Delawares followed to a sufficient distance from their own encampment, and then halted for orders, apprehensive of being led into an ambush. As both parties secreted themselves, the woods were again as still and quiet as a mild summer morning and deep solitude could render them.

The calm but still impatient Uncas now collected his chiefs, and divided his power. He presented Hawkeye as a warrior, often tried, and always found deserving of confidence. When he found his friend met with a favorable reception, he bestowed on him the command of twenty men, like himself, active, skillful and resolute. He gave the Delawares to understand the rank of Heyward among the troops of the Yengeese, and then tendered to him a trust of equal authority. But Duncan declined the charge, professing his readiness to serve as a volunteer by the side of the scout. After this disposition, the young Mohican appointed various native chiefs to fill the different situations of responsibility, and, the time pressing, he gave forth the word to march. He was cheerfully, but silently obeyed by more than two hundred men.

Their entrance into the forest was perfectly unmolested; nor did they encounter any living objects that could either give the alarm, or furnish the intelligence they needed, until they came upon the lairs of their own scouts. Here a halt was ordered, and the chiefs were assembled to hold a "whispering council."

At this meeting divers plans of operation were suggested, though none of a character to meet the wishes of their ardent leader. Had Uncas followed the promptings of his own inclinations, he would have led his followers to the charge without a moment's delay, and put the conflict to the hazard of an instant issue; but such a course would have been in opposition to all the received practises and opinions of his countrymen. He was, therefore, fain to adopt a caution that in the present temper of his mind he execrated, and to listen to advice at which his fiery spirit chafed, under the vivid recollection of Cora's danger and Magua's insolence.

After an unsatisfactory conference of many minutes, a solitary individual was seen advancing from the side of the enemy, with such apparent haste, as to induce the belief he might be a messenger charged with pacific overtures. When within a hundred yards, however, of the cover behind which the Delaware council had assembled, the stranger hesitated, appeared uncertain what course to take, and finally halted. All eyes were turned now on Uncas, as if seeking directions how to proceed.

"Hawkeye," said the young chief, in a low voice, "he must never speak to the Hurons again."

"His time has come," said the laconic scout, thrusting the long barrel of his rifle through the leaves, and taking his deliberate and fatal aim. But, instead of pulling the trigger, he lowered the muzzle again, and indulged himself in a fit of his peculiar mirth. "I took the imp for a Mingo, as I'm a miserable sinner!" he said; "but when my eye ranged along his ribs for a place to get the bullet in— would you think it, Uncas—I saw the musicianer's blower; and so, after all, it is the man they call Gamut, whose death can profit no one, and whose life, if this tongue can do anything but sing, may be made serviceable to our own ends. If sounds have not lost their virtue, I'll soon have a discourse with the honest fellow, and that in a voice he'll find more agreeable than the speech of 'killdeer'."

So saying, Hawkeye laid aside his rifle; and, crawling through the bushes until within hearing of David, he attempted to repeat the musical effort, which had conducted himself, with so much safety and eclat, through the Huron encampment. The exquisite organs of Gamut could not readily be deceived (and, to say the truth, it would have been difficult for any other than Hawkeye to produce a similar noise), and, consequently, having once before heard the sounds, he now knew whence they proceeded. The poor fellow appeared relieved from a state of great embarrassment; for, pursuing the direction of the voice—a task that to him was not much less arduous that it would have been to have gone up in the face of a battery—he soon discovered the hidden songster.

"I wonder what the Hurons will think of that!" said the scout, laughing, as he took his companion by the arm, and urged him toward the rear. "If the knaves lie within earshot, they will say there are two non-composers instead of one! But here we are safe," he added, pointing to Uncas and his associates. "Now give us the history of the Mingo inventions in natural English, and without any ups and downs of voice."

David gazed about him, at the fierce and wild-looking chiefs, in mute wonder; but assured by the presence of faces that he knew, he soon rallied his faculties so far as to make an intelligent reply.

"The heathen are abroad in goodly numbers," said David; "and, I fear, with evil intent. There has been much howling and ungodly revelry, together with such sounds as it is profanity to utter, in their habitations within the past hour, so much so, in truth, that I have fled to the Delawares in search of peace."

"Your ears might not have profited much by the exchange, had you been quicker of foot," returned the scout a little dryly. "But let that be as it may; where are the Hurons?"

"They lie hid in the forest, between this spot and their village in such force, that prudence would teach you instantly to return."

Uncas cast a glance along the range of trees which concealed his own band and mentioned the name of:

"Magua?"

"Is among them. He brought in the maiden that had sojourned with the Delawares; and, leaving her in the cave, has put himself, like a raging wolf, at the head of his savages. I know not what has troubled his spirit so greatly!"

"He has left her, you say, in the cave!" interrupted Heyward; "'tis well that we know its situation! May not something be done for her instant relief?"

Uncas looked earnestly at the scout, before he asked:

"What says Hawkeye?"

"Give me twenty rifles, and I will turn to the right, along the stream; and, passing by the huts of the beaver, will join the Sagamore and the colonel. You shall then hear the whoop from that quarter; with this wind one may easily send it a mile. Then, Uncas, do you drive in the front; when they come within range of our pieces, we will give them a blow that, I pledge the good name of an old frontiersman, shall make their line bend like an ashen bow. After which, we will carry the village, and take the woman from the cave; when the affair may be finished with the tribe, according to a white man's battle, by a blow and a victory; or, in the Indian fashion, with dodge and cover. There may be no great learning, major, in this plan, but with courage and patience it can all be done."

"I like it very much," cried Duncan, who saw that the release of Cora was the primary object in the mind of the scout; "I like it much. Let it be instantly attempted."

After a short conference, the plan was matured, and rendered more intelligible to the several parties; the different signals were appointed, and the chiefs separated, each to his allotted station.

CHAPTER XXXII.

"But plagues shall spread, and funeral fires increase,
Till the great king, without a ransom paid,
To her own Chrysa send the black-eyed maid."
—Pope.

During the time Uncas was making this disposition of his forces, the woods were as still, and, with the exception of those who had met in council, apparently as much untenanted as when they came fresh from the hands of their Almighty Creator. The eye could range, in every direction, through the long and shadowed vistas of the trees; but nowhere was any object to be seen that did not properly belong to the peaceful and slumbering scenery.

Here and there a bird was heard fluttering among the branches of the beeches, and occasionally a squirrel dropped a nut, drawing the startled looks of the party for a moment to the place; but the instant the casual interruption ceased, the passing air was heard murmuring above their heads, along that verdant and undulating surface of forest, which spread itself unbroken, unless by stream or lake, over such a vast region of country. Across the tract of wilderness which lay between the Delawares and the village of their enemies, it seemed as if the foot of man had never trodden, so breathing and deep was the silence in which it lay. But Hawkeye, whose duty led him foremost in the adventure, knew the character of those with whom he was about to contend too well to trust the treacherous quiet.

When he saw his little band collected, the scout threw "killdeer" into the hollow of his arm, and making a silent signal that he would be followed, he led them many rods toward the rear, into the bed of a little brook which they had crossed in advancing. Here he halted, and after waiting for the whole of his grave and attentive warriors to close about him, he spoke in Delaware, demanding:

"Do any of my young men know whither this run will lead us?"

A Delaware stretched forth a hand, with the two fingers separated, and indicating the manner in which they were joined at the root, he answered:

"Before the sun could go his own length, the little water will be in the big." Then he added, pointing in the direction of the place he mentioned, "the two make enough for the beavers."

"I thought as much," returned the scout, glancing his eye upward at the opening in the tree-tops, "from the course it takes, and the bearings of the mountains. Men, we will keep within the cover of its banks till we scent the Hurons."

His companions gave the usual brief exclamation of assent, but, perceiving that their leader was about to lead the way in person, one or two made signs that all was not as it should be. Hawkeye, who comprehended their meaning glances, turned and perceived that his party had been followed thus far by the singing-master.

"Do you know, friend," asked the scout, gravely, and perhaps with a little of the pride of conscious deserving in his manner, "that this is a band of rangers chosen for the most desperate service, and put under the command of one who, though another might say it with a better face, will not be apt to leave them idle. It may not be five, it cannot be thirty minutes, before we tread on the body of a Huron, living or dead."

"Though not admonished of your intentions in words," returned David, whose face was a little flushed, and whose ordinarily quiet and unmeaning eyes glimmered with an expression of unusual fire, "your men have reminded me of the children of Jacob going out to battle against the Shechemites, for wickedly aspiring to wedlock with a woman of a race that was favored of the Lord. Now, I have journeyed far, and sojourned much in good and evil with the maiden ye seek; and, though not a man of war, with my loins girded and my sword sharpened, yet would I gladly strike a blow in her behalf."

The scout hesitated, as if weighing the chances of such a strange enlistment in his mind before he answered:

"You know not the use of any we'pon. You carry no rifle; and believe me, what the Mingoes take they will freely give again."

"Though not a vaunting and bloodily disposed Goliath," returned David, drawing a sling from beneath his parti-colored and uncouth attire, "I have not forgotten the example of the Jewish boy. With this ancient instrument of war have I practised much in my youth, and peradventure the skill has not entirely departed from me."

"Ay!" said Hawkeye, considering the deer-skin thong and apron, with a cold and discouraging eye; "the thing might do its work among arrows, or even knives; but these Mengwe have been furnished by the Frenchers with a good grooved barrel a man. However, it seems to be your gift to go unharmed amid fire; and as you have hitherto been favored—major, you have left your rifle at a cock;

a single shot before the time would be just twenty scalps lost to no purpose—singer, you can follow; we may find use for you in the shoutings."

"I thank you, friend," returned David, supplying himself, like his royal namesake, from among the pebbles of the brook; "though not given to the desire to kill, had you sent me away my spirit would have been troubled."

"Remember," added the scout, tapping his own head significantly on that spot where Gamut was yet sore, "we come to fight, and not to musickate. Until the general whoop is given, nothing speaks but the rifle."

David nodded, as much to signify his acquiescence with the terms; and then Hawkeye, casting another observant glance over his followers made the signal to proceed.

Their route lay, for the distance of a mile, along the bed of the water-course. Though protected from any great danger of observation by the precipitous banks, and the thick shrubbery which skirted the stream, no precaution known to an Indian attack was neglected. A warrior rather crawled than walked on each flank so as to catch occasional glimpses into the forest; and every few minutes the band came to a halt, and listened for hostile sounds, with an acuteness of organs that would be scarcely conceivable to a man in a less natural state. Their march was, however, unmolested, and they reached the point where the lesser stream was lost in the greater, without the smallest evidence that their progress had been noted. Here the scout again halted, to consult the signs of the forest.

"We are likely to have a good day for a fight," he said, in English, addressing Heyward, and glancing his eyes upward at the clouds, which began to move in broad sheets across the firmament; "a bright sun and a glittering barrel are no friends to true sight. Everything is favorable; they have the wind, which will bring down their noises and their smoke, too, no little matter in itself; whereas, with us it will be first a shot, and then a clear view. But here is an end to our cover; the beavers have had the range of this stream for hundreds of years, and what atween their food and their dams, there is, as you see, many a girdled stub, but few living trees."

Hawkeye had, in truth, in these few words, given no bad description of the prospect that now lay in their front. The brook was irregular in its width, sometimes shooting through narrow fissures in the rocks, and at others spreading over acres of bottom land, forming little areas that might be termed ponds. Everywhere along its bands were the moldering relics of dead trees, in all the stages of decay, from those that groaned on their tottering trunks to such as had recently been robbed of those rugged coats that so mysteriously contain their principle of life. A few long, low, and moss-covered piles were scattered among them, like the memorials of a former and long-departed generation.

All these minute particulars were noted by the scout, with a gravity and interest that they probably had never before attracted. He knew that the Huron encampment lay a short half mile up the brook; and, with the characteristic anxiety of one who dreaded a hidden danger, he was greatly troubled at not finding the smallest trace of the presence of his enemy. Once or twice he felt induced to give the order for a rush, and to attempt the village by surprise; but his experience quickly admonished him of the danger of so useless an experiment. Then he listened intently, and with painful uncertainty, for the sounds of hostility in the quarter where Uncas was left; but nothing was audible except the sighing of the wind, that began to sweep over the bosom of the forest in gusts which threatened a tempest. At length, yielding rather to his unusual impatience than taking counsel from his knowledge, he determined to bring matters to an issue, by unmasking his force, and proceeding cautiously, but steadily, up the stream.

The scout had stood, while making his observations, sheltered by a brake, and his companions still lay in the bed of the ravine, through which the smaller stream debouched; but on hearing his low, though intelligible, signal the whole party stole up the bank, like so many dark specters, and silently arranged themselves around him. Pointing in the direction he wished to proceed, Hawkeye advanced, the band breaking off in single files, and following so accurately in his footsteps, as to leave it, if we except Heyward and David, the trail of but a single man.

The party was, however, scarcely uncovered before a volley from a dozen rifles was heard in their rear; and a Delaware leaping high in to the air, like a wounded deer, fell at his whole length, dead.

"Ah, I feared some deviltry like this!" exclaimed the scout, in English, adding, with the quickness of thought, in his adopted tongue: "To cover, men, and charge!"

The band dispersed at the word, and before Heyward had well recovered from his surprise, he found himself standing alone with David. Luckily the Hurons had already fallen back, and he was safe from their fire. But this state of things was evidently to be of short continuance; for the scout set the example of pressing on their retreat, by discharging his rifle, and darting from tree to tree as his enemy slowly yielded ground.

It would seem that the assault had been made by a very small party of the Hurons, which, however, continued to increase in numbers, as it retired on its friends, until the return fire was very nearly, if not quite, equal to that maintained by the advancing Delawares. Heyward threw himself among the combatants, and imitating the necessary caution of his companions, he made quick discharges with his own rifle. The contest now grew warm and stationary. Few were injured, as both parties kept their bodies as much protected as possible by the trees; never, indeed, exposing any part of their persons except in the act of taking aim. But the chances were gradually growing unfavorable to Hawkeye and his band. The quick-sighted scout perceived his danger without knowing how to remedy it. He saw it was more dangerous to retreat than to maintain his ground: while he found his enemy throwing out men on his flank; which rendered the task of keeping themselves covered so very difficult to the Delawares, as nearly to silence their fire. At this embarrassing moment, when they began to think the whole of the hostile tribe was gradually encircling them, they heard the yell of combatants and the rattling of arms echoing under the arches of the wood at the place where Uncas was posted, a bottom which, in a manner, lay beneath the ground on which Hawkeye and his party were contending.

The effects of this attack were instantaneous, and to the scout and his friends greatly relieving. It would seem that, while his own surprise had been anticipated, and had consequently failed, the enemy, in their turn, having been deceived in its object and in his numbers, had left too small a force to resist the impetuous onset of the young Mohican. This fact was doubly apparent, by the rapid manner in which the battle in the forest rolled upward toward the village, and by an instant falling off in the number of their assailants, who rushed to assist in maintaining the front, and, as it now proved to be, the principal point of defense.

Animating his followers by his voice, and his own example, Hawkeye then gave the word to bear down upon their foes. The charge, in that rude species of warfare, consisted merely in pushing from cover to cover, nigher to the enemy; and in this maneuver he was instantly and successfully obeyed. The Hurons were compelled to withdraw, and the scene of the contest rapidly changed from the more open ground, on which it had commenced, to a spot where the assailed found a thicket to rest upon. Here the struggle was protracted, arduous and seemingly of doubtful issue; the Delawares, though none of them fell, beginning to bleed freely, in consequence of the disadvantage at which they were held.

In this crisis, Hawkeye found means to get behind the same tree as that which served for a cover to Heyward; most of his own combatants being within call, a little on his right, where they maintained rapid, though fruitless, discharges on their sheltered enemies.

"You are a young man, major," said the scout, dropping the butt of "killdeer" to the earth, and leaning on the barrel, a little fatigued with his previous industry; "and it may be your gift to lead armies, at some future day, ag'in these imps, the Mingoes. You may here see the philosophy of an Indian fight. It consists mainly in ready hand, a quick eye and a good cover. Now, if you had a company of the Royal Americans here, in what manner would you set them to work in this business?"

"The bayonet would make a road."

"Ay, there is white reason in what you say; but a man must ask himself, in this wilderness, how many lives he can spare. No—horse,"* continued the scout, shaking his head, like one who mused; "horse, I am ashamed to say must sooner or later decide these scrimmages. The brutes are better than men, and to horse must we come at last. Put a shodden hoof on the moccasin of a red-skin, and, if his rifle be once emptied, he will never stop to load it again."

"This is a subject that might better be discussed at another time," returned Heyward; "shall we charge?"

"I see no contradiction to the gifts of any man in passing his breathing spells in useful reflections," the scout replied. "As to rush, I little relish such a measure; for a scalp or two must be thrown away in the attempt. And yet," he added, bending his head aside, to catch the sounds of the distant combat, "if we are to be of use to Uncas, these knaves in our front must be got rid of."

Then, turning with a prompt and decided air, he called aloud to his Indians, in their own language. His words were answered by a shout; and, at a given signal, each warrior made a swift movement around his particular tree. The sight of so many dark bodies, glancing before their eyes at the same instant, drew a hasty and consequently an ineffectual fire from the Hurons. Without stopping to breathe, the Delawares leaped in long bounds toward the wood, like so many panthers springing upon their prey. Hawkeye was in front, brandishing his terrible rifle and animating his followers by his example. A few of the older and more cunning Hurons, who had not been deceived by the artifice which had been practiced to draw their fire, now made a close and deadly discharge of their pieces and justified the apprehensions of the scout by felling three of his foremost warriors. But the shock was insufficient to repel the impetus of the charge. The Delawares broke into the cover with the ferocity of their natures and swept away every trace of resistance by the fury of the onset.

The combat endured only for an instant, hand to hand, and then the assailed yielded ground rapidly, until they reached the opposite margin of the thicket, where they clung to the cover, with the sort of obstinacy that is so often witnessed in hunted brutes. At this critical moment, when the success of the struggle was again becoming doubtful, the crack of a rifle was heard behind the

---

*The American forest admits of the passage of horses, there being little underbrush, and few tangled brakes. The plan of Hawkeye is the one which has always proved the most successful in the battles between the whites and the Indians. Wayne, in his celebrated campaign on the Miami, received the fire of his enemies in line; and then causing his dragoons to wheel round his flanks, the Indians were driven from their covers before they had time to load. One of the most conspicuous of the chiefs who fought in the battle of Miami assured the writer, that the red men could not fight the warriors with "long knives and leather stockings"; meaning the dragoons with their sabers and boots.

Hurons, and a bullet came whizzing from among some beaver lodges, which were situated in the clearing, in their rear, and was followed by the fierce and appalling yell of the war-whoop.

"There speaks the Sagamore!" shouted Hawkeye, answering the cry with his own stentorian voice; "we have them now in face and back!"

The effect on the Hurons was instantaneous. Discouraged by an assault from a quarter that left them no opportunity for cover, the warriors uttered a common yell of disappointment, and breaking off in a body, they spread themselves across the opening, heedless of every consideration but flight. Many fell, in making the experiment, under the bullets and the blows of the pursuing Delawares.

We shall not pause to detail the meeting between the scout and Chingachgook, or the more touching interview that Duncan held with Munro. A few brief and hurried words served to explain the state of things to both parties; and then Hawkeye, pointing out the Sagamore to his band, resigned the chief authority into the hands of the Mohican chief. Chingachgook assumed the station to which his birth and experience gave him so distinguished a claim, with the grave dignity that always gives force to the mandates of a native warrior. Following the footsteps of the scout, he led the party back through the thicket, his men scalping the fallen Hurons and secreting the bodies of their own dead as they proceeded, until they gained a point where the former was content to make a halt.

The warriors, who had breathed themselves freely in the preceding struggle, were now posted on a bit of level ground, sprinkled with trees in sufficient numbers to conceal them. The land fell away rather precipitately in front, and beneath their eyes stretched, for several miles, a narrow, dark, and wooded vale. It was through this dense and dark forest that Uncas was still contending with the main body of the Hurons.

The Mohican and his friends advanced to the brow of the hill, and listened, with practised ears, to the sounds of the combat. A few birds hovered over the leafy bosom of the valley, frightened from their secluded nests; and here and there a light vapory cloud, which seemed already blending with the atmosphere, arose above the trees, and indicated some spot where the struggle had been fierce and stationary.

"The fight is coming up the ascent," said Duncan, pointing in the direction of a new explosion of firearms; "we are too much in the center of their line to be effective."

"They will incline into the hollow, where the cover is thicker," said the scout, "and that will leave us well on their flank. Go, Sagamore; you will hardly be in time to give the whoop, and lead on the young men. I will fight this scrimmage with warriors of my own color. You know me, Mohican; not a Huron of them all shall cross the swell, into your rear, without the notice of 'killdeer'."

The Indian chief paused another moment to consider the signs of the contest, which was now rolling rapidly up the ascent, a certain evidence that the Delawares triumphed; nor did he actually quit the place until admonished of the proximity of his friends, as well as enemies, by the bullets of the former, which began to patter among the dried leaves on the ground, like the bits of falling hail which precede the bursting of the tempest. Hawkeye and his three companions withdrew a few paces to a shelter, and awaited the issue with calmness that nothing but great practise could impart in such a scene.

It was not long before the reports of the rifles began to lose the echoes of the woods, and to sound like weapons discharged in the open air. Then a warrior appeared, here and there, driven to the skirts of the forest, and rallying as he entered the clearing, as at the place where the final stand was to be made. These were soon joined by others, until a long line of swarthy figures was to be seen clinging to the cover with the obstinacy of desperation. Heyward began to grow impatient, and turned his eyes anxiously in the direction of Chingachgook. The chief was seated on a rock, with nothing visible but his calm visage, considering the spectacle with an eye as deliberate as if he were posted there merely to view the struggle.

"The time has come for the Delaware to strike!" said Duncan.

"Not so, not so," returned the scout; "when he scents his friends, he will let them know that he is here. See, see; the knaves are getting in that clump of pines, like bees settling after their flight. By the Lord, a squaw might put a bullet into the center of such a knot of dark skins!"

At that instant the whoop was given, and a dozen Hurons fell by a discharge from Chingachgook and his band. The shout that followed was answered by a single war-cry from the forest, and a yell passed through the air that sounded as if a thousand throats were united in a common effort. The Hurons staggered, deserting the center of their line, and Uncas issued from the forest through the opening they left, at the head of a hundred warriors.

Waving his hands right and left, the young chief pointed out the enemy to his followers, who separated in pursuit. The war now divided, both wings of the broken Hurons seeking protection in the woods again, hotly pressed by the victorious warriors of the Lenape. A minute might have passed, but the sounds were already receding in different directions, and gradually losing their distinctness beneath the echoing arches of the woods. One little knot of Hurons, however, had disdained to seek a cover, and were retiring, like lions at bay, slowly and sullenly up the acclivity which Chingachgook and his band had just deserted, to mingle more closely in the fray. Magua was conspicuous in this party, both by his fierce and savage mien, and by the air of haughty authority he yet maintained.

In his eagerness to expedite the pursuit, Uncas had left himself nearly alone; but the moment his eye caught the figure of Le Subtil, every other consideration was forgotten. Raising his cry of battle, which recalled some six or seven warriors, and reckless of the disparity of their numbers, he rushed upon his enemy. Le Renard, who watched the movement, paused to receive him with secret joy. But at the moment when he thought the rashness of his impetuous young assailant had left him at his mercy, another shout was given, and La Longue Carabine was seen rushing to the rescue, attended by all his white associates. The Huron instantly turned, and commenced a rapid retreat up the ascent.

There was no time for greetings or congratulations; for Uncas, though unconscious of the presence of his friends, continued the pursuit with the velocity of the wind. In vain Hawkeye called to him to respect the covers; the young Mohican braved the dangerous fire of his enemies, and soon compelled them to a flight as swift as his own headlong speed. It was fortunate that the race was of short continuance, and that the white men were much favored by their position, or the Delaware would soon have outstripped all his companions, and fallen a victim to his own temerity. But, ere such a calamity could happen, the pursuers and pursued entered the Wyandot village, within striking distance of each other.

Excited by the presence of their dwellings, and tired of the chase, the Hurons now made a stand, and fought around their council-lodge with the fury of despair. The onset and the issue were like the passage and destruction of a whirlwind. The tomahawk of Uncas, the blows of Hawkeye, and even the still nervous arm of Munro were all busy for that passing moment, and the ground was quickly strewed with their enemies. Still Magua, though daring and much exposed, escaped from every effort against his life, with that sort of fabled protection that was made to overlook the fortunes of favored heroes in the legends of ancient poetry. Raising a yell that spoke volumes of anger and disappointment, the subtle chief, when he saw his comrades fallen, darted away from the place, attended by his two only surviving friends, leaving the Delawares engaged in stripping the dead of the bloody trophies of their victory.

But Uncas, who had vainly sought him in the melee, bounded forward in pursuit; Hawkeye, Heyward and David still pressing on his footsteps. The utmost that the scout could effect, was to keep the muzzle of his rifle a little in advance of his friend, to whom, however, it answered every purpose of a charmed shield. Once Magua appeared disposed to make another and a final effort to revenge his losses; but, abandoning his intention as soon as demonstrated, he leaped into a thicket of bushes, through which he was followed by his enemies, and suddenly entered the mouth of the cave already known to the reader. Hawkeye, who had only forborne to fire in tenderness to Uncas, raised a shout of success, and proclaimed aloud that now they were certain of their game. The pursuers dashed into the long and narrow entrance, in time to catch a glimpse of the retreating forms of the Hurons. Their passage through the natural galleries and subterraneous apartments of the cavern was preceded by the shrieks and cries of hundreds of women and children. The place, seen by its dim and uncertain light, appeared like the shades of the infernal regions, across which unhappy ghosts and savage demons were flitting in multitudes.

Still Uncas kept his eye on Magua, as if life to him possessed but a single object. Heyward and the scout still pressed on his rear, actuated, though possibly in a less degree, by a common feeling. But their way was becoming intricate, in those dark and gloomy passages, and the glimpses of the retiring warriors less distinct and frequent; and for a moment the trace was believed to be lost, when a white robe was seen fluttering in the further extremity of a passage that seemed to lead up the mountain.

"'Tis Cora!" exclaimed Heyward, in a voice in which horror and delight were wildly mingled.

"Cora! Cora!" echoed Uncas, bounding forward like a deer.

"'Tis the maiden!" shouted the scout. "Courage, lady; we come! we come!"

The chase was renewed with a diligence rendered tenfold encouraging by this glimpse of the captive. But the way was rugged, broken, and in spots nearly impassable. Uncas abandoned his rifle, and leaped forward with headlong precipitation. Heyward rashly imitated his example, though both were, a moment afterward, admonished of his madness by hearing the bellowing of a piece, that the Hurons found time to discharge down the passage in the rocks, the bullet from which even gave the young Mohican a slight wound.

"We must close!" said the scout, passing his friends by a desperate leap; "the knaves will pick us all off at this distance; and see, they hold the maiden so as to shield themselves!"

Though his words were unheeded, or rather unheard, his example was followed by his companions, who, by incredible exertions, got near enough to the fugitives to perceive that Cora was borne along between the two warriors while Magua prescribed the direction and manner of their flight. At this moment the forms of all four were strongly drawn against an opening in the sky, and they disappeared. Nearly frantic with disappointment, Uncas and Heyward increased efforts that already seemed superhuman, and they issued from the cavern on the side of the mountain, in time to note the route of the pursued. The course lay up the ascent, and still continued hazardous and laborious.

Encumbered by his rifle, and, perhaps, not sustained by so deep an interest in the captive as his companions, the scout suffered the latter to precede him a little, Uncas, in his turn, taking the lead of Heyward. In this manner, rocks, precipices and difficulties were surmounted in an incredibly short space, that at another time, and under other circumstances, would have been deemed almost insuperable. But the impetuous young men were rewarded by finding that, encumbered with Cora, the Hurons were losing ground in the race.

"Stay, dog of the Wyandots!" exclaimed Uncas, shaking his bright tomahawk at Magua; "a Delaware girl calls stay!"

"I will go no further!" cried Cora, stopping unexpectedly on a ledge of rock, that overhung a deep precipice, at no great distance from the summit of the mountain. "Kill me if thou wilt, detestable Huron; I will go no further."

The supporters of the maiden raised their ready tomahawks with the impious joy that fiends are thought to take in mischief, but Magua stayed the uplifted arms. The Huron chief, after casting the weapons he had wrested from his companions over the rock, drew his knife, and turned to his captive, with a look in which conflicting passions fiercely contended.

"Woman," he said, "chose; the wigwam or the knife of Le Subtil!"

Cora regarded him not, but dropping on her knees, she raised her eyes and stretched her arms toward heaven, saying in a meek and yet confiding voice:

"I am thine; do with me as thou seest best!"

"Woman," repeated Magua, hoarsely, and endeavoring in vain to catch a glance from her serene and beaming eye, "choose!"

But Cora neither heard nor heeded his demand. The form of the Huron trembled in every fibre, and he raised his arm on high, but dropped it again with a bewildered air, like one who doubted. Once more he struggled with himself and lifted the keen weapon again; but just then a piercing cry was heard above them, and Uncas appeared, leaping frantically, from a fearful height, upon the ledge. Magua recoiled a step; and one of his assistants, profiting by the chance, sheathed his own knife in the bosom of Cora.

The Huron sprang like a tiger on his offending and already retreating country man, but the falling form of Uncas separated the unnatural combatants. Diverted from his object by this interruption, and maddened by the murder he had just witnessed, Magua buried his weapon in the back of the prostrate Delaware, uttering an unearthly shout as he committed the dastardly deed. But Uncas arose from the blow, as the wounded panther turns upon his foe, and struck the murderer of Cora to his feet, by an effort in which the last of his failing strength was expended. Then, with a stern and steady look, he turned to Le Subtil, and indicated by the expression of his eye all that he would do had not the power deserted him. The latter seized the nerveless arm of the unresisting Delaware, and passed his knife into his bosom three several times, before his victim, still keeping his gaze riveted on his enemy, with a look of inextinguishable scorn, fell dead at his feet.

"Mercy! mercy! Huron," cried Heyward, from above, in tones nearly choked by horror; "give mercy, and thou shalt receive from it!"

Whirling the bloody knife up at the imploring youth, the victorious Magua uttered a cry so fierce, so wild, and yet so joyous, that it conveyed the sounds of savage triumph to the ears of those who fought in the valley, a thousand feet below. He was answered by a burst from the lips of the scout, whose tall person was just then seen moving swiftly toward him, along those dangerous crags, with steps as bold and reckless as if he possessed the power to move in air. But when the hunter reached the scene of the ruthless massacre, the ledge was tenanted only by the dead.

His keen eye took a single look at the victims, and then shot its glances over the difficulties of the ascent in his front. A form stood at the brow of the mountain, on the very edge of the giddy height, with uplifted arms, in an awful attitude of menace. Without stopping to consider his person, the rifle of Hawkeye was raised; but a rock, which fell on the head of one of the fugitives below, exposed the indignant and glowing countenance of the honest Gamut. Then Magua issued from a crevice, and, stepping with calm indifference over the body of the last of his associates, he leaped a wide fissure, and ascended the rocks at a point where the arm of David could not reach him. A single bound would carry him to the brow of the precipice, and assure his safety. Before taking the leap, however, the Huron paused, and shaking his hand at the scout, he shouted:

"The pale faces are dogs! the Delawares women! Magua leaves them on the rocks, for the crows!"

Laughing hoarsely, he made a desperate leap, and fell short of his mark, though his hands grasped a shrub on the verge of the height. The form of Hawkeye had crouched like a beast about to take its spring, and his frame trembled so violently with eagerness that the muzzle of the half-raised rifle played like a leaf fluttering in the wind. Without exhausting himself with fruitless efforts, the cunning Magua suffered his body to drop to the length of his arms, and found a fragment for his feet to rest on. Then, summoning all his powers, he renewed the attempt, and so far succeeded as to draw his knees on the edge of the mountain. It was now, when the body of his enemy was most collected together, that the agitated weapon of the scout was drawn to his shoulder. The surrounding rocks themselves were not steadier than the piece became, for the single instant that it poured out its contents. The arms of the Huron relaxed, and his body fell back a little, while his knees still kept their position. Turning a relentless look on his enemy, he shook a hand in grim defiance. But his hold loosened, and his dark person was seen cutting the air with its head downward, for a fleeting instant, until it glided past the fringe of shrubbery which clung to the mountain, in its rapid flight to destruction.

## CHAPTER XXXIII.

> "They fought, like brave men, long and well,
> They piled that ground with Moslem slain,
> They conquered—but Bozzaris fell,
> Bleeding at every vein.
> His few surviving comrades saw
> His smile when rang their loud hurrah,
> And the red field was won;
> Then saw in death his eyelids close
> Calmly, as to a night's repose,
> Like flowers at set of sun."
> —Halleck.

The sun found the Lenape, on the succeeding day, a nation of mourners. The sounds of the battle were over, and they had fed fat their ancient grudge, and had avenged their recent quarrel with the Mengwe, by the destruction of a whole community. The black and murky atmosphere that floated around the spot where the Hurons had encamped, sufficiently announced of itself, the fate of that wandering tribe; while hundreds of ravens, that struggled above the summits of the mountains, or swept, in noisy flocks, across the wide ranges of the woods, furnished a frightful direction to the scene of the combat. In short, any eye at all practised in the signs of a frontier warfare might easily have traced all those unerring evidences of the ruthless results which attend an Indian vengeance.

Still, the sun rose on the Lenape a nation of mourners. No shouts of success, no songs of triumph, were heard, in rejoicings for their victory. The latest straggler had returned from his fell employment, only to strip himself of the terrific emblems of his bloody calling, and to join in the lamentations of his countrymen, as a stricken people. Pride and exultation were supplanted by humility, and the fiercest of human passions was already succeeded by the most profound and unequivocal demonstrations of grief.

The lodges were deserted; but a broad belt of earnest faces encircled a spot in their vicinity, whither everything possessing life had repaired, and where all were now collected, in deep and awful silence. Though beings of every rank and age, of both sexes, and of all pursuits, had united to form this breathing wall of bodies, they were influenced by a single emotion. Each eye was riveted on the center of that ring, which contained the objects of so much and of so common an interest.

Six Delaware girls, with their long, dark, flowing tresses falling loosely across their bosoms, stood apart, and only gave proof of their existence as they occasionally strewed sweet-scented herbs and forest flowers on a litter of fragrant plants that, under a pall of Indian robes, supported all that now remained of the ardent, high-souled, and generous Cora. Her form was concealed in many wrappers of the same simple manufacture, and her face was shut forever from the gaze of men. At her feet was seated the desolate Munro. His aged head was bowed nearly to the earth, in compelled submission to the stroke of Providence; but a hidden anguish struggled about his furrowed brow, that was only partially concealed by the careless locks of gray that had fallen, neglected, on his temples. Gamut stood at his side, his meek head bared to the rays of the sun, while his eyes, wandering and concerned, seemed to be equally divided between that little volume, which contained so many quaint but holy maxims, and the being in whose behalf his soul yearned to administer consolation. Heyward was also nigh, supporting himself against a tree, and endeavoring to keep down those sudden risings of sorrow that it required his utmost manhood to subdue.

But sad and melancholy as this group may easily be imagined, it was far less touching than another, that occupied the opposite space of the same area. Seated, as in life, with his form and limbs arranged in grave and decent composure, Uncas appeared, arrayed in the most gorgeous ornaments that the wealth of the tribe could furnish. Rich plumes nodded above his head; wampum, gorgets, bracelets, and medals, adorned his person in profusion; though his dull eye and vacant lineaments too strongly contradicted the idle tale of pride they would convey.

Directly in front of the corpse Chingachgook was placed, without arms, paint or adornment of any sort, except the bright blue blazonry of his race, that was indelibly impressed on his naked bosom. During the long period that the tribe had thus been collected, the Mohican warrior had kept a steady, anxious look on the cold and senseless countenance of his son. So riveted and intense had been that gaze, and so changeless his attitude, that a stranger might not have told the living from the dead, but for the occasional gleamings of a troubled spirit, that shot athwart the dark visage of one, and the deathlike calm that had forever settled on the lineaments of the other. The scout was hard by, leaning in a pensive posture on his own fatal and avenging weapon; while Tamenund, supported by the elders of his nation, occupied a high place at hand, whence he might look down on the mute and sorrowful assemblage of his people.

Just within the inner edge of the circle stood a soldier, in the military attire of a strange nation; and without it was his warhorse, in the center of a collection of mounted domestics, seemingly in readiness to undertake some distant journey. The vestments of the stranger announced him to be one who held a responsible situation near the person of the captain of the Canadas; and who, as it would now seem, finding his errand of peace frustrated by the fierce impetuosity of his allies, was content to become a silent and sad spectator of the fruits of a contest that he had arrived too late to anticipate.

The day was drawing to the close of its first quarter, and yet had the multitude maintained its breathing stillness since its dawn.

No sound louder than a stifled sob had been heard among them, nor had even a limb been moved throughout that long and painful period, except to perform the simple and touching offerings that were made, from time to time, in commemoration of the dead. The patience and forbearance of Indian fortitude could alone support such an appearance of abstraction, as seemed now to have turned each dark and motionless figure into stone.

At length, the sage of the Delawares stretched forth an arm, and leaning on the shoulders of his attendants, he arose with an air as feeble as if another age had already intervened between the man who had met his nation the preceding day, and him who now tottered on his elevated stand.

"Men of the Lenape!" he said, in low, hollow tones, that sounded like a voice charged with some prophetic mission: "the face of the Manitou is behind a cloud! His eye is turned from you; His ears are shut; His tongue gives no answer. You see him not; yet His judgments are before you. Let your hearts be open and your spirits tell no lie. Men of the Lenape! the face of the Manitou is behind a cloud."

As this simple and yet terrible annunciation stole on the ears of the multitude, a stillness as deep and awful succeeded as if the venerated spirit they worshiped had uttered the words without the aid of human organs; and even the inanimate Uncas appeared a being of life, compared with the humbled and submissive throng by whom he was surrounded. As the immediate effect, however, gradually passed away, a low murmur of voices commenced a sort of chant in honor of the dead. The sounds were those of females, and were thrillingly soft and wailing. The words were connected by no regular continuation, but as one ceased another took up the eulogy, or lamentation, whichever it might be called, and gave vent to her emotions in such language as was suggested by her feelings and the occasion. At intervals the speaker was interrupted by general and loud bursts of sorrow, during which the girls around the bier of Cora plucked the plants and flowers blindly from her body, as if bewildered with grief. But, in the milder moments of their plaint, these emblems of purity and sweetness were cast back to their places, with every sign of tenderness and regret. Though rendered less connected by many and general interruptions and outbreakings, a translation of their language would have contained a regular descant, which, in substance, might have proved to possess a train of consecutive ideas.

A girl, selected for the task by her rank and qualifications, commenced by modest allusions to the qualities of the deceased warrior, embellishing her expressions with those oriental images that the Indians have probably brought with them from the extremes of the other continent, and which form of themselves a link to connect the ancient histories of the two worlds. She called him the "panther of his tribe"; and described him as one whose moccasin left no trail on the dews; whose bound was like the leap of a young fawn; whose eye was brighter than a star in the dark night; and whose voice, in battle, was loud as the thunder of the Manitou. She reminded him of the mother who bore him, and dwelt forcibly on the happiness she must feel in possessing such a son. She bade him tell her, when they met in the world of spirits, that the Delaware girls had shed tears above the grave of her child, and had called her blessed.

Then, they who succeeded, changing their tones to a milder and still more tender strain, alluded, with the delicacy and sensitiveness of women, to the stranger maiden, who had left the upper earth at a time so near his own departure, as to render the will of the Great Spirit too manifest to be disregarded. They admonished him to be kind to her, and to have consideration for her ignorance of those arts which were so necessary to the comfort of a warrior like himself. They dwelled upon her matchless beauty, and on her noble resolution, without the taint of envy, and as angels may be thought to delight in a superior excellence; adding, that these endowments should prove more than equivalent for any little imperfection in her education.

After which, others again, in due succession, spoke to the maiden herself, in the low, soft language of tenderness and love. They exhorted her to be of cheerful mind, and to fear nothing for her future welfare. A hunter would be her companion, who knew how to provide for her smallest wants; and a warrior was at her side who was able to protect he against every danger. They promised that her path should be pleasant, and her burden light. They cautioned her against unavailing regrets for the friends of her youth, and the scenes where her father had dwelt; assuring her that the "blessed hunting grounds of the Lenape," contained vales as pleasant, streams as pure; and flowers as sweet, as the "heaven of the pale faces." They advised her to be attentive to the wants of her companion, and never to forget the distinction which the Manitou had so wisely established between them. Then, in a wild burst of their chant they sang with united voices the temper of the Mohican's mind. They pronounced him noble, manly and generous; all that became a warrior, and all that a maid might love. Clothing their ideas in the most remote and subtle images, they betrayed, that, in the short period of their intercourse, they had discovered, with the intuitive perception of their sex, the truant disposition of his inclinations. The Delaware girls had found no favor in his eyes! He was of a race that had once been lords on the shores of the salt lake, and his wishes had led him back to a people who dwelt about the graves of his fathers. Why should not such a predilection be encouraged! That she was of a blood purer and richer than the rest of her nation, any eye might have seen; that she was equal to the dangers and daring of a life in the woods, her conduct had proved; and now, they added, the "wise one of the earth" had transplanted her to a place where she would find congenial spirits, and might be forever happy.

Then, with another transition in voice and subject, allusions were made to the virgin who wept in the adjacent lodge. They compared her to flakes of snow; as pure, as white, as brilliant, and as liable to melt in the fierce heats of summer, or congeal in the frosts of winter. They doubted not that she was lovely in the eyes of the young chief, whose skin and whose sorrow seemed so like her own; but though far from expressing such a preference, it was evident they deemed her less excellent than the maid they mourned. Still they denied her no need her rare charms might properly claim. Her ringlets were compared to the exuberant tendrils of the vine, her eye to the blue vault of heavens, and the most spotless cloud, with its glowing flush of the sun, was admitted to be less attractive than her bloom.

During these and similar songs nothing was audible but the murmurs of the music; relieved, as it was, or rather rendered terrible, by those occasional bursts of grief which might be called its choruses. The Delawares themselves listened like charmed men; and it was very apparent, by the variations of their speaking countenances, how deep and true was their sympathy. Even David was not reluctant to lend his ears to the tones of voices so sweet; and long ere the chant was ended, his gaze announced that his soul was enthralled.

The scout, to whom alone, of all the white men, the words were intelligible, suffered himself to be a little aroused from his meditative posture, and bent his face aside, to catch their meaning, as the girls proceeded. But when they spoke of the future prospects of Cora and Uncas, he shook his head, like one who knew the error of their simple creed, and resuming his reclining attitude, he maintained it until the ceremony, if that might be called a ceremony, in which feeling was so deeply imbued, was finished. Happily for the self-command of both Heyward and Munro, they knew not the meaning of the wild sounds they heard.

Chingachgook was a solitary exception to the interest manifested by the native part of the audience. His look never changed throughout the whole of the scene, nor did a muscle move in his rigid countenance, even at the wildest or the most pathetic parts of the lamentation. The cold and senseless remains of his son was all to him, and every other sense but that of sight seemed frozen, in order that his eyes might take their final gaze at those lineaments he had so long loved, and which were now about to be closed forever from his view.

In this stage of the obsequies, a warrior much renowned for deed in arms, and more especially for services in the recent combat, a man of stern and grave demeanor, advanced slowly from the crowd, and placed himself nigh the person of the dead.

"Why hast thou left us, pride of the Wapanachki?" he said, addressing himself to the dull ears of Uncas, as if the empty clay retained the faculties of the animated man; "thy time has been like that of the sun when in the trees; thy glory brighter than his light at noonday. Thou art gone, youthful warrior, but a hundred Wyandots are clearing the briers from thy path to the world of the spirits. Who that saw thee in battle would believe that thou couldst die? Who before thee has ever shown Uttawa the way into the fight? Thy feet were like the wings of eagles; thine arm heavier than falling branches from the pine; and thy voice like the Manitou when He speaks in the clouds. The tongue of Uttawa is weak," he added, looking about him with a melancholy gaze, "and his heart exceeding heavy. Pride of the Wapanachki, why hast thou left us?"

He was succeeded by others, in due order, until most of the high and gifted men of the nation had sung or spoken their tribute of praise over the manes of the deceased chief. When each had ended, another deep and breathing silence reigned in all the place.

Then a low, deep sound was heard, like the suppressed accompaniment of distant music, rising just high enough on the air to be audible, and yet so indistinctly, as to leave its character, and the place whence it proceeded, alike matters of conjecture. It was, however, succeeded by another and another strain, each in a higher key, until they grew on the ear, first in long drawn and often repeated interjections, and finally in words. The lips of Chingachgook had so far parted, as to announce that it was the monody of the father. Though not an eye was turned toward him nor the smallest sign of impatience exhibited, it was apparent, by the manner in which the multitude elevated their heads to listen, that they drank in the sounds with an intenseness of attention, that none but Tamenund himself had ever before commanded. But they listened in vain. The strains rose just so loud as to become intelligible, and then grew fainter and more trembling, until they finally sank on the ear, as if borne away by a passing breath of wind. The lips of the Sagamore closed, and he remained silent in his seat, looking with his riveted eye and motionless form, like some creature that had been turned from the Almighty hand with the form but without the spirit of a man. The Delawares who knew by these symptoms that the mind of their friend was not prepared for so mighty an effort of fortitude, relaxed in their attention; and, with an innate delicacy, seemed to bestow all their thoughts on the obsequies of the stranger maiden.

A signal was given, by one of the elder chiefs, to the women who crowded that part of the circle near which the body of Cora lay. Obedient to the sign, the girls raised the bier to the elevation of their heads, and advanced with slow and regulated steps, chanting, as they proceeded, another wailing song in praise of the deceased. Gamut, who had been a close observer of rites he deemed so heathenish, now bent his head over the shoulder of the unconscious father, whispering:

"They move with the remains of thy child; shall we not follow, and see them interred with Christian burial?"

Munro started, as if the last trumpet had sounded in his ear, and bestowing one anxious and hurried glance around him, he arose and followed in the simple train, with the mien of a soldier, but bearing the full burden of a parent's suffering. His friends pressed around him with a sorrow that was too strong to be termed sympathy—even the young Frenchman joining in the procession, with the air of a man who was sensibly touched at the early and melancholy fate of one so lovely. But when the last and humblest female of the tribe had joined in the wild and yet ordered array, the men of the Lenape contracted their circle, and formed again around the person of Uncas, as silent, as grave, and as motionless as before.

The place which had been chosen for the grave of Cora was a little knoll, where a cluster of young and healthful pines had taken root, forming of themselves a melancholy and appropriate shade over the spot. On reaching it the girls deposited their burden, and continued for many minutes waiting, with characteristic patience, and native timidity, for some evidence that they whose feelings were most concerned were content with the arrangement. At length the scout, who alone understood their habits, said, in their own language:

"My daughters have done well; the white men thank them."

Satisfied with this testimony in their favor, the girls proceeded to deposit the body in a shell, ingeniously, and not inelegantly, fabricated of the bark of the birch; after which they lowered it into its dark and final abode. The ceremony of covering the remains, and concealing the marks of the fresh earth, by leaves and other natural and customary objects, was conducted with the same simple and silent forms. But when the labors of the kind beings who had performed these sad and friendly offices were so far completed, they hesitated, in a way to show that they knew not how much further they might proceed. It was in this stage of the rites that the scout again addressed them:

"My young women have done enough," he said: "the spirit of the pale face has no need of food or raiment, their gifts being according to the heaven of their color. I see," he added, glancing an eye at David, who was preparing his book in a manner that indicated an intention to lead the way in sacred song, "that one who better knows the Christian fashions is about to speak."

The females stood modestly aside, and, from having been the principal actors in the scene, they now became the meek and attentive observers of that which followed. During the time David occupied in pouring out the pious feelings of his spirit in this manner, not a sign of surprise, nor a look of impatience, escaped them. They listened like those who knew the meaning of the strange words, and appeared as if they felt the mingled emotions of sorrow, hope, and resignation, they were intended to convey.

Excited by the scene he had just witnessed, and perhaps influenced by his own secret emotions, the master of song exceeded his usual efforts. His full rich voice was not found to suffer by a comparison with the soft tones of the girls; and his more modulated strains possessed, at least for the ears of those to whom they were peculiarly addressed, the additional power of intelligence. He ended the anthem, as he had commenced it, in the midst of a grave and solemn stillness.

When, however, the closing cadence had fallen on the ears of his auditors, the secret, timorous glances of the eyes, and the general and yet subdued movement of the assemblage, betrayed that something was expected from the father of the deceased. Munro seemed sensible that the time was come for him to exert what is, perhaps, the greatest effort of which human nature is capable. He bared his gray locks, and looked around the timid and quiet throng by which he was encircled, with a firm and collected countenance. Then, motioning with his hand for the scout to listen, he said:

"Say to these kind and gentle females, that a heart-broken and failing man returns them his thanks. Tell them, that the Being we all worship, under different names, will be mindful of their charity; and that the time shall not be distant when we may assemble around His throne without distinction of sex, or rank, or color."

The scout listened to the tremulous voice in which the veteran delivered these words, and shook his head slowly when they were ended, as one who doubted their efficacy.

"To tell them this," he said, "would be to tell them that the snows come not in the winter, or that the sun shines fiercest when the trees are stripped of their leaves."

Then turning to the women, he made such a communication of the other's gratitude as he deemed most suited to the capacities of his listeners. The head of Munro had already sunk upon his chest, and he was again fast relapsing into melancholy, when the young Frenchman before named ventured to touch him lightly on the elbow. As soon as he had gained the attention of the mourning old man, he pointed toward a group of young Indians, who approached with a light but closely covered litter, and then pointed upward toward the sun.

"I understand you, sir," returned Munro, with a voice of forced firmness; "I understand you. It is the will of Heaven, and I submit. Cora, my child! if the prayers of a heart-broken father could avail thee now, how blessed shouldst thou be! Come, gentlemen," he added, looking about him with an air of lofty composure, though the anguish that quivered in his faded countenance was far too powerful to be concealed, "our duty here is ended; let us depart."

Heyward gladly obeyed a summons that took them from a spot where, each instant, he felt his self-control was about to desert him. While his companions were mounting, however, he found time to press the hand of the scout, and to repeat the terms of an engagement they had made to meet again within the posts of the British army. Then, gladly throwing himself into the saddle, he spurred his charger to the side of the litter, whence low and stifled sobs alone announced the presence of Alice. In this manner, the head of Munro again drooping on his bosom, with Heyward and David following in sorrowing silence, and attended by the aide of Montcalm with his guard, all the white men, with the exception of Hawkeye, passed from before the eyes of the Delawares, and were buried in the vast forests of that region.

But the tie which, through their common calamity, had united the feelings of these simple dwellers in the woods with the strangers who had thus transiently visited them, was not so easily broken. Years passed away before the traditionary tale of the white maiden, and of the young warrior of the Mohicans ceased to beguile the long nights and tedious marches, or to animate their youthful and brave with a desire for vengeance. Neither were the secondary actors in these momentous incidents forgotten. Through the medium of the scout, who served for years afterward as a link between them and civilized life, they learned, in answer to their inquiries, that the "Gray Head" was speedily gathered to his fathers—borne down, as was erroneously believed, by his military misfortunes; and that the "Open Hand" had conveyed his surviving daughter far into the settlements of the pale faces, where her tears had at last ceased to flow, and had been succeeded by the bright smiles which were better suited to her joyous nature.

But these were events of a time later than that which concerns our tale. Deserted by all of his color, Hawkeye returned to the spot where his sympathies led him, with a force that no ideal bond of union could destroy. He was just in time to catch a parting look of the features of Uncas, whom the Delawares were already inclosing in his last vestment of skins. They paused to permit the longing and lingering gaze of the sturdy woodsman, and when it was ended, the body was enveloped, never to be unclosed again. Then came a procession like the other, and the whole nation was collected about the temporary grave of the chief—temporary, because it was proper that, at some future day, his bones should rest among those of his own people.

The movement, like the feeling, had been simultaneous and general. The same grave expression of grief, the same rigid silence, and the same deference to the principal mourner, were observed around the place of interment as have been already described. The body was deposited in an attitude of repose, facing the rising sun, with the implements of war and of the chase at hand, in readiness for the final journey. An opening was left in the shell, by which it was protected from the soil, for the spirit to communicate with its earthly tenement, when necessary; and the whole was concealed from the instinct, and protected from the ravages of the beasts of prey, with an ingenuity peculiar to the natives. The manual rites then ceased and all present reverted to the more spiritual part of the ceremonies.

Chingachgook became once more the object of the common attention. He had not yet spoken, and something consolatory and instructive was expected from so renowned a chief on an occasion of such interest. Conscious of the wishes of the people, the stern and self-restrained warrior raised his face, which had latterly been buried in his robe, and looked about him with a steady eye. His firmly compressed and expressive lips then severed, and for the first time during the long ceremonies his voice was distinctly audible. "Why do my brothers mourn?" he said, regarding the dark race of dejected warriors by whom he was environed; "why do my daughters weep? that a young man has gone to the happy hunting-grounds; that a chief has filled his time with honor? He was good; he was dutiful; he was brave. Who can deny it? The Manitou had need of such a warrior, and He has called him away. As for me, the son and the father of Uncas, I am a blazed pine, in a clearing of the pale faces. My race has gone from the shores of the salt lake and the hills of the Delawares. But who can say that the serpent of his tribe has forgotten his wisdom? I am alone——"

"No, no," cried Hawkeye, who had been gazing with a yearning look at the rigid features of his friend, with something like his own self-command, but whose philosophy could endure no longer; "no, Sagamore, not alone. The gifts of our colors may be different, but God has so placed us as to journey in the same path. I have no kin, and I may also say, like you, no people. He was your son, and a red-skin by nature; and it may be that your blood was nearer—but, if ever I forget the lad who has so often fou't at my side in war, and slept at my side in peace, may He who made us all, whatever may be our color or our gifts, forget me! The boy has left us for a time; but, Sagamore, you are not alone."

Chingachgook grasped the hand that, in the warmth of feeling, the scout had stretched across the fresh earth, and in an attitude of friendship these two sturdy and intrepid woodsmen bowed their heads together, while scalding tears fell to their feet, watering the grave of Uncas like drops of falling rain.

In the midst of the awful stillness with which such a burst of feeling, coming as it did, from the two most renowned warriors of that region, was received, Tamenund lifted his voice to disperse the multitude.

"It is enough," he said. "Go, children of the Lenape, the anger of the Manitou is not done. Why should Tamenund stay? The pale faces are masters of the earth, and the time of the red men has not yet come again. My day has been too long. In the morning I saw the sons of Unamis happy and strong; and yet, before the night has come, have I lived to see the last warrior of the wise race of the Mohicans."

BOOKS PUBLISHED BY

EX FONTIBUS COMPANY

# CONTENTS

CATALOGUE LISTING AS OF APRIL 10, 2019

BOOKS PUBLISHED BY

# EX FONTIBUS COMPANY

*http://www.exfontibus.com*
*contact@exfontibus.com*
*http://www.facebook.com/exfont*
*exfontibuscompany@gmail.com*

*Our books are sold on our own website, at Amazon.com,*
*& through other retailers*

*Get the latest news on our page!*

**SACRED TEXTS—SCRIPTURE, LITURGICAL TEXTS, AND PRAYER**

*Biblia Sacra—The Holy Bible in Latin and English [3 vols.]*
A beautiful parallel Latin/English edition of the Bible of the medieval Catholic Church, using the Latin of the Clementine Vulgate and the English of Douay-Rheims Challoner Revision. **Vol. 1** includes the Pentateuch (Genesis, Exodus, Leviticus, Numbers, Deuteronomy) and the Historical Books (Joshua, Judges, Ruth, Samuel/Kings, Paralipomenon/Chronicles, Ezra/Nehemiah, Tobit, Judith, Esther). **Vol. 2** contains Job, Psalms, Proverbs, Ecclesiastes, the Song of Songs, Wisdom, Ecclesiasticus (Ben-Sirah), Isaiah, Jeremiah, Lamentations, Baruch, Ezechiel, Daniel, Hosea, Joel, Amos, Obadiah, Jonah, Micah, Nahum, Habakkuk, Zephaniah, Haggai, Zechariah, Malachi, Machabees. **Vol. 3** contains the entirety of the New Testament.

*Biblia Sacra—New Testament and Psalms in Latin and English*
An elegant smaller volume containing only the New Testament and the Psalms. [This fourth edition enlarges the formerly-cramped font.]

*The Septuagint, with Apocrypha, in English (Second Edition)*
The Septuagint (LXX), the ancient Greek translation of Jewish sacred writings, is of great importance in the history of both Judaism and Christianity. Translated from Hebrew and other originals in the two centuries before Jesus, the Septuagint

provides important information about the history of biblical text. It captures a moment in time, illuminating for us how Greek-speaking Jews of that time read and interpreted the Hebrew Scriptures that they translated. In its time, it made the Jewish Scriptures accessible to peoples and cultures outside of Judaism through *koine* Greek, the common language of the Mediterranean world. The Septuagint was the Bible of Greek speaking Jews; it was the Bible of the first Christians. It is cited in the New Testament and by the great luminaries of early Christianity. In this edition of the famed translation by Lancelot C. Brenton, many archaisms have been removed and personal pronouns rendered consistent with modern English—yet without sacrificing any of the accuracy, power, or beauty of the original translation. [This second edition corrects several errors from the first edition.]

## *Kyriale Romanum*

Gregorian chant has long transmitted the mystery and majesty of the Catholic liturgical tradition. Newly republished, the Kyriale Romanum of 1961, preserves between its covers an invaluable patrimony of ancient and medieval chants for the Ordinary of the Mass that can be used with both the extraordinary (1962) and the ordinary (post-1970) forms of the Roman Missal. It collects from the Graduale the most frequently-used chant settings throughout the liturgical year, with eighteen mass settings, six credos, and numerous settings for feasts and holy days, including the solemn procession on the feast of Corpus Christi. This beautiful and affordably-priced volume is of great value to all who wish to encounter this venerable musical tradition of the Roman Rite.

## *The Prayerbook of Ælfwine of Hyde*

Decades before the Norman conquest of England in A.D. 1066, a Benedictine monk at Hyde Abbey named assembled a small prayer book from the tradition of early Saxon Christianity. That monk, who later became Abbot of Hyde, passed to his heavenly reward but fifteen years before the influx of Norman culture from France would reshape the prayer and liturgical tradition of English Christianity. The prayers that are preserved in his book bear witness to the zeal and vigor of early English Christianity, with a poetry that stirs the soul over ten centuries since first they were prayed.

ST. IRENÆUS OF LYONS

## Against Heresies and Other Writings

The complete text of *Against the Heresies*, with fragments of other writings. Available nowhere else as a standalone volume. Bishop St. Irenaeus of Lyons wrote his *Against Heresies* ca. A.D. 180 to preserve the Christian rule of faith against the Gnostic heresy. To vindicate the Incarnation against the Gnostics, he described and attacked their principal doctrine: the evil origin of the natural world. Affirming the unity of Old and New Testaments, the goodness of the Creator and the created world, and finally the mystery of divinization whereby human beings are elevated into the divine life, the saint produced an outstanding example of early Christian biblical theology. For the early Fathers, doctrines were taught to safeguard the confession of God's saving love revealed through His Incarnation as Jesus Christ. Of such work there is no better example than Irenaeus, disciple of Polycarp, disciple of John the Evangelist.

ORIGEN OF ALEXANDRIA

## Against Celsus (Contra Celsum)

This is Origen's great apologetical work, undertaken in answer to the attack on Christianity by the pagan philosopher Celsus. The text that Origen composed to refute Celsus's self-styled Λόγος ἀληθής (*True Discourse*) consists of eight books, and belongs to the latest years of his life. It has always been regarded as the great apologetic work of antiquity; and no one can peruse it without being struck by the multifarious reading, wonderful acuteness, and rare subtlety of mind that it displays. A great work, well-deserving the notice of the students of Apologetics and of Early Christianity in general.

ST. ATHANASIUS OF AELXANDRIA

## Essential Writings on the Incarnation [Forthcoming]

In collaboration with Christian Classics, an imprint of Ave Maria Press of Notre Dame, Indiana.

ST. AMBROSE OF MILAN

## Theological and Dogmatic Works

These works present the thought of St. Ambrose, the bishop whose preaching first renewed St. Augustine's interest in Christianity. Included in this volume are several of Ambrose's works on the chief doctrines of the faith: "The Mysteries," "The Holy Spirit," "The Sacrament of the Incarnation of Our Lord," and "The

---

* Chronological listing.

Sacraments," including his famous teaching on the transformation of bread and wine into the Body and Blood of Christ.

### ST. BASIL OF CÆSAREA

## Ascetical Works

Saint Basil the Great writes concerning the spiritual life, the discipline of the passions and growth in illumined love, by which the soul rises to union with God.

## Exegetic Homilies

Basil the Great, of Caesarea, here offers homilies on the creation of the cosmos (the Hexameron, or the Six Days), God's providential ordering of the world, and on selected Psalms. A great work of early Christian biblical exegesis and a monument of patristic theology, now available in an attractive and affordable edition.

### ST. JOHN CASSIAN

## On the Incarnation of the Lord, Against Nestorius

Near the end of his writing career, Cassian the monk was commissioned by an archdeacon—the future Pope Leo the Great—to write a reply to the Christological positions of Nestorius, who saw in Christ two subjects, that of the Word and that of the man Jesus. Cassian's foray into ecclesiastical controversy, a cannonade of arguments from the Scriptures and the early Fathers, offers a blusteringly-effective representation of the general Christological views of East and West. Unsurprisingly, for one such as Cassian who was so concerned with the heights of Christian sanctity, it places special emphasis on the distinction between Christ's divinity and the indwelling of the Word in the saints—for the full divinity of Christ is what indeed makes it possible for *Christ* to be said to dwell within those saints who tread the heights of union with God. What he lacks in the precision of an Athanasius or a Maximus the Confessor, Cassian more than makes up for in the passion of his argumentation.

### ST. GREGORY THE GREAT

## Dialogues

In the series of dialogues that he patiently holds with his deacon Peter, St. Gregory describes a vision of sacred stability in an unstable world; this stability is to be found in the saint's life, lived in the love of Christ and anchored in the power of God. Through tales of miracles and examples of charity, including a famous dialogue on heaven, hell, purgatory, and the power of the Mass, Gregory illustrates the guiding hand of providence in the life of the saint and in the divine power manifest in that saint's deeds and words. Through these stories he aims to teach his readers to offer themselves on the "altar of the heart" as a living sacrifice of love in union with the sacrifice of Christ on the Cross.

## Moralia in Job (Morals on the Book of Job) [3 vols.]

Pope Gregory the Great (r. 590–604) wrote his *Moralia*, or moral homilies on Job, one of his greatest works, before his accession to the See of Peter. Seeking a life of contemplation, Gregory had retired to a house on Rome's Caelian Hill, forming the monastic community of St. Andrew's. Shortly thereafter, however, he was sent obediently but unhappily to Constantinople as papal nuncio (*apocrisarius*) at the court of the Byzantine emperor. There too he gathered a small community to whom he delivered his famed homilies on Job. For Gregory, Job is a figure of Christ, who suffered innocently—not for his sins but for the increase of his merits and the salvation of others by love. These homilies span Christian doctrine, from Creation to final Judgment, from the height of angelic hierarchies to the innermost depths of the human soul. Confident that the Holy Spirit has not idly chosen the words of Scripture, Gregory finds a depth of allegory out of which he draws a brilliant picture of Christ, whose humanity must mark our own and whose Cross is our path to eternal rest. A beautiful meditation on suffering, on the path from fear to love, and on the healing and glorification of the individual soul which, as a member of Christ's body, comes to participate in the life of the holy Trinity. When Gregory was elected bishop of Rome just a few years later, he would continue to draw on and to develop the teaching herein, to guide the spiritual lives of his flock amidst the terror-filled final dissolution of the Western Empire. The teaching of the *Moralia* became a source for the doctors of the middle ages, including Hugh of St. Victor, St. Thomas Aquinas, St. Bonaventure, and many others. Western Christianity today owes an incalculable debt to the homilies that Gregory preached to his small circle of ascetics so many years ago.

## ST. JOHN OF DAMASCUS

## Writings

St. John Damascene, among the greatest of the Eastern fathers during the patristic age, produced his work *The Fount of Knowledge* as a summary of Christian philosophy and theology. It is one of the most important works of the Greek patristic age. Included are "The Philosophical Chapters," "On Heresies," and the justly-famous "Exact Exposition of the Orthodox Faith"—a veritable *Summa* of the doctrine of the Eastern fathers. Now available in an attractive and affordable edition.

HUGH OF ST. VICTOR

*On the Sacraments of the Christian Faith (De Sacramentis).*
Hugh of St. Victor (1096–1141) was a renowned medieval philosopher, theologian, and mystical writer. Because of his great familiarity with the works of St. Augustine, he is sometimes called "the Second Augustine." His work *On the Sacraments of the Christian Faith (De Sacramentis Christianae Fidei)*, composed about 1134, is his masterpiece as well as his most extensive work. It is a veritable *Summa*, a dogmatic synthesis unrivaled in Hugh's time.

By "sacrament," Hugh means not only grace-giving ceremonial signs and actions but also all "mysteries" of the Scriptures, the natural world, and the Church by which God elevates humankind into His life. Hugh's theology draws on Augustine, Gregory the Great, Anselm, and Abelard; and Hugh was also in contact with Bernard of Clairvaux. In the *De Sacramentis*, Hugh separates all of history into the "work of creation" and the "work of restoration." The work of Creation is the triune God's creative activity, the natures of created things, and the original state and destiny of humanity. Hugh's description of the Six Days of Creation is heavily influenced by Augustine's exegesis of Genesis. Divine Wisdom is the archetypal form of creation. The creation of the world in six days is a "sacrament," that is, a spiritually-illuminating mystery for man to contemplate. God's forming order from chaos to make the world is an instruction that guides human beings to rise in love from their own chaos of ignorance to become creatures of Wisdom and therefore beauty. This kind of mystical-ethical interpretation is typical for Hugh, who finds Wisdom's instruction everywhere in creation and in the Scriptures.

The work of Restoration includes the Incarnation of God the Son "with all its sacraments." Here the word "sacrament" refers to the means of salvation that flow from the Incarnation itself, including what are now called the traditional "seven sacraments." Hugh reflects on the mystery of God's freedom—why the Son came into the world even though this was not strictly necessary. Over all, Hugh's work is both an exegetical treatise and a work of spiritual instruction—an example of the inseparability of doctrinal reflection and spiritual growth as understood by this great twelfth-century theologian.

NICHOLAS OF CUSA
*Speculative Theology [Forthcoming]*
Translated by Jasper Hopkins.

*Early Sermons [Forthcoming]*
Translated by Jasper Hopkins.

*Didactic Sermons [Forthcoming]*
Translated by Jasper Hopkins.

*Last Sermons: 1457–1463 [Forthcoming]*
Translated by Jasper Hopkins.

ST. CATHERINE OF GENOA

*The Treatise on Purgatory*
St. Catherine of Genoa's treatise gives her teaching on the repentant soul's purification by the fire of God's divine love. A beautiful meditation on both the love of God and Christian perseverance.

**THEOLOGY—MODERN AND HISTORICAL**\*

JEAN DANIÉLOU, S.J.

*From Shadows to Reality: Studies in the Biblical Typology of the Fathers*
From the first centuries of its existence, the Church has interpreted the historical events recounted in the Old Testament as being "types" or "figures" of the events of the New Testament and of the sacraments instituted by Jesus Christ. Jean Cardinal Daniélou, one of the foremost Catholic scholars of the twentieth century, and a theologian especially concerned with the relationship between history and the Christian revelation, examines in this book the typological interpretation of the Fathers of the Church and their contemporaries during the first three centuries of the Christian era. Among examples he discusses are the crossing of the Jordan by the Israelites as a type of baptism, Rahab as a type of the Church, and the fall of Jericho as a figure of the end of the world. The complex interpretations of Adam, the flood, and the sacrifice and marriage of Isaac are also described in full and commented on. The work is divided into five books entitled "Adam in Paradise," "Noah and the Flood," "The Sacrifice of Isaac," "Moses and the Exodus," and "The Cycle of Joshua". Each book is divided into chapters discussing the various types and the interpretations of Irenaeus, Clement, Gregory of Nyssa and their contemporaries, including Philo.

ÉTIENNE GILSON

*The Philosophy of Saint Bonaventure [Forthcoming]*

---

\* Alphabetical listing.

ARTHUR F. KRUEGER

## *Synthesis of Sacrifice According to Saint Augustine: A Study of the Sacramentality of Sacrifice*

Sacrifice is, for Augustine, simply that life of love that is both the perfect worship of God and the core of participation in His divine life. Arthur Krueger's is the only book-length study of this central theme of Augustine's theology. Krueger considers the bishop of Hippo on sacrifice and priesthood, both in the abstract and in the concrete sacrifices of the Old and New Testaments. He particularly investigates these themes in their relation to Augustine's notion of sacrament, which Krueger presents as a "binding and synthesizing concept" at the heart of the great theologian's sacrificial teaching.

EMILE MERSCH, S.J.

## *The Whole Christ*

In the Scriptures, both the Savior in heaven, alive without suffering as victor over death, and the suffering Christians dragged to prison by Saul, are depicted as constituting together one man, who is, therefore, as Augustine called it, the "Whole Christ." In that mystic unity, Christ, the Incarnate Word, is the Head. We are the members. As for His sake the members suffer persecution He suffers in them, and on the contrary, as He is the Incarnate God they in turn are divinized through their union with Him. Through this same union they are, as co-members, most intimately united also with each other; and finally through their union with Christ as the second Person of the Triune God they are united with the Godhead, with the Most Blessed Trinity. This, Emile Mersch tells us, is the mountain peak of revealed religion, a teaching that pierces into the heavens far beyond our earthly ken. To seek understanding thereof is to ascend into fuller life with Christ. He unfolds this teaching by recourse to Scripture, to the early Church fathers, and to the great doctors of the Catholic tradition.

## *The Theology of the Mystical Body*

As a sequel or companion to *The Whole Christ*, this doctrinal, speculative study endeavors to investigate how and in what measure all dogmas can be seen as discoursing of the "whole Christ"—to ascertain whether dogma is always and everywhere Christ. Emile Mersch writes: "*We would see Jesus* (John 12:21). We are setting out in search of the truth which Christ has brought. Our aim is to see Christ who is the truth, to see Him in it and it in Him. For the truth is like a great panorama that shows forth what He is, depicting Him in His divinity, in all mankind, and in Himself, and nothing but Him. Is He not light and life?"

JOHN HENRY NEWMAN

*Oxford University Sermons*

Newman's fifteen sermons on faith and reason, sanctity, and the development of doctrine; preached before the University of Oxford between A.D. 1826 and 1843 by John Henry Newman.

AIDAN NICHOLS, O.P.

*Epiphany: A Theological Introduction to Catholicism (Second Edition)*

Now in its second edition. Renowned Dominican theologian Aidan Nichols presents the Catholic faith as a unique source of illumination for the good, the true, and the beautiful. That faith, he argues, is destined to be, and humbly offered as, light for all peoples. It was as "light" that that the babe Jesus Christ was hailed by the aged prophet Symeon when he was presented in the Jerusalem Temple. The Church, too, has applied the term "epiphany"—shining forth—to his first, pre-verbal contact with the Gentiles, as his mother held him out to the "magi," the representatives of the non-Jewish nations. Thus the title of this book.

The book is a theological "Introduction" because one could hardly encapsulate all the illuminating richness Catholic Christianity can offer. Still, Nichols skillfully weaves into his own work a truly-catholic gathering of other great lights from the tradition.

This is a traditional theology and, as Nichols writes, "a consciously non-liberal theology, but not, I think, an illiberal one, for its subject is the generosity of God in his revealing Word and sanctifying Spirit. . . It is not a neutral work, since it aims to arouse a 'Christian maximalism' and the boldness to seek in Catholicism's theological tradition inspiration for present and future."

This second edition corrects some errors in the original.

EDWARD DENNIS O'CONNOR, C.S.C.

*The Dogma of the Immaculate Conception [Forthcoming]*

A history of the dogma of the immaculate conception, given in a series of scholarly papers published half a century after the dogma's promulgation. Long out of print but useful to the novice and the specialist alike, this volume takes the long view of Church history and tradition, showing a doctrine's development in action.

JOHN SAWARD

*The Way of the Lamb (Second Edition) [Forthcoming]*

MATTHIAS SCHEEBEN

## Mariology (complete in one volume)

Writing in the nineteenth century, Matthias Scheeben forged a new creative synthesis of the teaching of the Fathers and of the scholastics. Scheeben's work had a decisive influence on later Catholic theologians such as Hans Urs von Balthasar. His primary theme is the nuptial union of God and the created order through the Incarnation, a marriage of heaven and earth that begins in the conception of Christ in the womb of the virgin Mary. Mary, therefore, is the temple in which God and humankind are reconciled. This and all that flows from it and preceded it by way of preparation is the subject-matter of his work Mariology. He draws together the teaching on the Incarnation, on deification, on the Marian dogmas, sacramental theology, and ecclesiology in a truly beautiful work. Originally published in two volumes, the entire work is gathered here in a single volume for the first time. It has been out of print for decades, now made available once more.

THOMAS G. WEINANDY

## Jesus the Christ

Father Thomas G. Weinandy—sometime Oxford tutor and later head of the Secretariat of Doctrine for the United States Conference of Catholic Bishops—opens the fascinating world of Christian theology to all readers. In clear language, he begins in Scripture to draw out the plan of salvation, leading the reader through the development of the Church's grappling with the glorious and paradoxical conviction: That no-one less than God Himself has lived nothing less than a human life. From within the life of the Trinity, to the womb of a young woman, to the Cross upon Calvary, the empty tomb, and the ascension into heaven, Fr. Weinandy unfolds the theological consequences of the Incarnation as the central belief of Christian faith in an understandable Catholic introduction to the theological wisdom of the ages. He hopes that it may be of use to every Christian who wants to understand Jesus and His work of Salvation better.

## HISTORY AND CONTROVERSIES

DOM JOHN CHAPMAN

## Studies on the Early Papacy

Dom John Chapman, fourth abbot of Downside Abbey, was a renowned scholar of early Christianity. On the question of the papacy in the early Church, he eschews selective apologetics in favor of a reasoned study of textual sources in the context of historical events. At these pivotal moments, he argues, the bishop of Rome both took and was expected to take a prominent and indeed authoritative role. This volume offers much substance to those who wish to take up the question of papal prerogatives. Chapman argues in favor of the Catholic claims, but does so with such care as a historian that his work has received high approval even from such an eminence as the famed Anglican historian Henry Chadwick who, in his own book on the history of the early Church, saw fit to recommend Chapman's work to readers interested in the question. There have been many successors to Chapman but few, if any, have engaged precisely with the matters that he discusses with such detail and clarity. His book, therefore, remains an important voice in the modern conversation.

EMILY HICKEY

### Our Catholic Heritage in English Literature of the First Millennium

(Originally entitled *Our Catholic Heritage in Pre-Conquest English Literature*). Ms. Hickey's reflections sweep us into a magical world of ancient epic, poetry, and allegory--by the verses of Cædmon and Bede; in stories of the Phoenix, the Cross, and King Alfred; in old runes and lost loves--in all of which one again and again discovers that Christ has been the narrative's subject all along. She writes: "This little book makes no claim to be a history of pre-Conquest British Literature. It is an attempt to increase Catholics' interest in this part of the 'inheritance of their fathers.' It is not a formal course, but a sort of talk, as it were, about beautiful things said and sung in old days: things which to have learned to love is to have incurred a great and living debt. I have tried to clothe them in the nearest approach I could find to their original speech, with the humblest acknowledgement that nothing matches that speech itself. If this little book in any way fulfils the wishes of those who have asked me for some thoughts on English Literature, I shall be glad indeed."

## LITERATURE—GREAT BOOKS AND GOOD BOOKS

Ex Fontibus Company is proud to present reprints of some difficult-to-find literary texts, such as Alexander Pope's translation of the *Iliad* and the *Odyssey*. However, our offerings are not limited to only the great books. We have also chosen to reprint some that are merely "good" books—yet not for that unworthy of our attention. Indeed, in his book *The Death of Christian Culture*, Dr. John Senior (1923–1999), founder of the once famed Integrated Humanities Program at the University of Kansas, offered a list of 1,0000 "good books" that prepare one to read the "great books." Among the "good" he includes such volumes as the Tarzan novels by Edgar Rice Burroughs:

> Taking all that was best in the Greco-Roman world into itself, Western tradition has given us the thousand good books as preparation for the great ones. . . . For us today, the [useful] cutoff point is World War I, before which cars and the electric light had not yet come to dominate our lives and the experience of nature had not been distorted by speed and the destruction of shadows....[These books are] part of the ordinary cultural matter essential for an English-speaking person to grow in.

Ex Fontibus offers the following—both good books and great—as points of entry into that heritage.

### ROBERT HUGH BENSON

## *Lord of the World*

> Interesting it must be to all to whom the deepest convictions of a man's heart are of moment. And in the artistic balance and taste of Father Benson's literary power every reader will find delight.
>
> —*The New York Times*

> Mr. Benson sees the world, . . . generations hence, free at last from all minor quarrels, and ranged against itself in two camps, Humanitarianism for those who believe in no divinity but that of man, Catholicism for those who believe in no divinity but that of God.
>
> —*The London Times*

> "The book as art is beautiful, delicately balanced, deeply inspired, intelligently executed.
>
> —*Putnam's*

One of Pope Francis's favorite novels, Benson's 1907 apocalyptic tale of the Antichrist is one of the first modern dystopias. Humanism has eliminated world conflict but practices a subtle barbarism upon the human mind. Religion is either suppressed or ignored. The Catholic Church, confined to ghettos, occupies an increasingly perilous position in the public square. The populace turns toward euthanasia as the solution to bodily pain and spiritual crisis. Meanwhile, a mysterious figure of apparent hope, Julian Felsenburgh, rises to become the head of a single world government. The plot follows a priest, Father Percy Franklin, who finds himself caught up in the final and increasingly open struggle between Antichrist and Christ. *Completely re-typeset with Latin phrases translated in footnotes.*

ROBERT HUGH BENSON

*The Dawn of All*

Benson's alternative to *Lord of the World*, this later novel vividly imagines the final peace of the world in the triumph of Christianity and the re-establishment of the Church at the center of daily life. A mysterious priest who cannot remember his own name, nor even anything of the past, must make his way as a Monsignor in a world undergoing a dramatic transformation in preparation for the return of Christ. The world itself becomes an image of the priest's soul. Benson himself writes: "In a former book, called *Lord of the World*, I attempted to sketch the kind of developments a hundred years hence which, I thought, might reasonably be expected if the present lines of what is called "modern thought" were only prolonged far enough; and I was informed repeatedly that the effect of the book was exceedingly depressing and discouraging to optimistic Christians. In the present book I am attempting — also in parable form — not in the least to withdraw anything that I said in the former, but to follow up the other lines instead, and to sketch — again in parable — the kind of developments about sixty years hence which, I think, may reasonably be expected should the opposite process begin, and ancient thought (which has stood the test of centuries, and is, in a very remarkable manner, being "rediscovered" by persons even more modern than modernists) be prolonged instead." As always, the story is rendered with suitable dramatic tension and—as is characteristic of Benson—a spiritual conflict of individual souls that matches the large-scale conflicts in the wider world. *Completely re-typeset with Latin phrases translated in footnotes.*

CHARLOTTE BRONTË

*Jane Eyre*

*Jane Eyre* (originally *Jane Eyre: An Autobiography*) was published in 1847 under the pen name "Currer Bell." The novel follows the emotions and experiences of its title character, including her growth to adulthood and her love for Mr. Rochester, the byronic master of fictitious Thornfield Hall. In its internalization of the action — the focus is on the gradual unfolding of Jane's moral and spiritual sensibility and all the events are colored by a heightened intensity that was previously the domain of poetry — Jane Eyre revolutionized the art of fiction. Charlotte Brontë has been called the 'first historian of the private consciousness' and the literary ancestor of writers like Joyce and Proust. The novel both reflects and heralds the literary movements of its day, containing elements of social criticism, with a strong sense of morality at its core, an individualistic protagonist, and explorations of class, romantic attraction, religion, and the social position of women.

EDGAR RICE BURROUGHS

### The Tarzan Novels, Vol. 1 (Five Novels), Second Edition

The Tarzan novels initiate the young person or the adult into the thrilling and sometimes terrifying world of nature, a world in which one can glimpse something of the eternal Beauty—undimmed even by the savage violence of man and beast. Welcome to the "primeval forest." This omnibus collection presents the first four complete novels of the thrilling adventures of Tarzan of the Apes, along with the collected *Jungle Tales* of Tarzan's early life. Son of an English Lord, raised by the savage apes that killed his father, found again by a civilization that he would never quite come to call his own, he was at home in the jungle in which he was reared. Swinging through the treetops, bane of lions, tamer of elephants, terror of cannibals, finder of lost cities, and beloved of the American woman Jane Porter, this knight of the forest, never trained in chivalry, was known to the outside world as John Clayton, Lord Greystoke—but to himself and the denizens of the jungle in which he grew up, he would be forever Tarzan, King of the Apes. Included in this volume: *Tarzan of the Apes*; *The Return of Tarzan*; *The Son of Tarzan*; *The Beasts of Tarzan*; *Jungle Tales of Tarzan*. A new introduction gives the history of Burroughs' novels and addresses certain points that later writers have rightfully questioned. [This second edition enlarges the previously-cramped font, for a more enjoyable reading experience.]

### The Tarzan Novels, Vol. 2 (Four Novels), Second Edition

This omnibus collection, second in a series, presents the next four novels of Edgar Rice Burroughs' enthralling Tarzan of the Apes. In *Tarzan and the Jewels of Opar*, the ape-man engages in a battle of wits and strength with a corrupt Belgian soldier, as they struggle to lay claim to the treasures of a long-lost colony of Atlantis—a struggle made more difficult by Tarzan having lost his memory! In *Tarzan the Untamed*, World War I disrupts the peaceful life of Tarzan with his wife Jane on their East African estate. Taking up once more the way of the savage ape-man, Tarzan vows vengeance against the German soldiers that he believes to have murdered his wife. His adventures take him through and across a deadly desert, fighting enemies all the way. In *Tarzan the Terrible*, Tarzan finds himself in the mysterious country of Paul-ul-don, an evolutionary island in the African jungle interior. Here dinosaur descendants and intelligent tailed ape-men live amidst fabulous lost cities. In *Tarzan and the Golden Lion*, our hero rebuilds his life in Africa, only to be abducted and held prisoner in the lost city of Opar, whose priestess would have him as her mate. Trekking through the legendary Valley of Diamonds, Tarzan finds himself followed by a mysterious man—who is Tarzan's own double! From his stirring descriptions of the jungle itself to his adept conjuring of scenes of action and mystery, Burroughs does not fail to deliver the thrilling narratives that have made Tarzan so very famous. [This second edition enlarges the previously-cramped font, for a more enjoyable reading experience.]

JAMES FENIMORE COOPER

*The Complete Leatherstocking Tales (2 volumes)*
Cooper's epic historical romances of frontier and Indian life in the early American days created a unique form of American literature. In two volumes five novels are collected, following the order of the stories' internal chronology (rather than historical publication order).
Volume I—*The Deerslayer*; *The Last of the Mohicans*.
Volume II—*The Pathfinder*; *The Pioneers*; *The Prairie*.

HOMER

*The Iliad, translated by Alexander Pope*
> The thing that best distinguishes this from all other translations of Homer is that it alone equals the original in its ceaseless pour of verbal music. . . . Pope worked miracles in highlighting the play of vowels through his lines. . . . Every word is weighted, with a pressure of mind behind it. This is a poem you can live your way into, over the years, since it yields more at every encounter.
> —"On Reading Pope's Homer," *The New York Times*, 6/1/1997

> Many consider [this translation] the greatest English Iliad, and one of the greatest translations of any work into English. It manages to convey not only the stateliness and grandeur of Homer's lines, but their speed and wit and vividness.
> —Daniel Mendelsohn, "Englishing the Iliad: Grading Four Rival Translations," *The New Yorker* Blog, 11/1/2011

For Homer to take his place among our classics it must be the case that a rendering could exercise the same spell over the collective ear as English-language poets. You could not memorize Fagles, or Lattimore—or Hobbes, a few phrases apart—while Pope, even at his least Homeric, is memorable. . . . Pope is not superseded.

—David Ricks, Kings College, London, *Classics Ireland*, vol. 4, 1997

When Alexander Pope's majestic translation of Homer's Iliad appeared between 1715 and 1720, it was acclaimed by Samuel Johnson as "a performance which no age or nation could hope to equal." Pope himself was only 25 years old. While other translations have since claimed distinction in this or that respect, Pope's translation remains unrivaled in its melodious beauty. This is the Iliad that has formed generations of British and American culture through a beauteous poetics that lends itself to easy recollection. With a clean and crisp text illustrated by the inimitable line drawings of Flaxman, this edition finally gives to audiences a fitting rendering of this monument of English verse which captures uniquely the song of Homer himself.

## *The Odyssey, translated by Alexander Pope*

The tale of Odysseus's return from the war at Troy, seeking Ithaca his home and Penelope his wife. Along the way he encounters the murderous Cyclops, the treacherous Circe, and the nymphs, gods, and goddesses who variously assist and impede his homeward journey. Many are his travails and dramatic his final homecoming wherein he joins battle with Penelope's erstwhile suitors. As with the Iliad, Pope, who had two collaborators on this project, renders Homer into a muscular and euphonious English poetry worthy of reading aloud. This volume is likewise illustrated by Flaxman.

J.-K. HUYSMANS

## The Durtal Trilogy

Joris-Karl Huysmans's trilogy of novels charting the religious and life journey of Monsieur Durtal, who once investigated a satanic order in decadent late nineteenth century Paris (*Lá-bas*, "The Depths" or "The Damned"), and now, turning toward God and becoming a Catholic, undertakes a mystical journey of sorts through a monastery (*En Route*; "On the Way"), the cathedral of Chartres (*La Cathédrale*, "The Cathedral"), and finally enters life as a Benedictine oblate (*L'Oblat*, "The Oblate"). This trilogy is intensely autobiographical, following the pattern of Huysmans's own life. Huysmans was an art critic as well as a novelist and thus the exquisitely constructed *Cathedral* has been used by generations of visitors as a guidebook to Chartres Cathedral. This edition offers the flowing translations that brought the original to an English-speaking audience, but with footnoted annotations explaining many of the erudite Huysmans's more obscure references to the artists, saints, and plant-life that populate the unfolding epic of Durtal's journey. Huysmans and his character Durtal are central to French author Michel Houellebecq's best-selling and controversial novel *Submission* (2015).

JOHN HENRY NEWMAN

## Callista: A Tale of the Third Century

Callista, a young and beautiful Greek girl, has just arrived with her brother in North African Carthage. Though she is a gifted young woman, she is unhappy with her life. Wooed by a troubled and lovesick young man named Agellius, Callista is drawn into his own struggle between a newfound Christian faith and the traditional pagan beliefs of his mother, a witch. After a terrible plague of locusts, a popular rage breaks out into persecution against the Christians and both Agellius and Callista must face for themselves the question of what indeed is the truth. Written by Newman after his reception into the Catholic Church, this novel of the early Church is surely a bright light in a flourishing nineteenth century genre that produced few classics and many mediocrities. Indeed, Charles Kingsley, whose later attacks prompted Newman's own *Apologia Pro Vita Sua*, had essayed an earlier effort at early Church fiction with the novel *Hypatia*. To Kingley's dismay, Newman's *Callista* had been received as the better work. *Callista* is rich in prose and vivid in its imagining of Christian life in the early Church.

Made in the USA
Middletown, DE
23 January 2020